Amish Country Crossroads

BEVERLY LEWIS

Amish Country Crossroads

3 BESTSELLING NOVELS IN ONE VOLUME!

The Postcard, The Crossroad, & Sanctuary (with David Lewis)

BETHANYHOUSE
MINNEAPOLIS, MINNESOTA

Published by Bethany House Publishers
11400 Hampshire Avenue South
Bloomington, Minnesota 55438

Bethany House Publishers is a division of
Baker Publishing Group, Grand Rapids, Michigan.

Printed in the United States of America

Library of Congress Cataloging-in-Publication Data

Lewis, Beverly, date-
   Amish country crossroads : 3 bestselling novels in one volume! : The postcard, The
crossroad, & Sanctuary (with David Lewis) / Beverly Lewis.
     p. cm.
   Summary: "The lives and love of Philip Bradley and Rachel Yoder captivate readers again
in this 3-in-1 edition of the popular series featuring The postcard, The crossroad, and
Sanctuary"—Provided by publisher.
   ISBN 0-7642-0186-7 (alk. paper)
   1. Bed and breakfast accommodations—Fiction. 2. Lancaster County (Pa.)—Fiction. 3.
Blind women—Fiction. 4. Journalists—Fiction. 5. Postcards—Fiction. 6. Widows—Fiction. 7.
Amish—Fiction. I. Lewis, David (David Gerald) II. Lewis, Beverly, date-Postcard. III. Lewis,
Beverly, date- Crossroad. IV. Lewis, Beverly, date- Sanctuary. V. Title.

   PS3562.E9383A6   2005
   813'.54—dc22
                                  2005021778

ABOUT THE AUTHORS

BEVERLY LEWIS was born in the heart of Pennsylvania Dutch country. She fondly recalls her growing-up years, and due to a keen interest in her mother's Plain family heritage, many of Beverly's books are set in Lancaster County.

A former schoolteacher, Bev is a member of The National League of American Pen Women—the Pikes Peak branch—and the Society of Children's Book Writers and Illustrators. Her bestselling books are among the C. S. Lewis Noteworthy List Books.

DAVID LEWIS grew up in Aberdeen, South Dakota. He met and married Bev in Colorado, where together they make their home in the foothills of the Rocky Mountains, enjoying their three grown children and one grandchild.

By Beverly Lewis

ABRAM'S DAUGHTERS

The Covenant
The Betrayal
The Sacrifice
The Prodigal
The Revelation

❖ ❖ ❖

THE HERITAGE OF LANCASTER COUNTY

The Shunning
The Confession
The Reckoning

❖ ❖ ❖

ANNIE'S PEOPLE

The Preacher's Daughter

❖ ❖ ❖

The Postcard • *The Crossroad*

❖ ❖ ❖

The Redemption of Sarah Cain
October Song • *Sanctuary**
The Sunroom

❖ ❖ ❖

The Beverly Lewis Amish Heritage Cookbook

www.beverlylewis.com

*with David Lewis

The Postcard

To Dave,

my beloved helpmate and husband.

To the memory of my dear aunt,

Gladys Buchwalter,

who, along with her co-worker in the Lord,

Dorothy Brosey,

led many souls—young and old—

to Calvary's Cross.

A cloud, unforeseen, skidded across the ivory moon and darkened his room, if only for a moment. He lit the kerosene lantern and set about rummaging through his bureau drawers, searching for something— anything—on which to write, so eager was he to pen a prompt reply to his beloved's astonishing letter.

Amish words poured from his joyous heart as he wrote on the back of a plain white postcard. . . .

Prologue: Rachel

❖ ❖ ❖

It's all I have to bring today,

This, and my heart beside,

This, and my heart, and all the fields,

And all the meadows wide.

EMILY DICKINSON (circa 1858)

I used to dream of possessing a full measure of confidence. Used to wonder what it would be like to have at least "a speckle of pluck," as Mamma often said when I was a girl.

Growing up Plain, I come from a long line of hearty women. Women like my grandmothers and great-grandmothers, who believed in themselves and in working hard, living out the old proverb "The Lord helps those who help themselves."

Yet, in spite of all that hereditary determination and spunk, I was just the opposite—overly timid and shy. Nearly afraid of my own voice at times. A far cry from the stories told me of my ancestors.

Elizabeth, my next oldest sister, seemed awful worried about me when, upon my sixteenth birthday, I was too bashful to attend my first Singing. Turning sixteen was an important milestone in the Amish community. The wonderful coming of age offered long-awaited privileges, such as socializing with boys, being courted.

Lizzy was so concerned, she confided in one of Bishop Fisher's granddaughters, explaining in a whisper so I wouldn't hear. "Rachel was born shy" came her tender excuse.

I *had* overheard, though the reason my sister gave for my perpetual red face didn't make me feel any much better. 'Least back then it didn't.

And it didn't help that all my life one relative or another felt obliged to point out to me that my name means *lamb*. "Rachel puts herself out, she does. Never mind that it costs her plenty," Lavina Troyer had declared at a quilting years ago. So my course was set early on. I began to live up to my father's distant cousin's declaration—working hard to keep the house spotless from top to bottom, tending charity gardens as well as my own, eating fresh in the summer months, putting up more than sufficient canned goods for the winter months, and attending work frolics.

Now that I've been married for over six years—a mother of two with another baby on the way—I've come out of my shell just a bit, thanks to my husband, Jacob, and his constant encouragement. Still, I wonder what it would take to be truly brave, to develop the kind of admirable traits I see so clearly in my eleven siblings, most of them older.

As for church, Jacob and I left the strict Old Order behind when we married, joining the ranks of the Amish Mennonites, which broke Mamma's heart—and she never forgot it! I 'spect she's still hoping we'll come to our senses and return someday.

Beachy Amish, that's what the non-Amish community ("English" folk) call us now—after Moses Beachy, who founded the original group in 1927. Our church does *not* shun church members who leave and join other Plain groups, and we hold public worship in a common meeting-house. Often our bishop, Isaac Glick, allows the preachers to read from the newly translated Pennsylvania Dutch version of the New Testament instead of High German, which the young people don't understand anyhow. We embrace the assurance of salvation, and we use electricity and other modern conveniences like telephones, but a few church members rely on horse-drawn carriages for transportation.

Still, we dress Plain and hold fast to our Anabaptist lifestyle. Besides my husband, I am most grateful that the Lord has seen fit to give me a confidante in my cousin Esther Glick. Confiding my deepest thoughts to my Pennsylvania-turned-Ohio cousin is always a joy. It seems easier to pour out my heart in a letter than face-to-face with any of my sisters. Esther and I had often shared our deepest secrets as youngsters—we go back as far as I can remember. Maybe further. I've heard it told that Esther's mother—Aunt Leah—and my mother experienced the first twinges of labor at the exact hour. So my cousin and I are a faithful reflection of our mothers' sisterly love.

Every Friday, without fail, I stop whatever I'm doing and write her a letter.

Friday, June 17

Dearest Esther,

It has been ever so busy here, what with the summer season in full swing. Jacob says we will soon have enough money saved to move to Holmes County.

Oh, I miss you so! Just think—if we do live neighbors to you, we'll quilt and can and raise our children together once more!

Tomorrow's a busy day at Farmers Market. Jacob has hand-crafted lots of fine oak and pine furniture for our market stand. He's worked especially hard at restocking the little wooden rocking chairs and toy trucks. Lancaster tourists snatch them right up—hardly think twice about opening their pocketbooks. We cater too much to outsiders, I fear. But then, tourism is our main industry these days. Not like it used to be when Lancaster farmland was plenty and not so dear. Things are changing rapidly here.

Remember the times I hid under the market tables at Roots and the Green Dragon? Remember how Mamma would scold? Every now and then, I look in the mirror and still see a young girl. Running alongside Mill Creek at breakneck speed, through glimmering shadows of willows and maple, I used to pretend I was the wind. Imagine that! I did enjoy my childhood so, growing up here in the country, away from the noise and bedlam of Lancaster.

Speaking of childhood, I see signs of friskiness in young Aaron. So much like Mamma he is, and only five! Annie, on the other hand, is more like Jacob—agreeable and companionable. My husband laughs when I tell him so, though deep down I 'spect he's awful pleased.

As for our next little Yoder, I do believe he or she will be a mighty active one. The way this baby wrestles inside me is a new experience altogether. I daresay the baby is a boy, probably another mischief in the making! Not a single one of my children shows any signs of shyness, like their mamma, and I 'spose I'm glad 'bout that.

Ach, forgive me for going on so.

Stopping, I adjusted the waistline of my choring dress, letting my eyes roam over the letter. *Jah,* I was downright uncomfortable these days. Oughta finish hemming the maternity dress I started yesterday. But first things first . . .

Jacob's itching to get his fingers back in the soil. Won't be long and he'll have his twenty-sixth birthday. I'm close behind at twenty-four, still young enough to hold on to certain dreams, you know, trusting the Lord to help make them come true. Even though we married young, we've worked mighty hard for a chance to buy some land, like you and Levi. We're both eager for that day—farming's im blud—in the blood.

Jacob's a good provider and a kind and loving husband. We're good friends, too, which isn't too often the case among some husbands and wives. (I have you to thank for setting us up. If it hadn't been for you, I might never have gone to my first Singing back when!) 'Course, I'd never want to return to my single days—ach! My face was always that befuddled pink. Remember?

When I look into Aaron's bright eyes, I can't help but see the hope of the future. Such a spirited disposition he has, and I am indeed grateful. When Annie points out the colors of a dewy rose garden at early morning or the changing sky at sunset (she really does have a keen eye for nature at just four)—it makes me stop and count my blessings. So very many!

Sometimes I think the dear Lord has showered too many wonderful-gut things down on me. But you know my reticent heart, Esther, that I do have much to be thankful for.

Mam and Dat are finally settled one hundred percent in their new place. Just didn't seem right, them moving out of the old farmhouse. But they're happy about the new business—Zooks' Orchard Guest House B&B—not far off Beechdale Road, on Olde Mill Road. I'm amazed, at their age (Mam's already sixty-three!), yet they want to do something completely different now that Dat thinks he's too old to farm. At least the homestead didn't change hands to strangers. It stayed in the family the way Dat always wanted. My two older brothers and their wives are keeping the place going. The dairy farm, too. I think my parents really do have a ministry to the weary traveler. Offering a retreat in the midst of Amish country is something more of us ought to consider.

Well, this is getting long, and news is scarce. Please write soon.

I remain your loving cousin,
Rachel Yoder

Ohio and Esther were both on my mind as I folded the letter, then placed the envelope on the buffet at the far end of the kitchen.

"Time for evening prayers," Jacob said, looking up from the *Budget*. He'd spread the weekly Amish newspaper out all over the kitchen table, open to the ads for carpentry tools.

"I'll go call the children." I watched from the back door as Aaron and Annie came running, their hands and faces smudged from digging in the dirt. "Pop's gonna read the Bible," I said, hurrying them to the sink to be washed up.

Jacob took the Bible down from its usual place in the corner cupboard and sat in his grandfather's old hickory rocker—his favorite chair. "Listen carefully, children," he said, his face tanned and smiling.

Aaron and Annie sat cross-legged at their father's knee. "What Bible story will it be tonight?" asked Aaron. Then, not content to wait for an answer, "Can we hear about David and Goliath again?"

Jacob grinned and ruffled the boy's head. "Something *friedlich*— peaceable—will do."

I pulled up a chair next to Jacob, grateful for our special time together. But the house was so warm, nearly too hot and humid to expect our little ones to sit still. Both the back and front doors stood wide open, the screen doors allowing circulation through the house, yet keeping out flies and other pesky insects. There had been an abundance of mosquitoes, my least favorite of the summer pests.

We listened as Jacob read from Psalm 128—a hymn of celebration, possibly sung by King David himself. Yet I found my thoughts drifting off to the move to Ohio. Probably wouldn't happen till the dead of winter. Still, the realization of our dream was fast approaching.

Jacob's soothing voice brought me out of my reverie. "'The Lord shall bless thee out of Zion: and thou shalt see the good of Jerusalem all the days of thy life.'" He paused, his eyes bright with affection as he looked over the heads of the children . . . at me. I felt a little giddy as our eyes met and locked.

Dearest Jacob, I thought, smiling back at him.

He began to read again. "'Thou shalt see thy children's children, and peace upon Israel.'"

I was delighted with the Scripture Jacob had chosen for this summer night. This balmy evening, brimful of peace and contentment, before the chaos and stress of market day. . . .

Once Aaron and Annie were safely tucked into bed, I scurried down the hall to Jacob's waiting arms. I recalled the words of the psalm, still clear in my memory. *Thou shalt see thy children's children. . . .*

Sighing, I smiled into the darkness. Ohio was just around the corner. At long last, we would see the desire of our hearts. The Lord willing, we would.

We talked into the wee hours, yet it seemed the night was young. "We have much to look forward to," Jacob whispered.

I felt a twinge of confidence. "A new beginning, ain't so?"

He gave a chuckle, and we sealed our love with a tender kiss before settling down to sleep.

There was no way I could've known then, but that night—that precious, sweet night—was to be our very last. Nor could I have foreseen that my sensitive, shy nature—a persistent hound throughout my life— would change my course and, in due time, plunge me into darkness and despair.

Part One

The best mirror is an old friend.

GERMAN PROVERB

One

❖ ❖ ❖

S omething as insignificant as sleeping past the alarm—getting a late start—always set things spinning out of kilter.

The hurrier I go, the behinder I get, Rachel thought, feeling awful frustrated about having to rush around. Quickly, she washed her face, glancing in the oval mirror above the sink. That done, she brushed her longer-than-waist-length hair, parting it down the middle and working it into the plain, low bun at the back of her neck, the way she arranged it each and every morning.

She had lived all her life in rural Bird-in-Hand, in the heart of Pennsylvania Dutch country. Her parents and siblings had found great fulfillment in working the land, all of them. But, as was their custom, only the youngest married brothers had been given acreage, divvying up sections of the original family farm. There was only so much soil to go around, what with commercialism creeping in, choking out precious land—the very reason Levi and Esther Glick had packed up and bid farewell to their close-knit families. All for the sake of owning a parcel of their own.

Still, the historic village and outlying area had offered everything she and her now-grown brothers and sisters ever wanted, and more. There was the grace of swaying willows, the tranquillity of clear, chirping brooks, the honesty of wide-open skies, and the blessing and abundant love of the People.

"Our Father God, thy name we praise," she whispered, starting the day—late as it was—with a prayer of thanksgiving.

Reverently, she placed the white prayer veiling on her head and turned to see her husband standing near the window, his tall, stocky frame blocking the path of the sun.

"We best hurry," she said, moving to his side. "Can't be late for market."

"We'll take the shortcut, then we won't hafta rush so," he said, drawing her close.

"The shortcut?" Rachel was cautious about the roads that led to the Crossroad—a dangerous intersection—where a number of fatal accidents had occurred in the past.

Jacob reassured her. "It'll be all right. Just this once." When she relaxed in his arms, he whispered, "What if we moved to Ohio a bit sooner?"

"How soon?" Her heart beat hard with excitement.

"Say late December . . . after Christmas maybe."

Delighted, she reminded him of her cousin's many letters. "Esther says there's still ample farmland where they are." She thought ahead, counting the months. "And the new baby'll be two months old by then, if I carry full term."

Jacob nodded thoughtfully. "A right gut time then, prob'ly."

Rachel couldn't deny that Esther's persistent letters had caused a stirring in her, and now to hear Jacob talk so!

"There's plenty time left to discuss the details." He looked down at her, his eyes serious. "The woodworking shop brings in nearly more business than I can handle, so we'll have enough money to make the move by December."

"The Lord willing," she whispered. God's will was always uppermost in their minds, yet she longed for the cutting sweet smell of newly mown hay and the earthy scent of cows herded into the barn, ready for milking.

Rachel's parents and both sets of grandparents, clear back to the sturdiest aging branches of the family tree, had been dairy farmers. Some of them had raised chickens and pigs, too, spending grueling hours in the field while they spread manure to insure bountiful crops.

According to snippets of stories she'd overheard growing up, there was only one of her ancestors who'd forsaken his upbringing. Considering the two hundred or so conservative folk connected to her through blood ties or marriage, losing a single member was ever so slight compared to some families. Age-old gossip had it that Great-uncle Gabriel, her mother's uncle, had turned his back on the Plain community sometime during his twenty-seventh year, long past the time a young man should've joined church, making his commitment before God and the People.

There were various spins on the story. Some said Gabe Esh was a self-appointed evangelist. Others had it that he'd been given a so-called "divine revelation"—only to die weeks later.

As far as Rachel was concerned, no one seemed to know exactly what happened, though she wasn't the sort of person to solicit questions. Truth was, most everyone closely acquainted with Gabe had long since passed through the gates of Glory. Except, of course, Old Order Bishop Seth Fisher and his wife, and Jacob's and Rachel's parents, though none of them seemed inclined to waste time discussing a "rabble-rouser," which was just what one of the preachers had said of Gabe in a sermon some years back. And there was Martha Stoltzfus—Gabe's only living sister. But the brusque and bitter woman refused to speak of him, upholding *die Meinding*—the shunning that must've been placed on him, for what reason Rachel did not know. Lavina Troyer was rumored to have been a schoolmate of Gabe Esh, though none of that was talked about anymore.

So there was a broken bough on Rachel's family tree, and not a single Esh, Yoder, or Zook cared to recall the reason for the fracture.

She headed downstairs to cook the usual breakfast for her dear ones. Abandoning thoughts of the past, she turned her attention to the future as she scrambled up nine large eggs, made cornmeal mush and fried potatoes, and set out plenty of toast, butter, grape jelly, and apple butter. Just knowing that she and Jacob and the children could move so far from home, that a Bible-based conservative group was expecting their arrival—or so Esther had said—filled her heart with gladness. The future was ever so bright.

Rachel and Jacob sat down with the children to eat, but the minute Jacob was finished, he dashed outside to load the market wagon. Rachel gently encouraged the children not to dawdle as she washed and dried the dishes.

Soon, Jacob was calling to them from the yard. "Time to load up the family. *Kumme*—come now!"

Rachel dried her hands and gathered up her basket of needlework. It was always a good thing to keep busy at market, especially if there was a lull, though that would hardly be the case on a summer Saturday. Tourists generally flocked to the well-known Farmers Market this time of year.

Spying the letter to Cousin Esther on the buffet, she snatched it up just as Jacob came indoors. "I think we're all ready," she said, shooing the children in the direction of the back door.

The Yoders settled in for a twenty-minute ride, by way of the short-cut. An occasional breeze took the edge off the sun's warm rays as Jacob hurried the horse. Still, they were forced to reflect on the day, allowing the primitive mode of transportation to slow them down, calm them, too. Truth be told, Rachel was glad they still drove horse and buggy instead of a car, like a few of her young Beachy relatives. The thought of buzzing highways and wide thoroughfares made her shiver with fright. She hoped and prayed Holmes County might be far less bustling.

"Plenty of time left," Jacob had said about scheduling their moving day. More than anything, she wanted to bring up the topic as they rode along. But she thought better of it and kept her peace.

It was Aaron who did most of the talking. Jabbering was more like it. After several minutes of the boy's idle babbling, Jacob reprimanded him. "That'll be enough, son."

Instantly, Aaron fell silent, but Rachel heard Annie giggle softly, the two of them still jostling each other as youngsters will.

Children are a gift from God, she thought, glancing back at the darling twosome. How very happy they all were in this life they'd chosen. And her husband's quiver was surely on its way to being full of offspring.

She allowed her thoughts to wander back to each of her children's home births. Seemed like just yesterday that Mattie Beiler, Hickory Hollow's most prominent midwife, had come at dawn to help deliver Aaron. Rachel kindly rejected her mother's suggestion to have a hex doctor come to assist—even after twenty hours of excruciating labor. Her firstborn would make his appearance when he was good and ready, she'd decided, in spite of Susanna's pleadings. For once, Rachel had spoken up and was glad of it.

One year and two months later, Annie, all sweet-like, had arrived with the mildest, shortest labor on record in the area—around midnight. No sympathy healer was hinted at for Annie's birth. And no midwife.

Rachel cherished the memories, yet tried to lay aside her ongoing concern over the powwow doctors. Especially one *die blo Yonie*—Blue Johnny. *Dokder* was the name the children called him, though she knew he was not a real doctor at all. Not Amish either.

The tall man with bushy brown hair came a-knocking on one door or another nearly every Tuesday afternoon. Last month, he'd come to the Yoder house quite unexpectedly. He'd reeked of the musty scent of pipe tobacco as he rubbed his little black box up and down her son's spine and over his shoulders, never waiting for Rachel's consent whatsoever. Yet in no time, he knew about a tiny wart, hardly visible, growing on Aaron's left hand.

"To get rid of it, just roast the feet of a chicken and rub the wart with them, then bury the chicken feet under the eaves of your house, and the wart will disappear," the man had said, eyeing her curiously.

Because of her wariness, Rachel never roasted any such chicken feet. She honestly wished she hadn't opened the door to Blue Johnny that day, what with Jacob working clear across the barnyard in his woodshop. Even so, she was too timid to speak up. Such folk, calling themselves faith healers—with charms for this and herbal potions for that—had frequently called on Plain folk for as long as she could remember. Some of them were Amish themselves, though the powwow doctors among her own family had died out years ago. She herself had been looked upon as a possible choice because of certain giftings manifest in her as a young child. But due to her extreme shyness, she had been passed over.

As for Blue Johnny, she felt uneasy around him and others who claimed "healing gifts," even though he'd graciously cured Lizzy of rheumatism years ago. He'd come to the Zook farmhouse and taken the disease away by tying a blue woolen yarn around her sister's painful limbs, repeating a charm three times. In the process, the man had taken the disease on himself. And she knew that he had, because he limped out of the house and down the back steps, while Lizzy was free of pain in the space of five minutes!

Most of the Plain folk in the area never gave powwow practices a second thought. Sympathy healers and folk medicine came with the territory, brought to Central Pennsylvania by early Dutch settlers. Such healers were believed to have been imparted gifts by the Holy Spirit and the holy angels, but there were others—a small minority—who believed the healing gifts were anything but divinely spiritual, that they were occultic in nature.

Rachel knew precisely where her own uncertainties concerning powwow doctors had come from—an old column in the *Budget*, the popular Ohio-based newspaper for Amish readers. There had been an article written by one Jacob J. Hershberger, a Beachy Amish bishop living in

Norfolk, Virginia, back in 1961. Esther had stumbled onto it when she cleaned out the attic before their Ohio move.

For some reason, her cousin had thought the article important enough to save, so she'd passed it along to Rachel and Jacob. The writer had spoken out strongly against enchantment and powwowing, describing such as the work of evil spirits. Jacob Hershberger had also admonished Amish communities everywhere to abandon their superstitious beliefs "handed down by godless heathen." He instructed them to "lay on hands, anoint with oil, call the elders of the church, and pray" for the sick as God's Word teaches, instead of turning to witchcraft—powwow doctoring.

After reading the column, Rachel initially wondered if there might be some truth to the notion that powwow doctors received their abilities from the devil rather than God. Could that be the reason she'd always had such a peculiar feeling around them? Yet if that was so, why didn't others in the community feel uneasy—the way she did?

Since Rachel didn't have the courage to speak up and share her apprehension with either her bishop or the preachers, she was glad she could confide in at least one other person besides Jacob. Esther was always kind enough to say, "Jah, I understand," or gently beg to differ with her. Esther was either black or white on any issue, and Rachel had come to trust that forthright approach. It was that kind of thoughtful and compassionate friendship they'd enjoyed throughout the years.

———

Rachel gazed lovingly at her husband's strong hands as he held the reins, urging the horse onward. She looked ahead to the narrow two-lane road, taking in the barley and wheat fields on either side. Bishop Glick's place, with its myriad rose arbors bedecking the side yards, would soon be coming up on the left-hand side. Then another two miles or so and they'd pass the stone mill and the homestead where she'd grown up amidst a houseful of people.

She marveled at the beauty around her—the sun playing off trees abundant with broad green leaves and the wild morning glory vines entwined along the roadside. Ambrosial fragrances of honeysuckle and roses stirred in the summer air.

"Will we miss Lancaster, do you think?" she asked Jacob softly.

He reached over and patted her hand. "We always miss what we don't have. 'Tis human nature, I'm sad to say." His was a knowing smile, yet his words were not of ridicule.

"Living neighbors to Esther and Levi will be wonderful-gut," she replied, thinking out loud. "We'll be farmers again . . . after all these years."

Her husband nodded slowly, his well-trimmed beard bumping his chest. "Jah, the soil tends to pull us back to it, I'd say. But I'm a-wonderin' if you and Esther don't have somethin' cooked up." Jacob looked almost too serious. "Maybe Levi and I oughta keep you and your cousin apart, for good measure."

Rachel didn't know whether to laugh or cry. "Surely you don't mean it."

He looked at her and winked. "You know me better'n that."

She had to laugh, the mere pressure of the moment bursting past her timid lips. "Jah, I know," she said, leaning her head on his strong shoulder. "I know you, Jacob Yoder."

They rode that way for a spell while the children twittered playfully behind them. She closed her eyes, absorbing the sounds of baby birds, newly hatched, and the rhythmic *clip-clop* of the horse. The familiar sound of a windmill told her they must be approaching her parents' homestead. She felt close to the earth; the back roads made her feel this way—riding in the long, enclosed market wagon, pulled by a strong and reliable horse down provincial byways that wove the farm community together.

It was the intersection at Ronks Road and Route 340—the Crossroad—that put the fear of God in her. But the junction was a good twelve minutes away and the unfortunate accidents long since forgotten. Thankfully, a traffic light had been installed after the last tourist car accident, making the crossing safer.

She would simply enjoy the ride, let her husband humor her, and put up with Aaron's increasing silliness in the back of the wagon. Then, once they settled in at market, she'd have the children run over to the post office and mail her letter to Esther.

Two

❖ ❖ ❖

With great expectancy, Susanna Zook watched through her front room window as an open spring wagon, drawn by a veteran horse, rumbled up the private lane to the Orchard Guest House.

Unable to restrain herself, she sailed out the screen door, letting it *slap-slap* behind her. She leaned on the porch post, catching her breath as her husband and his English friend climbed down from the wagon and tied the horse to the fence post, then proceeded to unload a large cherrywood desk.

Home at last! she thought, reliving the recent weeks of haggling with the Mennonite dealer over the handcrafted piece. The minute she'd caught sight of the fine tambour desk on display at Emma's Antique Shop she had coveted it, secretly claiming it for one of their newly refurbished guest quarters. She *had* thought of asking her son-in-law Jacob Yoder to make one, perhaps even suggest that he inspect the desk—see what he could do to replicate it. Something as old and quite nearly perfect didn't often show up in shop windows. Such handsome items usually ended up at private estate sales and family auctions.

Rumor had it that the rolltop desk had been in old Bishop Seth's family, unearthed and in disrepair in his wife's English nephew's shed up near Reading. Someone at the store let it slip that the 1890s desk had been restored in recent years, though when Susanna pushed for more background information, she was met with vague responses. She soon discovered that it was next to impossible following up on former antique owners.

Watching from the porch, Susanna held her breath as the men tilted, then lifted the enormous desk off the wagon. She could picture the space she'd set aside for its permanent new home. Upstairs in the southeast bedroom—newly painted and papered—ready for an overnight guest. All four of the other bedrooms had been completed in just a few short weeks after she and Benjamin had taken possession of the historic structure.

The architectural mix of colonial red brick, typical white porch, and country green shutters was both quaint and attractive, made even more fetching by the gentle backdrop of nature: the apple orchard and mill stream beyond the house to the north, a pine grove to the south, as well as expansive side and front lawns. Relatives and friends had come to help fix up the place, and in a few weeks, the rambling two-story house was ready for tourists.

Sighing with sheer delight, she watched as Benjamin and his friend hauled the desk up the red-and-pink-petunia-lined walkway. "It's awful heavy, jah?" she called.

Ben grunted his reply. It was obvious just how burdensome the ancient thing was, weighing down her robust man—her husband of nearly forty-five years.

She hadn't brought up the subject, but she figured Ben had encouraged her to purchase the desk as a sort of anniversary gift. "It's not every day a find like this shows up at Emma's—walks up the lane and into your house," he'd said, with a twinkle in his eyes.

She knew then he honestly wanted her to have it, and she was tickled pink. But then, Benjamin was like that, at least about special occasions. He, like many farmers, didn't mind parting with a billfold of money, so long as it made his wife happy. And Susanna had never been one to desire much more than she already had, which, for an Amish farmer's wife, was usually plenty, especially when it came to food, clothing, and a roof over their heads. Just not the worldly extras like fast cars, fancy clothes, and jewelry, like the modern English folk.

She held the door open as the men hoisted their load past her and into the main entryway. Deciding not to observe the painstaking ascent to the upstairs bedroom, she made herself scarce, going into the kitchen to check on her dinner of roast chicken, pearl onions, carrots, and potatoes.

When she was satisfied that the meal was well under way, she went and stood at the back door. Their new puppy, a golden-haired cocker spaniel, was waiting rather impatiently outside—as close as he could get to the screen door without touching it with his wet nose.

"You're just itchin' to come in, ain'tcha?" she said, laughing as she pushed the screen door open just wide enough to let him scamper past. She shooed away the flies, thinking that she'd have to go around with her flyswatter now, hunting down the pesky, germ-ridden insects. How she hated them!

Still amazed that Benjamin hadn't nixed her idea of having a house pet, she freshened the puppy's water dish, chattering with pleasure as he lapped up the cool refreshment. She'd grown up believing that animals—wild animals and farm animals alike, as well as dogs and cats—were meant to live outside in a barn or some other such place. Never in the house. So when she'd spotted the beautiful pup at the pet store, she didn't quite know why she changed her mind, wanting to raise an animal indoors. Maybe it was the dejected, yet adorable way the puppy had cocked his head to one side, as if to say, "Won'tcha please take me home?"

In the end, Benjamin was more than generous about purchasing the sad-eyed thing, giving Susanna full sway with the decision. Maybe he was softening in his old age, though he was just in his mid-sixties. Still, she assumed the purchase of a pet was somehow a joint retirement present to each other, possibly for optional companionship should one of them die in the next few years. How very strange such a house pet might seem to any of the People, especially when a host of cats and dogs were multiplying themselves monthly back on the farm they'd left to Noah and Joseph, their youngest sons, and their wives.

"Copper, baby, come here to Mamma," she cooed down at the shining eyes and wagging tail. "You want a treat now, don'tcha?"

The dog seemed to agree that a midday snack was quite appropriate and followed her across the commodious kitchen, complete with all the modern conveniences, and stood near the refrigerator, wagging his bushy tail, eager for his treat.

She was secretly glad they'd bought a house with electricity already installed. And the modern kitchen—what would her sisters and cousins give to live like this! Thank goodness Bishop Seth had given special permission to conduct their B&B business this way. Only one requirement: She and Benjamin were not allowed the use of electricity in their private quarters, and, of course, there was to be no television or radio anywhere in the house, which was quite all right with Susanna. Such worldly gadgets made too much racket for overnight guests anyway.

She heard her husband and his friend chatting on the upstairs landing. *Gut*, she thought. They must be finished with the weighty chore.

"Here we are, pooch." She handed Copper a pale green treat in the shape of a miniature bone. Leaving the kitchen and rounding the corner, she hurried through the breakfast room, situated in the center of a plant-filled conservatory, then through the formal dining room. There, she met up with the men.

"Your writing desk looks mighty nice," Ben said, jerking his head toward the stairs. "I daresay, if I hadn't seen it squeeze past the door-jambs, I wouldn't have believed it myself."

"*Denki*, Ben." She included her husband's friend in her thanks, offering him hot coffee and a sticky bun and inviting him to stay and sit a spell. But the man declined, shaking both his head and his hands, backing away toward the front door.

Ben stood there with a silly grin on his face. "Well, go on now, Susie. You know you're just achin' to have a look-see."

She *was* eager. "Jah, I'll get up for a peek at it." And with that, she hastened up the stairs to the well-appointed guest room. Her eyes found the desk immediately, and she stood a moment, admiring the central placement on the long, papered wall. "It's *lieblich*—lovely," she whispered, heading for the linen closet in the hall where she kept cleaning supplies.

Before she set about dusting the desk, she pulled up a chair. After sitting down, she proceeded to roll back the rounded wooden covering, peering into every nook and cranny. Each little drawer and opening was just as she'd remembered, and she thrilled at the opportunity to own such a magnificent piece. "I will not be proud," she said aloud. "I will be thankful instead."

She dusted the organizer, complete with pigeonholes, and all the intricate woodwork where dust might've found lodging. Taking her time, she polished all the compartments except for one wide, thin drawer off to the left. She jiggled and pulled, but there was no budging the tiny niche, and she made a mental note to have Jacob take a look.

It was after she had finished polishing the desk, as she made her way down the hall to the stairs, that she heard the wail of a siren. The dismal sound came closer and closer, then swept past the turnoff to Beechdale Road, just south of them on Highway 340. Momentarily she cringed as she often did when she heard an ambulance or a fire truck in the area. But she dismissed the worrisome thought and went about the task at hand—preparing the noon meal for her husband.

Three

❖ ❖ ❖

Jacob brought the horse and wagon to a complete stop, waiting first in line for the light to change at the Crossroad. "There's much traffic today," he mentioned, his eyes fixed on the highway.

"Public schools are out already," Rachel said, seeing the cars whiz past them on Route 340. "Tourists are here from all over."

"'Tis gut for business." Jacob looked at her quickly, then back at the road just ahead.

"Jah, and for us movin' to Ohio sooner," she replied with a nervous titter, eyeing the busy intersection.

Aaron, behind them, pretended to be attracting tourists, laughing as he talked. "Come on, now, folks, have a look at these handmade toy trains and helicopters! You won't find toys like this anywhere else in the whole wide world."

Glancing around, Rachel saw her son holding up the wooden play-things, one in each hand. "Dat's crafts won't last long today," she replied.

"If we ever get through this light, they won't," Jacob muttered.

Just then, an unexpected gust of wind snatched Esther's letter out of Rachel's hand, and it floated out the window and somersaulted—end over end—landing on the roadside to the right of the wagon.

"Aw, your letter," Jacob said.

"I'll run 'n get it right quick," Rachel said and got out before Jacob could stop her. But the wind played chase, sending the envelope into the field, and she stumbled after it, glancing over her shoulder to see if the light was still red. *Gut*, she thought, seeing that it was, and hurried to catch the stray envelope.

Just as she rescued the letter, pushing it down into her apron pocket—just at that moment—she turned and saw the horse rear up, spooked by traffic.

"*Himmel*, no . . . no," she whispered, running back toward the road, her heart in her throat.

Jacob was involved in a contest of wills, holding the reins firmly, pulling back hard. But the mare was up . . . up on her hind legs again, neighing loudly and shaking her long black mane.

"Hold steady, girl," Rachel begged, clenching her fists at her sides, helpless to do a thing.

She could see that Jacob was trying his best to control the horse, but after moments of struggle, the frightened animal lunged forward, still snorting and stomping.

Rachel screamed, but her cries did not keep the mare from pulling the market wagon forward into the busy intersection. In a split second, a surge of terrifying sounds filled the air—brakes squealing, car horn blaring. The noises accompanied a speeding car as it crashed broadside—Jacob's side—into the wagon.

Rachel stood gasping, frozen in place, as she witnessed the impact, seeing with her own eyes the market wagon splinter apart like so many toothpicks. Oh, dear Lord, her family . . . how could they possibly survive the crushing blow?

Moments passed. Everything around her fell silent.

Suddenly, strength returned to her legs. She began to stumble across the field to the accident scene, sobbing as she searched for her precious little children and dear, dear Jacob.

Rachel combed through the wreckage, calling frantically, "Aaron! Annie! Mamma's here. Aaron . . . Annie! Can you hear me?"

Unable to find her children, she wrung her hands, running here and there, nearly insane with dread.

Continuing her search, she winced at the sight of her husband lying in the highway, surrounded by dozens of damaged toys and mangled wood and metal from the shattered market wagon. She knelt on the road, its blacktop blistering her knees as she lifted her husband's battered face to hers. Lovingly, she cradled him as if he were a small child. "Oh, Jacob . . ."

He moaned pitifully as she held him, though she dared not rock or move him the slightest, so badly hurt he was. "Lord, please let my husband live," she prayed with trembling lips, all the while looking about her for signs of her little ones.

Jacob was breathing; she could feel the slow and labored movement of his chest. Still, she was frightened, alarmed by the gashes in his head, the torn shirt and suspenders. She hesitated for a moment, then touched the wound in his left shoulder, allowing her hand to linger there as if her touch might bring comfort. That shoulder had supported her weary head on countless nights as they lay talking into the wee hours, whispering in the darkness of their Ohio dream as they planned their lives together with God's help. Jacob's shoulder had soothed her when, at nineteen, she'd experienced the first unfamiliar pangs of childbirth.

Now . . . she heard voices as if there were people near, though she couldn't tell for sure, so murky and muddled things seemed, like a dream that she was actually living, unable to sort out the real from the illusory. She thought she might be dying, too, so dizzy and sick she was.

A distant siren sang out, moving toward her with a peculiar throbbing motion. The rhythm of its lament seemed to pulse up through the highway, into her body as she held Jacob close.

Compassionate hands were touching her husband, lifting his eyelids, putting pressure on his wrist. Then he was being carried away from her on a long stretcher. She felt faint just then and lay down in the road. "Where are my children?" she managed to say. "I must find my little ones."

"Several paramedics are with them." This, the voice of a man she did not know. "What are your children's names?"

"Aaron and Annie Yoder," she said softly, the life withering within her.

"And your husband?"

She attempted to speak his name, but pain—deep and wrenching—tore at her, taking her breath away. Then everything went black.

When she came to, she felt a cool hand on her pulse, followed by a sharp, brief prick in her arm. Though she had no sense of time, she knew she was being lifted onto something smooth and flat, the sun blinding her momentarily. The movement caused her great pain, and when she heard pitiful moaning, she realized that it was she herself.

"You're suffering from shock" came a voice in her ear. "We're going to take good care of you . . . and your unborn child."

The overwhelming emotion was that of helplessness as she was transported through the air, though she had no idea where she was being taken or who was taking her.

"Mamma!" a child cried out.

In her disoriented state she could not identify the source of the utterance, though something inside her wrestled to know. "Aaron?" she mumbled, beginning to shake uncontrollably. "Oh, Lord Jesus . . . help us, please."

A warm covering embraced her body, and for a fleeting moment, she thought her husband's strong arms were consoling her. Then came stark flashes of bewildering images. Two roads meeting, a horse lurching, children screaming . . .

"No . . . no," she said, fighting off the visions. Yet they persisted against her ability to stop them.

The sound of rushing feet startled her back to the here and now. Where *was* she? Struggling to raise her head even the slightest, Rachel tried to take in her surroundings, feeling horribly and completely alone. The noises about her ceased and outward awareness faded with the deep, prevailing pain in her womb.

The wail of a siren jolted her nerves, and gradually she gave in to the attentive urgings of those around her. *Relax . . . rest . . . please rest. . . .*

She sensed that she was weakening, letting go—surrendering to the tremendous pain. And fear so black and ferocious, such as she had never known.

In the hours following the accident, Rachel was unable to divide reality from haunting impressions. She knew only one thing: Her parents were near, along with several of her brothers and sisters and their spouses. Her semiprivate room at Community Hospital was lovingly cushioned with Plain folk, close relatives with concern stamped on each face.

Suffering the ill effects of her miscarriage, Rachel was finally able to speak the burning question in her mind. "Where are Jacob . . . and Aaron and Annie?"

Her parents stood on either side of the bed, their faces grim. "Annie's doin' fine," her father said. "Her right arm is broken and there are bruises, but she will be all right."

"What about Jacob and Aaron?" came her frightened reply.

Such a look passed between Mam and Dat that panic seized her, and she thought she might faint. "I must know about my family!"

When neither parent responded immediately, she felt something rise up in her. Something strong and defensive. "Please tell me what happened. I must know *everything*," she pleaded.

Their pallid faces told the dreadful truth. "I'm sorry, my precious daughter," Dat said at last.

"You don't mean . . ." She paused, trying to breathe enough to speak. "Jacob isn't . . ." She simply could not voice the impossible word. "Is Aaron. . . ?"

Mamma nodded slowly, eyes glistening. "Jacob and Aaron died in the accident."

"It's a miracle of God that Annie is alive," added Dat, his voice sounding strangely stiff.

Mam took Rachel's hand in her own. "We'll stay right here with you, till you're released to go home."

Home . . .

Rachel moaned; her whole body shook. Home could never be the same for her. Not without Jacob and Aaron. Overcome with grief, she closed her eyes, blocking out her mother's somber face. Mam's words were compassionate and true, yet Rachel could not comprehend a single one.

Jacob . . . Aaron dead? How can this be?

Her head throbbed with the truth, like a cumbersome weight against the long, flat hospital pillow. How it pained her to lean back. No matter what she did, her head ached, and her heart anguished for her dear ones. She wished she might've held her sweet little Aaron as he lay suffering on the road. It plagued her that he had died alone at the accident scene, that he might've called out for her—"Mamma, oh, Mamma, I'm hurt awful bad!"—or worse, that he could not utter her name at all.

She placed her hands on her womb, her flat, lifeless womb, longing for her unborn child as well.

More than anything, she wished to join her husband, her son, and their tiniest little one in heaven. Life without Jacob would be ever so lonely. Unbearable. Life on this earth without her darling boy would be intolerable. How could she face the years ahead? How could she bear the pain, missing them so?

Someone wearing white floated into the room, and although Rachel assumed it was the nurse coming with a sedative, a blanket of numbness fell over her before she ever felt the needle penetrate her skin.

Esther and her husband arrived the next afternoon. They had hired a Mennonite van driver to rush them from Holmes County to Lancaster. In the space of half a day, they'd come.

The reunion was a tearful one, and Rachel repeatedly searched Esther's dewy brown eyes, taking in the familiar rosy cheeks and the oval shape of her cousin's face. Esther had worn her best blue cape dress for the occasion, though her black apron was a bit wrinkled from the trip. "You'll need someone to look after you and little Annie for a while," she insisted, kissing Rachel's forehead and holding her hand. "Levi and I will be more than happy to stay till you're back on your feet."

"I'm so glad you're here."

"I came to help, to bear your sorrow," Esther pledged. "Levi and I can stay as long as need be." She explained that their children were with close Amish friends in Holmes County.

"I don't know what I'd do without you," Rachel said, her voice breaking. "Didja know that I must've written you a letter the night before the accident? But I don't remember writing it now. Mamma found it in my apron pocket." She motioned to the small closet. "It's in there somewhere," she said before giving way to a fresh spasm of grief.

Esther hugged her cousin. "Shh. I'm here now. We'll get through this, jah?"

When Rachel was able to compose herself, Esther sat on the edge of the hospital bed, their hands clasped. They talked quietly of Annie and how glad they were that the child had been spared, along with Rachel. "The Lord surely kept the two of you alive for a special reason," Esther said, her eyes still wet with tears.

Rachel didn't quite know what to think of that—being kept alive for a *special* purpose. God's sovereign will was not to be questioned, of course. Yet it was difficult to hear Esther go on so, especially when Rachel sincerely wished the Lord had taken her home to Glory, too.

Why *had* God let her live?

Mamma and Esther moved quietly to the window, encouraging Rachel to rest a bit. She heard the lull of their discreet whispering— Jacob's or Aaron's name slipping into the air every so often—but, honestly, she did not care to know what was being discussed. Funeral plans, most likely.

With the thought of such a thing—a funeral for her dear ones—horrifying mental pictures flashed before her eyes: the car roaring into the wagon, Jacob's body broken beyond recognition. She shook her head as if to shake off the visions, shutting her eyes tightly against the persistent images. "No!" she cried out.

Mam and Esther turned their heads. "What's that, dear?" Mam called to her. And Esther rushed to Rachel's bedside again.

She breathed heavily as the painful memories slowly receded. Then suddenly a new insidious notion sprang at Rachel—that the accident had been her fault. *Hers.* Taking a deep breath, she blurted, "I never heard the alarm! We slept through. If we hadn't overslept—if I'd heard the alarm clock like always—we'd never, *never* have taken the shortcut. We wouldn't have been at the Crossroad, and Jacob and Aaron would be alive today."

"Mustn't trouble yourself," Esther was saying, stroking Rachel's arm. "Mustn't go blamin' yourself."

But Rachel felt she had to express herself while this one memory was still alive in her. "We were rushing to market . . . requiring the horse to gallop. Oh, Esther . . ."

"The accident wasn't your fault," her cousin repeated. "Believe me, it wasn't."

Mam was on the other side of the bed now, leaning over to reach for Rachel's free hand. "The horse became frightened and leaped into traffic, is all."

"I . . . I don't remember any of that," she confessed as she wept. "How do you know this?"

"There were witnesses," replied Mam. "People saw what happened and told the police."

This was the first she'd heard any talk of police and witnesses. Why, the whole thing sounded like some made-up story.

Esther continued to hover near. "You mustn't dwell on what *was,* Rachel. Think on the Lord . . . how He watched over you and Annie," she said, her eyes filled with concern and love. "We will trust the Lord for His continued watch over you. And all of us will pitch in and help, too."

"Jah," she said, feeling calmer, knowing that what Esther said was precisely true. Still, she felt she was going through the motions, agreeing with Mam and Esther, yet not feeling much conviction, if any. She was now intended by God to be a widow, to raise Annie, her only child.

By herself.

Esther remained close as Mam looked on. "Rest now," she urged, squeezing Rachel's hand. "Please, just rest."

She wouldn't rest much, not the deep, life-giving rest that comes from a long day of toil. She would nap, but it would not—could not— possibly be restful.

———

That night, Rachel was alone for the first time. Mam and Esther had left Rachel to sleep, but her slumber was fitful and intermittent. Terrifying visions continued to haunt her as she fought to repress the nagging remnants of memories involving the accident, repeatedly refusing to see the sights her mind thrust upon her.

Giving up, she turned on the bedside lamp to read her New Testament, only to find that the room remained engulfed in hazy darkness. She blinked her eyes, trying to brush away whatever it was, assuming that her eyes were overly tired, strained perhaps. Slowly the darkness subsided.

She had been reading her New Testament only a short time when the words began to rill together like a gray smudge on the page. Thankfully, the distortion lasted only a few seconds, then cleared up. She said not a word to the night nurse but fell into a troubled sleep, the Testament still open in her hands.

Hours later, she awoke to a night sky, a starlit view from her hospital room. Getting up, she wandered to the window, looking up at a shimmering half-moon. "Oh, Jacob, I wish you hadn't had to die," she whispered. "You were such a peaceable man. Why did you and Aaron have to go that way?"

Her dreams just now had been filled with more nightmarish images. A horse—a sleek bay mare—lay sprawled out on a highway. Dead. And what might've been an Amish market wagon was twisted and on its side, all burst to pieces. She shuddered anew and rejected the repulsive visions. She would not, *could* not allow herself to see the memories that had torn her world apart. Yet with the shunning of images came shooting head pains, like long needles piercing her skull.

She closed her mind to the recollection of distant screams as well. The ear-piercing cries of a child.

Aaron? Annie?

Turning from the window, she limped back to her hospital bed, though it afforded little comfort. Once again she fell into a troubled sleep, dreaming that she was searching about her on the road, the sharp pain in her womb and the spasms in her head keeping her from moving much at all. She saw Jacob lying helplessly, wounded and bleeding. She began to cry out in her sleep, awaking herself with a jolt, only to find that the dimly lit hospital room had turned hazy beyond recognition.

The next morning, Rachel was sitting in a chair near the hospital bed, wearing her own bathrobe that Esther had so graciously brought to her from home, when the nurse carried a large breakfast tray into the room.

"Good morning, Rachel," the nurse greeted her, though Rachel could make out little more than a filmy white shape.

"Gut mornin' to you," she replied, not able to determine where the coffee or juice or eggs or toast were located on the tray. She didn't feel much like eating anyway, so she sat silently till Mam and Esther began coaxing her to "just taste something."

"Honestly, I'm not very hungry."

"Ach, now, what a nice selection of things," Mam prodded discreetly.

"Looks mighty tasty to me, too," Esther said, getting up and picking up something on the tray—maybe a glass of juice or milk; Rachel couldn't be sure. "Here, why don'tcha just have a sip?"

Though she felt they were treating her like a reluctant toddler, Rachel went along with the suggestion, reaching out toward the shadowy figure. But she fumbled and missed making contact, and the glass crashed to the floor. "Oh, uh, I'm awful sorry."

"Rachel? What'sa matter?" Mam asked as Esther wiped up the mess.

"I guess it's my eyes . . . I've been havin' a bit of trouble, that's all."

"What sort of trouble?" asked Esther.

"Just some blurriness every so often . . . it comes and goes."

"Well, have you told the doctor about this?" Mam wanted to know.

Rachel sighed, feeling awful about the broken juice glass. And terribly uneasy having to answer so many questions. What she really wanted was to be left alone to grieve her husband and son. "I hate to bother anyone about it, really. Prob'ly nothing much at all."

But when the nurse came in to pick up the tray, Esther inquired anyway. "What could be causing Rachel's eyes to blur up?"

"Can you describe your symptoms, Rachel?" asked the nurse.

"I don't see so clearly anymore. Everything's all murky."

"Do you see light and shapes?"

"Jah, but it's a lot like lookin' through a cloud."

Esther spoke up just then. "Doesn't seem normal, her having foggy vision—not after a miscarriage, does it?"

"Well, I'll certainly mention this to the doctor," the nurse said. "He'll probably want to do a preliminary check on Rachel's eyes, then, if necessary, refer her to an eye specialist."

"Thank you ever so much," Esther replied.

When the nurse left the room, Rachel reached out for her cousin's hand and squeezed hard. "Thank *you*," she whispered.

The doctor wasted no time in coming. He marched into the hospital room carrying Rachel's chart, a stethoscope dangling around his neck. "I hear you're experiencing some eye discomfort."

"No pain, really. Things are just all blurry."

"Well, we can't have you going home like that, can we?" he said casually, lifting her left eyelid and flashing a pen light into it. "Just exactly how much can you see now?"

Rachel struggled to describe her vision loss as the doctor led her through a series of probing questions.

"I don't need to tell you that you've been through a lot, Rachel. You're still reeling from having witnessed something no one should ever have to see. You'll need time to recover."

Recover?

She couldn't see how she would ever recover from such a loss as this. And she didn't want to be reminded of the grim accident scene. No, she desperately wanted to forget.

"But what would cause her eyes to blur?" asked Dat, sitting on the other side of the room, pressing for more explanation.

"I couldn't say for sure, Mr. Zook, but from what Rachel has just told me, the disruption in her vision may be related to what we call post-traumatic stress."

"How long will it go on?" Dat asked, his voice sounded thinner now.

"My guess is no longer than a week" came the cautious reply. "Only in rare cases does it persist. But if it does continue, I'd recommend you see an eye specialist and . . . perhaps a psychiatrist who specializes in grief counseling.''

Rachel's vision was blurry, but she could see well enough to notice the nervous glances exchanged between Mam and Dat. Esther listened quietly, her gaze intent on the doctor.

He continued. "I'm confident that with love and support of those close to her, Rachel should recover very soon if this is, indeed, the reason.''

Rachel mentally replayed the doctor's strange description of her condition. It sounded as if he thought she needed a head doctor. *I'm not crazy*, she thought.

Dat and Mam quizzed the doctor for several more minutes before he left to make his rounds, and Rachel took some comfort in his comment that her eyes would likely return to normal soon.

No longer than a week. . . .

In all truth, she was so discouraged by grief and the suppression of dreadful memories, her eye problem seemed almost trivial by comparison.

Four

❖ ❖ ❖

The joint funeral for Jacob and young Aaron was delayed a full twenty-four hours, making it possible for Rachel, though sickly and sorrowful, to attend. Her parents and siblings—and Jacob's family—lovingly surrounded her. And there was Esther, attentive as ever.

Rachel needed help walking to and from the buggy and into the Yoders' farmhouse. There had been times after her hospital release when her vision actually seemed to be improving. Today, however, things were rather dim again.

A blistering sun beat down on the People, nearly two hundred strong, as they traveled for miles—most of them by horse and carriage—to gather at the farmhouse of Jacob's father, Caleb Yoder. The Yoders, both Caleb and his wife Mary, had wanted the funeral at home, due to the tragic nature of the deaths and the fact that it was a combined funeral for father and son.

"Has nothin' to do with us bein' Old Order," Caleb had assured her. "A home setting always makes for better." He said this with eyes hollow, his wrinkled face gray as death itself.

Rachel knew enough not to question, for Caleb Yoder was not a man to tolerate interference. And she wouldn't have thought of doing so anyway. Being submissive was a result of having been the last daughter in a string of siblings prob'ly. And one of the twelve character gifts her father liked to talk about. Benjamin Zook believed certain traits were handed down through all families, through the ages. "Old" gifts, he chose to call them. Values such as generosity, responsibility, serenity, and simplicity. And, yes, submission.

Three expansive rooms had been prepared by removing the wall partitions so the People could see the preachers from any corner. The air was thick with heat and humidity as folks gathered, sitting on closely spaced wooden benches the length of each room. Women sat on one side of the house, men on the other. A large number of Jacob's English woodworking clients and friends also showed up to pay their respects. The house was filled to capacity, chairs being added here and there at the end of a bench row, squeezing in an additional person wherever possible.

Rachel sat stone-still, facing the coffins—one large, the other heart-breakingly small—seated with her relatives, Jacob's and Aaron's closest kin. Her back to the minister, Rachel recalled the painful, nagging memory of how they'd scurried about that last morning. She held her daughter close, letting Annie lean back against her, careful not to bump the broken arm. Rachel was glad her little one was still small enough to hold on her lap this way. There was something comforting about embracing a child, and she thought perhaps it was because she had lost the tiny baby growing inside her.

While they waited for the service to begin, she struggled with her circumstance, wishing she could go back and unravel the hours, relive their last morning together. A thousand times a day she wished it.

What was it Jacob had said—that they had plenty of time? She dismissed her keen thoughts for now, till her dear ones were safely buried in the ground, though the tragedy was as real to her as the precious child in her arms.

The People waited silently, reverently, for the designated hour. Then the various clocks in the house began to strike nine times, and the first minister in a lineup of several preachers removed his straw hat. The others removed their hats in unison.

The first preacher chose a spot, standing between the living room and kitchen. Rachel didn't have to turn and try to focus her eyes on him; she knew the scene by heart, from having attended a number of traditional Amish funerals. It was her place to face forward, to keep her eyes, though cloudy and dim, on the handmade pine coffins.

"The gathering here today is an important one," the preacher began. "God is speaking to us—all of us—through the death of our brother and his young son."

Rachel listened intently, adjusting Annie's position on her lap. Her little daughter might never even remember this solemn day, but Rachel wouldn't have considered not bringing her.

The preacher continued. "We do not wish either our brother Jacob Yoder back into this life or his son, Aaron, but rather we shall prepare ourselves to follow after these departed ones. Their voices are no longer heard amongst us. Their presence no longer felt. Their chairs are empty; their beds are empty."

He expounded on the grimness of dying in one's sins, though Jacob Yoder had chosen that good and right path—the only way a just and upright Amishman could stand before God on the Judgment Day, assured of where he stood for all eternity.

Their presence no longer felt . . .

Rachel stared over Annie's shoulder, down at her own black dress and apron. It was a blessing in disguise that the Lord had allowed her to be this calm and sedate at Jacob's and Aaron's funeral. By not looking so much at the small coffin, slightly wider at the shoulders and narrowing at both ends, she was able to keep her emotions in check. Her firstborn lay silent and still inside that box, dressed in crisp white trousers and shirt. She had combed his hair gently, though she hadn't had the courage to push his little feet into the "for good" shoes before the funeral. Rather, she had kept the black shoes, putting them away in her own bedroom closet. There was something dear about the feet of a child. So Aaron would be buried stockingfooted, in clean black socks. Not something the Lord would mind, she was sure. To the contrary, she was almost positive her Aaron would be running barefoot in heaven—his father, too. It was what they were most accustomed to. Jesus would see to it that their feet were washed and cooled at the end of each day in Paradise.

As for the untimely deaths, she did not question God, for she had been taught to believe that His supreme will was above and over all. Yet the utter sadness had already begun to carve out a hole in her heart.

Their chairs are empty. . . .

The second minister stood to give the main address. "We come together this morning, united in spirit under the blessing of God, our heavenly Father, to bury our brother, Jacob Yoder, and his young son, Aaron Yoder." His words reverberated through the long front room of the farmhouse.

Rachel missed the spirit of her church. It was sadly absent here today, though she'd refused to insist on her opinion. Caleb and Mary Yoder had had their say as to the type of funeral service. Still, she would have been more inclined to have at least Aaron's service at the familiar meetinghouse, where she and Jacob and the children attended Sunday school and church, packed out each week with Amish Mennonite friends and relatives. By the looks of things, the folk had turned out strong for the somber occasion, despite the traditional service. She would not have been so bold as to request a separate funeral anyhow.

What's done is done, she determined, paying close attention to the Scripture reading from John, chapter five.

"'Verily, verily, I say unto you, the hour is coming, and now is, when the dead shall hear the voice of the Son of God: and they that hear shall live.'" The preacher read through the verses until he came to the thirty-fourth. Then he began to expound on the reading, saying that the text spoke of passing from death unto life.

When the People turned and knelt at their benches, Annie folded her hands in spite of the arm splint and leaned in close to Rachel. As the preacher prayed, Rachel realized for the first time since the accident that her knees were awful sore. She kept her eyes closed for the lengthy rote prayer, yet she reached down and pulled her dress away from her legs, touching curiously the blistered areas on her knees. She wondered how on earth the welts had gotten there, what had happened to cause them, having no recollection of ever scraping her knees . . . or burning them.

The People stood for the benediction. There had been no music, which seemed awful empty and even more sorrowful to Rachel. She loved the rich harmonies of a cappella singing. Another sigh slipped from her lips, and she hoped Jacob would forgive her for not having the sort of funeral service he would've preferred. When it came time for her to pass on to Glory, she would try to explain the sticky situation to him. Jacob would understand, she knew.

It was then, thinking of heaven again and the hope of seeing her husband someday, that her tears began to flow, unchecked. Try as she might, there was no stopping them, even as the preacher recited the ages of both Jacob and his son—the only formal obituary statement given at the end of the funeral.

"Jacob Yoder's memory is a keepsake, as is his son's. With that we cannot part. Their souls are in God's keeping. We will have them in our hearts," the preacher said finally.

We always miss what we don't have. . . .

Rachel wept silently, accompanied later by uncontrollable sobs at the graveside service. Quickly, little Annie was surrounded by Rachel's mother and sister Elizabeth as the pallbearers began to shovel gravel and soil, filling the graves.

The thumping sounds of the dirt hitting the coffins made Rachel quiver, and she was grateful for her mother-in-law and cousin Esther, who held on to her, standing with their arms linked through hers as the traditional hymn was read and the men removed their hats one last time.

That night Rachel slipped Aaron's black shoes under the covers, on Jacob's side. Then, when she got into bed, she reached over and held the shoes near her heart, thinking of the little barefoot boy with the bright, happy eyes . . . and his fun-loving father. She knew she would not speak of this deed to anyone. Not to Esther or to Mam.

It was her secret. Hers and God's.

Five

❖ ❖ ❖

In the days that followed, Rachel was beholden to Esther for her care and supervision. Overwhelmed with despair, she slept around the clock some days, only to become too dizzy to stand when awake. So Esther cooked and cleaned and sewed, doing the things Rachel would normally have done if she'd felt strong enough.

By the end of the week, Rachel got out of bed due to sheer will-power, helping with a few chores indoors. She was grateful, especially, for Esther's loving attention to Annie and for her cousin's fervent prayers for Rachel as well.

"Can Esther stay with us, Mamma?" Annie asked as Rachel tucked her in for the night.

"'Twould be nice." She sat on the edge of the bed, touching her little one's brow. "But Esther and Levi must return to Ohio soon to care for their own family."

Annie was silent for a moment, her blue eyes the color of the summer sky. "Is God taking care of Dat and Aaron?"

"Jah, my *liew*—dear one, the Lord is taking gut care of them." She kissed Annie's cheek and held her in her arms long past the child's bedtime.

"I miss Dat and Aaron," Annie said, sniffling.

Sighing, Rachel fought the urge to weep. "I miss them, too, but we'll see them again in heaven."

After tucking Annie into bed, Rachel stood in the doorway, lingering there. Often, since the funeral, she'd questioned the wisdom of leaving her child to fall sleep alone. As hard as it was for *her* to sleep peacefully, she hoped Annie wasn't struggling that way, too.

"Don't think twice about bringing Annie into your room to sleep once in a while," Esther said when Rachel mentioned it to her privately. "The dear girlie's feeling awful alone in the world—and she's still just a baby, really. She needs to know that her mamma doesn't mind sharing that great big bed."

"She's blessed with many relatives who love her," Rachel added quickly, knowing full well that Annie would never want for fellowship. She would grow up completely loved and looked after by the whole of their church community, Beachy Amish and Old Order alike.

"Annie is not to be pitied," Esther commented. "And neither are you. Pity parties can only last so long, then one must put a hand to the plow, so to speak. Life goes on."

For you it does, Rachel thought, suppressing the idea as having been spiteful, then immediately asking the Lord to forgive her. She knew her cousin meant well. There was no doubt in her mind about Esther's motives.

Once Esther and Levi had departed for Ohio, Rachel allowed herself to confront the extent of her loss, agonizing over the guilt that hung weighty in her mind. She sat up in bed each and every morning, greeting the dawn just as the sun was about to break over the horizon, though not without tears. Her outward mourning was her soul's response to the pain in her heart—especially at night—though she purposely put on a smile for Annie during the daylight hours.

Mam seemed wise to what was happening, though, and one morning while helping Rachel with her gardening, Susanna broached the subject. "Your eyes are forever swollen and red. Are you crying for Jacob and Aaron or for yourself?"

Rachel felt her heart constrict, wondering how to explain the pain inside. The guilt was present with her always, along with such feelings of worthlessness. "I should've been the one to die," Rachel replied, tears choking her voice.

Mam's expression was filled with tender concern. "It is not for us to question God's ways."

"Jah" was the only answer she could give, though she thought of telling her mother the truth, that she wished she might die even now.

"We must trust the Lord to work His will among us," continued her mother. "Each of us must come to accept it in due time."

In due time . . .

Rachel's eyes filled with tears. "It is not so hard to submit to the will of God." She paused, having to breathe deeply before she could go on. "It's knowing that things might've been—*should've* been—different, oh, so much different." She could not attempt to describe the ongoing gnawing in her heart, that she felt responsible for the accident. Accepting the deaths of her beloved ones would have been far easier had it not been for that singular fact.

"Time to move on, Daughter, past your agony," Mam said, though such a pat answer was nothing new. "For Annie's sake, you must."

In essence, her mother was saying the same things Esther had spoken to her before leaving—time's up on the pity party! Say what they may, she wondered how either of them might be coping with the unexpected and violent deaths of their own husbands. Cautious not to brood, Rachel pushed the thought out of her mind and prayed for grace to bear the loss, as well as the correction of her elders.

She trudged up the back steps and into the kitchen, carrying a large plastic bowl filled with mounds of leaf lettuce and a fistful of new carrots from the garden. Her vision shifted and the room seemed to float about. Things cleared up again just as quickly, and she wouldn't have thought much about it, except the English doctor had said all this would go away. *Less than a week*, he'd said. Well, now here it was two full weeks since the accident, and her eyes were still playing tricks on her.

She and Mam began to chop green peppers and cucumbers for a salad. But when the fuzziness returned, Rachel was hesitant to say anything, holding her knife silently. The blurring lasted much longer than usual, and she pushed the knife down hard into the butcher block, waiting. The longer the fog prevailed, the harder her heart pounded. Still, she attempted to stare down at a grayish-looking green pepper.

"What's wrong, Rachel?" Mam said. "You all right?"

She blinked repeatedly, trying to shake off whatever was causing the frustrating distortion. Steadily, she directed her gaze downward at the knife she knew was in her hand and the pepper on the cutting block, willing herself to see clearly, to focus on the shapes. Hard as she tried, she was engulfed in a misty world of grays and whites.

"Rachel?" She felt Mam's hand on her arm. "You're pale. Come sit for a spell."

She released the paring knife and followed Mam to the rocking chair—Jacob's favorite. She thought if she did as Susanna suggested and sat there, relaxing and fanning herself for a bit, everything would be all right soon enough.

Sitting in the hickory rocker, she realized how very dismal things had been these past weeks, pining for Jacob's jovial nature. Oh, how she missed his hearty laugh! She missed other things about him, too. But it was the thought of his good-natured chortle that brought more tears.

"Ach, Rachel, must ya go on so?" Mam was saying. Yet she stood behind the rocking chair, stroking Rachel's back.

"I hafta tell you something, Mam," she said softly, wishing she knew where Annie was just now. She felt the swish of her mother's long dress against the chair and heard the patter of her bare feet against the linoleum floor.

Susanna seemed to understand, taking her hand and squeezing it. "If you're thinking of your miscarriage . . . well, believe me, I *do* know how you're feeling, Rachel." And she began to explain the empty sadness associated with the loss of a baby born years ago.

Rachel listened, though she continued to weep. "What I want to tell you isn't about the baby I lost," she whispered. Then, pausing, she asked, "Is Annie anywhere about?"

"Why, no, she's outside playing in the side yard—out diggin' in the dirt. You know, the way she and Aaron always . . ." Susanna stopped. "What do you *mean* asking if Annie is near? Are ya still having trouble with your eyes?"

"Well, right now, I can't see much of anything."

"I think we oughta have Blue Johnny come and take a look at you. He's been known to heal a wheal in the eye within twenty-four hours," Mam was quick to reply.

Rachel flinched at the mention of the pipe-smoking hex doctor. "I don't believe there's anything growin' in my eye, Mam. It's just that my spirit's awful troubled . . . I can't shake it off."

"If I told your pop this, he'd say you're crying your eyes out. Plain and simple. That's just what he'd say."

Rachel blinked again and again, holding her hands out in front of her now, turning them over, trying to see them clearly. Still, she could not make out even the contour of her own thin fingers. "What's *really* causing this?" she pondered aloud. "Do you believe what the hospital doctor said?"

"You witnessed a *greislich*—terrible thing, Rachel. And if you ask me, I don't think it's something we oughta be foolin' with. Why don'tcha let me contact Blue Johnny?''

"I'm sorry, Mam, but no.'' She felt herself straighten a bit, determined not to let Susanna get the best of her, in spite of her distorted sight.

True, the powwow doctors were much cheaper—most of them worked for nothing—that was common knowledge, and most of the time they were quite effective. Still, she hadn't made a practice of calling on them and wasn't much keen on starting now.

Mam's voice rose in response. "I wouldn't be so quick to turn up my nose at the powwow doctors. 'Specially if you keep havin' trouble.''

Rachel leaned her head against the rocking chair. "I think I'd rather go back to an English doctor, if I go to anyone. Besides, Jacob . . .'' She paused. "Well, if my husband were here, he'd prob'ly tell me to stay far away from Blue Johnny.''

"But Jacob's not here to see what you're goin' through, Daughter. He'd want what's best for you, jah?''

What's best for me . . .

She figured it was just as well she hadn't told Mam about the sharp, penetrating pain that came sometimes at night, just after she lay down to sleep. It came most often with the sound of horses and carriages *clip-clop*ping up and down the road. And it came with the recurring noise of an automobile motor. She feared that one day the pain might come and stay put, with no relief ever again.

Sighing, she got up from the rocking chair, her vision having cleared up somewhat, enough to find her way to the back door and call Annie inside for lunch.

Truly, she might not have gone to bed so early that evening— might've put off giving in to fitful sleep—had she known the needlelike affliction would grow nearly unbearable.

She sat up the next morning to watch the sun rise, the very dawn she had always greeted with joy. In an instant, the tormenting images returned, and she cried out in agony, renouncing them. "No! I *will not* see these things. I will *not* see!'' She repeated it again and again, closing her eyes, shutting out the persistent mental pictures as she rocked back and forth.

How long she remained crumpled in her bed, she did not know. But when at last she opened her eyes and ceased her weeping, the earliest rays of morning had turned to a dark and dreary shade of charcoal.

She swung her legs over the side of the bed and stood up, groping her way across the room to the window. She and Jacob had stood and looked out together on this very spot, their last hours together. Yet no longer could she make out the rows of neatly tilled farmland beyond. So cloudy were the trees, the four-sided birdhouse, and even the neighbor's silo that they might not have existed at all.

The darkness persisted as she attempted to dress, then brush and part her long hair. No longer could she see the golden brown hues of her tresses. Neither outline nor color was visible in the mirror. Only murky, shadowy images shifted and waved, taunting her.

She had to call on past memory to place her prayer veiling in the correct location. Fear and panic seized her as she let her fingers guide the *Kapp*. Jacob and Aaron were never coming back, no matter the amount of hoping. Her life as Jacob Yoder's wife was a thing of the past. *This* was her life now. She'd had everything—*everything* right and gut and lovely—and all of it had been swept away in a blink of time. Why, she did not know, nor did she feel she could question the Almighty. Yet in the quiet moments—just before falling asleep—she had allowed herself to think grievous thoughts of anger and fear, sinful as they were.

Feeling her way along the wall, she stumbled back to the bed. This, the bed she and Jacob had shared as husband and wife. She dared not permit herself to recall the love exchanged here, nor the dreams spoken and unspoken. Denial was the only way she could endure the heartache of her life.

She made an attempt to smooth out the sheet and coverlet, to fluff the lone pillow. But the fiery pain in her head stabbed repeatedly, and in the depths of her troubled heart, she perceived that the light had truly gone from her eyes. Even as tears spilled down her cheeks, she resigned herself to the blindness, that self-imposed haven where no painful image could ever intrude.

"What's done is done," she whispered.

The Postcard

Part Two

Midway this way of life we're bound upon,
I woke to find myself in a dark wood,
Where the right road was wholly
lost and gone. . . .

DANTE

The Lord is slow to anger, abounding in love
and forgiving sin and rebellion. Yet he does not leave
the guilty unpunished; he punishes the children for
the sin of the fathers to the third and fourth generation.

NUMBERS 14:18, NIV

Six

❖ ❖ ❖

Two years later

Philip Bradley checked into the first Amish B&B he could find off the main drag. Somewhat secluded and picturesque, Olde Mill Road was the kind of setting he'd wished for—made to order, actually.

The Lancaster tourist trade was like a neon sign, attracting modern-day folk who longed for a step back in time to the nostalgic, simple days—by way of shops offering handmade quilts and samplers, crafts and candles, as well as buggy rides and tours of Amish homesteads.

But it was the back roads *he* wanted, earthy places where honest-to-goodness Amish folk lived. Not the establishments that lured you with misnomers and myths of painted blue garden gates and appetizers consisting of "seven sweets and seven sours." Above all, what Philip wanted was to get this assignment researched, written, and turned in. Bone-tired from the pace of recent travels, he thought ahead to his writing schedule and deadlines for the next month.

At twenty-seven, Philip was already weary of life, though he wouldn't have admitted it. Even as a youngster he had been reticent to call attention to himself—the private side of Philip Titus Bradley, that is. His public image was a different story, and though he had risen to the top tier of feature writers for *Family Life Magazine*, he clung hard to his privacy, guarding it judiciously.

Sitting on the four-poster canopy bed, Philip stared out the window at a cluster of evergreens. The open space to the left of the pines captured his attention. In the distance, he spied a white two-story barn, complete with silo. A gray stone farmhouse, surrounded by tall trees, stood nearby. He wondered if the place might be owned by Amish. His contact, Stephen Flory of the Lancaster Mennonite Historical Society, had informed him that nearly all the farms in the Bird-in-Hand area were Amish-owned. The minute it was rumored that an English farm might be for sale, a young Amishman was sure to knock on the door, inquiring about the land and offering the highest bid.

Philip raked his hands through his thick dark hair, gazing at the streams of sunlight pouring through the opening in the tailored blue drapes, its gleaming patterns flickering against a floral wallpaper of blues and greens. The large desk had caught his eye upon entering the room, and now as he studied it, he fancied that if he were ever fortunate enough to own such a piece, it, too, would be made the focal point of its surroundings. Though such a colossal desk would be out of sync with the contemporary decor of his upper Manhattan apartment.

It was odd how the desk, centrally situated on the adjacent wall, seemed remarkably fashioned for the room. Lauren would *not* have agreed, however, and he chuckled at the fortuitous notion. Thank goodness they'd parted ways long before this present assignment. Were they still dating, she would be totally disinterested in his Lancaster research. On second thought, she might have made some crass remark about the back-woodsy folk he planned to interview.

Lauren Hale had been the biggest mistake of his adult life. She had completely fooled him, displaying her true colors at long last. To put it bluntly, she was an elitist, her intolerant eyes fixed on fame and fortune.

Nor had Philip measured up to Lauren's expectations. She had had a rude awakening; discovered, much to her amazement, that beneath his polished journalistic veneer, there was a heart—beating and warm. And no amount of wishful thinking or manipulation could alter that aspect of his character. So thankfully, he had won. He had let her have her way that final night, let her break up with him, though he'd planned to do it himself had he not been so completely exhausted from the recent European trip.

Philip observed the antique bow-top bed. King size. *Handmade canopy*, he thought, noting the delicate off-white pattern. Thanks to his vivacious niece, he knew about stitchery and such.

Young Kari had pleaded with him to let her accompany him on this trip. She'd giggled with delight when he called to say he was flying to Lancaster County. "That's Dutch country, isn't it?" she exclaimed. "And aren't there horses and buggies and people dressed up old-fashioned?"

"They're Amish," he'd told her.

"*Please*, take Mom and me with you, Uncle Phil. We'll stay out of your hair, I promise."

Regrettably, he had to refuse, though it pained him to do so. He made an attempt to explain his deadline. "You wouldn't have any fun, kiddo. I'll be busy the whole time."

"Won't you at least *think* about it and call us back?" She was eager for some fun and adventure, though she needed to stay close to home, follow through with her homeschooling—the sixth-grade correspondence course her parents had recently purchased. Public school just wasn't what it used to be when *he* was growing up in New York City. He had tried to get his sister and brother-in-law to see the light and allow him to assist them financially to get Kari into one of the posh private schools, but to no avail. They had joined a rather evangelical church and gotten religion, or the equivalent thereof, thus their desire to protect and groom Kari in the ways of God. Which wasn't so bad, he'd decided at the outset. After all, it hadn't been very long ago that he himself had knelt at the altar of repentance and given his boyish heart to the Lord, though too many dismal miles and even more skirmishes with life had since altered his spiritual course.

Before hanging up the phone, he'd promised his niece another trip instead. "Some other time, maybe when I go to London, I'll take you and your mother with me . . . when I'm not so tired."

"Tired of living and scared of dying?" She was a spunky one. "Okay, Uncle Phil, I'll take whatever I can get . . . if that's a promise. About London, I mean."

In no way did he wish to think ahead to the overseas assignments. Not then and not now.

He knew if he gave in to the abrasive feeling behind his eyes and the overall lassitude of the moment, he might not awaken in time to conduct any research or write a single sentence. Which now, as he considered the idea, seemed an exceptionally grand way to dispose of three days.

It was the notion, however, that he might miss out on the candlelight supper included in the night's lodging that caused him to rouse himself and forego the possibility of a snooze. Mrs. Zook, the hospitable owner's wife, had promised pork chops fried in real butter. Bad for the arteries but tasty on the tongue. The woman, who'd insisted that he call her Susanna, had welcomed him with such enthusiasm that he wondered at first if he were the only guest staying the night.

He discovered, soon enough, that the historic dwelling was solidly booked through October. "Most of the smaller rooms, that is," Susanna Zook had told him. Such was the Zooks' Orchard Guest House. A popular B&B indeed.

In dire need of a shower, he pushed himself off the comfortable bed, noting the handmade Amish quilt. He carried his laptop across the room to the handsome desk. The rolltop portion had already been pulled back, as though a welcome sign were attached. He was glad for the desk's spacious accommodations and would use every inch of space it could afford.

After setting up the computer, he turned his attention to unpacking. He would stay three days, depending on how solid his research connections were, though he'd called ahead to the Lancaster Mennonite Historical Society, setting up a specific appointment with Stephen Flory, a research aid, who, in turn, had promised a private interview with a "talkative Amish farmer." In addition to that, the owners of the B&B certainly seemed like a good possibility. They appeared to be retired farmers, though he couldn't be positive. There was something intriguing about their gracious manner, their kindly servant mentality. Only hardworking farmers emulated such character traits, or so his grandpap had told him years before. Grandfather Bradley had informed him about farm folk back when Philip was a boy, visiting his daddy's parents in southern Vermont. What a spread they had just outside Arlington, not far from Norman Rockwell's former home.

On first sight of Grandpap's place, his seven-year-old heart had actually skipped a beat or two. He immediately envied anyone who lived under a sky that blue and wide. And what enormous trees! Not a single towering building to block the sunlight, no blustery canyons created by skyscrapers that swayed in the wind. His heart felt free on Grandpap Bradley's land.

Philip's grandfather had built the hideaway in New England as a summer cottage, on the steep bluffs overlooking the Battenkill River. The five-room house possessed all the knotty-pine appeal a city boy might imagine, though prior to that first summer, Philip had had no knowledge of vacation spots of this sort. Especially summer places where lofty trees swept the expanse of sky instead of finger-thin structures—ninety or more stories high—and vegetable gardens were planted firmly in rich mahogany soil instead of imported box gardens on top of drafty penthouse roofs.

And there were llamas. Grandpa had a penchant for the long-
necked, hairy creatures, and though they were gentle enough, Philip
never quite got over the feeling, even as a teenager, that he ought to give
the animals a wide berth. He'd read that llamas sometimes spit if they
were aggravated or apprehensive. Young Philip could hardly begin to
imagine the slime of a llama's spittle on his face. Such an experience,
he'd decided early on, was to be avoided at all costs.

The oversized cottage was a replica of surrounding farmhouses,
though less opulent and more quaint, in keeping with the unpretentious
charm of the red Chisselville Bridge, the covered bridge not more than
a mile away. Philip particularly enjoyed the miles of hiking trails and
wilderness cross-country skiing near his grandparents' home. In summer, he pretended to be an explorer in those woods; in winter, just the
opposite—he launched search-and-rescue missions for imaginary folk.

His grandmother's African violets were always on hand to cozy up
the southern exposure of the large breakfast nook. From everything he'd
read about Amish kitchens, the one set back in the hills of Vermont
might have easily rivaled any Old Order kitchen, complete with buck
stove and long wooden table and benches. He was yet to find out, of
course, because the modern and convenient kitchen where Susanna Zook
prepared supper, was, no doubt, a far cry from the turn-of-the-century-
style kitchens he hoped to discover.

After he showered and dressed, he wandered downstairs for afternoon tea. Passing the parlor area, he caught sight of a young woman
dressed in a long gray dress and black apron, dreary as any mourning
clothes he'd ever seen. Yet it was the color and appearance of her hair
that caught his attention—subtle flaxen rosettes mingled with light
brown tones, parted down the middle and pulled back in a low bun,
partially hidden by a white see-through head covering. She sat motionless, her hands folded gracefully in her lap. He thought at first that she
might be asleep but saw that her head was erect, eyes open.

A small girl, wearing a long dress of pale green, her honey brown
hair wrapped in braids around her head, came running past him and
into the room. She was as cute as she was petite, and he was compelled
to stand still just to see what she would do next.

Sweetly, the young woman turned and reached up to touch the
child's pixielike face. "Ach, Annie, it's you."

"Jah, it's me, Mamma. Do you want somethin' to drink?"

"A glass of water will do," the woman answered, her hand still resting on the child's cheek. "Thank you, little one."

The encounter was like none Philip had ever seen. Yes, he'd felt the hand of his own mother on his brow, but to stand back and observe such a tender gesture from afar was pure poetry.

Moments of compassion were worth watching—savoring, too—even if one felt entirely removed from those involved. He had experienced a similar emotion the first time he'd seen a boy and girl holding hands as they ran down the steps of the Eighty-sixth Street subway station, laughing as they tried to squeeze through the turnstiles together. Moments like that, he'd decided, were priceless in the overall scheme of things.

Even if it were only his innate journalistic curiosity, he found himself drawn to the scene, especially to the woman, though her child intrigued him as well. Not one to gawk, however, he turned and made his way to the common area, featuring a bonnet-top highboy with slipper feet, as well as two sofas and several wingback chairs. A primitive butter churn stood sentinel in one corner, near a wood-burning fireplace.

Susanna Zook, the plump Amish hostess and owner's wife, had encouraged him upon his arrival to make himself at home. "Feel free to read, relax, and mingle with the other guests," she'd said. So he located the pleasant room, complete with floor-to-ceiling bookshelves built in across one wall and a marble-topped coffee table with ample reading material—all this within yards of a well-appointed dining room. He congratulated himself on having made an excellent choice for his stay, sight unseen.

A young couple was curled up on a settee near a fireplace marked by eighteenth century delft tiles, quietly exchanging intimate glances. He greeted them, then settled down in a chair to thumb through a Lancaster tourist guide.

"Oh, there you are again, Philip." He looked up to see the round and jubilant face of his congenial hostess. "Would you like something to drink?" she asked. "I can get you coffee, tea, a soft drink, or a glass of milk."

"Black coffee, thank you."

"Don't forget to save room for supper, served promptly at five o'clock, two nights a week—Mondays and Wednesdays," Susanna replied, including the couple in her remark. "You're always welcome to help yourself to snacks, before and after supper. Anytime, really." She turned to a corner table, arrayed with a variety of cheeses and fruit, chocolate chip cookies, and scones. "Homemade specialty breads are also handy, if you know where to look for them." She opened a cabinet door under the table, producing a wooden tray of additional delicacies. "Now, let me get you that cup of coffee. Black, you say?"

He nodded, sinking back into the chair just as the little girl he'd seen in the parlor came scurrying through the room, carrying a tall glass of water.

"Careful not to spill," Susanna called to her, then turning to Philip, said, "That's Annie, our six-year-old granddaughter. She's busy as a honeybee."

"I can see that." As they engaged in small talk, he listened carefully, paying close attention to the inflection of the woman's unique speech pattern. "Does Annie live with you?" he asked when there was a lull in the conversation.

"Both she and her mother do."

He waited, thinking that an explanation might be forthcoming. Was Annie's mother divorced, a young widow . . . what? But no clarification was given, and Philip decided it was none of his business anyway.

The Amishwoman turned toward the kitchen, and it was then he noticed the midcalf length of her blue cape dress and black apron, similar to the style of the younger woman's. She wore, also, the accompanying white netting head covering made familiar to moviegoers by Hollywood's portrayal of Lancaster County Amish. The see-through cap was referred to as a prayer covering by non-Amish folk; a Kapp or veiling by the Amish themselves. That much he knew.

He had a strong desire to get chummy with some Amish folk; maybe even volunteer to help pitch hay somewhere. Simple enough. It was what he was paid to do, his *gift*, or so his young niece had mischievously informed him last time he'd visited. Yet he knew he'd have to temper his questions, choose each one carefully, especially those he asked the Amish directly. He had been warned by his sister, who had been corresponding with an Amish pen pal near Harrisburg for several years now. Drained and wondering why he'd even agreed to this assignment, he now wished he had grilled Janice in more detail. Mainly, though, he had been caught up in his own affairs—too busy as always to delve into his only sibling's casual friendships.

"Most importantly," Janice had advised, "you must prove that you're a trustworthy sort of guy before *any* Amishman will give you the time of day. And I'm not kidding.''

He had appeased her by listening with one ear, thinking that when he arrived in Lancaster, there would certainly be folks who'd be willing to talk. For money, if for no other reason. But now that he was here, had been offered a sampling of the conservative lifestyle, had met Susanna and observed Annie with her mother, he was having second thoughts about the silver-tongued approach. Maybe his sis knew what she was talking about. Lest he start out on the wrong foot, maybe he should mention to Susanna or her more reticent husband that Janice was close friends with one of *their* relatives. After all, weren't all Amish connected by blood or marriage? Yes, maybe some old-fashioned name-dropping would open a few doors for him.

He wracked his brain, trying to remember the name of the Harrisburg woman, Janice's pen pal. Was it Stoltzfus? Something fairly uncommon.

Scanning the room, he observed the brown tufted velvet chair and settee. Not exactly the most vigorous choice of color for such a grand room, considering the large tan hooked rug beneath his feet. Although coupled with the backdrop of yet another floral wallpaper pattern, the earthy tones actually worked.

He was beginning to wonder if Plain folk purposely chose to decorate their homes a whit better than they adorned themselves, though the bright blues and purples he'd seen several Amishwomen wearing as they scurried about Bird-in-Hand Farmers Market weren't entirely unattractive. At least, he hadn't seen anyone else sporting the dismal gray that Annie's mother wore as she sat alone in the parlor, completely still.

He took note of the pink- and cream-colored hurricane lamp. Antique, no doubt. Most everything in the house was of the Victorian era. That, or New England Country. Susanna surely had an affinity for old things, same as his sister. He wondered how the two might get along if ever they were to meet.

Culture clash, he thought, suppressing the urge to laugh. Then again, they had the potential to get on famously, especially since it was Janice who'd told him in no uncertain terms to slow down and live. The Amish seemed to know how to enjoy a slow-paced life. ''You're rushing through life, Philip, and it makes no sense . . . especially since you seem so absolutely miserable,'' Janice had said.

''But I *need* to keep busy,'' he'd responded, a bit put out. ''I function best that way." He'd laughed, but he knew the truth. If he stopped working so hard, stopped filling up every second of his life with appointments and interviews and social events, he'd have to think. About the state of his life, for instance.

"I'd rather die than sit around twiddling my thumbs," he'd tossed off, hoping to end the uncomfortable Q and A.

"So you're addicted to work, is that it?" Janice never quit. She always pushed until he clammed up. "You know what I think? I think you're running from yourself, and if you slow down, you're afraid you'll have to take a long, hard look at who Philip Bradley really is."

Nailed again.

Truth was, of course, he *did* long for a simpler, slower life. But it was easier, by far, to keep running on this insane but safe treadmill called life, going faster and faster, never allowing himself to stop.

Susanna startled him slightly as she came with a generous mug of steaming coffee on a saucer. "Here we are. Feel free to take it to your room if you like." She glanced about her. "Or you may stay here . . . for as long as you wish. We also have a number of footpaths, leading to the orchard and beyond, to Mill Creek. It's a wonderful-gut afternoon for a walk."

"Thank you, I'll keep that in mind . . . and I'll look forward to supper as well." He offered a smile to the friendly hostess, and to the cozy couple who paid him no mind.

"I think you'll be mighty pleased with the pork chops." Susanna's smile was warm.

"Yes, I'm sure I will," he agreed, heading toward the stairs and to his room high above the parlor—that room where he had witnessed the sort of thing most writers would give their eyeteeth to see. A heartfelt, unposed portrayal of love between two human beings. Little Annie and her mother, no doubt.

He thought of his photographer friend on staff at the magazine. Henning would travel any number of miles if assured of such a tender photo opportunity. The vision of the child and mother was implanted in Philip's memory, and as part of his research, he decided to write the description, along with his emotional response to it. In fact, as he rehearsed the maternal scene, he realized with sudden enthusiasm that he was eager to begin.

Mighty happy, indeed, he thought, letting the quaint expression sink in. The Pennsylvania Dutch twaddle might take some getting used to, but he would be mindful of his sister's admonition and be a trustworthy kind of guy. The instant this assignment was finished, he would think about taking a much-deserved vacation. Janice would be happy to hear of it. So would Kari, who might even be allowed to sneak off with him to Vermont and hide out at Grandpap's old summer cottage. A pleasant thought, though he doubted he could ever bring himself to pull off such a fantasy.

First, though, the assignment—Plain folk and their family traditions. Tonight at supper, he would get his research rolling by saying all the right things. And hopefully he could get Susanna Zook talking. Maybe Benjamin, too.

Then he remembered Susanna's adorable granddaughter. *"Busy as a honeybee,"* the woman had said of the child.

Annie's perfect, he thought.

Seven

❖ ❖ ❖

S usanna poked a sharp meat fork into the pork chops, testing them for tenderness. "We'll have us a right fine supper tonight," she said, nearly singing the words. "Wouldja care to join us, Rachel?"

Rachel, who was counting out the utensils with Annie's help, shook her head. "Nothing's changed, Mam. I don't eat with our guests at breakfast, so I wouldn't feel comfortable joining in at supper. You know how I feel about eating with strangers."

"Strangers—*so en lappich Wese*—such a silly matter! Our guests are no longer strangers once they hang their hats in the vestibule." She sighed, a trifle exasperated.

Rachel wore a pained expression. "I'm all right, just keepin' to myself."

Susanna feared she'd hurt her daughter's feelings. "Well, then I'll leave it up to you." Which was pretty much the way things turned out most of the time—leaving Rachel to wallow in her grief. Had it not been for Annie, full of vim and life, Rachel might never wander any farther than their property, in either direction. She wondered, too, if her daughter would ever think to be wearing dresses of blue or purple again, instead of the humdrum gray of mourning. 'Course if she couldn't see, then what did it matter?

"Annie and I will have supper in the parlor, with the door closed," Rachel said softly. "It's all right with you, ain't so, Mam?"

"No, Daughter, it's *not* all right." She was surprised at herself, revealing her true feelings at long last. She probably should've said something a year or more ago, after the appropriate time for mourning had ceased. But Rachel's grieving seemed endless, and she worried that her daughter was downright content with it.

The peculiar symptoms of lingering blindness bothered her almost as much as her daughter's indifference to life. She viewed Rachel's condition as something other than a true affliction. A Philadelphia doctor—an eye specialist—had conducted a battery of tests, even attached sensors to Rachel's head. Measured her brain-wave activity no less, and had found nothing physically wrong. Not mincing words, he'd said there was no medical basis for Rachel's inability to see. According to the tests, her brain was actually registering sight!

He'd termed Rachel's problem a conversion disorder—a hysteria of some sort—like hysterical blindness, which the specialist said sometimes comes on a person who has witnessed something so appalling that the mind chooses to block out visual awareness. He had also mentioned studies of refugees from Cambodia, mainly women, who, after being forced to watch the slaughter of their families, experienced one form of this hysteria or another, including temporary blindness, deafness, or paralysis. "I've heard of cases lasting as long as ten years or more," the English doctor had told them, "but that's very rare."

Susanna sighed, thinking back to that trip to Philadelphia and the specialist's peculiar comments. Honestly, she *had* suspected something mental, and to compound her suspicion, Rachel continued to shy away from talk of powwow doctors, which wasn't the only thing her poor, dear daughter was disturbed about these days. She also avoided talk of the accident that had taken her husband's and son's life, even to the point of excusing herself and fleeing the room if the slightest comment was made. And she'd shielded Annie from the truth, too. Rachel sidestepped, no matter what, the possibility of stirring up perplexing memories in both herself and her little girl. Emotionally wounded, Rachel was a bit *ab im Kopp*—off in the head. And though time seemed to have run out for Rachel's sight ever returning, Susanna hadn't given up hope of a full recovery. One way or the other.

Overall, her daughter was a joy to have around. In fact, inviting her and Annie to move in with them two years ago was the best thing Susanna and Ben could've done for their daughter, granddaughter, and for themselves. Rachel cheerfully pulled her weight with the housework, especially helping with the numerous loads of laundry. She was a good cook, too, and helpful in the vegetable and flower gardens close in toward the house. She was always more than happy to lend a hand; a diligent worker, no getting around it. But the spring in her step was long gone.

Rachel reminded them frequently to avoid the Crossroad, and Susanna understood, for she was loath to go near it as well. This meant they had to spend precious time driving horse and buggy out of the way, going west on Route 340—away from the accident site—then south on Lynwood Road to attend church and to visit several of Susanna's sisters, cousins, and Lavina Troyer, too, for quilting frolics and such.

Avoiding the Crossroad was one of the few things Rachel requested. It made no sense, really, especially since she couldn't see much of anything. But they humored her—at least on that matter. Something else bothered Susanna to no end. It was Rachel's insistence that she attend her *own* church—the Amish Mennonite church she and Jacob had chosen—though there were times when it simply didn't suit. So more often than not, Rachel had to be content with Old Order preaching services at one aunt's house or another.

Despite the random inconveniences, Susanna had reconciled herself more and more to doing certain things Rachel's way. When all was said and done, wasn't it the least she and Benjamin could do for their disabled daughter?

"Mam?" Rachel's voice interrupted Susanna's brooding. "You're ever so quiet."

"Jah, I 'spect I am," she replied, wiping her hands on her apron. "I didn't mean to snap at you. Honest, I didn't."

Rachel fidgeted, gathering up the dinner plates. "'Spose I had it comin', really."

Annie glanced up; her blue eyes blinked several times thoughtfully. Then she got up quickly, calling for Copper, who came bounding into the kitchen through the doggie opening in the screen door. The girl and the dog scampered outside.

"Don't go off too far now," Susanna warned. "Supper's almost ready."

"Ach, she needs to run a bit," Rachel said. "Annie's been cooped up all day."

"And what about *you*, Daughter?" Susanna stood at the back door, watching the early autumn haze as it settled over the apple orchard. "Why don'tcha go out and sit in the sun for a bit? Fresh air will do you gut."

Rachel sighed. "Maybe tomorrow."

Susanna turned, watching her daughter place freshly laundered cloth napkins, dinner plates, and the supper silverware on the wooden tray. Then, slowly, Rachel moved toward the dining room, shuffling her bare feet across the floor, feeling her way as she'd come to do.

Maybe tomorrow . . .

Susanna had tired of Rachel's *alt Leier*—same old story. Would tomorrow ever come? she wondered. And if so, what would it take to move Rachel past her complacency?

Somewhat annoyed, she opened the screen door and went out to sit on the flagstone patio in the waning sun, watching Annie and their lively pet run back and forth through the wide yard. They chased each other around and through the oval gazebo.

There was a hint of woodsmoke in the air, and Susanna relished the scent, breathing it in. A flock of birds flapped their wings high overhead, and she suspected they were making preliminary plans to head south.

She delighted in the hydrangeas just beginning to turn bright pink, spilling long and bushy into the yard beyond the house. Soon they'd bronze with age as September faded. The lawn was still green, but she could see it beginning to lose its lush color, leaning toward autumn dormancy. When had *that* happened? she wondered. The circle of seasons was evident all about her, an inkling of the fall brilliance—reds, oranges, and golds—to come.

Annie was smack-dab in her springtime, while Susanna and Benjamin were fully enjoying the early winter of their lives.

But Rachel . . . where was *she*? To look at her, you'd think she was older than all of them put together! Yet Susanna forced herself to dwell on the bright side and silently rejoiced that her widowed daughter possessed a resolute spirit. The girl was ingenious when it came to needlework, especially crocheting. Why, she'd designed the prettiest pattern for several of the bow-top canopy beds upstairs and seemed right joyful in making them. When the womenfolk gathered for apple picking or canning, Rachel put herself in the middle of things, always a smile on her face. It was at such times Susanna suspected the key to bringing Rachel out of her shell was keeping her hands busy. 'Least then her mind couldn't torment her so.

"Come along now, Annie," she called, chuckling at the girl's antics. So like her mother she was, playing and enjoying the out-of-doors. Or how her mother *used* to be, was more like it.

Rachel had always been the last one to come dragging into the house when the dinner bell was rung, back at the old homestead. As a girl, she'd rather have stayed outside, even all night long, than come inside to a hot house in summer, or, as she liked to say, to the *dunkel Haus*—dark house in winter. Young Rachel had decided that houses were dismal places of retreat compared to the shining meadows and ample pastureland surrounding the large farmhouse. Even now, Susanna surmised that Rachel missed the farm where she'd romped through the fields of her childhood, helping her older brothers and sisters work the soil and bring in the harvest.

Getting up, Susanna called to Annie again. "Bring Copper with you, please. Time to wash up for supper."

"Already 'tis?" Annie asked, eyes wide. "Seems like we just come out here."

"Jah, I 'spect it does." And she headed into the house.

Susanna found Benjamin washing up as she hurried into the kitchen. "Smells gut, jah?" she said, greeting him.

"It's bound to be *appeditlich*—delicious—if *you're* doin' the cooking." His smile stretched across his tawny, wrinkled face. He wore his best white shirt and tan suspenders, all dressed up for supper. It was his gray hair that looked a bit oily, and she suspected he'd been out working all afternoon in his straw hat, tidying up the front lawn. The man never tired of odd jobs, whether it was around the B&B or over at the old homestead, helping his sons work the land.

"We're full-up in the guest quarters tonight," she told him, turning her attention to the meal at hand.

"Yes, and I do believe we've got ourselves a big-city reporter in residence." Benjamin reached for the towel and dried his hands.

"A reporter? *Here*? Are you sure?"

He smiled, slipping his arm around her waist. "Sure as the sugar maple turns crimson. I sniffed him a mile away. Philip Bradley's the name, and you best be watchin' what you say at supper, hear?"

Ben oughta know, she thought. He'd smelled a rat before, not from visitors up north or anywhere else for that matter. But she'd seen his God-given gift in action many a time. It was the gift of discernment, all right. He could pretty much tell who was who and what was what before anyone fessed up to much of anything. And Susanna, well, she liked it just fine that way. Jah, she'd be mighty careful what she said from now on.

'Twould never do to have some dark-headed English reporter

snooping around here, living under their roof and writing stories that weren't one bit true—or slanted at best. Wouldn't do, a'tall.

They'd had more than their share of false reporting. Amish were forever being featured in one newspaper or another, especially after that drug business broke last summer. But for the most part, far as she was concerned, the reporting was heavy on exaggeration and sensationalism. She'd never known a single Amish teenager doing drugs of any kind. *Net*—never! 'Least not in their church district. English newspapers were cooked up by many a misguided writer, hoping to turn a few heads and make a dollar. When it came right down to it, a body had to stick to what they believed—wrong or right. And that was that.

Eight

❖ ❖ ❖

Philip stared at his laptop computer screen, scanning the description he'd written before supper. *Before* the cordial hostess—Mrs. Susanna Zook—had decided to give him a rather cold shoulder. At first he had just assumed that her detached manner during the meal was due to the fact that both she and her husband were busily engaged in conversation with a number of other guests, three couples from the Midwest who seemed rather ignorant of the Plain lifestyle and who fairly dominated the evening's chatter. This turn of events had suited him fine because he merely had to listen to the responses given by Susanna and Benjamin, though occasionally guarded, to learn tidbits of Amish tradition.

Interestingly, the most fascinating aspect of the evening had been the grand entrance made by Annie Yoder, introduced by Benjamin as their "littlest helper." She was as candid and bright as his own niece had been at the coy age. However, he did not hold out false hope of making friends with the Zooks' granddaughter. The B&B owners had become somewhat cautious around him, and the obvious shift in their demeanor had him utterly intrigued.

First thing tomorrow, he would wander down the road to the village shops—see if he could eavesdrop on some of the locals prior to his formal afternoon interviews. In leafing through the tourist handbook, he'd noticed that several Bird-in-Hand stores—among them Fisher's Handmade Quilts and the Country Barn Quilts and Crafts—offered genuine Amish quilts, wall hangings, and other handcrafted items. Folks at country stores often stood around, conversing while they drank coffee or sipped apple cider. Most likely, there would be some Amish person he could connect with in the immediate area *before* his interview with

Stephen Flory's contact, unless, of course, he was able to get things back on an even keel with Susanna Zook.

What *had* he said or done to make the Zooks so suspicious?

———————

"Ach, you're not sittin' very still," Rachel chided her daughter. She let her fingers run down the long, silky tresses, weaving Annie's hair back and forth, doing her best to make a smooth braid.

"It's awful hard to sit still, Mamma."

Rachel understood. "'Twas hard for me, too, at your age."

"It was?"

"Oh my, yes." She remembered the many times her mamma had asked her to stop *rutschich*—squirming. "That was long before you were born," Rachel added.

"How old were you when it started . . . the rutsching, I mean?"

She had to laugh. "Well, ya know, I was born with the wiggles most prob'ly. Was forever running through your *dawdi* Benjamin's farmland—makin' mazes in the cornfields an' all. Just ask him."

Annie must've moved again because Rachel lost hold of the braid. "Ach, where'd you go to?"

"I'm right here, Mamma. Right in front of you." There was a long pause, though Rachel heard Annie's short, breathy sighs. "How much of me can ya see just now?"

A pain stabbed her heart. "Why do ya ask?"

"'Cause I wanna know."

Rachel didn't know how to begin to tell anyone the truth, let alone her own little girl. And her heart thumped against her rib cage, so hard she wondered if Annie might be able to see her apron puff out.

"Mamma? Won'tcha tell me what you see?"

She moaned, resisting the question, not wanting to say one word about her blindness. "I . . . it's not so easy to tell you what I see and what I don't," she began. "If I lift my hand up to your face, like this—" and here she reached out to find Annie's forehead, allowing her fingers to slip down over the warm cheeks and across to the familiar button nose—"if I do that, I can see you in my own way."

"But what if I got up real close to you, like this," said Annie. "*Then* could ya see my face without feeling it?"

Sadly, Rachel knew enough not to try. "Sometimes I see light flickers, but that's only on good days. It doesn't matter, really, how close you sit to me, Annie; I don't see any part of your face at all.''

"What about my eyes, if I make them great big, like this?"

Rachel suspected what her daughter was doing. "Are your eyes as big as moons?'' she asked, playing along.

"Jah, very big moons.'' Annie giggled.

"And are they big and beautiful *blue* moons?'' she asked quickly, hoping to divert Annie's attention.

"How'd ya know, Mamma? Jah, they're blue!'' Annie was in her lap now, hugging her neck. "Oh, Mamma, you *can* see me! You can!''

She waited for Annie to settle down a bit. "No, I really can't see your face. But I *do* know how beautiful and blue your eyes are. I saw you the night you were born, and I saw you every day of your life until . . .''

"Every day till what, Mamma? Till the accident?''

Rachel sucked in air suddenly, then coughed. Someone had reminded Annie about the Crossroad, about that horrible day. Surely they had, for her daughter, at only four years of age, would never have remembered without someone prompting her.

Who?

It was then that she actually tried to force herself to see, that very moment as she pulled her darling girl into her arms, holding her close. She tried so deliberately that it hurt, like knowing there was surely a light at the end of a long, long dark tunnel. Knowing this only because people told you it was there, and trying so hard to see it for yourself.

Leaning forward . . . straining, with Annie still tight in her embrace, Rachel strove to catch a glimpse of the minuscule, round opening—the light—at the end of the blackness, *her* blackness. At the end of the pain.

"Why can't you see, Mamma?''

"I . . . well . . .'' She couldn't explain, not really. How could she make her daughter understand something so complicated?

"Mamma?''

She felt Annie's tears against her own face. Oh, her heart was going to break in two all over again if she didn't put a stop to this. "Now, ya mustn't be cryin' over nothing at all,'' she said, stroking the tiny head.

"I won't cry,'' Annie said, sniffling. "I promise I won't, Mamma, if *you* won't.''

Again, the pain cut a blow to her heart. How did Annie know about Rachel's tears? Had she heard what her grandfather used to say, back before they'd come to live here? Was Benjamin still telling folk that his daughter had cried her eyes out—that's why she couldn't see? 'Course, no one in their Plain community really and truly believed what the English doctor had said—not anymore anyway. He'd said Rachel's sight would return quickly, but it hadn't. No amount of wishing or hoping could make it so.

"Will you promise, Mamma?" Annie said again.

"I can't promise you for sure, but I'll try at least."

"That's wonderful-gut. Because we've got us some pumpkins to pick tomorrow. Won'tcha come help me?" Annie wrapped her slender arms around Rachel and hugged her hard.

"Maybe I will," replied Rachel, hugging back. "Maybe tomorrow I will."

———

Philip was contemplating his interview questions, crafting them wisely as his sister had recommended, even getting them down in longhand for a change. Stopping, he stared at the desk, tinkering with his pen. He noticed the many cubicles and cubbyholes, realizing that most men probably would not have concerned themselves over the size of a compartment to store paper clips, staples, and the like. But he was one to enjoy a systematic approach to order, and the current location of his computer work station and filing cabinets in his home office were not conducive to anything akin to organization.

In the process of opening and closing the various drawers and investigating the nooks in the magnificent desk, he acquired the notion that his system was too limited, at best.

Where can I locate such a desk? he wondered. Almost immediately he decided against inquiring of Susanna or Benjamin Zook. Perhaps someone at the Country Store might be able to direct him to an antique auction or estate sale. Yes, that's what he might do after his interviews tomorrow. The plan of action, though rather simple, gave him a surprising surge of energy. Not to say that he wasn't still thoroughly worn out, but the idea *was* a grand one.

Just as he thought he might head downstairs to have another look at the tourist guide before turning in for the night, he tugged on a rather flat, thin drawer. No more than two inches deep, it was ideal for fine stationery or a slim stack of computer paper.

The drawer was entirely stuck. He tried opening it again. It didn't

move one iota. More struggling brought no result. The drawer was simply not going to budge.

"That's strange," he said aloud. Then, getting down on his knees,
he peered under the desk, trying to see what was causing the drawer to
malfunction, if anything.

The ceiling light, along with the several lamps on either side of the
desk, cast a dense shadow on the underside of the desk. So much so that
he got up and went over to the reading lamp on the table beside the bed
and unplugged it. He carried it over and plugged it into the outlet near
the desk, then removed the lampshade so that the light bulb was
exposed. He felt like a Boy Scout—though he'd never been one—on an
adventure of some sort.

Squatting down, he shone the light directly under the desk, into the
inner recesses, hoping to see what was jamming the drawer. As he held
the light steady, he spied something sticking out beneath a seam in the
wood. He reached for it, holding the lamp in the other hand. Just what
it was, he couldn't be sure. But he was determined to find out.

Reaching up, he made a jiggling motion, discovering that the item
was heavier than typical writing paper, more like card stock. He peered
closer, trying to see how to dislodge it.

Getting up, he placed the lamp carefully beside his computer, then
began to work on the narrow drawer again, wiggling it from this angle.
"Out with you," he grumbled impatiently, and carefully, little by little,
he coaxed the drawer out of its too-snug spot.

Once free, the drawer was clearly empty. But it was within the far
end of the slot that the problem lay. He reached his fingers into the
narrow mouth and tugged.

The culprit proved to be a wrinkled plain postcard, slightly torn and
yellowing around the edges. The stamp had begun to fade, but the postmark—May 17, 1962—was clear enough. So was the writing, though the
message looked to be a foreign language. What it was he did not know,
since they were words he'd never seen. Possibly German. Could it be
that this was Pennsylvania Dutch, the language of most Old Order
Amish?

Philip was curious, but he had more important work to accomplish
here than obsessing over a crumpled postcard. "Ach, such awful important work," he said, mimicking some of the phraseology he'd heard
repeatedly during supper.

Then an idea came to him, possibly just the thing to get Susanna

Zook talking again. He would produce the postcard tomorrow, sometime prior to breakfast, before the other guests came downstairs. Perhaps in a private encounter, she might even offer to decipher the message, though he would never be so forward as to ask.

More than likely, the postcard belonged to the Zooks. Something
they might be quite glad he had uncovered, or perhaps it was worth
nothing at all. Yet he wondered how long the card had been lodged in
the drawer. Even more fascinating—how had it found its way into the
dark confines of the old desk in the first place? In his line of work, he
was constantly asking the "Five W's" of good reporting—Who? What?
Why? Where? and When? *How* was never to be over looked, of course.

Nine

❖ ❖ ❖

P hilip was restless.

The night was exceptionally warm for mid-September, though too early to be classified as Indian summer, since the first frost had not yet occurred. He rolled out of bed to open the window, then switched on the ceiling fan, hoping the night breeze and the whirring sound might help him drift off again. Not accustomed to sleeping in total silence, he searched the room once again for a clock radio, anything for a little background noise—something to soothe his wakefulness.

There was not even an alarm clock, let alone a radio. And no TV. Such were the heralded benefits of a back-roads bed-and-breakfast—peace and tranquillity accompanied by nighttime silence, broken only by a multitude of night insects, including some loud crickets.

Philip lay on the bed, concentrating on the vigorous chirping outside the window. Listening to the rhythm in the crickets' song, he noticed after a while that the various cadence patterns gradually began to correspond with each other. He'd read of this phenomenon, kindred to clock pendulums on the same wall aligning themselves over a period of time.

For one ridiculous moment, he thought of Lauren Hale. How fortunate for him that they had parted ways. To think that he might have begun to match the ebb and flow of *her* spirit and general approach to life was appalling and made him roll out of bed again to shake himself. He should've known better than to get involved with a stubborn, self-absorbed young woman.

Thoughts of the ill-fated romance made him more unsettled than before, and he decided to turn on the light, thoroughly disgusted with his insomnia. Perhaps his body was too tired, too wound up to relax; that had occurred on any number of occasions in the past.

Pacing the floor, he caught a glimpse of the postcard on the right side of his laptop, where he'd placed it before retiring. He picked it up, studying the steady hand of the writer. The addressee was a Miss Adele Herr, and though the street number and name were illegibly smudged, the city and state—Reading, Pennsylvania—were remarkably clear. The message was signed simply, *Gabe*.

Post-office issued, the card seemed in fairly good shape, but then, it may have been kept from the light for who knows how long. Nevertheless, he sat at the desk and scrutinized the handwriting, the unfamiliar prose stirring his interest.

He leaned back in the chair, his long legs sprawled out before him, taking in the country-red apothecary chest on the opposite wall, the wide-plank pine floors scattered with braided oval rugs, and the tall highboy. Even the ceiling fan had the appearance of being bent with age. If he hadn't known better, he might've suspected that he'd been tricked somehow—transported back in time. He wondered if, on some subconscious level, the discovery of the postcard had indeed roused him from slumber—the soul-deep slumber of spirit that had marked him for too long, despite the frenetic rhythm of his days.

———

Rachel turned in her sleep, aware that a window was being opened in one of the guest quarters at the far end of the house. In her drowsiness, she reached for her daughter, who often slept next to her these lonely nights. Annie had a small single bed across the room but didn't often start out the night sleeping there. Annie much preferred falling asleep next to her mother, and Rachel didn't mind at all.

"Annie?" she whispered, sitting up.

"I'm here, Mamma" came the reply from the foot of the bed. "It's too hot to sleep."

"Well, let's open the window, then."

"Open them *all* up," Annie suggested.

"Gut idea." Getting up, Rachel counted four short steps to the first window. In an instant Annie was next to her, pushing against the wooden panel, helpful as always. "There, that's better, ain't so?" she said, breathing in the clean night air.

They stood in the window, enjoying the breeze as it sifted through the screen and caressed their faces. "Sometime I wanna sleep outside all night long. Beside the creek, maybe," Annie said. "What do ya think of that?"

Rachel chuckled softly. "Well, I must admit that I had the same bee in my bonnet back when I was your age."

"So then you might let me fall asleep under the sky so I can listen to the hoot owls and the crickets and—"

"Careful not to raise your voice," she interrupted her daughter. "We have guests in the house tonight."

"Sorry, Mamma. But we have guests in the house most *every* night, except come winter, ain't so?"

"Jah, and it's a wonderful-gut way for all of us to make a livin' these days. Besides that, we can be a blessing to tourists."

"Jah, the tourists," the girl whispered.

Rachel hoped her little one didn't resent the never-ending flow of B&B guests. "We have much to offer our English friends."

"'Tis what Dawdi Ben says, too." Annie reached for Rachel's hand and led her back to bed. "I'm gettin' sleepy now."

"*Gut Nacht*, dear. See you in the morning."

Annie was silent for a moment, then she said, "Will ya, Mamma, really? Will ya honestly *see* me? There ain't nothin' wrong with your eyes, is there?"

"Well, where'd you get a silly idea like that?"

"Joshua says."

She knew well and good young Joshua, Lizzy's middle son, had probably overheard some adult talk here and there. The boy was too rambunctious for his britches. "What else is Joshua saying?" she asked, nearly in a whisper.

Annie was suddenly quiet.

Rachel felt awkward, pushing for answers from one so young. "Annie? You all right?"

"I surely don't wanna tell a lie, Mamma."

"Well, then, we best drop the whole thing right now," she said, slipping into bed, leaving the sheet and coverlet off for now. 'Least till the breeze from the window cooled things off a bit.

But she was wide awake. Couldn't sleep a wink, even long after Annie's breathing became slow and even. Poor, dear child . . . what she'd had to suffer. All because of an unfortunate accident that might easily have been avoided if they hadn't had to take the shortcut. *If only*

I hadn't slept through the alarm, she thought.

Lying there in the stillness, Rachel realized that she'd never forgiven herself. She felt sadly responsible for Jacob's and Aaron's deaths, and the truth of it bewildered her daily. As for her inability to see, she had rather adapted to her level of blindness these two years, feeling her way around the boundaries of her familiar world—the realm of her lonely existence. Truth be told, she felt right safe in the cocoon she'd spun for herself, but it broke her heart not to see her only child growing up. There were times when she missed roamin' freely outdoors, taking long walks on deserted roads, strollin' through orchards and meadows, seein' the new baby lambs in the spring. On occasion, she actually questioned her resolve not to visit Blue Johnny or other sympathy healers, her desire to see springin' up in her more and more these days.

A waft of cool air blew in the window, and as she listened to the sounds of the night, she noticed that the crickets' chorus seemed noisier than usual. Had it not been for the fact that there were several roomers in the house, she might've sneaked downstairs and sat out on the back patio, inhaling the rich, spicy fragrance of the humid night. Recently, on two separate occasions—though Mam would've been downright surprised—Rachel had slipped out into the night, unable to sleep due to the warm temperatures. And missing Jacob. Tonight she might've risked doing so again, but Dat had warned that a New York reporter was snooping around—staying right here under their noses, of all things. Fact was, Dat had gotten wind that a well-respected tour guide in Lancaster had made plans to take the big-city fella to have a confidential chat with a local Amishman, come tomorrow afternoon.

"Best be watchin' yourself . . . what you say, anyhow," Dat informed her before supper.

'Course she agreed to be cautious, though it wouldn't require much of a change on her part. Occasionally she helped out in the Gift Nook, their gift shop, an addition on the north side of the house. She preferred her role as the silent helper, and Dat and Mam pretty much allowed her to live her life that way. Looking after Annie was her one and only aim.

Turning in bed, she faced the window and wished she might dream of Jacob holding her or whispering adoring words in her ear. Jah, she would like that right nice. But her dreams weren't always romantic ones. Frequently, there were taunting nightmares in the middle of the night— dreadful visions of things that never, ever could be. Jumbled-up, hideous images that made no sense at all.

She knew that on the other side of those grisly pictures was her sight—her full and clear vision—but she was unwilling to allow herself to walk through the foggy maze to get to the sunlight.

Dozing off, she listened to the night sounds, and they mingled together with her thoughts till the crickets seemed to chirp in unison *Jacob . . . Jacob . . .*

Ten

❖ ❖ ❖

P hilip rushed through his usual early-morning routine—shaving, showering, dressing—eager to chat with either Susanna or Benjamin before breakfast. He tucked the postcard into his shirt pocket and headed downstairs.

"Good morning," he said, offering a broad smile as his hostess met him in the common room.

"Didja have a good night's sleep?" Susanna inquired, not waiting for his reply. Instead, she turned her attention to arranging some croissants and doughnuts on a tray.

"I slept quite well, thanks." He did not say that he'd lost several hours in the *middle* of his sleep, however.

She turned and glanced out the window. "Looks like it'll be a right nice day today."

"Yes." *Right nice indeed*, he thought, wondering if now was a good time to show Susanna the postcard he'd found buried deep inside the old desk.

"Will you be needing anything besides coffee just now?" she asked, clearly in a hurry to get back to the kitchen and breakfast preparations.

"Coffee's fine, thanks."

"Would there be anything else, then? There's sticky buns and things on the table." She gestured toward the tray behind him.

Before she bolted, Philip decided to plunge in. "I, uh, found something stuck in the desk in my room." He reached into his pocket and pulled out the postcard. "This was caught behind one of the drawers."

She took the card, glancing at it casually. "Well, for goodness' sake." She pushed her glasses up, tilting her head back, and began to read. "'My dearest Adele . . .'" Her voice trailed off, and though her lips continued to move silently, her eyes began to blink. "Oh . . . uh, that's all right. You'd better keep it." She pushed the postcard back into Philip's hand.

"Is something wrong?" he asked, concerned that her face had grown quite pale.

She shook her head back and forth, muttering something in what he guessed was Pennsylvania Dutch. Her voice had turned raspy. "You'll hafta excuse me. I've got sausage in the oven." And with that, she left the room.

He stood there, holding the innocuous postcard in his hand, and stared at the handwritten note. *My dearest Adele . . .* Why would a message that began so beautifully affect someone in such a strange manner? He really didn't know what to do with the postcard now that she had rejected it. But his curiosity was definitely heightened, and he decided the missive legitimately belonged to him since she'd actually invited him to keep it.

Hurrying back upstairs to his room, he copied the message as best he could, in case Susanna might have second thoughts. He wanted to know more; wanted to know what had disturbed her enough to stop reading and toss the postcard back in his face.

His mind was whirling, and he made a quick call on his cellular phone. "Stephen?" he said when his Mennonite contact answered. "Thought I'd let you know I'm in town."

"When did you get in?"

"Yesterday afternoon. I'm in Bird-in-Hand, at the Orchard Guest House B&B. Do you know the place?"

"Oh yes. Great spot to get away from it all, I hear."

His gaze dropped to the postcard. "Thought I'd check in, make sure we're still on for this afternoon."

Stephen chuckled. "I've got a live one for you. You're going to like Abram Beiler. He'll answer all your questions."

"Sounds good. Let's meet for lunch—on me."

"I can get away by twelve-thirty or so. You're not far from Plain and Fancy Farm, just down the road, east on Route 340. You'll see it on the left side—can't miss it—just before you get to Intercourse."

"Good enough." Then impatient to know, he said, "I was wondering if you happen to understand Pennsylvania Dutch?"

"Well, I don't speak the language, but Abram does. What do you need?"

He mentioned the postcard briefly.

"Sure, Abram will help you out. And if he can't, there are several translators here where I work."

"That's good to know. See you soon." Philip put the postcard and his own written copy of it in his briefcase, then went and stood in front of the window, looking out at the expanse of Amish farmland in the distant morning mist. Closer in, toward the area of the backyard, he noticed for the first time since he was a boy that there were water droplets shining atop the grass, some creating tiny rainbows in the early-morning light.

On a sudden impulse, he stooped down and got his nose up next to the screened-in open window, inhaling the pungent smells, a hint of spice in the air. His view encompassed the apple orchard, with a glimpse of the creek beyond. Mill Creek, it was called, according to his map. He would have to go exploring sometime before he checked out. His sister would be surprised to hear that he'd actually taken some time for himself on this trip.

Getting his fill, he left the room and stood out in the hallway, leaning his ear toward the stairway, listening for the other guests. It would be wise to wait until there were plenty of people gathering for breakfast before heading back downstairs.

He thought he probably looked quite peculiar standing there, eavesdropping that way, especially to the little Amish girl who came hurrying toward him.

"Hullo, mister."

"Hello, Annie."

Her eyes popped open wide. "How do you know my name?" she asked in an ecstatic whisper.

"Your grandmother told me, that's how," he whispered back, just as enthusiastically. "What do you think of that?" He had the urge to reach out and poke her arm playfully, but he resisted, lest he scare her off.

Her face was bright with a smile, and today she wore a tiny white head covering similar to Susanna's adult-sized one. "I never heard nobody talk like you do."

"Never met anyone from New York City, then, did you?"

She shook her head slowly, and just the way she did, Philip remembered her grandmother, Susanna, doing the same thing, the same way, after reading the postcard. "Are you from New York?" asked Annie, still grinning.

"Born and raised in the Big Apple. I'm what you call a city guy, but"—and here he squatted down, placing himself at eye level with the darling child—"I have to tell you a secret."

"A secret? I like secrets." Her light brown eyebrows rose higher.

"Then I'll tell you." He lowered his voice. "I'm not much for big cities. They're noisy and busy and—"

"Why'd you come here?" she interrupted. "To find bigger apples?"

He couldn't help himself—he laughed. Such an adorable child. He would have six or seven little girls just like this if ever he found the right woman to marry. "I came to meet *you*, Annie."

"You did?"

"Yes." He straightened now to his full height. "Would you like to go down to breakfast with me?"

"Okay, but I can't eat with you. You're a guest, and I live here all the time." She turned and bounced toward the stairs. "Just follow me, mister."

"My name is Philip," he said, jumping at the chance to introduce himself. Might be beneficial later.

"Mr. Philip," she replied. "Mamma would want me to call you *Mister* first."

"That's okay with me." And he followed her down the steps, congratulating himself on having made a new friend. A special little friend indeed!

Rachel waited till after all the guests had cleared out of the breakfast area before asking Dat if she could talk to him. "It oughta be somewhere private," she said.

"Well, then, we'll walk outside. How's that?" Benjamin said, finding her walking cane.

She didn't have the energy to resist his suggestion. After all, it had been weeks since she'd ventured farther than a few short walks with Annie.

Dat guided her to the back door, and once they were outside, she brought up the topic that had troubled her. "I don't rightly know how to begin."

"It's not necessary to mince words with me, Rachel."

Fresh smells of autumn filled the air, and she remembered her promise to Annie to help gather pumpkins. "I oughta make this short," she continued. "But I'm thinkin' that besides young Joshua, someone might be giving Annie an earful—about certain things, you know?"

"Well, now, if you mean the accident, I think I know exactly what you're askin'."

For a fleeting moment, she wished she could see Dat's face, witness the way the smile lines had carved deep furrows at the corners of his mouth, see the sincerity and goodness in his eyes. Surely he had not been the one to tell Annie. Ach, surely not.

"She's still so young, ain't? And a mite small for her age, too," Rachel added.

"Jah, she's that. Still, it's time you sit her down and talk things out with her, tell how her father and brother died . . . from your point of view. Best not to keep her in the dark any longer."

She wondered if he'd said it that way—*in the dark*—to drive home a point. But she thought better of it. 'Twasn't her place to be questionin' her father. After all, she was under his protective covering and guidance as a single woman, in spite of the fact that she was raising a child.

"So *has* Annie overheard things from you and Mam?"

"Not overheard . . . outright *told* her," Dat replied, his voice stern yet soft. "If it makes you uneasy, then I 'spose you'd best be tellin' your daughter what *you* remember."

She sighed. "I don't remember anything. Not one thing." It was absolutely true, and with all her heart, she wished he hadn't questioned her. "In all of two years, nothin's changed, Dat."

"I don't doubt you. You've always been a woman of integrity, pleasing to the Lord. Bless you for that. But I beg to differ with you on Annie bein' talked to about the accident and all that it summons forth." Benjamin Zook had spoken, and there would be no pushing the issue. His word stood, and she resigned herself to respect and conform to his opinion.

They walked a bit farther, down the gravel footpath through the orchard. She breathed in the sweet aroma around her, felt the warmth of the sun on her face, and wondered why she didn't come outside more often.

Dat guided her, turning her around at the end of the walkway, and step by step they headed back to the yard and to the house. "It's gut to see ya come outside for a spell," he said. "The sun and air's gut for you."

"Mam and Annie are always saying the same thing."

"Well, it's high time you listened," he said, chortling.

"Jah, you're right about that." They laughed together, heading inside again. Rachel felt no animosity toward her father for bringing it up, but she wondered how to approach the subject of the accident with Annie. And when?

———

Susanna was upstairs, stripping the sheets from the beds in the southeast room—Philip Bradley's room. She knew enough not to meddle in his business, wouldn't think of poking around in a paying guest's personal affairs. Still, she was mighty tempted to go a-fishin' in the dresser drawer, searchin' for that there postcard. Why on earth hadn't she taken it and ripped it up when she had the chance?

Ach, she'd behaved so . . . *ferhoodled*, her sisters would be sayin' if they knew what she'd done—and right there in front of that reporter-writer fella, no less. Benjamin would be terrible disappointed in her, too. Thing was, she had no plans to tell anyone of the postcard from that lunatic uncle of hers. Best if Gabe Esh had never been born Amish, let alone to be found writing such things. No wonder the Old Order had had to treat him like a shunned man—and this before he'd ever joined church, though at nearly thirty, his kin had perty much given up anyways. Well, she wasn't gonna let this keep on a-botherin' her all the live-long day.

Now . . . where would a big-city reporter put a thing like an old postcard? She honestly didn't want to go a-lookin' for it, but the more she thought of it, the more she knew she oughta at least try and retrieve it. And the sooner the better.

First place she looked was in the trash can near the desk, though she had no real hope of finding anything. Truly, by the curious look on Philip Bradley's face, she 'sposed he might just go off and ask someone to translate the message on the postcard for him. 'Course, then again, she easily could've misread his expression. She stood up and took a deep breath, deciding it was best to just forget the whole thing. Surely there was nothing to worry about anyhow.

Hastily, she put fresh sheets on the bed, dusted the furniture, and dry-mopped the floor. Rachel could finish up in the bathroom, replace the old soap and soiled towels with fresh, and wipe down the shower.

Her arms loaded up with sheets, she ran into Annie in the hall. "Mammi, Mammi, I know a secret!" the little girl said.

"Oh, is that right?" she muttered, hoping that whatever her granddaughter had to say wouldn't take too awful long.

"Mr. Philip wants to be a farmer, I think. He don't like city noises with big apples and he—"

"Who?"

"You know, that tall New York fella . . . with the funny-soundin' talk." Annie's face was alight with glee.

"You were talkin' to Philip Bradley?" she broke into the prattle.

"He's real nice, Mammi. Honest, he is."

She wondered what else *Mister* Philip had told the child. "Why don'tcha help me get these sheets downstairs," she said, wanting to change the subject.

Annie giggled, playing horsey with the tail end of one of the sheets. "I'll help you. Giddy-up!"

She didn't say it, but she wondered how long before one of them—either Benjamin or herself—would have to ask Annie not to talk so openly or get too chummy with the English guests that came their way. Especially those that came a-callin' from the newspapers and whatnot all.

Eleven

❖ ❖ ❖

Philip spent part of an hour at the County Barn, which was in reality a renovated tobacco shed on an Amish farm. The place still had that faint, sweet pipe-smoking odor. He looked around for a while, paying more attention to various British tourists than to any one item in the entire shop.

Next, he stopped off at Fisher's Handmade Quilts and, for the first time, actually took notice of the intricate patterns and highly colorful pieces that went into making an Amish quilt. He thought again of Kari and felt bad that he had rejected his niece's plea to accompany him here. Sure, she and Janice would have had a good time—he would've seen to it—but he wondered how things might've turned out with them having to tag along to his interviews and all. Too late now.

The restaurant was humming with tourists. Philip registered his name with the hostess, waiting for Stephen Flory. He reached inside his sports jacket and felt the postcard there, while around him sightseers chattered about candle barns and basket lofts. The recent drug bust, involving two young Amishmen, seemed to be the biggest buzz on visitors' lips.

He had questioned Bob Snell, his editor, when given this assignment, asking why a follow-up feature on the drug incident wouldn't be a good idea. "Amish family traditions—that's what I'm after," Bob had insisted.

So Philip's story was to be a "soft" spread, covering the customs and rituals of the American Old Order family unit. He liked the idea of focusing on Christmas and other holiday traditions, though he'd read that the Old Order bishops didn't encourage putting up trees or stringing up colored lights either inside or out, steering members away from worldly holiday merriment. In fact, the common practice of exchanging gifts was largely ignored in some church districts, except, of course, in the case of small children. Gift giving was especially impractical among families with many children.

He thought of Annie and wondered if she might tell him what gifts she had received for Christmas *last* year, though he couldn't count on having another opportunity to converse with her. Philip had noticed the guests at breakfast, all of them eager to hear more about Amish life. Some of them actually seemed interested in quitting their day jobs and moving to the community. One woman said she'd like to talk with an Amish elder about how to join the church.

He thought it a bit boorish of the woman, talking that way, though Susanna didn't seem flustered by it. In fact, she seemed genuinely interested in helping the woman understand the transition involved. "Going Plain ain't so easy for outsiders. Most *Englischers* who come our way, thinking they're ready to join church, last, oh, a couple of months, if that. Some fit in better than others, though, so it's hard to know for sure who'll keep their vow and who won't."

The thoroughly modern woman's spirits had not been dampened one iota by Susanna's comments, and he'd heard her tell another guest after breakfast that she was very serious about becoming Plain. "I can't wait for someone to teach me to quilt—that's going to be lots of fun."

Lots of fun . . .

He couldn't imagine the woman even remotely fitting into a work frolic, or so the Amish called their quilting bees. She had fake fingernails as long as any he'd seen, airbrushed hot pink and silver with gemstones glued to the tips. How did she expect to be able to produce the tiny stitches required to create the colorful, expensive quilts hanging in all the tourist traps around Lancaster? He wanted to ask her if she was willing to abandon her personal glamour—nails, lipstick, and dyed hair—for the good of the Amish community. However, he thought better of it and kept quiet. Yet he wondered about Susanna's comment—*Some outsiders last only a couple of months.*

What made the difference? Was it background that made it easier for some folk to "fit in better than others"? And what of the baptismal vow? Did modern folk just assume they could make a haphazard promise to God and the Amish church, only to break it if things didn't work out? Something akin to modern-day marriage vows, he supposed.

"Excuse me. Are you Philip Bradley?" A tall blond man in his mid-thirties approached him with a warm smile.

"Yes, I am. And you must be Stephen Flory."

They shook hands in the crowded entrance to the dining room. "A popular place," Philip commented, glancing around.

"You should see it in the summer. Lancaster is swarming with out-of-state folks. It's one of the top five tour-bus destinations. Isn't it amazing, the draw the Amish have?"

Philip nodded. "I read somewhere that one tourist actually thought the Amish were actors, hired by the county to pull in tourism dollars."

Stephen laughed. "You'd think folks would be more savvy. But then, if you've never seen the likes of horse-drawn buggies and mule-powered plowing, I guess a person might wonder."

Philip heard his name being paged, along with several others. "Our table's ready," he said, falling in step with the other man. "After that hearty breakfast Susanna Zook served this morning, I must confess I'm not very hungry."

"Susanna's an excellent cook, I hear."

"Aren't most Amishwomen?" Philip said, following the restaurant hostess into the large dining room.

After a light lunch and some preliminary talk—a few basic questions from Philip regarding the Amish—they rode in Stephen's car to New Holland, a seven-mile trip north of Intercourse.

"I wasn't sure what to expect when I arrived here," Philip admitted. "If it hadn't been for a quick phone chat with my sister, I'm afraid I would be even more ignorant of Amish ways. I thought I was coming to research a people who embraced a Quaker-like religion, but I'm finding out there is much more to them."

"They live out their faith daily," Stephen replied. "It's a lifestyle . . . a total culture. But they'd be the first to tell you they aren't perfect."

They pulled into a dirt lane and spotted a man who had to be Abram Beiler, sitting on the L-shaped front porch. A wide straw hat sat atop his hoary head, and he wore a black vest over a long-sleeved white shirt. His gray-white beard was long and untrimmed.

"Looks like Abram's ready for Sunday-go-to-meeting," Stephen commented, turning off the ignition and straightening his tie. He turned to Philip, lowering his voice. "Before we go in, you should know that Abram's straddling the fence between the Old Order and maybe Beachy Amish, I don't know. He and several other families are a little upset with their bishop and some of the preachers."

"Why is that?"

"Some problems in the church district," Stephen explained. "Half the community sides with the bishop's recent sanctioning of cell phones and pagers. The other half's rankled over it."

"Cell phones . . . are you kidding?"

Stephen shook his head. "They seem to be testing the waters, so to speak."

Philip had to admit he hadn't heard any of this, though he found it quite interesting. Rather humorous, too. "Does Abram own a cell phone?"

"Amish farmers aren't the ones using them. It's the woodworkers and blacksmiths, but especially the women who own craft and quilt shops. I have to tell you, Philip, the Plain community is changing by leaps and bounds."

"Oh" was all Philip said. Seemed to him that a farmer could benefit from a cell phone as well as anyone else.

Abram was coming down the front porch steps as they got out of the car. "*Wie geht's*, gentlemen. Name's Abram Beiler. I come from a long string of Beilers—even got me a cousin down in Hickory Hollow. A bishop, he is."

"Pleased to meet you, Abram," said Stephen, shaking the Amishman's hand. "I'm Stephen Flory, and here's Philip Bradley, the writer I told you about . . . from up north a piece."

"New York City, ain't?"

"That's right," Philip chimed in, extending his hand and receiving the man's strong grip in return. "Good to meet you, Abram. Nice of you to agree to talk with us."

"Ain't nothin' really. 'Tis always fun meeting up with interesting Englischers." He chuckled and motioned for them to follow him into the house.

The front room was as sparsely furnished as Philip's sister had said an Old Order Amish living room would be. Two hickory rockers sat side by side near the corner windows, as well as a tan couch with a purple and black afghan folded neatly over one arm. A number of multicolored rag rugs adorned the unstained pine floor, imparting a dry, silvery look. One especially large rug—a circular one in the middle of the long room—boasted nearly every color of the rainbow. There was a scenic calendar on the north wall, but no other decorations or pictures.

On one small table in the corner, two kerosene lamps stood at perfect attention.

Abram promptly went to the kitchen and brought out a straight-backed cane chair for Philip. Stephen and Abram sat in the matching rockers.

"Ask away," said Abram, pulling on his scraggly beard. "You ain't the first fella with questions about us Amish folk."

"It's not always easy finding the right person to interview," Philip was quick to say.

"Jah, I 'spose that's true."

Philip began his conversation inquiring of daily family traditions, then worked his way to Christmas and Easter. He discovered, quite pleasantly, that there was another holiday observed by Lancaster County Amish—"Second Christmas" on December 26, a day set aside to visit with relatives and friends, offering yet another respite from work.

Abram was quick to point out that New Year's Day was little cause for much celebrating in Amish circles, albeit the People made note of the passing of another year. There was no special church meeting on New Year's Day, but "the young people sometimes use it as an excuse to have a school program," he added with a wry smile.

Irreconcilable differences in marriage were discussed next. "When a man and woman can't make things work out together, they might up an' separate," Abram explained, "and if they do, one or both will like as not leave the community. But those who do stay understand clearly that there'll be no remarryin'."

This led to a question-and-answer session on early-morning prayers, as well as lively talk around the table every night. "We all work together," Abram continued. "In the fields—plowin' and plantin', sowing and harvesting. In the barn—the milkin' and cleanin' up. But we play hard together, too. Games like volleyball and baseball are big around here. We'll often gather in the yard just to watch the sun go down of an evening. When everything's said and done, family's all we got."

"How many children do you and your wife have?" Philip asked.

"Fifteen—eight boys and seven girls—and that gives us eighty-five grandchildren, with plenty more on the way."

Stephen spoke up. "Enough to start your own church district?"

The threesome laughed at that, but Philip presumed Stephen's comment wasn't too far afield. He asked several more wrap-up questions, then glanced at his watch and was amazed to see that two hours had passed so quickly. The answers to his numerous questions had come so effortlessly, he was, in fact, astonished when he arrived at the end with such success. "I'm grateful for your time, Abram," he said, closing his notebook and feeling confident he had covered all the bases.

"If ya think of anything else, just come on out and see me. Gut enough?"

Philip nodded. "That's very kind of you." He could certainly see a resemblance between affable Abram Beiler and his own deceased grandpap. Miles apart in culture, however. "Oh, before I forget, I wonder if you might be able to translate something for me?"

"Why, sure—so long as it ain't French," said Abram with a snigger. "I know only two languages. One's the English I butcher daily, the other's Amish. How can I help ya?"

Philip pulled out the postcard and showed it to the old gentleman. "Any idea what this says?"

"Let's have a look-see." Abram took out a pair of reading glasses and slipped them on the tip of his nose. He began to read silently, his silver eyebrows rising over deep-set eyes. "My, my . . . I believe what you've got here is a love note, among other things." He smiled briefly, the wrinkles creasing hard around his eyes.

Philip had suspected as much, based on Susanna Zook's reading of the greeting.

Abram looked at the front of the postcard and leaned forward, eyeing the postmark through his reading glasses. A frown furrowed his brow, and he removed his glasses. "Well, *was der Dausich, Deixel!*— what the dickens! You know, it sure seems like I've heard tell of this fella. I think this here's that preacher-boy who caused such a stir years ago."

Philip was astounded that Abram seemed to know the writer.

"Jah," Abram was saying, "and the sign-off, 'Gabe,' matches up with Gabriel Esh, the young man I'm a-thinkin' of. Honestly, I believe he went by Gabe quite a lot, if I'm right about this."

"Do you know anything more about the man?"

"Well, I 'spose there's a way to double-check, but it sure seems like young Gabe died over a Memorial Day weekend. Most all of Lancaster County was whispering 'bout it." He nodded his head, touching the postmark with his pointer finger. "Jah, Gabe Esh died just two weeks after this here postcard was mailed, if I remember rightly."

"Gabe *died?*" Flabbergasted, Philip knew he'd have to follow up on this. First thing tomorrow, he'd make a trip to the library and look up the obituaries for deaths that had occurred the weekend of Memorial Day 1962.

Abram was rocking in his chair now, fidgeting with the card. "Somethin' seems mighty strange about this," he said, waving the postcard in the air.

"What's that?"

"Why on heaven's earth did Gabe Esh write a love note in Amish . . . to an English girl? Don't make any sense." Then a smile creased his ruddy face. "Unless, of course, 'twas a code of some kind."

"Maybe Gabe didn't want anyone to know what he'd written—at the postcard's final destination, that is," Stephen piped up.

Philip made a mental note of everything, thinking that this might be the seed for a much bigger story, not just a two-page soft spread. Perhaps even a lead story!

"Gabe's girlfriend surely could read Amish, if that's what you're thinkin'," Abram spoke up, grinning at Philip.

"Why, yes, as a matter of fact, I *was* wondering that!"

They had another hearty laugh, but because Philip sensed the Amishman's restlessness, he asked again for the translation. "I want to jot down the words as you read," he said, anxious to hear the message, more so now than before. Gabe Esh's postcard had become far more intriguing than anything he'd planned to write for the magazine. In fact, more fascinating than anything he'd come across in recent travels.

"Would you mind reading it to me slowly?" Philip said, his pen poised over his notepad.

Twelve

❖ ❖ ❖

Rachel walked hand in hand with Annie down the narrow road, enjoying the rumble of the pony cart just ahead. They had single-handedly filled a small wagon with small and medium-sized pumpkins. 'Course, Dat had come along later to help with loading up the biggest ones.

"I think Dawdi Ben's gonna beat us home," Annie said, giggling. "Let's run just a bit?"

"Oh, Annie, it's best that I walk."

"But Mammi says you used to run fast as the wind when you were little. Was that so long ago?"

Rachel had to chuckle at that. "Not so long ago, no, but . . ."

"C'mon, Mamma. Take my hand and skip just a little. Please?"

Skipping was safe enough. Sure, she could skip down Olde Mill Road this once with her daughter. "Keep holding my hand," she said, lifting the walking cane in the other.

"Are ya ready?" Annie asked.

"*Fix un faerdich*—all ready!" She moved awkwardly at first, trying to keep up with her energetic girl. Every so often the cane bumped the road, throwing her off balance, but she stayed upright. The jaunt took her back to the many foot races she'd enjoyed with her brothers and sisters out on the dusty mule roads that crisscrossed between Dat's cornfields, tobacco fields, and pastureland. Usually, she was the winner of such events, though occasionally her brother Noah might beat her by a hairsbreadth at their homemade finish line. Then it was up to Joseph or Matthew to intervene and decide once and for all who'd really and truly come in first.

Those free and easy days of youth were long past, and she felt some regret that there was no longer much fellowship between herself and a good many of her siblings and their spouses. Nowadays, she had more connection with her mother's sisters and cousins, and there was always Lavina Troyer, the garlic-lovin' distant cousin on Dat's side of the family. It was a regrettable situation all around, but many of Rachel's brothers and sisters had simply chosen to stay away. She sensed it was because she hadn't given in and gone to the powwow doctors, seeking help for her eye condition—or *mental* condition, as some had surely concluded.

In spite of all that, she'd preferred to let bygones be bygones, settling into her snug and happy life with Dat, Mam, and Annie, never thinking much ahead to the future. Or the past.

"Ach, I'm winded," she confessed at last, slowing down while Annie ran ahead. Rachel heard her daughter's bare feet smack against the pavement, distinguishing that sound from the gentle rumble of the pony cart. If someone had told her that one day her sense of hearing would be this acute, she might've laughed. Within just a few months of her eyes clouding up, after the accident, she'd been able to hear an owl calling to its mate and tell how far away the creature was. She could also make out the buggies going up and down Beechdale Road to the west of them—things nobody else could hear. Though she didn't take pride in her heightened hearing ability, she was ever thankful to God for allowing her this compensation.

"What'll we do with all those pumpkins?" Annie called, running back to her and tugging on her apron. "Can we set up a vegetable stand in front of the house? Can we, Mamma?"

Rachel was still catching her breath. "Sounds like fun, but we'll hafta see what Dawdi says. Don't wanna scare off any tourists, now do we?"

"Might bring *more* guests," Annie suggested. "And I'd tend the stand, 'cause I don't mind talkin' to Englischers one bit. Some of them are right nice."

"Like Mr. Philip, maybe?"

Annie giggled. "Mammi Susanna told you, didn't she? *That's* how you know!"

"Jah, I guess I should 'fess up and say that I heard 'bout your little chat with our guest. But you know what?"

"Let me guess," Annie squealed. "He's gonna move clear from New York and come here and farm."

"Well, now, that's what *you* told your grandmother is more like it."
She knew it was true.

"Well, Mr. Philip said so . . . I think."

She figured Annie had completely misunderstood whatever conversation she'd had with the reporter man. More than likely, Mr. Bradley had said something more on the order of being tired of big-city living— something like that. The child was known to exaggerate now and then.

"Maybe it's time we had a little talk about your chats with the B&B guests," she said, walking faster again.

"Do I talk too much, Mamma?"

She didn't want to discourage Annie's friendly nature—wouldn't think of hindering her that way. Yet there was an unspoken line between the People and outsiders that should never be crossed. She understood this fully; so did everyone around here. But how on earth was she to make such things clear to an outgoing six-year-old?

"I'll try not to be such a *Blappermaul*—blabbermouth. I'm awful sorry, Mamma."

Rachel's heart ached for her little one. "No . . . no, you're not to blame, dear. You have a wonderful-gut neighborly way aboutcha. That part mustn't change . . . not ever. But I want you to think about not gettin' too thick—too overly friendly—with outsiders. Do ya understand?"

"Jah, I think so."

"Gut, then." They walked another quarter mile or so to the Orchard Guest House. There was a slight chill in the air, though still unseasonably warm for the fourteenth day of September. She heard a distant song sparrow warbling its tune near Mill Creek, and she reveled in the outing Annie had planned for her today. Because she'd enjoyed herself so much, she decided to go for a walk again. Tomorrow, prob'ly.

"We're home," Annie said, leading her around the back to the kitchen door where Copper greeted them with doggie licks and jumps and excited yips.

Mam had warm chocolate chip cookies waiting, and Rachel busied herself, pouring tall glasses of milk for everyone while Annie recounted all the happenings of the afternoon.

"I do believe some things are settled with Annie now," Rachel told Mam before supper.

"Oh?"

"On our walk home we had a nice chat about the English guests."

She told Mam how nice the day had been, spending time outside.

"I see your cheeks ain't nearly so pale. You best get out and go walkin' again real soon."

She was glad she'd gone, mostly for Annie's sake. Mam would always be pushing for more from her. That's just how Susanna Zook was and always had been.

"We wanna sell some early pumpkins," Annie piped up. "Out on the front lawn."

"*We?*" Rachel laughed. "Don't you mean *you* want to?"

Annie was giggling, slurping her milk. "Well, what do ya say, Mammi Susanna? Isn't it a gut idea?"

"Ask Dawdi about it," said Mam.

Annie continued. "You mean you don't wanna clutter up the front yard?"

"That's not what I said," Mam retorted.

Rachel sensed what was coming. Her mother would require her to reprimand Annie—make a point of belittling the girl in front of her elders.

"I think it's high time for some rebuke" came the stiff words.

"Annie, please come with me," Rachel said, getting up and tapping her cane across the floor. "We best wash up now."

She and Annie headed off to the stairs, and Rachel used her cane and the railing to guide her, letting the child run free this time. And just for this moment, she wished the two of them had stayed longer out in the sunshine and the fresh air.

Silently, Philip reread the postcard's translation as Stephen drove him back toward Bird-in-Hand.

> *My dearest Adele,*
>
> *What a joy to receive your letter! Yes, my feelings remain the same, even stronger, but I should be the one to bridge the gap between us and leave my Amish ways behind—for you, my "fancy" dear girl.*
>
> *God is ever so faithful. Pray for me as I continue to expose the kingdom of darkness.*
>
> *Soon we'll be together, my love.*
>
> *Gabe (Philippians 1:4–6)*

Philip wondered what the Scripture reference might be and asked Stephen if he knew offhand.

"Sure do. It's one of my favorites. Would you like me to quote it?"

Oddly enough, he did. "Please do."

"'In all my prayers for all of you, I always pray with joy because of your partnership in the gospel from the first day until now, being confident of this, that he who began a good work in you will carry it on to completion until the day of Christ Jesus.'"

"Wow, what a mouthful," Philip said, wishing now he hadn't asked.

"Verses to base a life on," Stephen said, nodding. "Gabe Esh must certainly have been a man of faith."

Philip stared at the line that stirred his curiosity most. "What do you make of 'the kingdom of darkness'?"

"Not so hard to say, really. Could be a reference to some local pow-wow practices." Stephen made the turn into the parking lot where Philip's car had been parked. "It's not commonly known by outsiders, but we Mennonites know that there are hex doctors, even today, among the Amish and other conservative circles, too, though some criticize it."

"Is that something pertaining to Native Americans?"

"Sympathy healing or the German term *Brauche*, as powwow doctoring is often called, has no direct association to Indian folk medicine. Its origins can be traced back to Swiss and Austrian Anabaptists who later immigrated to America. But Plain folk weren't the only ones who got caught up in the healing arts. Pennsylvania Germans practiced it, too."

"So . . . are you thinking that Gabe Esh considered powwowing as part of the kingdom of darkness?" Philip's interest was clearly piqued.

"It's quite possible . . . but who's to know for certain?"

Philip was reluctant to go on, unwilling to wear out his welcome. "I've kept you much too long, but getting back to the powwow issue— we're not talking witchcraft here, are we? I mean, don't Amish folk subscribe to the Christian way? Don't they read the Bible, pray—the things most Protestants do?"

"Old Order Amish follow the *Ordnung*—a code of unwritten rules. That, I would say, is quite different from what you just described. In fact, powwow doctoring is a type of white witchcraft—conjuring—and I assure you the spirits invoked are not godly ones." He paused, then continued. "One thing's for sure—don't expect to find an Amishman willing to discuss any of this."

"I appreciate the warning," Philip said, extending his hand. "Again, thanks for everything."

Stephen shook his hand cordially. "You know where to reach me if you have further questions."

"I'll see that you get a copy of the story when it runs."

"Yes, do that." And Stephen was gone.

Philip located his rental car and drove west toward the turnoff to Beechdale Road. He thought back to his interview with Abram Beiler. The old farmer hadn't mentioned the Ordnung, hadn't said a word about rules either. But overall, Philip was pleased with the favorable reception from both Stephen and Abram.

It was the postcard's entire message that plagued his thoughts, not so much the mention of evil deeds—although that aspect was intriguing—but the endearing phrases. Gabe Esh must have loved Adele Herr beyond all reason to be willing to abandon his People for her. They must have been true soul-mates, though he despised the term so overused in recent years. Heart-mates . . . yes, that was better. The ill-fated lovers had apparently belonged together, culture clash or no, though Gabe's untimely death had kept them apart forever.

One thought nagged at him. *How could such a declaration of love have been buried in an old desk?* Something as compelling as an Amishman pledging to leave his People for his beloved—why was such a message not found among Miss Herr's most precious possessions—in a fragrant box with other love letters and notes? Surely Gabe's sweetheart would have treasured the postcard for a lifetime, possibly the last correspondence between them.

Soon we'll be together. . . .

The tender words haunted him as he drove back to Orchard Guest House and long into the night.

Thirteen

❖ ❖ ❖

S usanna poured out her heart to Benjamin before retiring. "I
shoulda had you look at that stubborn drawer in the antique desk
upstairs a long time ago," she said, brushing her hair. "You
know, the one we bought over to Emma's?"

Her husband grunted his answer from under the sheets.

She knew better than to push the issue, late as it was. Benjamin's
brain perty near shut down around eight-thirty every night. No gettin'
around it. The man's body clock was set to wind down with the chickens, from all those years of farming. "Never mind, then," she whispered, about to outen the lantern light.

"What's that?" Ben asked, lifting his head off the pillow to stare at
her.

"Ach, that writer fella you warned us about found an old postcard
written by my scoundrel uncle."

"Gabriel Esh? You don't say."

"I saw the postcard with my own eyes."

"Your uncle Gabe, your mother's little brother?" Ben asked again,
pulling himself up on his elbows. "Glad we had sense enough to disown
him back when. It's a real shame, a blight on the whole family . . . and
the community, too, the way he carried on."

"Lavina stuck up for him, remember?" Susanna sputtered. "The
only one around these parts who did, that I know of."

"Lavina's a crazy one, she is," said Benjamin. "*Nadierlich*—naïve as
the day is long."

Surprised that Ben was coherent enough to pay any mind to her ramblings, Susanna seized on the opportunity. "Cousin Lavina has a right
gentle way about her, though. Folks seems to know better than to med-

dle with her opinion. They just leave her be, really."

"Leave her be? The way most our grown children have turned a deaf ear toward Rachel, you mean?"

Her heart pricked at Benjamin's words. "What's important now is that postcard Gabe wrote—a love note to his English girlfriend. If that don't beat all."

"Well, what'd it say?"

"Don't have it no more."

"But you said you found it, didn'tcha?"

"Philip Bradley did," she insisted. "He brought it down and showed me this morning before breakfast, but I was so flustered when I saw it, I didn't wanna have nothin' to do with it, so I gave it back to him."

"You did *what*?" Ben's face had turned redder than any beet she'd ever peeled.

"I told him I had no use for it."

Ben shook his head. "Well, didja read any of it?"

"Mostly romantic prattle. I didn't care to read it really." She wasn't sure she should say more—especially the part where Gabe had asked Adele, his English sweetheart, to pray that he might uncover more of the sin and darkness in the community.

"That's all it was, then—just a love note?"

Ben knew her too well to let this drop. True, he wouldn't go 'round tellin' folk that he'd smelled a rat in his own bedroom, but if she didn't come clean and confess everything, he'd probably know anyways. Insight from God was right strong in Ben. Everybody knew it was. One of the many old "family" gifts Benjamin believed in.

"Well, jah, there was more," she said at last, a bit reluctant to own up. "Gabe wrote something about evil spirits at work among the People. 'The kingdom of darkness,' I think was how he put it."

Ben motioned for her to come to bed. "Aw, that's *alt*—old news, Susie. Long ago dealt with. Nothin' to worry about now, I'd say."

"'Sposin' you're right." She knew she'd sleep ever so much better now, just hearing her husband say that there was no need to be concerned, this wonderful-gut man who knew far more about the intangible things of life than most anybody. If Ben Zook said it, most likely it was true.

Philip stayed up late, writing the first draft of his Amish family article on his laptop computer. Every detail, each cultural nuance that Abram Beiler had mentioned fit together like a jigsaw puzzle, and when Philip was satisfied with the initial draft, long past midnight, he decided this assignment had been one of the easiest he'd ever undertaken. Quite possibly the most enjoyable in recent months.

But it was the message on the postcard that energized him. Tomorrow morning he would drive downtown to Duke Street, to the Lancaster County Library, and begin his research on Gabriel Esh's death. Perhaps someone in Bird-in-Hand would know something of the man's life as well. After all, the postmark had originated there.

Young Annie crossed his mind, but he rejected the idea of pursuing a small girl with such serious questions. Surely Susanna Zook's young granddaughter would not have been told stories involving a preacher-man who'd planned to leave the Amish for a modern woman. Philip resolved to be more cautious around the Zooks, especially prudent with Annie—that is, if there was to be another encounter with the precocious child, though he had left some space in his article in case he was able to chat with her about Christmas gifts. Annie had an uncanny way about her, delightfully attractive. She was gifted in all the social graces, especially for one so young. And strikingly pretty, as beautiful as the woman whom he'd observed touching the child's cheek. Annie's mother, he was sure.

The more he pondered it, the more he realized he could not leave just yet. He would discuss with Susanna Zook the possibility of booking the room for a few more days. Yes, he would take care of that small matter tomorrow, immediately after breakfast.

———

Rachel crept downstairs to the parlor, her tape recorder in hand. She'd waited till the house was quiet, until Annie had fallen asleep. A taped letter to her dear cousin was long overdue. Already two weeks had passed since she'd received Esther's ninety-minute cassette recording in the mail. How wonderful-gut it had been to hear from her. Working the land, sowing seed—and this with Esther side by side with Levi and their children. She could just picture all of them out in the field with the mules, the smell of manure and soil mixed together, the sun shining down on their heads.

The scene in her mind made her awful lonesome for Jacob. She figured if he were alive today, she, Aaron, Annie, and the child she'd miscarried would be doing the selfsame chores together as a family . . . out in Ohio.

Closing the door to the small room, she located the electric outlet under the lamp table and plugged in the recorder. Then she felt for the masking tape where Mam had marked the Record button. She pushed it and sat on the floor next to the recorder, pulling her long bathrobe around her.

"Hullo, again, Esther," she began, holding the tiny microphone close to her lips. "It's been ever so long since I talked to you this way. I can't begin to tell you what a busy time we've had this fall, what with the steady stream of out-of-town tourists. But, then, you must surely have the same thing there in Holmes County, right?

"I haven't been too happy about certain things that I 'spect are goin' on behind my back. I wouldn't be surprised if Mam went to visit Blue Johnny last week. Maybe she even stood in for me, the way she used to have Elizabeth and Matthew do for ailing elderly folk now and then. Anyways, there was one day when she was gone for the longest time, and I honestly felt somethin' right peculiar come over me. But, of course, none of the powwow magic worked on me, because I have very little faith in it. I memorized the Bible verses in Jeremiah you read in your last tape to me. 'Blessed is the man that trusteth in the Lord, and whose hope the Lord is. For he shall be as a tree planted by the waters, and that spreadeth out her roots by the river, and shall not see when heat cometh, but her leaf shall be green.'

"Anyways, when Mamma finally did come home, she kept a-hummin' the same tune—sayin' the words over and over again. I never asked her about it, but I sure thought somethin' was up. Like maybe Blue Johnny gave her some charms to say around me.

"Oh, I wish you could come visit again. I wanna talk to you more about that article by Jacob Hershberger. You remember how we discussed it up one side and down the other, back when my Jacob was still alive? Well, I can't put my finger on it, really, but there seems to be something to what that Hershberger fella wrote so long ago. Seems to me he's right, though Dat would prob'ly make a big fuss if he knew I was talkin' to you about such things.

"Well, it's gettin' late, so I best sign off for now. Send me a tape back real soon, ya hear?

"I love you, Esther. Take gut care now, all right? Tell Levi and the children I said hullo, just don't let anyone else listen to this. And I promise to do the same when I hear next from you.

"Ach, I come near forgettin' to tell you that Annie and I spent the afternoon picking pumpkins over at the neighbors. They promised to give us whatever we picked, so we've got us a pony cart full. The pumpkins felt so smooth and round in my hands, I could almost *feel* the deep orange color, though I wouldn't say that to anyone but you, Esther. Certain folk 'round here might get the wrong idea and start thinkin' they oughta come to *me* for their amulets and charms. Honestly, I want nothin' to do with powwow doctoring. You know my heart in this.

"Well, back to the afternoon, which took me by surprise. I felt that I'd gone right back to our pumpkin-pickin' frolics when we were little girls. Oh, I wish you and Levi had never left here. Any chance of you returning to Lancaster County? Never mind, that's not fair to ask. Of course you wanna stay put there in Ohio. I'd give just about anything to have land . . . with Jacob and Aaron still alive to help farm it. But we all know that wasn't God's will.

"The Lord be with you, dear Esther. From your cousin in Pennsylvania."

Rachel pressed Stop and then ejected the tape from the recorder before unplugging it. She slipped the "letter-tape" into her bathrobe and carried the recorder upstairs.

Her fondest memories of Jacob made her cry, and when it was time for her bedtime prayers, she only had tears to say.

———

Philip thought he heard talking in the room below him. He couldn't be sure if what he heard was a woman's voice or a child's, but something was going on downstairs in the parlor.

For a fleeting moment, he wondered how many secrets the walls of this house had witnessed. Were there others, like the mysterious postcard, hidden elsewhere? What about compartments in old furniture? He'd read once about a late–1700s Rhode Island desk and bookcase combination that had sliding panels, concealing six separate hiding places. He suspected that his brain was tired, thus the curious notions.

After turning out the light, he got into bed. A piece of the moon shone through some scraps of clouds, the faint light filtering in through the window. The crickets were more subdued tonight, making it possible to overhear, but not decipher, the soft words spoken in the room below. A woman was talking alone, to herself perhaps, Philip decided just as he fell asleep, though he was too drowsy to determine if the sounds were merely part of a dream or not.

———————

Susanna was altogether dumbstruck at the things her daughter was saying in the quietude of the parlor. She had been thirsty in the night and needed some water. Tiptoeing out to the kitchen, she'd heard Rachel's voice, of all things.

What in the world? she wondered, starting to open the door, then realized that Rachel was prob'ly up making a late-night recording to Esther.

Instead of interrupting, she leaned her ear against the door, listening to the most revealing one-sided conversation she'd ever heard tell. Jah, she knew of Rachel's and Esther's plan to send taped messages back and forth once a week. In fact, she'd encouraged the idea, thinking it would give Rachel someone to pour out her heart to, though she wished her daughter might share her thoughts with someone besides Esther. Someone like her own mother, although she wouldn't have admitted to being envious. Never!

But this . . . this idle rambling about Blue Johnny! How *could* Rachel have known where Susanna had gone last week? *Puh!* The girl must be a diviner, as receptive and open to intangible things as the water witchers and powwow doctors themselves. After all, her daughter had been just six, around Annie's age, the first time someone handed her a hazel twig—a dowsing fork—and, praise be, if it didn't start a-jerkin' like nobody's business, right there in Rachel's tiny hands. 'Course, then she was so awful young she couldn't be expected to go chasing after well water with other dowsers. Which was prob'ly just fine, what with past years of community strife over the use of black magic or hexing having finally died down.

Still, the more she thought about it, the more she suspected she was right about the *real* reason for Rachel's resistance to sympathy healers these many months. Nay, most all her life.

Susanna shivered with excitement. Could it be that her youngest daughter had been rejecting the inclinations in her own mind—the uncultivated giftings of a full-fledged powwow doctor—all along? Supernatural gifts were often passed from one generation to the next, and in spite of the folk who condemned powwowing practices, the age-old giftings continued to flourish through the blood lines, though kept hush-hush to outsiders. Mediumistic transference—from one powerful dowser or powwow doctor to a younger member of the community or family—was another way the "miracle" gifts were passed on.

Susanna wondered if Rachel had shied away from Blue Johnny out of bashfulness, though she didn't see why Rachel should be afraid, if she was. After all, it was considered a high compliment to be chosen, anybody knew that. If her guess was right, he'd had Rachel in mind all these years, wanting to bestow the full mediumistic transference to her.

Susanna nearly burst out laughing. Here was a young woman who'd willed herself not to see, of all things! Her highly sensitive, reserved Rachel—why in the world hadn't she thought of this before? Her very own daughter had all the makings of a *Brauchfraa*—powwow doctor— and to think that she was most standoffish around one of their best-known healers of all!

'Course, it would be prudent for Susanna not to be mistaken about any of this. She decided to get Benjamin's opinion on the matter. Ben would understand her suspicions, maybe even stamp his approval on them.

Tomorrow, just as soon as breakfast was served to the B&B guests, she would find out and settle the whole thing in her mind. Once and for all.

Fourteen

❖ ❖ ❖

Philip had often noticed during his years of research that librarians seemed to subscribe to a most gracious and accommodating code of behavior. More so than any other profession he could think of. "Why, certainly," they'd say. "I know well that particular book." Or . . . "Why, yes, I just spotted that reference for another library patron."

Patron? The word conjured up visions of the wealthy elderly who made huge annual donations to well-known organizations. Never anonymously, however.

Philip stood in line to request microfilm for the *Lancaster Intelligencer Journal*—for the last fifteen days of May 1962. Unwittingly, he made the comparison between the amicable qualities of most librarians and the lack of such traits of his former girlfriend. Not that Lauren held any residual influence over him. No, what their relationship had granted him—literally—was the realization that he was now able to describe in words the kind of woman he wanted to marry someday.

First and foremost, she must be a lady, someone mannerly and appreciative. He also did not think much of married women who felt they had to invent their husbands. He had decided the day after Lauren and he broke up that if ever he was to marry, the girl would have to be demure—a nice change. A young woman who allowed him to lead, though he was no tyrant. In the two years he'd spent dating Lauren, the role of leadership—something he believed a man and woman ought to share equally—had been totally usurped. Was it old-fashioned to long for sweet submission in a mate—and be willing to give it as well? His own mother's humble approach toward his father had worked beautifully for their marriage, and when asked to give their formula for a lifetime of happiness, they often referred to Bible verses, pointing to characteristics such as meekness—a give-and-take relationship. That, he would be quick to acknowledge, had never once occurred with his former girlfriend.

"How may I help you?" asked the librarian, bringing him back to the task at hand.

He made his request and waited, wondering where he might meet up with the sort of girl he'd decided he must have, or be content to remain a bachelor. Would she love books and research as much as he? Perhaps she might be a librarian or, at least, a library *patron*. He grinned at his own thoughts.

When the librarian had located the particular microfilm spool, she was all smiles. "Here we are." She handed it to him.

"Thank you," he said, his mind on the data he held in his hand. The mystery of the postcard had gripped him beyond belief.

The obituary stated that the twenty-seven-year-old man had died on Sunday, May 30, 1962, and been laid to rest in Reading, Pennsylvania, though his place of birth was listed as Bird-in-Hand. Why Reading and not Lancaster County, somewhere close to his family? Philip found it equally interesting that no services had been offered for the young Amishman. Why?

According to the obit, Gabe had been the only son born to John and Lydia Esh. His surviving sisters were many: Mary and Martha—twins—Nancy, Ruth, Katie, Naomi, and Rebekah. There was no way of knowing Gabe's birth order, though the thought of being the only brother of seven sisters made Philip break out in a sweat.

While there, he looked up the name *Herr* in the Reading phone book. To his amazement, he discovered page after page of Herrs. He decided that, if necessary, he would go to the trouble of driving to Reading at some point and put his investigative skills to the task. But first he wanted to drop in at the Old Village Store in Bird-in-Hand, nose around a bit, get acquainted with some of the local folk.

He left the library, briefcase in hand, and walked a block down sun-dappled cobblestone sidewalks to his rental car. Then, driving to King Street, he turned east and rode past long red-brick blocks, reminding him somewhat of the famous Beacon Hill row houses of Boston. He passed the Conestoga View County Home, then veering left, took Route 340, also known as the Old Philadelphia Pike.

The sun had climbed the sky while he was inside the library, turning hot enough for Philip to push the AC dash button. The day was as bright as any September day he recalled in recent years, and while driving along the busy road, he realized just how inspired he had become since arriving here a scant two days ago. He made a mental note to phone his sister and let her know that he had been surprisingly revitalized on this trip. He guessed what her response might be. She would say she wasn't surprised, that he'd needed to experience a simpler, less-harried pace. She might also encourage him to go a step further and get in touch with his Maker. After all, Pennsylvania had long been considered a "God-fearing" state, due to William Penn's influence, offering land to immigrants in search of religious freedom.

Glancing in the rearview mirror, he noticed a horse and carriage trailing behind him as he came up on the old, abandoned Lampeter Friends Meetinghouse. The horse and buggy followed him down the pike, past the Bird-in-Hand Fire Station on the left and the Greystone Manor B&B on the right, then under the railroad bridge. He definitely wanted to thank his editor for having shoved the Amish assignment down his throat. Yes, he would do just that the minute he stepped foot back in the magazine office.

Philip began to formulate a strategy for gathering answers to his growing list of questions. To start with, he hoped to meet with at least one of Gabe's seven sisters. Surely, out of all those Esh women, one would have settled in the Lancaster area.

The Old Village Store was coming up on the left-hand side of the road. The prominent sign out in front—complete with well pump adjacent to it—declared the date of establishment as 1890. The inverted U-shaped, barnlike buildings had intrigued him earlier this morning when he first drove past this stretch of road. A store with such origins might have some folk connected with it who'd known Gabe Esh or his family, someone who might be willing to direct him to the right people. Hopefully even one of the Esh sisters; perhaps one who may have had a soft spot in her heart for the young man for whom no one had cared to conduct even a memorial service.

Susanna and her younger sister Leah were friends on two important levels. On the first and most significant, they were intimate sibling-friends; on the second, they were farmers' wives, or at least had been once. Now that Susanna was busy running an Amish B&B, she regretted not being able to get out to near as many quilting frolics.

On the first level, the sisters shared memories. They grew up learning the importance of patience and submission to God, the Amish church, and their elders. They sewed together, helped their mamma cook, made beds, mended their brothers' socks, swept the kitchen, hoed the vegetable and flower gardens, washed the clothes, raked the front and side yards, and put up as many canned goods as any other hardworking sibling team around. When they got married, nothing much changed. They still worked from dawn to sunset, never stopping to rest or think of themselves. It was always "put others before yourself"— their mother's motto for all her children, especially the girls. So they were prime examples of Mamma's strict upbringing.

On the second level, Susanna and Leah had given birth to a good percentage of their offspring in nearly the same months of the year, for all but two sons. (Rachel and Esther had come into the world on the exact same day, like twins carried by different mothers.) Now the two sisters enjoyed sharing stories or chatting over common gossip in each other's kitchens, usually with a cup of black coffee or iced tea, depending on the season. Or, here lately, they might slip off into town together, stop at the Bird-in-Hand Bakery, and secretly splurge on Grandma Smucker's giant cinnamon rolls, though they could've easily made some at home, had they cared to. The idea of getting out and away from what was forever expected of them was the main thing that compelled them out for a half hour here or there, especially now that most of their children were grown and gone. Leah's two youngest girls were courtin' age—Molly, seventeen, and Sadie Mae, nineteen—still living at home and anxiously awaiting the right carpenter's son or farmer's boy to ask them to "go for steady or so."

When Susanna and Leah weren't planning the next quilting or apple butter frolic, they were discussing their many grandchildren, commenting on whose offspring reminded them of which brother or sister. Or, in some cases, aunts or uncles.

But today Susanna had felt the need to make a quick run over to see Leah about something far removed from grandchildren and the like. "Somethin' I need to tell you," she'd said right out the minute her sister motioned her into the long, sunny kitchen.

"You feelin' all right?" Leah asked, her big brown eyes narrowing a bit as they met Susanna's.

"Never better." Susanna fanned herself with the flap of her long apron.

Leah pulled out a chair for her, and the two of them sat at the table with a tall glass of iced tea, eyeing each other and ready to giggle like schoolgirls. "This must be some juicy gossip I don't know about. I've never seen your face so flushed."

"Well, I wouldn't go so far as to say it's gossip, but what I have to tell you is mighty interesting, for sure and for certain."

Leah's eyes brightened. "I'm all ears."

"Will you hear me out before you say a word?"

Leah indicated that she would with a smile and a nod.

Then, taking a deep breath, Susanna began to relay the conversation she'd had with Benjamin, first thing after they were up and dressed, as she couldn't bear to wait till after the B&B guests had their turn at the breakfast table. "I coaxed Benjamin outside onto the back patio, and here's what I said to him. It's beyond me how I coulda missed somethin' this special all this time. 'Course he wanted to know exactly what I was thinking, but I hafta to tell ya, Leah, I think—and Ben agrees—that our Rachel is someone Blue Johnny's got his eyes on."

Leah's mouth dropped open. "But he's a man in his fifties, and he ain't even Amish, so how on earth's that gonna work out?"

Susanna laughed right out loud. "C'mon, now, think 'bout what I'm sayin' here. In no way am I referrin' to marriage. The man's old enough to be Rachel's father, for pity's sake! What I'm tryin' to tell ya is that I think she's gonna be our next powwow doctor."

"Rachel is?"

Susanna shared with her sister regarding the giftings she'd noticed in Rachel off and on her whole life. "Anyone who's as sensitive to things like she's always been—making herself blind and all—well, I'm tellin' ya, she's bound to be next. You just wait and see."

Leah shook her head, smiling. "And to think you're her mother and all."

"Oh, don't go giving honor where it ain't due. It's nothing I've done."

"You gave birth to her, didn'tcha?"

"And eleven others, but none of the rest showed any signs of the abilities Rachel's got." Susanna stopped to sip some tea. "To tell you the truth, I'm a-thinkin' the healing gift must've skipped a generation—stopped with Uncle Gabe when he died. But to think now it's showin' up again, and right under my nose, for goodness' sake!"

"Well, what's Rachel think of all this?" Leah asked, tracing the pattern on the green-checkered oil cloth.

"The poor dear's fightin' her natural-born inclinations, rejecting the gifts like I've never seen the likes of it since—"

"Don't tell me!" Leah blurted.

"Jah, you know exactly who I'm talking 'bout. I'm afraid she's an awful lot like our uncle Gabriel, except he was far more outspoken and fired up. Bold to a fault—and look where it got him. Honest to goodness, Rachel would be right content to sit in the parlor and crochet afghans most every day if it wasn't for Annie. Someone besides me oughta tell her that courage ain't the lack of discouragement or fear but the might to push forward in spite of it."

"Ach, you're soundin' more like a sage than a guest-house owner." Leah laughed, her round cheeks turning pink. "Does Annie ever coax Rachel outdoors?"

"Jah, they were out pickin' pumpkins over at the neighbors' just yesterday."

Leah rose and freshened their drinks, then sat back down. "You don't think she's scared, do ya?"

Susanna was shocked that her sister would say such a thing. "Afraid of the transference or just accepting the whole idea of being a powwower?"

"Well, you know what folks were sayin' back when Gabe was preachin' all that about wickedness among the People—evil spirits in the community and all. I remember overhearing a lot of it from our parents, and honestly it makes a body think twice about some of what was going on back then . . . and still is."

Susanna huffed at her sister and tapped her fist on the table. "Now, you listen here and listen gut. There ain't no way on God's green earth that what the powwow doctors are doin' is wrong or comin' from the devil. They're helping folk, plain and simple, and that's just right fine with me." She went on to recite the healings of Bishop Seth's deaf great-grandson and Caleb Yoder's second-degree burns. Even Benjamin's driving horses had been cured of ulcers when the local veterinarian couldn't do anything. She knew she didn't have to, but she reminded her sister of Lizzy's bad rheumatism. "It's gone for gut now, ain't? So how could something like that be wrong?"

Leah nodded her head slowly, and Susanna felt it was time she oughta be leavin', now that things were back on somewhat of an even keel between them.

"Are you planning to go to Lavina's tomorrow?" Leah wanted to know. "Some of us are gettin' together to make applesauce, then put up some pickled beets. You could come after you serve breakfast to your guests."

Susanna headed for the back door. "I'll see if Rachel wants to."

"Tell her Molly and Sadie are goin'."

Calling her good-byes over her shoulder, Susanna wondered why Leah had mentioned her unmarried daughters—Molly and Sadie Mae. The younger girls, along with all the rest of Leah's daughters, not including Esther out in Ohio, had written Rachel off after the accident. Susanna figured she knew why, too. None of their Amish kinfolk honestly believed that Rachel's vision problems had anything to do with the English doctors' explanations. Some of them prob'ly thought she might be faking her blindness, yet if they lived with Rachel and saw how she shuffled through the house, reacting the way a truly blind person would, they'd know. Truth be told, she herself had tested Rachel of sorts, flicking dishrags at her every so often. But every single time Rachel never so much as blinked an eyelash. So Susanna was convinced that her daughter couldn't see much—knew it beyond a shadow of doubt. She just had no idea why her eyes hadn't cleared up long ago like the hospital doctor had said they would.

Well, for now she wasn't gonna fret over what Leah's grown children—or hers and Benjamin's for that matter—thought of Rachel. Leah was prob'ly laughing up a blue streak over Susanna's idea that Rachel had inherited miracle-working powers. She'd seen the skeptical gleam in her sister's eye. Leah would be tellin Molly and Sadie Mae 'bout it, too. "Why, Susanna's girl can't even make *herself* see, so how's she gonna heal anybody else?"

Jah, that's what Leah was saying about now. But Susanna didn't much care. Her sister and all the rest of her Esh relatives—Zooks, too— just might be in for a big surprise one day. Maybe sooner than anyone expected.

———

Less than forty-eight hours earlier, on Monday, Philip had been going about his life—rushing here and there, gathering information for assignments, writing rough drafts, revising them, handing them off to his line editor—in general, eking out a living the only way he knew how. But here it was Wednesday, and too much had happened for him to merely fly home with his tidy and tight feature article in hand. He'd landed the perfect story, and if he could satisfy his reporter's curiosity and make everything fit, perhaps he would write a major spread—a human interest piece based on the postcard's message that would surpass anything he had yet contributed. That is, if he had any success in finding one Miss Adele Herr.

The postcard, after all, belonged to Gabe's sweetheart, wherever she might be. He would take some extra time—between assignments—to locate the lady.

He pulled into the designated parking area in front of the village store side of the complex of buildings and walked across to the hardware store. He noticed the large red pop machine standing to the left of the entrance and almost bought a can of soda, but he was distracted by a pay telephone with a phone book dangling on a chain on the opposite side of the door. On impulse he looked up the name *Herr* in the book, discovering there were almost as many listed here as in the Reading phone book. *Must be a popular German name*, he thought. Locating Adele Herr, especially if she had married, could take some time. While he had the book in his hands, he checked on the name *Esh* and discovered that *that* name was also common to the area.

Closing the book, he headed inside to find the most rustic setting he'd seen in years. The hardware shop was a typical country store, complete with wood-burning fireplace and bare wood floors. Every imaginable gadget was on display—an impressive array of items—from hand tools to shovels, nails, screws, and brackets of every conceivable size. Antique furniture, scattered around the store, caught his eye, and he wondered if a place like this might sell old writing desks, though he wouldn't have thought so. Not a hardware store. But as he strolled the aisles, he decided to inquire about antique furniture as a way of striking up a conversation with one of the clerks—if he could locate one.

"May I help you, sir?"

He turned to see a short little man with an eager smile. "Yes, I hope you can," Philip said. "I noticed your antiques . . . are any of them for sale?"

"I'm sorry, but no. They're just to give the old place some atmosphere, you know."

Philip glanced at the wide plank floors. *As if it needs atmosphere*, he thought, returning the man's smile.

They talked about the weather, how mild and warm it was for this late in the season—a real plus for the tourist business. "We have lots of tourist trade around here. This store's always busy in the summer and fall. Folks like to come to Lancaster to see the leaves turn colors, you know, especially on toward October."

Philip asked where he might find an antique desk. "Something on the order of a rolltop. Know of anything like that?"

The clerk scratched the back of his neck, wrinkling up his face. "Seems to me Emma had an old piece like that back a few years ago. Wouldn't have any idea who bought it, though. You could check with her about it."

"Emma, you say?"

"She's down just apiece, off the pike here"—he was pointing east—"then south on Harvest Road. You'll see her sign . . . says Emma's Antique Store."

"Thanks, I'll check there," said Philip. "By the way, you wouldn't happen to know of any Amish folk named Esh around here, would you? I'm looking for one of Gabriel Esh's sisters. I understand he had seven, two were twins. Ring a bell?"

The man grinned from ear to ear. "Asking for Plain folk named Esh is like lookin' for a needle in a haystack, so to say."

Philip nodded. "This man, Gabe Esh, was only twenty-seven when he died—nearly forty years ago. Supposedly, he was a renegade preacher." Philip was so eager it was all he could do to restrain the flood of questions he wished to ask.

The clerk held up his finger, glancing over his shoulder. "Hold on there, just a second. Let me ask someone who might know better about this."

Hope fading, Philip idly picked up a tiny gadget for curtain rods, hoping to blend in with the other customers. Still, dressed in slacks and sports coat, he looked every whit the part of a New York reporter. What *had* he been thinking to make himself so conspicuous?

When the clerk returned, he had a thin, gray-haired woman with him. She was cheerful enough—seemed to want to help, too. "Joe, here, tells me you're looking for the Esh sisters?"

"Why, yes, I am." Philip realized she was waiting for something more from him, some reason for her to offer information to a total stranger. "I'd like to talk with someone related to the late Gabriel Esh. Someone who might've known of his love interest, a Miss Adele Herr."

The woman's eyebrows arched over her inquisitive blue eyes. "Well, in that case, I suppose you should go on over to see Martha Stoltzfus. She runs a quilting barn down off Lynwood Road. There's a big white tourist sign out front. You can't miss it."

"This Martha Stoltzfus—is she Amish?"

"Old Order through and through. She's one of the twins, Gabe's youngest siblings, 'cept Mary's gone now, like all the others."

"Thanks for your help," he said. "I appreciate it very much."

"I'll call Martha and let her know you're coming. She doesn't take too well to non-Amish men, though. Just be sure and take a close look at those quilts of hers—some of the finest around Lancaster. And tell her Bertha Denlinger sent you."

He thanked both the woman and her short male sidekick and headed out the door, stopping to buy a can of soda on the front porch of the store. "Too easy," he said, pulling open the can and having a long swig in celebration.

When he returned to the car, he discovered that Stephen Flory had left a message on his cell phone's voice mail. "How goes the investigation?" The recording revealed a strong interest in Philip's work.

He phoned Stephen back before pulling out of the parking space. "I'm heading off later to an Amish quilt barn to chat with one of Gabe Esh's sisters."

"So . . . you're hot on his trail," Stephen remarked with a slight chuckle.

"After that puzzling postcard message, I had to know more of the story. I've arranged to keep my room at the B&B through Saturday."

"Sounds interesting, your visit with Gabe's sister. Maybe you can fill me in sometime." The man was more than eager to be included, and rightly so. After all, he had gone out of his way to introduce Philip to Abram Beiler yesterday afternoon—with the appropriate pay, of course—but the matter had become more than an extension of his job, it seemed. Stephen Flory was hooked.

But Philip preferred not to be put on the spot, having to invite Stephen along to meet Martha Esh Stoltzfus, though the man was cordial enough—and fine company. He just didn't see the need to alarm the Amishwoman needlessly with *two* strange men showing up at her place of business. That was one sensible excuse, at any rate. "I'll give you a complete report, if you'd like." It was his awkward, yet fastidious way of sidestepping the issue.

Stephen seemed reluctant to hang up, and when he pressed for more details, Philip finally mentioned having been to the library, "where I discovered some interesting facts."

Admitting that he, too, had read and copied the obituary that morning at his place of work, Stephen demonstrated far more than a passing interest in the story behind the postcard. "Turns out one of my colleagues knows something of Gabe Esh and his precarious relationship with his family and the Old Order community. From what my friend says, the young man was more than a rebel in the community. He was outcast among his people. They out-and-out shunned him . . . and he wasn't even a church member. How do you figure that?"

It was Philip's turn to be curious. "So you *do* have something on him?" he joked.

"Maybe we should pool our resources."

"Tomorrow . . . you name the place."

"The Bird-in-Hand Family Restaurant has a good menu. I'll meet you there for supper." So it was set. The two would attempt to piece together the puzzle of Gabriel Esh's life.

Meanwhile, Philip needed some fresh air and a change of clothes— something casual that would give him the appearance of a relaxed sightseer instead of a journalist. He drove down the road, drinking his soda as he headed back toward the turnoff to Beechdale Road. Noticing how clear and blue the sky was, he thought it a good idea to get out and enjoy the morning. Susanna had kindly suggested the walking path through the orchard a number of times since he'd checked in. Now would be as good a time as any.

Pulling into the lane at the Orchard Guest House, he parked the rental car on the far north side, in front of the Gift Nook just off the main house. He wondered if the boutique had been a *Dawdi Haus* at one time—an addition built to house aging Amish grandparents, so he'd learned.

He turned off the ignition and shed his sports coat, heading around the side of the house, past lavender and rose-pink asters standing sentry along a floor of old bricks. He was able to put a name to the large flowers because he'd heard his grandmother mention their names more than once as a boy. "Asters are as showy as can be," she would say of her favorite annuals.

Philip paused to take in the well-manicured back lawn, noticing an antique-style wooden wheelbarrow overflowing with red geraniums and white nasturtiums. His gaze lingered on an oval gazebo with its crested roof and vines trailing up its lathed posts in the front. Something out of *Better Homes and Gardens*.

Beyond the gazebo, east of the yard, the gravel footpath beckoned to him by way of colorful pots of hybrid fuchsias—deep pinks, reds, and purples—their bright heads nodding in a row. He strolled past a white resin birdbath and decided he wouldn't take time to change clothes before his walk. The breezes were warm and tantalizing, and he knew from having stared out the second-story bedroom window that far beyond the orchard a creek awaited him. He wanted to sit beside its banks, the way he and Grandpap had often sat when he was a young boy. Wanted to contemplate the remarkable morning, to collect his thoughts before the visit with Gabe's sister.

Just southeast of the B&B, farmers were cutting tobacco. Rachel didn't have to see it to know. The smell was fondly familiar, pungent with memories of playing near the tobacco shed with Esther while their fathers and brothers worked hard to cut and store the moneymaking crop come September and October every year.

She wanted to go walking out to Mill Creek while Mam was out visiting Aunt Leah. The creek, which ran diagonally across her father's property, was running full due to recent rains, Dat had said at breakfast. She had never ventured so far on the property and decided today was the day for some adventure.

"Wanna go for a gut long walk?" she asked Annie, finding her cane in the umbrella stand just inside the back door.

"Mamma? Are ya sure?"

"I'm sure."

"But you usually say you'd rather stay inside."

"I know, but it's high time I got out more," she admitted. "Besides it's a perfect day for a walk, ain't so?"

"Can we take Copper along?" Annie asked, scurrying about.

"Not such a rowdy dog. He might lead us astray." She laughed but meant every word.

She heard Annie's feet slide against the floor. "You can't be comin' along with us this time," Annie was telling the dog. "You best wait till Mammi Susanna gets back. Maybe then I'll take ya for a walk."

"That shouldn't be too long now," added Rachel. "So are we ready?"

They headed outside, past the flagstone patio, making their way through the wide backyard toward the direction of the orchard. The grass felt cool on her bare feet, and she thrilled to the buzzing of bees and the intermittent chirping of birds, some close in trees, others farther away. "Tell me what you see, Annie."

"Well, there's hardly any clouds . . . except for one tiny little one at two o'clock."

Rachel chuckled at her daughter's use of the traditional time positioning to describe the cloud's location. "Tell me what it looks like. Is it a double dip of ice cream or puffs of cotton batting?"

Annie was laughing now. "It's none of those things, Mamma. It's like an upside-down tooth. Just like the tiny little tooth I lost last month. Remember?"

"Jah, I remember." She thought about Annie's tooth, how easily it had come out while Annie bit into a Macintosh apple—their very own. "Now, what else do you see?"

"Birds. There's a robin over near the creek. Oh, we hafta be quiet . . . I think he's taking an air bath." She was silent, then—"Jah, that's what he's doing, picking away at his feathers."

"That's how they clean themselves," Rachel said, recalling her own fascination with birds, especially baby birds in the spring.

"Hold my hand tight now, Mamma. We're gonna cross the footbridge."

"Is the bridge very plain?" she asked.

"Not so plain, really. There's a nice wide place to walk. It's all wooden, not painted any color—just the wood color, you know. But the best part of all is two people can walk side-by-side on this little bridge."

Rachel's heart sang as she tapped her cane with one hand and gripped Annie's hand with the other. "Can we stop in the middle?"

"Two more steps to go . . . there." Annie led her to the wooden railing.

"Tell me about the creek. What's it look like today? What color is it?" Rachel leaned on the railing, then placed her hand on her daughter's back, feeling the restless muscles between the child's shoulder blades.

"It's blue from the sky and brown from the dead leaves on either side—and it's purple, too, all mixed up together. And there's dancing pennies on the water, just a-floatin' downstream. Oh, Mamma, we'd have lotsa money if I could take a bucket down there and dip it up."

"The pennies are really the sunshine twinkling on the creek, ain't so?" Rachel said.

"No . . . no. You mustn't spoil the picture." Annie threw her arms around her mother. "There's pennies in there, Mamma. You should see 'em."

"Jah, pennies . . ." Rachel smiled. "I don't know 'bout you today." They stood there silently, listening to all the sounds around them.

"Think of the prettiest place you ever saw before you couldn't see anymore," Annie whispered.

"I've got a right gut place in mind." Rachel thought of the time she and Esther had gone wading in the Atlantic Ocean.

"Tell me about it," Annie said, giggling. "I wanna know."

Rachel described the cold sting of the water on her bare feet, the foamy white edges of the tide as it rolled up toward her and Esther, splashing over their ankles. "It was prob'ly the pertiest place in the whole world."

"I wanna go to the shore someday. Do you think we could?"

"Maybe . . ." She had no idea when that might be—if ever again—but she didn't want to discourage her little one. The girl was filled up with a love for God's creation.

"Now it's your turn. Tell me about the pertiest place you've ever seen." She tickled Annie's neck.

But Annie stiffened just then. "Ach, there's someone sittin' over yonder," she said softly. "Oh, never mind, it's just that tall Mr. Philip. He's over there near the creek bank, throwing twigs into the water." Before Rachel could tell her daughter not to call to him, Annie did just that. "Hullo, there, Mr. Philip!"

"Hi again, Annie. It's a beautiful day, isn't it?"

The man's voice sounded altogether kind, not what Rachel had expected from a fancy reporter-writer. And snoop. Still, she felt terribly unsettled being out here, so far from the house, with Annie calling attention to them like this.

"It's a right nice day, all right," Annie replied.

Rachel held her breath, hoping the man wouldn't answer her this time. "Let's head back to the house," she whispered to Annie.

"Take my hand, Mamma."

All the way back, on the dirt path through the orchard, Rachel felt uneasy. She wanted to be left alone with Annie on this, her first visit to Mill Creek and the footbridge.

Left alone . . .

The motto of the past two years.

To get her mind off herself, she thought of the blue and purple creek with its dancing pennies. Annie was cute that way, describing things in such a fresh, interesting manner.

"Denki, Annie," she said, almost without thinking.

"For what?"

"For going with me on our beautiful walk. I enjoyed the creek pennies, especially."

"Me too, Mamma. Maybe I'll go back and dip up some of them. Then you'll believe they're for real."

"Promise me you won't go back there alone," Rachel blurted.

"I won't go by myself. I'll take Copper with me, if Mammi Susanna says it's all right."

Rachel guessed they'd be puttin' lunch together here before long. That would keep the girl from running back to the footbridge . . . and to Mr. Philip. Why on earth did she have to be so downright gabby with strangers? Rachel bit her lip but didn't say a word. She figured she'd said enough already.

All the way back through the apple trees, Rachel heard the clear song of the brook. She felt the warm, dry dirt under her feet and was ever so thankful for the day.

He was crouched along the bank of the creek, tossing pieces of sticks into the stream, when he first noticed Annie with the young woman. They were leaning on the footbridge railing, peering into the water below. The girl was talking about the brook, it seemed, pointing and laughing.

The woman, whom he was increasingly sure was Annie's mother, placed her hand gently on the child's back, eyes closed as she faced the sky. The sun on the water made tiny round jewels of light, and he noticed it especially because Annie was gesturing toward it.

Yet his eyes were drawn back to the beautiful woman, her face still raised to the heavens. In spite of her gray dress and black apron, he found her breathtaking, and he might've continued to stare if it hadn't been for Annie's enthusiastic greeting.

Only after he had called back to her did Philip begin to understand why the child seemed to stand so close to the woman, why Annie took the hesitant woman's hand and guided her safely, step by step, away from the bridge and back to the orchard path.

Annie's mother was *blind*. The realization struck him hard, and he shrank from it, thinking he must be mistaken, wanting to be wrong for Annie's sake. For her mother's.

Long after they'd gone, he sat beside Mill Creek, beholding brown clumps of earth as they curled around the mossy banks. He watched with pleasure the delicate shadows made by lofty maples, their yellow-green leaves trembling in a soft flurry of air, and he gazed at silver sunbeams falling atop a riffle of water on smooth gray rocks—seeing with new eyes.

Susanna picked up the reins and called, *"Hott rum!"* instructing the horse to move out to the right. The path that led home was a straight strip ahead with a yellow do-not-pass line running down the middle. Stretching out flat and narrow, the road skirted the edge of the white fence that ran along Gibbons Road, where a red Amish schoolhouse stood, facing east. She relived bygone memories of having dropped off two or three of their sons at a similar one-room school on raw, wintry days while riding along with Benjamin and the boys in their horse-drawn sleigh. Oh, so many years ago.

Roadside flower beds of orange, yellow, and red blossomed as edging along rows of cabbage or sweet corn, the typical Amish way to fancy up property borders. The bishops had no say in how a farmer's wife "dressed" her flower gardens—couldn't keep nature from shouting with color. Susanna smiled to herself, privy to the unspoken reason why many of her Amish neighbors chose such a profuse variety of hues. Some of the crimsons, yellows, and oranges clashed—colors they were forbidden to wear, all of them.

Her thoughts roamed back to her conversation with Leah, then back to Rachel. How could she get her timid daughter to see the light about Blue Johnny? She could smooth the way and talk to Bishop Seth Fisher or one of their preachers about it maybe. But, no, it'd be best coming from Benjamin, though she knew he wouldn't be one for taking sides.

The man was easily persuaded when it came to his blind daughter, though he wouldn't think of letting his partiality show, 'specially in front of his other adult children. Susanna suspected he'd had a favorite these many years. As for Annie, well, there was no getting 'round it, the child was a favorite of them both, even though Susanna wished she could do something about Rachel's unwise, forbearing approach with the little girl.

Making the turn onto Olde Mill Road, she waved and called a greeting to Rebekah Zook, both her neighbor and cousin by marriage, on her husband's side. "Another nice day, ain't so?"

Rebekah looked up from her yellow spider mums and waved. "We could use some rain one of these days."

"Jah, rain," Susanna agreed, craning her neck to peer at the blue sky out of the buggy.

The mare bobbed her head, pulling the carriage toward home. Susanna settled back in the carriage, thinking more about Rachel, ever so glad she'd taken the time to stop by and see Leah.

For better or worse.

Fifteen

❖ ❖ ❖

T he Quilt Barn was filled with handmade goods. King- and queen-sized bed quilts hung from the rafters, smaller wall-hangings and samplers hung on wooden stands, and table runners of every color and shade were displayed on a number of tables, along with place mats, napkins, and potholders.

One wall hanging especially caught Philip's eye. It was the King James Version of one of the Scripture verses from Gabe's postcard: *He which hath begun a good work in you will perform it until the day of Jesus Christ.*

Philip didn't give it a second thought and went in search of something authentically Amish to take back to his sister and niece. He was playing tourist, hoping to ease his way into a chat with the owner. A bright-colored quilted apron seemed to have Janice's name on it, and he carried it over his arm, heading for the next section of goods. He had to look longer to find something he thought Kari might like, finally settling on a faceless Amish doll, though he couldn't be sure that Kari, knowing how she liked to embroider, might not end up making cross-stitched eyes, nose, and mouth on the doll dressed in the traditional cape dress and apron.

When he went to pay for the items, he introduced himself to the elderly woman behind the counter. "I'm the man Bertha Denlinger sent over . . . from the hardware store," he said, offering the woman a hearty smile.

"She called me not long ago."

He waited for her to say that she was indeed Martha Stoltzfus, but she leaned hard on her cane while adding up the amounts on a small calculator. "That'll be forty-two dollars and fifty-five cents."

He pulled out his wallet and paid with a fifty-dollar bill, hoping to buy some time with the woman while she made change. "Bertha Denlinger said you might be able to help me locate someone"—he paused—"if you're Martha Esh Stoltzfus, that is."

She didn't blink an eye, just looked him straight in the face and said, "Bertha should learn to speak for herself."

"I see," he said, not sure how to proceed. "Well, if it's not a good time, I can certainly come back."

"Come . . . go, do as you please, but I'm tellin' ya right now, there's nothing more to be said about my dead brother and that wicked woman of his."

He chose to ignore her terse remark. "How can I get in touch with Adele Herr? I have something important that belongs to her."

She snorted. "That woman dropped out of the picture a long time ago. Last I heard, she's dead."

"Are you sure about that?" He wished the question hadn't come out sounding so brash.

"She hasn't been heard of since her father died of a heart attack."

"Her father?"

"Jah, a Baptist minister up in Reading."

"Would you happen to know when Adele passed away?" he asked, softening his approach.

"Couldn't say." She clammed up after that, sitting down behind the counter, still leaning on her cane, her long blue dress nearly touching the floor.

"Uh, this may be a strange question, but why wasn't your brother buried in Lancaster? Why Reading?" It was an assertive question, no getting around it, but he felt it might be his last stab.

"Now, you listen here." She'd lowered her voice, teetering forward on her chair. "We don't make a habit of speakin' much 'bout shunned folk—dead or alive—around here, so it'd be best now for you to be goin'."

She doesn't take too well to non-Amish men. . . .

"I'm sorry to have upset you, Mrs. Stoltzfus." His attempt was met with utter silence, and for the old woman's sake, he was glad the other customers were not within earshot.

———

Rachel helped Mam clear away the lunch dishes. "I can look after the Gift Nook tonight, if you want," she offered.

"You sure?"

Rachel heard the surprise in her mother's voice. "Jah, and Annie can help me with prices and things. We'll do that for you; give you some rest for a change."

"That's right nice of you, Rachel. I think I could use a bit of peace and quiet tonight. S'been quite a morning."

"We had a busy morning, too," Annie piped up.

"Well, what're ya waitin' for? Let's hear all about it," Mam said across the table.

"To start with, Mamma and me stripped down all the beds upstairs. We dusted and mopped and cleaned the bathrooms. Then we went walkin' . . . clean out to the end of the footpath, to the mill bridge."

"Is that so?" Mam seemed pleased.

"Jah, and we saw pennies—lotsa them!"

"I think ya best tell Mammi Susanna whatcha *really* saw today, Annie," Rachel cut in just then.

"It was pennies! Hundreds of tiny pennies a-skippin' down the creek."

Rachel waited for her darling child to 'fess up, though she wouldn't have pushed for an end to this fantasy. Not yet anyways. Annie was having too much fun.

"Let me guess," Susanna said. "Was it very sunny out?"

"Jah," Annie replied.

"And was it about noon, when the sun's straight up in the sky?"

"Jah."

"Then, I do believe what you saw out there in the creek was the sunlight dancing on the water. Am I right?" Mam's voice wasn't the least bit harsh, and for that Rachel was thankful.

She could just imagine her daughter nodding her little head ever so slowly, head tilted down a bit, and big blue eyes looking up as innocently as she ever had back when she was only four years old. Annie was a dilly, she was.

"How'dja know that, Mammi? And you weren't even there," said Annie, as serious as anything.

"Oh, I've lived many a year if I've lived a day, so you ain't tellin' me anything new. There's nothin' new under the sun, I tell you."

Rachel was perty sure her little one was thinking Mammi Susanna might be wrong about that. That those shiny, bright pennies were as new as new could be. 'Course, if you'd never seen such a thing as glory-lights on a brook as it flowed joyously downstream, you just might be thinking the same thing.

———

Emma's Antique Shop was a thing of beauty. Well organized and attractive, the place was an antique shopper's paradise. Even the smallest items such as dinnerware, tea sets, and odd dishes had been carefully arranged for display. On one wall, there were decorative plates with tiny crack lines indicating age as well as character. Stacked up in a corner hutch, odds and ends of turn-of-the-century yellowware caught his eye. The pieces reminded Philip of Grandma Bradley's old set, the same grandmother who sang to her African violets to make them grow. There was also an abundant assortment of sea green apothecary bottles, he noticed, and he was reaching for one of them when a cheerful voice rang out, "Let me know if I can help you find something."

He turned toward the register, searching for a face to match the engaging female voice. "I'm looking for a rolltop desk," he said, wondering where Emma might be.

Slowly, a young Mennonite woman emerged from behind the long counter. She wore a print dress in a tiny floral pattern, high at the throat and sleeves with lace trim at the wrists. Her prayer veiling was different from the formal caps he'd seen on older women. Shaped more like a bandanna, only white and edged with lace, it hung down gracefully in back. "Oh my," she said, rolling up a dust cloth. "Someone oughta clean under there once in a while." She broke into a smile then, catching his gaze. "It's a desk you want? Now, let me see." She glanced around the large room. "I know I've got one coming in next week. Would you care to see it then?"

"Well, I'm from out of town, but I thought if you had something available, I'd take a look."

"I'm sorry about that," she said, coming out into the aisle. "What was it you were looking for exactly?"

He described to her the old desk in the bedroom at the Orchard Guest House. "It's magnificent."

Emma's eyes lit up. "I know that desk! I sold it to Susanna Zook myself."

He was surprised at the coincidence, and this on the heels of having just encountered the most discouraging Martha Stoltzfus. "I've hoped to find a desk similar to it ever since I first laid eyes on it. Wouldn't it be nice if it had a twin somewhere?"

"Maybe somewhere in England there's another one just like it, though I doubt it." She was grinning, nodding her head. "No . . . no, that desk was one of a kind, let me tell you."

A light switched on in his brain, and he knew he had to stick his neck out about the desk's origins. "Would you happen to know where it came from . . . I mean, before you acquired it?"

"As a matter of fact, I stumbled across it in a run-down secondhand store in downtown Reading, of all things. Not a soul there seemed to have any idea how old it was, and let me tell you, it was in sad shape when I bought it for a little bit of nothing. Now, don't you tell any of this to Susanna Zook, you hear?"

Philip nodded his promise, delighted to meet someone so cordial and willing to chat.

"Before that, a lady in the store seemed to think Bishop Seth's nephew by marriage had it holed up in a shed somewhere, waiting to be hauled off. And before that, I honestly don't know."

Philip had to ask. "Who's Bishop Seth?"

"Oh, I almost forgot you're not from around here." She took a slight step backward before continuing. "Seth Fisher is the oldest Amish bishop living in Lancaster County. Last I heard, he was ninety-three. They call him the 'anointed one'—guess that's what his first name means. Anyway, it's hard to believe it, but most of his wife's family— her brothers and sisters, at least—were never even Amish, never joined church, I mean. Now, isn't that something?"

Philip nodded.

The woman continued. "From what I know, Seth Fisher's wife's nephew, who had the desk, was a Baptist minister, of all things. I've for- gotten the man's name, but I think he pastored a church up in Reading somewhere. Anyway, that's about all I know of Susanna Zook's desk."

Philip's head was spinning with more information than he might've hoped for. "Do you have a business card?" he asked, out of the blue, thinking that he might actually call the friendly woman and see if he couldn't purchase an old desk from her sometime. If not next week, another time. And he told her so.

"Oh my, yes." She turned back to the counter. "I've got plenty here. How many do you want?"

"One is fine," he said and thanked her for her help, though he did not reveal just *how* much help the woman had been.

———

Rachel tapped her cane across the hardwood floor in the common area of the B&B, following Annie. "We're gonna have fun tonight," she said, feeling her way to the Gift Nook. "We could sell some of those creek pennies of yours maybe, in the gift shop, ya know."

"Ach, Mamma, you're pokin' fun!"

Laughing, Rachel unlocked the door and right away smelled the scented candles and other fragrances, a mishmash of odors, though she detected peach and strawberry real strong.

"What's on sale tonight?" Annie asked, standing beside her behind the small counter.

"Nothin's on sale, but everything's *for* sale!"

"Oh, I get it," replied her daughter. "Jah, I like that."

Rachel could hear Annie's pencil making circles on a pad of paper. "What's that you're drawing?" she asked.

"Can ya guess?"

"Maybe it's pennies? From the creek?"

Annie laughed. "Not that again, Mamma." She quieted down quickly as a customer walked in. The footsteps were heavy, more like a man's tread.

"Well, it's you again, Annie" came the man's voice. "We seem to keep running into each other, don't we?"

Rachel recognized the mellow voice and felt herself stiffen. Feeling awful shy, she wondered if other guests had come in, too, or if the man was by himself.

"I don't mind it one bit, Mr. Philip. You can talk to me anytime ya want."

"That's nice to know. Thank you, Annie."

"We have all sorts of souvenirs in here," the girl said, "case you wanna take somethin' back to New York."

"Annie dear," whispered Rachel. She truly wished her daughter might remember the things they'd discussed on the way home from pumpkin-pickin' yesterday.

"I almost forgot, Mr. Philip. I'm not 'sposed to be talkin' so awful much. My mamma says so."

Ach, Annie, must ya go on so? thought Rachel, not only feeling shy but terribly awkward now as well.

"And is this your mother?" the man asked.

"Jah, she's Mamma." The next thing Rachel knew, Annie's hand was on hers, pulling on it to shake with Philip Bradley. "Mr. Philip wants to meet you, Mamma. He's real nice, so it's all right if I talk to him this much, jah?"

Rachel smiled at her little chatterbox. "Hullo, Mr. Bradley," she said, feeling the warmth of his handshake before releasing it quickly.

"Please, call me Philip. Mr. Bradley is much too formal for my taste."

"See, Mamma, I told you he was real nice."

She honestly wished Annie would stop talking altogether, though she wouldn't have embarrassed her daughter for anything. "There's lots of handmade items in the shop," she managed to say, hoping Mr. Bradley wasn't looking at her but had turned to see what was available maybe.

"Yes, I noticed," he replied. "And who's responsible for making these lovely things?"

"Oh, Mamma makes most everything in here," Annie volunteered. "She can crochet as gut as anybody 'round Lancaster."

"I believe that must be true" came the courteous response.

Rachel hadn't realized she'd been clenching her hands during the conversation with Philip Bradley and Annie—a three-way chat to be sure. She willed herself to relax. *There's no reason to be so tense,* she decided, though she wondered how long the man would stay in the tiny shop just talking and not looking.

"Do you wanna buy something for your wife or children?" asked Annie.

"That's very nice of you to ask, but I'm not married."

"Oh," said Annie, "that's too bad."

"Well, I don't mind being single. It's not such a bad thing." He was silent for a moment. Then—"I wonder if you might be able to tell me something, Annie? Something about how you celebrate Christmas. That is, if it's all right with your mother."

"Is it, Mamma?"

Rachel had no idea what on earth the man might want to be asking about Christmas, so she didn't know if it was all right or not.

But before she could speak, the young man said, "I'm working on a story for a magazine about Amish family traditions, and I have only one question to finish the story. Do you mind if I ask Annie what she received for Christmas last year?"

Rachel almost laughed out of pure relief. This wasn't going to be so hard after all. "Well, I guess so. If Annie can remember."

"'Course I remember, Mamma. I got this right here in my hand—a great big pad of rainbow papers and a set of colored pencils. *Des is ewwe es Allerbescht.*"

Rachel knew Annie had been right surprised to get the thick pad of paper, but she really didn't expect her to say what she did just now. Especially not in front of an Englischer, for goodness' sake!

"What's *des is ewwe* . . . mean?" asked the man.

"Oh, I'm awful sorry, Mr. Philip. I just said, 'This is the best of all,'" Annie explained.

"I'll write that into my article, if you don't mind," he said with a quiet laugh. "And I think I'll have one of these crocheted angels to take home with me . . . uh, Mrs. . . . ."

Rachel thought he was waiting for her to say her name, to introduce herself, but surely she must be mistaken. Quickly as it had come, she dismissed the silly thought.

"It's five dollars and fifty cents," Annie said, helping the way she usually did.

"And I'm giving you a ten-dollar bill," Philip said.

He knows I can't see, Rachel thought, opening the register and making the correct change. The idea that he might have observed her and Annie this morning out at the creek made her feel even more uncomfortable. She handed the money to Annie to give to Philip Bradley, then felt for the box of tissue paper under the counter and began to wrap the crocheted angel.

"Do you sew, too, Annie?" Philip asked.

"A little bit."

"I saw some quilts today over at Martha Stoltzfus's quilting barn."

"Jah, I've been there. Mamma and Mammi Susanna go there sometimes to make big quilts for the tourists."

"I think my niece would be a good quilter, too," he said. "She likes needlework."

"What's her name?" asked Annie.

"Kari, and she wanted to come with me to visit Lancaster. I know she would like you and your mother . . . if she had."

"Oh, bring her along next time maybe."

He chuckled. "You know what? I believe Kari would enjoy that very much."

Rachel heard several more guests wander into the shop just then and she breathed a sigh of relief. The conversation with Annie and the Englischer had gone on much too long.

"I'll see ya tomorrow," Annie said, and Rachel assumed that Philip Bradley had waved or made a motion toward the door.

"It was wonderful to see you again, Annie and . . ."

Rachel held her breath. He *was* waiting for her to mention her name!

"Mamma's name is Rachel," Annie filled in the silence.

"Very nice to meet you, Rachel."

And with that, he was gone.

Sixteen

❖ ❖ ❖

Philip thought he'd like to go to Reading and locate the cemetery where Gabe Esh was buried, but before heading out the next morning, he happened to notice Susanna changing the table runner in the dining room. The house was almost too quiet, so he assumed that most of the guests had already checked out, though he heard the soft *clink* of silverware in the kitchen.

Tentatively, he stepped into the large room where a long pine farm table, stained ruby red, was surrounded by his favorite style of antique chair—the comb-back Windsor. On the wall opposite low, deep-silled windows, a tall, slant-backed cupboard, housing a set of white china, graced the space.

"Excuse me, Susanna," he said, getting her attention. "I don't mean to bother you, but I'm curious about a particular man, Gabe Esh, who wrote the postcard—the one I showed you yesterday. Would you happen to know if his fiancée is still alive?"

Her face went ashen at the mention of the card. "I . . . uh, I don't have any idea what happened. . . ." She caught her breath and tried to continue. "His fiancée, you say?"

"Yes—Adele Herr. Do you know what may have become of her?"

Susanna shook her head repeatedly. "Honestly, I wish you'd never found that . . . that horrid thing," she was saying, her face turning from white to pink. "I wish you'd just leave things be. It's none of your business, really it ain't."

"Please forgive me. I didn't intend to upset you this way."

She pulled a chair out and had to sit down. "It's not the kind of thing you wanna delve into, Mr. Bradley, and I'm sorry that I didn't come across that postcard myself. Seems to me I oughta be askin' you for it back." Her final sentence had turned into a bit of muttering, but Philip had heard nevertheless.

"I'm just trying to put some pieces together, that's all. I wouldn't think of causing trouble," he assured her.

There was a sudden commotion behind Susanna—young Annie, coming into the common area from the kitchen, carrying an armful of soiled cloth napkins, place mats, and dish towels. "Mammi Susanna, I think I need some help," the child said, about to drop the load.

"Here, let *me* help you," he said, taking the pile from her. "Just head me in the right direction."

"That would be around the corner, down the hall, and down the cellar steps," Susanna said rather tersely. "And I must say, since we bought this house, I've never, ever allowed a guest to help thisaway."

He heard the edginess in her voice and knew she was more upset over the postcard questions than his assistance with Annie's load of dirty linens. Yet she followed him down the hall and on down the cellar steps, with little Annie close behind.

In the end it was Rachel's daughter who saved the day, diverting Susanna's attention away from Philip's questions. "Mamma needs ya just now."

Susanna responded by showing him where to put the laundry items. "Thanks for helpin' my granddaughter out," she said, heading for the stairs.

Philip knew the woman expected him to follow, and follow he did, up the stairs and into the hallway. When he came to the second flight of stairs, he turned and made his departure to the southeast guest room.

———

Susanna's reaction to the boarder's questions had flustered her no end. Even worse, Rachel must've overheard part of the conversation in the dining room, and now that Susanna was in the kitchen, Rachel wanted to know how Mr. Philip Bradley knew about her great-uncle.

"I couldn't believe my ears—I honestly thought I heard him askin' about your uncle, Gabriel Esh," said Rachel, frowning.

"Jah, you heard right, but you also must've heard me say that it's not nobody's business what went on back forty years ago. That includes you, my dear. Besides, it ain't right to be talkin' so awful much about a dead man under the shunning."

"Why *was* your uncle shunned, Mam?" Rachel seemed to be looking right at her, and even though Susanna knew her daughter couldn't make out her face or her frame, she almost wondered now as she stood there if the young woman's sight had suddenly returned. *Himmel*, there was almost a bold look on her daughter's face, and it got her thinking how to smooth this whole ridiculous dialogue over, bring it to a quick end.

"No need us wastin' precious time talking 'bout what's over and done with," she said softly, hoping her tone might quell the matter. She surely didn't want to open that can of worms.

Rachel stood near the sink, the breakfast silverware in her hand. Susanna fully expected her to turn back to the task of drying the knives, forks, and spoons, but Rachel shuffled past her, without reaching for her cane, sliding her bare feet along the floor, the utensils and dish towel still in her hands. "Where're you going, Daughter?"

When there was no reply, she decided to let things drop. No way, nohow, did she ever want Rachel to inquire about Gabe Esh again. Not the way her daughter seemed so hesitant toward the area healers. Not the way she'd wavered about Blue Johnny these many years.

Rachel sat on the deacon's bench in the entryway, waiting for the New York man to come downstairs. She didn't rightly know how she would find her voice and ask the stranger what she wanted to know. It was a hard thing to cross the unspoken line the People had drawn between themselves and outsiders. Yet all her life she had wished for someone to talk to her about the mysterious great-uncle on her mother's side. But just about the time she'd get up a speckle of pluck to ask, the wind was knocked out of her courage.

The last time she'd almost stuck her neck out and asked about Gabe Esh was the day she'd ridden along to town with Dat, nearly a month ago. They'd been talking about this and that, most anything that came to mind; her father had spilled the beans and said he'd purchased a set of Bible tapes for her to listen to. "Don't be tellin' anyone 'bout it, though," he'd said.

She'd come that close to blurting her question out. In all her days, she'd never known or heard of a person being shunned for no gut cause. Surely there must be some important reason why.

Another time she thought of asking someone like her cousin Esther to write a letter to Bishop Glick—Esther's husband's grandfather—since she figured the bishop would surely know about Gabe's shunning, but she didn't want to step on Esther's toes, using her that way. If Bishop Glick was the sort of man her Jacob had been, she might've felt she could speak to him privately—in the presence of his wife, of course—but the bishop was rather reserved, not someone you could just walk up to after a preachin' service and ask a question like that. Bishop Glick was as reticent, folks said, as she herself was. Still, Rachel wondered what things he might know—what others in the community knew but weren't saying.

"Good morning, Rachel." Hearing her name spoken by a man jolted her out of her musing.

"Oh, hullo," she said, almost forgetting why she'd sat here so close to the front door.

"Have a nice day, and tell Annie I said good-bye."

Philip's kind voice encouraged her to reply. "Are you leaving?" she said, then realized what he meant, that he was saying 'good-bye' just for the day.

"No . . . no." He laughed, and she felt her cheeks heat at her blunder. "I'm paid through until Saturday. Can't let a terrific room like that slip through my fingers."

She didn't quite know how to respond to that, but she was surprised that she was able to get any words out at all. Here she was talking to the sophisticated New York guest. "May I . . . I mean, would it be all right . . . if I ask you a question?"

"You certainly may. What is it, Rachel?"

She was taken a little by surprise, the way he said her name—kind and gentle-like. "I heard you talking to my mother about Gabe Esh a little while ago."

"Yes?"

"How did you know him?"

"Well, I didn't know him at all. I found an old postcard in the desk upstairs . . . in my room, which he wrote forty years ago."

"A postcard . . . from Gabe Esh? Who was he writing to?"

"Here, let me show it to you. Maybe *you'll* know more about this. It's written in Pennsylvania Dutch, but I'll read the translation to you."

Slowly, he began. Rachel was silent, listening intently. "Oh my, what a mysterious and beautiful message," she said when he finished.

"Do you know who Adele Herr was?"

She shook her head. "Sorry, I've never heard of her. But I, too, am curious . . . been wanting to know more about my great-uncle . . . for many years now."

"Gabe was your great-uncle?"

"Jah, on Mam's side of the family."

"I didn't know."

"Well, what did my mother say about her?"

He was silent, and she wondered why. Then he said softly, "Your mother seemed quite troubled by this, so perhaps you should speak to *her*. I don't want to cause problems."

She was quite taken aback by his sincerity. "Thank you, Mr. Bradley. That is very kind."

"Philip—remember? I don't quite know how to react to anything more formal."

He'd said precisely the same thing last evening, and she felt foolish about having forgotten. "I apologize, Philip," she said, enjoying the sound of his name.

"That's quite all right. And, if it should work out for me to relay to you any information I might uncover today—about your uncle—I will certainly do that."

"Denki," she said, almost without thinking. "Thank you very much."

"Well, it's another warm day. Maybe you and Annie will go for another walk."

"Oh, I don't know about that. We'll be makin' applesauce and picklin' beets today," she said, aware that the silverware and dish towel were still in her hands. "There may not be much time for walkin'."

"Well, then, good-bye," he said and was out the door before she realized that she'd talked nearly a blue streak to a stranger. And an Englischer at that.

Rachel was standing at the back door, waiting for Annie to fill Copper's water dish outside. She heard Mam scurrying about the kitchen, straightening things up before they headed off to Lavina's.

"I don't know what you were thinkin', talking to Philip Bradley thataway, Rachel. It was like you were just tarryin' there for him to come downstairs."

She wondered how much her mother had overheard, though she didn't think it was much to worry about. "He seems nice enough" was all she said.

"He's a snoop, and he's got his gall nosin' into our family business."

Rachel said nothing, knowing from past experience it was best not to egg Mamma on. Susanna hadn't heard everything Philip had said, though now to think of it, Rachel could scarcely believe the conversation had taken place at all. What *had* come over her to speak to a stranger like that? She'd told him something she'd never told a soul on earth except Cousin Esther, for goodness' sake! So now Mr. Philip Bradley knew just how curious she was about Gabe Esh, and that she had been all her life.

On the buggy ride to Lavina's, she second-guessed herself, worrying that she'd made a mistake talking to a stranger. One thing was sure—he had the nicest-sounding voice she thought she'd ever heard. And wonder of wonders, he was on his way to dig up information about Gabriel Esh. And Adele Herr.

Adele Herr ain't Amish, she thought.

Could it be true that Gabriel Esh had had an English sweetheart, like the postcard seemed to indicate? Was *that* the reason for his shunning?

Philip took Interstate 176 to Reading, eager to get there as soon as possible. He wanted to have plenty of time to locate Gabe's grave marker, if there was one, before heading back to Lancaster in order to meet Stephen Flory for supper at the Bird-in-Hand Family Restaurant. He also wanted to do some checking, see if anyone in the area might have known Adele or knew the date of her passing. Ultimately, if need be, he could search back microfilms for a death notice, but he much preferred the human connection. The tenderness with which the postcard's message had been written and the fact that the postcard itself had been entrusted to him were, perhaps, the driving forces behind his desire, spurring him on to locate both Gabe's final resting place and Adele herself, though he feared the lady might also be deceased.

Between Plowville and Green Hills he wiled away the miles, talking to his sister on his cell phone. "Thought I'd check in and let you know your brother's still alive and kicking."

"How's the article coming?" asked Janice.

"Nearly finished."

"You're always in a rush, aren't you, looking ahead to the next project? Never take a minute to sigh."

"Not this time. I'm actually thinking of joining up with the Amish." He laughed. "So . . . how would you and Kari like to come help me run a bed-and-breakfast in Pennsylvania?"

"In Amish country?" She was hooting. "What would Ken say?"

"Just get him here, then we'll tell him. I'm not kidding—it's beautiful."

"Hey, you're sounding like your old self. What's happened? Did you meet a girl?"

He snorted. "Like I need one more failed relationship."

"Don't get sarcastic with me. You just sound so good . . . well rested or something."

"I like that—the rested part."

"Kari misses you," said Janice. "Maybe you can give her a call when you get home tomorrow."

"Didn't I tell you? I'm staying till Saturday . . . rescheduled my flight and everything."

"How come?"

"I'm on a fast track to solving an old, old mystery. What do you think of that?"

"Doesn't sound like you, Phil. What's going on?"

"Hey, that's interesting—you're starting to sound worried, more like the old Janice."

"You're bad," she said. "What are you *really* doing there?"

"No joking, I'm playing detective with a forty-year-old postcard as my guide, and if you don't think this is fascinating, you'll just have to wait and read the book."

"Are you sure you're all right, Phil? You didn't just say you're planning to write a book, did you? You can't sit still long enough to tie your shoes. What is it . . . a novel?"

"I'm toying with the idea, that's all." He wouldn't let her get the best of him.

They talked for a few more minutes, then he hung up to look at the map, glad that Janice hadn't chosen this phone chat to lecture him about slowing down, getting married, joining a church.

His mind wandered back to the peculiar scene in the entryway of Zooks' Orchard Guest House. Annie's beautiful, blind mother had clearly been waiting for him, sitting there on an old deacon's bench just to the right of the front door. It struck him as odd even now—that she had wanted to ask about Gabe Esh—and the way she had brought up the subject almost seemed as if her mother's uncle had been kept a deep, dark secret. Martha Stoltzfus had also given the same impression.

Something had startled him about seeing Rachel sitting in the foyer, holding silverware in one hand and a white dish towel in the other, so quiet and still—the way he'd seen her in the parlor with Annie that first day. He'd initially shrugged it off, thinking she may have been merely resting, not waiting to speak to him at all. He hadn't known why a thought like that might cross his mind. Rachel, after all, had not a single reason to speak to him. She was Amish, and from everything he'd gleaned of Plain women, they didn't go out of their way to talk to outsiders.

So he'd just assumed she was catching her breath. Nothing more. He also had the feeling that Susanna Zook took advantage of her daughter and any and all help she could get around the place. Husband Benjamin included. The man was constantly weeding the garden or trimming the lawn, working the acreage just as he surely must have worked his farm for many years. Farming was probably in the retired man's blood— couldn't help but be—and Philip had an inkling he knew what that might feel like, though he'd never had a real chance at plowing or planting sunup to sundown. He would have been happy to have the experience of such a day, though; had even attempted to keep up with his grandpap several summers in a row at the Vermont cottage, there being a good amount of land behind the house.

The Amish B&B family—the Zooks and their daughter and granddaughter—certainly made up a unique nucleus of people. Three generations under one roof. He didn't know why it bothered him that Rachel was blind. Perhaps it was because her daughter was so vivacious and alive, so outgoing. And where was Rachel's husband? Dead? Divorced? Hardly, according to Abram Beiler, who had said all the area bishops spoke out severely against divorce. "We turn lemons into lemonade, but no divorcing 'round here," Abram had said during the interview.

Philip hadn't realized it until just this moment, but he was indeed interested in knowing more about the entire Zook family. Only two days remained. Could he tend to Gabe Esh and Adele Herr *and* learn more about the Zooks in such a short time?

"Mmm, delicious," Rachel said, smelling bushels of tart Macintosh apples as they walked through the screened-in porch at Lavina's. The fresh apple smell covered Lavina's usual garlic-ridden kitchen odor.

"We're here—anybody home?" called Mam, guiding Rachel inside.

"Hullo . . . hullo! Smell them apples, Rachel? I'm tellin' ya they're the best apples this year, ain't?" Lavina said as Rachel, Annie, and Mam made their way to the kitchen.

"It's a gut day for making applesauce, too," Mam chimed in. "Not so warm as it's been."

"How's Annie?" Lavina asked.

"Wonderful-gut!" replied Annie herself. "And I brought some extra raw sugar. In case we run out."

Annie's enthused response was met with laughter, and by that Rachel knew that most of the group had assembled. She didn't hold out any hope of hearing a "hullo" from either Molly or Sadie Mae, even though Mam had informed her of Leah's comment—that the girls were coming.

Rachel was just content to be around Lavina again. It had been a gut long time since she'd worked in the dear woman's kitchen, soakin' up some of the older women's unique perspectives on life, love, and family, among other things.

"Here, Mamma, can you hold this for me?" It was Annie pushing the bag of sugar into Rachel's hand. Applesauce, the way they made it, needed a good dose of sugar to mix with the delicious tartness of the Macintosh. Nothin' like homemade applesauce, especially made at Lavina's house. 'Course, her father's cousin was no ordinary woman. Something didn't seem quite right about her, though it had never bothered Rachel a bit. Spending time with her all day—canning or quilting—was always pleasant. Lavina had a sweet, giving spirit, and that's what came shining through, when all was said and done.

Rachel had overheard talk of a mental condition, when first she'd come to make apple butter in late October, years ago. She was only thirteen when one of her cousins remarked that Lavina was one of "God's special children," as if she were a product of a marriage of first cousins, but that wasn't the case. Rachel didn't understand the label at that time—not where Lavina was concerned—because she'd never had reason to think there was anything wrong with her father's cousin before then. Sure, Lavina had never married, but that didn't mean there was something amiss with her mind.

Rachel set about washing a bushel basketful of apples, helping several others while Mam, Aunt Leah, Molly, and Sadie Mae began pulling

out stems and quartering the clean ones, preparing to boil them, skin
and all. She felt she understood Lavina a lot better these days. Certain
of the People had called *her* mental, too, and all because of her reluctance to go to the powwow doctors. She knew what they said behind her
back. She may be blind, but she wasn't stupid.

They were boiling the apples, a whole batch of them at once, when
Lavina let slip the most peculiar thing. She said it loud enough so everyone heard. "Martha Stoltzfus had herself an English visitor yesterday
afternoon, and you'll never guess who that stranger was asking 'bout."

"Who?" Leah spoke up.

"Gabriel Esh, of all people," Lavina replied. "Nobody's had the grit
to bring up his name in nigh onto forty years."

Rachel perked up her ears. "Who was the stranger?" she said so
softly she didn't expect to be heard.

"Some fella named Philip Bradley is what I heard," Lavina replied.
"And I got it straight from Martha's mouth—hers and Bertha Denlinger's—ya know, up at the hardware store."

They all knew. Lavina didn't have to say where Bertha was workin'
these days. Fact was, the women—both Martha and Bertha—had a neg-
ative outlook on life, far as Rachel was concerned. Neither one of them
ever seemed to look on the bright side of things. Not anything; not ever.

Most amazing was how Mamma kept mum during all the talk at
Lavina's. Rachel was mighty sure if she hadn't witnessed it for herself—
if she hadn't been present to know how tight-lipped Mam was being
about their New York B&B guest—well, she might not have believed it.
Truth was, Mam prob'ly wouldn't be volunteering one thing, wouldn't
want the women to know her guest was nosing around, stirring up
something that was best left alone.

But, then again, maybe it would turn out that it was a right gut thing
that Philip Bradley had found that postcard and poked around after all.

'Course, all that remained to be seen. . . .

———————

The stone wall surrounding the Reading cemetery reminded Philip
of a cemetery he'd visited in England many months before. It was the
old-world setting he recalled—ancient trees with gnarled roots extended
and exposed, leaf-filtered sunlight, and the overall serenity of grave-
stones. Weathered granite markers commingled with tall, stately head-
stones—some with angels, some with crosses. The day had been much

different, however, with drizzle and fog, not like the sunny Pennsylvania morning he was presently enjoying, with temperatures high in the sixties.

He parked the car and got out, not knowing where to begin his actual search. He could walk down each row of markers, he supposed, but that could take all day. Then he spied the groundskeeper, a tall, thin, older gentleman, edging a circular section of lawn just below the crest of a hill.

Eager to make contact with him, Philip quickened his pace. "Excuse me, sir."

The old man stopped his work and leaned on a medium-sized headstone, mopping his brow. "Hello," he replied.

Philip said, "I wonder if you might be able to help me locate the marker for a Gabriel Esh."

"Gabriel . . . like the angel?"

Nodding, Philip realized he hadn't thought of the name being linked to the heavenly host. "According to an old obituary, he's buried in this cemetery."

The man's face was tired and drawn. "Yes, I know who you're talking about. He's buried seven rows over, in that direction." He pointed to the north. "It's quite peculiar, really, when you think of it."

"What's that?"

"For all the years I've worked here, except the last two, Gabriel's burial plot was covered with flowers, dozens of them . . . every year on his birthday."

"January seventh," Philip said, remembering the birth date on the obit.

"That's right, in the dead of winter. I tell you it was the strangest thing to be out here plowing snow off the walkways, and there'd be all those flowers, piled up on the grave—like the first crocus of spring when it pushes up through the ice and cold." He was nodding his head. "The oddest thing you'd ever want to see, but it wasn't my imagination. Those flowers kept coming every year like clockwork, and then, one year, they stopped."

"Any idea who was sending them?"

"All I know is, it was the same florist bringing them. A person in my business doesn't overlook something like that."

The old gentleman seemed glad to tell the name of the florist, and Philip jotted it down, thanking the man for the information. He hurried back to the car and drove several miles, following the gardener's specific directions.

The flower shop was tiny, crowded with white flower-filled buckets. Philip made his way through the maze, heading for the woman behind the cash register.

Except for one shopper, the place was empty. The customer's transaction took a few minutes and was done. When the florist offered to assist him, Philip found himself studying the woman, ticking off questions in his head. *Could she have been the one taking flowers to Gabe's grave? What could she tell him about the sender?*

"How may I help you, sir?" the middle-aged woman asked.

"I'm here not to purchase flowers but to ask about someone who must have been one of your faithful customers. I'm interested in knowing the name of a particular sender of large amounts of flowers. Every year, for a number of years . . . always on January seventh."

The woman pushed her long brown hair back away from her face. "Well, I'm the new owner here. I've only worked the shop about two and a half years, so I'm probably not the person to help you."

"Are you saying you have no records for someone purchasing flowers every January? For a Gabriel Esh's grave?"

Her face brightened with recognition. "You know, that name sounds very familiar to me. If I remember correctly, the sender was a woman. . . ."

Philip had to know. "Is there any way to check on that customer? Is the former owner of this shop in the area?"

"I'm really terribly sorry. If my memory serves me well, I believe the sender was ill . . . no, possibly deceased. Yes, I believe she passed away around the time the flowers stopped being ordered."

He felt the air go out of his chest and could not speak for the blow. With a wave of his hand, he gestured his thanks and found his way out of the shop, back to his car.

So Adele Herr was dead after all. She must have passed away the year the flowers ceased coming, just as grouchy Miss Martha Stoltzfus had said. But he hadn't paid attention. He'd pushed ahead, determined to find Adele Herr at all costs. And here, to think she'd died two years or so ago.

I should be the one to leave . . . my Amish ways behind. . . .

The poignant message, though safely tucked away, continued to trouble Philip. He would not have the pleasure of meeting Gabe's beloved, would not experience the joy of returning the postcard to its rightful owner.

He drove through the outskirts of Reading and made the turn onto the southbound ramp, heading back to the interstate. It was then, as he settled in for the drive to Lancaster, that he was struck with a sorrowful thought. Was it possible, could it be that Adele had breathed her last without ever laying eyes on the postcard?

Seventeen

❖ ❖ ❖

I t had been coming on toward midafternoon, and the sky was beginning to cloud up like it might rain any minute. Susanna hoped they could get home before a gully-washer descended—them without umbrellas and all.

"Smells like rain's comin'," Annie said from the backseat of the carriage.

"Jah, and it's a gut thing, too. It's been almost too warm for this time of year, ain't?" Rachel observed.

Susanna breathed in the damp smell a-stirrin' in the air, thinking that now might be the right time to talk to Rachel about her God-given gifts. She'd had a chance to mention it briefly to Benjamin, getting his word on the situation, and he'd given her the go-ahead. "Tell her just to be open, if nothin' else," he'd said. "She oughta at least think on the idea of receivin' the healing gift from Blue Johnny, if that's what he's got in mind."

So she humored her daughter a bit. "I'd hafta agree with you on the weather these past few weeks. A body hates to see it frost too early in the season, but I'm ready for a little nip in the air myself."

They rode along quietly after that, Susanna hoping Annie might nod off and give the women a chance to talk heart-to-heart. A number of years had passed since such a thing had happened between them—back before Rachel had married Jacob Yoder and joined up with the Beachy church. It wasn't that she and her youngest daughter didn't have much to say to each other; 'twasn't that at all. There was far more to it, and she 'sposed it had a lot to do with Rachel having been so close to her husband, Jacob Yoder. 'Course, she wouldn't be one to fault the couple for having had such a bond. But it did seem mighty unusual to have a relationship like that with a man.

As for her and Benjamin, their marriage was right suitable. Ben was a gut provider, no question about that, all the years of farming an' all. But to share her heart and soul with him would seem unnatural somehow; the furthest thing from her mind. How much easier to confide in another woman—an aunt or close female cousin—someone who truly understood how you felt, how you thought.

A light rain began to fall, coming down like a mist and without a smidgen of wind. The moisture made the vegetation along the road look greener. The leaves on the maple trees, too.

Susanna glanced over her shoulder at Annie, who had fallen asleep, sure enough. It was high time to forge ahead, and she did, opened her mouth up and got the words said right out. "Rachel, I know you may be opposed to what I wanna say, but I feel I should say it anyhow."

Rachel didn't move or speak, so Susanna continued. "When you were just a girl, I recognized some real special things in you, Daughter. Gifts from the almighty God, I'd say. But I wasn't the only one who noticed. Our bishop did, too, and so did the faith healers around here, 'specially after you held that water-witching stick and it came alive in your little hands. Remember that?"

Rachel winced. "Mamma, you're gonna talk about Blue Johnny. I know that's what you're workin' up to."

Susanna wasn't too surprised to hear Rachel speak up so; the young woman had been throwin' out her opinion quite freely here lately. "Blue Johnny's only the half of it," Susanna went on. "There's so much more for you to consider than whether or not you should go to him about your sight. To begin with, I'm a-thinkin' Blue Johnny has his eye on you, Rachel. I think he has you in mind to pass his healing powers to."

Rachel frowned. "Do ya really *think* so?"

"Jah . . . I do."

Her daughter was quiet for a spell. Then, "I never told you this, but Cousin Esther says powwowing is wrong—black as sin. She and Levi believe the angel of the Lord is siftin' through families, showing certain ones 'bout sins of their ancestors. They're even willin' to be the only ones in the family who repent and renounce those sins. And Esther says if they hafta stand alone in this, they will."

"Well, I'll be," Susanna muttered, figuring now was as gut a time to shut her mouth as any. But she sure didn't like hearing that Esther and Levi Glick, way out there in Ohio, were the ones filling her girl's head with this nonsense. What was the matter with them? Maybe somebody from the church here oughta set 'em straight, and if no one was up to the task, she wouldn't think twice about volunteering.

"Esther wants to be pure and spotless before the Lord, wants to clean house in her heart, with God's help." Rachel seemed too talkative all of a sudden. "Clear back through the generations of her and Levi's families, they wanna tidy up spiritually, so to speak."

"Well, that's *their* business, I'd hafta say. Just you remember that the gift transference from one healer to another is a sacred honor. You oughta know that by now. There's nothin' a bit sinful 'bout it, neither."

"But Esther says—"

"Your cousin's wrong," Susanna cut in. *Esther this and Esther that* . . . What on earth would Leah think of all this! Honestly, she hadn't heard any such blather since her preacher-uncle was alive and causin' an uproar amongst the People. "Seems you oughta be takin' a closer look at yourself, Daughter."

"What're you sayin'?"

She sighed. "If you ask me, it's your inclination toward the powwow gift that's makin' you blind."

Rachel gasped. "How can you say such a thing?"

"I've hit the nail on the head, and you know it."

Looking as if she might cry, Rachel confessed, "I'm all mixed up 'bout bein' tried for with Blue Johnny, really I am. Esther believes one thing; you say something else altogether. I just don't know what to think anymore."

Susanna felt her chest tighten, and she picked up the reins. Best they be gettin' on home. She didn't know how much more of this she could stand to hear.

Lord o' mercy, she thought. It was downright uncanny the way Rachel was spoutin' off Esther's heretical quibble—sounded like Gabriel Esh all over again, back from the dead.

———

Benjamin sat all of them down in the upstairs sitting room, Annie included, and read from the Bible. "'These six things doth the Lord hate; yea, seven are an abomination unto him: a proud look, a lying tongue, and hands that shed innocent blood, a heart that deviseth wicked imaginations . . .'" He paused for emphasis, then continued on, "'. . . feet that be swift in running to mischief, a false witness that speaketh lies, and he that soweth discord among brethren.'"

Rachel was perty sure Mam had filled Dat in on the comments Esther had made about powwowing and the evil thereof, thus the reason for the impromptu Bible-reading session. And the tone of reproof in Dat's voice.

"Can we hear the story of Samuel, when God calls to him in the temple?" Annie piped up.

"Jah, gut idea," Susanna said.

Rachel was silent, sitting next to Annie. *"It's your inclination toward the powwow gift that's making you blind. . . ."*

Mamma was wrong about what she'd said in the buggy, coming home from Lavina's! The more Rachel thought about it, the more Mam's statement upset her. She felt downright fatigued after spouting off so much in the buggy, defending her cousin thataway. Jah, she felt nearly as drained as she had after holding that dowsing fork in her little hands, twenty-one years ago.

And here Dat had just read a passage in Proverbs—nothin' whatsoever pertaining to Esther's and Levi's desire to forsake and repent of the past sins of their family. She truly felt she had been wrongly reprimanded, treated as a child. A *Sindhaft*—sinful child.

An astonishing thought crossed her mind: Had Gabriel Esh felt the selfsame way back long before she was ever born? He'd been shunned . . . but for what reason? For speaking out against sin? She had no way of knowing for sure, except for the hints Philip Bradley had dropped this morning on his way out the door.

While Dat read the Bible, she pondered these things silently.

––––––––––

"The Reading trip turned out to be a waste of time," Philip told Stephen Flory as the two men opened their supper menus. "Except for meeting an elderly gentleman in the graveyard."

"What do you mean?" Stephen blinked with anticipation.

"The groundskeeper had an interesting tidbit about Gabe Esh. Said flowers had been delivered and put on Gabe's grave every year on the man's birthday by the same florist shop."

"January seventh?"

Philip smiled his answer. "Too bad I didn't come to Pennsylvania and find the postcard two years ago."

"Why's that?"

"The flowers stopped coming about then."

Stephen leaned back in the booth, his arms crossed over his chest. "Let me guess—you traced the flowers to the florist and found nothing."

"I found something, but not what I wanted to hear." He inhaled deeply. "Adele Herr passed away a while back, it seems." He explained that both Gabe's sister and the florist had indicated they were aware of Miss Herr's death. "It's a closed door, I'm sorry to say. And I wonder if for some reason Adele never received the postcard in the first place."

"Let's double-check her obituary. Reading, right?"

Philip hadn't thought of doing that. "Sure, let's find out when and where she died." He took a drink of his water. "By the way, didn't you say you had something, from someone at your work?"

Stephen nodded slowly. "I don't know how it would be possible to track this down, knowing how tight-lipped the Amish are, but my colleague's friend seems to think that Gabe Esh was disowned by his father."

"For what reason?"

"Something to do with his resistance to a powerful bishop, though I don't know who."

"What kind of father would renounce his only son?" Philip asked, closing his menu.

"Your guess is as good as mine," Stephen said, his face solemn.

The waitress came to take their orders. Afterward, Philip was preoccupied with the unknown circumstances surrounding the postcard and its message. More than ever, he was determined to get to the root of the story.

———

Susanna brought the mail inside, eyeing a tape mailer from Ohio. She assumed the package was another one of those spoken "letters" her niece and Rachel had been sending back and forth. She thought of listening to the tape first, before giving it to her daughter, but didn't dwell on that notion, knowing she wouldn't be able to live with herself for doing such a thing.

"Here's something for you." She placed the small package in Rachel's hand.

"From Esther?"

"Must be. The postmark's Ohio."

Rachel's face burst into a rainbow of a smile, and Susanna knew something was up. 'Course, then again, maybe not. Maybe the two women were just eager to correspond. It was just the idea of Esther reading all those Bible passages to Rachel that got her goat. Certain sections of Scripture were sanctioned by their bishop for use in personal reading and meditation. Seemed to her Rachel and Esther—Levi, too— had launched off on their own private exploration of God's Word. Didn't seem right, really. Too much like the Mennonites' way, but she wasn't about to consider that just now. She had enough problems of her own to take on the world, the flesh, and the devil.

Rachel decided to wait till later to listen to Esther's tape recording. She couldn't tell for sure, but it seemed Mam might be too interested in what it had to say. She'd had enough of a run-in with her mother and felt a bit hemmed in. So she decided to wait for sleep to fall over the house before ever listening to Esther's tape-letter.

She had an idea that it was time to talk with Annie about some personal things. *Other* things besides the fact that the child was too friendly with strangers; it seemed to her that Annie hadn't made any big mistake by talking to the New York City writer. No, Philip Bradley came across as right trustworthy. 'Course, you could never be too sure of that, 'specially with outsiders.

What she needed to bring herself to do was tell Annie the things Rachel remembered about Jacob and Aaron. About their life together before the accident, because evidently there was really nothing else she could add to what Dat had already told his little granddaughter. It appeared to be no secret that Dat and Mam had taken it upon themselves to bring up the subject of the accident with Annie.

So tonight, just as soon as the supper dishes were washed and cleared away, she would sit down with her little daughter and share with her the recollections of the wonderful-gut days. Days marked with laughter and sunshine, sounds of woodworking comin' from the barn, and smells of sawdust on the floor. Playful bickering between brother and sister, and the life-giving movement within Rachel's womb.

Jah, the best days of her life . . . gone forever.

The drive to the Reading cemetery had been for the express purpose of locating Gabe Esh's tombstone, and Philip had ignored it altogether, he realized as he drove the short distance back to the Orchard Guest House B&B. There he had stood just seven rows of markers away from the Amishman's grave. Yet he'd turned on his heels to follow the interesting but dead-end lead to the florist shop.

Why he hadn't taken time to stop and pay his respects at the cemetery was beyond him. Now as he thought about it, he concluded that he had made an error in judgment, though at the time, it seemed the right thing to do—chasing after the unknown person responsible for yearly outpourings of love.

He wouldn't beat himself up over it, and he dismissed it as he pulled into the B&B driveway, noticing an abundance of cars. *The place is booked solid*, he thought, getting out of the car and wondering what he would do tomorrow to kill some time. Perhaps a bit of sightseeing was in order. No, what he really wanted to do was pitch hay with some Amishmen. Get a feel for more things Amish.

As for tonight, he would take a fresh look at his article before retiring. With the inclusion of Annie's Christmas tablet and colored pencils, and the addition of a strong yet heartwarming wrap-up, he was actually finished with the piece. He would email it to Bob first thing in the morning.

Heading to his room, he greeted Susanna, who forced a smile and nodded. *What a difference*, he thought, remembering the uncommon cordiality at the outset, followed by the more frosty treatment just hours after his arrival.

He wouldn't let it get the best of him. The thing he most wanted to do in the time remaining was to show continued kindness to Rachel—that is, if he should meet up with her again—and to be attentive to the little girl. He felt the child had been sorely cheated by fate. No father—at least no mention of one—a blind mother, and an overbearing grandmother. Annie's grandfather seemed disconnected to the family, though he assumed well his patriarchal position. Philip couldn't imagine the man going fishing with Annie—if Amish children even did such things with their elders. No, Benjamin Zook took more of a passive role with his exuberant grandchild, letting the women in Annie's life have the say-so. Yet the child displayed a sense of security and happiness. It made no sense, but then, life was rather senseless most of the time, he conceded.

Rachel stayed put in her bedroom till after Annie was sound asleep. She got down on her hands and knees and rummaged around, trying to locate the electrical outlet near the bed, hoping she wouldn't cause too much noise and alert Mam. She didn't want Susanna to know she was still up, not this late, and she wanted complete privacy in listening to Esther's tape.

As it turned out, there had been no time to talk heart-to-heart with her little one as she'd planned. Mam had requested another round of Bible reading after supper. Dat had obliged, though it was apparent by the monotone that his heart wasn't much in it. Mam's doing, for sure.

Once Annie was bathed and dressed in her nightgown, it was too late to get such a serious talk started. Too late for a little girl to drift off to dreamland, thinking of the daddy she'd lost to death and the bright-eyed older brother no longer alive to tease or play with her.

So their talk would wait till tomorrow, after breakfast prob'ly. That's what Rachel decided and felt better about it. She hoped and prayed the dear Lord would guide her words, help her say the things that truly should be said, according to Dat and Mam anyways.

Sliding the volume down all the way to the lowest setting, she pushed the tape into the recorder and began to listen for the soft voice of her cousin.

Dearest Rachel,

I couldn't wait a minute longer for a letter from you, so I'm starting this tape now. It's Monday night, September thirteenth, and the house is as quiet as it ever gets around here, I 'spose. I trust everything's all right there with you, that you're healthy and Annie's well, too. Guess you're busy during the fall tourist season, and we are, too, but in a different way. I've put up more applesauce than ever; pickles, corn, succotash, and more chowchow, too.

Levi's been visiting with our preacher quite a lot this week. God continues to show us individually—and in the church body here—the importance of identifying generational sins and repenting of them. More and more, different ones in our church district are coming forward to confess patterns of family sins. What a joy to know that our prayers and testimony of faith are making a difference.

How're Susanna and Benjamin? We're praying for your parents more than ever, that the Lord will work in their hearts through His Word and through the nudging of the Holy Spirit, and that old

Bishop Seth will wake up to the truths of the Gospel. We must pray that the Lord will plant a hunger in him for God's Word, then he could encourage the People to search out the Scriptures. It's not so farfetched, really. We've been hearing of a real stirring—jah, a breakout of revival—amongst Plain circles in many areas. So we can pray and know our prayers are more powerful than anything we might do or say.

It's gettin' awful late now. I hear Levi a-snorin' so loud he's gonna shake the bed frame loose. That actually happened once. You should've seen the look on his face when he woke up with the mattress sliding toward the floor! It was a right funny sight to behold.

James, Ada, Mary, and Elijah are growin' like weeds—I can hardly keep them in clothes. I'm not complainin', but it keeps a body goin' in circles, trying to keep up with all the sewin' and whatnot all.

Before I sign off, I want to leave you with a verse from Second Corinthians, chapter two, verse fourteen. Here it is: "Now thanks be unto God, which always causeth us to triumph in Christ, and maketh manifest the savour of his knowledge by us in every place. For we are unto God a sweet savour of Christ, in them that are saved, and in them that perish. . . ."

That part about us being a sweet savour or fragrance to God is so encouraging to me . . . and you, too, ain't? I'll be sendin' you another preachin' tape from our pastor's sermon soon.

Well, I need my sleep for tomorrow's work. Blessings to you, dear cousin. And just as soon as you can, please send me a tape back. Give your darling girl a big hug from Cousin Esther.

Rachel turned off the recorder and hid the tape under her pillow. It was a wonderful-gut feeling to know that Esther, too, would prob'ly be listening to a tape tomorrow—the one Rachel had made for her two nights ago.

As she climbed into bed, she remembered the cutting, cruel thing Mam had said to her—about her special giftings being the reason Rachel was blind. And she wondered what Esther would think if she told her.

To soothe herself, she thought of the beautiful verse her cousin had quoted on the tape recording. *For we are unto God a sweet savour of Christ. . . .*

The words comforted her as she plumped her pillow and lay down. The day had been as trying as any recently, and the Scripture from Esther was just what she needed to think on as she entrusted her sleep, and her dreams, to God.

Eighteen

❖ ❖ ❖

O n another day the early-morning landscape might have had a
mark of lackluster, but in the predawn hour, Philip found
himself seized by the awakening countryside. He walked
west to Gibbons Road, then south to Beechdale, toward an iron-gated
entrance to Beechdale Farm, relishing the quietude, the peace of his surroundings. What he wouldn't give to bottle up the tranquil setting and
carry it back with him to New York.

Standing along the road in the midst of daybreak gold, he considered
his life as one might at the conclusion of it. Where had he been heading
these twenty-seven years? Would the path he was treading lead him out
of his feature writer's cubicle to a senior staff writer's office? Was *that*
what he wanted? What of the fading thrill of the chase—the journalistic
hunt—the lonely hours and days of writing one assigned article, followed by yet another? How could such a life be Frost's road "less traveled by" that truly "made all the difference"?

The sun inched past the horizon, casting lengthy shadows over the
fence palings, spilling them across the road. He longed for a stroll down
one of the wagon paths he'd spied earlier, especially one bordered by
identical cornfields on either side. Not willing to trespass, he continued
walking south on Beechdale Road, toward Highway 340 and the village
shops of Bird-in-Hand. No real direction to his journey. No viable reason to be out and roaming this early, except that he had awakened hours
before his usual "rise and shine." Not having had adequate exercise in
the past days, he'd slipped out of the house before the slightest indica-
tion of life was in evidence, meaning Susanna Zook had not made her
presence known at the hour of his departure.

Stopping again, he propped his foot on the lower rung of a roadside fence, aware of the heavy dew on grass, foliage, and rust-red marigolds. He contemplated the hustle and flurry awaiting him at the magazine upon his return. Normally after finishing an assignment he would look ahead, ready to embark on the next. But over the past months his passion had waned to the point that he had mentioned to his mother that he might be considering a career change.

"At *your* age?" she'd replied, indicating with a grin that he was much too young to be disillusioned with his work.

"It's a mad chase all the time. Maybe it's just me. . . ."

"And maybe it's the *city* that doesn't agree with you. Lots of folk don't handle commotion well. Manhattan might not be your cup of tea, Phil."

Mom knew him about as well as anyone. She was right on, several counts' worth. He wasn't happiest among the glitz and the hubbub of big city life. "What would it be like to have a truck farm somewhere?" he'd blurted.

His mother's eyes lit up. "Now that would make your grandpap smile."

Shaking his head, he changed the subject to an upcoming European trip. "Pipe dreams."

"You must be having one of those days, right?"

Indeed, he'd confessed to having had a frustrating week in general. Not often he admitted something like that to her. Dad, maybe. Never Mom. Didn't need to; she always knew.

A lone horse and buggy came up behind him, the spirited mare stepping out smartly as it pulled a gray boxlike carriage on its tall, oversized wheels, *clip-clopping* toward the intersection of Beechdale and Route 340. It stopped, then crept out, clattering onto the main highway.

He'd never contemplated what it would be like to ride in an Amish buggy or any carriage, for that matter. The pace was problematic, he decided. Except, of course, if he'd never experienced the power and speed of a car. Yet Abram Beiler had said the Amish liked the *inconvenience* of horse and buggy travel because it let them "stop and smell the roses" of life, allowed them to feel the pith and the rhythm of their unsophisticated, sylvan reality.

His cell phone rang just then, interrupting the repose. "Phil Bradley here."

"Sorry I'm calling so early." It was Janice.

"It's not early here," he joked. "I've been up for two hours."

"Everything all right?" Naturally, she would assume something was wrong.

"I'm out on a ramble across a deserted byway and a wooded bower and—"

"Phil, you sound strange. You sure you're okay?"

"I'm okay if you're okay."

"No, seriously, I need to know when you're due in tomorrow."

"I'll have to let you know. My flight information's back at the B&B."

"So. . . . you really are out on a walk this early."

"Ramble."

"Whatever."

He didn't think he could do justice, describing the sky just now. "I wish you could see the sun coming up. This place is nearly as captivating as Vermont, I guess."

"You're way out there, aren't you?" she remarked with a laugh. "Okay, I'll wait for your call later. But don't forget, unless, of course, you'd rather take a cab into the city."

"I vote for the welcoming committee. How is Kari doing?"

"Just waking up. I'll tell her you said hi."

"Yes, do that."

"Well, I'd better get busy here. Enjoy your last day in the bush."

"Don't worry. I'll talk to you later, sis."

He clicked off the phone and planted himself in the grassy eaves between the road and a potato field, staring through distant black trees as the sun made its glimmering ascent. Never had he witnessed a more awe-inspiring sight as this. Never had he felt so unsettled, glimpsing the panorama of his life.

Susanna made note of Philip Bradley's absence at the table. The man was clearly sleeping in, and she wasn't about to take breakfast up to a lazy man. He'd just have to miss out.

"After bit, Dat and I have to make a quick run over to Smoketown," she informed Rachel. "But we won't be gone for long, I don't expect."

"Annie and I will be all right here. Take your time, Mam."

"I won't leave you with all the dishes, and I'll help strip down the beds before we go."

"That's fine, and I'll wash down all the showers while you're gone," Rachel said, gathering up two plates of eggs and bacon, one for herself and one for Annie. She picked up the heavy tray and started to shuffle toward the parlor. "You know where to find us."

"Wait . . . let me do that for you." Susanna intervened, taking the long wooden tray from Rachel, carrying it into the parlor room, where Annie was already drinking a glass of milk, a white ring above her lip. "There you are, girlie. How wouldja like some bacon and eggs with your glass of milk?"

Annie nodded, pulling her chair up to the sofa table she and Rachel always used for their private meals. "Can I take Copper out for a little walk after breakfast?"

"Don't see why not," Susanna replied, glancing at Rachel. "S'okay with you, Daughter?"

"If you stay away from the creek, Annie. You know what Dawdi Ben says about that. There's a couple hornets' nests down there, remember?"

"Jah, I remember. I spied 'em one day when Joshua came to visit."

Susanna said, "Well, just so you obey your mamma. Copper's leash is hanging out on the back hook, you know."

"Denki, Mammi! I'll take gut care of your doggie, I will."

She set the eggs and bacon and the smaller plates piled high with toast on the table, then removed the tray and headed for the kitchen. "Annie's gonna have herself a nice morning," she told Ben as he came through the kitchen on his way outside.

"A gut day to be outside," Ben called over his shoulder to her.

"Jah, a right gut day to be alive," she whispered, hurrying around to finish up the breakfast for the guests. She hadn't given Esther Glick's tape a second thought. Not till just now, and she didn't rightly know why. Maybe it was Rachel's somewhat subdued manner in the parlor. Maybe it was nothing, really.

———————

"Annie, honey," Rachel began hesitantly, when they were alone, "I wanna tell you what I remember about your father and brother."

The parlor was quiet, though she could hear Annie's soft breathing. "Dawdi Ben and Mammi Susanna already said how they died. Car hit 'em . . .'cause the horse got spooked."

"I didn't wanna talk about the accident so much as I thought we could share our favorite memories about Dat and Aaron.'' She felt a lump in her throat and was afraid she might lose control.

Annie was silent.

''You all right, honey?''

There were sniffles just then. ''I don't remember anything,'' said Annie. ''I tried plenty of times to think what my brother and Dat looked like, but it's all fuzzy in my head.''

Like my eyes, thought Rachel.

''Well, then, let me tell you about the things I remember. Our wonderful, happy days together . . . all of us.'' She told of long walks on summer afternoons, of taking the pony cart and filling it with hay on a sweet September night, and watching the lightning bugs dance up and down all over the meadow. ''Dat loved nature, and Aaron, too. We were gonna buy us a big farm in Ohio, near where Esther and Levi live.''

''We were? I didn't ever know that.''

''Your father wanted to have dairy cows just like my brothers Noah and Joseph do.''

''You mean over at Dawdi Ben's old place?''

''That's right. But we're here now—you and me—with your grandparents, and God's takin' care of us.''

''And we're helpin' lots of tourists have a place to sleep at night, ain't so, Mamma?''

''Jah, we are that.'' She hoped this little talk with Annie might satisfy her father's request. ''Is there anything you want to ask me?''

''Why'd you go blind, Mamma?'' came the sincere words. ''Dawdi Ben says you weren't even in the buggy when the car hit us, so how'd you get blind?''

''Oh, honey, I wish I could tell you.''

''But you don't remember—that's what Dawdi says. You can't remember nothin' much about that day.''

''I know *one* thing,'' she was able to say. ''I'm ever so thankful that you weren't hurt too awful bad, that you were safe. God protected you . . . for me.''

Annie's little arms slipped around her neck. ''Oh, Mamma.''

Rachel felt Annie's warm tears on her face. ''I'm so sorry, little one . . . so very sorry. I should've never brought this up.''

Annie whimpered against her neck, not saying anything. All the while, Rachel held her precious girl in her arms, rocking her and humming a hymn.

After Annie had calmed down some, Rachel stood at the kitchen counter with Esther's tape, preparing to roll out dough for piecrusts, which Mam had prepared before leaving the house. Annie, bound and determined to take Copper for a short walk, had left not but five minutes before. Rachel figured she oughta keep her hands busy awhile; keep her mind busy, too, by listening again to her cousin's encouraging tape recording while she rolled out the dough.

The talk with Annie had upset them both, though she hadn't cried the way her darling girl had. What *was* she thinking, rehashing those things with one so young? She wouldn't harbor bitterness toward Dat for prompting such a conversation, no. She'd forgive him for bringing it up in the first place, for pushing her beyond her better judgment.

Just then, she heard pounding noises in the cellar. Sounded like something amiss with the washing machine, and she hurried down to check.

He had done a lot of walking in his day, but never so far on an empty stomach. Upon his return to the guesthouse, Philip was glad to find a few sticky buns left on the corner table in the common area. Susanna hadn't forgotten him, even though she seemed to be distancing herself from him. He stood in the front window, looking out while he devoured the fat, juicy pastry, licking his fingers clean when he was finished.

Only his rental car remained in the designated parking area, and he assumed he must be the only guest still around. The house seemed devoid of sound, too quiet, as he made his way upstairs to his room. Where was everyone?

He was surprised to see his room already clean, the bed made and towels freshened. "No time wasted around here," he muttered, heading for the closet. The postcard lay hidden in Philip's briefcase, and though he had uncovered only a few links to Gabe and Adele, he found it impossible to dismiss the young Amishman's urgent message. In his hands he held the final remnant to a long-ago love story, compelling and heartrending. One that he might never fully know. The realization struck him anew.

Sitting at the desk, he relocated the narrow drawer—the one that had been stuck—where he'd first discovered the postcard. Mentally, he ticked off a summary of the facts: Emma, at the antique shop, had acquired the desk two years ago, followed by the new owner, Susanna Zook. Evidently, the postcard had been placed inside the desk at some point prior to Emma's discovering the piece at the secondhand store in Reading—before Susanna ever laid eyes on it. Which meant the postcard must have managed to arrive safely in Reading at its intended destination. *Then why had Adele discarded such a message?* The question burned into his brain.

Philip wished he could offer the postcard as a remembrance to someone close to Adele Herr. Someone who might have loved her as a sister or dear friend. Surely, there was someone alive who had been devoted to the woman.

He went to brush his teeth; he had to get the sugary residue from the sticky bun out of his mouth. After doing so, he connected his cell phone and emailed the Amish family article to his editor in New York. He shut down his laptop, thinking that somehow or other he'd like to give Rachel a report of his trip to Reading, if that was even possible without Susanna overhearing. He went to the wall of built-in bookcases, scanning the choices and deciding on an old classic. He was just getting comfortable when he heard the sound of high-pitched barking. The commotion persisted until he was drawn to the window to see what was causing a dog to carry on so.

Below him on the patio, Rachel was floundering with her cane, trying to find her way while bumping into one flower pot after another. "Annie!" she called again and again.

He rushed downstairs, and when he burst out the back door and caught up with Rachel, he saw that she was weeping. "Annie!" she called pitifully. "Annie, where are you?"

But there was no answer, only the frenzied barking in the distance.

"Rachel, it's me, Philip Bradley," he said calmly, so as not to startle her. "What's happening?"

She was pushing her feet through the lawn, her cane swinging back and forth. "Annie went walking the dog . . . she hasn't come home for the longest time. Now Copper's barking out by the creek, and I'm terribly frightened."

"I'll look for Annie. Will you wait here?" he said, concerned that Rachel might stumble and fall.

"Please, bring her home to me." Her face was streaked with tears.

"I'll find her." He turned and ran toward the dog's yelping, through the apple trees, past the gravel walkway, over the footbridge, and to the opposite side of the creek. "Annie!" he called. Behind him he could still hear Rachel's distressed cries for her daughter.

The little girl sat in a heap of crumpled leaves on the bank of Mill Creek, her long rose-colored dress soiled, her white head covering in her hand. The dog was crouched near her, howling till his bark was nearly ragged.

"Annie, are you all right?" Philip hurried over to her, noticing a reddish swelling on her face.

"Oh, Mr. Philip, I got stinged so awful bad."

He saw that she had been crying and was rubbing her cheek where the swelling had extended past the wound itself. Searching for a stinger and finding none, he suspected that Annie had been stung by a wasp.

"I didn't . . . disobey Mamma, Mr. Philip . . . honest, I didn't. Copper got away from me, and I had to . . . run and catch him." She was wheezing now, and he recognized the dangerous asthmatic symptoms. His niece, Kari, often had such flare-ups, but this was different. Annie must be suffering from an allergic reaction.

"Ach, my head hurts, too," the little girl cried.

"Let's get you home. Your mamma's worried about you." He was concerned about her labored breathing and gathered the child into his arms. Dashing over the footbridge and through the orchard, he kept saying, "I'll take care of you, Annie. Don't cry, honey."

The braids that wound around her head began to fall loose as he ran with her toward the house. The dog nipped at his heels behind him, barking incessantly.

When he was within yards of the house, he caught sight of the girl's mother. "Quick, Rachel, hold on to my arm," he called, hurrying over to her. "Annie's been stung. Let's get you both inside."

When Rachel and Annie were safely in the kitchen, Rachel leaned down to listen to her daughter's breathing.

"Does Annie have asthma?" Philip asked, still holding the child with Rachel hovering near.

"No . . . not asthma," Rachel whispered.

"Is she allergic to wasps or bees, that you know of?"

"This has never happened before." Rachel stroked Annie's face, letting go of Philip's arm.

"She needs a doctor right away, unless you have an inhaler, something to open an airway.'' The child was starting to go limp in his arms. ''Where's the nearest hospital?''

''I'll call 9-1-1,'' Rachel said, her hand shaking as she reached for the phone.

''There's no time for that. You'll have to trust me. I can get Annie to a hospital faster than waiting for an ambulance.''

Rachel grimaced. ''The Community Hospital is the closest one.''

Philip lost no time in getting Annie and her mother into his rental car. Nor could he spare a moment to consider Rachel's possible aversion to riding in a modern-day conveyance rather than the familiar horse and buggy.

On the way, Rachel whispered to the child in her first language, kissing her forehead every so often. She sat in the backseat, cradling Annie in her arms.

Philip pushed the speed limit where there was less traffic, hoping a policeman might spot him and escort them to the emergency room. He sensed a dire urgency as he stole glances at Rachel and her child in the rearview mirror. Annie's continual struggle to breathe worried him so much he dialed 9-1-1 on his cell phone and alerted the hospital that they were on their way.

The closer they came to the downtown area, the more congested the traffic became, slowing their pace. For the first time in many years, he found himself praying under his breath.

Nineteen

❖ ❖ ❖

With great apprehension, Philip made himself pick up a sports magazine and thumb through it, impatient for some word—anything—on Annie's condition. He glanced up now and then to watch people coming and going. People watching. It was one of his favorite pastimes, though under the circumstances, he would much rather have been in an airport or any other public place. Hospitals made him nervous.

How was Annie doing now? The little child had looked absolutely miserable there by the creek bank when first he'd found her. And her breathing was terribly wispy, threadlike, continuing to be so as he carried her into the emergency room entrance not twenty minutes ago.

And what of Susanna Zook and her husband? Had both of them left the house? It seemed a bit strange that they would leave their blind daughter home alone with the rambunctious child, but then he didn't know their routine well enough to cast blame. The truth was, a little girl's life was hanging in the balance even as he sat here in the ER waiting room. He wished he could do something to guarantee that young Annie would survive the ordeal, come out of it unscathed. But it was difficult to erase the visions of her gasping for air, her tiny lungs giving out no matter how fast he had been willing to speed down the streets of Lancaster.

It was while he was recalling the morning's chaos that he realized he didn't know Rachel's last name. Couldn't be the same as her parents, or could it? She must surely have been married at one time or other. He took out his pen and a small tablet—the one he carried with him everywhere—and began jotting down all the things he *did* know about Rachel, though for no special reason. Instead of doodling like some folk, he often wrote lists of words, characteristics of people, or one-word descriptions of places. Though he had never actually put pen to paper and attempted to write a novel, he'd toyed with the idea often enough. And he had dozens of such character and setting lists in a file at home just waiting for the moment when he might actually get serious about fiction writing. If ever.

Rachel trembled inwardly as she held Annie's limp hand in the emergency room. A number of nurses and the ER doctor surrounded them, administering the initial treatment—a shot of epinephrine, a muscle relaxant to aid in opening airways, and a bronchodilator, a fancy name for an inhaler, Rachel was told.

She imagined the doctor listening with a stethoscope to Annie's lungs, to make sure the constricted airways were beginning to open, though she continued to hear her daughter's raspy breathing.

"Is Annie gonna be all right?" she asked, her own chest feeling somewhat tight.

"The doctor wants to observe Annie for several hours, just to make sure she's clear before we release her," one nurse said. "You got her here just in time."

"Has Annie ever had a reaction like this from a sting?" the doctor inquired.

"Never before."

"If she is ever stung again, the second reaction is often more severe than the first. I'd recommend an epi-kit to keep with Annie wherever she goes."

"What's that . . . an epi-kit?"

"It's a wallet-sized case with a spring-loaded syringe similar to the shot we just gave your daughter. If Annie should ever experience similar symptoms, she or you can easily poke it into her thigh, or most any place on her body—even through her clothes. It could save her life," said the doctor with an ominous note of warning in his voice. "You can get one from your family doctor."

"I'd be interested in having something like that handy," Rachel said, wishing they *had* a family physician who was a real medical doctor.

Later, when she sensed she was alone with Annie, she leaned down and put her ear against the small chest. The crackling in Annie's lungs was beginning to subside.

"Can I sit up now, Mamma? I feel ever so much better."

"Why don't we wait till the doctor comes back." She cupped Annie's cheeks in her hands. "I'm so glad the Lord was with us."

"I feel awful jittery, Mamma."

"Jah, you're much better, but try to sit still so you won't fall off the examining table."

When the nurse came back, Rachel asked about Annie's sudden surge of energy. "She seems terribly restless."

"It's quite normal for her to feel a bit hyper, just until some of the adrenaline wears off."

Over a period of two and a half hours, there was repeated checking on the part of various nurses. Later, the doctor returned to discuss the benefits of allergen solutions or vaccines "to prevent a similar situation from occurring in the future. Hyposensitization is a long-term treatment by which an allergen is injected into the patient at regular intervals, at ever larger doses," he explained. "The body builds up a tolerance over time—three to five years in the case of wasp and bee stings. You may want to consider the desensitization route where Annie's concerned, especially if she plays outside a lot, or more specifically, in the vicinity of a creek, where bees and wasps tend to gather."

"I'll talk it over with my parents," Rachel replied.

"Well, I think Annie's ready to go home. She may seem tired after the shot wears off. Have her take it easy today," he suggested, then paused a moment. "Excuse me, I don't mean to be forward, but you look very familiar to me. Have you ever been treated at this hospital?"

"Well, yes . . . two years ago I had a miscarriage."

"I thought I remembered you and your family . . . yes, I remember quite clearly now." He was silent again. Then, "How is it that you are still blind, Mrs. Yoder?"

"On my best days I see shadows, but other than that, I don't see much of anything."

"But your vision . . . how can this be?"

She told him that she'd consulted a specialist. "He said my brain was recording images, yet I don't see them."

"Have you had any treatment?"

"What do you mean?" She'd heard there were professionals who offered hypnosis and other forms of psychotherapy. Such things didn't interest her—sounded like hocus-pocus to her, and there was far too much of that going on already.

"Would you like a referral for a psychiatrist friend of mine? I think he could help you."

Suddenly, she felt coerced—put on the spot—though she supposed she ought to be open to a truly medical remedy since she wasn't too sure about the alternative doctoring in the community. "I . . . uh, hadn't thought about it really."

"Well, here's my card if you should decide to try it."

She felt the business card against her hand and accepted it with her feeble thanks.

When Susanna and Benjamin returned home, Susanna spied the flour and the rolling pin on the kitchen table, wondering where Rachel could be. She checked the upstairs rooms, then the parlor again. Searching the cellar, as well, she called for Rachel and Annie, who was apt to come flying through the house most any time now. "Rachel . . . Annie . . . are you here? Where are you?"

When there was no reply, she rushed back to the kitchen, only to see Benjamin outside with the dog. "The dog's here, at least."

"Any sign of Rachel or Annie?"

"I checked the footpath . . . nothing."

Unwilling to entertain panic-ridden thoughts, she spun in circles as she stood on the flagstone patio. "Well, it looks like Rachel or *somebody* was rolling out a couple o' pies, so where on earth could they be?"

"Gone for a walk maybe?" came Ben's reply. "I wouldn't be too worried."

"With dough spread out all over the table? I don't believe Rachel would do such a thing—leave the kitchen in such a mess."

"Well, you know how Annie is. She's been coaxin' her mamma out in the sunshine these past few days."

"But Rachel would've made her wait a bit—till the pies were filled and in the oven at least." Susanna felt mighty uneasy and ran back inside. That's when she happened to notice that Philip Bradley's car was no longer parked out front. "Himmel, he didn't kidnap 'em, did he?" she muttered, knowing she best not tell Ben what she was thinking just now.

When the phone rang, Susanna was out of breath. "Zooks' Orchard Guest House. Susanna Zook speaking."

"Mamma! I'm ever so happy you're home."

"Rachel, where are you?"

"At the hospital. Annie had a horrid wasp sting, and Philip Bradley drove us to town."

"Philip Brad—"

"It's all right, Mam. Annie's breathing is much, much better now. The color's come back in her cheeks, too. . . . But we nearly lost her."

Susanna put her hand to her forehead. "My, oh my, you gave us a fright, leavin' the house thataway. We hardly knew what to think, Dat and I."

"Annie's gonna be all right—that's what matters," Rachel said. "We have so much to thank the Lord for."

Gathering her wits, Susanna offered to have Benjamin call a Mennonite van driver. "We'll come get you."

"No . . . no, that's all right, really. Mr. Bradley's here with us. He'll bring us home when it's time."

Mr. Bradley this, and Philip Bradley that. . . . Thank goodness the man was checking out tomorrow!

Once Annie was stabilized and given the okay to leave, Philip guided Rachel to the accounting window. There, he learned of Rachel's last name for the first time. Yoder. So—she was Rachel Yoder. He found himself wanting very much to remember.

She requested that the bill for treatment be mailed to Benjamin Zook. "Annie and I live with my father," she said, explaining that she had rushed out the door without money, not even a purse. "We don't carry medical insurance. It's *das alt Gebrauch*—the Old Way of doing things."

No insurance? Philip was stunned. How risky, especially raising an adventuresome child like Annie. Upon further investigation, he discovered that Amish folk didn't buy insurance of most *any* kind. They took care of each other through individual donations and the Amish Aid Society, a fund set up primarily for the purpose of aiding their farmers in the case of losses due to lightning, storms, or fires.

In the frenzy of leaving the house to get Annie to the ER, Rachel had evidently forgotten to bring along her cane as well. Now both Annie and Philip walked on either side of her, guiding her safely out to the car. What an odd-looking trio they must appear to be to anyone observing— Philip wearing modern attire, Rachel in her mourning dress—black apron and white prayer veiling—and young Annie still wearing the smudged rose-colored dress.

"I think you best be thankin' Mr. Bradley for savin' your life," Rachel said as they walked.

"*Philip,*" he reminded her. "Call me Philip."

"Ach, I forgot already."

He laughed softly, thinking about her obvious hesitation with his first name. "Does a guy named 'Mr. Bradley' sound like someone who goes around saving little girls from wasp stings?"

Annie peeked around her mother's long dress at him, grinning. "You're funny, Mr. Philip. I like you. I wish you would stay 'round longer."

"Maybe I'll have to come back and visit again, how's that?"

She seemed satisfied with the idea, bobbing her little head up and down. Annie had a peachy glow about her now, probably from the adrenaline in the shot. Her hair had been neatly rebraided and wound around her head while in the emergency room. Rachel's doing, he assumed.

After they were settled in the car and heading back toward Bird-in-Hand, he heard Rachel tell Annie, "Never since the accident have I been so frightened as today."

"You mean since Dat and Aaron died?" Annie replied, next to Rachel in the backseat.

"Jah, since then."

Philip was stunned and spoke up, "Someone in your family was killed?"

"A car hit our market wagon, and my father and brother died," Annie said. "I was only four, so I don't much remember. But I broke my arm."

Unbelievable! To think that Rachel's husband and child had died so horribly. No wonder the young woman continued to wear her drab mourning clothes. How had Rachel and Annie been spared such an accident? He'd seen an Amish buggy up close enough to touch on his early-morning walk. The thought of a car ramming into a fragile rig like that, why, there was no way a person could survive an impact involving three tons—

"If anything had happened to you today," Rachel was saying to her little girl, "I could never have forgiven myself. Never."

"But it wasn't your fault I got stung by that mean old hornet,"

Annie insisted. "And Dawdi Ben says it ain't your fault about the accident at the Crossroad, neither."

Now it was Rachel who was silent, and Philip drove for several minutes without glancing once in his rearview mirror.

The sun bore down on the hood of the car as Philip drove Rachel and Annie Yoder back to Bird-in-Hand, to their home at Orchard Guest House. He thought of another Orchard House, though not an inn open to overnight guests. It was the Massachusetts home of Louisa May Alcott, a favorite author of his niece. He had taken Kari, along with her parents, on a tour of the old place on the outskirts of Concord. Set back in the woods, off a narrow, tree-lined road, stood the big brown house where the classic novel *Little Women* had been penned in 1868.

The call from Stephen Flory to his cell phone came quite unexpectedly as Philip was approaching Smoketown. "I think you're going to be very interested in something, Philip."

"What's up?"

"Believe it or not, a woman in Reading —residing in a nursing home—is willing to tell you what she knows of Gabe Esh and Adele Herr."

"You're kidding."

"The ailing woman's name is Lily, in case you wish to pursue the lead."

"Do I ever!" He thought Rachel might be fascinated to hear this. "Sounds too good to be true."

"The connection came from a very reliable source right there in the Bird-in-Hand community—a friend-of-a-friend sort of thing—so you can believe it."

"Thanks, Stephen. I'll call you later, okay?"

"By the way, I'm still checking on that obit for you," Stephen added. "If Adele Herr died anywhere in Pennsylvania, I should be able to track down the death notice."

"Maybe this Lily in Reading can fill me in. Thanks."

"Give me a call when you can. I'll have more details for you."

Philip wondered how Susanna Zook would react when he asked to rebook his room. Again. As for juggling his flight schedule—that is *if* the Reading visit forced him to extend his stay—he might decide to take the Amtrak back to New York. At any rate, he'd have to give Bob Snell another call. Janice too.

"I may have some interesting news for you about your mother's uncle by this evening," he told Rachel, glancing over his shoulder.

"What do you mean?" she asked a bit hesitantly.

"A friend of mine put his feelers out and has a lead on someone who seems to know the woman Gabe wanted to marry. Looks like I'll be heading back to Reading this afternoon, hopefully."

Rachel was quiet. He wondered if she might have inquired more were it not for Annie seated next to her, looking wide-eyed. And now quite bushy-tailed.

"Sometime I'd like to tell you what I discovered in Reading . . . at a cemetery there," he said discreetly, even though Annie was hardly paying attention to the conversation.

Back at the Amish inn, Philip phoned his editor and left a message on his office phone. Next, he called Janice, who offered to pray for him while he was having some much needed "R 'n R." Downstairs, he waited for three other guests to complete the check-out process, expedited efficiently by Susanna Zook.

"I don't suppose it would be possible to lengthen my stay," he said as he paid his bill in full.

Susanna shook her head stiffly. "We're sold out up through the next full month." She flipped through a black leather notebook. "Sorry."

She offered not a word about his having befriended her daughter and granddaughter. No show of gratitude, though Philip wasn't looking for it. Still, he thought she seemed rather pleased that her B&B was fully booked—that there was not even a square inch left for one Philip Bradley.

He returned to his upstairs quarters to pack his bag. Finished with that small chore, he closed his laptop and carried his personal belongings to the front door, not bothering to call a good-bye to either Rachel or Annie, though he would have liked to, providing Susanna hadn't been hovering there, waiting for him to exit. She was so eager to see him out, in fact, she opened the door as if shooing out a nasty fly.

Outside, Benjamin was stooped over in the hot sun, weeding a long bed of low-growing cushion mums of red, yellow, and bronze. He looked up from his crouched position and nodded. "Didja enjoy your stay with us, Mr. Bradley?" the man asked, scratching his beard.

"Very much, sir. Have a nice day."

"And the same to you" came the tentative reply.

Philip proceeded quickly to his car, eager to phone Stephen Flory for more details regarding Lily, the friend of Adele Herr. Before pulling out of the driveway, he chatted by cell phone with Stephen about the location of Fairview Nursing Home and whom to contact once he arrived there. Also the phone number. "Any suggestions on a place to stay around here? Or maybe even Reading, if need be. I've been booted out."

"No kidding." Stephen seemed amused.

"It seems Benjamin and Susanna Zook were more than eager to have me vacate the premises."

"And why is that?"

He chuckled. "It's a mystery, unless they were put out with me for saving their granddaughter's life."

"Excuse me?"

"Never mind. Not important."

Stephen had a suggestion. "Why don't you come stay with us? We have a spare room in our basement. Think it over and let me know."

"Thanks, I appreciate the offer," said Philip. "I'll see what I can do about getting in to see Lily this afternoon."

"Better call ahead . . . find out the visiting hours."

"I'll do that and get back with you about the invitation. I just might take you up on it."

"Very good."

They hung up, and Philip immediately dialed the phone number for the Fairview Nursing Home in Reading. He had a good feeling about this visit.

Part Three

Love is intensity, that second in which the doors
of time and space open just a crack. . . .

OCTAVIO PAZ

And it shall come to pass, that before they call,
I will answer; and while they are yet speaking,
I will hear.

ISAIAH 65:24, KJV

Twenty

❖ ❖ ❖

The middle-aged receptionist greeted him warmly, almost too enthusiastically, as if she encountered few opportunities to welcome visitors.

"I've come to see Lily," he told the woman with red, shoulder-length hair. "My name's Philip Bradley."

"Ah yes." She pushed up her glasses. "And how is it you're related to our Lily?"

"No relation. I'm a friend of a friend, you could say." He thought about it, wanting to be absolutely truthful. "Actually, I have in my possession an old postcard that belonged to someone I understand Lily—your patient—knew well." He reached into his sports coat pocket, displaying the pictureless card and the English translation stuck to the front with a Post-it note.

The redheaded woman accepted it, glancing at the postcard briefly. "I'll give this to her and see if she's still up to having a visitor." She stood up then, and he saw that she was a short woman. Possibly only five feet tall or less. Shorter than his niece. "Can you wait here for just a moment?"

"I'd be glad to." He chose a comfortable chair in the small, fern-filled sitting area and found himself browsing through several magazines and waiting once again.

The receptionist returned sooner than he expected. "I'm afraid Lily's not feeling well after all. She's simply not her best today, though she had agreed to see you. Perhaps another time."

His heart sank. "Tell her I hope she's better very soon."

The petite woman walked to the door with him. "Again, it's a shame you made the trip for nothing."

"No . . . no, I understand." Before leaving, he wrote his cell phone number on one of his business cards. "You can reach me at this number anytime." So determined was he to meet with Adele's friend, he had already made up his mind to be available for her. No matter what time of day—or night—Lily might be able to see him.

Rachel and Mam made chowchow together after slipping three apple pies into the oven. "Annie's her happy self again," Rachel commented. "I can't begin to say how awful worried I was."

Susanna didn't reply but continued chopping cauliflower and celery to add to a large bowl of cut green and yellow beans, sliced cucumbers, lima beans, diced carrots, and corn. The ingredients would be cooked till tender, then salted and drained. Next came chopping and more salt for the green tomatoes and the red and yellow peppers. A syrup made from vinegar, sugar, celery seed, mustard seed, and other spices was brought to a rolling boil and mixed with the many vegetables. Rachel especially liked to add onion to their chowchow.

"I guess Annie will be stayin' far away from them hornets' nests from now on," Mam blurted. "A hard lesson to learn, to be sure."

"Jah, but she says she wasn't disobedient. Copper just got away."

"Still, she oughta be punished for it."

Rachel didn't have the heart to consider such a thing, not after her little one's suffering already today. "In case she ever gets stung again, I wanna get her an epi-kit."

"A what?"

Rachel explained what the doctor had said at the hospital. "It could be the difference between life and death."

"That's real silly, 'specially when Blue Johnny can do the same thing, prob'ly. And you could, too, if you stopped bein' so stubborn about receiving the blessing."

Rachel chose to ignore the comment. "If you'd heard Annie wheezin' and all—why, it was downright frightening." She paused, thinking she shouldn't say much more about this. "One of the nurses said we got Annie to the hospital just in time. Honestly, I don't know what we would've done if Philip hadn't helped us."

Again, Susanna clammed up.

Rachel hadn't found conversation with Mam to be very agreeable; she was a woman who fought against most everything a person had to say, it seemed. So when Mam was silent, there was usually an important reason for it. But just now, Rachel had no idea at all what was causing her mother to be so upset at Philip Bradley. None whatsoever.

"Philip Bradley's making another trip to Reading," she ventured, changing the subject, hoping Mam might not fly off the handle.

"What the world for?"

"Something about a cemetery up there . . . and a woman in a nursing home who knew Adele Herr."

Mam nearly choked, carrying on so bad Rachel ran some water into the sink and filled up a glass real quick.

"Are you all right?"

"I'll be right fine when Mr. Bradley's long gone, that's what!"

Rachel was shocked. What had caused this hostility toward the kind and gentle young man?

––––––––

Philip attended church on Sunday with Stephen and his wife, Deborah. The interior of the meetinghouse was marked by stark simplicity: a small, raised platform with center pulpit, windows of clear glass, and modest light fixtures overhead. There were long wooden pews occupied by Mennonite worshipers—women and small children on the left side; men and older boys on the right. Most every woman wore a head covering of some kind or other. Some of the men wore plain black coats with no lapels, and collars similar to a liturgical collar.

So Stephen Flory was a Bible-believing, conservative Mennonite. Philip should have suspected as much, given the warm hospitality and congenial spirit exhibited by both Stephen and his wife. He took the knowledge of it in his stride. After all, the man had generously opened his home to this virtual stranger. "Stay as long as you like," he'd said upon Philip's arrival back from Reading. "We're always glad to have guests around here."

Deborah, a pleasantly plump brunette, had agreed, nodding her head and smiling her welcome. "We don't always get folk in from New York City."

He returned her smile, thinking he must be quite a spectacle here. It was as if Lancaster County residents didn't often get to see someone from the Big Apple. Glad to have the company, especially in view of the easy camaraderie between himself and Stephen, he was more than happy to go along with their church plans.

It was the pastor's sermon that caught him off guard. A message about the role of the Christian in spiritual warfare. When Philip inquired of the Scripture references later with Stephen, he was told that the pastor was well versed in intercession. "He's new here, but he's on fire. Wants to see us move forward in what we believe to be the end times before Jesus returns for His church."

Philip hadn't heard anything so straightforward, not even during his churchgoing days as a boy. But he was polite and listened. It was the least he could do for his host and hostess.

After church, he was treated to a superb dinner in the Flory home: roast beef, mashed potatoes and gravy, green beans, corn on the cob, coleslaw, Jell-O salad, and angel food cake. Table conversation centered around small talk mostly, but an occasional comment was made about the young, new pastor.

Just as he leaned back, realizing that he had enjoyed Deborah Flory's cooking entirely too much, Philip's cell phone jingled. He excused himself and took the call in the living room. "Hello?"

"Philip Bradley, please."

"This is he."

"I'm the receptionist at the Fairview Nursing Home in Reading. Lily is asking for you. Would it be convenient for you to come see her today?"

"Why yes, I can leave here within the hour."

"She says, 'The sooner the better.'"

"Very good. Tell her it will be 'sooner.'" He didn't think to ask if the woman would mind if he made a tape recording of his visit. He was thinking of Rachel just then, knowing that the young blind woman might enjoy hearing Lily's answers to his many questions. He would wait until he got there to ask permission.

Meanwhile, he thanked Deborah for the delicious dinner. "I'll treat the two of you to a meal before I leave."

"It's a deal." Stephen nodded, beaming. "Have a safe drive and a pleasant afternoon."

"Hopefully, Lily won't turn me away this time." He meant it as a joke, but he was more than ready for the solution to the postcard's mystery, hoping Lily might clear up a number of things for him. For Rachel, too.

Rachel sat close to Annie on the preaching bench at Lavina's. It was the older woman's turn to have service at her house. The second sermon seemed ever so long—longer than usual—but maybe, Rachel thought, it was because she had other things on her mind. Things like wanting to sing praises to God for giving her Annie back to her, for sparing her little one's life. She wished it might've been possible for her to attend her Beachy church this morning, but Dat said they were runnin' late— his pat excuse, it seemed—and she went along with it. Still, she day-dreamed about the more evangelical service going on up the road apiece.

Letting her mind wander, she thought about Mam's unfriendly comments toward Philip Bradley. She didn't know why it bothered her so that her mother didn't think kindly on the man who'd saved Annie's life. From everything she knew of him, Philip was good-hearted and trustworthy. It seemed there was a strong undertow of ill will toward their former guest. Maybe it was best he left when he did, but she wondered how she was ever to hear what he'd discovered in the cemetery in Reading. And what of the possibility of Philip talking to a woman who knew Gabe's English sweetheart? She wished she might be told some-thing, if not from Mam and Dat, then Philip Bradley.

She dismissed those thoughts in time for the benediction, followed by Lavina's brothers and other men rearranging the benches in the front room, making ready for the common meal.

As much as she loved the People here, she missed the fellowship of those friends and relatives at her own Beachy church. And she missed Esther on this day particularly, anxious to answer her cousin's recent tape with one of her own.

It was Lavina's strange remark to her that got Rachel thinking more about Philip Bradley and the "lead" on Adele Herr he supposedly had uncovered in Reading. "Someone's soon gonna hear the truth 'bout Gabe Esh," Lavina whispered in passing as she carried a stack of plastic plates across the kitchen.

There wasn't any question in Rachel's mind that Lavina was the one whispering because she recognized the familiar smell of garlic on her breath. What was going on that the older woman seemed to know— about Philip Bradley's plan to go to Reading? Or did she?

Rachel was downright befuddled; she couldn't quite put two and two together.

By the time Philip made the turn into the long, wide driveway leading to the Fairview Nursing Home, the digital clock on the dash glowed
three-fifty. He hoped the ailing woman might be well enough to see him
this time. Parking the car, he reached for his briefcase, where he kept
his portable tape recorder. If all went well, he'd soon have Lily on tape,
answering his questions about Gabe Esh's life and the story embracing
the postcard. Such a format was ideal for a blind woman, though he
knew his visit here was more to satisfy his own curiosity than to present
a tape to Benjamin and Susanna Zook's daughter.

"Oh, good, you're here," said the same receptionist, looking up, her
green eyes smiling. "Lily's waiting for you."

"Thank you." He followed the slight woman down a long, narrow
hall with private rooms on either side. An occasional wheelchair was
parked next to the wall, but he saw no children or families and wondered
how a sickly, elderly person might feel, banished to such a place.

The woman stopped at a doorway marked Rm. 147. "I'll be happy
to introduce you."

"I'd appreciate that," he said, waiting for her to enter the sunny
room.

A woman with pure white hair and round, rosy cheeks sat propped
up with a myriad of pillows in a hospital-style bed. She wore a blue
satiny bed jacket that brought out the azure in her eyes. Behind her, on
the wall, a large bulletin board was filled with birthday cards.

Cheerfully, the receptionist announced his entry. "The young man
I told you about is here to see you, Lily. His name is Philip Bradley."

"It's very nice to meet you, Lily." He offered his hand, and the delicate flower of a soul offered hers.

"Your name is Philip?" came the fragile voice.

"Yes."

"Please, pull up a chair and make yourself at home."

"Thank you."

When he was settled, she said, "Can you tell me where you found
this postcard?" She held it in her thin, wrinkled hands.

"I certainly can. While I was staying at an Amish bed-and-breakfast
in Lancaster this week, I discovered it caught under a drawer in an
antique rolltop desk . . . in my room."

"Antique rolltop, you say?"

"I was told it dates back to the 1890s. A beautiful cherrywood
finish."

She was quiet for the longest time, only her eyes blinking, as if assimilating the information he'd offered. "Adele's mother once owned a desk like that," she said softly.

"Then you knew her well?"

A smile crossed her face. "Ah yes."

He was hesitant to spoil the moment by asking if he could tape-record their visit, but he mustered up enough professional oomph to do so. "I hope you won't mind."

"It's all right, I guess." She sighed, and Philip noticed dark circles under her eyes. "Perhaps it *is* time someone heard Adele's story."

"Most likely, someone besides myself will listen to this tape," he explained. "Rachel, the grand-niece of Gabe Esh . . . her mother's uncle."

Lily tilted her head and stared at the window. "I knew a girl named Rachel once. She was a sweet little thing—an Amish girl—one of Adele's students at the one-room school where she substitute taught one year. But then, there were many Plain girls named Rachel in Lancaster County—probably still are."

He switched on the Record button just as Lily mentioned the Amish schoolhouse. "Do you mind if I state the date of our conversation before you begin?"

Offering a slight smile, she agreed. "Are you sure you're not a newspaper reporter, Mr. Bradley?"

He'd come too far and too often for this meeting to fall through the cracks. "One thing I'm *not* is a newspaperman." He was glad that he could honestly say so, though writing for a magazine hardly exempted him from the category.

"So, Mr. Bradley, what is it you would like to know about Adele?" she asked.

The question took him by surprise. "There is much about Gabe's situation I don't understand. An Amish farmer told me he died soon after writing the postcard, yet Gabe was buried *here* instead of Lancaster. That seems very strange to me, given the circumstances."

"Yes, I suppose it does."

"I'm also curious to know why the man was shunned by the Amish community when, according to various folk in Bird-in-Hand, he never joined the Amish church." He stopped, thinking he might have thrown out too many questions at once. "Maybe we should start with how *you* came to know Adele Herr."

The white-haired woman looked toward the window and seemed to lose herself there. "Adele and I were . . . quite close at one time."

He settled back in his chair, eager for the answers. "Then you must have known Gabe Esh as well?"

She nodded, closing her eyes for a moment, still clutching the postcard. "If it's Gabe you're interested in," she said, opening her eyes with a smile, "then perhaps I should take you back to the very beginning. . . ."

Twenty-One

❖ ❖ ❖

The day Gabriel Esh was born, a fierce snowstorm with up to forty-mile-an-hour winds swept through Bird-in-Hand. John and Lydia Esh had been blessed, at long last, with their first son. His seven older sisters were in attendance at the home birth, in one way or another. The older girls boiled water and ran errands for the midwife; the younger girls played checkers near the wood stove in the kitchen.

Shouts of "It's a boy!" rang through the farmhouse. The eldest dashed outside in knee-deep snow to ring the bell, announcing the news as a strong wind blew the message through the Amish community.

It didn't take long for his parents to see that Gabriel was an unusually sensitive child. Not the sort of rough-and-tumble son John Esh had long wished for, and not much good on the farm, he was so slight.

Along about his seventh birthday, things began to change for the quiet, blond-haired boy. He'd gone out with three of his older cousins—much older, in their teens—and was tramping around between the rows of corn at the far end of Bishop Seth Fisher's cornfield when he felt a peculiar burning sensation in his hands and a mighty downward pull, enough to halt him in his tracks. He battled against the unseen force that seemed to come from the ground beneath him.

Painstakingly, he was able to battle against it, moving his hands, palms flat out in front of him, while the other boys ran ahead. The hot tingling continued until young Gabe thought his hands might be reacting to a low-voltage current somewhere in the ground. He hadn't ever watched a man go dowsing for water across a field, but he'd heard enough stories about it, growing up in Lancaster County. Folks called dowsers did this sort of thing all the time, deciding where to drill for water or locating minerals, hidden treasures, and lost objects like keys and other things. But from the stories he'd heard, it was usually older men or women who were the ones out water-witching, not young boys half scared of their own voices.

When his cousins realized Gabe wasn't trailing along behind them, one of the boys came back for him. Seeing Gabe's hands trembling to beat the band, the boy shouted to the others. "Come, see this! Looks like we got ourselves a new little water-witcher in the family."

Gabe didn't like what he was feeling. The electricity flying through his hands made him think he might be close to being electrocuted. He clapped his hands, trying desperately to make them stop twitching. At last, he folded them as if in prayer, pulling them close to his chest, and stepped back. He stared in awe at the ground, knowing it belonged to Bishop Seth. "*Vas in der Welt?*—what in all the world?" he whispered.

"There's gotta be a water vein below us," Jeremiah, the oldest cousin, said. "We best mark the spot and tell the bishop."

"He'll be right happy to hear 'bout this," said his brother with glee.

The boys, all three of them, started laughing and hooting, jumping up and down, and getting right rowdy about the find. "Maybe there's a gold mine under our feet," said one. "If there is, we'll be richer 'n snot."

Then Jeremiah quit leaping long enough to say, "Wait a minute. Bishop Fisher's lookin' for someone to pass the powwowing gift on to, ain't so?"

"I heard Pop say he's a-huntin' for a young woman for the transference. It's been ever so long since we had *die Brauchfraa*—a lady powwow doctor—'round these parts. That's prob'ly why."

"No . . . no, it don't matter, just so long as the person's got a trace of the gift already. And lookee here who it is!" He was pointing to Gabe and laughing.

Soon all the boys were gathering around him, pretending to be sick or faint, begging him to chant or make up a charm over them.

Gabe ignored them, letting his hands drop to his sides. He shook them hard, feeling all wrung out—like he needed to lie down. "I'm goin' home now," he muttered.

"Oh no, you ain't. We're takin' you to see the bishop."

Gabe started running, fast as his little legs would take him, straight through the cornfield and down the dirt lane to his dawdi's side of the house.

He had outrun Jeremiah and the others that day, but it was just the

beginning of folks taking notice of him. Word spread quick as lightning
about the "wee dowser" in their midst, and Gabe couldn't go anywhere—school or church—without somebody comin' up to him and
makin' over him, like he was special or something. Maybe it was
because the bishop got a well driller to come out and sink a shaft in the
corner of his cornfield. Lo and behold, if he didn't discover a water vein
at twenty-five feet!

Seven years later, around the time Gabe turned fourteen, Preacher
King took him aside, came right into the schoolhouse and escorted him
outdoors. "Bishop Fisher wants to have a word with you, son."

"Me?"

Preacher looked over his shoulder comically. "Well, he sure ain't
askin' for *me*."

Gabe ran his fingers up and down his suspenders, then took off his
straw hat and looked it over good. "I didn't break the Ordnung, did I?"
He shouldn't have let the tears well up in his eyes, this close to being a
young man and all, but he was mighty worried he'd gotten himself into
some trouble. Random transgressions happened all too often in the community, seemed to him—folks making a mistake about the width of a
hat brim or the kind of hobbies they might choose.

"Best be gettin' yourself up to the bishop's and find out," said
Preacher King. "But I'd say it's nothin' to fret over."

Preacher's laughter and the urgent, ominous look in his eyes made
Gabe feel uneasy. He'd overheard some of the Mennonite teenagers
talking disapprovingly about powwow doctors, that they were conjurers
or hex doctors, but he'd never witnessed the "evil eye" as some of them
cautioned. That day he felt something keeping him back, telling him *not*
to go see the bishop, something as powerful as the pulling force in his
hands the day he'd walked in that water-rich cornfield. Yet there was a
fight raging inside him—another voice just as strong, nagging him to get
going, urging him to obey the man of God.

"I don't know what's-a-matter with me," he told Lavina Troyer, a
tall and skinny blond girl in the eighth grade. "I feel God callin' me to
somethin'—I just don't know what. But everyone says I have this here
gift, and if that's true, I should obey and see the bishop 'bout it, right?"

Lavina stared a hole clean through him. "This may sound like tom-
foolery, but do you ever pray 'bout things before you just up and do
'em?"

It was the single most absurd thing he'd ever heard, but then most folk he knew figured there was something worse than wrong with Lavina. She struggled hard with book learning at school; most everywhere else, too, it seemed. Though she was getting close to courting age, he wondered if any boy would ever have her. 'Course, then again, if she chewed peppermint gum 'stead of them awful garlic buds, maybe that would help. But that was the least of his worries.

Yet Gabe couldn't dismiss Lavina's remark, and instead of running off to see Bishop Seth Fisher like Preacher King said to, he hurried on home after school, out to Dat's barn, and knelt down next to a hay bale and talked to God as if He might even care to be listening. That prayer and the feeling that followed turned out to be the downright oddest thing he'd ever encountered. When he quit praying, there was an awful ache in his belly, low in the pit of his stomach, like he hadn't eaten in over two days. He was one hungry boy, but when he went in the house and gulped down a handful of oatmeal raisin cookies and the tallest glass of milk you ever did see, none of it seemed to satisfy him.

The hollowed-out feeling persisted, even as he crawled into bed that night. Instead of saying a silent rote prayer the way he was taught to do, he whispered into the darkness a prayer that came straight from his young heart. It was all about how he wanted God to fill him up inside, to make his life count for something more than just working the land, raising dairy cows, and marrying and having a family like his pop and mamma and their dat and mam before them. He wanted a mission to carry out, something far different from the powwow doctoring everyone said he was destined for. He wanted to do something holy and good for Jehovah God.

When he finished his prayer, the emptiness inside was filled with something strong and true. He knew God would answer.

Gabe figured he couldn't tell just anybody what he'd done, 'least not his family. But he did feel homelike enough with one person to tell her about his prayers because he figured Lavina Troyer wouldn't go squealing on him, on account of her childlike way. But it went deeper than that. He felt he could trust Lavina with most any secret. She was the kind of older friend he'd wished he'd had in a *brother*, but God had seen fit to bless him with a houseful of sisters. Maybe that was why he felt at ease around Lavina.

"I'm right proud of you, Gabe," she said when he told her at recess about the praying he'd done.

"You don't hafta be proud, really. I'm just doin' what I believe is God's will."

Her eyes went banjo-wide. "You sound like you've been talkin' to the Mennonites."

He wondered what she meant by that and decided to investigate. Soon he had two fast friends, Paul and Bill—not brothers but cousins—both of them saved and baptized Mennonites. For the next couple of years, he spent as much time with them as he could, sneaking off to Bible studies, even attending Sunday school and church on the People's off Sundays.

He was constantly having to avoid certain farmers who kept after him to come help them locate the best place to dig a well or plant a new tree on their land.

And there was Bishop Seth Fisher. "You're runnin' from God Almighty," the tall, imposing man with graying beard and penetrating dark eyes said after a preaching service at the Esh home one Sunday afternoon. "If I were you, I wouldn't be surprised at nothing, the way you're acting. Out-and-out *glotzkeppich*—blockheaded you are, Gabriel Esh."

Gabe didn't think twice about the bishop's vague, yet somewhat threatening, pronouncement. He wasn't frightened or intimidated by it and wouldn't consider going to meet Seth Fisher privately at the man's home because of it. In fact, Gabe was more determined than ever to follow the new calling on his life. The calling of God.

There came a day of testing, when his own mother was so ill with a high fever and convulsions, Gabe's father declared that her brain might burn up if Gabe didn't at least attempt to exercise some of his supernatural powers over her. But Gabe refused, petitioning God to heal his mamma, quoting the New Testament as he offered a fervent prayer. Angry, John Esh went out and brought Bishop Seth back to the house with his powwow cures and remedies instead.

By the time Gabe was twenty and showing no signs of taking the expected baptismal class necessary to become an Old Order church member, the People wondered if they might be losing one of their own to the world. Bishop Fisher was enraged over the situation—this haughty course the wayward young man had set for himself—and it was mighty clear to everyone that Gabe was avoiding the bishop like a plague. "John Esh's son won't amount to much of anything if he don't

join church," the bishop was reported to have said to Preacher King, who in turn told Gabe's father.

So John took his son aside one winter afternoon while the womenfolk were having a quilting frolic. Gabe's father walked him out to the barn, to the milking house. "You know, Gabe, we named you Gabriel for a very gut reason."

"What's that, Dat?"

"Well, honestly, I handpicked the name myself on account of it being your great-grandfather's name before you. You see, son, Gabriel means 'God is my strength'—right fitting for a scrawny lad such as yourself."

He'd heard the story often enough, though never the part his father was about to reveal.

"Your great-grandfather, old Gabriel Esh, was a powerful healer in the community, looked up to and revered by everyone whose life he touched. He died at the ripe old age of ninety-seven, but long before he did, he graciously passed on his gift to Bishop Seth, the bishop we now have."

"Why didn't he transfer the gift to someone in our family?" Gabe asked, knowing that was the way things usually happened.

"Because the woman—your grandmother's sister and *your* great-aunt Hannah—who was most expected to receive it died in childbirth. There was no one else in the Esh family with the same inclinations toward the 'curious arts,' so the gift fell to our present bishop."

Gabe contemplated his father's explanation. "Ain't it true that my great-grandfather could've chosen *anybody*, even someone with no inclination at all?"

"Jah."

"Then why Bishop Fisher?"

His father looked down at his work boots. "Seems that after your great-aunt passed away, there was a lot of pressure comin' from Seth Fisher's elderly grandfather for Seth to have the gift. And that's just how it went."

"What sort of pressure do ya mean?" Gabe asked, eager to know. Because he, too, had felt a burden, almost an obligation, to follow through with Preacher King's invitation "to go and see the bishop," even now, after all these years of avoiding the austere man.

"I 'spose it's not for us to say, really."

"But there must be a reason why you think that, Dat."

John Esh shook his head, exhaling into the cold air. "It's just a downright shame that you ain't interested in the bishop's blessing, son. 'Twould give us another healer in the community, and the good Lord knows we sure could use more than one." He paused, wrinkling his face up till Gabe thought he saw the man's eyes glisten. "Such a wonderful-gut honor it would be to the Esh family, havin' our son become the new powwow doctor."

So it was the family Dat was thinking of! Gabe should've known, but he had no idea the "blessing" was so important to his parents.

"God's called me to preach," he said boldly. "To expose the wickedness in high places."

His father's mumblings were not discernible as the farmer walked away, kicking the stones in the barnyard as he headed back to the warmth of the house.

That brought the discussion to a quick end, though Gabe often wondered about the things Dat had said. He searched the Scriptures even more vigorously, together with his Christian friends. It was becoming clear to him that there were certain patterns in families, ways of thinking or behaving that seemed to influence as many as three and four generations from the original sin of a particular family. Some patterns affected the continuation of blessing in a lineage; others gave full sway to chronic sickness and money-related troubles, relationship problems, and barrenness. And there were those who seemed accident-prone or who had emotional or mental breakdowns, all of which seemed to run in families.

On the other hand, there were folk in the community who seemed to enjoy prosperity and health, happy relationships with both their spouses and parents, and had their quiver full of many children. He was so intrigued by the lessons he was learning, he began to teach others, and not long after that, he discovered a column in the *Budget*, written by an Amish bishop in Virginia. The writer spoke out against the patterns of wickedness in the conservative communities, going so far as to say that the black deeds of sympathy healers and powwow doctors were from the bottomless pit itself. The writer's ideas confirmed everything Gabe himself had come to believe.

Week after week, Gabe devoured the columns by Jacob Hershberger and even wished he could go to Virginia and meet the Beachy Amish bishop. But an urgency gripped his spirit, and he began to share the liberating truth of the power of Jesus Christ to break generational bondages to all those who would listen.

There were some in his community who wagged their tongues about the formerly shy and reticent son of John and Lydia Esh. What had happened to transform the frail boy into a self-appointed evangelist, driven and outspoken? Was it truly God's power that had changed him?

Bishop Seth seethed in anger at having been scorned these many years, more determined than ever to set Gabe straight on the path of his "true calling." Now approaching his mid-fifties, Seth Fisher was more than eager to get the young man alone in a room, just the two of them. The community was ready for a young healer, someone who could carry on the gift into the next generation and beyond. John Esh's only son was the bishop's first choice, though he had his eye on a teenager outside the Amish community, a humble boy nicknamed Blue Johnny.

Lavina Troyer was present, along with her mother and sisters, that warm April day the People had a barn raising at Preacher King's place. The preacher's barn had been destroyed by a lightning bolt six weeks before, and without the aid of telephones or email—though announcements were given in local church districts the Sunday before the scheduled event—word spread, and four hundred men from the county showed up to help build and raise a new barn in a single day.

Gabe, too, was on hand to assist, though no longer living in his father's house due to his unwillingness to join the church. One of his new friends, Paul Weaver, had taken him in, and together the two were working for Paul's father in a carpenter apprenticeship.

The women brought all kinds of food to eat, as was their custom. One church district of women brought meat loaf and white potatoes. Another group brought macaroni and cheese, bread pudding, and sweet potatoes. Other food included roast beef, chicken, ham, stewed prunes, pickled beets and eggs, doughnuts, raisins, applesauce, cake, and lemon pies. Theirs was a set dinner menu for a barn raising, and often the women had to plan ahead for up to seven hundred workers.

So Lavina was there, along with all the women from the Bird-in-Hand Old Order district, including young Leah Stoltzfus and her sister, Susanna Zook, both women with toddlers and babes in arms.

It was Bishop Fisher who took Gabe aside and ordered him to climb the beams and help fit the pieces together at the pinnacle of the wooden skeleton, high above the concrete foundation. Lavina pointed Gabe out to her sisters and cousins. "Watch him work," she said of the light-weight and nimble-footed man who had confided his prayer secret to her years back. She kept her eyes focused on the young fellow dangling perilously in midair.

Right before the nine-thirty snack break, she saw him slip and fall; watched in horror as he skimmed the long beam, breaking his downward course on something that slashed open his side. She cried out when she saw the gash give way to dark red blood. She sped across the yard to the place where he lay, now surrounded by the workers and Bishop Fisher.

"He's hurt awful bad!" she hollered, and one of the women held her back, though she fought them off, thin as she was.

Gabe groaned, still conscious, holding his left side and feeling the sticky substance against his fingers. The bishop knelt beside him and placed his hand on the open wound, whispering something, though neither Gabe nor Lavina could make out what.

"I want no powwowing done . . . on me," Gabe managed to say.

Bishop Fisher straightened, glaring down at him as he lay there in great agony. "Gabriel Esh, you will repeat after me: 'Blessed wound, blessed holy hour, blessed be the virgin's son, Jesus Christ.' And you will repeat it three times."

Gabe refused. "I choose the healing power of . . . Jesus, my Lord and Savior over . . . your charms . . . and incantations."

This infuriated the bishop, who proceeded to place his thumb inside Gabe's wound. "Christ's wound was never—"

"No! You will not pronounce . . . your witchcraft on me." He paused to gather his strength, to breathe, though it was excruciating, every breath torturous. "In the name . . . of the Lord Jesus Christ, I command you, Bishop Fisher . . . to stop." It was all he could do to raise his voice this way, knowing full well that he was dangerously close to death.

The bishop bent low and whispered, "Choose to receive the blessed gift at this moment . . . or bleed to death."

Gabe could no longer speak, so weak was he from the loss of blood.

"Call an ambulance!" someone shouted in the crowd. "For pity's sake, call for help!"

Gabe recognized Lavina's voice and silently thanked God for his feeble-minded friend as he slipped into unconsciousness.

Lavina was the one who ran and pulled an unsuspecting horse out of Preacher King's barn and rode it bareback to the non-Amish neighbors' to place the emergency call. No matter that she had done so poorly in school and didn't have herself a beau, she could dial the operator.

And she did just that, saving Gabe's life.

Lily stopped her story, her eyes bright with tears. "I'm sorry, I guess I got a bit emotional just now."

"No . . . no, that's quite all right." Philip was glad she'd paused from her story so he could check on his tape recorder. Sure enough, it was time to flip the tape over. Before pressing the Record button, he asked if she was feeling up to continuing.

"If you hand me that glass of water, I think I'll be able to go on, at least for a while."

Philip was glad to hear it, as he was eager for more, and promptly handed the glass to the woman. She drank slowly, taking several long sips. Then, returning the glass to Philip, she began once again.

The Lancaster countryside was ablaze in sugar-maple reds and autumn-radiant oranges, golds, and yellow-greens the year Adele Herr filled in for Mary King, who had been the children's Amish instructor for a little more than two years. Mary, Preacher King's daughter, was getting married, which meant no more schoolteaching, and it was unfortunate because the students had grown attached to her.

It didn't take long, however, for them to switch loyalties and reattach themselves to a bright-eyed brunette woman with a jovial smile and good sense of humor. The children took it upon themselves to make Adele feel right at home, bringing jars of homemade applesauce, beans of all kinds, carrots, corn, beets, sauerkraut, and jellies. In no time, they taught their new teacher to read and speak their language, too.

One day after school, there was a ruckus going on outside the boys' outhouse. Thirteen-year-old Samuel Raber and his stocky younger brother, Thomas, had their fists up, ready to take each other on. Adele rushed outside to put a stop to it, but the boys were all fired up, hungry for a good scrap. "I'll fight ya to the finish!" Samuel shouted, swinging the first blow.

Thomas, who was about the same size, hollered back and swung, too. The two were having it out, right there near the boys' outhouse and the tree swing.

No amount of insistence or pleading on Adele's part could defuse the situation. She was ready to throw up her hands, not knowing what to do, when across the school yard a tall and slender young man came bounding toward the boys. His denim carpenter overalls exhibited a composite of sawdust and what appeared to be smudges of paint and possibly mustard. His yellow hair, cropped around his head, peeked out from under a straw hat. "Sam . . . Tom . . . time to head on home!" the man called to them, breaking up the fight.

Immediately, Samuel and Thomas ran toward the red schoolhouse, glancing over their shoulders as if they thought they'd better run for their lives.

She didn't quite know what to say to the handsome blond man, but she brushed her hands against her skirt and smiled her thanks. "That was truly amazing," she said, finding her voice.

He smiled back, and she noticed the apple green color of his eyes. "Those boys are my sister's youngsters, and she asked me to come down and fetch 'em for her. They're gut boys, really, just full of boundless energy, as you must surely know."

"I've never had any trouble with them until today," she said, glancing at the sky. "Must be a change in weather coming. Sometimes a falling barometer does strange things to children." She smiled back at him.

"Well, weather or no, I'll see to it that they don't cause you any more bother."

"I'm glad you came, because I was about to have someone run and get the bishop."

"No . . . no, you don't wanna do that," he replied, his smile fading.

She didn't tell him that Bishop Fisher was her great-uncle—one of the reasons she was able to land the substitute teaching position. "Why not?" she asked.

"It's a long story." He quickly removed his straw hat and introduced himself slowly and politely. "I'm Gabriel Esh, but my friends call me plain Gabe, and you can, too." His gaze held hers.

"Well, it's very nice to meet you, Gabe. My name is Adele Herr, and I'm filling in for Mary King until next spring."

"Ah yes, she's to be married next month."

"Well, supposedly the wedding hasn't been 'published' yet, but word has it she's tying the knot with the bishop's grandson real soon."

"That she is," he said, still holding his hat in his hands. "Are you from around here?"

"Reading's my home, though I attended Millersville State Teachers' College, so I'm familiar with this area."

Gabe nodded, smiling again. "We don't often get outsiders to teach our children."

"Then I suppose I was in the right place at the right time, though the parents and the board did scrutinize me, I must say."

"Warned you not to instill worldly wisdom in the minds of their offspring?"

She was surprised. "Why yes. In fact, those were their exact words."

The boys emerged from the schoolhouse, carrying their lunch pails and looking as sheepish as they were besmirched. "We're sorry, Miss Herr," Samuel offered.

"Jah, sorry," said Thomas, his face beet red with embarrassment.

Gabe said, "You boys run along now. Your pop needs your muscle power in the barn."

"Good afternoon, Miss Herr," called Samuel, running.

"Good-bye, Miss Herr," Thomas echoed.

"You won't be havin' any more scuffling out of those two," Gabe promised. He flashed a heartening smile again before excusing himself, then ran to catch up with his nephews.

"Well, one never knows what a day will bring forth," Adele muttered to herself, heading toward the schoolhouse steps.

Adele had her first outing with Gabe two days later. She was twenty-six, and he one year older. Folks had said that Gabe would never settle down and marry till he found a girl who'd be willing to put up with his incessant preaching, his roaming all over the county proclaiming the Gospel. Adele was glad he was still single, because she had been waiting a long time for a man like Gabe Esh to come along and catch her fancy. Only trouble was, he had been raised on an Amish farm, and she was a refined and thoroughly modern Baptist.

Love, they say, is blind, yet she wasn't so sure she wanted to jump into such a peculiar relationship with both eyes closed. So she kept them wide open as they headed off north in Gabe's open buggy, the only transportation he had, what with him still a carpenter's apprentice, with little hope of owning a woodworking shop because of all the traveling he did.

They spent an early evening together, that first date, walking along a wooded area. Ideal for a picnic. And what a picnic it was! Complete with every possible food a young man would enjoy; Adele had seen to that. She even asked Gabe's sister, Nancy—the mother of Samuel and

Thomas—to nose around a bit and find out what sandwiches he liked best. Turned out that beef tongue was his favorite, with plenty of Swiss cheese, mayonnaise, and lots of mustard.

After the meal, they hiked farther into the woods, stopping to rest on a stone fence, about three feet high. The sun, sinking fast, shimmered over the rocky surface, providing a warm and cozy spot on that October eve.

"I hope to have a place like this someday," he'd said rather confidently. "It would be ideal for a spiritual retreat, where folks could come and get away from the humdrum of their lives and meet God."

"It's real pretty here." She held her breath though, hoping he wouldn't rush things and say something about the two of them owning a place like this together. Instead, he reached for her hand and they sat in awkward silence. Several orioles flapped their wings and chirped down at them, but she paid them little heed. Her hand fit perfectly in Gabe's, like a glove. Honestly, it was hard to think of anything else.

When Gabriel stood up, she did too, and they walked hand in hand all the way into the deepest part of the forest, where red sugar maples were so high they had to crane their necks back to see the tip-tops. They laughed together, trying to catch a squirrel, though when Gabe cornered the furry gray creature and put his hand down into a tree hole, she worried that he might get bit. That was the first sign she knew she cared, possibly a little too much.

A few days later, they went for another walk, and the day after that they drove Adele's car to Honey Brook for hamburgers, where no one knew either of them, though folks gawked at the likes of him in his Amish getup and her in a best dress and pumps.

After that, Gabe dropped by the schoolhouse several times a week, usually after school. He said it was to check up on the wood stove or help with anything that might need to be fixed, but, of course, there wasn't anything needing his attention . . . except Adele herself. She struggled with her feelings toward him, wondering how such a relationship could possibly work in the long run. Yet her heart longed for his, Plain or no, and they spent joyous hours together, sharing each other's dreams. They talked of everything under the sun, except that one painful thing, too caught up with each other to broach the chasm that kept them truly apart.

Gabe accompanied her with the children on several snowy field trips in late November, and she observed him with the younger students, especially, noting how they seemed drawn to him. "I love the small ones," he said later when she brought it up. "Maybe it's 'cause I never had any little brothers or sisters—since I was the caboose."

It was early in December, a night when Gabe had borrowed his friend's car for a hymn sing in Strasburg. They were listening to the radio, soft music in the background, enjoying the quietude of the moonlit evening, when Gabe said, "I don't know if you know it, Adele, but I believe I must be fallin' in love with you."

Her heart leaped at his words, yet she felt she could not return his ardent affection. Although she cared for him deeply, she could not offer him hope of more than friendship. She knew, as sure as she was a modern woman—"fancy," as he called her—the two of them must remain merely good friends, lest they break each other's hearts.

Gabe was silent for the length of time it took to drive her home. When he pulled into the long, narrow lane of the Troyer farmhouse where Adele was renting a room, Gabe stopped the car and turned to her, reaching for her hand. "I know we've managed to avoid talkin' out our cultural differences, but perhaps with God's help we could work through our future . . . together."

Her eyes clouded with tears. "As much as I care for you, Gabe, as my dear, dear friend, I don't see how we . . ." She paused, struggling with her choice of words. "Oh, Gabe, we're worlds apart, you and I."

"Jah." His eyes held her gaze. "Yet I believe the Lord surely must've brought us together for a purpose."

Adele didn't know what to say to that. Gabe was especially sensitive to God and His ways; she knew it by observing his life and the way he truly relied on the Lord, walking wholly in tune with Him.

"I'm glad for *one* thing," she replied, fighting tears. "We're brother and sister in the Lord, therefore we belong to each other in the family of God. You know what I'm trying to say, don't you?"

"That if we can't be together as husband and wife, at least our spirits are knit together in the Lord?"

"Yes," she whispered. It *was* a comfort of sorts. Still they struggled with their background differences in the weeks that preceded Christmas, never so much as exchanging an innocent hug or kiss on the cheek, though Adele secretly longed for his embrace.

Adele did not anticipate her father's severe reaction to her friendship with Gabe, during the Christmas holiday. Evidently, word had gotten back to Reverend Herr via Bishop Fisher that Adele was spending lots of time with one of the Amish fellows in the Bird-in-Hand area. This nearly spoiled their family celebration, especially hers and her ailing mother's. "I suspect that you're in love with this . . . this Plain farmer," her father said one evening at supper.

"Gabe and I are true friends" was all she would admit, though with each day of separation came an intense desire to see her Amish friend again.

Upon her return to Bird-in-Hand, Adele told Gabe that she was the grand-niece of the bishop. "Seth Fisher married my father's aunt—that's how we're related. There was a break away from the Amish several generations back," she explained. "Most of my father's people are Baptists. Isn't that interesting?"

"And very unusual, seeing as how they all came from the same Ana-baptist roots." Gabe actually took the news of the connection to his People as an encouraging sign. "We're not so far apart, maybe after all."

She smiled at his attempt to dissolve the gap between them. "Three generations ago someone was shunned, excommunicated from the Amish church. I don't see how that's such a good thing."

They joked about it—that they were nearly distant cousins in a vague sense—and Gabe continued to stop by after school or made arrangements to spend time with Adele nearly every day.

For four bliss-filled months they enjoyed somewhat of a dating rela-tionship, though purely platonic, until mid-April, the end of the Amish school year. Three days before she was scheduled to return to Reading, Gabe invited her on a final buggy ride.

"I chose Dat's oldest horse for tonight on purpose," he confessed to her, giving a quiet laugh. "This way we'll have plenty of time to talk."

The night was warm, filled with the sweetness and the promise of springtime. "I wonder what you'd say if I told you I'd like you to think about marryin' me," said Gabe, his eyes intent on her as the horse pulled them forward into the starry night.

Again her heart was drawn to him. "I . . . I *do* care for you, Gabe," she said softly, "but . . ."

Before she could say more, he moved close to her, gathering her into his arms. "Please, my dearest one, you mustn't decide tonight."

"Oh, Gabe, I wish . . ." She yielded to his warm embrace as his lips found hers.

"I know," he said breathlessly. "I know, my darling fancy girl." And he kissed her again.

She snuggled close to her beloved, under the dim covering of a partial moon, and knew in her heart of hearts there could never be another night like this. She would return to her father's house and never see Gabe Esh again. As fond as they were of each other, their love was not meant to be.

They rode in utter silence, except for the occasional snort of the mare and the quaint *clip-clop* against the road. Adele watched the moon come and go under a smattering of clouds, a lump in her throat and a tear in her eye. "Gabe, I don't have to wait to give you my answer. The past months have been the most wonderful of my life. I thought I'd never meet someone like you, someone gentle, who loves children, someone sensitive to the Lord and to me. Oh, Gabe, we both know it can never be."

"Shh, don't say any more. I understand why you feel that way, Adele, but I also believe that if we are both willing, we could make it work." He held his "fancy" girl close to his heart as they watched the moon slide under a cloud, oblivious of what was to come.

———

Lily sighed, still clutching the postcard. "Not long after that night, Gabe witnessed of God's saving power to one Amish farmer too many."

"What do you mean?" asked Philip.

"He went over to Benjamin Zook's place, and right there in front of his uncle and aunt and their four little children, Gabe preached to them of Jesus."

"Benjamin Zook? You don't mean the husband of Susanna Zook?"

"Yes . . . yes, I believe that *was* her name. Do you happen to know them?"

"They are the owners of the Amish guesthouse where I discovered the postcard, and the parents of the young woman of whom I spoke— one of the reasons I made this tape recording. Susanna Zook was related to Gabe Esh."

Her mouth dropped open. "I'd forgotten, but yes, I believe she was Gabe's niece."

Philip was struck by the connection. "What happened at the Zooks' farm when Gabe witnessed?"

"Well, Benjamin was so put out with Gabe's condemnation of powwow doctoring that he went immediately to the bishop and complained. It was Ben Zook who began making the first loud noises toward getting Gabe excommunicated and shunned."

"But if he hadn't ever joined the Amish church, how could such a thing happen?"

She sighed deeply. "As far as Bishop Fisher was concerned, Ben Zook's outrage was the ammunition he needed. One irate farmer and one spurned bishop made for the kindling that was to ignite a roaring fire, to burn Gabe out of the community."

Lily's room had grown dim with the setting of the sun, and Philip was surprised that her tale had lasted well over an hour.

"Do you mind if we stop for now?" Lily said, looking wan. "I'm quite weary."

Philip turned off the tape recorder and thanked the lady for her time. "I hope you will rest now." He stood to go.

She shook her head. "You come again tomorrow, Philip," she said almost in a whisper. "I'll finish the story then."

"Wild horses couldn't keep me away," he confessed.

She extended her hand to him and squeezed it lightly. "You're a good man, Philip Bradley. Why don't you bring along Gabe's grand-niece tomorrow. I'd like to meet her."

He thought it interesting that Lily wanted to meet Rachel, though he had no idea how he might persuade the young woman to accompany him to the nursing home tomorrow. Would Susanna Zook even allow him to speak to her daughter again? That was *one* hurdle he wasn't sure he was willing to attempt.

Twenty-Two

❖ ❖ ❖

Philip stopped briefly at the Orchard Guest House on his way back to Stephen Flory's home. Susanna answered the door, looking quite startled when she saw who was standing on her doorstep. "I'm full up, Mr. Bradley," she said before he could even speak.

"I'm not here about a room. I'm here to see Rachel, if I may."

Susanna stood her ground, not budging an inch. "I'm afraid Rachel's not available at the moment."

He toyed with handing over the tape to her, hoping it might find its way into Rachel's hands, but he was no fool. "I'll wait until she *is* available, if you don't mind."

"Well, if you'll excuse me, I have guests to attend to."

Just then Annie spotted him and came running toward the door. "Mr. Philip," she greeted him with a grin. "You came back!"

"Well, yes, I did. But not to stay."

"Do you wanna see where the wasp stinged me? Do ya?"

He leaned over to inspect the tiny mark on her cheek. "All better, looks like to me."

She was grinning, looking up at him with adoring eyes. "Mamma says you saved my life, didja know that?"

He couldn't help smiling now, even at Susanna who appeared to be guarding the doorway with her round personage. "I was very glad to help."

"You did more than help me," the child insisted.

Chuckling, he stood up only to come face-to-face with Annie's mother. "Oh, hello, Rachel."

"I heard Annie talking so loudly, I had to come and see for myself."

"Mr. Philip's here, Mamma!" Annie tugged at Rachel's sleeve.

Rachel smiled; Susanna scowled.

"Hello again," he said. "I stopped by briefly to loan you something from the woman I visited in Reading today—the one who knew Adele Herr."

With that, Susanna turned on her heel, leaving Rachel, Annie, and Philip standing there together. "I think you will enjoy hearing the story of your mother's uncle . . . and his beloved." He gave the tape to her. "I also believe it will answer your questions, and then some."

"Thank you," she said. "I'm very gut at running a tape recorder— it's one of the ways I communicate best."

"Wonderful." He paused, thinking how he should present Lily's invitation. "Before I leave, there's one other thing," he said quickly, keeping an eye out for Susanna Zook, who was bound to return in a huff with Benjamin and order him off. "Lily would like to meet you. She's invited you to come and hear the rest of the story . . . in person."

"Lily?"

"Yes, Adele Herr's close friend. The woman in the Reading nursing home."

"When?"

"Tomorrow afternoon. Would you like to ride along with me?"

"I . . . I don't care much for cars," she said, more cautious now.

"Well, if it's any consolation, I'm a very careful driver."

She thought for a moment. "I might sit in the backseat, if that's all right with you."

"Not a problem."

Rachel's face broke into a spontaneous smile. "Then, jah, I'll go there with you."

Philip could think of nothing else during his restaurant stop for supper. Rachel Yoder had actually consented to accompany him to meet the dear friend of her great-uncle's fiancée. Why should he be excited about something so perplexing?

———————

That night, Rachel listened to Lily's recorded story with rapt attention and interest. She was amazed at the parallels between herself and Gabe Esh—his childhood matching hers so completely, though *he* had become a straightforward and courageous teenager and young adult. What had caused him to change, she did not know, just as the People in his day didn't seem to understand either.

She figured she couldn't pick Dat's brain about all that he had heard and seen during the early days of Gabe's "preaching," but she wished she were bold enough to do just that. So much more she wanted to know about the man who had obviously rocked this community forty years ago.

One thing was sure about her parents, though—she noticed they seemed more united recently—'least since Philip Bradley had come to stay at the B&B. Was it because of finding the postcard? She wondered about that till the tape began to make a bumping sound in the recorder, and she turned it off.

The sixty-minute tape seemed to last only a few minutes, and she could hardly wait to hear the rest of the woman's story. To think that her own father had been partially responsible for Gabriel Esh's outrageous shunning. Mighty shocking, it was.

She wondered, too, what Esther and Levi might say about all this if they knew. But she would wait to tell her cousin till after her visit with the Reading woman. Then tomorrow night she would make another taped letter for her Ohio cousin. Such interesting news she would have this time!

After supper, she thought only of the hapless lovers, Gabe and Adele, wondering what was to become of their short-lived relationship, though she knew it could never come to fulfillment due to Gabe's untimely death.

Even though it would mean riding in a car yet another time and traveling with a near stranger, she could hardly wait to meet Adele's friend face-to-face.

Susanna would have liked to have had a fit once that Mr. Bradley left. She had restrained herself because of Annie, however, and it wasn't the easiest thing in the world, what with her granddaughter carrying on so about the man who'd saved her life, for goodness' sake!

"It's downright saucy, him showin' up on our front steps," she ranted to Benjamin in the privacy of their own quarters.

"Why didn'tcha just shut the door on him?" Ben said, looking a bit peeved.

"I'm a kind woman, that's why."

"Then you best not be complainin' to me."

Susanna was put out with her husband. She reached for a bed pillow and pounded at it, pretending to fluff it but gut.

Things seemed to be unraveling around her, and she felt somewhat helpless about it all, beginning with the handsome and tall, smooth-talkin' reporter. Whatever was he thinking, coming back to their inn thataway? Brazen, he was, insisting on talking to Rachel, a widow still in mourning. Couldn't he see how wounded the poor girl was? Couldn't he see that she was suffering, missin' her husband?

"It's beyond me what the man wants with our Rachel," she let slip, not even realizing that she suspected any romantic interest on the part of Mr. Bradley.

Ben shook his head and got out of his chair. "I'd say you're bor-rowin' trouble, Susie. Ain't no way a good-lookin' fella like that is inter-ested in our daughter; Plain and blind she be."

Susanna dismissed their conversation; she didn't have time for such speculatin'. Other things were brewing in her mind just now.

Susanna waited till Benjamin was clearly asleep, then made her way downstairs to phone a Mennonite van driver a few miles up the road, asking him to come pick her up. It was still plenty early in the evening for what she had in mind. Early enough to pay a visit to a longtime friend. . . .

———

Rachel heard the gentle sound of a car's engine idling in front of the B&B just as she was beginning to nod off. She gave it nary a thought, as quite often a traveler or two would arrive as late as nine-thirty of an evening, coming to book an available room. Usually, though, it was Mam who took care of things after the supper hour, because Dat wasn't much gut to anyone after about eight-thirty or so.

Annie had decided to "be a big girl" tonight and, of her own accord, had gone to sleep in her little bed across the room. Yawning, Rachel lay down and stretched out a bit. She missed Jacob more than usual—hav-ing more space in bed upon first retiring and all—and reached for the extra bed pillow and drew it close, hugging it to herself.

A mixture of familiar smells—pungent, yet musty—met Rachel's nostrils, urging her to consciousness, but she felt serene and too relaxed to rouse herself, assuming the pipe tobacco must surely be commingled with her dream.

It was the dreary murmurings, a man's monotone, that startled her out of sleep. "Who's there?" she whispered, fearful of waking Annie.

The chanting continued, and she recognized the voice of Blue Johnny.

"*Was in der Welt*—what in all the world?" Rachel gasped, pulling herself up to a sitting position in bed. She clutched her pillow, wondering how this could be. Blue Johnny, here, in her bedroom?

Then, slowly . . . miraculously, her eyes began to behold a hazy vision of a small girl, curled up on a bed against the wall. Long honey-colored braids fell loosely over the tiny shoulders and back.

What was happening? Was her sight returning?

"Annie?" she managed to say. Then she groped her way out of bed and was met by the blurred figure of a tall, bushy-haired man and Mam, too, holding a large lantern, its golden light spilling over the room. "Why are *you* here?" she whispered.

His features were impossible to identify, yet a radiant glow had settled over him, from the lantern light, no doubt. His dark eyes were silent, hollow pools. "You know I have the power," said Blue Johnny. "And *you* have it, too, Rachel Yoder. You can heal, just as I can."

She felt helpless to oppose the echo of his words. They flowed like warm oil over her sensitive being, enveloping, entrapping her very thoughts. Yet something deep within fought to free her from his sway, and she forced her misty gaze away, searching the room for Annie.

With a whimper, she stumbled to her daughter's bedside and knelt there, stroking the long, silky braids, seeing her little one as through a veil, for the first time in two long years—the skin, fair as a dove; the cheeks, pink as a rose petal. How beautiful her young daughter appeared to her hungry eyes, how very lovely. Or was it just her own imaginin'? It was as she cherished Annie with her cloudy sight that she thought she saw something of Jacob in the little girl. Jah, just the slightest glimmer of his dear, dear face.

"Best not waken her," Mam said.

Even as she continued to touch her daughter's satiny hair, she recalled Lily's tape-recorded story, the amazing account of her own great-uncle Gabe. How the young man with giftings similar to her own had refused the powwow doctors of his day, had rejected the strong inclinations that had come through the bloodline of his family—*her* family—how he'd stood firm against the Old Order bishop.

"No," she heard herself saying, as if in a dream. "I will not accept this sort of healing . . . and the transference neither."

"But, Daughter . . ." Mam was weeping now.

"Don't be foolish, Rachel," Blue Johnny spoke up then. "You don't want to miss out on your little girl's growing-up years, now do you?"

Rachel turned and raised her voice to him. "I'd rather be blind forever than choose the devil's gift."

Annie began to stir, and as quickly as the shadowy vision had come, her sight left her once again. "Please, just go now," she told Blue Johnny.

"Ach, Rachel . . ."

"Make him leave, Mam."

Leaning hard against the bed, she reached for her child's little hand and held it.

"Just remember, Rachel, I have the power to give you full sight," Blue Johnny reminded her. "Someday . . . someday *soon*, you'll come looking for me. Mark my words."

Someday soon . . .

She cringed, forcing the impact of his unholy words from her head, relieved to hear footsteps exiting the room. Then, when the upstairs had become still once again, she rubbed her eyes, thinking that the encounter might've been just a dream. A terrible, awful one at that.

Twenty-Three

❖ ❖ ❖

P hilip felt it awkward for Rachel to sit in the backseat on their trip to Reading, as if he were a chauffeur for an Amishwoman, for pete's sake. Nevertheless, this was the arrangement the blind woman had agreed on, and he found himself stealing glances in his rearview mirror.

At one point, while waiting for a traffic light to change, he caught himself staring at her, wondering what Rachel's hair might look like down, flowing over her shoulders and back, freed from the severity of the bun and head covering she always wore. Free and graceful, and perhaps a bit wavy, as there were hints of some curl whenever a strand of hair fell loose from the twisting on the side, leading back to the bun.

"I think you'll like Lily a lot," he said, making small talk to ease the tension he could feel emanating from her.

Rachel was silent.

"Gabe and Adele seem like real people to me."

"Jah, they do." Her mouth curved up slightly, then resumed its somewhat taut position.

He wondered if she might be feeling more than a little uneasy, perhaps even fearful. "I'm driving well below the speed limit," he offered.

She nodded but still did not speak.

He let it drop, deciding the woman needed space, time to adjust to the ride. After all, it hadn't been so long ago since she'd lost her husband and young son . . . because of an automobile.

Rachel rode in the backseat of Philip Bradley's car, sensing that he wanted to put her at ease. But she preferred to remain silent, thinking on Lily's riveting story. Honestly, she found it right surprisin' that her own father had been involved in settin' Gabe up for the most unjust

Twenty-Three

❖ ❖ ❖

Philip felt it awkward for Rachel to sit in the backseat on their trip to Reading, as if he were a chauffeur for an Amishwoman, for pete's sake. Nevertheless, this was the arrangement the blind woman had agreed on, and he found himself stealing glances in his rearview mirror.

At one point, while waiting for a traffic light to change, he caught himself staring at her, wondering what Rachel's hair might look like down, flowing over her shoulders and back, freed from the severity of the bun and head covering she always wore. Free and graceful, and perhaps a bit wavy, as there were hints of some curl whenever a strand of hair fell loose from the twisting on the side, leading back to the bun.

"I think you'll like Lily a lot," he said, making small talk to ease the tension he could feel emanating from her.

Rachel was silent.

"Gabe and Adele seem like real people to me."

"Jah, they do." Her mouth curved up slightly, then resumed its somewhat taut position.

He wondered if she might be feeling more than a little uneasy, perhaps even fearful. "I'm driving well below the speed limit," he offered.

She nodded but still did not speak.

He let it drop, deciding the woman needed space, time to adjust to the ride. After all, it hadn't been so long ago since she'd lost her husband and young son . . . because of an automobile.

Rachel rode in the backseat of Philip Bradley's car, sensing that he wanted to put her at ease. But she preferred to remain silent, thinking on Lily's riveting story. Honestly, she found it right surprisin' that her own father had been involved in settin' Gabe up for the most unjust shunning ever. No wonder Mam had reacted so severely upon Philip's first inquiring of her. No wonder Rachel's own questions about Gabriel Esh had always been met with guarded remarks.

And what about that dream-vision or whatever it was last night? She'd experienced such a mighty bold feelin'—rare to be sure—risin' up powerful-strong within, and she knew it must've come from hearing the story of Gabe's stand against wickedness in the community.

So, praise be, over the span of years, godly Uncle Gabe had touched her, influenced her to make the decision, once and for all, to turn away from her wavering over Blue Johnny and the other "healers." Cousin Esther would be right proud of her.

Rachel could hardly wait to hear the rest of Lily's story. . . .

If Susanna had a hissy fit over Rachel talking to Philip, well, today she liked to have the tremors. After that no-gut New Yorker man came and stole her girl away, Susanna just spun herself in circles every which way, rushin' all over her kitchen, tryin' her best to hunt down stew fixin's, forgetting that most everything she needed for it was downstairs in the cold cellar.

Annie seemed as perplexed at her as Benjamin, and the minute the stew meat, potatoes, onions, carrots, and celery were all chopped up and pushed into a big black kettle, Susanna got off her feet and had to fan herself to beat the band, even though Annie kept on saying, "S'not the least bit hot in here, Mammi Susanna."

Lily was perched in the midst of even more pillows than yesterday when Philip and a staff nurse guided Rachel into the older woman's room. But she was smiling as if she had been waiting for their visit with great anticipation.

"I've brought Rachel Yoder with me," Philip said, introducing the two women.

"Very nice to meet you, Rachel," said Lily, extending her thin hand.

Philip watched as Rachel's hand met and clasped Lily's briefly. "I got to hear all about my great-uncle last evening," said Rachel, slipping her hand into her pocket and holding out the tape for Philip. "It was the most interesting story I've ever heard, I think."

"For me, too," Philip added quickly, taking the tape from Rachel.

The nurse located an extra chair so Rachel and Philip could sit while they visited, eager for the continuation of Lily's account of her friend and Gabe Esh.

Lily seemed transfixed by Rachel, and Philip found it intriguing that she would study the blind woman so carefully. "I must tell you something, Rachel," she said at last. "You look very much like your mother's uncle."

"I do?" Rachel said.

"Yes, very much," replied Lily. "In fact, the resemblance is as striking as if you had been his own daughter."

Rachel's eyes appeared to be focused on her lap, but not seeing. "No one has ever told me that."

"I suppose not," Lily replied softly, that faraway look creeping into her gaze once again. "It is truly remarkable. And it is a compliment to you, because Gabriel Esh lived up to his name in that he had the face of an angel. At least Adele thought so."

Philip felt as if he were witnessing the melting away of years as Lily, a peer of Adele Herr's, and the distant relative of Adele's loved one sat in the same room together. It was as if they had come *across time* to this very moment.

He noticed that someone had pinned Gabe's postcard to the center of Lily's bulletin board. Obviously, having it in her possession meant a lot to the woman, and Philip was glad he'd had the opportunity to deliver it.

"Let's see," Lily said, "where did I stop yesterday?"

"The shunning," both Philip and Rachel blurted together, which brought smiles all around.

"Yes, the shun imposed on Gabe was the most shameful thing that had ever happened in the church community," Lily remarked. "It tore the Old Order district into pieces."

"What do you mean?" Rachel asked softly.

Lily turned her head toward the younger woman. "Gabe's shunning fragmented the People. I'd never seen or heard of anything so divisive happening among the Amish before. It shook the core of the community."

Rachel sighed audibly. "That may be the reason for so many Amish Mennonites and New Order Amish in our area now. Many of my own relatives are no longer Old Order, as well."

Lily nodded thoughtfully. "I'm not surprised to hear that."

Rachel was silent, sitting with her hands folded in her lap. But Philip could hear her shallow breathing in the chair next to him and wondered what was going through her mind.

"I don't think I told you that it was Lavina Troyer who rented a room to Adele the year she taught at the one-room Amish school," Lily said.

Rachel seemed surprised. "*Lavina* did?"

"But offering the English schoolteacher a place to stay wasn't the only demonstration of Lavina's kindness. She was far wiser than most people gave her credit for, but I'm afraid I've gotten ahead of myself. . . ."

Lavina had gone the second and third mile to befriend Adele Herr. She lived alone in her deceased father's farmhouse, bequeathed to her after his passing. At twenty-eight, she was now considered an *alt Maedel*—a maiden lady—among the People, and because she had more than enough room and needed the extra income, she offered to rent out part of the upstairs to the English schoolteacher.

On one of Adele's last days in Bird-in-Hand, at the end of the school year, Lavina was busy cutting off the cream from a gallon jar of old milk when Adele came into the kitchen. A refreshing April breeze was blowing in the window, and the smell of fields and dirt and dairy cows wafted in right with it.

Adele dropped her teacher's notebook on the table and stood staring out across the barnyard. The sun shimmered off the pond south of the barn, casting shadows on a gentle slope that moved upward to scattered willows circled around the sparkling water. "Oh, Lavina, I'm going to miss this beautiful place, and all the children, too," she blurted.

"Well, I hope y'all be missin' me, too," Lavina said, wide-eyed and grinning.

Adele turned and looked at her friend. "Of course I'll miss you. You've been so very good to me. I don't know how to thank you, especially for teaching me all the tricks of the trade—the many canning and cooking hints, and needlework, too."

"We should be thanking *you* for your gut work with our youngsters." The Amishwoman smiled sweetly. "You'll hafta come back and visit sometime. Maybe when you can stay longer, jah?" There was a twinkle in her gray-blue eyes.

"That's very kind of you, Lavina. Thank you." But Adele knew she could never come back to Bird-in-Hand. She headed upstairs to pack up the few things she'd brought with her to Amish country.

There was a private meeting of the deacons, Preacher King and one other preacher, and Bishop Fisher that night. They planned how to oust Gabe Esh from their midst, talking over the way to expedite things the following Sunday when the church membership would gather after the preaching service.

Preacher King went along with Bishop Fisher's idea to put it to a vote of the People, to forego approaching the rebellious young man in the usual scriptural way, giving Gabe a warning and opportunity to repent. But then, what was there for him to repent of? He'd had a differing view of the Bible from theirs, and he'd refused the powwow gift from the bishop—that's what it amounted to. They'd have to keep a lid on this. If word leaked out beyond the Lancaster community, out into neighboring circles, Plain folk might frown on not only their procedure for shunning, but also the reason for it.

Gabe drove his horse and carriage right into Lavina's yard the day Adele was scheduled to leave. He caught her just as she was loading up her car. "I wanted to come over to say good-bye," he said, helping her lift several medium-sized boxes into the trunk.

She hardly knew what to say. Here was the man her heart had always longed for, and yet she had refused him, rejected his marriage proposal on a most romantic carriage ride.

"Will you pray for me, Adele? For the work God's called me to do?" His eyes searched hers.

She found herself nodding. "Of course I will."

"May I write to you from time to time?" he asked, reaching for her hand.

She thought about that. "Only if you write in Pennsylvania Dutch, okay?"

Gabe didn't question her reasoning, just seemed glad that she would agree. "We'll always be friends, jah?" he said, removing his hat. "Always?"

"In our fondest memories, yes," she replied. "I'll never forget you, Gabe Esh. Never as long as I live."

Gabe moved toward her, his eyes shining. "I love you, Adele," he said once more. "Always remember that."

She longed for one last embrace but felt herself backing away. "I'm sorry, Gabe," she said, reaching for the car door. "I'm so very sorry. . . ."

His eyes were sympathetic and tender, yet the muscles in his jaw twitched repeatedly. "I'm mighty glad the Lord brought us together, even as friends, Adele dear. And I will miss you . . . for always."

She tried to swallow the throbbing lump in her throat, escaping to the privacy of her car before tears spilled down her cheeks uncontrollably. Closing the door, she pushed the key into the ignition, blinking back tears, struggling with the shift. Then slowly, she pulled away, waving a tearful farewell to Lavina who had just come out to sit on the porch.

But it was the vision of a dejected blond man, standing alone in the sun next to a chestnut-colored mare and an open courting buggy, holding his straw hat in both hands, that she was to remember for all her days.

Three long letters arrived from Gabe the first week after Adele returned home. She was thankful he'd remembered to write them in his native language. Her father's indignation over what he perceived to be a continuing relationship had been the main reason for her strange request—that Gabe's letters be written in Pennsylvania Dutch. Yet her response to her friend's correspondence was utter silence.

For two more excruciating weeks, his letters came, but she did not answer them, though they were not filled with declarations of devotion. The young Amishman had honored her heartbreaking decision, filling his missives instead with the things of the Lord, page after page of testimonials of souls finding salvation and divine healing in some cases. Her wonderful Gabe, unfairly shunned, was following God's call on his life, working with a Beachy Amish preacher outside Bird-in-Hand.

Adele began to look forward to hearing from him nearly every other day, though to reply might encourage him, she feared. So she refrained from answering his letters, though it tore at her heart to keep her silence.

In the early part of May, her mother, who had been ill for years, slipped away to heaven in her sleep. Her death was a blow to Adele, and it set her thinking about the brevity of one's life and how each day was unquestionably a divine gift. Her mother's passing also forced her to evaluate her own life in the light of eternity.

So the day after her mother's funeral, Adele crept into her mother's former sitting room and penned her first and only letter to Gabe. As she wrote, she felt as if a dam had broken loose within her, and she realized without a doubt that not only did she love Gabe enough to commit her affection to him, she was now willing to submit to the Plain lifestyle in order to share his life and ministry.

May 14, 1962

Dear Gabe,

Your precious letters, all of them, are gathered around me on my mother's rickety old rolltop desk as I write. My heart can no longer bear not to respond to you.

Although I said before I left that it seemed impossible for us to be together, I know now that I do not want to live my life without you. I am willing to abandon my modern lifestyle for you, dear Gabe, if need be.

Since we've been apart, I have come to understand that in spite of our contrasting backgrounds, we do share life's most important commonalities, you and I. We are similar in our zeal for God, our love for the spiritually lost, and, of course, we both enjoy nature— yes, I miss our many walks together. And we are drawn to children. . . .

If you still feel about us the way you did the night of our last buggy ride, then my answer is yes. I will wait intently for your reply.

With all my heart, I do love you!

Your "fancy" girl,
Adele

Lovingly, Adele assisted her father in sorting through her mother's clothing, furnishings, and personal effects in the week that followed, donating much of it to charity, although the wobbly rolltop desk was put out in the shed, waiting for an antique dealer to haul it away.

Adele waited breathlessly each day for Gabe's response, but none came. Days passed, and still there was no word from the smiling, blond Amishman. She thought that perhaps he hadn't received her letter, though it was not returned stamped "Undeliverable" or any such thing. A thousand times she considered composing another in the event that the first had ended up in a dead-letter file somewhere. But she chose to wait instead, praying that all was well with her dear Gabe, hoping that his silence was not evidence of his waning affection or, worse, that he no longer cared at all.

Late in the afternoon, on Sunday, May thirtieth—two weeks and two days after she had written her letter to Gabe—Adele received a phone call from Lavina Troyer, telling her that Gabriel Esh's life and ministry had been cut short in a car accident. "He was on his way to a preachin' service . . . over near Gordonville," the young woman stammered tearfully. She went on to say that his family would not be offering a funeral service or a burial site "due to the shunnin'."

Stunned and heartbroken, Adele took to her bed with such grief as she'd never known. Lavina arranged to bury Gabe with some of her own money, which originally had been invested by an older brother and set aside for a possible dowry. With the help of a New Order Amish friend's connection at the Lancaster Mennonite Historical Society, she purchased a grave plot and headstone in a Reading cemetery, giving her former school chum a proper burial.

Adele joined the young Amishwoman on the grassy slope, where the two stood just below the headstone, taking turns reading Gabe's favorite Scripture passages at this, their private service. Lavina glanced toward the sky when she said, "Gabe was prob'ly just too gut for this old world, and the Lord God heavenly Father saw fit to take him home." Adele was inconsolable and fell into Lavina's arms, promising to keep in touch "no matter what."

In the years that followed, Adele remained single, throwing herself into her instruction of children, filling up the empty years with her teaching duties and that of caring for her aging father. She never found the kind of love she had experienced with Gabriel Esh and could not forgive herself for having let him go.

Occasional letters were exchanged with Lavina, the unpretentious, simple-minded Amishwoman with a heart bursting with charity and goodness, who, in her own naïve way, had loved Gabe, too. Because of Lavina's compassionate decision to bury Gabe in Reading, Adele was able to visit her beloved's grave, just blocks from her father's house.

Weeks later, Adele heard from Lavina that Adele's letter had been found among Gabe's personal effects, though it was little consolation.

Every January seventh, Adele ordered abundant flowers, which she placed on Gabe's grave, commemorating the day of his birth. But after a time, a shadow fell over her spirit, and her faith faltered. She spent her remaining years pining for what might have been, disappointed with God, disappointed with herself.

A hush fell over Lily's room as she spoke the final words of the heartbreaking story. Rachel brushed tears from her face, and Philip coughed softly, composing himself as well.

"Adele rarely spoke of Gabe after his death," said Lily. "She saved each of his letters, memorizing them over the years. They were her only link to him."

Philip stared up at the postcard tacked neatly to the bulletin board above Lily's head. How ironic that something so small and seemingly insignificant at first had brought the three of them together on this autumn afternoon.

When Lily's nurse came into the room with medication, Philip and Rachel quickly stood and said their quiet thank-yous and good-byes. Philip gathered up his tape recorder, wishing they might've had time to discuss the remarkable tale with Lily. He also wished he'd thought to ask her how she knew Adele Herr but assumed, upon further reflection, that the women had probably met while at the Millersville college or had been close teacher friends. Philip felt, however, that he and Rachel had already presumed to take up a good portion of Lily's afternoon, and it was apparent that the retelling had taken much out of the dear woman. No, it was time to go.

Philip and Rachel settled in for the drive back to Lancaster, with Rachel sitting in the front passenger seat this time. He'd helped her get situated there after their visit with Lily, and Rachel hadn't refused, although he didn't think she was sure at first exactly *where* he'd put her. It seemed a better choice than the backseat. This way, they could talk more readily about Adele and Gabe, if they chose to.

"We should've asked Lily when her friend passed away and where Adele was buried as well," Philip mentioned when they got onto one of the main roads.

"Jah, and it's a pity, really, that Adele died without knowin' Gabe's answer. Receivin' that postcard would've changed her life, ain't so?"

Philip glanced at the young woman sitting next to him. How shy she had seemed when he first met her, yet she was becoming more comfortable with him, he thought. "I have a feeling the postcard would have changed everything, for both Adele *and* Gabe."

She nodded, remaining quiet for a bit. Then—"Why do you 'spose Gabe's message never found its way to Adele?"

He'd pondered that question himself during Lily's recounting of the story. "Well, I really don't know, but it's possible Adele's father, angered by yet another message from the Amishman, impulsively shoved it deep into the old desk that was to be hauled away. But that's only speculation—my spin on it. Who's to know, except that the postcard *had* been jammed into one of the narrow desk drawers."

Her jaw dropped momentarily. "Caught in a drawer, you say?"

"Yes, and remember Adele had sat to write her one and only letter to Gabe on a dilapidated, old rolltop desk? Must be the same one."

"Sounds to me like you missed your calling, *Detective* Bradley."

He chuckled a little. "It's what I do—gather all the facts for a story. So I guess you could say I *am* a detective of sorts. As for Adele's mother's desk—according to Emma at the antique store in Bird-in-Hand, it *did* come from Reading. She was able to trace it back to a Baptist minister's old shed."

"So you did some right-gut checkin' up on the desk, then." Her face broke into a genuine smile, and she let out a little chortle, then caught herself, covering her mouth quickly.

Philip said, "I feel satisfied now, knowing what I know about Adele's and Gabe's love."

"It's ever so surprising that the desk came full circle, so to speak, ending up in my father's house—right under your nose."

Rachel's comment was insightful, and he agreed with her, glad that she'd come along to hear her great-uncle's story on this mild September day.

The sun was creeping ever higher as he made the turn past the white stone wall and into the old cemetery. Towering trees like giant watchmen with wide arms were strewn out randomly across the grassy hillside. "I hope you don't mind, Rachel, but I thought we could make a quick stop . . . to visit Gabe's final resting place."

"I don't mind."

"I was here once before, but I'm afraid I got sidetracked. Now that we've heard the full story, it might be nice to see Gabe's headstone for ourselves." He meant the epitaph, though he had no idea if the Amishwoman would even have thought to inscribe Gabe's marker except for the name, date of birth, and date of death. Yet he wanted to see for himself, and he sensed Rachel was just as curious.

He hurried around the car and helped her out, gently taking Rachel's hand and wrapping it through his arm, while she used her cane with the other. Then, guiding her as carefully as if she were a fragile doll, they walked together over the paved pathway. Getting his bearings, he spied the general location of Gabe's marker, where the groundskeeper had directed him four days earlier. His heart quickened as they made the turn and strolled over a slightly sloping path of grass, under a shining sun.

Gabe's marker was unadorned, devoid of crosses and angels, as were others near it. Only slightly weathered, it was rounded at the top, a plain tombstone befitting an Amishman. "What's it say?" Rachel asked, her arm still linked through his.

Slowly, his eyes scanned the inscription as he read the words, silently at first:

GABRIEL ESH
Born January 7, 1935
Died May 30, 1962
Shunned by men, Blessed by God.
Loved by Adele Lillian Herr.

Philip was deeply moved as he read the words on the headstone aloud to Rachel. She was especially still, her eyes open in the dazzling light of the sun. A breeze skipped across the grass, rippling her skirt and apron, and for a moment it seemed as if she could actually see.

"Will you say Adele's *full* name again," Rachel said softly.

Philip looked down at the marker once again. "Adele Lillian Herr."

She breathed in quickly, gripping his arm.

"Are you all right?" He placed his hand over hers, consoling her.

"Jah, I'm fine, really. But I think maybe you missed somethin' important—it's there for all to see."

"What do you mean?"

"Lily . . . short for Lillian, ain't so?"

He was stunned by this beautiful blind woman's insight. Of course—Lily was Adele Herr!

Twenty-Four

❖ ❖ ❖

I t seemed as if they stood there for hours, motionless, lost in thought, absorbing their discovery of Lily's true identity.

When they finally turned from the gravesite to walk away, both were contemplative, seized by the poignancy of the moment. Philip wondered why Lily had wanted to keep her identity hidden. Why hadn't she wanted them to know?

Continuing to make their way down the gentle slope, he took great care to point out the uneven places beneath their feet, for Rachel's sake, then fell silent again, considering the events of the day as they approached the car.

It was Rachel who spoke first, breaking the near-reverent stillness—and when she did, it was as if she were reading his thoughts. "Lily didn't want to be known as Adele, 'least not to us." She sighed audibly. "She must've suffered terribly—losin' Gabe thataway—must've felt she had to mark time, keep standin' still, not movin' forward at all in life, choosin' her middle name instead. It was a way to hide—go into her-self—protect herself from the awful pain."

Philip was struck by Rachel's profound evaluation. *She seems to speak from experience*, he thought.

She stopped, turning to face him, though her eyes were downcast. "I know all too well what Lily . . . Adele, has gone through her whole life long. She simply couldn't move forward with livin'. That's the reason for her secrecy."

As Philip helped her into the car, he wondered what secrets Rachel may have pushed down into her own soul, hidden from the light.

The sun slipped behind a cloud just as he started the car and headed back in the direction of Lancaster, making it easy to concentrate on the road and on the lovely, perceptive young woman by his side.

"Adele *did* get Gabe's message of love before she died," he heard Rachel saying. "She got it just in the nick of time."

Soon they fell into a rhythmic and pleasant ebb and flow of conversation such as he had not recalled ever engaging in so fully with a woman. They talked and laughed about each other's childhood and religious training, their parents and siblings, their hopes and dreams. . . .

And Rachel shared with him her dedication to Jesus Christ and how she loved to listen to Bible tapes and occasionally the taped sermons sent her by Esther, her Ohio cousin. "Walkin' with Jesus makes all the difference in the world."

Philip found himself lost in conversation with the intuitive and bright woman, and by trip's end, he had nearly forgotten that she was both blind and Plain.

———

Stephen Flory and his wife seemed pleased to be treated to supper that evening. Philip touched on the high points of his and Rachel Yoder's visit with Lily, "who quite amazingly turned out to be Adele herself."

"No wonder I couldn't find her obituary," Stephen joked.

Philip nodded. "No wonder . . ." He told them he would be heading back to New York tomorrow. "I'll catch the first train out," he said.

"So your work here is done?" Stephen wore a boyish grin.

"I believe I have the makings of a terrific human interest piece." He was thoughtful. "I don't know exactly what I'll do with Gabe's and Adele's story, but I'm sure it'll come to me . . . in time."

"Maybe after it simmers awhile," Deborah spoke up.

"Maybe . . ."

———

Rachel was ladling out the chicken corn soup for supper when her thoughts drifted back to Philip Bradley. She supposed she oughta be caught up in the astonishing story she'd heard over the past two days— one on tape, the other in person. But she didn't feel it was so wrong to focus mental energy on someone as kind and appealing to her as was the writer from New York. Mighty interesting, he was, especially for an Englischer.

She found herself wondering about his human interest story on Gabe and Adele, but she had little hope of ever bein' able to read it. Not unless Susanna would agree to read to her, and if not, maybe when Annie got a little older. Still, she felt awful sorry for him havin' to return to such a busy place as New York. She'd allowed herself to enjoy the strength in his arm as he led her through the cemetery where Gabe lay buried and the smell of his subtle cologne, something she'd never smelled on Jacob—never. Which wasn't to say she didn't like it a lot.

Something about Philip Bradley made her feel alive again, like she didn't want so much to mark time anymore. Like she could begin to think about movin' ahead a bit. One tiny step at a time. Jah, and she felt ever so confident with him by her side.

Yes, now that she thought of it, Rachel was mighty glad he'd picked their Orchard Guest House B&B in the first place. . . .

Twenty-Five

❖ ❖ ❖

While waiting at Lancaster's Amtrak station for his train to
arrive, Philip toyed with the idea of calling Rachel. He hadn't
stopped thinking of her once since he'd dropped her off last
evening. And he didn't think it was so much a romantic thing he felt;
he just wanted to hear her voice one more time. So he took the risk of
getting Susanna Zook on the other end and called anyway.

"Orchard Guest House" came the soft, sweet voice.

"Rachel?"

"Yes?"

"It's Philip Bradley, the man who—"

"I know who you are," she interrupted, surprising him.

"Just wanted to say good-bye before my train leaves. And it was
very nice to meet you—to get to know you."

"That's gut of you to say, Philip. I pray you'll have a safe trip home.
May the Lord bless you always."

He smiled at her quaint expression. "And you, too," he said without
even thinking. "Oh, and please tell Annie good-bye, too. I hope her
wasp sting is healing nicely."

"Jah, it is."

He heard some commotion in the background—voices, as if someone
wanted to use the phone. "Is something wrong?"

She fell silent.

"Rachel?"

"No, it's *not* Rachel, and you're not to bother our daughter again,
you hear?"

He felt his eyebrows jump up. "I'm sorry, but I was having a conversation with—"

"Not anymore you ain't" came the terse reply. "And for your information, Rachel's not blind . . . not really. She suffers from a mental disorder, some sort of hysteria. So it ain't in your best interest, I wouldn't think, to search out a . . . a woman such as Rachel."

Philip was dumbfounded. "I understood she was blinded in the accident."

"Well, you're quite *wrong!*" the woman said emphatically. "She's mentally impaired . . . doctor says so."

Mentally impaired?

Rachel was far from it, and Philip knew it without a doubt. Susanna was obviously disgusted with him and rightly so. He'd taken her helpless, widowed daughter out of the city, exposed her to the heartwarming story of their wayward ancestor, brought her safely home, and was only interested in saying an innocent farewell. "I'm terribly sorry to have bothered you, Mrs. Zook."

"Jah, and so am I." And with that, she hung up the phone.

Once his bags were safely secured in the baggage compartment above his head, Philip browsed through a magazine he'd purchased, though not seeing either the ads or the articles presented.

He could not shake the words Susanna Zook had fired into his ear. Rachel not really blind? How could that be?

What kind of woman would make up such things about her own daughter? He dismissed the strange statements, assuming they were the product of a desperate woman's defense—to keep her widowed daughter safely secluded from the outside world. Surely that was all Susanna was attempting to do.

Instead, he chose to concentrate on Rachel's spiritual declaration, some of her final words to him on the phone.

May the Lord bless you always. . . .

Rachel's voice echoed in his thoughts as the train pulled away from the station, past warehouses and industrial buildings. Within minutes, the landscape became gloriously different. Visions of nature's beauty and simplicity framed the picturesque farmland and gentle, rolling hills, all of it representative of his Lancaster County experience.

Leaning back, he realized anew the wonder of God in his life—the grace and goodness he'd let fall by the wayside of his hectic existence, smothered and choked out by his own personal goals and ambitions. He thought of a young boy, kneeling at the altar of repentance, his heart innocent and true.

Lord, forgive me, Philip prayed silently. *Thank you for waiting for me to come to my senses.*

Lulled by the swaying of the train, he closed his eyes and thought of the delicate woman with an occasional curl in her honey brown hair. What a delightfully old-fashioned young lady. Her innocent approach to life was refreshing, and Rachel's adorable little daughter—well, they were quite a pair.

Please, Lord, watch over Rachel and Annie. . . .

Philip caught a cab to Times Square, checking in with his editor before heading to his cubicle. "Wild and wacky stuff," Bob said, chewing on a pencil. "Do people really live like that?"

"You'd have to see it to believe it, but yes, they do, and quite cheerfully, I might add."

He purposely did not mention the human interest piece. He liked Deborah Flory's suggestion about letting it simmer for a while. Trudging back to his small enclosure, he felt as though he could use some simmering, too. Not this week and not the next, but when the leaves started to change in Vermont.

He picked up the phone and dialed Janice. "I'm back," he said. "Is Kari around?"

"She's standing right here, dying to talk to you."

"Well, put her on."

"Uncle Phil, hi! It seems like forever since we talked."

"Forever—yeah, I know." He stared at a wide bank of windows just beyond the next row of cubicles, spying the sides and tops of buildings, one column of them after another, as far as the eye could see. "Do you and your mom want to watch the leaves change with me?"

"In London?"

"In Vermont . . . at Grandpap's cabin in the woods."

"But you promised London," she insisted.

"London can wait."

"Okay, if Mom can get away."

"She'll say yes, trust me," he said. "It's been a long time since I sat still and watched green turn to red. Maybe too long . . ."

———

Philip was packing for the trip to Vermont when the doorman rang his apartment. "You have a registered letter downstairs, Mr. Bradley. Would you like the mail carrier to bring it up?"

"I'll come down. Thanks."

When he had signed for the letter, he noticed that the return address was Fairview Nursing Home in Reading, Pennsylvania.

"Lily?" he said aloud, waiting for the elevator.

Quickly, he opened the long business-style envelope and discovered a typewritten letter addressed to him.

Dear Philip,

I was quite relieved that Shari, our receptionist, had saved your business card. I never could have found you, otherwise, to properly thank you for Gabe's postcard . . . and for your visits.

Perhaps by now you know that I am Adele Herr. I didn't intend to deceive you, but years of great sorrow and denial on my part had taken their toll, and I grew to trust few people. I must confess that I have lived an embittered, hopeless life, and by your coming, I know how wrong I was.

The postcard is a reminder of God's faithfulness to me, that He had His hand on me from the beginning, though I allowed great disappointment to rob me of my faith. I have given myself to my Lord and Savior once again.

So thank you, Philip. The message from Gabe, though quite belated, has altered my life and given me a reason to live.

I wish you well, my friend.

Sincerely,
Adele Herr

Philip refolded the letter, his heart filled with gladness, and he thought again of the Scripture reference Gabe had so aptly placed next to his signature, some forty years ago.

He who began a good work in you will carry it on to completion until the day of Christ Jesus. . . .

Epilogue

❖ ❖ ❖

Things seem a bit unsettled 'round here since our New York guest left for home. Mam's on edge more than ever, 'cept she still does insist on having frequent prayer times as a family, where Dat reads one pointed Scripture passage or another, directed toward me.

There's plenty of apple-cider makin' and apple-butter churnin' in the area, and I have to say that I hope we'll be making some candied apples, too. 'Least for Annie's sake.

We're hosting ever so many more guests, now that it's peak foliage, and I'm right grateful to be keeping busy. Still, it's mighty hard to tidy up the southeast guest bedroom or take a walk with Annie over the footbridge without thinking of the young man from New York. Seems the longer time goes, the harder it is to believe everything that happened while Philip Bradley was here.

Most surprising is the story behind it all—how a humble young fella, born sensitive and timid as anybody, mustered the courage to stand up to Bishop Seth Fisher and all the preachers, too! In the end, the obvious heir to the powwow "gift" chose to follow the call of the Cross, becoming a joint heir with Jesus.

It's a pity that Gabe died so awful young, missin' out on his sweetheart for a lifetime. I 'spect sometime here real soon, they'll be meeting again over yonder for all eternity. Gabe was surely right, after all, 'bout what he wrote: *Soon we'll be together, my love.*

Thinking 'bout the Glory streets and that wonderful-gut heavenly reunion to take place over yonder, I'm surprised that Jacob doesn't come to mind just now. Still, it's Philip Bradley who takes up much of my thoughts here lately, though not a soul must ever know—not even Cousin Esther—how brave I felt when I was with him. And even though he's a fancy Englischer and long gone, just thinking back to the way he said my name—like it was right special somehow—how we laughed together on the ride home from Reading, the way he saved Annie's life . . . well, every speckle of that memory leaves a right pleasant feeling.

Every so often, I catch myself thinking: Wouldn't it be something if Philip came back around—workin' on some project or another? 'Course, the way Mam talked to him on the phone—grabbing the receiver out of my hand like she did and tellin' him I wasn't really blind, that I was mental—who knows what he thinks 'bout me now? Well, next time—if there ever *is* a next time—maybe I won't be so timid-shy around him. Maybe not . . .

I still don't know if that dusky vision of little Annie was real or not, don't know if Blue Johnny ever truly came to my room that night. Mam refuses to talk about it, so I 'spect it *did* happen. I do know *one* thing, though: Powwow doctoring is not of God. For sure and for certain.

Thanks to Lavina, we've been attending my former church again. Clear out of the blue, the dear woman offered to pick up Annie and me in her little carriage for Sunday preaching at the Beachy church. I'm learning as much as I can about God's healing plan for His children, trusting, too, for His perfect timing for me. Esther sends me wonderful-gut Scripture verses on our taped letters, back and forth. I've still got plenty of growin' to do in the Lord before I discover all He has planned for me. But I do have a strong feeling that the postcard was sent by an unseen, yet divine hand, arriving at just the right time—across the years—winging a message of truth to each of us.

News travels fast amongst the People, so it's not surprisin' how many folk have heard Gabe's story. In a way, he's still preachin' the sermon God gave him back when, maybe more powerfully than ever before. Sometimes I think my great-uncle must be looking down from on High and smiling at the way the Lord has overcome evil with good. Here in Lancaster County, we call that Providence.

Acknowledgments

Space doesn't allow me to describe the way in which this story took root in my heart, but I can say with assurance that God planted the seeds in me, regarding my study of various types of "sympathy healings," to include powwow doctoring and other kinds of alternative healings. Out of my inquiry came a better understanding of the "curious arts" and the tools that Satan uses to seduce and ensnare.

I don't often talk about my writing "pilgrimage"—the process by which I craft a novel—but I can say that the Holy Spirit is always on time, preparing the way for research and inspiration as well. And without certain key people of God, this book would be languishing in a file.

So it is with great appreciation and thanksgiving that I recognize my wonderful husband and first editor, Dave, who literally made it possible for me to meet book deadlines. Always my friends and discerning editors, Barb Lilland, Anne Severance, and Carol Johnson offered gracious support and prayerful encouragement; so did BHP editorial, marketing, and publicity teams. My parents, Reverend Herb and Jane Jones, helped with numerous book resources and prayer, along with other prayer partners: Barbara Birch, Alice Green, Carole Billingsley, Jean Campbell, Judy Verhage, Bob and Aleta Hirschberg, and John and Ada Reba Bachman.

Special thanks to nurses Kathy Torley and Rita Stull, who answered medical questions. I am also indebted to Marianna Poutasse, curatorial assistant at Winterthur Museum, who shared her knowledge of antiques.

In addition, I extend heartfelt gratitude to the countless readers who have written to me this year, offering prayers of encouragement, sharing Scripture, and requesting more stories. May the Lord bless and keep each of you always.

The Crossroad

This book is lovingly dedicated
to my parents,
Herb and Jane (Buchwalter) Jones,
whose zeal and devotion to God
have both inspired and encouraged me
throughout my life.

Together, they pastored
Glad Tidings Temple
in Lancaster, Pennsylvania,
during my growing-up years.

Prologue: Rachel Yoder

❖ ❖ ❖

All my life I've been drawn to wooded landscapes—thick green groves of maple and sycamore. And weeping willows, 'specially those growing alongside the creek bed. As a young girl, I often crept out of the house just as the sun's glorious first rays peeped over distant hills, running lickety-split through dawn-tinted shadows of lofty tree umbrellas. Those early-morning ramblings, and the carefree way I felt in the midst of the woodland, gave me cause for living.

Now, as a young widow and mother, I'm reasonably content to help my parents run the Orchard Guest House, instruct my six-year-old daughter, Annie, in the ways of the Lord—and the Beachy Amish church—and help out wherever I can amongst the People, doing my best to keep up with sewing, quilting, gardening, canning, cooking, and cleaning house with *Mam*, in spite of things being the way they are with my eyes.

Here lately, I've begun to miss my morning run more than ever, but I daresn't mention it to Mam or *Dat*, or they might start pressing me to pay a visit to Blue Johnny or one of the other powwow doctors in the area. Far as I'm concerned, that subject's settled, 'cause at long last I know the whole story behind my great-uncle Gabe Esh—on account of an innocent little postcard, of all things. So I know in my heart of hearts, sympathy healing and Blue Johnny's "black box" just ain't for me. Not for any of us, really.

Ach, such a time we've had here lately. On Thanksgiving Day my young nephew Joshua Beiler nearly drowned in the frigid pond back behind Bishop Glick's house, where a wedding of one of the bishop's granddaughters had just taken place. I 'spect Josh was just itchin' to crack through the ice, knowin' how Lizzie's boy carries on sometimes.

My Annie said Cousin Josh was "a-flailin' and a-squealin'," carrying on to beat the band about getting himself soaked and freezin' cold. Well, it was nothing short of divine intervention that our Mennonite neighbor was out driving past the pond 'bout the time Josh skidded out of control and slammed through the surface into the frosty water below. *Jah,* the boy's life was spared, and it's a right *gut* thing, too, this side of Christmas and all.

Back last week, we had us a time while some of the women were over at Lavina Troyer's—my father's distant cousin—butchering chickens. Honest to goodness, if one of the teenage boys—who was helping chop heads off, defeather, and char the birds—didn't cut off one of his own fingers in the process. 'Course, someone had the presence of mind to wrap the finger, along with the missing piece, and hasten him off to the Community Hospital.

Then yesterday our cocker spaniel puppy, Copper, knocked over the birdbath in the backyard, breaking several terra-cotta pots along the walkway. Mam scolded the poor thing up one side and down the other; really, 'twas a shame the way she laid into him. But that's her way of handling most any conflicting situation—take the bull by the horns and show 'um who's boss.

Other than those mishaps, we've had a real pleasant autumn, I'd say. But just the other day, Mam remarked that she hated to see the "chillin' winds come and benumb the posies."

'Course, I agreed with her, though I can't actually see the nipped blossoms any more than I can make out my own little girl's features, but I *do* remember how the early frost used to make bedding flowers turn dark and shrivel up.

Mam and I, with some help from Annie, who pushed up a kitchen chair to stand on, baked a batch of molasses cookies to serve to our B&B guests at our afternoon tea. We topped the morning off with a steamy mug of hot cocoa, and all the while Mam bemoaned the fact that snowy months were just around the corner.

My heart feels more like the onset of springtime, though I don't exactly know what's come over me. Even little Annie seems to notice the bounce in my step. Mam, on the other hand, acts as though she's downright put out with me, and if what I 'spect is true, she has it in her head that the fruit basket got upset back in September when a New York City journalist paid a visit here at the Orchard Guest House. I'll have to admit, Philip Bradley *did* raise quite a ruckus, findin' Gabe Esh's love note the way he did. But I believe God put that old postcard in Philip's hands, and, honestly, I don't care what the People say or think, or anybody else for that matter. Out-and-out timely was his discovery of Great-Uncle Gabe's story—hushed up under a covering of mystery far too long.

"Rachel," my father said to me last night at supper, "you have no idea what that New York fella did, comin' and diggin' up the past, finding Gabe's note thataway. No idea a'tall."

Oh, but I *did* know. For sure and for certain, Philip was the best thing that had happened here in Bird-in-Hand in recent years, and whether or not the journalist ever returned to do research or write more Plain articles was beside the point. Fact was, he'd changed the entire landscape of a gut many lives. 'Specially mine.

note the way he did. But I believe God put that old postcard in Philip's hands, and, honestly, I don't care what the People say or think, or anybody else for that matter. Out-and-out timely was his discovery of Great-Uncle Gabe's story—hushed up under a covering of mystery far too long.

"Rachel," my father said to me last night at supper, "you have no idea what that New York fella did, comin' and diggin' up the past, finding Gabe's note thataway. No idea a'tall."

Oh, but I *did* know. For sure and for certain, Philip was the best thing that had happened here in Bird-in-Hand in recent years, and whether or not the journalist ever returned to do research or write more Plain articles was beside the point. Fact was, he'd changed the entire landscape of a gut many lives. 'Specially mine.

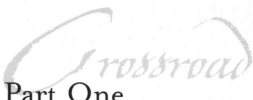

Part One

'Tis the gift to be simple,
'Tis the gift to be free,
'Tis the gift to come down
Where we ought to be.
And when we find ourselves
In the place just right,
'Twill be in the valley
Of love and delight.
When true simplicity is gain'd
To bow and to bend
We shan't be asham'd,
To turn, turn will be our delight
'Til by turning, turning we come round right.

—SHAKER HYMN, 1848

One

❖ ❖ ❖

Manhattan's skyscrapers jeered down at him as he flung open the door of the cab and crossed the narrow, congested street. Behind him, yellow cabs zigzagged in and out of indefinable traffic lanes, blaring their horns. Side by side, late-model cars, shiny limousines, mud-splashed delivery trucks, and pristine tour buses waited for the light to change, exuding puffs of exhaust. Each contributing to the chaos typical of New York City's business district.

The glassed entrance to the Lafayette Building, where the editorial offices of *Family Life Magazine* were located on the thirty-fourth floor, revolved with an endless tide of humanity, ebbing and flowing.

Pulling his overcoat against his tall lean frame, Philip Bradley pushed through the crush of the crowd, leaning into the bitter December wind. At the portico, he nodded to the Salvation Army volunteer with the red velvet Santa suit, ringing a small but mighty brass bell, the *plinking* of which added to the hubbub.

"Merry Christmas," the would-be Santa called to Philip, and the young journalist stuffed a five-dollar bill—his first contribution of the season—into the donation box.

"Bless you," Santa sang out.

May the Lord bless you always. . . .

The words had echoed in Philip's brain these past months, and immediately his thoughts sped back to the unassuming and beautiful Plain woman he had met while staying at an Amish B&B in Lancaster County. A young widow with a delightful little daughter named Annie, Rachel Yoder lived in the quiet farming community of Bird-in-Hand. While on assignment for the magazine, he had gone to research Amish Christmas customs, staying—by mere chance, he'd thought at the time—at Rachel's parents' Orchard Guest House on Olde Mill Road.

"May the Lord bless you always," had been Rachel's parting words, and the impact of her blessing and gracious Christian witness had resonated unceasingly in his mind. So much so that Philip had begun to read his Bible again, after years of indifference; even attended church services with his married sister and family, the very church he had once privately sneered.

Inside the atrium-style lobby, businessmen and women bustled to and fro, their well-polished shoes clattering and scuffing against gleaming tiled corridors.

The security guard addressed Philip with a nod and "Morning, Mr. Bradley." He returned the smile and greeting, making his way toward the elevators, where a large cluster of people extended out to the atrium itself.

Though not an impatient man, Philip glanced at his watch, wondering where he *might've* been in the early-morning scheme of things if he hadn't left his apartment twenty minutes earlier than usual. He made a mental note to give himself an extra ten tomorrow. It might help alleviate his increased feelings of stress, what with traffic surging in ever-increasing swells—weekly, it seemed.

Philip shifted his briefcase, waiting for his turn in the elevator, recalling a recent predawn stroll—a ramble, he'd called it—while in Amish country. There had been something exceptional about that particular day; the memory lingered fondly in his mind. Something about the quietude, the beauty of witnessing the sun's lustrous, silent rise over the horizon, breaking upon distant hills, spilling a rose-stained glow across the earth.

Something ever so special, he thought, recalling an Amish expression. He couldn't seem to shake the images and emotions of that singular short week, and he did not know why. Was it the tranquil, slower pace of things he longed for? The farm-fresh aroma of cows and soil?

Philip found himself thinking of Rachel, missing her—though in a non-romantic sort of way, he was absolutely certain. They were worlds apart, and both he *and* Susanna Zook—Rachel's determined mother—had recognized the all-important fact at precisely the same moment. Nevertheless, the enticing thoughts prevailed to the point that he had to shove them aside lest he not focus sufficiently on his journalistic assignments.

"Bradley!" a man called through the crowd, standing a few feet from the elevator doors.

"Hey, Henning," Philip replied with a grin. Richard Henning was a lead photographer for the magazine. Red-haired and sporting a goatee, he was a brilliant artist, if not a little overzealous at times. But most New York photojournalists were known to be pushy and demanding. They had to be.

"Just caught your Amish piece. Keep it up, and I'll be working for *you* someday," Henning said.

"You could do worse," Philip joked.

The elevator door opened and they followed the crowd inside.

Philip turned to Henning and whispered, "So . . . you liked my Christmas feature?"

"Yeah, yeah, but the photos were weak. You didn't give 'em much to work with. That's what I wanted to talk to you about."

"Uh-oh. Here we go." Philip chuckled.

"No, this is good. Hear me out. I'm thinking about a photo essay . . . featuring the Amish."

At the mention of the Plain People, a number of heads turned. Henning dropped his voice. "I think we could get Farrar, Straus & Giroux interested if you're on board."

Philip cringed. Most likely, the young photographer had no knowledge of Plain folk and their ways, probably didn't know they would shy away from being the subject of a photograph.

The elevator doors opened at the thirty-fourth floor, and the mass of humanity poured out. He followed Henning past the law offices of Abrahms and Hampshire to the double doors of *Family Life Magazine*. They opened to an enormous room of congested cubicles housing busy writers and copy editors. The entire floor was abuzz with the low but steady hum of computers, ringing phones—cell and otherwise—and human voices, people scrambling here and there. Philip waved at several co-workers in his section, then turned to Henning and motioned to his cubicle.

Henning started off in the opposite direction. "Give me a minute!" he shouted, and then he was gone.

Philip's writing space was clogged with vital paraphernalia: newspaper clippings, snatches of notes for interviews and email addresses, and an occasional phone number. His computer stood ready, centered on his desk, a telephone off to the left, and his married sister's family portrait—framed in oak—to the right of a wide red canister of pens and pencils. The picture included Janice, her light brown hair pulled back on one side, her tall blond husband, Kenneth, sporting a jovial smile, and their perky, flaxen-haired daughter, twelve-year-old Kari.

A bespeckled brunette in a navy blue pantsuit knocked on his partition just as Philip was logging on to the computer. "Great piece, Phil."

Looking up, he smiled at Beth, a top-notch copy editor for the magazine. "Thanks . . . but *you* make me sound good."

"So, any truth to the rumor?" she asked, ignoring the kudo.

Philip scratched his chin. "Okay, I'll bite. What rumor?"

"That you're joining the Amish." She stood at attention in the doorway, as though waiting for an answer.

"My buggy permit hasn't shown up in the mail yet. Until then, all plans are on hold."

Beth laughed. "Don't ask me to ride with you." She wiggled her fingers at him, then headed across the room.

Philip turned back to his desk and thumbed through his Rolodex, locating the address for his late-afternoon interview. Congressman Thomason, New York state senator. A man who, at the age of fifty-eight, had become an adoptive father. The perfect feature for next June's Father's Day issue.

Meanwhile, Henning had returned looking like a hungry puppy. He sat in a chair in the corner of the cubicle, slurping a cup of coffee, and staring intently at Philip.

"I know that look," Philip said.

Henning's smile turned dubious. "So . . . I come up with these incredible ideas, and all you want to do is shoot them down. That's what our friendship's come to?"

Philip sighed dramatically. "Okay, let's hear it."

Henning's smile broadened, and he affected his best Ross Perot impression. "Here's the deal."

Philip groaned.

"In a nutshell—I set up the photo shoot; you write the copy. Subject matter: the Amish."

"It's been done."

"Not like *I* can do it," Henning replied. "We go more in depth, maybe find an Amish family that'll take us in for a few days. Up close and personal. None of this superficial and pretentious stuff. We'll bring more humanity to the subject."

"With pictures," Philip muttered.

"Lots," Henning replied without skipping a beat. "The way I see it, this Amish thing's a hot button. People are just plain nuts about the plain and simple." He laughed at his own word play. "Everyone's yearning for the earthy, the back-to-basics approach to things . . . to everything."

What the man said rang true. Maybe the unending emphasis on technology *had* backfired on the entire human race. Were we, all of us, craving a simpler life, a slower pace?

Philip studied Henning. "Count me out this time."

"That's it? Just like that, you dismiss it?"

Shaking his head, Philip said, "I don't feel comfortable about any of it."

Henning rubbed his pointer finger back and forth under his nose. "I don't follow, Phil. I thought you were smitten with the Plain culture. Bob says it's all you talk about . . . Amish this, horse and buggy that."

Bob Snell, their editor, had every reason to regurgitate Philip's own enthusiasm to Rick Henning. "Most Amish disapprove of photographers," Philip explained. "It wouldn't be such a good idea to sneak around with your high-powered lens, taking shots of folk who've chosen to disconnect from the outside world, which just happens to include free-lance photographers."

Henning's jaw dropped. "Are you saying I can't zoom in on the eighteenth century, standing halfway across a pasture?"

"There's a difference between *can't* and *shouldn't*." Philip inhaled, then expelled the air loudly.

"Hold on a minute. Couldn't we try to get their permission—at least make some attempt?"

Philip wasn't surprised at his friend's persistence. "Whose permission?" he asked.

"*You* met some Amish folk—some you interviewed, right? Just get their consent. How hard can that be?"

Philip thought of little Annie Yoder and her widowed mother, Rachel; the stiff-lipped Susanna Zook and her bearded husband, Benjamin. He shook his head, staring hard at the bridge of Henning's long nose. "You really don't get it, do you, Richard? We're outsiders to the Amish world—two men they'd never be willing to trust, especially one with a camera poised and focused. Sorry, I'm not interested in exploiting their lifestyle to make some extra bucks."

"But the Amish exploit themselves. You've seen the tourist ads out in Ohio—tourism is a big part of their livelihood."

Philip stood his ground. "There are limits."

"All right, have it your way." Henning got up to leave. "But I'll be back."

Philip crumpled his coffee cup and threw it, but Henning ducked and scampered down the hallway.

Philip turned his attention to the project at hand—writing three pages of upbeat, family oriented questions for Senator Thomason. Something to engage and inspire the middle-aged politician, questions to set him at ease, make him feel altogether comfortable chatting about the toddler-aged Romanian twin girls he and his wife had recently adopted. Philip promptly set to work, putting Henning and the ridiculous proposal out of his mind.

Two

❖ ❖ ❖

R achel Yoder sat next to Lavina Troyer in the older woman's enclosed Amish buggy, wrapped in a woolen lap robe. She heard the gentle clatter and *clip-clop* of a passing horse as they headed south on Beechdale Road toward Lavina's house for a morning of baking. Just the two of them.

"Nothin' gut ever comes of deceit," Lavina said out of the blue.

Rachel listened intently. She had become slightly better acquainted with her father's somewhat eccentric relative recently. The discovery of an old postcard had drawn the two women together.

"Awful shame . . . the People payin' no mind to Gabe's preachin' back when."

Of course, Rachel supposed a gut many *had* given it some thought, seeing as how there was a hearty group of Amish Mennonites 'round here these days. She patted her mittened hands together against the cold, attempting to warm them under the blanket. "Uncle Gabe had a right gut heart," she said.

"Not one bit timid 'bout preachin' the gospel neither . . . long afore you was born."

Rachel thought on that. "I'm wonderin' something." She paused a moment, deciding if this was the right time to tell the woman 'bout the promptings inside her. Most everyone looked on Lavina with pity. Even Bishop Seth Fisher did, because she was slow in her mind, had to think right hard 'bout reading and writing, and needed more time than most to process her answers. Proof was in the fact that she failed near every school test she took all through eighth grade, be it true or false, multiple choice, or fill in the blank.

"Well . . . cat got your tongue?"

Lavina was trustworthy. Rachel knew it sure as anything, yet something kept her from speaking her heart. "You won't laugh if I tell you?"

"Never onct laughed at Gabe an' his secret prayers."

Rachel was truly glad to be able to share openly with someone 'bout her mysterious relative, the young man born as hesitant and shy as she, but who'd become mighty bold, rocking the community with his teachings against powwow doctoring and superstitions. Lavina was one of the few Plain folk around who knew the whole truth about Gabriel Esh, yet looked on past events in a sympathetic manner—in light of the spiritual, too, which wasn't all too common among the People.

Lavina had begun to attend the Beachy church, Rachel knew, turning her back on *das alt Gebrauch*—the Old Ways—though at the present time she was allowed to continue fellowship with many of the womenfolk from her former church district, even hold work frolics at her farmhouse. Some folk just assumed she'd upped and joined the Beachy group because of the way she was and didn't know any better.

But in the past weeks since Lavina had been driving her horse and buggy over to pick up Rachel and Annie for church, Rachel had begun to understand the woman more—what made her tick and all. Jah, Lavina's faith had nothin' whatever to do with her being slow. After all, the Good Book said "except ye . . . become as little children, ye shall not enter into the kingdom of heaven." So folks could flap their jaws all they wanted 'bout Lavina being backward, but when it came down to it, the gray-headed woman was the most accepting, kindest person Rachel knew. More so than her own mother, though Rachel assumed Susanna Zook was more peeved than uncaring these days.

"If'n ya ain't comfortable tellin' me, well . . . it's all right," Lavina spoke more softly now.

"That's kind of you." Rachel breathed in the frosty air, sure that Lavina would never tell a soul. Not if Rachel asked her to keep it under her bonnet, so to speak. She forged ahead, taking a deep breath. "I've been praying about seein' again . . . that the Lord might bless me with my sight."

Lavina said nary a word.

"I've been using Scripture tapes to memorize Bible verses 'bout divine healing, till it sinks in deep."

"Hate to think what some are sayin' 'bout your blindness, Rachel. Mighty distressing, 'tis."

Rachel knew. Even her own kinfolk figured she was as daft as Lavina was empty-headed. "But I truly *want* to see again," she said with boldness. "And in God's time, I believe I will."

She felt comfortable revealing this to Lavina, ever so glad the woman wouldn't be gasping or boring a shameless hole in her. Jah, it was right gut to express her desire because a strong and nagging feeling reminded her that the path to recovery might be a long, difficult row to hoe.

"I'll be prayin'" was all Lavina said as the horse pulled them forward toward the intersection of Beechdale Road and Route 340.

Rachel felt her muscles relax now that she'd shared one of her deepest longings with a sister in the Lord. Her *other* secret desire must remain veiled, shrouded in silence forever.

———————

Several batches of whoopie pies were ready to be stacked in the freezer by close to midmorning. All the while, Rachel continued to talk to Lavina, though mostly a one-sided conversation, it was. "What wouldja think of goin' to visit Adele Herr?" she asked.

Lavina was slow to reply. "Are ya sure . . . you wanna go to . . . to Reading?"

"I thought we could hire a Mennonite driver. Make a morning of it."

"An awful long ways," Lavina said. "I . . . I just don't know."

"We don't hafta decide this minute, do we?" Rachel chuckled softly, a bit surprised at her own resolve. "Let's think on it. If the Lord sees fit for us to go, we can take some goodies along. Maybe a basketful to share with the rest of the nursing home folk. Spread 'round some Christmas cheer."

Again Lavina remained quiet for the longest time, and while Rachel washed up, she wondered if she might've pushed too hard. Maybe she'd best back off the subject of visiting her great-uncle's former English fiancée. Maybe it had been too long for Lavina since the pain of those past days, the wounds too well-healed to risk scraping open again.

Rachel set about humming awhile, drying her hands and praying that the Lord might give her wisdom to know how to ease the fear in the poor dear, though she couldn't say for sure that she herself wouldn't be right bashful about traipsing off to parts unknown, really and truly.

"Adele always did like my apple butter," Lavina said at last.

Shuffling her feet and using her cane, Rachel felt her way across the linoleum floor of the large kitchen. She knew its setup—where the table and benches were positioned; the wood stove, sink, counter space, and battery-powered refrigerator, too—as well as she knew the kitchen at home. Long about now the sun should be pouring in real strong through the east windows, near the long trestle table. Sure enough, as she perched on the wooden bench, she felt the warmth caress her back.

"Had a letter from Adele . . . a few weeks back," Lavina said.

Rachel was surely glad to hear this interesting tidbit. "Well, if it's any of my business, what did she have to say?"

"Doctor's givin' her a different medicine. Seems to be helpin' some."

Rachel was curious, though she was too hesitant to ask. Had Adele mentioned anything of Philip Bradley in her letter?

But Lavina was off on another tack. "Sometimes I wonder if'n folk who knew 'bout Adele and Gabe's affection for each other . . . ever questioned why me 'n her never visited through the years," she remarked.

"I've wondered that myself."

"Me 'n Adele didn't write all that much—mostly just Christmas cards and birthdays."

Rachel perked up her ears. The woman was talking up a blue streak!

"'Twasn't my idea for Adele to stay put in Reading—not come to visit me none. But . . . well, we'd killed off her one and only love, so 'course she wouldn't wanna come back—not here."

"But you invited her plenty, didn'tcha?"

Lavina was quiet again, then she replied, "Adele was happiest teachin' school close to home."

Rachel could understand that. She, too, was a homebody. "Did she ever leave Reading?"

"Far as I know, never did." Lavina sighed and her breath sputtered a bit. "Doubt she ever forgave the bishop for Gabe's dyin' an' all."

"For goodness' sake, why *not*?"

"We're sharin' secrets today, ain't? So I got one of my own." Lavina drew in another deep breath. "It's been a-troublin' me for years, now."

Rachel felt herself tense up, wonderin' what was coming next.

"Adele did write me onct . . . 'bout the bishop and Gabe."

"She did?"

"Jah. Guess I oughta try 'n look for it . . . so's you know for yourself what I mean," Lavina said, excusing herself.

Rachel heard the quick footsteps on the stairs, and after what seemed like a long time, the woman returned. "Listen here to this. Back in 1963—one year after Gabe's death—Adele wrote this to me."

Lavina rattled the letter and, with great effort, began to sound out the words: " 'Something tells me things were . . . horribly strained between Bishop Seth Fisher and Gabe . . . prior to the accident. You may not know it, but Gabe once told me . . . that the bishop had . . . threatened his life on more than one occasion.' "

Rachel was aghast. "Threatened his life? Whatever for?" She thought back to Adele's story. What had *she* said about any of this?

" 'Twasn't any secret . . . some of the People thought the bishop put a hex on Gabe." Lavina's voice trembled momentarily.

Rachel felt breathless all of a sudden, as though someone had knocked the air out of her. "The *bishop*? A *hex*? I hate hearin' suchlike."

"Well, I, for one, never believed it. 'Least I didn't *want* to. And now it's mighty hard to know for sure, really."

"What with most everyone who knew anything 'bout it long passed on to Glory?" asked Rachel.

"Jah."

"Bishop Fisher's still alive," Rachel offered, hoping to draw more of the story from the one and only person who might know something 'bout her great-uncle's untimely death.

"Well's . . . there's no talkin' to *him*."

"I 'spose. The way Gabe upped and died . . . I hafta say I thought it seemed awful peculiar," Rachel replied. "Too abrupt it was, and right after he'd started preachin' so strong against powwow doctors and all. Does seem right suspicious, really."

"Best to just leave it be."

Leave it be. . . .

Lavina's words churned in Rachel's mind. Her own father had said something similar when she'd asked questions about Gabe's unjust shunning and ultimate excommunication. Rachel knew from Adele's lips the stand Dat and others had taken in their hush-hush approach to Gabe's ousting.

The women's talk eventually turned to domestic matters. "Are you comin' to Aunt Leah's for the quilting frolic next week?" Rachel asked.

"If'n I don't up and kick the ol' bucket. That, or they make the shun worse on me than 'tis already." Lavina laughed a little, making Rachel feel even more uneasy.

"I don't think we oughta talk 'bout untimely deaths or shunnings,"

Rachel was quick to say. "We best guard our lips."

"Well, now, I think you're right, prob'ly."

"The Lord's been showin' me some things in the Scriptures that have pricked my heart here lately."

Lavina spoke up. "Talk has it your cousin's spoon-feedin' you *her* beliefs."

"I don't have to guess who's sayin' those things." Rachel knew, sure as anything, Mam and Aunt Leah were the ones, prob'ly. "It won't be long and the People will know for sure and for certain. What I believe ain't just from Esther . . . it's deep in *my* heart, too."

"Your great-uncle would be shoutin' for joy . . . if'n he could see you now—one of his own family standin' up for Jesus right under Bishop Seth's nose. Just goes to show . . . no matter how hard the ol' enemy tries to stamp out the torch of truth, God always raises up someone to carry it along."

Rachel wished she could see the heavenly glow that surely must've settled over Lavina's long and slender face. Why, she'd never in all her days heard the backward woman express herself so easily, so sensibly.

Lavina rose and poured black coffee and served some homemade cinnamon buns. "I think you may be right 'bout spreading 'round some Christmas joy . . . up there in Reading."

Rachel's heart leaped up. "So you *do* wanna visit Adele?"

"Didn't know it before this minute, but, jah, I believe I do!"

Rachel didn't know what had come over her father's cousin, but she didn't plan to question Lavina's decision.

"I'll do some bakin' to take along, then." Lavina made a slurping sound in her coffee. "It'll be ever so nice, seein' the dear English girl again."

Dear English girl. Rachel had to smile at the remark. Of course, the older woman would remember Adele Herr as the young Baptist who'd come to fill in at the one-room school those many years ago. "Adele seemed like such a nice lady when I met her back in September. But I think it was right hard on her, tellin' the saddest story of her life."

They fell silent for a time, and Rachel relished the coffee bean aroma filling the kitchen.

It was Lavina who brought up Adele's letter again. "She's been gettin' letters—even postcards—from her friend in New York."

"Would that be . . . the journalist who came last fall?" Rachel carefully kept her tone matter-of-fact.

"That's who. Said Philip's become almost like a son. And he's goin' to church again, readin' his Bible, too."

"Well, I'll be. . . ." Rachel licked the syrup from her fingers.

"Seems them two are becoming fast friends . . . since he's the one who found Gabe's postcard, 'n all."

"I'm not surprised, really," Rachel replied. And lest she give too much away, she hushed right up. Wasn't anybody's business how often her mind traveled back to the early autumn days, when Philip Bradley had been a guest at the B&B.

After they'd finished drinking a second cup of coffee and devoured more than their share of sticky buns, Rachel rose to wash her hands. She was more than grateful she'd come to Lavina's today. Seemed to her the Lord was working in *both* their lives! Honestly, she thought it would be ever so nice if Philip Bradley would send *her* a letter. 'Course, the way Mam told him off on the phone that final day, the man would have to have nerves of steel to consider such a thing!

Three

❖ ❖ ❖

K ari opened the door nearly the instant his finger pressed the doorbell. "Uncle Phil!" she squealed, as though she hadn't seen him in years. She threw her arms around his neck, and he leaned down, hugging her.

"How's my sunshine?"

She let go, stepping back, then twirled about to model her long floral skirt, blond hair fanning out around her shoulders. "What do you think? I made it without any help from Mom."

"Wow, is *this* the sewing project you told me about?" He eyed the new skirt. "So . . . along with your *other* talents, you're a seamstress, too."

Kari beamed, still posing a few feet from the arched entrance to the dining room, where the table was set with Janice's best dishes and tall white tapers, already lit for supper. Kari had chosen the perfect backdrop to show off her newly acquired domestic skill.

"Hey, wait a minute. I think I may be underdressed for this occasion." He unbuttoned his overcoat, pulling it open slightly to gaze down comically at his own clothing—dress slacks and a sweater.

Kari giggled at his antics, her blue eyes twinkling.

"You're just fine, Phil." Janice breezed into the living room, reaching for his coat. "Let me take that for you."

Philip exchanged a glance with Kari while his sister hurriedly hung up his coat in the entryway closet. "Hope you're hungry," she called over her shoulder as she sailed back to the kitchen.

Kenneth Milburn, his brother-in-law, emerged from the hall study. "Good to see you, Phil. How long has it been?" He thrust out his hand, and Philip returned the warm handshake.

"Weeks, I'm afraid," replied Philip.

"Too long," said Kari, still spinning. "It's about time for the London trip, don't you think, Uncle Phil?"

"London?" he teased, knowing she was definitely counting on him to follow through on an earlier promise.

Ken smiled. "Give your uncle a chance to catch his breath," he admonished with a wink. Then, turning to Phil, "I've heard nothing but good reports about your Vermont vacation. Kari and Janice talked of it for days. And it was educational, which was a real plus."

Kari followed her dad to the sofa and curled up on one end, while Philip took the wing-back chair across from them. "Dad thinks most *everything* in life should be educational." Kari grinned at her dad. "We toured Robert Todd Lincoln's estate, where one of Abe Lincoln's three remaining stovepipe hats just so happens to be on display. Can you believe it? Mom and I had Uncle Phil take our picture next to it. For posterity."

Philip chuckled. "Don't forget the Norman Rockwell exhibit in Arlington," he prompted her. "That was also *educational*."

She took the cue, describing the magazine cover illustrations for *The Saturday Evening Post* they had enjoyed. "We found lots of surprises in Vermont when we stayed at Great-Grandpap's cabin."

Philip remembered. They *had* discovered some fascinating treasures on their daily treks through the woods. Things like a rusty horseshoe, old pennies, red and yellow leaves, and aluminum cans imbedded along the trail, which they picked up and deposited into Kari's backpack to be recycled later. But it was the chatter between him and his niece that he recalled as being the most rewarding aspect of the trip. For some unknown reason, she had been curious about the Amish and their plain attire—especially the women's clothing—so he had attempted to describe the details he remembered: the length of Susanna's and Rachel's dresses, the colors—not mentioning Rachel's choice of gray for mourning—the cape-style bodice and high-necked, full-length apron, and, of course, the white head covering. "Not a sign of makeup," he'd told her. "But, it's funny, you really don't notice."

"Is that because their cheeks are naturally rosy?" Kari had asked.

He thought about that. "Well, yes, I suppose they are."

"Must be all the gardening they do."

He let his niece think the latter, though he knew for a fact that Rachel Yoder had not been one to expose her face to the sun. Yet she was beautiful—pink-cheeked—nevertheless.

Kari had been so excited upon hearing his account that while they were still in New England, she decided to look for some fabric to sew a long skirt. He'd gone with Janice and Kari to a fabric store, following them around as Kari looked for the "perfect print." The material instantly reminded Philip of another flower print dress he'd seen while in Bird-in-Hand. It was very similar to Emma's dress, the Mennonite woman who owned Emma's Antique Shop.

So here was Kari, presently modeling the finished project. "It's as pretty as you said it would be," he told her. "I'd say you could compete with any Plain woman I know!"

With that, she burst into laughter again, and he felt the heat creep into his face. "Oh, so you *do* know a lady in Lancaster County." She turned away, calling for her mother. "Mom! Guess what—Uncle Phil has a secret love in Amish country."

Secret love . . .

When no reply came from the kitchen, Philip was more than relieved. No sense exposing that part of his Pennsylvania sojourn. He preferred to keep his passing interest in Rachel Yoder under wraps. That way, there could be no misunderstanding.

"What sort of grade did your mom give you on your sewing project?" he asked, changing the subject rather naturally.

"B-plus." Kari shrugged. "Mom doesn't believe in perfection, you know."

Philip wondered how his sis was managing the home-schooling program she and Ken had chosen this year. "How're you doing in language arts?" Dramatically, he pulled out a pen and tiny note pad from his shirt pocket.

"Oh, so you're going to take notes?" Quickly, Kari fluffed her hair. "Is this an interview?"

"Just checking up, that's all."

Her face shone with delight. "Tell Uncle Phil how school's going, Dad."

Ken nodded, smiling. "Janice gives Kari plenty of writing assignments, if that's what you're concerned about."

"Glad to hear it." His niece had real writing talent, quite a surprising way of expressing herself. "Tell me about some of your essays." He knew they existed because she'd dropped hints several times on their hiking trips.

"She's written some excellent poetry, too," Ken spoke up.

"Oh, Daddy, *please*."

"No, really, hon," Ken added. "I believe you may be following in your uncle's literary footsteps."

Philip had begun his early writing career by jotting down free verse during adolescence. He preferred to think of that youthful time as purely a phase, mainly because he had felt caught up in the tension of those turbulent years. But when he emerged safely into his early twenties, it was journalism that called to him. Not poetry.

He put his pen and note pad away. "So you're going to be a girl after my own journalistic heart."

"I'm not a girl, Uncle Phil. I'm almost a teenager!"

"Hang on to your youth, kiddo." With that, he found himself pummeled with sofa pillows. Even Ken joined in the trouncing, picking up pillows and tossing them to Kari.

It was Janice's dinner bell and "Time to wash up for supper" that brought their rambunctious play to an end.

"We're having pork chops," Kari announced after they'd taken turns washing hands.

"Really? Where'd you get the recipe?" Philip asked, nearly forgetting himself.

Janice's brown eyes shot daggers across the table. "What do you mean, *where*? It's *my* recipe . . . I've been making it for fifteen years," she jived him.

He would not reveal his thoughts—that Kari's innocent announcement and the tantalizing aroma of broiled pork chops had sent him drifting back to another supper, served with an astonishing array of colorful and tasty side dishes, freshly baked bread and real butter, various condiments, and sumptuous desserts.

It was well after supper when Philip brought up the subject he had been researching on the Internet—the treatment for various hysterical disorders. Especially blindness. He hadn't fully understood Susanna Zook's comments on the phone the day he'd called Rachel to say good-bye. But after mulling it over, pieces of the full picture were beginning to come together. He was especially curious about any information Ken might have, as he was a nurse and rubbed shoulders with doctors on a daily basis.

"Tell me what you know about conversion disorder," Philip said later as Kari helped Janice clear the table.

Ken scratched his chin, leaning back in his chair. "It's rare, but we see it on occasion at the hospital. Why do you ask?"

Philip hesitated, uncertain how to proceed. How much should he reveal? How much of Rachel's situation did he really know? "I think I may have come across a case of hysterical blindness . . . in Lancaster County."

Ken frowned, apparently concerned. "Do you know what caused it?"

"Not all the particulars, but the person *did* witness the death of two family members and her unborn child."

Janice emerged from the kitchen with dessert plates. "Was this *someone* Amish?" she asked.

Nodding, Philip hoped he wouldn't have to say much more. He wouldn't feel comfortable discussing Rachel Yoder—even with his family.

"There really isn't any treatment other than psychiatric care," Ken said, shrugging. "It would depend on the cause of the conversion disorder and the extent of denial and repression."

This sort of terminology had been used on the various Web sites Philip had located when he did his investigating late at night on forms of hysteria—the term Rachel's mother had mentioned. At the time, though, he'd just assumed she was merely flinging angry words. But the more he thought about it, the more he believed that Susanna had not misrepresented the situation to him at all.

"I don't know about the denial angle." He didn't want Ken or Janice to guess just how much time he had already spent on his net-search. Fact was, the pace with which he had kept at it—feverish at times—had cost him more than a few nights of sleep.

Yet something urged him to find a way to help Rachel Yoder. She was missing out on her daughter's life, her precocious little Annie. And as much as he loved children, he was dismayed by that fact alone. So he had worked diligently over the past months, reading accounts of patients who'd received various kinds of intervention, though he assumed Rachel would be resistant to anything involving hypnosis or other forms of New Age therapy.

So he would continue to seek out medical opinions, talk to Ken and Janice—in a vague sort of way—and most of all, to pray. At some point he would decide how he should go about contacting the Amish widow. That is, *if* he chose to reach out to her directly. He'd thought of sending information her way, though with Rachel unable to see, the data might very well fall into her parents' hands, serving no purpose whatsoever.

Recent correspondence with Adele Herr had shed some light on the fact that Adele and Lavina Troyer, Adele's longtime Amish friend, still kept in touch through letters. He had actually considered Lavina the better choice for getting the information to the Bird-in-Hand area but had yet to do anything.

Ken's comment brought him back to the conversation at hand. "I'd recommend your friend getting some group grief counseling, for start-ers."

Grief counseling . . .

It was almost impossible to imagine Rachel seated in a circle of chairs, surrounded by non-Amish folk, pouring out her heart amid strangers, both by way of their cultural differences and because she seemed quite shy. No, he couldn't imagine her attempting such a thing. Too, the way he perceived the Amishwomen's interconnectedness in the community, no doubt there was a close bond of candor and affection among the womenfolk. More than likely, Rachel had already talked out her memories, her sorrow, and the ongoing emotional feelings of loss.

"I've read that grief counseling can help a person know they aren't going crazy—that they are experiencing the same sort of symptoms as other members in the group," Ken added.

"That, along with a feeling of camaraderie," Janice spoke up, pulling her hair back away from her face, only to let it fall down over her shoul-ders again. "No one should face a grief situation entirely alone."

"Just so the person doesn't become too dependent on the group," Ken interjected, "so much so that he or she gets 'stuck,' continuing to focus on the grief event rather than growing beyond it."

"Guess I'll have to go to work with you sometime . . . so you can introduce me to your shrink friends," Philip quipped.

Ken responded to Philip's jest with a hearty laugh. "The only so-called shrinks I know are brain surgeons."

That got all three of them laughing, just in time for Kari to serve up Janice's surprise dessert of the evening—apple pie a la mode, warm from the oven. The cinnamon-rich smell tickled his memory again, buttering the Lancaster County scenes in his mind's eye with vivid sensory rec-ollections.

———

Philip turned the key in the lock, opening the door to his thirtieth-floor Upper Manhattan apartment. On the wall of windows, he noticed the reflection that crept up from the streetlights far below. They cast a silvery glow over the living room walls, tables, and sectional.

He double-locked the door. Then, instead of turning on the lights, he allowed his eyes to grow accustomed to the dim surroundings. Feeling his way across the wide tiled entrance and toward the living area, he was able to make out more of the furnishings—the long chalk-colored sectional and matching chair, as well as the artsy decorator touches he had scouted out at various bazaars and art exhibits over the past few years. In the absence of interior light, the longer he groped his way toward the windows, the more he was able to see.

He stood near the central window and stared down at the still busy street, ablaze with red and yellow bands of color. He thought of Rachel, blind by choice, though in no way to blame for it. And he thought of bright-eyed Annie, offering her own sight—her little-girl perspective—on their noncomplicated world. It was not his place to attempt to alter things for them, to stick his nose back into their lives on the slim premise of making things better. Besides, Rachel might not embrace the prospect of regaining her sight as something better at all, although he would certainly assume so. No doubt she had been a sighted person prior to the accident that took her husband's and son's lives. Yet she *had* seemed somewhat content with her state, though he could only speculate on the matter, due, perhaps, to the fact that he'd scarcely had time to really know her. But, surprisingly, what he had discovered about her—her lack of artifice and pretense—well . . . simply put: He missed Rachel's old-fashioned mannerisms.

In his world, where women willingly and purposefully climbed corporate ladders, it was refreshing to learn that meekness and gentleness were alive and well in the heart of Pennsylvania Dutch country.

Even despite the rousing and interactive discussion with Senator Thomason this very afternoon—thoroughly enjoyable, since he himself craved the writing life—Philip recognized that in the depths of his soul he truly longed for something fresh and new. So he had come upon an unexpected fork in the road of his journalistic career—aware of his own talents, yet desirous of a saner pace and setting in which to work. He had shared these concerns openly with Lily—Adele, as she now insisted on being called—in a recent letter, detailing his soul-searching, explaining how the aspects of life in the village of Bird-in-Hand had strongly appealed to him. He'd let her know, too—as a young man might share with his own mother or father—his purposeful return to his faith, his renewed journey to know the Lord. And he *had* mentioned this to his parents as well. But Adele . . . well, there was just something about the woman that allowed him to be completely candid with her.

Adele had replied within a few days of receiving his heartfelt letter. *All of us, at one time or another, must make a choice,* she'd written back. *I'm delighted to know that you are relying on God's help with your 'fork in the road,' as I should have, back when I lost my way spiritually.* Her comment had been a direct reference to having allowed the disappointments of life to lead her astray. Philip had read and reread the passage so many times, he'd come to memorize it.

Thankfully, he wasn't standing at such a crossroad, but when the time came for him to choose a life-mate, he would hope to make his decision based on God's will.

One thing for sure, in the next weeks he would make a conscious effort to fight off the impulse to entertain even the most subtle thoughts of a plain and simple country Christmas, possibly a few stolen hours with Rachel and her young daughter in the delightful farming village.

From his perspective—where he stood this night—Rachel Yoder and her People were light years away. . . .

At last he turned from the window, disallowing himself the luxury of the track lighting overhead to guide the way to his writing studio, even closing his eyes to experience something of what it might be like *not* to see.

Then, fumbling about, he located his office chair, desk, and the computer and monitor, permitting his fingertips to direct him. Eyes tightly shut, he felt his way to the On button, then waited for his computer to boot up. Even before opening his eyes, Philip's thoughts raced ahead to his nightly research of conversion disorder, namely blind hysteria.

Four

❖ ❖ ❖

W hat're we gonna do for you on your birthday?" Susanna Zook asked her younger sister, Leah, as the two women darned socks in Leah's warm kitchen.

"Ach, ya know better'n to bring up such a thing," said Leah, flashing her brown eyes.

"Well, why not? A body only turns sixty once."

"And fifty-nine once, too!" Leah, on the round side of plump, stood up and laughed over her shoulder as she prepared to pour another cup of hot black coffee.

Susanna shook her head. "Oh, go on. You can't mean it."

"I'm sayin' what I mean, Susie. You just listen to me 'bout this birthday nonsense." Leah placed two steaming mugs on the table. "Seems to me a person oughta have a say in how she celebrates—or doesn't."

"S'pose we oughta do something *extra* special for a stubborn sort like you," Susanna shot back.

"Mark my words, if there turns out to be a party or some such thing, I'll know who's to blame." She wagged her finger in Susanna's face.

"*Himmel*, then, if ya really and truly don't want nothin'."

Leah's face broke into a broad smile. "That's what I want. No cake, no pie . . . no nothin'."

"Well, what if we sang to you at the frolic—how 'bout that?" She knew she was pushing things past where she oughta.

Leah kept her eyes on her mending. "You just never quit, do ya?"

"So . . . if you aren't sayin' we *can't* sing to you, then I 'spose that means we *can*." She'd made her pronouncement.

Leah clammed up for a good five minutes, so Susanna figured it was time to bring up another subject. Best not to allow festering thoughts to continue. Still, she didn't see any harm in honoring her youngest sibling's sixty years on God's green earth. It wouldn't be like they were behaving like the Mennonites, partying and such 'bout a birthday. No, they'd just have a nice excuse to fix a big meal and invite everybody over.

"Well, you'll never guess what I heard Rachel a-mumblin' to herself yesterday," Susanna said as casually as she could.

Leah glanced up, grunted, then stuck her head right back down, paying close attention to her poised needle.

Susanna took the grunt as a go-ahead to talk about something unrelated to birthday dinners. So she did. "*Ich hab mich awwer verschtaunt*— Was I ever surprised! Rachel was saying, 'I will see . . . I will see!' over and over in her room. Don't quite know what to make of it, really."

"I don't see how that's so surprisin'. After all, you kept tellin' me— for the past two years or so—that she's made herself blind, didn'tcha?"

"Jah, I've said as much."

"Well, maybe then she can make herself see again, too. What do you think of that?" Leah was truly serious and looked it in the face, the way her dark eyes were so awful intent on Susanna.

"If you ask me, I think Rachel's gone *ferhoodled*." Susanna hushed up real fast, though, realizing what she'd just said. Didn't wanna let on too much 'bout her daughter's state of mind, 'specially the way Rachel seemed so awful bouncy these days . . . like she was in love or some such thing.

"What do you mean, Sister?" Leah asked, still sending forth a powerful gaze.

Susanna was cornered—had to say something or leave it up to her sister's imagination, which, in the end, might be even worse. "Ach," she pressed onward, "you know how it is when a body gets eyes fixed on something they can't have."

Leah brightened. "Are we speakin' of romance?"

Susanna swallowed hard, worried 'bout what she'd gone and gotten herself into. "Well, I couldn't say that for sure. But"—and here she dropped her sewing in her lap and gave Leah a grim look—"Rachel's a bit perplexed, I'm a-thinkin'."

"Over a man?"

She shrugged. "Who's to know."

"Well, I think *you* know," Leah piped up. "And truth be told, you oughta make positively sure that Mr. Bradley never comes pokin' his nose 'round here anymore."

Susanna was surprised that her sister seemed to know exactly what she herself was thinking. And it *was* true. Philip Bradley best not come looking for her daughter anytime soon. That, in fact, must *never* happen. The girl was much too vulnerable these days, what with her comin' out of mourning just now, wearing the usual Plain colors of blues and greens again. Even the purple dress had up and appeared here lately— the day Lavina came and took Rachel over to her place, just the two of them.

"Don't 'spose you'd know of a Plain widower 'round Lancaster who might be lookin' for a right gut wife . . . and stepdaughter," Susanna said.

"Well, now, if that don't beat all."

"What're ya sayin'?" Susanna wondered if she'd opened her mouth too soon.

"I think I might know of someone." Leah's face looked quite a bit rosier than Susanna had seen it in weeks. Almost as if her sister had stood outside pickin' sugar peas or tomatoes or shellin' limas for hours in the sun.

"So . . . what widower is it that's lookin' to marry a second time?" She thought it best not to hold her breath, make her face go white or whatnot; it would never do for Leah to know just how she felt 'bout losing her daughter and granddaughter to marriage. And most likely to an older man at that.

"Name's John Lapp—a right nice Amishman down in Paradise, though it might be a ways too far . . . for courtin' and all. And then again he's Old Order, so I don't know how that'd work, what with Rachel leanin' toward the Beachy group."

Paradise . . .

Susanna felt herself sighing with relief. Jah, the town was prob'ly too far away for a romantic encounter, 'specially for horse-and-buggy Amish. Still, if she hadn't brought up any of this to Leah, the word might never have had a chance to spread 'round the area. 'Course, now she couldn't go and stick her foot in her mouth and ask her sister not to say anything.

"Best just to let the Lord God set things up," she managed.

"Jah, but a little help from His children wouldn't hurt none, don'tcha 'spect?"

Leah had her but good.

The sun clouded over around the time Susanna got in her buggy and prepared to head home to Benjamin. She glanced at the sky, wondering if the weatherman's prediction would prove true 'bout the first snowstorm of the season. Wasn't that she minded the snow so much. It was the wind whipping at her face that she had to put up with when she rode horse and buggy somewhere or other. Here lately, she'd gotten more accustomed to calling a van driver to take her places—mostly for trips into Lancaster and sometimes down to Gordonville to buy quantities of fabric on sale for Benjamin's pants and shirts and little Annie's slips and things. Rachel, it seemed, had plumb wore out her gray mourning dresses. 'Twasn't any wonder, seein' as how she'd put on the same ones over and over again for the past two and a half years.

Jah, it was high time Rachel threw away her old clothes or made rag rugs out of 'em, 'cause her mamma had been thinkin' of sneaking them dresses out of her daughter's room and making sure they disappeared. Rachel couldn't see anyway and wouldn't know the difference.

Susanna couldn't be sure, but she thought her daughter might just be getting to the place where she'd listen to some advice 'bout some of her ongoing quirks and whatnot. Folks were starting to talk here lately 'bout the amount of time Rachel was spending with Lavina, who was under the *Bann*—the shun—for breakin' her baptismal vow, goin' off to the Beachy church on account of Rachel and Annie. Susanna and Ben had never approved of Rachel and her beloved Jacob headin' off to the Beachy church, but least her Rachel hadn't broken any vows, never having been baptized in the first place. Still, all that time spent with Lavina couldn't be any gut for Rachel, really, even though she and Lavina *were* kin in a far-removed sort of way.

Truth be told, Susanna was worried that some of Lavina's peculiar ideas and ways might rub off on Rachel. The poor girl sure didn't need that.

Rachel redd up the entire upstairs, cleaning bathrooms, shaking rugs, dusting and sweeping under each bed. Then she ironed every last one of her father's shirts and pants and even cooked up a pot of chicken and dumplings before she slipped the corn bread batter into the oven and hurried upstairs to make a tape-recorded "letter" to her Ohio cousin, Esther Glick.

She saw to it that Annie was occupied downstairs at the kitchen table, making her little drawings with her favorite crayons, before Rachel closed the bedroom door and turned on the recorder.

Hello, Esther!

Greetings from chilly Bird-in-Hand.

Scarcely could I wait to share with you today—you just have no idea how excited I am! Last Thursday, I spent part of the morning with Dat's relative, Lavina Troyer. Anyhow, she and I got to talking, and she agreed to go with me to visit my great-uncle Gabe's former fiancée, Adele Herr. Remember, I told you how that New York writer came to stay with us, and he took me to meet Adele? Remember, too, how she told all 'bout what happened here to Gabe when he wouldn't go along with Bishop Fisher, wouldn't accept the unholy "healing gift" the bishop wanted to pass on to him? The same way I didn't wanna have anything to do with Blue Johnny and his black box?

Well, I've been thinking long and hard 'bout what it'll take for me to get my sight back, and I hafta tell you, Esther, it's become ever so important to me here lately. Something new is happenin' inside me. I truly want to see again. Not just because it's so hard bein' blind in a sighted world—it ain't that a'tall. I want to see so I can raise Annie, and more than that, I want to see again so I can be a better witness for the Lord.

You might be thinkin' that I want to take Gabe Esh's place in ministry, and that could be what God's callin' me to do. I don't know for sure or for certain, not just yet, but I'm trusting the Lord to show me, day by day, what He would have me do for His glory.

I know you and Levi are doing your part out there in Ohio to spread the Good News. Well, I want to do the same. I believe, as you do, that we don't have much time before the Lord says, "Come on up a little higher."

Don't forget how much I enjoy hearing those sermon tapes of your pastor. Whenever you can, will you please send some more?

Wait just a minute, I believe I hear Annie callin' me. I best run down and check on her.

I'll finish this later. . . .

Pressing the Off button, Rachel left the tape recorder on the floor near her dresser and scurried out of the room and downstairs to Annie.

"I've been wonderin' where you were," the child fussed.

"Sorry, dearie. I was taping a letter to Cousin Esther."

Annie sighed. "Do ya think they'll ever come back and live here again?"

"Esther and Levi will prob'ly stay put in Holmes County. But, jah, I wish they'd move back," Rachel was quick to add.

"They like farmin', don't they?"

She nodded. "Workin' the land's the best thing for a farmer."

Annie was quiet for a moment. "Will *we* ever get to farm, Mamma?"

"Well, now, you know we live with *Dawdi* Ben and *Mammi* Susanna so we can help them make a living . . . with the English guests."

"Are we gonna stay with 'em forever?"

Forever . . .

Rachel hadn't thought of that. She'd felt ever so content for the longest time, just going on the way she and Annie had been living.

Annie whispered, "Maybe someday we could farm, too, like Cousin Esther and Levi."

"Are you hopin' that we'll move to Ohio and live with your young cousins—James and Ada, Mary and Elijah?"

"Well, it *would* be lotsa fun havin' other kids my age, unless . . ." Annie grew silent again.

"Unless what?"

"Well . . . I don't mean to speak out of turn, but it would be awful nice to have some brothers and sisters someday, like my cousin Joshua has, you know?"

Lizzy, her older sister, and her husband had a good many children and another baby on the way. "In order to give you little brothers and sisters, I'd be needing a husband, and you know that's impossible," Rachel reminded her daughter.

"'Cause Dat got killed in the car wreck?"

"That's right."

"But does that mean you can't marry somebody else?"

Annie's childish question took her off guard. "Well, I guess I *could* marry again, if the Lord saw fit."

"Why don'tcha, Mamma? Then you can have some brothers and sisters for me—and some more cousins for Joshua, too."

Rachel had to smile at her darling girl. "It's not as easy as just sayin' it."

"What do you mean, Mamma?"

She sighed, wondering how on earth to explain that one person couldn't just decide to up and marry. "It takes *two* people—a man and a woman—who love each other very much."

"So . . . all's we need is one more—the man—right?" Annie was giggling now. "I think I know where the other *one* can be found."

"Where's that?" Rachel asked absentmindedly.

"New York City."

Rachel's heart leaped at the mention of Philip Bradley's hometown. "What in the world gave you such an idea?"

"Mister Philip did," Annie replied.

Rachel was flustered beyond all words. "What . . . whatever do you mean?"

"Oh, I almost forgot you couldn't see what I saw, Mamma."

She wasn't clear on what her daughter was saying. And she was beginning to feel uncomfortable with her father sitting just around the corner at the end of the sunroom. "We best keep our voices down," she whispered.

"Nobody's near," Annie volunteered.

Rachel grinned at her girl's insight—another one of those traits passed down through the family. Only this wasn't a questionable one, like some of the "gifts" on her mother's side, beginning as far back as Gabe's great-grandfather, Ol' Gabriel Esh, a powerful conjurer in the area. No, God was going to use Annie for His glory and honor. Rachel honestly believed that and had begun to pray blessings over her daughter, till such time as Annie herself could give her heart and life fully to Jesus.

"I saw something in Mister Philip's eyes, Mamma . . . the way he looked at you. There was something wonderful-gut 'bout it."

Rachel felt the heat rising into her cheeks. "Well, I don't know how that could be."

"*I* do, Mamma. He must've seen in you what Dat saw a long time ago."

She leaned down and wrapped her arms around Annie. "You're sayin' the silliest things, I daresay."

"No . . . no, I ain't makin' it up. I saw what I saw!"

Sitting down, Rachel held Annie on her lap. "Listen to me, honey-pie. Mr. Bradley is an *Englischer*. So there's just no way in the world Mamma could marry him." She couldn't bring herself to speak further of romance or whatever it was her darling girl had in her little head. "I believe it's time we stopped talking 'bout this and get something to eat. What do you say?"

But Annie didn't budge. She leaned against Rachel and began to whimper into the bodice of her apron.

"What is it, little one?" She kissed the top of her daughter's head, holding her close.

"I miss him, Mamma. Mister Philip . . ."

'Course, she couldn't openly agree. She couldn't tell her precious girl that for some reason or other, she, too, felt the selfsame way about Philip Bradley of New York City.

Five

❖ ❖ ❖

The weatherman hit the nail on the head 'bout the snowstorm, turned out. Susanna was mighty glad the quilting at Leah's wasn't till tomorrow morning, 'cause the sky was awful heavy with the grayest-looking clouds she'd ever seen. And the snow! Goodness' sakes, it was comin' down!

So for today, she and Rachel would keep the kitchen cozy and warm with plenty of pie-bakin' and cookie-makin'. Rachel had asked if she could take one of the pies to a friend of hers, though she hadn't said just who or where. Fact was, her daughter was too quiet most the morning, Susanna thought, but she decided not to press for reasons. No, she'd bide her time.

Annie entertained Dawdi Ben in the not-so-sunny sunroom, where the B&B guests always took their breakfast of a morning. Now that it was deep December, the Zooks were without a speck of overnight folk. Susanna was honestly enjoying the break from her hectic schedule of cleaning up after one guest or another, making sure every room in the house was ready at all times. And they *were* ready, but it was nigh unthinkable that anybody in their right mind—especially an out-of-towner—would attempt to make his way up Gibbons Road and on over to Olde Mill Road to their secluded property nestled along Mill Creek.

Annie came into the kitchen just then. "Dawdi Ben says he's awful thirsty," she announced.

"Well, let's get him a nice cold drink." Susanna moved to the sink and let the water run a bit.

"He's mighty hungry, too," Annie said, her blue eyes shining mischievously.

"Well, now, I wonder what he's hungry for?" Rachel chimed in. "Go ask him."

The child turned and scampered out of the kitchen.

"Aw, he's playin' with her," Susanna whispered to Rachel. "She'll come back wantin' a piece of pie, you watch."

A right curious look came over Rachel's face, and Susanna caught herself gazing in wonderment at her grown daughter. It was an honest-to-goodness glow! Susanna couldn't quite remember seeing Rachel look so radiant. Well, no she *did* recall, now that she thought 'bout it. Back when Rachel was sixteen and had first met up with Jacob Yoder. Jah, that's when it was. . . .

Annie soon returned to tell them just what Susanna had predicted. "Dawdi Ben wants to have the first taste of apple pie, if that's all right with Mammi Susanna, he says."

The two women burst out laughing.

"What's so funny?" asked Annie, eyes wide.

"Aw, honey, we're not makin' fun of you, not a'tall." Susanna waved her hand, still laughing so hard the tears were coming. "I think it's 'bout lunchtime here, perty soon."

Annie, bless her heart, looking ever so perplexed, turned and went to report to her grandfather.

Rachel stooped to pet Copper, and while she did, Susanna heard her whisper something 'bout it snowing so hard the puppy would hafta stay in the house all day. "Just like all the rest of us."

"'Tis awful cold out," Susanna ventured, hoping to draw her daughter into conversation.

"Jah, and from what Lavina says, we'll prob'ly hafta hitch up a sleigh to the horse so we can get to Leah's tomorrow."

Susanna peered out the window. "Well, if it keeps a-comin' down like it is, we'll have us a white Christmas this year."

"Would be nice, wouldn't it?"

Nodding, Susanna caught herself, realizing anew that her daughter could not see even the slightest movement. "It's *wunnerbaar*—wonderful—to see you wearing colors again," she said softly. "And green suits you right fine."

Rachel's face broke into a smile. "*Denki* . . . it's gut of you to say so."

It was then that Susanna wondered if the color of the dress had been the reason for Rachel's radiance. Or was it that she'd gotten so used to the drab grays and blacks that she'd forgotten how rosy-cheeked Rachel could be in blues and greens?

"I daresay you'll be the talk of the frolic tomorrow," she said. "The womenfolk ain't seen anything but mourning clothes on you for so long."

Rachel didn't say a word, just sat quietly at the table, still stroking Copper's back.

"This is an awful nice change for you." Pausing for a moment, she was eager to press on. "Does this mean you're movin' past your grief?"

Blinking self-consciously, Rachel replied, "I doubt anyone ever gets over the grief of losin' a beloved husband and child, Mam. I just don't see how."

So Rachel's choice of colors didn't mean what Susanna thought . . . hoped, really.

"I get ever so weary of folks starin' hard at me," Rachel blurted out. "I can *feel* their stares."

Susanna was somewhat surprised at this admission. But she needn't have been, now that she thought on it, for she herself had witnessed some of the womenfolk lookin' on Jacob Yoder's widow with eyes full of pity.

"Lavina's one of the few who doesn't," Rachel remarked. "She may not be very smart 'bout book learning, but in other ways she's wiser than us all."

Susanna was disturbed to hear that assessment of her husband's rattlebrained cousin. Just how wise Lavina was, well, that was perty obvious after all these years. "She oughta know better'n to push the bishop's hand on the probationary shunning, really. Attending the Beachy church, and all."

Rachel exhaled audibly. "Lavina wants to follow the Lord just like the rest of us. Maybe more so."

"Well, whatever does *that* mean?" Susanna was feeling a bit put out.

"She's searching for truth in the Scriptures . . . just like Esther and Levi and I. Lavina's as hungry for the gospel as Dat is for the first piece of your apple pie."

Susanna didn't quite know what to say to that. So she kept quiet, waiting—ear tuned—for the oven timer to *ding* and interrupt the flow of this nonsense talk.

———

Rachel was happy to have a chance to finish her taped letter later in the afternoon before supper preparations. She waited till Annie fell asleep for a nap, then reached for the tape recorder, beginning where she'd left off.

I'm back again, Esther. I had to stop a bit and do some baking with Mam, and before that Annie and I got into quite a long conversation, but now I'll take up where I left off.

I've been meaning to ask: Do either you or Levi know anything 'bout how Gabe Esh died? The reason I ask is Lavina said something right startling to me the other day—about Bishop Seth Fisher and Gabe's death. Don't know if I oughta say it on tape and all, but some folk 'round here evidently were suspicious of the reason for my great-uncle's death back then. If you happen to know something, will ya tell me? I'll leave it up to you if you wanna put your answer on tape or not . . . or you could tell me sometime when you're visitin' here, which just got me thinking how nice it would be if you and Levi and the children could come to Lancaster for Christmas. Will you think about it, at least?

Well, the Lord bless and keep you and your little ones. I miss you, Esther. Really, I do! I best sign off for now.

Your Pennsylvania cousin,
Rachel

———

Leah Stoltzfus found *great* pleasure in telling her youngest daughters, Molly and Sadie Mae, the news that their widowed cousin, Rachel Yoder, had "turned a corner" on her grieving.

"What's it mean, then?" Sadie Mae asked, brown eyes wide with wonder. "Surely, she won't start showin' up at the singings on Sunday nights. She's too old for such things!"

"Well, no, but it does mean you and your sister can start spreadin' the word on her behalf," Leah was quick to say, enjoying the flurry her news had caused.

"So now there's *another* woman lookin' for a husband?" Molly's mouth dropped open. "I'd say we'd best keep it quiet."

Sadie Mae pulled up a chair near the wood stove. She looked more than a mite worried, her forehead creased with concern. "Ain't even enough fellas for us girls of courtin' age. You know it's true, Mamma."

Her Sadie had a point, but that didn't stop Leah. "I heard tell of a Paradise widower eager to marry."

"How old is he?" asked Molly.

"A farmer?" asked Sadie Mae. "Most all the young women wanna marry a farmer."

"Who's got plenty of land," added Molly.

The girls burst into laughter.

"He's not so old. Not a farmer, neither." Leah sighed, wondering if she should continue. After all, the thirty-year-old blacksmith was a distant cousin to Gabriel Esh, her own uncle, though the blood lines were thinned way out, even enough for one of her own daughters to consider John for a possible husband. Thing was, John Lapp was known to have an occasional temper flare-up, wanted things done just so; Leah wouldn't have wished that type of fella on either of her darlings. Besides, he was too old for her girls, prob'ly.

But now, Rachel Yoder was another story altogether. Leah wondered if someone like the smithy Lapp might not be a gut idea for her widowed niece, the way Rachel seemed so awful unsettled and all. 'Course if it was *her*, there would've been no getting her into a courtin' buggy with the likes of one John Lapp.

"Just ain't that many widowers 'round here, Mamma," Molly spoke up again. "Rachel's twenty-six now, ain't so?"

"Close to twenty-seven . . . birthday's a-comin' in February."

"Maybe she's too old to get married again," Sadie Mae offered. "After all, look at Lavina. She never seemed to mind being an *alt Maedel*."

"Some mind more than others," she said, keeping an eye on her girls' faces.

"The older men get snatched up the minute a wife dies, you know," offered Sadie Mae. "But I'm thinkin' that maybe Rachel ain't much interested in marrying again. After all, she's blind."

Molly nodded her head. "But Rachel can perty much do what any of us can."

"And to think we used to say she was touched in the head," said Sadie.

"Seems to me a woman who's grieved so awful hard for her first husband might just not be able to let herself love another." This from Molly.

"Jah, but think of poor little Annie," said Sadie. "Can you imagine goin' through life without even *one* brother or sister?''

Molly snickered. "Bein' the only child of the family? Jah, I'd like to know what that'd be like.''

The girls exchanged snooty glances. Leah was outdone with the both of them. "Now, girls, quit your bickerin', for pity's sake.''

Sadie Mae rose and hurried out to the utility room off the kitchen. Molly, in turn, headed upstairs, her feet much too heavy on the steps.

"Well, now, the word's out about Rachel," Leah muttered, turning her attention to finishing a cross-stitching pattern on a pillowcase. "Won't be long till Paradise comes a-callin'.''

Six

❖ ❖ ❖

Such a perty snowscape Annie had not remembered seeing in all
her six years. Perched on Mamma's lap in the horse-drawn
sleigh, she took it upon herself to describe every detail. "There's
white everywhere. Looks just like sugar frosting!"

"Are the trees covered with white, too?" asked Mamma, both of
them wrapped in woolen blankets.

"The branches look like ice cream Popsicles, without no chocolate,
all coated with ice the whole way 'round each branch. Honest, they do."

"And the fields? Tell me about the wide-open spaces."

"I wish I had some black paper to draw on right now. I'd make the
snow with a white crayon—so someday when you see again, you can
remember this day."

Mammi Susanna snorted like the horse, but Annie kept on. "I'd
make my drawing look just like the neighbor's field and their yard, too."

"Rebekah Zook's yellow spider mums are but a memory," Susanna
said with an absentminded sigh.

"How do *you* see the snow today, Mammi?" Annie asked.

"Ach, snow's snow," her grandmother replied, waving her mittened
hand in the air. "But I *would* say it's the worst storm we've had in a
decade or more."

"A decade?" Annie asked. "How long's that?"

"Ten years," replied her mother.

"That's a gut long time," Annie said, thinking of Mister Philip just
then. The nice man from New York had said he'd have to "come back
and visit again."

Seemed to her *that* was a decade ago.

Rachel couldn't help but worry about the tone in Susanna's voice.

Sounded to her like Mam was still peeved 'bout something.

"Whatcha wantin' to draw the snow for? So your mamma can look at it *if* her sight comes back?" Mam said out of the blue.

She is still angry at me, Rachel thought. And she was perty sure why. Susanna had sneaked Blue Johnny, the area's conjurer/healer, into Rachel's bedroom, without her permission, back six weeks ago. Had him chant over her. Prob'ly used his black box, too—the one that was supposed to tell what was wrong and cure it. Both.

She knew it was true, 'cause she'd gone to her father to check, and Dat had told her so. It was just what she'd expected, anyways. Blue Johnny *had* given her a glimpse of sight that night. It hadn't been a dream at all. So now Mamma was going to keep stewin' about it. More so over the fact that Dat had spilled the beans than the short-lived miracle the powwow doctor had performed.

Rachel, having refused the healing, was glad about her bold decision. The dark and shrouded happening had caused her to consider her healing in the light of Scripture. And thanks to Esther, she was doing just that. Truth was, she was beginning to stand on the promises of God for her sight, which she believed might just occur any day now. Whenever the Lord saw fit to bless her with full vision once again.

"I'm gonna draw a picture of snowy cornfields for Mamma. When I get to Great-Aunt Leah's, I will," Annie said, bringing Rachel back to the matter at hand.

"That's right nice," she whispered to her little girl. "Now, just leave it be."

Susanna slapped the reins and called for the mare to move along faster. Rachel thought it foolish to make such a request of the animal in this weather. After all, the road must surely be snow-packed and ever so difficult for the horse to make passage. A gut thing they didn't have far to go.

The buzz at the quilting frolic was about Rachel's coming out of mourning. "She looks the picture of health," said one of her mother's cousins.

"Jah, and she's got her little one to think of, too," said another. "So . . . we know what that means, prob'ly."

Rachel was aghast—the women talking so openly about her state of singleness. Later she discovered that Mam was also upset—more vexed than surprised—though it only served to compound the problem of Susanna's sour perspective.

All the while, the women cut, sewed, and pieced, preparing to make a large quilt—the dahlia pattern—sitting twelve strong around the frame. Rachel entertained the children in the kitchen, doing her share of piecework, though it wasn't complicated.

"Mamma *ain't* gettin' married again," she heard Annie whisper to one of the other children.

"How do you know?" came the coy reply.

"I just know."

Rachel held her breath, wondering what to say or do to counter the childish exchange. But just as she was about to interfere, to distract the girls, Lavina came into the kitchen.

"All ready . . . for our trip tomorrow?" asked the older woman.

Rachel nodded toward the sound of Lavina's voice. "What do you think about going in all this snow?"

"Well's . . . if'n you'd rather not go . . ."

"Let's see what the weather's like tomorrow. I called the nursing home yesterday afternoon, and the receptionist said Adele's very excited to see you."

"And you, too . . . surely she is."

Rachel smiled, wishing she could see the look on the woman's face. "You're just as eager as I am, I'm thinkin'." She leaned forward, talking more softly. "I asked Esther if she knew anything about what you said the other day."

Lavina was silent.

"About the problems between Bishop Fisher and Gabe." She wasn't comfortable spelling things out, not with children playing at her feet.

"Best be careful . . . who you talk to," Lavina warned, and she was gone.

Her words rang in Rachel's memory for more than an hour, till mid-morning, really, when quilters broke for refreshments.

It was the continued chatter about various Plain widowers in the Lancaster area that made Rachel feel *naerfich*—nervous. No, it was worse than that. She was downright jittery. Truth was, she had no interest in marryin' again. 'Least of all to an older man, off in another township.

After lunch, while generous portions of white-as-snow cake and chocolate mocha pie were being served, Lavina observed the determined look on Susanna Zook's round face. Smack dab in the middle of the kitchen, Susanna started warbling the birthday song for Leah, encouraging everyone to join in.

Leah, quite befuddled, folded her arms over her ample bosom, trying to be polite. She didn't scowl really, the way she had on certain other occasions in the past. Her face flushed an embarrassed pink, and Leah simply avoided eye contact with her older sister. But it was all too clear the birthday girl was peeved, just not letting on too awful much, for the sake of company, prob'ly.

Keeping her peace, Lavina watched the amusing situation unfold. Slipping behind the long kitchen table, she located Rachel and stood silently behind the younger woman's bench, listening to the chatter but not entering in. She was a shunned woman amidst the Old Order. Soon her six-week probationary period would be up, and she'd have to decide whether or not to offer a kneelin' confession before old Bishop Fisher, the preachers, and the church members.

Just now, as she was thinkin' things over, she realized she wasn't much sorry for her actions—attending the Beachy church with Rachel and Annie. That was all her transgression had amounted to. She didn't see how she could turn her back on the prayerful atmosphere and God-inspired sermons each and every Sunday. Besides, she was learning new things about divine grace and love, and how to gain freedom in the Lord.

So if she *didn't* bend her knee in repentance, she'd have to put up with being shunned, though she guessed the People wouldn't treat her as harshly as Hickory Hollow's district had one young woman, Katie Lapp. The church members here would be kinder, seeing as how she was slow in her mind. Still, she'd have to bear the shame of being the only shunned person in her entire family.

Spending time with Rachel here lately had softened some of her pain. Rachel Yoder was about as dear to her as anyone in the community, aside from a few elderly relatives and many, many nieces and nephews. 'Twasn't such a surprise that Rachel was so sweet neither. Lavina should've known it, having worked closely with many a Yoder and Zook at pea-snappin', apple-cider makin', and corn-huskin' bees over the years. Jah, she'd watched Rachel grow from a wee girl in a sheer white pinafore apron and tiny head covering, to a blushing young bride, whose light brown eyes shone at the slightest glance from Jacob Yoder.

She had just never had the opportunity to get to know Rachel all that well, due to the wide age span between them.

Now that Gabe's story was more out in the open, so to speak, Lavina felt she could talk freely 'bout it with Rachel. And tomorrow she'd be visiting Adele Herr, too. Face-to-face after forty-some years.

The thought of seeing the woman Gabe had loved, after such a long time, gave her a peculiar feeling in the pit of her stomach. Still, she wanted to please Rachel by going. Sure, the visit might stir up sad feelings, but more than that, she knew it would be a chance to share the pain of another hurting woman.

She leaned down and asked Rachel, "Want another piece of pie?"

Rachel nodded. "But why are ya hiding?"

"Thought this was as gut a place as any to be . . . out of the way, ya know."

"Because of *die Meinding*?" Rachel asked softly.

"Jah, the shun."

"Wish there was no such thing," Rachel spoke up. She was quiet for a moment. Looked to be studyin' on somethin'. Then, "Come to think of it, I'd like some ice cream on my pie this time, if you don't mind."

Lavina reached for the younger woman's dessert dish. "Don't mind a'tall." She scurried off to do the favor. Honestly, she wished she could help Benjamin and Susanna's widowed daughter even more. She'd do just about anything to help Rachel get back her sight. Till such a thing was even possible, she figured her best choice was to be as gut a friend to the young woman as possible. Agreeing to ride to Reading and visit Adele was a nice start.

Lavina knew why she'd hemmed and hawed at Rachel's initial suggestion to see Adele. Only one reason, really. She'd written few notes and letters to Adele Herr over the years. And, well, she felt embarrassed at her lack of correspondence skills, though she would've been glad to visit with the woman face-to-face on any number of occasions. Fact was, she'd suggested regular visits early on, soon after she and Adele had buried Gabe's body in the cemetery just blocks from the Herr family home. House-to-house visiting was the Amish way—what she was most used to—but Adele had said in a letter that she felt uncomfortable returning to Lancaster County, and for a gut many reasons.

Something else pricked her mind as Lavina waited for a turn at the chocolate mocha pie. Adele Herr was the woman Gabe—*her* Gabe—had loved, proposed to, and longed to marry. Not his first companion and buddy. Not the tall and lanky Plain girl in the grade above his. Still and all, Lavina knew he *had* loved her just the same. In his own, wonderful-gut way, he surely had.

As a young boy he'd displayed his quiet affection when they were in school together. Sixty years ago. And she'd saved the get-well cards he'd made for her, kept them in a treasured, yet crude, wooden box, also handcrafted by Gabe Esh. Sick with the flu one winter, and other times, too—when she was ill with chicken pox and the croup—she welcomed his little cards, sometimes rhyming, sometimes merely signed with his boyish scribble, under a backdrop of cornfields in summer, swollen creeks in springtime, or woodlands in autumn.

Gabe had been her one and only hope for love, and just 'bout the time she thought he might actually take her for a ride in his open court-ing buggy, the English girl from Reading had come along, filling in as a substitute teacher at the nearby one-room schoolhouse. It was Adele who'd caught Gabe's attention back then. Hadn't seemed fair either.

In the early days, she remembered trying her best to appear to be "normal" for Gabe's sake. Whatever that was she didn't know, 'cept what she observed in the folk who were of average or higher intelligence. She remembered practicing her speaking skills, gazing into the pond just south of her father's barn, on a day with not a stitch of a breeze in the willows that circled the shining water. There, in the water, she'd seen a slight face and gray-blue eyes staring back, framed by her white netting *Kapp* atop her wheat-blond hair.

She'd gone to study her reflection—since Mamma wasn't all too happy 'bout mirror-primping and such. While she sat by the pond, she had asked herself one question after another, pretending to be her class-mates, tryin' her best to think up the answers. When the experience was past, she believed her practicing had paid off. 'Least *that* summer it had, 'cause Gabe asked if she wanted to go fishing, and would she help him gather worms for some bait?

She remembered having to push answers out of her mouth quick as she could that sunshiny day. "Jah, I'll go with ya," she'd said, scared he'd up and change his mind. "Betcha I can dig worms faster 'n you!"

He'd taken her comment as a challenge, like most any eleven-year-old boy. So they'd spent one whole afternoon digging for fish bait, her hands wrist-deep in mud, grabbing hold of one slimy earthworm after another. 'Course, every bit of the mess and mud was worthwhile, sharin' the day with the handsomest Amish boy on the face of God's earth!

A slice of chocolate pie and vanilla ice cream in hand, she scurried back to Rachel. Placing the dessert in front of her, Lavina thought how blessed she was to be getting better acquainted with a woman who resembled Gabe, not only in looks, but in temperament and deed. Why, it was downright uncanny, come to think of it. And here, with talk of Blue Johnny eager to pass his powwow doctoring gift—and the evil "black box"—to someone younger, well, it made her honestly wonder 'bout family ties, generational sins, and all. The very things Rachel's cousin Esther had been sharing with Rachel by tape. Some of the things Rachel Yoder now believed.

She touched Rachel's shoulder gently. "Want some coffee . . . to go along with that second helpin'?"

Rachel smiled her thanks. "Pie's fine for now."

Lavina, still bending over, whispered, "Leah's birthday song set me thinkin'. . . ."

"Oh?"

"Tell you tomorrow . . . on the trip to see Adele."

"I won't forget," Rachel said, finding her fork. "What 'bout the snow? Is it still comin' down hard?"

Lavina turned to look out the window. Sure enough, the snow had begun to slow a bit. "Seems like the Lord above might be smilin' down on us, come tomorrow."

"He blesses us *every* day. Snow or no snow," Rachel replied with a nod.

Just then Annie came in carrying a picture she'd made of a snow-covered field with gray clouds overhead. Three birds in one corner of the sky. "Look-ee here," the little girl said. "I drew a wintertime picture. It's for when Mamma can see."

The drawing reminded Lavina again of Gabe's third-grade artwork. Along with his homemade cards, she'd saved his drawings, too, storing them away in the hand-hewn box to be cherished all her life.

Rachel spoke up, "Jah, hang on to your drawing, Annie, dear. 'Cause I *will* see it someday. I truly believe I will."

Lavina couldn't help but smile as Annie hugged her mamma's neck. She felt the familiar twinge of sadness for all the little ones never born to her. "Come along, now, Annie," she said. "Did ya get yourself a slice of your aunt Leah's choc'late pie?"

Grinning, Annie showed a missing front tooth. "Jah, I had more than one. *Appeditlich*—delicious!"

Like mother, like daughter, Lavina thought, now more eager than ever to share Gabe's drawings with someone. Someone like the deceased man's great-grandniece—Annie Yoder.

And possibly Adele Herr. . . .

———

The day had been long and arduous, filled with rewrites, interviews, and follow-ups, yet Philip sat in his apartment, gathering together the many snippets of information he'd found while in Pennsylvania. Each was directly related to Gabriel Esh's fascinating story, one of rejection and betrayal among his own people. It was the story he had uncovered while innocently jiggling a stubborn drawer in the recesses of an antique desk in his room at the Amish guesthouse.

He smiled to himself at the myriad of notes he'd jotted down—even on a paper napkin from the Bird-in-Hand Family Restaurant. Having gone to the Lancaster County area to do research on behalf of the magazine, he'd returned home with numerous ideas and observations on the Amish culture. That uncomplicated community of the People, where respect for each other's opinions and privacy was a daily occurrence, where a person was expected to be conscientious, civil, generous, and responsible. Where the wholesomeness of rural life abounded. Where time seemed to stand still.

Upon locating the business card from Emma's Antique Shop, he studied the address and phone number, noting there was no fax number or email address. Emma, a young Mennonite woman, had given him the card after he'd browsed there, looking for an antique rolltop desk similar to the one at the Amish B&B. Emma had informed him that the desk was one of a kind, yet he'd hoped to find something comparable. He had searched various New York antique shops and prestigious stores in and around Columbus Avenue, near Lincoln Center, on weekends, then later in Vermont, where he and his sister and niece had gone to enjoy the autumn foliage. But he had found nothing to compare with the magnificent piece in his former guest bedroom at Benjamin and Susanna Zook's B&B.

He felt the urge to pick up the phone and call the Bird-in-Hand antique shop to inquire as to other desks Emma may have procured recently.

Too late in the season, he decided, changing his mind. He recalled that stores in the Lancaster area, especially those catering to tourists, were often closed during the winter months.

Philip leaned back in his chair, his hands clasped behind his head. Sighing, he looked around the apartment-sized writing studio. Tall custom-made cabinets of white oak graced one full side of the room. Shelves lined with handcrafted contemporary pottery and wrought-iron art, purchased from juried artisans, reminded him of his travels. Behind him, a silkscreen silhouette of oval leaves, pale yellow and green, juxtaposed the unadorned wall. To his right, a bank of windows allowed daylight to flood the room, and at night reflections from a thousand windows flickered across to him. Usually, he preferred to keep the designer blinds open at all hours. Tonight, however, he rose after a time and pulled the cord, blocking out the enormity of the population, noise, and vibrations of the city that surrounded him, threatening to strangle him.

Sitting down at his desk once again, he thought of Lancaster County, where farmers talked to their cows and went to bed with the chickens. A world set apart. And not so surprisingly, a place he missed more than he cared to admit.

He stared at the telephone, wondering if it was too late to make a phone call to Reading, Pennsylvania. He wanted to talk again with his new friend, Adele Herr.

Seven

❖ ❖ ❖

For as long as she remembered, Rachel had awakened early, at the pre-rooster-crowin' hour. Bone-chilling cold no longer greeted her first thing on a winter morning, however. Not in the toasty-warm bedroom she and Annie now shared at the Orchard Guest House B&B.

Growing up in Dat's drafty old farmhouse was another story. There the wood floors were as cold as a frozen pond, and she'd discovered it firsthand. As a child she'd stuck out a brave big toe on more than one occasion. Quickly, she would retrieve her bare foot and slide it back under the warm quilts, all the while shivering at the thought of facing the morning. Pleading for one or more of her older sisters to bring her a pair of long johns—and warm socks—she waited for her requests to be granted, putting up with occasional teasing. So she dressed *before* actually emerging from bed, similar to the way she lived most of her youthful days, shy and retiring.

This December morning a bitter wind had blown about flakes of light snow, reminding her anew of those childhood days. She'd gotten up early as usual and bundled up for the trip to Reading, accepting the arm of their usual Mennonite driver—Calvin Witwer—who'd come for her at the door.

"It's not snowing as much now," he said as they made their way to the waiting van.

"Are the roads cleared off, then?"

"Plowed and sanded. Shouldn't have any trouble getting to where you wanna go." Calvin helped her inside the warm vehicle, and they were off to pick up Lavina.

Rachel's thoughts ambled back to the first time she'd ever gone anyplace with her father by herself. It, too, had been a wintry day. Mid-January. She had been 'bout eight, prob'ly, and had need of some needles and thread for a practice quilt she was making with her sisters, Lizzy and Mary.

"*Kumm mit!*" Dat had called to her, offering to stop at Beiler's Country Market on the way to Bird-in-Hand.

"All's I need is some sewin' needles and thread," she'd replied, skipping down the back porch steps to the waiting carriage.

Mamma had come to the back door, calling that it was all right to go. "Have a gut time with your pop."

Rachel, silent as always, had realized just then that none of her sisters or brothers—or Mam—were comin' this morning. Just her and Dat.

"Well, now, hop in, Rachel. I'll take-a-you along." And Dat helped her up into the enclosed gray buggy, covering her real gut with several warm lap robes.

She remembered feeling a bit more grown-up than she'd ever felt before in her young life. To think that Dat was taking her for a buggy ride to the store, and all by herself. Well, now, must he be thinkin' his little girl was ready for such an adventure on a snowy day?

The horse had trotted slower than usual, but that didn't seem to bother Dat. He was gentle and kind to the animal, letting the mare set her own pace. And, funniest thing, Dat talked a blue streak, never stoppin' once to ask her a thing, though, 'cause she was just too shy to answer him. But that day, *that* day, she had begun to change her mind 'bout having a conversation with adults. Talkin' with a grown-up didn't seem all that frightening anymore.

Maybe it was the way the snow fell quietly, like a curtain 'round them, as they made their way down the long road. Or maybe it was Dat's voice lulling her, oh so steadily, keepin' her mind off herself for once—she didn't know, really—but something stuck in her childish mind 'bout that wintry ride to market.

When they arrived at the little country store, already there were two buggies parked out front. The folk who shopped here, her mamma had always said, liked cookin' from scratch, as if there was any other way. And the shop owner, Joe Beiler, seemed to know it, too. So after locating the exact sewin' needles she wanted and three colors of fine thread, she wandered over to the dry goods section while Dat chewed the fat with Joe.

What she discovered made her eyes pop out nearly. Why, there was an amazing amount of beans—seven kinds in all—and ten different noo-dles, along with six varieties of flour. All sorts of dried fruits, too, including raisins and dates. Nuts and oodles of other dry goods were on display along the long wooden counters. Things like white, brown, and confectioners' sugar; baking powder, salt, pepper. Countless types of seasonings, grains, and cereals, too.

'Course, there were baked goods, in direct competition with Grandma Smucker's Bakery. But that didn't stop Joe Beiler from offer-ing the ooey-gooiest cinnamon rolls this side of Ronks Road. And she found out just how tasty they were, thanks to Joe's wonderful-nice wife coming over and chattin' with Rachel.

"Well, now, look-ee here at you," the blue-eyed woman said. "You must be Ben Zook's littlest girl."

She hadn't known whether to nod her head or just blink her eyes at the pudgy Mrs. Beiler.

"Cat ain't got your tongue, has it?" she asked.

Rachel shook her head.

"I've got just the thing to make ya smile, girlie." The owner's wife motioned for Rachel to follow her. "As long as you live, you'll never taste any sticky buns better'n Nancy Beiler's."

So . . . Rachel found out her name, and she never forgot it, 'cause that day Nancy Beiler insisted that Rachel was the "pertiest little girl" she ever did see.

"And whenever you want yourself a free samplin' of my sweets, well, you just call me Auntie Nancy, and I'll come a-runnin'."

Rachel figured, without ever speakin' a word, she'd just stumbled onto the nicest person in the whole world. And she never, ever forgot the way those sticky buns melted in her little mouth. She just never did. From that day on, Auntie Nancy kept her word 'bout the free samples, too. She even came through on the day before Rachel's weddin' to Jacob Yoder, too, along with every other time she stopped in to say "hullo."

Every so often, Rachel thought 'bout Auntie Nancy, wonderin' what had become of her—'cause for the past year or so, nobody ever talked of Joe's wife. Rachel 'sposed it was none of her business, but still, she wondered.

"Do you ever hear tell of a Nancy Beiler over off Stumptown Road?" Rachel asked, finding her voice long enough to ask the driver.

"Last I heard, Joe quit stocking the bakery part of the store."

"Oh? Why's that?"

"His wife left the Old Order."

That surprised her. She hadn't heard of any shunning over in that area. "When was this?"

"Couple of years ago, if my memory serves me well. Mrs. Beiler went and joined the New Order Amish folk over near Gap."

"I wish I knew where she lived," Rachel said softly. "I miss seein' her."

"Well, I believe I could find out for you, if you want me to."

She was glad to hear it and told him so, and she couldn't help but smile 'bout that wonderful-gut *first* time at the country market. Just Dat and his little Rachel, on a cold and snowy January day.

When the two women were settled into the backseat, they got their offhand prattle all talked out—Lavina, in her slow, measured way; Rachel, prompting her when her mind took to wanderin'.

"You were going to tell me something today," Rachel reminded her after a time, keeping her voice low.

Lavina was quiet for a bit before she spoke up. "I've been thinkin' . . . 'bout Bishop Fisher. That's what I wanted to tell you."

"What about the bishop?"

"His eternal soul" came the unexpected reply. "But I don't know just what to do 'bout what I'm a-thinkin'."

"Well," Rachel said, "what would *that* be?"

"I've been prayin' for the old bishop."

Rachel wasn't afraid to admit that she was, too. "In fact, I've been wonderin' when a gut time might be to talk to him, just so he doesn't try 'n talk me into accepting Blue Johnny's powwow gift—the transference, you know."

Lavina was still.

Rachel whispered, "You don't think he'd do that—try 'n force me, do you?"

After another long pause, Lavina replied, "I don't 'spect anyone can force a body to receive a gift—holy or unholy."

Rachel thought on that. "I'd hate to see the powwowing thing get stirred up 'round here. After what happened between Blue Johnny and me, well, I'd say a visit to the Old Order bishop would have to be intended by God, pure and simple."

"Don't blame you none for thinkin' thataway." Lavina's voice sounded strained.

Rachel wondered if the woman was nervous 'bout a visit to the ninety-three-year-old church leader. "You okay?"

"Don't 'spose I'll be if'n I *don't* follow the Lord's biddin' and speak to ol' Seth Fisher . . . afore his next birthday. 'Tis comin' up here real soon."

So *that's* what was bothering Lavina. She was worried the old man might die without hearin' the truth 'bout God's Son and soul salvation, full and free.

"Let's not wait, then, if you feel the Lord nudgin' you," Rachel suggested.

"Don't see how I could do it alone. I'm a shunned woman, ya know. Doubt Seth Fisher would give me the time o' day."

"I'll go with you." The words had flown out before she'd even had a chance to think what she was gettin' herself into.

"Denki, Rachel. Had a feelin' you'd see eye to eye."

Unsure her parents would agree with any of what she and Lavina were cooking up, Rachel leaned against the seat, praying silently. *Dear Lord, help me not get in over my head with all of this. Please, will you lead and guide Lavina and me? Amen.*

"I declare, if that shunned woman ain't up to somethin', well, then I ain't Susanna Esh Zook!" She rushed down the stairs, one frustrating thought after another tumbling in her mind.

"Not for you to be worryin' over," Benjamin called down from the second-floor landing, holding a wrench in his hand.

Susanna knew if she kept it up, sooner or later little Annie might put two and two together and figure her grandparents were fussin' over Rachel and Lavina. "We best talk this over in private," Susanna replied, standing at the bottom of the long stairway. She would give her husband the final say.

"You're right, Susie. We oughtn't cause a scene in front of you-know-who," Ben said, then he went to finish repairing the shower head in one of the guest bathrooms.

Susanna just couldn't get it out of her head that Lavina was influencing Rachel to keep in touch with that fancy woman up there in Reading, slippin' away to death in a nursing home, of all places. Amish folk wouldn't think of abandonin' their ailing and elderly. Plain and simple. They made a home for them right under their own rooftops.

'Course, then again, Adele Herr had no real firsthand knowledge of the Old Ways, and 'twas understandable, seein' as how she'd turned down Gabe's proposal of marriage. Just as well, though. The People would have shunned her right along with the young preacher-man. And would've shunned Gabe all the harder for marryin' outside the church. As it turned out, the troublemaker had got himself killed on his way to speak at a church somewheres in Gordonville. No doubt it was God's way of quieting the voice of a disobedient soul, though she *had* heard various accounts of the "why" behind the accident.

Still, 'twasn't something Susanna cared to discuss, not even with her wise and discerning husband. Both she and Benjamin preferred never to air the superstitious nature surrounding Gabe Esh's untimely death. Jah, best those things be kept buried, and she figured they would be, too, considering old Bishop Fisher was comin' up on ninety-four years. Once he passed, only one other person besides Benjamin and Susanna herself even knew of the strange circumstances surrounding Gabe's death. A good thing, too. 'Twasn't something a snoopy New York reporter could get ahold of and sink his teeth into. As far as she knew, her sister Leah was the only other person with even the slightest knowledge. The secret was safe with the four of them. For sure and for certain.

Sighing, Susanna's thoughts flitted from one problem to another. For all she knew, Rachel and Lavina were prob'ly jabberin' right now during their ride north 'bout all the things Philip Bradley had set in motion when he discovered that no-gut postcard. Things that oughta be kept hush-hush and forgotten. Just the fact that the problem was bein' talked 'bout by Rachel, Lavina, and who knows how many others bothered Susanna no end. She just knew the old bishop was prob'ly havin' himself a fury over some of the rumors going round—gettin' a-stirred up over 'um.

Oh, she could still kick herself for not snatchin' up the postcard right out of the young man's hands! What on earth had kept her from it? Seeing the message, written in Pennsylvania Dutch, of all things, to that wicked Baptist girl who'd torn the community upside down, inside out. Falling in love with the very hope of the Amish church, no less. Well, if it hadn't been for Gabe Esh gettin' his worldly eyes on Adele Herr, who knows just how the powwow doctoring in the area might be flourishing these days? 'Twasn't that they didn't already have several folk healers. It was just that the community had grown, what with couples having upward of eight children or more, in some cases. Jah, they truly needed another *Brauchdokder*—powwow doctor—and with the many giftings her daughter possessed, surely someone other than herself oughta be able to persuade Rachel to accept the revered position. Surely.

———————

At Fairview Nursing Home, Lavina sat next to Rachel in the small, yet sunshiny, room marked Rm. 147—the very room Adele Herr had called home for the past two years and some odd months. A single hospital bed flanked one wall. The patient was dressed for the visit, wearing a pale pink bed jacket around her slender shoulders. The color brought out the slightest hint of pink in her cheeks, though Lavina was sure the rosy hue had been dabbed on, prob'ly, the way most fancy folk—women—did. Adele's eyes were just as blue as ever, and her smile was the same as it used to be.

At the far end of the room, plants hung gracefully near a window with wide blinds for its covering, no curtain. A dresser with a gilded antique oval mirror sat just beyond the bed, so that the mirror faced out. And Lavina thought it was a gut idea, too—not havin' to look at yourself if you were so awful thin and ill. Mirrors were far too revealing, 'specially at her and Adele's age. Best just to leave them be, a cold reminder of the youth everyone must lose, sooner or later.

Jah, it was a right gut thing Rachel had brought her here today. Otherwise, she'd have never recognized the meager little woman perched amidst her bed pillows. She figured, though, the reason Adele Herr looked to be so different wasn't necessarily age. No, she just wasn't the selfsame girl who'd come to rent a room at Lavina's farmhouse forty years ago. It was mighty clear to see that the disappointments of life had brought the biggest changes on Adele's face.

Lavina had squeezed the dear woman's hand the minute she set foot in the room, not waiting for Rachel to take the lead. "You have Rachel here to thank for this visit," she insisted. "It was *her* idea to come and pass 'round some Christmas cheer."

Rachel spoke up, blinking as she seemed to look around, though not seeing. "But *Lavina* was eager to bring her tart and tasty apple butter along . . . for you and your friends here." Both Rachel and Lavina had brought baskets filled with mouth-watering homemade sweets.

Adele smiled, seemingly amused. "Well, what does it matter *which* of you decided? The fact that you're both here is a blessing to me. A joyous pre-Christmas blessing. You'll never know how pleased I am to see you again, Lavina. And you, too, Rachel."

"Didja want us to call you Lily or Adele?" asked Rachel out of the blue.

The older woman sighed, smiling. "I understand why you might wonder about that, Rachel, but to tell you the truth, I prefer Adele. The name Lily was a crutch. I don't have to hide behind my middle name anymore. The Lord has freed me from those insecurities. Even the nursing staff has agreed to change my name, so to speak!"

Lavina truly hoped she wasn't staring just now, but she couldn't seem to keep her eyes off the woman in the hospital bed. Was this really Adele Herr—Gabriel Esh's old sweetheart? She studied the features even more closely. Could this be the selfsame young girl who'd come to Bird-in-Hand those many years ago, filling in at the schoolhouse? She'd changed more than Lavina thought such a beauty ever could. 'Course, they were each growing older, and who was *she* to be thinkin' any such haughty thoughts, with plenty-a wrinkles spreading across her own face? Enough to share with Adele *and* Rachel—both!

Combed into a short bob, Adele's former chestnut brown hair was now snowy white, nearly silver-hued. 'Least, certain ways she turned, it looked thataway.

Lavina could hardly sit still, anxious to join in the conversation. But she listened as Adele brought up Philip Bradley, the reporter from New York she'd heard 'bout from both Adele's letters and from Susanna Zook while making apple cider a few weeks back.

"I've been giving some thought to possibly inviting my new friend Philip for a visit," Adele announced, her eyes shining.

"Nice thing to do," Lavina spoke up.

Rachel said nothing.

"He could come for our Christmas party," Adele continued. "Maybe he would like to write an article on all us old folks."

Lavina noticed the sudden flush on Rachel's face and wondered what *that* was all about.

Adele glanced up at a bulletin board, not far from the side of the bed, and pointed to a slightly yellowed card. "There's the postcard Philip found, and it's changed everything . . . absolutely *everything*." She went on to say, "Philip is such a forthright person. And, you know, he's following the Lord again."

"You mean he wasn't before?" Lavina asked, feeling awkward

because Rachel had hardly said a word.

"He wrote that he'd strayed from his first love, his commitment to Christ . . . as a boy." Adele turned and seemed to observe Rachel, and at one point Lavina's eyes met Adele's. The two women shrugged, but Adele went on. "Philip's attending a men's Bible study twice a week, I believe he said. He's full of questions in his letters, and more recently he's started calling long-distance."

Rachel spoke at last. "What sort of questions?"

"Life questions, he says," Adele answered, catching Lavina's eye once again. "He's preparing himself for ministry."

Lavina wasn't exactly sure what that meant. "Gonna be a preacher, then?" she asked.

"Not a preacher, I don't think. But he feels called to something— just *what*, he's determined to find out. And from our exchange of letters, I believe it's safe to say he's open to God's leading."

Lavina found this information to be mighty interesting, but more than that, she wondered what on earth had come over Rachel. Why had she closed herself up like this? Was it something one of them had said out of turn?

She observed the beautiful blind woman, thinking back to when Rachel had first blushed crimson. Then she remembered, and the startling realization caught her truly by surprise.

Hearing Adele speak of Philip in such glowing terms had Rachel nearly beside herself. She felt her face growing warm as Adele commented on the New Yorker's attributes. Jah, she'd also experienced Philip's straightforwardness, among other things. And she was ever so glad to know he'd returned to his faith in the Lord. In fact, she was a bit surprised to hear that he might've neglected his childhood covenant to God. But it was Adele's mention of her possible Christmas invitation that had flustered her so. She knew it was the thought of Philip coming to visit his ailing friend—here in Reading. Why, it was only a hop, skip, and jump down to Lancaster. 'Course, that would be silly to think he'd come see her, too. He had no way of knowing how very often she thought of him, how she remembered his well-chosen words, the way he seemed so taken with Annie . . . and with her, too.

Lavina's words jarred her back to the visit at hand, and she straightened in her chair, taking a deep breath. Oh, she hoped the red had gone from her cheeks, lest either woman discover her most guarded secret.

"I hafta take all the blame for what was written on Gabe's head-stone," Lavina was saying. "Poor fella couldn't speak for himself . . . but he must've knowed how much ya loved 'im, Adele."

Rachel thought it right honest of Lavina, admitting her truest feelings to the woman whose heart was awful close to giving out. She, on the other hand, couldn't begin to think of revealing *her* feelings. No, it wouldn't be prudent for her to voice any interest in Philip. The correspondence was ongoing between Adele and him, and she could fully understand why the man had reached out to the kind and gentle woman. Ever so nurturing, Adele Herr was like a wise older relative to Philip. And Adele, in turn, had obviously found a dear friend, as well.

She was truly happy for their friendship—anything to bring a little joy to a woman who'd lost so much early on in life.

Still, Rachel wished she felt more at ease just hearing his name unexpectedly, let alone being told that he'd called Adele Herr and discussed "life questions." Such comments made her truly long to know him better—even to *see* his face. But, of course, regainin' her sight was a matter for the good Lord—and Him alone.

Eight

❖ ❖ ❖

Friday, December 17

Dear Philip,

How are you? Keeping your head above water with your many assignments, I trust? You have my prayers, as always.

It occurred to me that you might be pleased with an invitation for a visit here. I know you have family in New York, but it never hurts to ask. At any rate, we're having a small informal get-together of sorts here on the night of Christmas. Several musicians are scheduled for the event, among them a string quartet of which I am quite fond. Another is an ensemble of singers. Sounds like fun.

Please don't feel pressured to make the trip. I don't know your plans, of course, and at this late date, I would probably be fooling myself to think that there might be the slightest hope of seeing you during the celebration of our Lord's birth. If, however, you are so inclined, you are certainly welcome!

On another note, I had the nicest visit from Rachel Yoder and Lavina Troyer yesterday morning. They came bearing gifts, just as the Wise Men of old. I don't know when I've enjoyed seeing someone as much as I did Lavina. The woman is every bit as sweet and compassionate as she was back when she "took me in" years ago. She was quite friendly and talkative, in her own way, and I do believe she may have begun to forgive me for being Gabe's first romantic choice. The way she smiled so at me—speaking of such things as her reason for adding my name to Gabe's gravestone—did warm my old heart.

Rachel Yoder, the dear, dear girl, brought a basketful of various home-baked items—sour cream chocolate cookies, sugar cookies, molasses drop cookies, date bars. Is your mouth watering? I do plan to pass the basket around at the Christmas party—yet another enticement for you to join me.

I had no idea that Rachel's blindness was due to trauma, and she mentioned the fact quite openly, I might add. Poor child, my heart goes out to her. But the good news is that she and her cousin in Ohio are "standing on the promises of God" for her healing. So Gabe's grandniece is believing for her sight to return. Isn't this the most wonderful news?

Please, no matter where you spend it, you must have a very special Christmas. Know that I appreciate your friendship so much, dear friend. May the Lord bless and keep you always.

> In Christ . . . I remain,
> Adele Herr

Philip didn't bother to read the letter a second time. Reaching for the phone, he sat at the desk in his home office and dialed the number for Fairview Nursing Home.

When one of the nurses put him through, he was met with a cheerful, strong voice. "Merry Christmas, Philip!"

"How'd you know it was me?"

She laughed softly into the phone. "No one else calls."

"Well, it's good to hear you're in such fine spirits. Must be the advent of Christmas."

"That . . . among other things."

"Such as?" He was eager for a good health report.

"To begin with, my doctor is cutting back very slowly on all of my medication. My old ticker is working better than it has in years."

"That's terrific news!"

"Yes, and I'm able to be up and out of bed, walking the halls. I even helped one of the patients address a few Christmas cards yesterday."

He was excited to tell her his plan. "Say, I received your letter . . . just now read it, and I'm taking you up on your invitation. I'm coming to your Christmas party."

"How wonderful, Philip!"

He heard the joyful ring to her voice. "You really *are* feeling better, aren't you?"

"For which I thank the Lord," she replied. "God has touched my life by bringing you into it . . . and Rachel, as well."

Philip thought about her remark and wondered what she'd make of it if he casually mentioned the research he had been conducting on behalf of, but unknown to, Rachel. Forging ahead, he said, "I've gathered some information, and it's interesting that you mentioned it in your letter . . . about Rachel's hysteria. . . ." He paused, inhaling a bit. "Did she bring it up herself when she was there?"

"Well, let's see . . . Yes, Rachel actually spoke freely of the emotional effects she's suffered since the accident. I think she soon may be ready to face her past head on, though I have no idea what that may involve."

"I have an idea," Philip said, not telling her that he'd talked with several therapists on Manhattan's East Side, upon his brother-in-law's recommendation. Philip felt he had a handle on the sort of questions a doctor might ask to permit the pain and the memories to resurface, the deeply submerged anguish of Rachel's loss. If he could just spend some time with her, he might be able to befriend her.

"I'm glad I wrote you about the Christmas program. Meanwhile, be careful not to work such long hours," she said, beginning to sound a bit tired. "It's not a good thing to burn the candle at both ends."

"It's what I'm used to. Besides, I'm working my way down a long list of assignments. I'll see you soon. Keep smiling."

"You're a wonder," she said.

"Good-bye, Adele."

"God is ever faithful," she said before they hung up.

He recognized it as one of the last lines of Gabe's postcard message to her.

Before heading out to the kitchen to heat up leftovers, Philip opened his file drawer and located a list of characteristics he'd observed in Rachel Yoder. He'd made the list while waiting at the Lancaster Community Hospital last September for word of Rachel's little daughter's wasp-sting incident.

Soft-spoken, mild-mannered, devoted to Annie were among the first qualities he'd written. Scanning the words, he recalled the beautiful young blind woman. If ever there was something he wanted to give at Christmastime, it was sight to Rachel Yoder!

Monday night meetings were a bit unusual, but Rachel wanted to go
to the preachin' service that had been called at the Beachy Amish meetinghouse. 'Specially since a visiting minister was passing through. "Lavina's picking me up," she told Mam, adding, "Wouldja be so kind to
tuck Annie in for me?"

"Well . . . how late do you 'spect to be?"

"I really don't know, but I wouldn't think too awful late."

Dat spoke up from the kitchen table, where he was having seconds
on cake, prob'ly. "'Course if he's one of them hellfire preachin' fellas,"
Dat said, "it'll be close to ten, which is mighty late for young women to
be out and about."

Ever so protective, Dat was. Yet she loved him for it. "You mustn't
be worryin'," she was quick to say. "Lavina's always careful, really she
is."

"Does she know enough to avoid the Crossroad?" Mam probed.

"Jah."

"Well, then, I 'spect you're set," Mam said. "Just make sure Lavina
watches the speed of the horse. We got us some nasty roads out there
tonight."

Rachel nodded, wishing there was some way she could convince Dat
and Mam both not to fret over her so awful much. "God's lookin' out
for us," she offered, hoping that would suffice. She found her cane and
shuffled out of the kitchen.

Ever so eager for more of God's Word, Rachel sat with Lavina near
the front of the meetinghouse, on the side with the women. She felt that
her spirit might soar, might need to be brought back down to her body,
hearing the things the minister was teaching. Spiritual defense—how to
put on the armor of God, as found in Ephesians 6, and how to enter into
God's protection—something she wished she'd known and understood
long before the accident that took Jacob's and young Aaron's lives. Oh,
if only her heart had searched for God's provisions back then. So much
might've been different had she known to commit herself to the rock of
ages, the mighty fortress, and her shelter in time of trouble.

All the way back to Beechdale Road she chattered to Lavina. "I
believe the Lord's gonna let me see again," she declared.

"Well, God bless ya, Rachel."

"Oh, He has . . . He already has."

Lavina was quiet again, while Rachel babbled on. She reached her hand out of the buggy, hoping to catch a few flakes. That's when Lavina made the remark that a certain widower "was at service tonight."

"Who wouldja be talkin' about?"

"John Lapp from Paradise Township. Ya heard o' him?"

"No, and I don't much care," she replied, guarding her words.

"Well, just so ya know, he was lookin' you over real careful-like."

"How'd he know who I was?"

"S'pose the word's got out, Rachel."

"What on earth does *that* mean?"

"You put away your mournin' clothes, now didn'tcha?"

"Doesn't mean I'm lookin' to remarry, though. Just ready to move ahead with my life some."

"You're awful young to be deciding such a thing . . . 'bout not remarryin'. Maybe you should be praying 'bout that."

"What would this John Lapp want with a blind woman?" she asked, wondering aloud.

"Now, Rachel, you oughta know better'n to say such a thing. You'd make any man a fine wife."

Rachel felt terribly uneasy. What was all this talk going on behind her back? She didn't want to know, not really. Still it was unnerving, hearing that someone was looking her over in terms of marryin' potential. She wasn't a sixteen-year-old Maedel—maiden—anymore. The whole idea of being eyed that way . . . ach, it just didn't set well. "You don't 'spose he'll come callin', do you?"

Lavina was slower to respond than usual. "I . . . would hafta say that's what he already done . . . tonight in church, so to speak."

She didn't quite know what to say to that. "He came to church to look at a woman? Why, that sounds downright sacrilegious, if you ask me."

"Maybe so."

"Well, it *is*," Rachel insisted, marveling at her own courage to speak her mind. And feelin' the better for it.

'Twasn't all that late when Rachel came in the front door. Even still, Mam was waiting up. "Glad to see ya home in one piece."

She accepted Mam's hug and gave her a peck on the cheek. "Honestly, I don't know when I've learned so much," she managed to say, trying not to think about the audacity of widower Lapp.

"How was the meetin'?" Mam asked, the weight of the question hanging in the air.

"Can I tell you in the mornin'?" Rachel said, feeling her way to the stairs. "All's I know is, I'm ever so heart-hungry for the things of God."

"Speaking of which, I forgot to give you a tape mailer. It came today."

"From Esther, prob'ly."

"Well, no, I believe it's from some reverend out in Ohio somewheres."

Rachel was overjoyed to hear it! Esther's pastor had sent along yet another sermon. She thought about staying up till midnight to listen to it. Jah, she just might do that. It would certainly be worth the weariness come morning.

Nine

❖ ❖ ❖

Not only did Rachel listen to the taped sermon, she played it twice before retiring for the night. And the next afternoon, another tape arrived. This one from Esther herself.

Rachel squeezed time out of her busy day—cleaning, baking bread, and washing clothes—in order to hear snatches of it. Yet she was more than eager to do so, for it seemed that Esther *did* know something of the superstitious nature of Gabe's death.

I've just been made privy to some shocking information, her cousin's words came strong and clear. Rachel was relieved that Esther had seen fit to position the highly personal information in the middle of the taped message. This way, if ever Mam was to eavesdrop on it, she would not discover what the two women were passing back and forth.

She continued listening, then was moved to tears as the strange story began to unfold.

> *Yesterday Levi had the chance, finally, to call his grandfather, your Beachy bishop, Isaac Glick. I just had no idea that Isaac would know one thing 'bout the events surrounding Gabriel Esh's death. But let me tell you, Isaac shared some terrible frightening things with my husband. I best be careful how I say this, 'cause I sure don't want to garble the truth. From what Isaac knows, Seth Fisher did put a hex on Gabe Esh! Now, I don't exactly know what sort of spell it was. All I know is the very next day, Gabe and his friend were driving in a car somewheres, and Gabe's friend hit a white dove. The friend turned deathly pale . . . terrified, to say the least. He told Gabe that in the religious circles he was akin to, killing a white dove was an omen, a sign that the person or persons would die unexpectedly, and soon.*

Gabe didn't know what to make of it, 'cause he, too, had heard of the powerful superstition. In fact, Gabe knew firsthand of people who'd died after an experience like that.

Oh, Rachel, if only your great-uncle had known to turn his back on such things—if only he'd known what we know now, that those who belong to the Lord can take authority over fears and false beliefs. I don't honestly know if Gabe feared the superstition, and his dread resulted in his untimely death. Only God knows for sure. But fear is such an open door, 'cause when we fear we're believin' the devil, whereas faith is believin' in what God says. The book of Job, chapter three, verse twenty-five says, "For the thing which I greatly feared is come upon me, and that which I was afraid of is come unto me." It may be that Gabe didn't understand how fear can open up a believer to front-line attacks from the ol' enemy. And you know, all that Gabe was doin' for the Lord—speaking out so strongly against the powwow practices—well, of course the devil was out to silence him.

Seein' as how Gabe had followed the Lord so closely, though, it's hard to understand how a hex of any kind could've affected him, really. We know, from some of the teaching we've had, that there are ever so many curses folk unknowingly put on each other. Even by things like jealousy, gossip, and rejection.

Even so, Levi and I both believe Gabe is in heaven with his Lord because of the stand he made. Honestly, we do.

Rachel brushed tears from her face. Not only was she shocked, but saddened and confused by her cousin's news. And she found herself wondering yet again why such past wicked activity had been hushed up.

Something rose up in her, and she felt so strongly that the darkness had to be exposed so that the Way, the Truth, and the Life could flood hearts that had been hardened by tradition and deceived by the devil. This, more than anything, she desired for her people. The spreading of the Light was what she also desired for the old, now ailing bishop, a former powwow doctor in the community. Jah, Seth Fisher needed to hear that the Light has come. That God's glory had appeared to at least one humble soul amongst the People . . . a distant relative of Gabe, the young man the bishop had despised enough to curse.

Yet Rachel truly felt she must be able to see, have her sight restored by the power of God—and not by powwowing—before she could ever approach the Old Order bishop. Why, surely, once her blindness was a thing of the past, the highly revered church leader would hear what she had to say—even if she *was* a woman. And she feared, in the shape he was in, his time on this earth was fast runnin' out.

She fell to her knees beside her bed, impulsively claiming one healing promise after another found in the Bible. She knew many of the passages by heart, quoting them aloud in her prayer, as she held fast to God's Word. Deep within she felt a sense of urgency, though she did not think she was demanding anything out of the ordinary from the Lord. No, she was merely acting on the Scripture tapes her father had purchased for her months before.

"Dear Lord in heaven, I ask that you heal me," she prayed. "Body, mind, and spirit. I know your Word says, 'Is any sick among you? let him call for the elders of the church; and let them pray over him, anointing him with oil in the name of the Lord.' Well, I ain't an elder, and I haven't had much faith for my healin' in the past—haven't much cared to see, really. So I'm here to present my eyesight to you just now, askin' you to heal me, as you promised. I am willing to go to the elders of our church, to be anointed with oil, if that is your will. In Jesus' name, Amen."

She lifted her head and opened her eyes, fully expecting to see clearly. But the room was a shadowy gray, and she was ever so disappointed, wondering if her ongoing condition had now become a permanent blindness, yet not allowing herself to dread that possibility.

After telling Mam the highlights of the church meeting the next morning, Rachel rushed off to her room between chores to pray fervently for her sight. "Dear Lord Jesus, I'm reminding you this day of your many promises to heal. In your Word—in Luke, chapter four— you said that you were sent 'to heal the brokenhearted, to preach deliverance to the captives, and recoverin' of sight to the blind, to set at liberty them that are bruised.' Well, Lord, I'm all of those things, ain't so? I'm brokenhearted over losin' Jacob and Aaron, my dear husband and little boy. I've been a captive awful long, too, 'cause of fear and bitterness, and I'm blind because I purposely blocked out every memory connected with the accident." She paused, brushing tears away. "I'm bruised, too, Lord, way deep in my spirit, wounded 'cause of my family's past sins. I know this from the Ohio pastor's sermon tapes that

Esther has him send. He teaches that ancestral sin brings curses and consequences on a family, whether a person believes in you or not."

Just then, it dawned on her why Bishop Fisher's hex might've actually worked on a Christian like Gabe and his friend. She just didn't know for sure, but she had a perty gut idea that Gabe had had no inkling how to battle such things as the sins of his forefathers. One ancestor, whom Gabe had been named after, was known to be the originator of the powwow doctoring in the whole community.

The more Rachel thought on it, the more she wondered if that might've been the problem—the lack of spiritual warfare. From what she'd learned, generational sins had to be identified, confessed, and renounced in order for curses to be put to death on the cross of Jesus. She knew this only because of Esther's pastor, out in Ohio, yet she was ever so thankful to God for bringin' such teaching into her life. If she could just pass it on to her parents, her eleven siblings and their wives and children, and 'specially to Bishop Fisher. She'd hafta keep praying 'bout that, 'cause she needed more courage to speak out to the People. The way Gabe Esh had spoken out so long ago.

"Mamma's spendin' lots of time upstairs," Annie informed Susanna.

"Well, now, you know your mam's busy with her personal correspondence, and all."

"Is it Cousin Esther in Ohio . . . that she's making tapes to?" Annie's round face was filled with questions. "Maybe we're movin' out there to live with Levi and Esther and their children."

"What the world, child? Where'd you get a notion like that?"

"Mamma and I talked 'bout it once." The little girl's words came out a bit lispy, due to a missing front tooth.

"I'd say that's just horse feathers."

"What do you mean, Mammi Susanna?"

She knew she'd better come up with something perty gut, or the bright child would catch on. "Well, it's like this. Your mamma feels right stuck here in Bird-in-Hand, prob'ly, what with her best cousin livin' in wide-open spaces out there in Holmesville. We always want what we can't have. That's just human nature, I'd say."

Annie looked at her with those big, innocent, blue eyes of hers. "I wanna live on a farm, too, just like Mamma does."

"Well, now, if that don't beat all." She couldn't say much more. Truth was, there wasn't nothin' better in the whole wide world, far as she was concerned. Nothin' better'n working the soil of God's good earth.

"I think someday we're gonna end up farmers," Annie said out of the blue.

"You really do?"

"Jah, 'cause I have a powerful-strong feeling."

Susanna perked up her ears at that. Could it be her granddaughter had some of the family giftings passed down through the generations? Could it be that Annie was next in line—after Rachel, of course. If this was true, she'd just received some mighty gut news indeedy. And so close to Christmas. Wait'll Benjamin heard 'bout this!

———————

Rachel began the next day with earnest prayer, not the silent rote prayers she'd been taught. She prayed with her eyes wide open, yet not seeing, waiting for the Lord to bless her with healing. Desiring her sight more than ever, she pleaded that God might grant her "a clear vision in time for Christmas. And what a *seelich*—blessed gift that would be," she prayed, once again repeating the promises of God, so determined to receive.

"I'm willin' to cross the horrible visions—to remember the accident that took Jacob's and Aaron's lives—to get to my sight. Whatever it takes, Lord. I want to see again!"

When her healing didn't come just then, Rachel rose, washed, and dressed for the day. She didn't want to admit it, but she was getting a bit impatient. After all, God didn't seem to be answerin' awful fast, especially now that she was wanting her sight, more than eager to see her little Annie-girl.

Wanting something so much; why, it was gettin' to be right unbearable. After all, when she'd willed herself to block out the images of the accident, refusing to see, her vision had begun to dim within just a short time. She just didn't understand why the Lord would delay His perfect plan for her life now that she wanted to be whole. Why?

It was as she made her and Annie's beds that the sharp shooting pain began. The needlelike sensations felt horrible, seeming to pierce her skull. The turmoil and horrendous ordeal of the past two years came flooding back with the pain. Oh, she never wanted to go through any of that ever again.

Cupping both hands around her head, she gasped, the agony nearly taking her breath away. "No . . . no, not this way, Lord. Please, not this way."

———

When Susanna wandered upstairs to redd up, she heard what she thought was moaning coming from the far northwest corner bedroom—Rachel's and Annie's room. "*Was is letz?*—What's wrong?" she mumbled, making her way down the hallway.

Standing at the door, she listened. Sure enough, it was Rachel, whimpering. She tapped on the door, anxious for a reply. "Are ya all right, Daughter?"

"Come in, Mam."

She opened the door to find Rachel lying on the bed, fully dressed. "What's-a-matter?"

Rachel's hands were pressed to her temples, and she was writhing in pain. "It's my head . . . I can't stand this pain."

"Well, forevermore," she whispered. "Will an aspirin help, do ya think?"

"No . . . no, not pills."

She sighed. Dare she mention Blue Johnny just now?

"Not powwow doctors either, Mam. Please don't even think of it."

Susanna shook her head in wonderment. There Rachel went again, saying her thoughts aloud, almost before she thought 'em. How she did it, Susanna did not know, but it was a sign of a true gift. That was for sure and for certain. "Do you want me to call a *medical* doctor, then?"

Rachel didn't answer right away but continued rocking back and forth as if she were being tortured. At last, she said, "I wish you would call Esther . . . ask her and Levi to pray."

"Clear out there to Ohio? Well, you must be crazy to ask such a thing. Do you have any idea how expensive that could be?"

"Cheaper than goin' to a hospital doctor," Rachel said, surprising Susanna at her spunk.

"Well, now, ain't you nervy today . . . pain 'n all?"

"Mamma, please forgive me. I didn't mean it in a bad way."

Susanna thought on that. "However you meant it don't matter none.

Truth is, I'm a-thinkin' it's long overdue for you to settle things with Blue Johnny. Once and for all."

"But, Mam—"

"Nothin' doing. You listen to me, Daughter. He's got the power to heal—sight, too. What in all the world do you think you're doin' refusin' him?" Susanna thought she might burst apart if she stayed in the room another second. So she bolted, leaving Rachel weeping great heaving sobs.

Lord'a mercy, was her daughter goin' backward, starting her mournin' time all over again? The thought of such a thing worried her sick. Never again did she want to go through the past two years, 'specially the first fifteen months or so. Rachel's grief had been like no widow's woe she'd ever known.

"I declare, I don't know what to do 'bout her," she muttered to herself as she hurried downstairs, only to bump into Annie, who looked right surprised to see Mammi mumblin' a mouthful of angry words.

"What's wrong?" the child asked.

"Your mamma's sick just now."

"I'll go up and help her."

"No . . . no . . . no, you best stay down here. Help me make a nice big lunch."

Annie's eyes glistened. "But how can I eat if Mamma's sick? I could never do it, Mammi Susanna. I just couldn't."

The way the child was carryin' on, you'da thought Rachel was dyin' or something. Then it struck her, hard as anything ever had. She knew what to do. "Jah, maybe you should go on up and comfort your mamma, Annie. Just lie down next to her and place your hand on her forehead and say these words three times, 'Tame thou flesh and bone, Mamma dear.' Then make three crosses with your thumb on her forehead, and let's see if you can't cure that ol' headache."

Annie got the biggest smile on her face and hurried out of the kitchen. Susanna couldn't help but grin, too.

Ten

❖ ❖ ❖

Rachel, still lying down, was prayin' hard and fast when another knock came at her bedroom door. "Who's there?" she asked, hoping Mam wasn't comin' up to pester her some more.

"It's me, Mamma . . . it's Annie."

"Oh, darling girl, come on in." She made an attempt to control herself and not let on how pain-ridden she really was.

"Mammi Susanna said I should help you." Annie's footsteps were light as she crossed the room to the bedside.

"Well, now, how are *you* gonna help me, little one?"

"Can I lie next to you?"

Rachel slid over, making room. Then, holding her breath, trying not to focus on the excruciating pain, she felt Annie place her warm hand on Rachel's forehead. "Whatcha doin'?"

"Feelin' your head. And . . . I'm makin' the cross on your forehead three times. Now I'm gonna say something over you."

"Like *what* are you thinkin' of saying, Annie?" She could feel the goose pimples popping out on the back of her neck. "Who told you to do this?" Rachel was provoked, 'cause she knew. Without a shadow of doubt, she did.

"Mammi Susanna said I might could cure you" came the tiny voice.

"Well, don't you believe a word of it!" Rachel sat up, wishing for all the world she could see her daughter. "What Mammi told you is very, very wrong."

"Why would she . . . why?" Annie sounded as though she might cry.

"Oh, it's ever so hard to explain," Rachel said. "But makin' chants over folk ain't what God has in mind for healin'. I know it sure as anything."

"But Josh, my little cousin, makes 'um."

Rachel sucked in her breath, then coughed. "What do you mean?"

"He talks like he's gonna be our doctor someday. It's what Aunt Lizzy keeps on tellin' him. I guess Mammi Susanna told her all 'bout curin' folks's sickness, too."

Rachel's head hurt from the penetrating pain. But it pained her more knowin' how the enemy of the soul was workin' overtime in the hearts of her dear relatives. "We hafta be prayin' for our healing, not lettin' Josh or anybody else make chants or spells over us. The Bible teaches against it. Do you understand?"

"Josh says it's 'the People's way.'"

"Well, that doesn't make it right. *God's* way is always best."

Annie seemed to be satisfied enough with Rachel's answer and didn't continue to question. She offered Rachel a kiss on the cheek and left the room.

Rubbing her temples, she breathed a prayer heavenward.

Rachel knew she had to make a choice. One way or the other. She didn't want to go back to the silent dark days of denying herself, tellin' herself lies. She'd been deceived by her own fears, too terrified to remember the truth of whatever it was she'd witnessed at the corner of Highway 340 and North Ronks Road—the Crossroad—where Jacob and Aaron had passed over into eternity.

She just might have to make herself ride horse and buggy down Ronks Road, coming to a complete stop at the deadly intersection. How she would do such a frightening thing, Rachel did not know. But such an experience was somehow wrapped up in her recovery. She felt sure it was.

———

Fully perplexed at Rachel's desperate state, Susanna told Benjamin she was going to call a driver so she could go into the village after lunch. "I need a bit of breathin' room," she admitted, grabbing her coat and boots. "You understand, jah?"

He looked up from his gardening magazine, frown lines evident. The clothes he wore—long-sleeved white shirt and black broadfall trousers—had been pressed nicely. Rachel's doing. "Are you perturbed, Susie?" he asked, closing the magazine.

She clenched her teeth, trying to maintain composure. "More than I care to say."

"Well, then, go ahead. Get it out of your system."

Susanna had no idea where she was actually headed. A cup of black coffee and Leah's listenin' ear might go a long way toward makin' her feel some better. "I won't be gone too awful long," she said softly.

"Over to Leah's?" he asked, getting up and comin' over to give her a hug.

"Prob'ly."

"Gut idea, if ya ask me." He kissed her lips, though they pouted in spite of the loving gesture. "I'll tend to Rachel . . . if she needs some tea or whatnot."

He went to the door with her when the driver arrived. "Now, run along and have yourself a gut time."

Oh, she would try to do that. Jah, she would. Anything would be better than stewin' in the house just now. Both she *and* Rachel needed space from each other.

Susanna figured she'd wait to fill Benjamin in on Annie's statement: "a powerful-strong feeling" that the girl and her mamma were gonna be farmers someday.

Puh! If that childish notion came true, well, she'd be right surprised. After all, 'twasn't enough land to go 'round in families much no more, in Lancaster County anyways. Where on earth were Rachel and Annie gonna find themselves land 'round here?

She attempted to calm herself, staring out the van windows at the white and wintry fields that rolled away from the snow-packed road on either side. Glistening-smooth, the street lay ahead, fraught with plowed snow, making for a straight and narrow path, scarcely wide enough to allow automobiles to pass.

In the distance, rolling hills of frosted ivory scattered across the southern ridge, and for a moment, Susanna had the strange notion that she'd like to go there, far away from home, and find a place of repose. Away from her grown daughter who was behavin' like a spoiled child.

She thought back to the days when Rachel was just a little girl—bashful as the day is long. A sweet and soft-spoken youngster, Rachel seemed eager to obey. Never once exerted her will, not that Susanna recalled. No, Rachel Zook had been the kind of girl most any Amish parents would be wonderful-glad to have as kin, 'cept that she had always been far different from the older five girls born to Benjamin and Susanna. Rebekah, Naomi, Susie, Mary, and Elizabeth possessed a confident and strong disposition, as did Susanna's own sisters and mother, and the generations of women before her. Stubborn women.

Why Rachel had been prone to faintheartedness, coming from a long line of such determined women, had always puzzled Susanna. But here lately, she had come to the conclusion that her youngest daughter was chosen, over all the others, to be the next powwow doctor in the community. Susanna had pondered this many times of late, but more and more she felt strongly that she was right 'bout this. The Almighty One had planted a receptive and humble spirit in Rachel for a right gut reason. She felt confident of God's plan for the blind woman. Wouldn't be long, either, till the rest of the People came to understand. She could hardly wait for Rachel herself to grasp the importance of the powwow "blessing," once and for all. As for Susanna, she would never rest till that day came.

Bells tinkled in the air as they came up on a horse-drawn sleigh, slowing so as not to spook the horse. A group of women from the Old Order church district were out for some fresh air; either that, or they were on their way to a work frolic somewheres. Not having been invited, she wondered where they might be headed.

When Susanna turned to look more closely, she spied Mary and Lizzy, two of her married daughters, and their teenage girls, Elizabeth Anne, Mary Beth, Katie, Susie Mae, Lydia, and Martha, along for the ride. Why hadn't she been included? But then again, she s'posed it was plain to see. Folks had declined to ask her to doin's, here lately, knowing full well she'd have to turn them down on account of her work at the B&B. First things first, she always liked to say. And she didn't feel too awful bad 'bout bein' passed over, not on a chilly day like this, anyways.

The more she thought 'bout the women, most of them from her own family and headin' off somewhere—lookin' mighty happy, too—she got to thinkin' that maybe Leah was gone to some frolic, away from the house.

Should've phoned out to their woodshed, she thought. Leah's husband or at least one of the older boys would answer out there. That way she could've found out if Leah was at home before ridin' all the way over there for nothin'.

Oh well, she didn't much care. Truth was, she needed the aimless ride in the frosty morning. Helped clear her head some, made her breathing come a bit more easy. And helped her stop dwellin' on the shenanigans her daughter seemed to be pullin' these days.

And my, oh my, those tapes from Ohio—they just kept a-comin', it seemed. Snow, sleet, or shine. Made her wonder, more than ever, what the two women had to say to each other. If she wasn't such a forthright person, well, she might just be tempted to "borrow" one of 'em and listen in for a change. . . .

Turned out Leah *was* home, and Susanna was mighty glad to see her younger sister. "I had to get out of the house for a while," she confessed.

"Rachel?"

"Uh-huh."

"Well, bless your heart, you'll hafta tell me 'bout it."

That was all it took for Susanna to open up and pour out her distress. "She's got a headache . . . carryin' on so, same as she did right after Jacob and Aaron died. Makes me think she's startin' to recall some of the accident."

Leah's face was tipped slightly, looking at her with keen interest. "You know how it is with certain widows and widowers—they just keep a-livin' the loss over and over. Maybe that's what Rachel's doin', too."

"Grief comes in waves. No question 'bout that."

"Jah, but that's not *our* way. The People don't usually carry on so."

The words jabbed at Susanna's heart. She heard the disdain in Leah's voice. Her sister thought Rachel wasn't behavin' like one of them. She was acting more like a modern, "fancy" woman, though she was Amish through and through.

"I daresay a visit from John Lapp of Paradise might change all that," Leah said with conviction.

"You don't mean . . ."

"I most certainly do. And I think you oughta out-and-out invite the smithy to supper some night soon. From what I hear, he showed up over at the Beachy meetinghouse last Monday night."

"John Lapp did?"

"Came lookin' for your Rachel."

"Are you sure now?"

"A gut many folk spied him there, saw Lavina and Rachel sittin' up close to the front, too. I got my facts straight on this, Susie."

She thought for a moment. "Hmm, now I just wonder what the smithy Lapp might be doin' for Christmas dinner?"

Leah was noddin' her head to beat the band, brown eyes a-smilin'.

'Course, Susanna was smart enough not to think of mentioning any of this to Rachel. No, it was better kept quiet.

"Speakin' of Christmas, I got a letter from Esther yesterday, and it looks like they'll be comin' in on Friday afternoon . . . Christmas Eve."

"First I heard of it," replied Susanna.

"I'm awful glad your Rachel said something."

"Oh, so maybe *that's* what them two's been cookin' up."

Leah frowned. "What do ya mean?"

"Well, I'd be lyin' to you if I didn't say that there's been a flurry of taped letters goin' back and forth between here and Ohio lately."

"You're thinkin' that Rachel might be needin' a visit with Esther, is that it?"

She nodded. "I'd say them cousins are as close as two women ever could be."

"Well, now"—and here Leah burst out laughing—"look how close their mammas are!"

Susanna had to smile at that. "And here I thought maybe there was something else a-goin' on."

"What . . . with the tapes?"

"Jah" was all she said. Didn't wanna stir up curiosity on Leah's part. Still, she couldn't help but think there was some mighty important reason for Rachel to be the one asking Esther and Levi to come home for Christmas. Had to be.

The Crossroad

Part Two

If a man therefore purge himself . . .
he shall be a vessel unto honour,
sanctified, and meet for the master's use,
and prepared unto every good work.

—2 TIMOTHY 2:21

Eleven

❖ ❖ ❖

The sound of busy feet, booted and crunching against polluted snow—shoppers running helter-skelter up and down Broadway and surrounding boulevards—filtered into Philip's head. He purposely kept his own pace, walking nearer the shops than the curb, noting that not a single person caught in the mad dash of holiday buying seemed remotely interested in peering into the exquisite windows along the avenue. Even the locksmith and pharmacy, ordinary merchandisers, were brimming with beleaguered buyers. The Broadway Nut Shop and Starbucks Coffee were crammed with people waiting in line for gift certificates or a quick snack to boost their spirits.

Christmas in New York City was precisely the place to be for many. Not for Philip. Not anymore. He could hardly wait to set out for less peopled climes. Namely, the village of Bird-in-Hand, population: 300.

He planned to leave Manhattan in two days by car, long before rush hour, on Christmas Eve. He had discovered, upon calling his travel agent, that there were any number of inn accommodations available in the Reading area this time of year. He would take his time driving to Pennsylvania, delirious with the idea of abandoning the bustling city for a few days. Typically, things were slow at the magazine between Christmas and New Year's, so the only hurdle had been in getting Kari to understand why he wouldn't be able to spend the holidays with her and her parents. His mother was visibly unnerved by the news, but he had promised her and Dad—Kari too—that he'd make up for being gone by hosting an exciting New Year's Eve party "at my place . . . or we'll go to Times Square and watch the ball drop, if you want to," he'd offered.

But Kari and her parents preferred to attend church for an old-fashioned "Watch Night" service. "There's a European choir," Kari said, her eyes dancing. "I know you'll love it, Uncle Phil. We'll have prayer and communion at midnight."

He actually liked Kari's idea better. So along with the rest of the family, he had agreed to "pray in" the New Year.

Janice and Ken had seemed rather surprised that he wanted to spend Christmas with Adele. But he assured them—all of them—that this was important and reminded them that he'd never missed celebrating the season with them, "not in twenty-seven years."

Time for a new approach to the holy days, he told himself as he slipped into a small corner bookstore, an out-of-the-way spot where he could drink some cappuccino and purchase a gift or two for his niece, a bookworm extraordinaire. He was also on the search for a picture book for Annie Yoder, whom he wanted to see again, almost as much as her mother, Rachel.

———

"I saw Mary and Lizzy and their girls heading over toward Hess Road, in a sleigh, no less," Susanna said while helping Leah wipe down cupboards and later, mopboards. "Thought maybe you'd be goin' out to the same frolic."

"Jah, I heard of it but didn't much feel like gettin' out today, not with the roads so awful."

"What's doin'?" Susanna was just too curious to let it drop.

"Bishop Seth's great-granddaughter's havin' a baby come late March, so some of the younger women were gettin' together to make a batch of crib quilts."

"Oh."

"Hope the old bishop lives long enough to see his first great-great-grandson."

"So . . . it's a boy for sure, then?"

"Well, the powwow doctor tested her with a penny tied to the end of a string, ya know."

"If that's the case, Bishop Seth can count on it, 'cause the powwow doctors ain't never wrong. They can even tell how many babies—twins, triplets, ya know—and the sex of each in correct order."

Leah frowned, her eyes wide. "Ever wonder why that is?"

"What?"

"The accuracy of them powwow doctors . . . what makes them right so often?"

Susanna shrugged. "Just the way it's always been."

"But *how* do they know so much? Must be some reason, I'm a-thinkin'."

Susanna didn't make an effort to explain. She didn't know for sure, really. Just that the "knowing" powers were passed from one person to another through the generations, same as other gifts of enchantment.

They continued with their cleaning chore, and Susanna came mighty close to bringin' up her concerns over Esther, who just seemed bent on a-fillin' Rachel's head with things she oughta forget. But she kept her peace and let the matter drop.

———

"Hope you get to feelin' much better, and right soon," Lavina told Rachel, offering her the cup of chamomile tea and honey she'd made in the Zook kitchen. "Between you and me, I think the Lord's speakin' to me . . . 'bout visiting the Old Order bishop in a couple-a days."

Rachel plumped a pillow behind her as she sat up in bed. "Is that why you came? To talk to me 'bout goin' along?"

"Honest, Rachel, I felt a nudge—strong as anything this mornin' while I was prayin'. Thing is, 'twouldn't be right—two unmarried women goin' to speak to the bishop."

"I was thinkin' the same thing." Rachel raised the teacup to her lips, her hands trembling.

"Who wouldja ask to go with us—what man?" She stood at the side of Rachel's bed, looking down at the poor girl, pale as the moon.

"Levi Glick would be the best choice, I'd hafta say, but I haven't heard for sure if they're comin' for Christmas or not."

Lavina studied awhile. "Oughta be prayin' . . . for the Lord's leading, ya know."

"If Dat was in the know 'bout spiritual things, I'd ask him."

"Well's . . . why not? Your father could hear the witness same time as the bishop does." Lavina hadn't thought of that before, but it was an idea worth thinkin' through.

"When wouldja wanna go?" Rachel took another sip of the tea, eyes squinted shut as if in terrible pain.

"Soon as you're able."

"Then I don't know if I can, really. The pain in my head's gonna hafta taper off a whole lot before I can think of goin' anywhere."

Lavina sighed, sitting on the edge of the bed. "Have ya tried a home remedy?"

"I rubbed oil of rosemary at my temples, but the pain seems to be comin' from deep inside my head . . . not like just any headache."

"You be fearful 'bout something, Rachel?" She suspected as much.

"Well . . . maybe I am." Rachel went on to tell her how she'd been praying, beseeching the Lord for her healing.

"Tryin' too hard, maybe."

Rachel cocked her head thoughtfully. "How could *that* be?"

"Rest in the Lord. Wait patiently for Him." It was the best advice Lavina could give.

"So I shouldn't keep remindin' God of His promises to heal?"

"Far as I understand, you don't hafta to remind your heavenly Father 'bout things He's said He'd do. The same way you don't hafta remind your dat when he says he'll take you somewheres. Just rest, Rachel. Your healin' will come in due time."

If she hadn't been in such pain, Rachel would've pressed the older woman. Lavina was sounding ever so much like a wise old sage of a lady, and far as she knew, there was only one woman like that 'round Lancaster County. She'd heard tell of Ella Mae Zook—one of her father's second or third cousins once removed—who lived down in Hickory Hollow a piece. Folk in that church district often called Ella Mae the Wise Woman 'cause she seemed to have answers to life's grittiest questions.

Your healin' will come in due time. . . .

Whoever heard? And how could Lavina know that for sure? Rachel thought long and hard 'bout it even after the kind and gentle woman took the empty teacup, with a promise to refill it, leaving Rachel alone in her room once again. But the more she thought, the more she just figured you had to be a bit slow in some areas to be as quick as Lavina Troyer was in others. Now, didn't that beat all?

Still, she didn't know how she could keep from reciting the biblical promises, those wonderful-gut Scriptures her cousin had sent her. How could she *not* pray the way Esther's pastor had taught on the sermon tapes Rachel loved to hear?

Ach, she was ever so puzzled now. Didn't quite know what to do, really.

Philip spied a vacant, overstuffed chair in the corner of the diminutive bookstore. He set down an armload of children's books on the table in front of him—children's poetry, a humorous takeoff on Noah and the Ark, a story about two Amish children who make Christmas preparations, several editions of Nancy Drew mysteries, and a collection of C. S. Lewis's *Chronicles of Narnia*. He also wanted to purchase something for Adele Herr. So many choices, so little time . . .

Glancing at his watch, he began to peruse the picture books and the other books he wanted to buy for Kari. He made his selections rather quickly, deciding on the set of the Lewis books for Kari and the book with the Amish setting for Annie Yoder, though he couldn't be certain of the accuracy of dialogue and information, or how Rachel's little girl might perceive the characters. Regardless, he would take the risk. The illustrations, after all, were quite eye-catching, and from what he remembered of Lancaster County, the artistic renderings seemed authentic enough.

He located a beautifully illustrated gift book, featuring American rural scenes, as well as a blank book for journaling—both for Adele.

On his way out of the store, purchases in hand, he spotted a book on the bargain table with a most intriguing title, *Gifts of Darkness*. Compelled to pick it up, he noticed that the author had been a Pennsylvania Amish preacher at one time. He was intrigued and decided, upon reading a portion of the first chapter, that he must have it for his growing collection of Plain books.

Not until he arrived home from work later in the evening did he discover the actual theme of the book. One of the chapters was entitled "White Witchcraft," and once again Philip was reminded that there were certain dark and secret rituals occurring under the guise of faith or "sympathy" healing in many Plain communities. Other than Adele Herr's story of Gabe Esh, he had not heard of occult practices associated with the Anabaptist people, so he read from cover to cover, not stopping until he had completed the entire book.

Most surprising was the seemingly honest approach the former Amish minister had taken in writing the book, revealing the grip of Satan in his own life, how he had been forced as a youth to "receive giftings passed down from an older female relative," as well as his path to spiritual freedom. The author recounted the steps the Holy Spirit had led him to take in order to be released from the enemy's stronghold.

After reading certain chapters a second time, Philip began to rethink the timing and his purchase of the book. No longer a believer in happenstance, he had recently entrusted his very life and future to the Lord. He began to pray on behalf of people everywhere who might indeed be under the "deceitful spell of the devil," as the Amish writer had stated. Philip had no one in mind, though he wondered later, while reheating leftovers in the microwave, if what he knew of Gabe Esh's story might have subconsciously triggered his encounter with the pocket-size book.

After a light supper, he began to pack for his trip. He was eager to share his find with Adele; even wondered if Rachel Yoder had ever encountered such practices in her present-day Amish community these many years since Gabe's death. Most remarkable were the steps to deliverance from generational curses and what the author called "familiar spirits" in families, and how to become free of bondage through the power of Jesus' name.

He was anxious to head for Pennsylvania, now more so than ever, praying that what he had just read might be something he could share with a needy heart. He recalled the unique sermon at the Mennonite church, back in September, where his historical society contact Stephen Flory and wife attended. It had been the first message on spiritual warfare he'd ever heard—how to make a rock-solid covenant to truth. "The very arrows intended for God's people shall enter into the evildoers' own hearts, 'and their bows shall be broken,'" the pastor had preached with reference to Psalm 37 from his unadorned pulpit in the meetinghouse.

At the time, Philip hadn't known what to make of such a sermon. Now, since renewing his faith and studying the Bible daily, his "eyes of faith" had been opened to redemptive truths. He could see the Lord's hand in his life so clearly these past few months and could hardly wait to share this teaching.

Closing his suitcase, he knelt beside his bed, the way he had often prayed as a boy. "Dear Lord, it has occurred to me that you have placed in my heart an urgency to minister. I cast myself on your mercy, thanking you for bringing me back to the Fold. It is my desire to commit my life, one hundred percent, to your work and to your kingdom.

"As for Rachel Yoder, if it is your will, allow me to present to her the information on conversion disorder. I entrust her sight to you, as well as her future. In Jesus' name I pray. Amen."

Rachel didn't wait till Annie was asleep to kneel at her bedside. She prayed with her daughter, her arm around her dear one. "Lord Jesus, I have never asked you for my healing in front of my little girl. But Annie knows now how much I want to see again . . . how badly I want to be whole, too—healed from the memory of what happened the day of the accident. She and I come before you just now, prayin' that you'll hear and answer our prayer."

Annie continued, quite unexpectedly. "I don't know how you're gonna do it, Lord, but Mamma really wants to see what I look like now. So could you do that for her? And could you do somethin' else, too, Lord? Could you please take away her awful headache? Amen."

Rachel nodded in agreement. Jah, it would be ever so wonderful to be free of the throbbing pain, especially that intense and thorny penetrating sensation that filled her entire day. The acute, raw pain that accompanied the return of terrifying visions.

Long after Annie was tucked in, the memories continued to present themselves. A horse rearing up on its hind legs . . . her dear husband struggling to control the mare. Screams of children . . . a car horn wailing . . . the hideous, grating sound of the crash.

She did not reject the visions as she had in the past, but made a futile attempt to shield herself from the persistent pain that seemed to accompany them. She was willing to walk through the nightmare, through the memory. Jesus had promised to be with her—even through the valley of the shadow of death.

Wrapping her arms about herself, Rachel rose and reached out to feel the wall, locating the windows across the room. "Oh, Lord Jesus, I want to remember what happened that day," she whispered. "Because I want to be healed . . . no matter what."

But she could speak no more, for the tears threatened to fall. Determinedly, Rachel waited with open eyes, hoping to regain her sight, to witness the moon's rise over the neighbor's barn, to see her beautiful child who lay sleeping.

Sometime later, Rachel groped her way back to bed and crawled in, curling up under the layers of quilts. She placed both hands next to her face, as if in prayer, her knees nearly touching her chin. Then she wept softly.

Much later, Rachel thought she heard voices, possibly Mam and Dat arguing. She wished to fall asleep without pain, either emotional or physical, yet she experienced great stress at the thought of her parents' fussing.

Getting up, she made her way down the long hallway, her hand on the wall as she counted her steps to the top of the staircase. Then, turning away from the stairs, she followed the voices and stopped well within earshot of their bedroom.

"I daresay our Rachel was the one who invited Esther and Levi home for Christmas. She wants to talk 'em into takin' her and Annie back to Ohio with them, prob'ly," Mam was saying.

"Well, now, how could that be?" Dat replied.

"You just see if I ain't right."

Dat was quiet now, and Rachel wondered if he had been talkin' in his sleep. After all, it was much too late for her father to be carryin' on any sort of intelligent conversation. Mam oughta know that!

"There's more," Susanna continued.

Rachel thought she heard something of a grunt, but she couldn't be sure. Still, Mam persisted.

"Annie's talkin' like she and Rachel must've discussed farmin' someday, so I'll betcha I'm right 'bout this."

Dat was beginning to snore. So much for a two-sided conversation. Poor Mam. She never knew when to quit!

"And . . . you listen here to me! Our granddaughter's showin' some interesting signs, I tell you, Benjamin. She might just be the next pow-wow doctor 'round these parts. If'n I can ever sneak her out of the house to see Blue Johnny. Or maybe Bishop Seth's the one to see before he passes on. . . ."

Rachel cringed, turning on her heels. She hurried down the hall as quickly as possible, though she didn't want to go fallin' headlong down the stairs. *That* would never do!

Back in her room, she knelt at her bedside again. "Oh, Lord Jesus, I need your help tonight! I don't even know how to pray 'bout much of what's on my heart just now, but I believe you know and you care. And protect Annie from what Mam might be planning to do. Mam needs you ever so much, Lord. She really does. . . ."

Susanna waited long into the night, past her usual bedtime, to slip into Rachel's bedroom and snatch up one of the tape recordings from

Esther Glick. She'd promised herself months ago she'd never do such a thing, listening in on her daughter's and her niece's personal "letters" to each other. Still, she figured the Lord God heavenly Father would understand and forgive her just this once. After all, it was high time she had an inklin' why on earth Rachel would ask Esther and Levi to return to Bird-in-Hand for Christmas.

Twelve

❖ ❖ ❖

Lavina sat on her big feather bed—her grandmother's ancient bed—with artwork strewn around her. *Gabe's* . . . when he was a young boy, back when he had shown occasional signs of actually caring about his friend, who just so happened to be a girl one year older and a mite skinnier.

Studying each picture closely—one, a pencil sketch of a two-story bank barn and silo in early summer; another, a rusty water pump with a lone daisy growin' to one side, nearest the handle. The third was her favorite—a watercolor picture of his father's meadow in full spring, with purple and pink wild flowers and sunny-yellow dandelions, too, all colorful and eye-pleasin'. She'd decided she wanted to take them—or at least color copies of them—along to show Adele next time she and Rachel paid a visit.

Next time? Well, she was hopin' she could get Rachel to go again real soon. In time for the nursing home's Christmas program, maybe. After all, sounded to her like Adele was going to invite Philip Bradley—the man whose name had caused Rachel to blush red as a ripe tomato. Jah, he was prob'ly coming down from New York for the special program. Sure as anything, made sense to get Rachel back there, too. That is, if she could bring up the idea without Rachel 'specting something was up.

For sure, she didn't much wanna to be playin' matchmaker. She'd come mighty close to urgin' young Adele to return to Bird-in-Hand one summer, forty-some years ago, just weeks before Gabe was killed in a car accident. Still, she knew without question that the English schoolteacher had dearly loved Gabe, without a smidgen of help or matchmakin' from an old maid, let alone a woman with only half her wits.

Carefully she gathered up Gabe's drawings, setting aside her three favorites. She wouldn't risk losing them; couldn't part with 'um, either. She would drive horse and buggy over to her married brother's place—he had a copy machine in back of his woodworking shop. Color copies would make a right nice Christmas gift for her friend. And 'twould be a gut excuse to return to the Reading nursing home . . . with Rachel Yoder.

She couldn't help but snicker as she headed to the hall closet to put on her warmest coat, artwork in hand.

————

The next day, Lavina made a point of goin' to see Rachel. Mainly it was to show little Annie the perty drawings Gabe had made so long ago. There was another purpose in her visit, though. She wanted to chat with Ben Zook 'bout accompanying her to see Bishop Seth Fisher, who folks were sayin' here lately was real bad sick with flu and other complications.

"High time he hears from *me* 'bout my shunning," she said as she sat in the Zooks' parlor, with both Susanna and Ben sharing a couch across from her. "'Least 'fore he dies, I believe I oughta go."

Ben put down his paper, looking over his glasses at her. "Well, now, I wouldn't be opposed to such a thing. That is, if you're goin' there to repent." He paused, his frown growing deeper by the second.

Susanna spoke up. "That *is* what you had in mind, ain't?"

Lavina felt flustered all of a sudden. She'd come to ask a favor, and Benjamin and his wife were puttin' her on the spot. "There's somethin' else I best be doing, too." She didn't go on to say that Rachel had agreed to go with her—to witness to the old bishop—but now that seemed out of the question, what with Rachel sufferin' so with crippling headaches.

Ben's face seemed even more ruddy than she'd remembered, but she figured it was due to the fact that he was vexed. She could be wrong, but she thought the color creepin' up in his neck and face prob'ly was just that.

His fingers worked up and down his tan suspenders, makin' her even more nervous. "Well, Cousin, what is it?" he pressed for her answer. "What's it ya wanna do?"

Avoiding his serious gaze, Lavina was wishin' she'd left well enough alone. Still, she believed God wanted her to speak to Bishop Seth. "Has the Lord God heavenly Father ever put somethin' strong in your heart, so powerful-strong you knew you best do something 'bout it?" Lavina managed to say as she sat there on Susanna's brown tufted settee.

Ben's face broke into a most pleasant smile, and for a moment she was relieved. "Why, sure He has, and I can tell you 'bout one of them times, too. It was back when Seth Fisher was one of our preachers and had just been chosen by lot to be our bishop." He stopped, inhaling slow and easy, as though he was enjoying the recollection. "I was no more than ten years old, seems to me."

Lavina wondered how old the *bishop* had been at the time, but she didn't have to wait more than a second to find out.

Ben continued. "Seth Fisher was close to forty years old, and one of our ordained preachers, when I felt led of God to help out the church's new leader . . . or soon to be."

Susanna's eyes were fixed on her man, prob'ly having heard this tale many-a-time. She nodded her head, listenin' like Lavina had never witnessed before, 'specially since Susanna Zook was known to be frisky at times, and quite a talker, on top o' that.

"Jah, I was just a boy when I assisted the man of God by hangin' a small bag of ingredients 'round a sick horse's neck. I watched Seth Fisher cure my uncle's best drivin' horse thataway."

Lavina wasn't too surprised to hear this. Plenty of youngsters had been eager to help the bishop—or anyone who had "magical powers"—down through the years.

"You can imagine my surprise when I thought he wasn't lookin', and I peeked into that there little burlap bag." Ben's smile was contagious, and Susanna was grinning, too. "I found nothin' but a handful of sawdust mixed with oats, of all things!"

"Still, the horse was cured," Susanna pointed out.

Lavina didn't think Ben's boyhood tale had much to do with being led of God, but she sure wasn't going to argue. Just listened, waiting for the man to agree or disagree on going with her to talk to the respected bishop. One of the two.

It was after Annie came into the parlor, telling Susanna that her mamma wanted to "talk to Lavina," that she remembered the drawings. "I've got something right nice to show you," Lavina said, getting up and heading for the stairs.

"What is it?" Annie asked.

"Perty drawings, that's what. I'll be right down, dearie."

Annie nodded and pranced out of the room. And Lavina hurried upstairs to see about Rachel, poor thing.

"You still sufferin', child?" Lavina asked, going quickly to the side of Rachel's bed.

Rachel kept her hands on a wet cloth that was wrapped 'round her forehead. "No need to worry over me, 'cause what I have to tell you is ever so important. My cousin Esther said some mighty interesting things on her latest tape."

"I'm all ears," Lavina said, perching on the edge of the bed.

Rachel's face was drawn, her eyes downcast. "I think you should know what Esther said 'bout the hex put on Gabe Esh." And she went on to tell her what was told to Esther's husband about Bishop Seth's "death charm." "Must've sprung out of Seth's anger against Gabe for not comin' under his authority. Gabe was a right stubborn fella—stubborn for God, you know."

Ach, she was shamed to hear such horrid things 'bout the man who'd led the People all these years. Lavina clamped her hand over her mouth when Rachel mentioned the hex and the encounter with the white dove.

"But remember, Lavina, the enemy will use anything—even superstitions—and you know how we Plain folk are 'bout that," Rachel added. "Esther says it's ignorance and irrational fear that make superstition work."

Lavina couldn't agree more. "Jah, but it's time we take back our families, our community, for God!"

Nodding, Rachel whispered, "I'll be prayin' for you when you go to the bishop, and I'm ever so sorry I can't go with you . . . on account of this horrible headache."

"I think your father's comin' with me. And I'm hopin' and prayin' he'll stay and listen . . . when I talk to Bishop Seth 'bout the hex . . . and the dove."

Rachel frowned. "What'll you say if the bishop asks you to repent for goin' to the Beachy church?"

Truth was, she couldn't show remorse. "The Lord will hafta give me the words to say. That's all I know."

Seemed to be what Rachel needed to hear, 'cause her face brightened, and for a moment, Lavina wondered if the pain in the poor girl's head just might be lettin' up some. "You just stay here and pray, and I'll go and do the speakin' for the Lord," she said before getting up and kissing Rachel's cheek.

"You can count on me," Rachel replied, still rubbing her forehead.

Lavina headed back downstairs to show Annie the perty artwork by the little's girl very own great-great-uncle Gabe.

———

The phone rang almost as soon as Lavina and Dat left by way of the front door. Rachel had heard the doors close behind them, and when the phone rang, she was glad Mam had stayed home. That way she wouldn't have to bother getting up to answer it.

Soon, though, it was Mam calling up the steps to her. "Rachel, are you up to talkin' to Mr. Witwer?"

She was sure their Mennonite driver must have some information 'bout "Auntie" Nancy Beiler. Maybe located her, though she wished the call had come on another day. When she felt better.

"Jah, I'll take it up here," she succeeded in saying loud enough to be heard. Hobbling down the hall, she sat on the small chair next to the phone table.

Turned out, Calvin Witwer *had* found where Nancy Beiler was living. "She's stayin' with her married sister, over near Gap."

"Really, so far away?" Rachel replied.

"I just now talked to her, and she says she wants you to give her a call sometime, when it's convenient."

She memorized the woman's number, still holding one side of her head with one hand, the phone cradled in the other. "I'll be glad to. Thank you ever so much, Mr. Witwer."

Hanging up the phone, it was all she could do to make it back to bed. Yet she'd promised to pray for Lavina, so she lay there on her back, her head stinging with every pulse of her heart, trying to make sense of her prayer. "Dear Lord, please help my father's cousin as she goes and talks to the old bishop 'bout you. Help her remember the deliverance prayer she learned from Esther's tapes."

She sighed, hesitant to ask the Lord for her healing again. "Help Seth Fisher show grace and mercy to Lavina . . . help her not to feel rejected if the shun is put on her for gut. Oh, Lord, just help her. And help me, too." That was all she said 'bout herself. She wanted to "rest in the Lord" as Lavina had instructed so wisely yesterday. With everything in her, she was trying her best to do just that.

So she would set her mind to resting. Then in a few minutes, she would get down on her knees and pray again, remembering her dear friend and relative, Lavina, whom God had called to testify for Him.

Thirteen

❖ ❖ ❖

The elderly bishop lay lifeless—gray 'round the gills—his bed marked only by the colorful blues and yellows of the quilts and the modest walnut headboard and footboard. His plain white nightshirt was visible, though only the neckline, as he was covered securely with a mound of blankets and quilts. His gray hair was damp with perspiration at the crown, and strands clung to his wrinkled brow. His beard, grizzled and untrimmed, was *schlappich*—disheveled. Overall, he looked downright wrung out.

The room was typically Plain with rag rugs scattered here and there—one rug on either side of the low double bed and a long narrow one directly in front of the dresser. A lone rocking chair sat near the corner windows across the wide hardwood plank flooring. Lavina noticed that the bishop's wife had draped her bureau mirror with jewelry—mostly glittery necklaces and bracelets. Truth was, many Amishwomen decorated their bedroom mirrors with colorful jewelry and shiny trinkets, since they weren't allowed to wear such things.

"I've sent for Blue Johnny and his black box," Rosemary Fisher said, her wrinkled face solemn and drawn as she stood near her husband's bedside.

Lavina hoped Rachel was callin' her name out to the Lord just now. Oh, she needed divine wisdom! She could scarcely hear the bishop breathing, but then she set her gaze on his chest and saw that it was rising and falling ever so slowlike.

She found herself concentrating on the beloved bishop, the tall, dignified-lookin' man who'd overseen her baptism into the Amish church back when she was only eighteen years old. Now he lay still as death, looking like a bag o' bones beneath the many bedclothes. "Is he conscious?" she whispered.

Rosemary shook her head. "He's been sleeping 'round the clock, so it's all right if you wake him." Then, she asked, eyeing Benjamin Zook, "Are ya here to confess for sinning . . . against the *Ordnung?*"

The sick man perked up a bit, his eyes fluttering open. Just in that instant, Lavina remembered how those serious dark eyes could pierce a body through, although just now there seemed to be a flicker of relief in his countenance. Mighty confusin' to Lavina, to say the least. She recalled, too, his stern preachin' voice, the way he used it to exhort the People.

"Lavina Troyer's here," Ben said softly, stepping back to allow her to move closer.

Rosemary also moved toward her, stooped over and leaning on a cane. "So you're here 'bout confessing, then?" She seemed anxious for an answer, her gaze intent on Lavina.

"I've come in the name of the Lord." Lavina was somewhat surprised at her own sudden boldness.

"That don't answer my question." The bishop's wife, feeble as she was herself, was unyielding, and Lavina couldn't blame her for wanting to protect her husband, as ill as he seemed to be.

"Jah, I'm here to 'fess up, all right. I own up to bein' right headstrong 'bout attending preachin's over at the Beachy meetinghouse. Guess I ain't been forthright with the bishop 'bout that, and I'm sorry. Should've spoken up weeks ago 'bout the way the Lord's touched my life over there . . . how He's taught me things I never knowed were in the Bible. Jah, I'm just sorry I didn't speak up sooner."

Rosemary took a step or two back, frowning and looking ever so befuddled.

"What's that, Rosie?" the bishop was saying, struggling to raise his head off the pillow. "What's the woman want?"

"Lavina Troyer says she's sorry," Rosemary told him. "She wants to tell you that—"

"I'm here to give you a message from the Lord who loves you, Bishop Seth," Lavina interrupted. All she could think to say was the Scripture passage in Luke she'd memorized just this week. She began slowly, deliberately, sayin' the words as clearly as she could. "'In the synagogue there was a man, which had a spirit of an unclean devil, and cried out with a loud voice, saying, Let us alone; what have we to do with thee, thou Jesus of Nazareth? Art thou come to destroy us? I know thee who thou art; the Holy One of God.'"

The bishop's eyes blinked several times, and a scowl settled on his brow. "What . . . what do you want with *me*?"

It was the pitch of his voice that made Lavina wonder. Didn't sound like Seth Fisher's voice at all. Sounded eerielike. Dark and distant, too.

She sensed an unusual heaviness in the air. Yet in spite of the troublesome oppression, she felt something else just as strong, if not stronger. She recognized the presence of God in the room. The very closeness of His Spirit.

"'Hold thy peace,'" she spoke the Scripture, "'and come out of him.'"

Without warning, the bishop began to shake and twist on his bed, winding the ends of his sheet into what looked like a coiled rope, holding on to it as if convulsing. His face broke out in heavy perspiration, and his eyes kept rollin' back in his head. Then he began to cough and sneeze repeatedly.

"What's happenin' here?" Ben Zook gasped, his face turning ashen.

"The power of God's on him . . . and evil spirits can't stay where God is," Lavina answered, praying silently all the while.

"Well, whatever it is, I best be gettin' Blue Johnny, but quick," Rosemary said, leaning hard on her cane.

"Won't be needin' him," Lavina was quick to say. Again, she was unsure where the words were coming from, so fearless were they. "Just wait a bit . . . and pray for God's peace to pour over him."

The bishop's wife scratched her salt-and-pepper head through her formal veiling.

Ben was shaking his head in amazement, staring at both Rosemary and Lavina. "This ain't 'bout the powwow gift, is it? This writhing and whatnot?"

Lavina explained as best she could. "If you're thinkin' I've got the conjurin' gift, no . . . no. But if you're a-thinkin' the magical powers— and the curses—are comin' out of the bishop just now, jah, I'm trustin' and believin' the Lord Almighty for that."

Ben's face turned from white to bright red, and he spun on his heels and fled the room. Rosemary stayed put, though, wiping her husband's brow with a cloth, trying to soothe him. "I'd heard tell of things like this," she muttered. "Just never seen it with my own eyes."

"Let's pray," Lavina said, not wanting to get caught up in idle talk. "God's been wantin' to deliver our bishop ever since Gabe Esh died of the hex."

Rosemary's mouth dropped open. "Whatever are you talking 'bout? How do *you* know 'bout. . . ?" She clapped her hand over her own mouth.

"The hex . . . the white dove . . . and the all-consumin' fear that surely must've killed Gabe and his friend that night on their way to Gordonville—that's what the Lord wants out in the open. Once and for all."

"But that happened a long, long time ago."

"Jah, but the Lord sent me to pray for Bishop Seth 'bout all that. I can't think of disobeyin' the Lord God, now can I?" Lavina could see the sick man was beginning to relax, sighing, and taking long, deep breaths. His eyes were still fluttering, but his expression seemed to be changing—softening—right before their eyes.

"I wanna pray for you, Bishop Seth," she said, leaning closer. "The Lord wants to save your soul 'fore He takes you home to heaven."

"Now, you wait just a minute," Rosemary spoke up, eyes casting fiery darts her way. "My husband don't need no soul-savin'. He's the bishop, for pity's sake!"

At that, Seth Fisher motioned with his finger to his wife weakly, but motioning all the same. "Closer," he muttered.

Rosemary, quite shaken, bent down while the bishop whispered something in her ear. "Well, I'll be!" She straightened to her full height.

But the bishop gestured to her again. "Come closer, Rosie."

Turning pale herself, the bishop's wife leaned down again to hear what her husband had to say.

Lavina was beginning to wonder if the Lord would allow her to finish the work He'd started here and was greatly relieved when Rosemary stood to her full height once again. Facing Lavina, her eyes glistened as she spoke. "My husband insists on hearin' what you've got to say."

"He does?"

"Jah, but best make it snappy."

Seth Fisher's voice was raspy and weak. "I had a vision earlier this morning . . . hours before you came. Never has such a dream haunted me like this one, and I didn't know what to make of it. But now I understand that it was God preparin' me, for I saw an angel of the Lord come to me, tellin' me that what I've been doin'—hexing and powwowing— is wrong, dead wrong." His voice, though thin, was every bit normal-sounding now.

"Don't wear yourself out, Seth," his wife spoke up, stroking his shoulder with her free hand.

But he persisted. "The vision was as real as you are standin' right here, I tell you." He looked right at Lavina. "God knew you would be comin' today to wake me up out of my sin-sickness . . . to cast the evil out of my soul."

The gray pallor was slowly disappearing. Even as the women stood over his bed, the color began to return to his face. A moment passed, and the room was still as night.

Lavina felt it was time for her to speak again. "Bishop Fisher, God wants to forgive you for the death-hex you put on Gabriel Esh," she said gently. "And for the way you've kept the People in the grip of the enemy all these many years."

The bishop's eyes grew moist, and a tear slid down his crinkled cheek. His deep brown eyes shone with compassion, like beacons in the darkness, yet he remained silent, not speaking for a gut long time.

At last, the words poured forth. "I've been waitin' for this day. Who would've thought the Lord God would send a simple-minded woman to me." He sighed, eyes closing. "But it don't matter, not no more. I'm ready to receive forgiveness."

"I can help you say a prayer," Lavina said, glad that she'd learned how to in the past weeks since attending Rachel's church. "Is that all right?"

There was no hesitation. Bishop Seth nodded his head, the muscles in his jaw relaxing as Lavina looked on him in mercy and kindness, this man who'd shunned her unfairly.

"Lord Jesus, I come to you," she said.

He repeated her words, slowly, purposefully.

"I believe you are the Son of God . . . the only way to the heavenly Father." She paused for him to recite the simple, yet all-important words.

"You died on a cruel cross for my sins, took my place there, and rose up from the dead." While the bishop repeated after her, she inhaled slowly. "It's high time I give up the fight against you, Lord. I won't resist you no more. I repent of all my sins. Take me, Lord, I'm your child . . . your servant from this day forth."

Rosemary was sniffling now, and Lavina wasn"t sure, but she thought the woman might be whisperin' the words right along with her husband.

"I'm askin' for your forgiveness, Lord . . . 'specially those sins of my forefathers, who passed down curses and their consequences on me and my children. Make us free from the sinful patterns of our ancestors, in Jesus' name."

The bishop recited every word without questioning her. Lavina continued her prayer. "I turn my back on the devil and cancel the claims wickedness once had on me. And I ask to be forgiven for Gabe Esh's death, for the evil that I harbored in my heart."

Not only did the bishop say the prayer after her, he cut in and finished it himself. "And, Lord God in heaven, I do ask to be forgiven for the *many* hexes and charms I called forth." He stopped to cough several times. "I pray you'll see fit to forgive me for denyin' the People your truth . . . all these years. And for not livin' up to my own name, Seth, which I understand means 'anointed one.' Jah, I want *your* anointing on me . . . now as I live out my final days."

Lavina held her breath, believin' that the Lord might keep him alive a bit longer because of the witness his life could be. . . .

"Please, Lord, heap blessin' on our bishop where once there was cursin'," Lavina ended the prayer. "In Jesus' name. Amen."

"Amen," Rosemary repeated, then reached over and gripped Lavina's hand. "Oh, dear girl, thank ya for comin' . . . today of all days."

"Thank the *Lord*." She didn't want to go on and on, not really, tellin' the bishop's wife 'bout the divine help she'd been given. She'd just have to let the Lord do His work in Rosemary's life.

The bishop breathed a long ragged breath and looked straight up at Lavina. "I saw the mercy of God's Son, Jesus, in your eyes today, Lavina Troyer. Bless you for coming . . . thou wise and righteous woman."

Lavina felt mighty happy and could hardly wait to share the miraculous account with Rachel. My, my . . . who would've thought?

Soon after, she left for home with Benjamin Zook, who was visibly shaken over the visit to the ailing bishop. He tried to put the blame on her for upsetting the poor man, but she turned a deaf ear to him. No, she wouldn't begin to argue the truth or describe what she'd seen with her own eyes as the bishop was released from the evil spirits that had controlled him for so long. And she didn't wanna spoil things by recountin' the blessed moment just now.

Lavina heard from the bishop's wife, later in the afternoon, that Blue Johnny had shown up at last, though his services "weren't needed . . . or wanted, neither one," Rosemary said when she phoned from an English neighbor's house. "Denki for whatcha did, Lavina. I can't say thank you enough for the miracle that happened between my husband and God today."

"What 'bout you, Rosemary?" Lavina was bold enough to ask. "Did you pray the prayer, too?"

There was a slight pause, then the bishop's wife admitted she had. "I've always followed my husband in whatever he chose to do, ya know, as married couples oughta."

"But you believed it for *yourself*, ain't so?"

"Oh, my . . . more than words can say!"

So Lavina hung up the phone and set about cleaning house and bakin' molasses bread, thanking the Lord for helpin' her lead two dear souls to Himself.

And she knew, without a shadow of doubt, the angels were rejoicin'—twofold—as they wrote down the bishop's and Rosemary's names in the Lamb's Book of Life!

Fourteen

❖ ❖ ❖

A festive tree, decorated with slip-glazed gingerbread figures, stars, hearts, angels, tiny mangers, and white twinkling lights, literally brushed the ceiling with its tip-top sprig.

Philip watched his niece busy herself with the gleeful task of distributing gifts to her parents, grandparents, and Uncle Philip himself. He had felt somewhat obliged to attend the pre-Christmas Eve gathering when his sister called with her "great idea to get the family together before you leave" and sounding nearly breathless with her pleading that he "must come." There was the promise of prime rib and, naturally, the family gift exchange.

And he had come, not so much reluctantly as chagrined that his impromptu travel plans had inspired Janice to throw a last-minute party.

He sat in the corner, nearest the tree, in the lone hand-painted Hitchcock chair, one of the many prized antiques his sister had collected over the years. Gazing about him, he took in the bank of windows to his right, where, in the near distance, a spectacular night view of midtown New York's skyscrapers shimmered against the black sky. Across the room, Janice had decorated a mock mantel, encasing a wide bookcase. On it was a splendid array of evergreen garlands, white candles of varied sizes, ivory roses, and pine cones lightly sprayed with fake snow. Scattered about the room, white poinsettias and fragrant paperwhite narcissus added to the simple, yet elegant, holiday decor. The coffee table, partially covered with a lace doily, was the showcase for dessert—a bundt cake with icing drizzled down the sides and powdery doughnuts to boot. "Homemade," Janice had insisted upon first carrying the silver tray into the room, followed by "oohs and aahs" from Philip's mother, especially. Ken, too, seemed impressed, as did Kari, whose wide eyes told the truth.

The word *homemade* caught Philip off guard, though he should have been prepared, but he wasn't. His thoughts went twirling away to Lancaster County, although Kari's interruption brought him back quickly.

"For you, Uncle Phil." She stood before him, holding a large, rectangular present.

"Thank you." He accepted the gift, then began his usual dramatic shaking of the box, leaning his ear down to determine if there were sounds emerging. "Hmm, *what* could be inside?"

"Not yet." Kari gave him a playful poke.

Philip's mother, sitting prim and proper in her white woolen suit and aqua blue brooch, smiled demurely, eyes shining. Dad, looking fit in his perennial red sweater vest, grinned when Kari handed him the family Bible.

"Time for the Christmas story, Grandpa," she said, recommending Luke's account.

He began to thumb through the pages. "Luke's my favorite, too."

Philip and Janice's father was a small wiry man, yet a "softie," as Kari liked to refer to her grandpa, Howard Bradley, a retired Long Island businessman. But when he read the Bible, the family paid close attention because he read with authority, as well as a semblance of tenderness.

The evening went smoothly as family get-togethers go, and when the slightest fussing about "too much money being spent on your parents this year" commenced from none other than Philip's mother, he rose and excused himself to get some more eggnog in the kitchen.

Janice joined him in a flash. "She makes the same comment every year," she whispered.

Philip poured his eggnog. "It's not important."

She nodded, shrugging. "So . . . when do you leave?"

"In the morning, as soon as I can get out of town."

Janice stepped back to survey her brother, hands on hips. "You're not yourself tonight, and I think you know what I'm talking about."

"Wouldn't have a clue." He made a serious attempt to mask his expression.

She eyed him curiously. "I read your Amish feature last week . . . nice work."

"Thanks."

"C'mon, Phil, there's more to that article than meets the eye. I *know* you."

"You're dreaming." He forced a droll grin and pushed past her, back to the living room and the merrymaking.

"Never been s' happy in all my life," Lavina exclaimed the next morning, bright and early, when she stopped by to visit Rachel. "After I got home from the bishop's yesterday, I hafta admit I felt like kickin' up my heels and dancin' a jig. 'Course, we don't believe in such things, but I felt like it, all the same."

Rachel had to smile at her friend's remark, ever so glad to hear the news of Bishop Seth's glorious conversion. She sat in a chair near the bed, still wearing her bathrobe and slippers. "I believe I prayed so hard for you while you were at the bishop's house that my head actually quit paining me," she said. "It's a miracle."

"That's wonderful-gut news."

"Jah, and just in time to help Mam get ready for Christmas dinner tomorrow, for which I thank the Lord. Mam says Esther and Levi and the children are comin' in from Ohio for a few days. It'll be a fun time for all of us—Annie, too, 'cause all she's talked 'bout here lately are her young cousins from Ohio, and when is she ever gonna get to see them again."

"They'll stay at Leah's?"

"My aunt and uncle wouldn't have it any other way," Rachel replied, excited to see her cousin and family again.

"So . . . sounds like Susanna's having Christmas dinner here this year."

"Jah, but we're all goin' over to Aunt Leah's and Uncle Amos's tonight after supper for hot cocoa and cookies. We'll sit 'round the kitchen, talking 'bout the olden days with all the relatives, prob'ly. One of our Christmas Eve rituals." Rachel enjoyed hearing the old stories, one after another, at such gatherings. Things like hearing how Great-Aunt So-and-So had fun helping her mamma sort potatoes back when, or the first flood of the twentieth century and how they managed to bale water out of the cold cellar, or the time Uncle Samuel heard about "Amish dirt"—as a young boy—and how dumbfounded he was to learn that such dirt held more than six times the water an average no-till field did, due to crop rotation and manure application.

'Course, then again, discussing such farm-related things might not be the best topic for discussion at Christmas. But if she knew Levi and Esther, there'd be plenty talk of farming and reminiscing over their childhood days in Lancaster County.

Remembering—one of the best things 'bout the Christmas season. And she had her own private memories to cherish, though they had nothin' at all to do with Christmas or any other holiday, for that matter. No, her memories of Philip Bradley had not a single connection to the Amish life and heritage.

———

"You did *what?*" Ben said, hurrying to close the bedroom door behind Susanna.

"You heard me right."

He shook his head, coming 'round the side of his plump wife. "Well, what's our Rachel gonna think of such a thing?"

"Ach, she'll be just fine with it." Susanna's eyes flashed with her connivings. "Besides, it's high time she meets someone."

"Well, now, I don't know 'bout that," he insisted, going to the window and looking out. "When's the smithy due over here, anyways?"

"Straight up noon, Christmas Day."

"And you called him?" he said, turning to look at his wife, still skeptical 'bout what she'd gone and done. Without asking his advice, of all things!

"*I* didn't call him."

"But you had a hand in invitin' him?"

Susanna pursed her lips, trying to smother a smile, it seemed. "John Lapp has received an invitation to dinner here." That was all she was gonna say 'bout the stunt she'd pulled. He knew it was, 'cause she flounced off to their private bathroom and locked the door with a resounding thud.

Knowin' there wasn't much he could do now, Ben left Susie to have her little snit if she wanted to. He headed on downstairs to sit and read *The Budget* by the fire. Soon it would be time to leave for Susanna's sister's place. He just hoped Leah's daughter and son-in-law, back home from the Midwest, would mind their manners and watch what they said 'bout their religious beliefs and whatnot. Why, he'd seen enough strange spiritual goings-on since yesterday at the bishop's house. And that thing Lavina did, quoting the "deliverance" Scripture over the bishop, or whatever it was she'd called it, well . . . he wished he'd never agreed to take her over there, causin' such a ruckus she had. Should've asked her what the world she was thinkin', annoying the poor ailin' man thataway.

Far as he was concerned, it was a gut idea to keep things solemn just a bit, seein' as how the People might hafta be laying their bishop in his grave soon, sick as he was.

Copper came bounding into the room just then, wagging his tail like nobody's business. "Well, hullo there, pooch," he said, bending down to pet him. "I 'spect you're lookin' for a nice Christmas treat, and I know of just the thing."

He rose with a grunt and marched out to the kitchen, where he knew Susanna kept tiny bone-shaped doggie biscuits. "There, now, that oughta make ya happy," he said, offering Copper a whole handful, not caring what his wife might say 'bout so many.

———

Philip unpacked his clothes and hung up the shirts and trousers quickly, hoping to discourage wrinkles. He didn't mind touch-up ironing, but only if necessary, and there were more important things on his mind today. Once he was settled in his room at the inn, he planned to make a surprise afternoon visit to Adele Herr. She wouldn't be expecting him until tomorrow evening, but a lady like Adele shouldn't be alone on Christmas Eve without the love of family or close friends. He would see to it that she laughed and enjoyed herself *both* days. After that, he wasn't sure of his game plan. He would trust the Lord to guide his every step. Whether or not his steps led him back to Bird-in-Hand remained to be seen.

The walkway leading to Fairview Nursing Home was trimmed with white lights, and along the porch, boughs of evergreen and an occasional lantern dressed up the outside, offering the warm home-away-from-home atomsphere. An enormous holly wreath, composed of white flowers, fake blueberries, and clusters of cinnamon sticks, provided the initial welcome as Philip pushed open the door.

Inside the foyer area, garlands of evergreen, bedecked with red velvet bows, hung over deep casement windows. A large multiroomed birdhouse made a showcase for colorful glass Christmas balls and was perched on a lamp table near a splendid tree adorned with strands of golden beads and red, white, and gold ornaments.

He heard laughter and muffled talking, and because the receptionist was nowhere in sight, he wandered down the hallway toward the sounds.

Philip spotted Adele first. The dear lady was seated in a chaise lounge, an afghan thrown over her legs. A harpist—a young girl not much more than twelve or so—had just begun "O Holy Night." Standing in the back of the sunny room, Philip folded his arms, listening in rapt attention to the angelic rendition, already glad he'd made the decision to come for the holiday.

When the carol was finished, he applauded with the rest of the patients, and, quite unexpectedly, Adele turned and glanced back at him, almost as if she'd sensed that he was there.

Quickly, he made his way to her. "Merry Christmas, Adele." He stooped down to greet her.

Her smile warmed his heart. "Oh, it's so good to see you again, Philip."

"You're looking well," he replied, accepting a chair from one of the nurses with a nod and a thank-you.

"I'm getting better, and the doctors are amazed." She folded her hands on her lap, grinning up at him.

He was about to make a comment, but a young boy was standing before them, ready to recite a poem. Philip felt as if he were playing hooky from his upcoming assignments, scheduled conference calls, and the like, but sitting here next to his surrogate relative, he felt rejuvenated by the message of the young man's poem and the musical performances that followed.

"What a lovely program," Adele said when it was over.

He agreed. "And to think you have something just as wonderful to look forward to tomorrow evening."

Her eyes brightened. "All I need is right here," she said, reaching for his hand and squeezing it.

Nodding, he continued to sit with her, welcoming her company. For two hours they engaged in animated conversation, talking about whatever Adele wanted to discuss, until supper was brought to her on a tray and he said his good-byes.

"I'll come again tomorrow," he told her, promising to bring "a surprise from the Big Apple."

"Well, what could *that* be?"

"That's *my* line," he said, describing the shenanigans he always pulled for his niece's sake.

"Then you must've celebrated Christmas already with your family."

He admitted that he had. "But the most special part of my Christmas this year is being here with you." Indeed, he'd wondered if this might not be the woman's last celebration of Christ's birth on earth, but as he gazed on her dear face, noting her bright eyes and rosy cheeks, he had a feeling that Adele might fool everyone and live a while longer. And he was elated at the prospect.

Susanna and Benjamin greeted their relatives as they made their way up the snow-swept walk. "*En frehlicher Grischtdaag!*—A Merry Christmas!"

"*S'naemlich zu dich!*—The same to you!" Amos and Leah called out in unison, meeting them with warm hugs and smiles at the kitchen door.

Amos took their wraps and disappeared into the front room with an armload of coats and scarves.

Leah leaned on Susanna's arm, chattering a mile a minute. "Come, have some sand tarts, sugar cookies . . . whatever you like."

Susanna made herself right at home, taste-testing her sister's cherry pudding first thing after they said their "hullos" all 'round, 'specially greeting Esther and Levi and their youngsters.

Leah and her daughter-in-law Lyddie Stoltzfus, along with an elderly aunt—Auntie Ann—on Leah's husband's side, had put a nice spread on the kitchen table, even used all the table leaves to extend it gut and long. 'Course, they wouldn't be sittin' down, but still there was plenty of room for an array of pastries, cookies, and cups of hot cocoa with marshmallows peeking over the tops.

Leah and Amos's married sons and their wives and children had come, and, of course, Sadie Mae and Molly were on hand, whispering and grinning from ear to ear, along with ninety-year-old Auntie Ann. In the middle of the kitchen stood Esther, Levi, and their brood, like they were on display after bein' gone all this time. Esther was just a-huggin' and a-kissin' Rachel and Annie, babbling to beat the band, standing right under a string stretched clear across the width of the kitchen. Little red and green paper bells hung from the string, and Susanna s'posed that Leah's grandchildren had made the decoration or brought it home from school. One or the other.

She decided it best to let them talk as much as they wanted. Get it out of their systems. 'Course, then again, she must be very wise and not let on that she'd listened to one of Esther's tapes late last night. Wouldn't let on one bit. Far as she was concerned, that business 'bout family patterns and sins of ancestors and whatnot was downright ridiculous—for the birds, really. Esther and Levi had gone and gotten themselves caught up in some mighty strange teachings. And she'd already planned to put her foot down if there was the least little bit of talk 'bout Esther and Levi cartin' Rachel and Annie off to Ohio!

Still, while making over her sister's wonderful-gut recipe, she couldn't help but overhear a little of what Esther and Rachel were sayin' to each other. Made her think back to that tape, and a little shiver came over her, recalling some of the Scripture verses. They were passages she'd honestly never heard of ever in her whole life. 'Course, if they were really and truly recorded in God's Word, well, then, she s'posed she oughta be lookin' them up and findin' out for herself. And once Christmas dinner was behind her tomorrow, that's just what she intended to do.

When all was said and done, it was the applesauce nut cookies that won her vote, if there was to be one. And she told Leah so. "I daresay you've outdone yourself, Sister."

Leah grinned, showing her gums, and reached out and hugged Susanna. "Well, if you must say so, then I'll hafta be sayin' Denki for it."

The People weren't big on giving compliments, usually didn't do it at all. Truth be told, Susanna felt mighty odd with all the attention being showered on Esther and Levi. My goodness, they were standin' there in the middle of everything awful long, though Leah and Amos didn't seem to mind a'tall. Prob'ly assumed the evening's visit was for this very purpose, to get reacquainted with their Ohio relatives.

At long last Susanna made a point of catchin' Molly's eye, and going across the kitchen, she stood with the seventeen-year-old girl, Leah's youngest, not too far from where Esther and Rachel were still gabbing up a storm. She whispered that she appreciated the "help" Molly and a certain boy cousin had given while over in Paradise Township not so many days ago. "It was right kind of you."

"Oh, it was nothin' really," Molly said, smiling. "I just hope everything works out tomorrow . . . for Rachel, ya know."

Well, Susanna hoped it more than anyone, but she couldn't be sure how her daughter would take to the outspoken smithy Lapp. 'Least not the way she seemed to be comin' into her own more and more these days. Susanna truly hoped she hadn't stuck her neck out too far, invitin' a near-total stranger for Christmas dinner.

Fifteen

❖ ❖ ❖

Lavina really wanted to take the copies of Gabe's artwork to Adele for a Christmas surprise. She'd even asked Rachel if she wanted to go up to Reading, but Rachel hadn't seemed much interested. 'Least she hadn't responded the way Lavina thought she might, seein' as how she was sure the young woman was sweet on one Philip Bradley. 'Course, it was best to let things happen as they might, in God's way and His time, too . . . if'n the friendship was meant to be at all. Besides, who was to say that Philip would come all the way down from New York City, anyways.

"Mam says we're havin' company from Paradise," Rachel told her, looking worried. "You don't 'spose it's—" She stopped right then, her face drooping.

Lavina gasped upon hearing it. "Don't think it could be the smithy Lapp, do ya? Not unless . . ."

"What?"

"Whoever'd do such a thing? Not your mamma!"

Rachel shook her head in dismay. "You must not know my mother very well, if you're askin' that. She's a conniver, she is. And I surely ain't the first person to tell ya so!"

Lavina thought on that and had to agree that Rachel was right 'bout at least one thing. Jah, Susanna was a schemer, all right. As for invitin' a stranger into the Zook house to share Christmas dinner, well, Lavina didn't have an opinion on that, really. Lots of Amish families had outside guests comin' in on Christmas Day, 'specially. Guess Rachel would just hafta wait and see what happened.

———

Rachel was awful glad to have Esther over for the noon meal. Levi and the children played checkers on the floor in the commons area with Annie—where B&B guests usually spent their time. Not *this* Christmas. It was the first year since they'd had overnight boarders that not a single lodger would be sharing the day or the feast. Rachel wasn't as happy 'bout *that* as she was to have more time with Esther.

The older women, all six of them, helped Mam put the finishing touches on the roasted turkey, stuffed with corn bread, and laid it out in the dining room on the longest platter Mam owned with all the trimmings: mashed potatoes and gravy, buttered homemade noodles, cut sweet corn, lima beans, cabbage slaw, sweet and sour pickles, two kinds of olives, and plenty of celery and carrot sticks. To top off the meal, there'd be enough pumpkin pie for seconds, ice cream, and a variety of cookies. Not to mention the many small dishes of candy and nuts scattered here and there.

Mam had made certain that the younger children—ten of them, including Annie and Joshua, Lizzy's little one—had places in the kitchen. "That way we won't worry who spills what," she'd said as Rachel and Esther worked to set the tables in both the kitchen and the dining room. There would be an overflow area, where folding tables would be used, but every detail of the dinner had been carefully planned, as Mam was known to do.

Only one aspect of the meal was left to be discovered, and Rachel encountered that rather abruptly when the doorbell rang. Just as they were preparing to sit down, she heard Dat's voice as he answered the door, welcoming someone inside.

"It's John Lapp . . . the blacksmith widower," someone whispered, though Rachel couldn't tell who, not for sure.

All she knew was that her stomach was churning and her face felt warm. What had Mam gone and done now?

She made herself scarce, hiding out in the kitchen as Dat went 'round introducing the smithy from Paradise like he was the most important guest under their roof, now that he was here, anyways. She didn't quite know how to act, seein' as how this man had been invited for *her* sake—unbeknownst to her and without her consent.

Was Mam so eager to have her courtin' again that she'd do such a thing? Why, it was beyond her how Mam could've gone and spoiled Christmas dinner for her like this. Now that she thought of it, she almost wished she'd agreed to go to Reading and visit Adele Herr with Lavina, after all. Maybe it wasn't too late for an afternoon visit. . . .

Philip arrived at the nursing home, bearing gifts. "It's looking like Christmas around here," he said, placing two colorful packages on the dresser near the foot of the hospital bed.

"Oh, Philip, what have you done?" Adele was sitting in a chair across from the bed, gazing at the gifts. "Those aren't for me, are they?"

"You and only you." He pulled up a chair and sat facing her, amused at her naiveté and childlike comment.

"What a blessing you are to me."

He thanked her, once again, for the spiritual encouragement she had offered during their months of correspondence. "I've learned so much from you, Adele, and in such a short time." He reached for his New Testament, pulling it out of his sports coat pocket. "I have a Scripture to share with you before you open your gifts."

Adele's eyes closed briefly; then opening them, she dabbed at her face with a tissue, apologizing. "Oh, look at me go on this way. For goodness' sake, it's Christmas morning, and my favorite person is sitting right here."

He reached for her hand. "It's all right, Adele."

She sighed heavily. "My eyes should be void of tears after all these years."

He shook his head, wishing to cheer her. "But they're joyful tears."

"Yes, I believe they are." She was smiling now, motioning for him to read from his Testament. "Don't mind me. I want to hear the verses you've chosen for Jesus' birthday celebration."

Locating the very passage his father had read two nights before, Philip shared the story of the first Christmas from Luke's gospel with the woman who had adopted him as her own, at least in her heart.

After they prayed together, he showed her the book he'd found in the small-scale New York bookstore. "It has an unusual title and topic, don't you agree?"

"Yes . . . yes it does," she said, turning to the back of the book. When she'd finished scanning the copy, she looked up. "*Very* interesting."

"If you'd like to read it, you may. I'd like to have your opinion, as well."

"Oh, I'll read it, all right, but this looks like a book that should be circulated among Plain folk."

He didn't know if she was thinking of any particular community, but one thing led to another, and soon they began to talk about Philip's investigation into conversion disorder.

It was Adele who first brought up the topic. "I've been thinking a lot about your hysteria research . . . with Rachel Yoder in mind."

"There's certainly a lot of information on the subject, and I've brought it with me. I just don't know exactly how to go about getting it to her."

"Keep in mind, Lavina Troyer's a good friend of Rachel," Adele remarked. "She might be able to help."

"I'd thought of Lavina," Philip admitted. "But I don't know her, only know *of* her."

"Well, seems to me, Lavina's a person who can be trusted. And I should know, because I lived in her house a good many years ago."

"True, Lavina might be the best choice. I'd wondered about mailing a packet of information to her, and would even be willing to write a brief letter to explain what I hoped she could do . . . for Rachel's sake."

"So you would ask her to read the contents to Rachel—is that what you're thinking?"

"Would Rachel think it presumptuous of me, sending it through Lavina?"

Adele glanced at the ceiling, then shook her head slowly. "I just don't know how Lavina would manage all those technical terms. But it *would* be a shame if all your work came to naught."

Philip wouldn't come right out and say he'd much prefer to deliver the data in person and discuss some of the ideas with Rachel directly. But how that might come about, he didn't know.

When Adele's turkey dinner arrived on a tray, Philip excused himself to go eat at the inn's dining room, where he was staying. "I'll return in time for the Christmas program this evening," he promised.

"Good idea, Philip, especially since the nurses will insist I have a nap after this sizable meal." She glanced at the generous portion before her and shrugged. "Have you ever seen so much food?"

He didn't have to think too hard to recall the six-course candlelight suppers he'd experienced at the Orchard Guest House B&B last fall. "Eat what you can, but don't overdo it," he suggested. She extended her arm, and he was glad to go to her for a hug. "Will you be all right until I return?"

"Never better. Now, you go enjoy yourself . . . wherever you're bound."

The glint in her eye made him wonder. Did she suspect that he might be headed to Bird-in-Hand for a short visit with Rachel? Did Adele know him *that* well?

————

They were sitting around the fire, tellin' one story after another—the children in the sunroom 'round the corner, playing games and sneakin' cookies—when Benjamin came up with a humdinger of a tale. 'Course, Susanna knew it was every bit true, but it was just so surprisin' to her that her husband would wanna reveal something so personal.

"Back in the days when corn huskin' bees were still goin' on 'round these parts, Susie and I showed up at one of them work frolics—not together, really. We was just gettin' acquainted at the time."

Susanna could feel the heat risin' in her face, and she wondered if it was such a gut idea for Benjamin to be tellin' this one in front of John Lapp, who most definitely had his eye on their Rachel. Why, from the time the womenfolk finished cleaning up the kitchen and joined the menfolk, who'd come into the front room to relax a bit, the smithy Lapp sat across from her daughter, just a-starin'. Truth was, his big brown eyes hardly strayed once since they all finished eatin' and come in here. 'Twasn't that John wasn't a right gut-lookin' fella, even though he was older than Rachel by three or four years, no doubt. He was clearly attracted to her daughter, and Susanna was ever so relieved 'bout that. Appeared as if her plotting might just pay off.

She watched the smithy, careful not to be caught staring. He was a tall, solid man. His dark hair was thinning just a bit on top, but his beard was thick and full, which implied that he'd been married and lost his spouse to death. 'Course, if folks hadn't known of his widower status, they'd be thinkin' he was married, due to the untrimmed beard and, of course, no mustache. The beard was their way of lettin' folks know who was hitched up and who wasn't.

She was gawkin' now, noticing his long fingers and callused hands. John Lapp was a hardworkin' blacksmith and the father of children—how many she didn't rightly know. 'Least if Rachel paired up with him and they eventually wed, little Annie would have herself some step-brothers and sisters, and prob'ly more, too, before long, knowin' how Rachel loved children. Sad thing, though, she'd be losin' her girl to another township if that happened. It was the one thorn in her flesh as she thought 'bout all this.

Benjamin continued his story. "Susie and I'd gone to this here Singin' over near Smoketown, and the older folk had departed for home along 'bout ten o'clock, so we knew it was time for a little pairing off and square dancin' amongst the young people. 'Course I knew that the folk games we often played to the tune of 'Turkey in the Straw' and 'Skip to My Lou'—on a fiddle, guitar, and a mouth organ or two— wasn't really considered dancin' by the Old Order." Ben stopped here and, right in the middle of the tellin', turned and asked John Lapp, "How 'bout your church district over in Paradise?"

"Jah, same as here," John said, nodding his head. "Most of the bishops are sticklers when it comes to any sort of dancin', you know, for the young folk. Same thing with music at them Singin's." He spoke with authority, like he was mighty confident 'bout his answer.

Susanna liked that, but she wondered 'bout his blunt approach. Almost sounded as though he had something to prove. She wasn't sure how that would set with Rachel, her bein' as timid as she was. Most the time, anyways. 'Cept here lately . . .

"Be that as it may," Ben went on, "Susie and I each took a corn shock—same as the other couples there—tryin' to see who could finish shocking their corn first. And wouldn'tcha know, it was *my* girl who found the red ear of corn, put there by the hostess, and she had no choice but to receive a kiss from her partner, which, of course, was me." Ben was glowing. "'Course, you all know who I ended up courtin' and marryin' soon after that."

The group burst out clapping. Even Rachel joined in, though she kept her face down, prob'ly because she didn't know precisely where John Lapp might be seated.

Susanna was startin' to blame herself for the whole setup. She'd clearly made her daughter miserable on Christmas Day. The smithy was no dummy, neither. Her own husband pullin' something like this? Why, she could hardly contain herself.

Straightening herself a bit and taking a few deep breaths, Susanna hoped her husband would start thinkin' of poor Rachel, how she might be feeling along 'bout now. As for John Lapp, she could tell he was a mite embarrassed, too, by the looks of them bright red ears peekin' out from under his brown hair.

Esther, bless her heart, saved the day for both Rachel and the smithy, changing the course of the afternoon. In a clear and strong voice, she led out in a well-known carol, followed by two more. And if anyone had asked Susanna privately, she would've agreed that singing "Joy to the World" and the other songs was a right gut move on her Ohio niece's part.

Jah, 'twas.

After carols were sung and several of Leah's and Susanna's married sons and their families headed back home for milkin' chores, Levi began sharing certain things from his heart. Listening more closely now, Rachel was ever so interested in hearing what Esther's husband had to say. He was explainin' some of the life-changing teachings he and Esther had discovered at their Ohio church, and began to read from the Old Testament book of Deuteronomy. "'Let not your hearts faint, fear not, and do not tremble, neither be ye terrified because of them; for the Lord your God is He that goeth with you, to fight for you against your enemies, to save you.'"

Levi went on to explain that "fear is the opposite of faith," and that "we" must turn away from it in the name of Jesus. "It's time we do spiritual battle against the enemy. But we mustn't shrink back in fear. We must keep our eyes set on the Lord—gaze on Him—as He leads us on to victory."

He was startin' to sound ever so much like a preacher, Rachel thought, and she wondered how her own parents would receive his forceful words . . . on Christmas Day, of all things.

And what of John Lapp? Was he hearin' some of God's Word for the first time, maybe? Honestly, she didn't want to give a second thought to the Paradise widower, not the way her heart beat for Philip Bradley since first meeting him. And, goodness' sake, the way John had dominated the conversation at the dinner table, well, she was right surprised at a stranger coming in and taking over like that, almost as if he was showin' off for the whole lot of them!

Just as she was wonderin' what she'd say if the smithy asked her to go with him somewhere, sometime, the doorbell rang.

"Well, now, who's this?" Dat said and went to the door.

Immediately Rachel recognized the man's voice. Philip had come back. Just like he said he would!

She sat still as anything, trying not to get her hopes up that he'd come to see *her*. No, she oughtn't to be so quick to think such a wonderful-gut thing. Still, her heart pounded with delight.

"Merry Christmas, Mr. Zook," Philip said, standing on the doorstep, his present for Annie tucked under one arm.

Ben eyed the gift. "I'm surprised to see you here . . . again."

"I was in Reading, visiting a friend, and wanted to drop by and wish you folks a Merry Christmas."

"Well, the same to you," Ben said, but he didn't budge an inch or indicate that Philip was welcome inside.

Philip tried but failed to call upon his journalistic skills, those used in interviews and research. "Are, uh, Rachel . . . and Annie at home?" A ludicrous question. Of course, they were home. It was Christmas afternoon! He struggled with what to say, having experienced the same cotton-mouthed situation months ago, when he'd come here the first time.

Ben glanced over his shoulder. "Jah, Rachel's home, but she's entertainin' company just now, and Annie's busy with some of her cousins." The man turned back to face him, eyes narrowed and brow furrowed, nearly hissing through his front teeth. "It's Christmas Day, for goodness' sake."

While Ben admonished him, Philip was able to see past him into the living room, where he spotted Rachel. She was sitting next to a woman about her age, someone who might be a cousin, perhaps, since they looked very much alike, only this woman had darker hair and eyes. But it was the man, a bearded Amishman in his thirties or so, who caught Philip's attention. He sat directly across from Rachel, gazing at her intently, as if awestruck. And understandably so. Rachel's face was aglow with color, and there was something more to it, although he couldn't pinpoint what. Nevertheless, it was obvious the blind woman was the object of *someone's* affection. Even a momentary observation was enough to see that.

"I . . . I guess I made a mistake in coming," he managed to say. "Merry Christmas, Mr. Zook." Philip turned to go, present still in hand, undecided as to whether to leave it or take it back to his car. So disconcerted was he that he had not a thought of what he might've said to Rachel—or little Annie—if he *had* been given the opportunity. And there was the pertinent information on conversion disorder in his briefcase, representing hours of work. . . .

Opening the back door to his car, Philip placed the lone Christmas present inside on the seat. Just as he was standing up to close the door again, he heard someone call out his name. Looking toward the house, he saw that it was Rachel's adorable daughter. "Well, hello there, Annie," he replied.

"You mustn't be goin' just yet, Mister Philip." She was running out the door and down the driveway.

He went around the side of the car to greet her, though he was cautious, touching only her head. "I should've called first, I suppose."

Annie's eyes widened and her mouth dropped open. "Why wouldja wanna do that on Christmas? Nobody calls first before they come. It's just fine to drop by. All the People do that 'round here."

"All the *People*," he echoed, standing up and noticing that both Ben and Susanna were standing in the doorway. "But, you see, I'm not one of the People, Annie."

The child seemed surprised at his remark and shook her head, her little white prayer bonnet slipping back slightly. "I think Mamma'd be ever so glad to see you," she whispered, leaning closer.

"Your mother has company today."

She wrinkled up her nose. "John Lapp, that's all 'tis."

"Oh, *Mister* Lapp, eh?"

"He's lookin' to marry Mamma, but I won't let him."

Chuckling, Philip backed away, thinking he ought to exit the premises before Benjamin came out and bodily shooed him off. "You're a lively one, Annie," he said, wishing there was a way to give her the present he'd purchased for her.

"Wait, you mayn't leave just yet," Annie said.

"Annie!" Susanna was calling from the front door. "Come inside, child. It's much too cold!"

Philip motioned for her to heed her grandmother's warning. The next sound he heard was Rachel's gentle voice. "Annie, dear, you best be comin' inside."

Reaching for the car door, he caught himself just before thoughtlessly waving to the lovely blind woman in the long blue dress and full-length white apron. "Merry Christmas, Rachel!" he called instead, relieved that her parents had moved back into the house.

"Same to you, Philip." She smiled at him from across the front yard. "Can you come in for a bit?"

Could he? That was the reason he'd come—but how was this precarious situation going to work itself out? He thought of the Amish suitor John Lapp and Rachel's crestfallen parents.

Annie reached for his hand and began to pull on him, attempting to bring him back up the driveway. "You hafta come in and sit a spell," the girl said. "You *hafta* . . . it's Christmas!"

"I do?" he teased, thankful for Annie's tenacity. He would get the opportunity to visit with Rachel, after all.

"We got cookies and candy and—"

"Candy? What kind?"

"Come see." And she continued to tug on his hand.

In Philip's entire life, only one other female had ever tried such a tactic with him—his niece, who was equally as spunky as Rachel's young daughter.

Philip's coming was the perfect remedy for gettin' John Lapp out of the house and on his way. 'Course, it was downright awkward, what with both men there in the same room. And no man, 'cept for her dear Jacob, had ever been interested in her back when she was courting age and able to see just fine. The present situation was ever so peculiar, and Rachel was more than relieved when the smithy bade his farewell, not only to her, but to everyone else in the room. Then, before actually leaving, he asked if he might call on her again. "Would that be all right?" he asked, so close that she honestly felt his breath on her face.

Stepping back, she gave him her answer softly, so as not to call attention. "I . . . I'll be thinkin' on it."

"Gut then, I give you a few days."

She didn't say "Thank you" or "Have a nice Christmas" or any such polite thing as he prepared to leave. Truth was, she could hardly wait for him to exit the house. And once he was gone, she wondered what on earth she would do now with Philip Bradley here again, the very man she'd found herself thinking of so often since the day he'd left. If she could've seen the expression on Mam's face, she may have been sheepish, but she was spared that. And Dat did his best to cover his tracks, and he made small talk with Philip, having been a bit aloof at the door. But it was truly Esther and Levi who were most kind.

About the same time as John Lapp left, Aunt Leah and Uncle Amos said they'd best slip out and get on home. And so did each of their married children and spouses and Molly and Sadie Mae, of course, which left only Esther, Levi, and their four children and Annie in the house with Philip and the elder Zooks.

The job of introducing Philip to Esther and Levi fell to Rachel. But Philip had a remarkable way of setting her at ease, once again, and did an excellent job of fillin' Esther and Levi in on his whereabouts, where he'd grown up, why he'd first come to Bird-in-Hand—to do research for a magazine article—and how it was that he'd come to write for a New York magazine called *Family Life*. Things like that.

She wasn't sure how it happened that they got to talking 'bout a book Philip had purchased in New York. Sounded like something she wished her own father might be willin' to read. All about the life of an Amish preacher who'd found himself caught up in age-old practices of powwowing and other occult activities. Philip didn't mention the title of the book, but he was asking if any of them had heard of it or knew the author, and he gave the name.

"Does sound familiar to me," Levi said.

"And it's high time we had someone Plain speaking out 'bout such things in our communities," Esther put in.

Dat was quiet; Mam, too, though she didn't stay put long, excusin' herself to go out and "check on the children," which she gave as her reason for leavin' the room.

"There *was* someone like that—someone who wasn't afraid to speak out against the witchcraft in high places," Philip said. "He lived here in the area a long time ago."

Rachel was worried over what Dat would think. What was Philip going to say 'bout Gabe Esh?

Fear is the opposite of faith. . . .

Just then, Dat cut in. "And that there fella got himself excommunicated and shunned for it, too. We have our ways, and that's that." Then he got up and marched out of the room, making the floor shake as he rumbled past her.

Fear not, and do not tremble. . . .

"I guess I shouldn't have brought *that* up," Philip was saying in an apologetic tone.

"No . . . no, don't be feelin' doubtful," Levi encouraged. "I believe that's one of the reasons these things keep bein' covered up and never discussed. I believe it's the reason we find so many of the People in bondage to darkness . . . to the evil one."

"Why don't I mail the book to you when a friend of mine finishes reading it," Philip offered.

"Jah, do that."

They talked awhile longer, mostly 'bout what they could do to band together in prayer for the community, though Rachel just listened, finding it interesting how very well Philip seemed to fit in with her cousins. In many ways, he was a man her family would approve of. Except for one glaring problem. He wasn't Plain. 'Course, then again, she was gettin' way ahead of herself. It wasn't as if they were courtin' or any such a thing.

All too soon, Philip mentioned that he needed to get back to Reading. "I came to visit Adele Herr for Christmas," he explained.

"Lavina and I were just up to see Adele a week ago Thursday," she offered. "Adele told us 'bout the Christmas program comin' up."

"That's where I'm heading now."

"Will ya tell her Merry Christmas for me?"

He was silent, but only for a second or two. "You could tell her yourself, if you wanted to," Philip said, surprising her completely.

"What . . . what do you mean?"

"Come with me to the program." He didn't wait for her answer, then added, "Adele would be delighted, I'm sure."

Is Philip speaking for himself, too? Rachel wondered, hesitating, not sure how to answer, really. After all, Esther and Levi wouldn't be staying 'round Lancaster for too much longer, and she really wanted to have some personal sharing time with her beloved cousin.

"Sounds like a gut idea to me," Esther chimed in.

"Jah, go ahead and have yourself a nice time," Levi added.

They must approve of Philip, she decided, finding the situation to be rather comical. A fancy New Yorker invitin' an Amish widow—a blind one at that—to a Christmas program at a nursing home, of all things! "Well, if Mam won't mind lookin' after Annie, I 'spose I could go."

"Ach, don't worry over Annie. I'll see to it she gets fed supper and has a gut time with her cousins," Esther offered. "And tomorrow, we'll do some catchin' up, just you and me."

Rachel paused, thinking that it was high time she told Esther what she'd been planning to do. "Uh, tomorrow, I'm lookin' to go to the Crossroad. Sometime after church." She hadn't got up the nerve to tell anyone before now, but she'd thought it through, all the same.

"How will ya get there?" Esther asked, sounding flabbergasted.

"You and Levi will take me, won'tcha?" she said, her voice growing softer, and a lump filling her throat. "I've been waitin' an awful long time."

"What's this all 'bout?" Levi sounded concerned.

"I wanna see again, that's what. I feel I hafta go to the scene of the accident. After all this time, I'm ready to face up to whatever happened there—every last bit." She didn't go on to say that she'd suffered severe headaches due to some of her memory returning. But she was past that and wanted to force herself to remember *everything*.

"Well, now, have ya prayed 'bout this?" Levi asked, sounding more like a father than her cousin's husband.

"Oh, I've prayed like nobody knows. And I believe the Lord's in it—me goin' to that intersection, in a horse and buggy . . . on Second Christmas." She wasn't exactly sure if Philip knew what "Second Christmas" was, but if he'd done a thorough job of researching Plain Christmas customs, he'd surely know that it was merely another day set aside for visitin' and relaxation in Lancaster County. 'Course, when it fell on a Sunday, like this year, the Old Order Amishfolk would have house church. Beachy Amish had church *every* Sunday in celebration of the Resurrection, like most Bible-based churches.

Just then Philip spoke up. "If you wouldn't think it too bold of me, Rachel, I'd be more than happy to accompany you and your cousins to the Crossroad."

Esther seemed to take the decision right away from her. "Jah, I think Philip *should* ride along."

Oddly enough, Rachel didn't resent her cousin for speakin' up that way. Not one iota.

———

Susanna had promised herself she would go and look up certain Scripture verses in the old German Bible once the busy day was behind her. But with Rachel off into the night with that Mister Bradley, she was lookin' after Annie. Esther hadn't stayed, but had given in when Susanna insisted she and Levi go on back to Leah's to bed down the children at their *own* mammi's house.

"Ach, are ya sure?" Esther had asked, indicating she wanted to help with Annie as she'd promised Rachel.

"No . . . no, you go on. There's no need for you to stay up all hours. Besides, who knows when Rachel will be back."

So Esther, Levi, and the children had got their coats on and scurried off, almost as if they'd been pushed out against their will.

Later, Susanna was fit to be tied when Annie started askin' her things like "Why's Mister Philip so awful nice to Mamma?" Those sorts of questions flyin' out of Annie's mouth served to rankle her all the more. And she could scarcely get the little one bathed and into bed fast enough.

"He brought a Christmas present along," Annie said as Susanna pulled up the quilts on the small bed. "I saw it."

"Well, now, I think you must be dreamin'."

"No . . . no, I *saw* some perty paper and a big green and red bow and—"

"Time for prayers now." She cut off the girl's chatter.

Annie blinked her big eyes. "Why don'tcha like Mister Philip?"

Susanna sucked in her breath. "I think you have no idea 'bout that man."

"Well, I think he's just 'bout the nicest I've ever met, Mammi Susanna."

"Your dawdi Ben's a *nice* man." She was desperate to turn the conversation 'round before lights out.

"But Mister Philip is, too."

"Guess I don't know him as well as you seem to."

Annie giggled. "Oh, I know him, all right." And she went on and on 'bout how the tall, smooth-faced Englischer had saved her life from the wasp sting she'd got down by Mill Creek, out behind the house. "He smiles real nice, and Mamma says he's followin' the Lord God heavenly Father. That makes him a gut man, don'tcha think?"

"*I* think you've talked quite enough for one night," she said, getting up and heading for the door.

"I'm sorry, Mammi. Honest, I am. I talk too much sometimes . . . even on Christmas, I 'spose."

"Ach, Annie, just say your silent prayers" was all she could think to sputter before flicking off the light.

Annie said her prayers all right, but they weren't her ordinary prayers. No, she said "prayers from her heart," just the way Mamma had been praying lately.

"Dear Lord Jesus," Annie began. "Please watch over Mamma tonight. Mister Philip, too. And thank you ever so much for bringin' him back for a visit. I'm thinkin' it's the best gift I could've ever had, come Christmas Day."

The Crossroad

Part Three

For, behold, the darkness shall cover the earth,
and gross darkness the people:
but the Lord shall arise upon thee,
and His glory shall be seen upon thee.

—Isaiah 60:2

Sixteen

❖ ❖ ❖

Rachel decided it was real thoughtful of Esther to pack a meal for both her and Philip. She was also completely dumbfounded when Levi had suggested that Philip check in at the Zooks' B&B for the night. "It'll save him from havin' to drive all the way back to Reading tonight." Not only was it surprising, but Philip had actually agreed to the idea, making financial arrangements on the spot with Mam—who was tolerant of the idea—before they ever left the house.

Mam, she was sure, had had a change of heart toward Philip. Possibly toward other things, as she had not lashed out at Esther and Levi when they were talking 'bout their church in Ohio and some of the teachings. She actually wondered if Mam wasn't mellowing somewhat. And if so, it had been a long time comin'!

So once again, Philip would stay temporarily in the southeast guest room—one of their very best. Rachel could hardly believe this was happening! 'Course, she knew better than to get her hopes up that anything would come of this visit. No, she would be foolish to assume such a thing. Philip was a busy man, and though she had no idea what a magazine writer did besides write stories to earn a living, well, she was perty sure he kept a fast pace in New York City.

They rode along in Philip's car, Rachel enjoying the easygoing conversation with this modern fella in the driver's seat. She still got little shivers when he said her name, though she found herself making an effort to shield her heart. She must make herself not care so much!

Together, they ate their sandwiches, then sang along with familiar Christmas carols on the radio. Later Philip said, "I bought a book for Annie . . . a Christmas present. I thought it would be all right."

"Jah, 'tis. And Annie does like her books."

"This one has full-color illustrations . . . set in Amish country," he explained. "It very well could be Lancaster County, though it doesn't say for sure."

"You're very kind," Rachel said, meaning it. Oh, how she meant it, but she guarded her response so as not to let on just how much.

They traveled awhile in complete silence, except for the soft radio music, until Philip spoke. "I don't know how to bring this up . . . wouldn't want you to misunderstand, but I've been doing some research. On your . . . type of blindness." He said it with empathy, almost apologetically.

Rachel felt a sudden rush of warmth to her face and neck. "Then you must be recallin' what my mother said that day on the phone— 'bout her own daughter bein' 'mental.'"

"I think I understand why she may have said that."

"Jah, I've forgiven her. Mam means well." She was eager to know what he'd discovered. "What did you find out . . . from your research, I mean?"

"Many interesting things." He paused for a moment, then continued. "Have you ever thought of talking to a professional, Rachel? For some initial counseling, perhaps?"

She didn't know how befitting it would be to tell him that she'd memorized many Scriptures dealing with divine healing but hadn't thought of counseling much at all. She wasn't sure if she should open herself up to this kind and ever so thoughtful Englischer. "I do happen to have the name of a therapist," she said softly. "From a doctor at Community Hospital."

"Then you've talked with someone?"

"Not a therapist . . . not yet."

Philip didn't speak again for a moment. Then, "What made you decide to go to the Crossroad?"

"I guess I've just been puttin' it off long enough now, that's all."

"But the day after Christmas . . . is there some special reason?"

"Has nothin' to do with it, really."

"This is a big step for you, Rachel."

She thought she might cry, hearing him speak so tenderly, as though he truly cared.

"All I know is I'm standin' on the Word of God. It may sound a bit odd to you, but I believe the Lord's been leadin' me to the Crossroad for a gut long time. My whole life changed there in a split second of

time." She felt a bit more comfortable now, sharing with him the accident story, at least the things she'd begun to remember just in the past
week. How Jacob had been driving the enclosed market wagon, their
precious little children—Aaron and Annie—sitting behind them, playing and cuttin' up a bit. "Honestly, I must've told Aaron to hush several
times, at least," she confessed. "But now, knowin' what I know, that it
was to be the very last day of his dear life, well, I'd give anything if I
could take back those words."

"Your little boy knew you loved him. I'm sure he did."

"Oh jah, he most certainly knew," she said, the strangest feeling
comin' over her now. "I can't change a thing by talking 'bout it, but I
just know it's better for me not to hold all those memories inside any
longer."

"Do you remember what happened?"

"Most everything, jah, except after the car hit the wagon. I don't
remember much at all after that." And she'd told no one 'cept Lavina
the extent of the horrendous pain she'd endured this week—days of
ceaseless headaches, stabbing pain through her skull. With the memories and the acceptance of them, though, the headaches had gone away
completely. At last.

Now she was anticipating the next step on the road to healing. Her
sight must surely return. Oh, she was ever so hopeful!

"I had wanted to be able to share some of the information I
gathered . . . with the possibility that it might help you see again,
Rachel." Philip trod gently, trusting she would understand that his
research was meant to be helpful, not pushy. "I prayed that the Lord
would guide me to know what to do." He went on to tell her he'd
thought of contacting Lavina, sending the materials to her.

"Well, it's a gut thing you came, 'cause Lavina's reading skills are a
bit limited, I must say."

He smiled at her insight. "You're right. I'm glad we could visit." He
sighed, thinking how relaxing it was to be in her company again. Rachel
Yoder was a pure breath of fresh air. She had it all over the erudite
women he worked with, and though they were articulate, witty, and
climbing the success ladder, they lacked Rachel's simple and refreshing
common sense, her ability to perceive the world in an uncomplicated
way. No wonder he'd thought of her off and on all these weeks.

He wondered what Adele would say about his bringing Rachel along to visit her on Christmas night. She was a wise one, his seasoned friend. No doubt she would suspect there was something happening between him and this beautiful Plain woman. But more important than initiating a romantic situation—out of the question entirely—his true goal was to help Rachel accomplish her own objective: regaining her sight. But he wouldn't interfere in her life while doing so. It was a fine line he must walk in his pursuit of Rachel's wholeness and ultimate healing.

So he would. But in the interim, he would continue to pray for God's leading.

Rachel waited in the car while Philip checked out of his room at the Reading inn. She found herself becoming giddy at the thought that they were to share the evening with Adele, enjoying a Christmas program, of all things. She'd always enjoyed music played on instruments but hadn't been much exposed to it in church or 'round the community. Amishfolk relied more on human voices for their music of worship. But to think that she would be hearin' a quartet of stringed instruments with Philip at her side, well, that thought made her as joyful as she'd been in two long years. Jah, she was perty sure this night would be most exciting.

———————

Opening the German family Bible, Susanna read the words she'd first heard on Esther's tape: *Our fathers have sinned, and are not; and we have borne their iniquities.*

Our fathers have sinned. . . .

She paused, thinking 'bout such a Scripture. How could it be that the sins of the fathers were passed down through the family? Through the bloodline?

We have borne their iniquities. . . .

She closed the Bible, wondering. Yet here it was, stated ever so clearly in God's Word. Right there in Lamentations—the Old Testament, of all things. She knew their preachers much preferred to admonish them from the Old Testament. Still, in all her days, she'd never heard a single sermon on any of the verses Esther had talked about on her tape to Rachel. Not one time. And why was that?

'Course, she'd be asking Benjamin 'bout this just as soon as possible. Right now the house was quiet and peaceful, what with Annie asleep and all of Leah's grand-youngsters finally gone, too. Ben would be snorin' up a storm here before long. The thought never crossed her mind to talk to Leah 'bout any of this. No, Leah was actin' awful strange these days. My goodness, for her sister to question the validity of the powwow doctors. Why, it was beyond her what would make Leah say such a thing. She knew better. 'Least, she oughta by now. Leah had lived a gut long time here in Bird-in-Hand, for goodness' sake—same as Susanna. Folks living 'round here had sense to believe in what they'd been taught. Down through the years, comin' straight from their fathers' lips and their grandfathers before them.

The sins of the fathers . . .

The words stuck in her head as she outened the lantern and slipped into bed. Her silent rote prayers seemed awful heavy this night, like stones weighting her down. And she didn't understand why, really, but she began to weep into her feather pillow, wishing she didn't feel this way—not on the night of the celebration of Jesus' birth.

"I do believe the Lord has His guiding hand on that young Englischer, Philip Bradley," Levi said as he and Esther prepared to retire for the night.

"Jah, I feel the same way," Esther replied. "That's the reason I encouraged Rachel to go along with him to Reading."

"I thought so." He paused, weighing his words. "I'm thinkin' it's a gut idea that Philip goes with us over to the Crossroad tomorrow . . . the four of us together."

"Why's that?"

"Let's just be prayerful as we take the horse and buggy down North Ronks Road. The Lord's impressed on me that this trip is necessary for more than Rachel's memory."

"Oh?"

"I believe Philip, too, has a need to make such a journey." He watched as Esther stood at the dresser, brushing her long flowing hair, without the prayer veiling. His wife's hair, thick and dark, was her glory, meant to be shared only with him.

Esther put down the brush and crossed the room to turn down the bed quilts. "I believe something else, too," she said softly.

"What's that, dear?"

"Rachel's falling in love again."

Levi didn't quite know what to make of that. Could be Esther was so in tune to her cousin, so close to her, that she could rightly make such a statement. As for himself, he could only pray that God would guide and direct his wife's blind and widowed cousin. Surely the Lord had a plan for Rachel Yoder's life, as well.

————

Rosemary Fisher sent for her grown children and grandchildren. The great-grandchildren, too. Clear as anything, the bishop was dying, and on Christmas of all things. It was like a blessed sign, and she sat near the bed, whispering a prayer as Seth's eyes fluttered.

"There's something I hafta say, Rosie" came her husband's words. With great effort, he began to reveal the truth behind the many hexes he'd put on folk during his lifetime. But it was Gabe Esh's death that troubled him most.

"Gabriel was one of *us*. . . ." Her dear, dear Seth struggled to breathe. "Mighty cruel . . . I was."

"The Lord God's forgiven you." She touched his brow, beaded with perspiration. "No need to struggle anymore."

He shook his head, making a futile effort to sit up. "I was bent on seeing Gabe dead . . . full up with loathing, I was. Wanted revenge . . . he turned his back on me." Weeping, he continued. "Don'tcha see, Rosie? Gabe never would've died that day, but I . . . I called up the spirits of darkness . . . enchantments against an innocent man."

His tears fell freely as he told, for the first time, how he'd seen a dusky vision of Gabe and a Mennonite friend, riding in a car toward Gordonville. How the accident took place just before the preaching service. "Just as I conjured it up to be."

"Ach, dear, must ya go on so?"

His voice was but a whisper now. "'Twasn't God showin' me them things that night. No, I sold out to the devil."

She listened, gripped by his sorrowful confession.

"And all because of a grudge," he murmured, his eyes pleading pools, searching hers. "Will *you* forgive me, Rosie, for my wicked ways?"

Brushing tears from her eyes, she nodded. "'Course I forgive you, and . . . so will the People."

He gripped her hand. "Tell them for me, will ya?"

Kissing his cheek, she felt his hand go limp in hers. "Jah, they'll hear the truth. I promise ya that."

Then, closing his eyes for the last time, her Seth—the People's bishop—passed through Glory's gate with a smile on his lips.

Seventeen

❖ ❖ ❖

Adele Herr seemed pleasantly surprised to see Rachel again, and Rachel, too, was delighted to spend time with the woman who might've become her great-aunt had Gabe Esh lived . . . and had Adele agreed to marry the young Amishman.

The nursing home Christmas program was unusually enjoyable, and as she sat with Philip and Adele, Rachel found herself wishing the evening might stay young, that it might not end. She was having such a wonderful-gut time here with her friends, even though neither was Plain. Yet it didn't seem to matter. She felt right at home with Philip and Adele because they belonged to the Lord.

After the program of instrumental carols came refreshments. Philip offered to get her some punch and cake, but she had not become accustomed to being waited on, in spite of her disability. So she went with him to the table, accepting his arm to guide her.

Walking slowly together, she recalled his cologne, that subtle scent that had first caught her senses off guard the day they'd strolled together in the cemetery, searching for Gabe Esh's gravestone. She felt now, as she had then, that Philip's coming had given her great courage. The pluck she'd always sought for—her whole life—and had never quite found. It wasn't something as frivolous as the smell of nice cologne on a considerate man—oh no, it was far more than that!

"Would you care for white or chocolate cake?" Philip asked.

She had to smile. He would have no way of knowing that she could *smell* the different choices from where she stood. "Chocolate, please," she said, allowing him to serve her, at least for the moment.

"Mints?"

"Thank you."

They made their way back to Adele, through the crowded room, together. Rachel carried her cake plate in one hand, the other tucked under Philip's strong arm. She'd had oh so many lovely dreams of walking with Philip this way, yet she'd never allowed herself to think twice 'bout ever spending more time with him.

Philip got her situated in a comfortable chair, then excused himself, leaving her alone with Adele, preparing to fill the older woman's order for white cake. "No punch, please," Adele insisted.

He chuckled at the comment. "Surely you'd like something to drink."

"Oh, I'll have my hot tea if there is any—"

"I'll locate some if I have to brew it myself." And Philip was off.

One bite of the chocolate cake, and Rachel recognized it as store-bought. What a difference between her own German sweet chocolate cake and the artificial taste of this one. 'Course, it should not be so surprising, as she sensed that not a stitch of butter had been put in the mixture. In all likelihood, *this* cake was straight out of a box. Still, she wouldn't think of saying so out loud. She could only imagine Mam's sentiments after biting into such a flat and disappointing dessert. She listened to the chatter of the patients in attendance, glad that Adele had, indeed, shared the homemade cookies both Rachel and Lavina had lovingly baked and brought days before.

Adele was content to sit quietly, and Rachel assumed that the older woman was tired from the long day, prob'ly. So she allowed her thoughts to drift back to the days when she was first learnin' to bake alongside her mamma. Amish mothers were bound and determined to pass on domestic skills to their young daughters just as soon as a little girl could hold a measuring spoon right steady. Being close to four years old, often she had to be called in from outside, where she loved to feed the ducks down by the pond. Oh, the happy, noisy creatures were always eager for day-old bread crumbs. They would come right up close to where she and Dawdi David crouched in the tall grass.

"Look-ee there at how hungry they are," her grandfather would say nearly in a whisper.

"What do they eat when we ain't here?" she had asked, peering down at the smallest ducklings.

"Ah, the Lord God heavenly Father watches out for 'um. You don't hafta worry 'bout that."

"But what do they *eat*?" she'd insisted.

"Bugs."

"Where from?"

"Floatin' on the surface of the water." And he'd point, sayin', "You'll see 'um if ya look hard enough."

Rachel scanned the pond, tryin' ever so hard to see the dead flies, mosquitoes, and whatnot. Ach, she hated the thought of the perty little downy ducks havin' to eat such awful-tastin' things as bugs. And she knew just how nasty they were, too, 'cause one of her big brothers had tricked her into eating an ant once. He'd rolled it in sugar, sprinkled cinnamon in his hand, and told her it was candy. But once the sweetness melted away in her mouth, she knew it wasn't no candy.

When she tried to *bapple*—tattle—on her brother, Mamma just shooed her off, back outside to Dawdi, who was always waitin' patiently for her to come and tell her troubles.

Dawdi David Zook was the quietest man she'd ever known, and she figured that's why she liked to feed the ducks with him. He was so silent the ducks came right up close, as if they weren't afraid of either of them—Dawdi or Rachel—neither one.

Till the summer she was ten, Dawdi lived in the *Dawdi Haus*, built on to the main house, after Rachel's grandmother passed on to Glory. And every single day, if it wasn't rainin', he'd gladly hike down to the pond with Rachel. Fact is, they went every day till the day he died.

Every so often he'd come out with what young Rachel decided then and there were wonderful-gut, important words 'bout life. She figured he wouldn't be 'round forever, and he prepared her for his passing by talkin' ever so softly—and joyfully—'bout heaven, "where Jesus is." He once told her that he "sneak-read" his Bible—from cover to cover in less than a year. "But that's my secret," he'd said with a serious look on his old, wrinkled-up face.

She had wondered then why such a thing had to be kept quiet, but she grew up to find out later. The Old Order preachers used select Scripture passages repeatedly, Sunday after Sunday. "Old favorites," Dawdi would say sometimes as he sat in the high grass, a stone's throw from the pond. Seems they didn't want the People reading the whole Bible on their own and tryin' to interpret the passages the way the Mennonites liked to do.

"Jah" was all Rachel would say whenever Dawdi whispered things like that, just enjoying her oldest living relative and the sounds of nature all 'round them.

So the outdoors was the place to be for her when she was but a young girl. Still was, 'cept now she wasn't free to run through the meadowland or the woods as she had when she was sighted. But, Lord willin', that was all 'bout to change. Come tomorrow.

When Philip returned with cake and tea for Adele, he asked Rachel if she'd enjoyed the music.

"It was wonderful-gut, jah."

"The string quartet reminded me of the kind of music there will surely be in heaven," Adele remarked.

"I wouldn't be surprised," Philip said. "But please don't plan on going anytime soon, all right?"

"You don't have to worry about that," Adele said, making a high-pitched clucking sound.

"You're feeling much better, ain't?" Rachel said, knowing it sure as anything.

"Why, yes, I believe I am, dear."

Rachel couldn't be sure, of course, but she thought Philip's eyes were on her just now. She wondered if he would talk more to her 'bout her sight problems on the drive home. Or would they talk of other things, maybe?

As much as she enjoyed visiting here with Adele Herr, she was actually anticipating the drive home, having Philip's attention all to herself. And even though she'd always been taught *not* to crave such attention, she did not think it displeasing to God—the way she felt just now.

Philip was reluctant to leave Rachel in the waiting area, but he wanted to assist the nurse in taking Adele back to her room. And he wished to have a few minutes alone with his dear friend.

"I believe you're fond of Rachel Yoder," Adele said when she was settled into her chair. "I see it in your eyes."

He didn't quite know how to respond. The truth was, Philip didn't know how he felt about Rachel, how he *should* feel. "I think you must be seeing things," he said at last, laughing off her comment.

"Well, I see what I see."

"If I can help Rachel regain her sight, that would be my greatest joy." He didn't reveal to Adele that he had invited himself to ride along in a horse and buggy to the Crossroad tomorrow afternoon. Adele might read too much into it. He was content to say nothing about his plans for the Lord's Day. Second Christmas, as Rachel had called it.

"You can say what you like, Philip, but I wonder if the same thing is happening between you and Rachel as happened with Gabe and me." She paused a moment, then continued. "I don't mean to sound bold, but do pray about Rachel. See what God has in store. Don't make my mistake and miss out on the love of a lifetime."

Adele's words took him by surprise. How she would have perceived any sort of emotional attachment between him and Rachel was puzzling, at best. But then, his own sister had questioned him on various occasions in her curious, off-the-cuff style.

So what *was* it that people sensed in him? His joyful countenance? His increased energy? A spring in his step? All of the above?

Philip had thought he was in love before, years ago, but things were completely different with him at that time. Surely, his feelings for Rachel Yoder were purely friendship, admiration. Nothing more. Certainly nothing on which to build a home.

"I believe you must be mistaken about Rachel," he told Adele.

She smiled a knowing smile, which Philip dismissed, and he began to wind down his visit. "I enjoyed your company very much, Adele. Thanks so much for inviting me."

"You mustn't wait until next Christmas to come again." Her azure eyes were bright with expectation.

"Oh, you'll see me long before that," he promised, taking her hand in both of his. "Shall we pray together?"

She agreed, and he bowed his head, asking the Lord to continue to give her health and strength and many blessings.

Before he could end the prayer, Adele whispered, "And, Lord Jesus, please lead and guide Philip's life and ministry. In Jesus' name. Amen."

She picked up the book *Gifts of Darkness*. "I do intend to read this, beginning tomorrow."

"Good. I'll give you a call in a couple of days."

Nodding, she smiled again. "We'll discuss the book then."

It was difficult to say his final good-bye, even though Philip fully intended to see her again. Soon. There was just something so comfortable about Adele. She seemed to know and understand him better than most of his own relatives.

"Merry Christmas, Philip," she called softly as he stood to go.

"Remember, seek God's will above all else."

God's will above all else . . . Her words followed him as he walked the long hallway, and as he looked ahead to the waiting area, his heart quickened at the sight of Rachel.

Eighteen

❖ ❖ ❖

S usanna's sleep was fitful. She tossed so much she worried she might wake up Benjamin, and that would never do. Slipping out of bed and heading downstairs, she went to sit in the parlor for a bit. She hadn't turned on the hall light, though she knew she oughta, 'specially since Ben was forever warnin' her not to "creep 'round the house at night in the dark." Well, they'd grown up thataway—with little or dim light, at best—so she figured she was used to it. Had only experienced the luxury of electricity for a little more than two years now, 'cause Bishop Seth had permitted it—due to the B&B. She and Ben had agreed it was best to continue with oil lamps in their own private quarters, obeying the bishop on the issue.

'Course, they'd just gotten word that Seth Fisher was dead now—and would be buried soon. She wondered who'd be drawin' the lot to fill his position in the church district. Any number of preachers 'round the area would do. But she hoped it might be God's will for Preacher King to be their new bishop, the man who'd helped them oust Gabe Esh ever so secretly forty long years ago. She couldn't help but think the People would be needin' a grieving period. Seemed only *kluuch*—prudent—that they not replace the bishop too soon, but she, bein' a woman, had no say 'bout such matters whatever.

All the talk in the community just now was that Bishop Seth had gotten salvation two days before Christmas, thanks to Lavina spreadin' the word 'bout it. Only thing was, the People—for the most part—didn't believe it, 'cause it sounded downright fishy. 'Specially comin' from a simple-minded woman. A shunned one at that.

When she'd asked Benjamin 'bout the day he took Lavina over to the Fishers', Ben had clammed right up, lookin' a mite peaked, too.

She'd wondered why and pushed for an answer.

"Ach, don't be so nosy, Susie," he'd chided her.

"I don't mean to be," she'd said softly.

"Well, ya are, and that's all there is to it!"

In spite of Ben's blunt retort, Susanna still s'posed there oughta be someone who knew what had happened while Lavina talked to the bishop on his sickbed. After all, where was Rosemary during all the supposed soul-savin' goings-on? Well, she'd just hafta go over and pay her respects to the bishop's wife before too long. Tomorrow after preachin' service, maybe.

Climbing back up the steps to their bedroom, she thought again of the Scriptures she'd read before retiring. They just kept a-goin' 'round and 'round in her head, and before she slipped under the covers again, she opened the old German Bible to the now-familiar passages. Just then, as she was reading, she thought of Rachel, wondering if she might not be talkin' to Philip Bradley 'bout all the Bible lessons she'd learned from Esther.

Susanna didn't quite know why the thought popped in her head just now, but she had a strange feelin' Philip was gonna be hearing 'bout them verses one way or the other. Why, the way Levi Glick had launched off on his view of Scripture and such things this afternoon— right there in the living room—she had a powerful feeling Rachel would also be sharin' some of the same things.

Here lately, it seemed her daughter couldn't stop talking 'bout the Lord, repentance, and whatnot all. Susanna had truly wanted to put a stop to it in the worst way, but something kept her from confronting Esther like she'd wanted to. Something *else* was keeping her from worrying so awful much 'bout Rachel tonight, too. Truth be told, she didn't know why she hadn't thrown at least a slight fit when Philip wanted to rent a room for the night. Why on earth had she agreed to take his reservation and his money?

What *had* come over her?

———

Before heading south toward the highway, Philip suggested they stop for coffee. "It's still early," he said, opening the car door for Rachel. "Are you hungry?"

"Let's see what's on the menu," she said, taking his arm.

He noticed for the first time that Rachel had come without her walking cane. Had she merely forgotten? Deciding not to inquire, he led her carefully into the restaurant, pointing out each step along the way.

Inside, they followed the receptionist to a table near the back of the restaurant. The woman looked them over rather indiscreetly. Philip supposed they did make an odd-looking couple—Rachel in her cape dress and apron, and he in his dress slacks and sports jacket. But then, how would anyone know for sure that they weren't simply brother and sister? The "brother" having left the Fold of the People—or never joined—and the "sister" . . . well, it was quite obvious where her church loyalties stood.

They sat facing each other in a padded tan booth. Philip leaned back, inhaling slowly as he studied the woman across the table. "I think it's time we had a real supper," he offered.

"I'm not *that* hungry," she replied, smiling.

"I suppose not, after cake and punch."

"And Esther's turkey sandwiches earlier," she reminded him.

"You'll have to tell Esther thank you."

She smiled unexpectedly. "You can tell her if you like. Remember, we'll all be goin' to the Crossroad tomorrow."

Philip wouldn't risk saying that he'd nearly forgotten the plans to ride in a horse and buggy, accompanying Rachel and her Ohio cousins to the busy intersection.

"Are you sure you're ready to go to the Crossroad, Rachel? I mean, do you feel comfortable with the thought?"

She blinked her eyes several times before she answered, almost as if trying to see him. "I believe I'm ready for whatever the Lord wants me to experience," she said softly.

Rachel's face was lovely and smooth; even without makeup she was truly beautiful. Eyebrows perfectly arched, cheekbones well formed, and lips . . . He stopped his analysis there. "I'll pray that the Crossroad will bring you the healing you long for."

"That's just what I've been asking the Lord to do. I believe He will heal me . . . tomorrow!" she whispered emphatically.

Such faith he had never witnessed. Rachel literally glowed with anticipation, and he felt, for a moment, that he, too, was catching her vision of hope. "More than anything, I wish that for you."

"Denki," she said, nodding her head sweetly.

And it was then he noticed again the gentle curl of her hair, where a strand or two had sprung free at her neck.

He almost told her how pretty she looked in the vibrant blue dress and white apron—Sunday attire, he supposed—instead of the gray and black mourning clothes he'd become accustomed to seeing her wear. But he caught himself, coming to his senses just as the waitress arrived at their table, bringing two water glasses and a fistful of clean utensils. "I'm very sorry, Miss," he said, begging for more time. "The lady and I haven't even looked at the menu yet."

The waitress glanced at them, offering the same shrewd smile that Adele had given him earlier. "I'll come back in a few minutes."

"I appreciate it," he said, realizing his mouth had suddenly become dry. He reached for his glass of water just as Rachel put her hand out, seeking her own glass. Without thinking how Rachel might react, he touched her hand lightly, guiding it.

"Oh!" Her face flushed instantly.

He wished to slow his heart, wished he could think more clearly. Could it be that Adele's assessment was correct? Was he actually fond of the blind widow before him? "Annie, uh . . . how's your little girl?" he blurted the ridiculous transition.

"Ach, a happy one, she is" came the sweet, yet baffled reply.

Each time Rachel answered, he attempted to think what her vernacular style reminded him of—aside from the initial conversations of the past fall—since first he'd met the reticent young Amishwoman. It was unlike any dialect he'd ever encountered anywhere. Except, perhaps, the "village talk" he'd come across during his school vacations spent in an isolated sector of southern Vermont. There he had listened in on a few old codgers, tottering friends of his grandpap. Folk who sat in ancient rocking chairs, watching the sun go down from their paint-peeled porches, sipping iced tea. Every summer night without fail. "Tip-top entertainment, yes, indeedy," one old gentleman had lisped through missing teeth, in regard to the sunset. Philip had never forgotten.

"Will Annie attend school next year?" he asked, shaking off thoughts of New England.

Rachel nodded. "She missed going this year by a few months, but I think she'll be ready come next fall."

"What a wonderful little girl."

"Jah, and she likes you, *Mister* Philip."

They laughed together, which broke the ice even more. And that was an excellent thing, he decided, because the way things had been going for the past few minutes, he was beginning to wonder if stopping off here for a bite was a mistake. Perhaps, talking while driving toward Lancaster might've been a better choice for them. But the truth was, he felt drawn to Rachel and wanted to get to know her better.

Shifting to his journalistic mode, he asked if she'd mind answering a question or two about the Plain life. "I know from the things Adele Herr shared about Gabe, there were one-room schoolhouses for the Amish children back in the sixties. Is that still the case?"

"Jah, they go through eighth grade."

"Then what, after that?"

She cocked her head as if recalling a distant memory. "Most of the boys work alongside their fathers, same as the girls do. We go back home to our mammas, learnin' how to can and quilt and keep house— that is, if we didn't already know how by that time."

"And if you did already know those things, what then?"

"There's ever so much to know 'bout woman's duties."

"Then are you saying that women and men have specific chores? That men, for instance, wouldn't clean or cook?"

Rachel actually giggled. "Not to laugh at you, but no, they wouldn't think of doin' our work. The men know what's expected of them; so do the women."

"And just what *is* expected of an Amishman?" He was aware of his own voice, that he was speaking much softer now, and he leaned forward, his elbows on the table, peering into Rachel's lovely face.

"Outside work," she replied. "A young boy is trained to work with his father and older brothers in the barn, the tobacco shed, the fields. That way, when the time comes for him to finish up with book-learnin', he can help farm the land or help his pop in the woodworkin' business or blacksmithing."

When she mentioned blacksmithing, he noticed she raised her eyebrows awkwardly, then shook her head as if she wished she hadn't alluded to that particular job. "What is it, Rachel?"

"Oh my." She looked positively flustered. "I don't know what came over me just now—bringin' up the job of a smithy and all."

"Because of John Lapp's visit?"

She put her hand to her throat. "Himmel! I'd never want to go anywhere with that man!" she confessed, spilling the words out like he'd never known her to do. "He is overbearing and outspoken. And Mam should've never invited him for Christmas dinner, for goodness' sake!"

"Your mother did?"

She folded her hands on the table in front of her. "It's our way. We often ask folk in at Christmas. But ever since I quit wearin' my mourning clothes, Mam has made it her duty to try 'n match me up with someone."

"Why is that so annoying?"

"I'm a grown woman. I can go 'bout my life without help from Mam."

"This must bother you a great deal." He could see from the frown on her face that it did.

"Jah, ever so much." Rachel sighed, then continued. "It's not such a carefree thing to be a young widow in the Amish community. People talk; they hope to put widowers together with younger women who've lost their husbands. All for bearin' more babies—future church members—especially the Old Order folk feel that way."

"So . . . the more children born, the better?"

"That's right."

The waitress was heading their way again, and they still had not looked over the menu. "What's your special tonight?" he asked the woman in the pale green waitress outfit.

"It's our Christmas special—chicken and dumplings" was the quick reply. "Would you care for that?"

"Does that sound good to you?" he asked Rachel.

She nodded her head bashfully, her eyes cast down, and Philip ordered the same. "With black coffee, please."

"I'll stick with water to drink," Rachel said.

Quickly, they resumed their conversation, and Philip was amazed that they'd fallen into the same comfortable dialogue they had experienced last fall on their drive home from the Reading cemetery. How was it that a young Amishwoman and a modern journalist could have this kind of rapport? How? He didn't understand in the least, but he knew it was a reality. Their spirits had found communion. Yes, he preferred that far better than the secular terminology of "soul-mates." More suitable for two people who loved the Lord and wanted, above all things, to serve and honor Him.

"Tell me 'bout the information you brought for me," Rachel said out of the blue. "On my blindness."

He was quite surprised, but pleased, that she had inquired about it and began to recount the information to the best of his ability. More than ever, he believed Rachel was ready to receive the help she surely needed.

During the drive back to Bird-in-Hand, Rachel explained for Philip what "ach" meant. He said he'd heard the word used often while in the Lancaster area and was curious.

"It just means 'oh!'—that's all."

"Oh."

"No . . . *ach*." He laughed at that, and she honestly didn't know what came over her to joke with him that way. 'Course she would never say she felt homelike with him. Prob'ly didn't need to, now that she thought 'bout it.

They fell to talkin' of less serious things. He wanted to know if she ever visited with Emma at the antique store in Bird-in-Hand village.

"Every so often Mam goes there to look at Emma's new items, but it's been a while now since I've gone. Why do you ask?"

"I've been thinking that I might order a desk, something similar to the one in the guest room where I'll be staying again."

"It's a nice piece," she said, though she'd never laid eyes on it, only dusted its pigeonholes. "Mam's mighty glad to have it."

"I can see why."

"Jah, it's a gut place to hide a postcard, right?" Again, they laughed together, and his chuckle was ever so joyful.

Their talk soon turned to Esther and Levi. "Wonderful people," Philip remarked. "Any chance they might return to the Lancaster area?"

"Funny you ask, 'cause I've been wishin' they'd come back. But I think it's out of the question. They've got the land they've always wanted in Holmes County," she explained. "And they waited an awful long time for it." She went on to say that one of her heart's desires was to farm again. "It goes without sayin' that we Amish have a cravin' for the soil." Unexpectedly, she thought of a comment her Jacob had often made—that he was born with dirt under his fingernails.

Philip said, "My grandpap on my father's side owned a large amount of acreage in southern Vermont, near the Battenkill River—the most beautiful place on earth, I thought as a boy. Grandpap built a summer cottage there, surrounded by trees and vegetable gardens. Whenever I go there, even now, it's a little foretaste of heaven. So I think I know what you mean."

Rachel had to smile at his comment. Something else they had in common, it seemed. "I don't know why, but I believe someday Annie and I will work the land again. But only the dear Lord knows how that's gonna come about."

"Trusting God for His plan isn't easy, is it?"

A little surprised at his question, she answered softly, "Lavina says to 'wait patiently for Him,' and, believe me, I'm learnin' to do just that. Every day of my life since I lost half of my family at the Crossroad."

"I can't imagine what you've gone through."

"You mustn't feel sorry for me," she was quick to say. "I don't seek pity."

"You've been courageous, Rachel."

His voice was tender just now, and she wished for all the world she could have one glimpse of his face. Surely he was a handsome man. Annie had said as much. Told her repeatedly, in fact.

"I've been meaning to ask you something," she said, eager to change the subject, get the focus off herself. "And if ya think I'm pryin', just say so, but I'm interested in hearing 'bout your preparations for the ministry. Adele mentioned to Lavina and me that you felt the Lord callin' you."

"I believe He is, but that's where trust comes in." Philip sighed, taking his time. "I'm praying daily for guidance."

"Does that mean you're not so happy with your writing job? At the magazine?"

"That may be too long a story for this particular night. Perhaps, though, we could have dinner together again before I leave?"

He was asking her to go with him somewhere, yet again! Oh, she wanted to say "Jah" without a bit of hesitation but knew it was best not to. "I don't know. I believe I oughta concentrate on first things first— the Crossroad . . . tomorrow."

Philip was quiet for the longest time, and she worried that she'd offended him. When he spoke, his words were gentle, yet somewhat disquieting.

"Your vision is more important than anything, Rachel. I wouldn't think of distracting you from that."

"No . . . no, I understand. Honest, I do."

"After the Crossroad, we can decide about having dinner or not."

She felt helpless to give a worthwhile answer, so she kept her peace. Best not to lead him on, anyways. What made her think that a man like

Philip would ever be content for long with a friend with such obvious . . . limitations?

Long past ten o'clock, Susanna awoke from a hair-raisin' dream. She sat straight up in bed, wiping the perspiration from her brow, attempting to catch her breath, which had been perty near snuffed out in the middle of all the nightmarish confusion. She'd dreamt the most peculiar thing, and its murky undercurrent was still pulling at her, even in her wakefulness. Blue Johnny and the newly deceased bishop, Seth Fisher, had been talkin' to her. The bishop was sending a warning from the grave, and Blue Johnny was trying to block it, rebuffing every word Seth Fisher was shouting out. There was screamin' and rantin'—all comin' from an angry Blue Johnny—worse than any nightmare she could've ever imagined.

She'd heard folks say that there was sometimes a meaning in a dream like this, but she daresn't think such a thing. No, 'cause she had a powerful-strong feelin' she knew just what the meaning was. Jah, she did. The bishop *had* found salvation, full and free—'least in the dream, he had—just like Lavina was spreading 'round amongst the People, but Blue Johnny was madder'n a hornet 'bout it. That's why he'd kept a-hollerin' to drown out the things the bishop was tryin' to say.

For the third time this night, Susanna crept out from under the bed quilts. This time she fell to her knees, clasping her hands in fervent prayer. "Lord God Almighty," she began, "if any of what I've read in the Bible tonight concerns me and the sins of my fathers, if any of it oughta be confessed and renounced, as my daughter keeps sayin', well, then, O Most High, I ask you to show me what to do. Amen."

She s'posed it was all right to talk that way to the Lord God heavenly Father, 'specially if no one was 'round, listenin' in on important things a body had to say.

Rachel felt sure she could trust her feelings for Philip, that she knew who he was deep inside, even after only a few visits with him. She also thought she understood what made him tick, so to speak, and that he was trustworthy as the day was long. Why else would she have allowed herself to be alone with an outsider on two separate occasions? Yet she could not grasp a sound reason why they had been brought together.

Did God intend them to be more than accidental friends?

Rachel knew she'd best cast the matter into God's hands. Let Him work things out. So she lay awake, long after talking to the Lord 'bout Philip Bradley and all that had taken place this Christmas Day. She thought 'bout John Lapp wantin' a bride younger than himself to bear him more children. And she sighed into the night, wonderin' what it would be like to be married again to someone of God's choosing. To someone as dear to her as the handsome blond husband she'd married at eighteen.

It was nigh unto impossible to think of the cocksure smithy that way. And as much as she liked Philip, she was ever so hesitant to consider an Englischer when it came to marriage. Yet beneath his "fancy" layers—speech patterns, intellect, and his perception of the world—she thought she saw glimmers of yearning. A longing for a more simple life. She saw it in the questions he asked, the way he drew her out. Besides all that, his patience seemed to have no end. And he had the ability to reassure her. She truly liked him for everything that set him apart from John Lapp. He was the sort of man her family would have smiled on had he been born into the Amish community—the thoughtful farm boy down Beechdale Road or Maple Avenue, harvestin' corn and baling hay along with his pop and brothers.

Oh, she knew his spirit, knew it through and through. Jah, with Philip she could see ahead to the future, her confidence being handed over to her, the doors of timidity cracking open and swinging wide at long last. Sun-filled days, a spread of land burstin' with crops, ponds a-plenty, and woodlands to run through at dawn. The Lord's name to be praised together with a man set on servin' Him, too. These were the things she wanted most out of life. Nay, needed.

But would Philip have understood these late-night thoughts of hers had she been able to put them into words? Prob'ly not. Still, she knew, deep within her spirit, Philip Bradley was a God-fearing man, full of faith. And he was ever so kind and playful with Annie. A right gut father he'd make! But would she be willing to go "fancy" for him?

Before she drifted off to sleep, she thought again 'bout what Philip had shared with her—therapeutic ideas, grief groups, and whatnot. All the information he had so kindly brought for her to consider. Yet she felt the Lord was prompting her to have the church elders pray over her, first and foremost. Emotional healing had been hanging in the balance far too long; her ability to see was bound up in it. She was ever so sure of that. It was time she mustered up the courage to follow through with biblical teaching, found in the book of James.

Come tomorrow, after the preachin' service, she would ask to be anointed with oil in the name of the Lord Jesus.

Nineteen

❖ ❖ ❖

The tiny gap, where Annie's front baby tooth had once been, caught Philip's attention as he helped the young girl and her mother into his car the next morning. He had offered to drive them to church during the course of breakfast, much to the unspoken astonishment of Rachel's parents. It seemed they, too, had church plans. But Susanna was quick to make the distinction between what she viewed as the wayward Beachy Amish and the Old Order. "*We* haven't forsaken the assembly and tradition of our forefathers," she'd said, eyes flashing. "We attend *house* church."

"Whose turn is it to have Preachin', then?" Rachel asked, diverting the subject almost effortlessly. Or so it seemed.

"Thomas and Mary Beiler," Susanna replied, then turning to Philip, she kindly explained. "That's my oldest living sister and her husband."

"And Thomas ain't no doubter neither," Benjamin piped up, bringing the conflict back into play. He was dressed for the day, wearing a pressed white shirt, tan suspenders, black broadfall trousers, and vest— "for gut" clothes—or so he'd said when first Philip was seated at the dining room table.

"Thomas is an upstanding Amishman," Susanna added, and it almost seemed as though they were united in an attempt to make a point. For Rachel's sake?

Rachel, who was sipping her coffee, did not so much as crack a smile. Philip assumed she was contemplating her visit to the Crossroad, this long-awaited day of days. Observing her more closely, he saw that she was pensive, even prayerful. He reached for his juice glass, recalling how, last evening, his hand had innocently guided hers to the water glass. Their first dinner alone. No matter what happened, he would

Nineteen

❖ ❖ ❖

T he tiny gap, where Annie's front baby tooth had once been, caught Philip's attention as he helped the young girl and her mother into his car the next morning. He had offered to drive them to church during the course of breakfast, much to the unspoken astonishment of Rachel's parents. It seemed they, too, had church plans. But Susanna was quick to make the distinction between what she viewed as the wayward Beachy Amish and the Old Order. "*We* haven't forsaken the assembly and tradition of our forefathers," she'd said, eyes flashing. "We attend *house* church."

"Whose turn is it to have Preachin', then?" Rachel asked, diverting the subject almost effortlessly. Or so it seemed.

"Thomas and Mary Beiler," Susanna replied, then turning to Philip, she kindly explained. "That's my oldest living sister and her husband."

"And Thomas ain't no doubter neither," Benjamin piped up, bringing the conflict back into play. He was dressed for the day, wearing a pressed white shirt, tan suspenders, black broadfall trousers, and vest— "for gut" clothes—or so he'd said when first Philip was seated at the dining room table.

"Thomas is an upstanding Amishman," Susanna added, and it almost seemed as though they were united in an attempt to make a point. For Rachel's sake?

Rachel, who was sipping her coffee, did not so much as crack a smile. Philip assumed she was contemplating her visit to the Crossroad, this long-awaited day of days. Observing her more closely, he saw that she was pensive, even prayerful. He reached for his juice glass, recalling how, last evening, his hand had innocently guided hers to the water glass. Their first dinner alone. No matter what happened, he would fondly remember that Christmas night.

Singing from the hymnbook at the Beachy Amish Church was somewhat similar to his own church, with the exception of the fact that each hymn was sung without musical accompaniment. Even so, Philip, who shared the hymnal with Levi Glick, found the harmonious, full sound of human voices entirely refreshing. He was glad, too, that Levi and his wife had chosen this house of worship today. A visitor in "secular" attire, he might have felt even more conspicuous sitting with the Plain men in their conservative dark coats and trousers had it not been for Levi, who welcomed him with a warm smile and friendly manners, putting Philip completely at ease.

In the middle of "O, for a Thousand Tongues," he happened to glimpse Rachel and Annie, sitting toward the front with an older woman, whom he assumed was Lavina Troyer, as well as Esther Glick and her two little girls. All the women and young children sat on the left side of the church aisle, the women in modest cape dresses—blues, purples, and greens—and white prayer veilings, as was their custom.

Verse five of the hymn was especially meaningful as he blended his voice joyfully with Levi's and the men around him.

> Hear Him, ye deaf; His praise, ye dumb,
> Your loosened tongues employ;
> Ye blind, behold your Savior, come;
> And leap, ye lame, for joy.

Philip contemplated Rachel's intended trip to the Crossroad, as she called it. During his short stay in Bird-in-Hand, he had become familiar with the junction of North Ronks Road and Route 340. In fact, on several occasions he had passed through on the main highway, noticing a line-up of horses and buggies at the red light. He'd thought it a wise and sensible move, installing a traffic light at that particular intersection. But to think that Rachel and her young family had experienced a fatal accident there was more than he cared to ponder. No wonder Rachel and Annie had been traumatized these many months. No wonder it had taken so long for the young widow to bring herself to this day. What courage—with God's help—she would have to muster to revisit the scene of the accident, sight or no, that had so altered her life! He would offer whatever support he could, though his guess was that Levi and Esther would be the key proponents. Yet he was going along. Had actually volunteered. And Rachel seemed altogether pleased.

During the last hymn, Rachel felt her faith rise up powerful-strong. *Ye blind, behold your Savior, come . . .*

She could scarcely wait for the church elders to pray for her. This was her day of deliverance. She believed it with all her might!

The pastor took his place behind a simple wooden pulpit immediately following the passing of the offering plate. There was no special Christmas music, no wreaths or decorations. Plain and off-white, the walls were devoid of crosses or pictures of Christ. A single small chandelier hung in the center of the aisle, offering sufficient light. The windows were clear, no stained glass here.

A gentle rustle of pages turning came as soon as the minister announced his sermon text. Philip, too, located the Scripture passage, a bit surprised that its focus was divine healing. He wondered if perhaps Rachel had had recent pastoral counsel, inspiring such a sermon topic the day after Christmas. Or was it that the pastor knew of Rachel's plan to visit the Crossroad this day?

He found himself paying close attention, yet, at the same time, wanting to be in an attitude of prayer. Philip concentrated on God's great mercy in sending Jesus as divine provision for the healing of mankind—accomplished by the beating Christ suffered prior to His death on the cross. Praying silently, he believed that this would indeed be Rachel's day of restoration.

Along with Rachel, several other church members met the elders and pastor in the altar area after the service. Philip stood in the back of the sanctuary with Levi and his four children, waiting without speaking for both Rachel and Esther to join them.

The elders anointed Rachel with oil, and Philip bowed his head, as well. *Lord Jesus, please give your child the desire of her heart . . . today, if it be your will*, he prayed silently.

After the elders' prayers, Rachel fully expected to be able to see, but when her sight did not return immediately, she felt she wanted to go straight to the Crossroad, postponing the noon meal "for just a short time," she told Esther and Levi in the church parking lot. "Would it be all right if we go now?"

Graciously, Lavina Troyer offered to stay at the church with the children, including Annie. Levi agreed to drive his in-laws' horse and buggy over to North Ronks Road and down to the Crossroad. As planned, Esther and Philip went along. Rachel's cousin guided her carefully across the driveway and into the enclosed carriage.

It was Levi who suggested that she sit in the second seat with Philip, behind him and Esther. She was taken aback by his insistence, yet she didn't question, doing as he requested. Surely, Levi wasn't in favor of encouraging her friendship with an outsider. Surely, he had her best interest at heart—sitting in the second seat was a way to cushion her a bit from the stark realities, maybe. From the return of memories that surely lay ahead.

By agreeing to go on this ride, Philip realized he was putting himself at risk, as documented in recent newspapers. Due to increased population and drivers impatient with slow-moving carriages on busy thoroughfares, more and more wrecks were occurring in Lancaster County. So here he sat, in a dilapidated old buggy, next to an attractive young woman, who was determined to see her way past the pain. Beyond the agony of the Crossroad.

Levi, their experienced driver—all the way from Ohio for Christmas—tapped the reins gently, and the horse pulled the carriage forward, out of the church parking lot and onto a two-lane road. If someone had told Philip—his sister, for instance—that he would spend the day after Christmas in such a peculiar manner, he would not have believed it. Yet he had volunteered only yesterday to go along on this, Rachel's journey to healing. The fact that he was here, hoping for the very best—praying too—meant that he must care more than he had let on to anyone. Most of all, himself.

———

Susanna waited till Rosie Fisher was alone to approach her 'bout what was on her mind. She offered her sympathy, then said, "Nobody seems to know, for sure and for certain, 'cept maybe Lavina, so I'll just up and ask ya. What happened the other day . . . at your place?"

"Well, *I* know 'cause I was there, but I don't rightly understand what happened, not really," Rosemary told her after Preachin' service at the Beilers'. "All's I know is Seth whispered to me that he wanted to hear what Lavina Troyer had to say. He didn't want me or anyone else to keep her from speakin' whatever was on her heart. And he said something else to me, too."

"What's that?" Susanna was all ears.

"Seth said the Lord God had prepared his heart for her visit."

"Well, I'll be," Susanna said, heading with Rosemary to the kitchen to help set up for the common meal. "If I hadn't heard it from you, I'd hafta say I wouldn't believe it a'tall."

The elderly woman nodded, her eyes shining. "I wisht you could've been there to see it for yourself. My husband's face was just a-glowin'."

"Where was Benjamin during all this?" She had to ask. Had to know what on earth went on that her husband hadn't witnessed any of what Rosemary was a-sayin'. Or wanted to forget, maybe.

"I daresay, if Ben didn't up and leave the room like a scared 'possum."

"Why, do ya think?"

"Well, a kind of glory come in and filled up the place."

Susanna didn't know what to make of this. "A *glory*, you say?"

"Jah, come right in and sent the evil a-spinnin' out."

"Evil?"

"Twistin' and a-turnin' right out of Seth. I saw it with my own eyes. He coughed and sneezed nigh unto thirty times."

"But what *evil*?" Susanna insisted.

"Them curses . . . all the years of hexin' and enchantments, that's what. My Seth got clear free of the powwowin', too, surprisin' as that might seem."

Susanna gasped. "What did you say?"

"The 'knowin' gifts' got prayed right out of him by your husband's shunned cousin. It was mighty surprisin'."

Susanna thought on that. Lavina castin' out wickedness? Why did Bishop Seth need such a deliverance as that? What was *wrong* with pow-wowing? The more she mulled over what Rosemary had just said, the more one certain Scripture came to mind. *Our fathers have sinned, and are not; and we have borne their iniquities.*

Was that verse the explanation for the bishop's need? Could it be? Well, now that she thought on it, she wished she *had* been on hand—at Seth Fisher's bedside—that day. She would've been downright interested to see what shunned Lavina had witnessed with her simple eyes and childlike understandin'.

She decided she'd be listenin' to Esther's tape yet again.

Snow-laden wheat fields met them on either side of the narrow road. In some places, large patches of frosted grass showed through, reminding Philip that one day, months from now, the pastureland would spring to life once again. The density of the snow and ice weighed down certain enormous tree branches as the horse pulled the buggy and its passengers down North Ronks Road. Philip began to wonder if Rachel were able to see the snowscape encompassing them, if she might not have associated the ice and heavy snow with her own personal state. That she, too, had been burdened with a ponderous mass.

Because Rachel was so silent, sitting next to him, he chose to accommodate her obvious need for quietude. Doing so, he created a mental picture—the best-case scenario for Rachel—that her sight would indeed be restored. Her life would return to normal, and the mission he'd hoped to accomplish would be fulfilled. He would go back to New York, proceed with his pursuit of Bible study and fellowship with the Christian businessmen of his community, and continue asking God for direction. He could throw himself back into his writing, even accept an occasional free-lance assignment.

Rachel, on the other hand, was sure to have many more opportunities to remarry. She wouldn't have to settle for the outspoken smithy from Paradise Township, after all. Even better, Annie would have a sighted mother once again!

God's will above all else . . .

"Why'd Mamma and her cousins and Mister Philip hafta go off without us?" Annie asked Lavina as they stood in the vestibule of the Beachy Church.

"Well, now, girlie, I think your mamma already explained that," she told the little girl with bright eyes.

"But how's goin' to the Crossroad gonna help Mamma see again?"

"Jah, I wanna know, too," asked young Ada, Annie's second cousin.

She wondered what more she oughta tell the children. Seemed Rachel had done a right gut job of sayin' what should be said. She sighed, wonderin' what she'd got herself into, offerin' to stay with the five little ones. "Sometimes a body's just gotta go back and see what's in the past . . . for their own selves," she said simply.

"But if Mamma can't see," Annie said, "how's she gonna do that?"

"Jah, Rachel's blind," James added. "Been that way for over two years now." And Mary and Elijah were shaking their wee heads in unison.

"I'd hafta say if God wanted Rachel to go in a buggy to the Crossroad, well, then, who are we to question that?"

That quieted them down, and Lavina went in search of a Sunday school lesson to read to her young charges. She'd have to sit them on the floor and pretend to be their teacher, something she'd always admired 'bout her old friend, Adele Herr. That's just what she'd do till Rachel and the others returned, and Rachel's sight was back to normal. Leastways, she'd be hopin' and prayin' for the dear girl. . . .

The morning had been breezy and cold when Philip first had awakened, the wind coming out of the north with a few flurries. But now a stillness fell over the region, gray and gentle, as if they in the buggy were nestled in the eye of a storm, protected from future fury; far enough removed, almost to be convinced that the storm did not exist at all.

His thoughts turned to Adele and her discerning reply to one of his recent letters, written before leaving New York. He had unburdened his soul, sharing his personal and professional concerns for the future.

I'm delighted to know that you are relying on God's help with your "fork in the road," she had said in her letter.

He didn't exactly know why her reply had continued to make such an impact on him. Was it because he had come to believe, as did Adele, that she had made an irrevocable life error? That she had missed God's will for her life forty long years ago? He cringed anew each time he recalled Adele's account of her refusal. Gabe's earnest love had gone unheeded; she'd broken the young Amishman's heart, rejecting his marriage proposal.

The four of them rode in unbroken stillness. He presumed Levi and Esther had immersed themselves in intercessory prayer on behalf of Rachel's healing. He, in turn, asked the Lord for divine help during and after the possibly traumatic journey they were embarking on, searching his own heart as he did.

As he opened his eyes, the wind began to blow again, pushing back the clouds. All at once the landscape and the road ahead were bathed in radiant light. Liquid gold spilled across the snow-packed road ahead, flowing across field and stream, casting a bold sheen over every farmhouse and barn as far as the eye could see. But most interesting was the effect the sudden burst of sunlight had on Rachel.

"The sun's just come out, ain't?" she whispered, leaning close to him.

Turning, he was amazed at what he saw. Her lovely face was wet with tears. "Yes, Rachel, the sun *is* shining," he said, trying to compose himself.

The noonday sun was ablaze in the sky, and he took for granted that he should have felt subconscious warmth. But beneath the layers of his fur-lined topcoat, Philip shivered.

Twenty

❖ ❖ ❖

Rachel kept her eyes closed, seized by the radiance around her, thinking that it might vanish. *Heart, you must not fear!* she commanded her timid spirit, recalling the verses in the Old Testament. *For the Lord your God is He that goeth with you. . . .*

Taking several slow, deep breaths, she asked the Lord to give her an abundance of courage for what she might remember, and that she would not be afraid to see again. *Please, dear Lord Jesus, help me get through to the other side*, she prayed silently. *To the other side of the Crossroad.*

Unexpectedly, a thought came to her—the term given the dangerous intersection had another meaning. 'Least for her, it did. The Crossroad could also mean the *road* to the Cross. Why she'd never thought of it, she didn't honestly know. The path to the Cross was ever so excruciating for the dear Savior. A grievance no one should ever have to endure, yet He chose to walk the way of it. Surely then, He would understand and see her through this day. Jesus himself would carry her to the brink of her memories, through the horrific visions she'd repressed and rejected. She pictured in her mind the Lord gathering her up, blind and tormented, into His own strong arms.

Brushing tears away, she fixed her heart on the painful journey the Lord had called her to. And she allowed herself to think back to the very day of the accident.

Two long years ago . . .

———

The day had been exceptionally hot for mid-June. But there was a breeze, which helped circulate precious little air through the enclosed market wagon. Jacob hurried the horse toward North Ronks Road. She was a bit on edge 'bout taking the shortcut to market, but Jacob reassured her that it was the best way "to make gut time." They'd gotten a late start, and she blamed herself for sleeping past the alarm, causin' this rushing 'round in the first place.

Leaning her head on Jacob's strong shoulder, she closed her eyes, enjoying the sounds of birds, crickets, and the cadence of the horse's hooves on the road. There was the humming sound of a windmill, too, and an occasional passing horse and carriage. In back, Aaron and Annie played happily.

In her hand, she clutched a letter, one she'd written the night before. It was to Esther, her close cousin, transplanted to Ohio from Bird-in-Hand, Pennsylvania.

———

"We're comin' up on the intersection," Esther said from the front seat. "Thought you should know."

"How much farther?" Rachel asked, her heart in her throat.

Levi answered. "A quarter mile or so."

She tried to settle back, cautiously thinking through—step by step—the events leading up to the accident, aware of Philip's presence. Yet she felt as if she might be floating through space and time, knowing full well she was conscious.

———

"Look at Dat's handmade toy trains and helicopters!" young Aaron was saying as they rumbled toward the Crossroad.

Jacob joked with his son, and right then the wind plucked the letter out of her hand. Sent it flying through the window. She told Jacob she'd get it "right quick," which she did. Jumped out while the traffic light was still red and chased the letter across the field.

When she retrieved it, she turned in horror to see the mare rearin' up, carrying on like their driving horse had never, ever done before. Jacob was struggling, trying to control the spooked creature. Oh, it was the most frightening thing she'd ever witnessed, and she felt her very breath go out of her lungs. And then the horse charged forward into a stream of traffic.

Just now, reliving the dreadful events, she fought her way through it, clawing her way out of what seemed like a long black tunnel. She agonized anew over not being able to locate her little children, their bodies surely wracked by pain, in shock. Searching, tripping over debris in the road, she kept callin' out their names, stumbling over Jacob's hand-made toys and the mutilated pieces of what had once been their market wagon.

A flash of light! Suddenly, Rachel remembered something sub-merged so deep in the recesses of her soul—ever so precious a mem-ory—one she'd lost, repressed with all the others.

She was kneeling on the hot blacktop, on the road, cradling Jacob in her arms. He was breathing, and she was oh so glad for that. He began to stir, looking up, his eyes fluttering open as he struggled against full sunlight.

"Rachel . . . I see the Lord Jesus . . . His arms are open wide . . . for *me*." Pausing, he breathed a ragged sigh, then coughed, wincing with the effort. "Heaven's here, radiant and bright . . . ach, it's so beautiful."

His eyes closed slowly, and she could feel the life draining from him. "Oh, Jacob," she whimpered, "I love you so. Please live. Stay with us. Please, don't give up."

Yet, in the stillness, as her husband lay dying, Rachel felt utter peace. Like a divine balm of Gilead, drenching her, warming and sooth-ing her very soul. She longed to linger in its indescribable glow, letting the amazing feeling flow over her. Jacob, her beloved, was going home to heaven right here in her arms.

The sweet reality filled her spirit, soul, and body. In that moment, she felt sure that nothing could ever move her again in such a profound way. She wanted to stay here for always, holding her husband just a handclasp from eternity. So close to that glorious hereafter, promised to all those who belong to the Lord. Heaven's door was near, at least for that one instant, and the glimpse of it was precious beyond words.

Her peace was short-lived as a crush of sounds flew at her—foot-steps, whispers—and hot, dense air flurried 'bout her as Jacob fell limp against her.

"Step back," someone commanded, and she felt an opening in the wall of commotion.

————

"Rachel . . . it's over," Philip said, reaching for her hand. "You've passed the Crossroad . . . to the other side." He could not go on, so filled with emotion was he. He continued to cradle her fragile hand in both of his, gently stroking, offering whatever comfort he could.

Esther turned around in the front seat, her hand reaching out for

Rachel's free one. "It's all behind you now, dear Cousin. The Lord is with you."

"Where are we?" Rachel murmured, tears spilling down her cheeks.

"Just south of the Crossroad, on Ronks Road," Esther explained. "Levi pulled off the road when you started to cry. We'll stay put here till you're ready to go again."

"You just say the word," Levi spoke up.

"I feel I hafta tell all of you what happened just now," Rachel began.

And the memories poured forth from her as if pent up for a lifetime. But it was the account she gave of her husband's heavenly homegoing that touched Philip most.

Rachel made several futile attempts to control herself, to make the tears stop. It didn't help that in spite of her faith-filled prayers, the return of her memory, and the striving she had felt in her spirit, she was still blind. Oh, there were the murky and occasional bursts of light at the end of the darkness, but as for seeing clearly, well, she simply couldn't. And she was ever so glad that neither Philip nor her cousins were asking her 'bout that.

Truth be told, she had come out on the other side in one piece, and yet there was only the gloom of reality. Jacob and Aaron were still in their graves, buried in the Amish cemetery on the hill. She was still a widow with only one of her children left living. No hope for a love like she'd had with dear Jacob Yoder.

No hope . . .

She began to sob in deepest despair, her body trembling with the truth she'd had to face. She covered her eyes with both hands, letting go of both Esther's and Philip's handclasp. Then she felt Philip draw her near as the horse and carriage continued down the road—away from the Crossroad. She gave way to his gentle touch, scarcely aware that her head had come to rest on his shoulder or that he whispered soothing words. In her grief, she also mourned the fact that Philip would be leaving soon, returning to his own world, where she did not belong.

"Your vision is more important than anything," Philip had said last evening. *More important . . .*

The memory of those words drowned out his compassion now. The carriage clattered onto Lynwood Road, heading toward the direction of the church. The long way back . . .

Lavina had read through all the Sunday school lessons and was makin' an effort to sing "Jesus Loves Me" on key when Annie asked where her mamma was. "I'm gettin' awful hungry," she said.

"Me too," young Ada added.

"My tummy's gonna cave in," Mary said, getting poked by her brother.

Lavina figured it shouldn't be too much longer now. "Let's count to one hundred in Dutch, and maybe they'll be back."

Elijah tried his best, but the four-year-old was havin' a hard time, mixing up the numbers. It reminded her of how troublesome counting had been for her back when she was a schoolgirl. "You'll hafta count along with your big brother," she suggested, knowin' how awful bad he felt.

He nodded and the other children were eager to help him. But it was Annie who seemed most distracted. She was clearly worried 'bout her mamma.

And now, as she thought on it, Lavina was, too.

Twenty-One

❖ ❖ ❖

I can't tell you how glad I am to have that ride over," Rachel told Esther in the privacy of her bedroom. "It was ever so frightenin', but I know now that I blocked out the most beautiful memory of all, right along with the horrifying ones."

"Jacob's homegoing?" asked Esther.

She nodded. "I just don't know how I could've rejected such an experience."

"Well, your heart was breakin', that could be why. Go easy on yourself, dear one."

"S'pose I oughta."

"Maybe the Lord saved this special memory just for today . . . when you most needed to remember," Esther said softly. "Ain't it true that God gave you Jacob for a short time, only to take him out of this present life to be with Him? I've thought so often since the accident that surely there was a lesson in it . . . for all of us, maybe."

"And I think I know now what that lesson might be."

Esther was silent, and Rachel reached for her cousin's hand as the women sat on the bed. "The lesson I believe the Lord would have me learn is not to take life's blessings for granted. The morning we drove to market for the last time, Jacob even said that we always miss what we don't have. I had to learn the hard way, I guess. Every single day's a gift from God."

"The Lord's grace is abundant . . . new every morning," Esther replied.

"And even though my sight hasn't yet returned, I still have hope that it will . . . in God's perfect time." Rachel truly wanted to believe it, fightin' hard against the hopeless feelings inside.

They sat quietly in the stillness of the bedroom, where both Rachel's large bed and Annie's little one had been neatly made with homemade quilts and Rachel's crocheted afghans.

"Wouldja like to talk about Philip?" Esther surprised her by saying. "A special young man, he is. Levi's very impressed with him . . . thinks he must surely have a call of God on his life."

Rachel thought on that. "But why should we talk 'bout him?"

"'Cause God's call is on *your* life, too, Rachel."

"I . . . I just don't know what you're tryin' to say, bringin' Philip Bradley up this way." Honestly, her mouth turned dry as cotton.

"Don't be shy 'bout prayin' for Philip, that's all. Could be that God has a plan for your lives . . . together."

She wondered if her feelings for Philip had begun to show. If that was why Esther had brought up the subject. She daresn't ask. Not even Esther must discover *this* secret.

Philip was enthusiastic to spend time with Levi. The house seemed nearly uninhabited at the present time, even though he knew the Glick children and Annie were off playing in the sunroom. He knew, too, that Rachel and Esther had disappeared upstairs. A good thing, presumably, what with Rachel's emotional state by trip's end.

They'd had a sumptuous dinner of baked turkey and ham, mashed potatoes and gravy, along with a number of side vegetable dishes, "wonderful-gut leftovers from Christmas dinner," Esther had said. It was amazing how she'd single-handedly whipped together such a meal while Rachel was resting.

The fact that Ben and Susanna were away from the house—having a meal with other Old Order church members—meant that Levi and Philip could talk more freely. And with the food cleared away and the kitchen cleaned up, he and Levi had the front room to themselves.

"I'd hoped to help Rachel regain her sight by coming," he ventured, specifying the information he'd discussed with Rachel. "Clearly, her sight hasn't returned, and I wonder if she might benefit from a Christian counselor, or even a secular therapist who has experience with such cases."

"Maybe." Levi smiled sympathetically.

"Do you know of anyone locally?"

"Well, I know that Rachel talked with her pastor's wife on several occasions."

"Is there a grief group she might join, as well?"

Levi frowned. "I don't know if she needs a group like that, really. Seems to me she's moved past her heartache over Jacob and Aaron."

Philip didn't press for an explanation but trusted the man's opinion. It was hard not to. Integrity emanated from Levi. "I hope I didn't stick my neck out with Rachel, sharing some of the materials I gleaned. I even went so far as to tell her about discussions I had with several New York psychotherapists."

"Well, how'd she take it?"

"Fine . . . just fine. But I hope she understands that I came to help . . . not to cause her confusion."

Levi eyed him curiously. "*Just* to help, is that it?"

He shrugged, uncertain of what to say.

"I think there may be more to it, Philip."

How Levi Glick, whom he had met only yesterday, seemed to know and understand Philip's personal struggle, he did not know.

The Lord's Day was turnin' off right nice as Susanna and Benjamin rode home from Preachin' service. Now it was much lighter, what with the sun shinin' bright and hard against a backdrop of snow and ice, nearly blinding. The road ran downhill past farmland, now dormant for the winter, and gently sloping yards of one Amish neighbor after another.

Susanna wondered how things had gone for Rachel, going in a buggy to the Crossroad, of all things. First time in well over two years. Well, her girl was in right gut company, so to speak. 'Least there was plenty of them, seein' as how Philip Bradley had gone, too, along with Esther and Levi.

She thought it best not to bring up the matter to Ben just yet. He'd been right quiet the past few days. Still, she'd been itchin' to talk to him 'bout Rosemary's account of the "deliverance" that had supposedly occurred at Seth Fisher's.

Susanna knew she oughta pick her conflicts carefully, this one weighin' mighty heavy on her mind. So she tilled the soil for discussion, hoping Ben wouldn't put up too much of a fuss. "Rosemary told me 'bout the bishop's change of heart before he died," she opened the subject. "Thought maybe you and I oughta be talkin' 'bout it, too."

"That's all well and gut, but I have nothin' to add."

"But you saw what she saw, didn'tcha?"

"'Twasn't a perty sight, Susie, I'm tellin' you."

"Well, the bishop told Rosemary that the Lord had been preparin' him for Lavina's visit. Now . . . what do ya think of that?"

Ben's eyebrows arched high and long over his eyes. "You don't mean it."

"That's what she said."

"Well, I'll be . . ."

Not permitting a delay in their conversation, she pushed onward. "Rosemary truly believes the bishop got salvation that day—and she did, too, she says . . . all thanks to Lavina's prayin' over them."

"Could be," Ben said.

"She's a true and brave soul, Lavina."

Ben nodded, his eyes beginning to glisten. "Maybe more than us all."

Whatever that meant, Susanna didn't much know. But she had a feelin' that her husband had made up his mind—had formed an honest opinion—of what went on at the Fishers' place. She was almost sure of it.

Benjamin looked weary from the long day, so she must leave off bein' overbearing. Quickly, Susanna dropped the matter with nary another word. Later, when her husband was well rested, she'd fish some more.

———

Philip was right about his hunch. Rachel *was* discouraged, and it was a wise move to invite her on a short walk to Mill Creek beyond the house. The same location where he had first realized that Rachel could not see. He'd gone that day to soak up some sun. In the midst of flaming autumn colors, he had crouched near the stream that ran across the Zooks' property, tossing twigs into the water. He hadn't forgotten how beautiful the young woman was, standing there on the footbridge that spanned the banks, with little Annie guiding her mother's every step.

Now it was *his* turn to lead the gentle lady whose cheeks were already pink from the cold, even though she was wrapped in a long black shawl and wearing her winter bonnet. "We won't be gone too long," he said, his eyes on the snowy path ahead. "I thought a short walk would do us both good." He didn't go on to say, "After your ordeal today." Instead, he added, "Actually, it's a nice excuse for us to have some time alone."

Philip noticed that she smiled at his comment, and it gave him the nerve to continue. The weather also served to brighten things a bit, though he knew Rachel could not see the brilliance of the sun as they walked, her arm in his.

"I've been thinking . . . I want to offer to make arrangements for you to see a doctor. There are several I know in New York, and with some help from my brother-in-law, I think we could pull some strings and get you in quickly."

She didn't respond or react to his gesture.

"I'm willing to do anything to help you. I could even take you back to New York with me, but you'll want to think about it, no doubt. And pray."

"I don't hafta think *or* pray," she said softly as they made the turn toward the footbridge. "New York City is your world. I have no desire to leave here."

He had assumed that she might turn him down, and no wonder. How would an Amishwoman—blind at that—manage in the middle of bustling Manhattan? He could hardly imagine her there.

"It was just a thought" was all he said.

"I appreciate the offer, Philip. It's awful kind of you."

Awful kind . . .

Was he? If he were truly kind, he might tell her how wonderful he thought she was. How very lovely. That her sweet and joyful spirit shone through her every action, word, and deed.

Yet if he said those things, he was unsure as to where they might lead. The truth of the matter was he did not know how to make the leap "back in time," so to speak, from modern life to the Plain. Even if he knew that he loved Rachel enough to marry her, even then he did not know if her feelings for him were the same.

They came to the highest point of the small bridge, and turning, they leaned on the railing. He peered down at the frozen layers of ice, though he could hear the current continuing its flow far beneath the surface.

"Tell me what you see," Rachel whispered near him.

"Sunlight and snow. And stark black tree trunks intermingled with tall evergreens."

"Are there birds?"

"A few crows here and there."

She sighed. "Come spring, this area is filled with birds, making nests and raisin' their young. . . ."

He allowed that thought to linger in the stillness between them, not daring to spoil the moment with a reply.

But Rachel had asked him to paint word pictures for her now. And so he continued. "The sky is as blue as a still clear pond. And the clouds are like cotton balls looming in the distance, which means it might be partly cloudy tomorrow."

She snickered. "You ain't a weather forecaster, are you?"

"That's one thing I'm not. Ask me about deadlines, political interviews, assigned columns, and revisions, but don't ask me about the weather."

"Funniest thing."

He glanced at her and saw that she was grinning. Rachel Yoder had a subtle sense of humor, and he laughed right out loud. "I'm going to miss this place," he declared, thinking that he could've gone one step further and said that he would miss her, too.

Everything had been going along just fine—even the weather was holdin' out—until Philip said what he did 'bout missing "this place." Once again, she wondered if he was trying to dodge the strong undercurrent between them. After all, if she felt it, surely he did, too. Yet, she couldn't be sure how such things worked between a man and woman, really. She'd been courted by only one man in her life. And that man was now with Jesus.

She wouldn't allow Philip's aloof comment to get her down. Fact was, he'd invited her to go walking. Just the two of them. And sometime here soon, it was up to her to give him an answer 'bout whether or not they should have dinner together. Uncertain how she should go about bringing the subject up, she let him keep describing the sky, the fields, and the neighbor's barn.

"You know, Rachel," he was saying, "I believe it was Esther's letter that spared your life the day of the accident . . . by blowing out of the wagon."

"I guess you're right, though I've never quite thought of it that way."

"God kept you alive for a reason, I believe."

She smiled. "Esther's always said that. So has Mam. But back then, it was much easier for me to wish the Lord had seen fit to take me to heaven, too."

"I understand why you might've felt that way," Philip replied. "But now that you've come this far, I pray that you'll accept the fact that God continues to be at work in your life."

That was the dearest thing he might've said to her. 'Specially today. "I fully intend to see again," she told him.

"I believe you will, too, and I won't stop praying for your healing till you do."

She thought it was interesting—his sayin' such a thing. Did he mean to keep in touch with her?

"Regaining your sight is very important to me."

There, he'd said it again. So . . . his interest in her as a person, sighted or not, had *not* brought him back to Bird-in-Hand. For sure and for certain, he had come out of sympathy. Pure and simple.

"I gave my heart to Jesus a long time ago," she said, feeling the need to say so. "It was right before Jacob and I married, and since then I've been learnin' that we can't always understand God's timing. So when you say that my sight is important, well, I know it's ever so much more important to God."

It was one of the most courageous statements she'd ever made. In fact, she actually believed she was becoming a mighty confident woman, the way she'd always wanted to be.

―――――

Susanna was fully aware that her daughter had gone out for a walk with Philip, but she wondered what on earth was taking them so long. Goodness' sake, they'd been gone twenty minutes or more. Still, the idea of the two of them together didn't get her goat near like it might've when Philip had first come here.

No, she was thinkin' more and more that she just might be able to turn him till he came 'round right, smack dab into their Plain community. 'Course, she had no idea what Benjamin would think of such a thing, havin' a fancy-turned-Plain son-in-law and all. But it wouldn't hurt none to ask him. Then again, she guessed she'd best wait to find out from Rachel if there was any hint of romance in the air.

Besides, she wanted to hear more from Ben 'bout the bishop's soul-savin' experience. Seemed to her if it was gut enough for the old bishop, maybe she—*they*—oughta consider it, too. She could hardly wait for her husband to wake up from his afternoon nap.

Their walk to the creek was coming to an end. Rachel could hear the sounds of the house—Copper yippin' in the yard, people moving 'round inside.

"Have you given any thought to having dinner with me?" Philip asked.

"When must you leave?" she asked, holding tight to his arm as they walked back toward the house.

"Tomorrow morning. I have several assignments due for the magazine, and some aren't even under way." He paused, and they strolled in silence for a moment. "I was thinking we could go somewhere quiet this evening, if you'd like."

She didn't really want to prolong the agony of parting, yet how on earth could she turn this wonderful man away? "That would be real nice, havin' dinner with you," she said at last.

"I'll call for reservations." There was genuine relief in his voice.

Still, she wished he didn't have to leave tomorrow. Or at all.

Twenty-Two

❖ ❖ ❖

Their dinner was a quiet affair at the historic Strasburg Inn in the colonial-style Washington House Restaurant. Elegantly appointed, the dining room was warm and inviting, resplendent in soft candlelight. Philip had requested a private table upon calling in the reservation and was pleased when he and Rachel were shown to a table in front of a draped window, made even more intimate by the crackling flames in the fireplace across the room.

"It's perfect," he told the hostess. "Thank you."

"Enjoy your evening," she said with a professional air and a smile. No impolite sidelong glances here.

"Lancaster County is one of the friendliest places I've visited," Philip said as they were seated.

Rachel smiled and nodded across the starched white tablecloth. "I'm not surprised. Lots of us here are God-fearin' folk. Maybe that's the reason. Pennsylvania got its start with people lookin' for a place to settle and worship God in their own way."

He hadn't thought of that. "I remember studying about William Penn in school. He was a devout Quaker who founded this state and made a colony for his fellow church members."

"And anyone else who wanted to join. You have a gut memory, I must say."

"Well, you know how it is. Certain things seem to stand out." Looking into her innocent face, sweetly aglow with candlelight, he realized anew that coming to Lancaster County and meeting Rachel would always be high on *his* list of "certain things."

Rachel was ever so curious. Halfway through dinner, Philip began asking repeated questions 'bout the Plain life. Was he actually thinkin' of joining conservative circles? Oh, she couldn't permit herself to think such thoughts, even if they were true. Couldn't let herself be hurt by hopin' for a future with Philip.

Still, she listened intently, then answered to the best of her ability, all the while enjoying the wonderful-gut dinner, as delicious as any she'd ever eaten in any restaurant. Her only regret was that she wasn't able to see the lovely surroundings, which Philip described so carefully, or . . . Philip himself.

What if she could see his face, smiling at her across the table? What then? Would she see God's Spirit shinin' out through his eyes?

Just then, he reached for her hand. "I really do want to keep in touch with you, Rachel."

Philip's voice and the caress of his hand made her heart leap up, and she knew she cared far too much. Oh my, ever so much! Tomorrow Philip would be leaving for New York. His home. She daresn't let on how she felt. Wouldn't be wise.

Rachel knew well the feeling of apprehension, and she was experiencing it now. "Wouldja mind orderin' me some coffee?" she said in a wisp of a voice, gently pulling her hand away.

Susanna stood outside the door to her daughter's room, deciding if she should knock or not. It was nearly too late to bother Rachel. She might even wake up Annie. Still, she *had* to talk to Rachel before she retired for the night.

"I hafta confess somethin' to ya," she whispered when Rachel opened the door a crack.

"What is it, Mam?"

"Please, will ya come downstairs?" Susanna stood in the hallway, waiting for Rachel to put on her slippers. Then she shone the lantern on the stairs as they made their way to the parlor.

"Is everything all right?" Rachel asked, frowning as she sat on the sofa.

"Oh, jah, everything's just fine . . . now 'tis." She wanted to cry and laugh all at once. But first she had to tell her daughter what had happened. "Your pop and I had ourselves a long, long talk tonight—with Esther and Levi. Right after you and Philip left, Dat opened up and told 'bout Bishop Seth's salvation. How he'd seen God's power reach down and deliver our leader on the bishop's sick bed."

"Dat said all that?"

Susanna put her hand on her chest, taking a deep breath before going on. "Seth was one of the main reasons the powwow doctoring has been goin' so strong in the community all these years. But I ain't telling you nothin' new."

"Mam, you sound awful excited," Rachel blurted. "How can this be?"

"I'll tell ya how." Susanna stopped to catch her breath again, so caught up with emotion was she. "Ach, I feel so wonderful-gut just now—washed clean through. I've been waitin' for you to come home so I could tell you what Dat said."

Rachel seemed eager to hear, sitting quietly with her hands folded in her lap.

"You know how you've been tellin' me, off and on, that the sins of the fathers are passed down to the third and fourth generation?"

"The Bible says so . . . wasn't me, so much."

"No . . . no, and that's all right. Dat and I talked things out right gut, and I hafta say that several days ago, I listened to one of them tapes Esther sent you. Borrowed it from your room and played it . . . several times over." She didn't wait for Rachel to reply, just kept a-goin' forward with what she had to get out before she might burst. "I wanna be ready for heaven like Bishop Seth. I wanna know my sins are forgiven, too . . . here on earth."

"Mamma?"

"Jah, you heard me right. I wanna be ready when Jesus comes back to catch His Bride away. Want my heart pure and clean, without any spot of sin."

"Oh, Mam, what are ya tellin' me?"

"That Dat said, 'We've been hearing 'bout salvation full and free our whole life long—from either Gabriel Esh or some Mennonite somewheres. So we ain't gettin' any younger, Susie. We should've turned our lives 'round back when we shunned young Gabe.'"

"Dat said that?"

"Every word. Then we prayed with Esther and Levi, followin' all the things they said to do—repenting of the known sins of powwowing and enchantment amongst our ancestors on both sides. Our *own* sins, too. Then we renounced the sins, and, ach, what rejoicing came over us both."

"Oh, thank the good Lord," Rachel whispered, leaning toward her, reaching for her hand. "Mamma, this is one of the happiest days of my life."

Susanna scooted over next to her daughter, and they fell into each other's arms, weeping for joy.

Rachel wanted to let the beautiful reality of the moment sink in. She certainly didn't want to think 'bout what lay ahead for her parents. They'd be shunned, sure as anything, if they spoke out, revealing to the People the things that had happened this night. 'Course, it would depend on the new bishop and the church membership, too. But the fact that Rosemary—the bishop's widow—had also received the gift of salvation, along with her husband, stood for quite a lot.

Here Rachel had hoped to be able to have her sight back by day's end. Instead, she was hearin' of the Light of God's truth shining into the very lives of her Old Order parents. *This* healing miracle, in the light of eternity, was far more important than her longed-for sight.

Many thoughts whirled through her mind as she stood near her bed. Too wide awake to sleep, she relived the evening with Philip, how he'd held her hand across the table, offered to "keep in touch," asked almost too many questions 'bout life in Amish country, and reminded her that "faith takes courage."

She realized anew how Philip's coming—Esther's too—had shown her just how much God must love her in spite of her blind state, that He invites each and every person to "see" through salvation by grace.

She pondered the divine work begun in her life, and her family's, on account of both Esther's tapes and Adele Herr's story of Gabe Esh. And her thoughts flew back to the very moment this afternoon when she recalled dear Jacob dying in her arms. How full of God's love he had been. How very precious the death of God's children . . .

Moved to tears, Rachel knelt beside her bed and poured out her heart to her heavenly Father for all the amazing things He had accomplished in her life. Then she added, "Lord, you know I've struggled and strived. I've stood on your promises for healing, but now I'm gonna do what Lavina said days ago. I'm gonna lay my head on my pillow tonight and simply *rest in you*. If I remain blind all my life, then that's the way I'll be. I just want more of you, dear Lord."

Twenty-Three

❖ ❖ ❖

First thing next morning, Mam offered to pray for Rachel. "After all my fussin' over Blue Johnny, I think it's high time to beseech the Lord God heavenly Father for your healin'."

Rachel didn't quite know what to make of the suggestion, but she gladly bowed her head, allowing her mother to pray that her sight might return "in your will . . . and for your glory. Amen."

"Denki," she whispered, embracing Mam.

"I won't give up neither," her Mamma said, her arms strong against Rachel's back. "We'll keep on prayin' and believin'."

That morning, hearing Mam's prayer, it seemed as if everything between the two of them had been near out of focus for a gut many years, and now, gradually, ever so slowly—and in God's timing—the picture was growing clearer. 'Least it appeared to be so.

She and her mother had come a long way in just a few days. And Rachel knew she had the Lord to thank for that. Mam was no longer her adversary. No, they were sisters in the Spirit! She also knew that they would never go back to the way things had been before, that they would move forward. From now on.

After helpin' Mam serve their one and only breakfast guest, Rachel left Philip and Dat chatting in the dining room and went to give Nancy Beiler a quick call. Rachel was ever so glad to actually talk to the dear woman who'd always insisted on bein' called "Auntie Nancy," after such a long time, too.

"Do you remember me?" she asked when the woman answered.

"Why . . . little Rachel, 'course I do! How in the world are ya, any-ways?"

"Oh, I'm thinkin' that we oughta sit down together and have hot chocolate and cookies here one of these days."

"Sounds like a gut idea to me."

They chatted 'bout some upcoming work frolics and such, then Nancy mentioned that she'd heard the "old bishop died . . . and on Christmas, too."

"His funeral's today."

"Is it true what we're hearin' . . . that Seth Fisher got the assurance of salvation before he died?"

"Lavina Troyer was there to see it, and so was Dat."

"Well, now, don't that beat all."

"It's wonderful-gut news, ain't so?"

Just then, Rachel heard Philip carrying down his luggage, so she said to Auntie Nancy, "Maybe I'll see ya at the bishop's funeral?"

"I'll try to come. Wonderful to hear your voice, Rachel."

"*Da Herr sei mit du*—the Lord be with you." Then she hung up, trying without success to quiet her heart. Philip was preparing to leave!

She'd learned long ago that it wasn't befittin' to let emotions rule you. 'Twas simply childish to get flustered over an Englischer leavin' town, for pity's sake! Rachel wasn't a child anymore. She'd been taught to "choke it down," if ever tears threatened to spill. 'Course, that was back when she was a little girl. Still, she'd "worn her feelin's on both sleeves" near all her life, as Mam often reminded. Wasn't because she wanted to; heaven knows, she didn't. It was just how she was by nature. The Lord knew her heart, and that was that.

As a child she had been told—by older sisters, and Mam too—that she could "squelch her emotions" by simply standing or sitting right still, putting her hands over her eyes, and shutting them "real tight." And if she did that and waited long enough, the lump in her throat would begin to go away, ever so slowly—but it *would* go away. "Sooner or later, your foolish tears'll dry up, too, never to fall," Lizzy had said.

But for Rachel to keep back the tears, she had to hold her breath a gut long time, too. Even then, sometimes that didn't much help.

This moment—here and now—had been a long time coming, really. For all the days and weeks she'd thought of Philip Bradley, dreamin' of him and sayin' a prayer for him—all that—only for him to be sayin' his good-byes. Again.

Yet she refused to let her tears be shed in front of him. Had to make them "dry up," 'cause Philip was here in the parlor with her just now.

She had to say "so long" without lettin' on that she cared so awful much.

"I wanted to say how much I enjoyed getting to know you better, Rachel," Philip was saying from across the room.

She nodded silently.

"I want you to know that I meant it when I said I'd be glad to set up an appointment for you with a doctor in New York City."

A psychiatrist, he means, she thought.

"If you decide differently, please let me know." He paused for a moment, and she felt the gloom hanging heavy. "I'll leave my business card here on the table for your parents . . . if they would be so kind as to give you the information. And . . . if ever you want to call . . . about that . . . I hope you will."

I hope you will. . . .

She heard his words, heartbreakingly distant, but what more could she expect? That he might rush to her side and take her in his arms? Tell her how much he loved her? That he wanted to be with her for always?

Just then, Annie came running into the room. "Oh, Mister Philip, you aren't leaving, are ya?"

Rachel couldn't bear to hear their exchange, their good-byes. As Annie scampered out of the room again, Rachel turned toward the latticed window she knew was there at the end of the private parlor. Her back to Philip, she shut her eyes "real tight" and squeezed her fist against her mouth. It was no use. The lump in her throat was enormous, overpowerin', really.

Amazingly, as she attempted to keep her emotions in check—the Amish way—she realized that she could make out the shapes of pine trees through the window, like seein' through the veiling of her prayer Kapp. Ever so slightly, the trees seemed more and more clear. And the longer she looked, the more distinct they became.

All the while, as Philip talked, she blinked, getting used to the light again, truly marvelin' at this wondrous thing that was happening. The murkiness, every bit of haze that had persisted since the accident, was beginning to fade away. It was as if a cloud or heavy film had been lifted slowly, gently from her eyes.

Little by little, colors were coming into view. She could see the forest green of the pines, the azure blue of the sky, the dazzling white of the snow—and shapes, edges, lines, shadows . . . all the many things she'd taken for granted before the light had dimmed.

Taking a deep breath, she focused on the grandeur of the sky, the texture of the underbrush along the creek, shadows made by the apple trees lined up in their orchard behind the house. Even the neighbor's silo and tobacco shed, more than a mile away, had become visible to her now. At long last, healing had come. She could see!

She wanted to turn and look into Philip's face—oh, with all her heart she struggled with the urge to behold him. She wanted to see for herself the fine features Annie had described, look for the sweet spirit shinin' out of his eyes. He was right there in the room—standin' ever so near.

But what if she did tell him, and then her sight failed her again? Like it had the night Blue Johnny tried to use his enchantments on her? Hadn't been long before her hazy vision was gone again, and the empty darkness was worse than before. And what if Philip pledged himself to her—thinkin' she could see—only to be shackled with a blind wife, after all?

"If it's all right with you, I'd like to call you sometime," Philip said.

"I . . . I just don't know," she managed, torn between giddy feelings over her renewed sight and sorrow over Philip's leaving. But she kept her gaze centered on the beautiful rich landscape beyond the window. She allowed her eyes to focus, ever so slowly, on closer objects: the windowsill, its white latticed frame—the center coming together in the shape of a cross. She looked with wonder at the Victorian marble-topped table—she'd gone with Mam to retrieve it from an estate auction years ago. She gazed fondly at the rose-colored hurricane lamp. Last of all, she stared down in complete astonishment at her own hands, folded tight across her waist.

Sighing, Rachel broke the silence. "Thank you for the offer, Philip—to help me get to a New York doctor. . . ." She paused, then, "Have a safe trip home. And may God bless you always," she said softly. Yet her heart longed to announce the remarkable miracle, cried out from the depths of her soul to let him know. She could see again!

All the months of waiting for this moment, and yet she knew it was ill-timed. She could not tell Philip the truth.

It was only after the front door closed that she allowed her tears to fall freely. Then she rose and went to stand in the gentle curve of the bay window—away from view—watching him walk to his car.

Rachel caught sight of his face, if only for an instant. "Dear . . . dear Philip," she whispered, thinking that Annie was surely right to say how good-lookin' he was. His chestnut brown hair shone in the winter sun. Taking a deep breath, she continued to watch as he started the car, backed it out slowly, and turned toward Olde Mill Road.

Now that he was gone, she began to second-guess her resolve. What had she done? Had she made the mistake of her life by not telling Philip what had happened? That her vision had returned? She was ever so sure he would've pledged his love if he knew she had her sight. Yet she had withheld the truth.

She heard footsteps just outside the parlor door. "Rachel?"

It was Mam.

"Oh, Mamma, I can see!" she exclaimed.

Mam frowned in disbelief. "You what?"

"My eyes are perfectly clear. I see your green choring dress and your old work apron. And you're scowlin' at me to beat the band."

"Well, praise be!" Mam rushed to hug her, then called for Dat and Annie. "Come, quick! The most wonderful-gut thing has happened!"

Rachel and Mam scurried out toward the hall as Annie came rushing in. "Annie, come here . . . let me look at you, my darling little one," Rachel called to her.

Annie blinked as the realization began to settle in. Her mouth dropped open ever so far. "Didja say . . . oh, Mamma, you can see?" Her daughter's eyes searched her own. "You *can*! You can!"

Rachel shed tears of great joy as she knelt down and let her baby girl hug her neck. "Oh, Annie, God made you ever so beautiful," she kept saying over and over. "Ach, you're the pertiest little girl I know."

"God answered our prayer," Mam said, all smiles as she stood over them.

Dat emerged from the front room, peering over his reading glasses. "Well, what's all the commotion 'bout?"

"It's 'cause of Mamma," Annie said, releasing Rachel and running over to her grandfather. She hugged him hard at the knees. "Mamma can see again. She can see me . . . and you, too!" Annie looked up at Susanna and then down at their little dog, who'd followed Benjamin into the hallway. "Ach, Mamma can see *everything*!"

"Well, bless the Lord God" was all he said, wearin' the downright biggest grin Rachel had ever witnessed on his face. "Bless the Lord."

Later, after the excitement began to dwindle some, Annie ran off to color, and Mam went to the kitchen, prob'ly to call Aunt Leah and

Esther with the news. Dat headed back to reading *The Budget*, but Rachel turned toward the parlor, searching for the business card Philip had left.

She spotted it—a small white rectangular-shaped card—lying on Mam's cherry tea table. Picking it up, she was tempted to look at it, to see the name of his workplace, what address it might be. But unsure of herself, she turned it over and over in her hand. Then, refusing the temptation to look at it, she began to tear it into tiny pieces. Scurrying outside, she threw the pieces into the trash can. Best not to be dwellin' on either Philip Bradley or his little card anymore.

Standing on the back patio, with her shawl wrapped tightly around her, she looked beyond the apple orchard, now stark against the blue, blue sky. Her gaze drifted to the snowy pathway leading to Mill Creek, where she and Philip had walked just yesterday. What had he said— that the walk was an excuse for them to have some time alone? Why had he said such a thing? Did he need an excuse? What had he really and truly intended to say there as they stood on the crest of the footbridge? Something important, something lovely . . . she was ever so sure of it.

She allowed her eyes to follow the outline of the oval gazebo, closer to the house, where ivy and morning glory vines adorned it clear up to the capped roof with greenery and splashes of color in early summer.

"So long, Philip," she whispered into the crisp cold air. "So long . . . forever."

Twenty-Four

❖ ❖ ❖

Love? Could this feeling for Rachel Yoder be *love*?

What was it anyway? Could *genuine* love make you feel this way—confused and troubled? And if so, how was a person ever to know if he or she had found the real thing—the one person with whom to spend the rest of one's life?

Philip pondered these thoughts as he traveled east on Route 340, then south on Harvest Road, to Emma's Antique Shop. Getting out of the car, he picked his way over the snow-packed walkway. Eager to see what was available in the way of an antique desk, he peered in the front window and was surprised to find a cherry wood rolltop desk, slightly smaller than the desk at the Zooks' B&B. Intent on getting Rachel off his mind, he opened the door and immediately spied the young Mennonite owner.

"Well, hullo . . . didn't expect to see you so soon again." She smiled so big her grin spread across her face. "And you just about missed me, too. I come real close to puttin' up my sign and goin' home to fix lunch for my hubby. I usually only stay open a couple hours in the deep of winter. But today, well, I had a feeling someone might drop by, lookin' to spend their Christmas money, maybe."

"Then it's good timing on my part."

She nodded. "What can I help you with?"

He motioned toward the antique desk. "I've been looking for a piece like that."

"Yes, I remembered what you'd said last time, so my husband and I went poking around at several different auctions in Massachusetts," she explained, leading the way to the desk, made in the late 1800s. "You didn't call back, so it's been sittin' here in the window since last September." She chuckled. "Must have your name on it."

"But is it in my price range?" he humored her.

"Well, I wouldn't be surprised if I came close to matchin' my price up with your pocketbook." She brushed a piece of lint off the top of it, patting the wood.

Philip liked Emma's jovial spirit. She was vivacious and cheerful, and her modest floral print dress seemed to emulate the meek and gentle spirit within. He thought if ever he was to make a lifestyle change, that honoring God by dressing more simply—conservatively, too—would be the least of his concerns. The more difficult thing, possibly: to embrace the Plain church as a covenant community, especially because he was a "secular" Christian in their eyes. Not so much from his own viewpoint, but from Plain church members who might be wary of his convictions. He would have to prove himself.

Catching himself again, he wondered why he was thinking this way. Was his subconscious working overtime? And if so, why?

Inspecting the desk, he noticed it had similar compartments to the old desk at the B&B—dovetail drawers and plenty of pigeonholes. "Nooks and crannies," Grandma Bradley liked to call them. But thinking of his grandmother sent his mind spinning back to Rachel and her quaint old-fashioned way of expressing herself. How was he ever to go on with his life if every time he turned around, he was thinking of the lovely and sweet young Amishwoman?

"What's your best price?" he asked, running his hand across the smooth surface.

"Since you traveled so far to look, I'll say $750."

The desk was in excellent condition, so he knew it was a good deal. Only slightly higher than what *she* must have paid. "I'll take it," he said impulsively, easily visualizing the piece in his apartment. His writing studio would be the perfect location. And a good thing, too; an excuse to rid himself of the useless computer desk he presently owned.

An excuse . . .

In his mind, he was back with Rachel, enjoying the invigorating walk through the snow, out to the frozen creek. There, he'd stood on the arched bridge with her, close enough to smell her hair, the fragrance of her beauty.

So why *was* he purchasing a desk and hauling it back to New York when his heart was here in Bird-in-Hand? Quickly, he dismissed the irrational thought that he ought to consider staying. He would return to

New York. No need to labor over that decision!

Having finalized the transaction, he told Emma he'd have to rent a small trailer to pull behind his car.

"Just as well," she replied. "Shipping costs are sky-high."

"Everything's high these days, but thanks for the excellent price. I appreciate it." He offered a smile. She had done him a favor.

It was as he was heading west toward Lancaster that he contemplated his own parents' long-lasting love affair, how workable and happy their marriage had been. Janice and Ken came to mind, as well, for he viewed his sister and her husband as a model couple. One of the essential ingredients for a good marriage was similarity of background and interests. He had read that tidbit any number of places.

Yet his and Rachel's backgrounds seemed foreign. How could their union possibly thrive and be blessed in the eyes of God . . . and man? And their interests? Other than eagerness to own land and farm, what else did they have in common?

Then the image of a precocious child came to mind. Blond, blue-eyed Annie. He had always wanted a houseful of little girls and boys for as long as he could remember. So he and Rachel shared a love for children. And they enjoyed talking together, spending time sharing openly. Most important, they had a strong desire to serve and honor the Lord in all things, and they both wanted to share the Good News, too. Now, thinking about it, he guessed they *did* have a number of mutual interests.

But what was he to do about it? Call Rachel when he arrived back in New York? Perhaps have a cordial chat on New Year's Eve? Start a letter-writing relationship? What?

All of us, at one time or another, must make a choice. The words Adele had written to him nipped his memory.

Turning on the radio, he was grateful for a Christian music station, hoping to drown out speculation. Wasn't it enough that he'd gone out of his way to demonstrate his caring—his keen interest in her well-being, wanting to help her see again? How many modern men would offer to take an Amishwoman to New York City, of all places? He'd stuck his neck out in making a ridiculous overture. The fact that she'd turned him down flat was probably a very good thing. And sensible.

Sure, he could admit that he cared for Rachel. This far removed from the Orchard Guest House B&B, he could. Safely en route to rent a trailer and journey home, he could. Philip knew, too, that she just assumed she'd never see him again, most likely. And rightly so. After all, he had refrained from declaring his love. Had not even made an attempt. Yet he had thought of her—missed her—nearly every waking minute from their first encounter until the present visit.

So . . . what significant things had kept him from proclaiming his love? His writing career, his parents, his sister and family—all these had definitely played a part in holding him back. Yet as he contemplated his mental list, he knew big city life was not consequential to him; rather, the contrary. His parents and Janice, Ken, and Kari would expect him to marry at some point. Possibly move away, as well. So they were not a hindrance.

New York had always been home. It represented all that he really knew. Haggling over who would snag the next cover story or feature piece. Flying in and out of foreign countries to interview ambassadors and political leaders. Frantically sketching out rough drafts, rewriting, revising—all to meet some crucial deadline. Climbing the corporate ladder to yet another level of stress and strain. Never having time to stop and breathe in the sweet fragrance of life. Worst of all, regularly lamenting the time spent in jockeying to achieve what *society* deemed success.

Sighing, he thought again of Adele and Gabe, how they had belonged together, yet sadly missed each other. Due to what? Adele's reluctance? Perhaps. But there was more to it, and he knew precisely what that was. Adele had been unwilling to face her need of Gabe, that he was the only man who could occupy that cherished place in her life. The only one. And she had been too reticent to make the leap.

Fear is the opposite of faith, Levi Glick had said on more than one occasion.

Philip turned up the volume on the dash radio, listening to a choral rendition of the old hymn—"I Surrender All." He had always enjoyed the pure, uncomplicated melody, even as a boy, but today the lyrics caught his attention most of all.

By song's end, he found himself humming . . . then singing, even after the music had ended. "All to Jesus I surrender, humbly at His feet I bow, Worldly pleasures all forsaken. . . ."

In the quietude, hearing his lone baritone voice fill the car, he sang out the words of joyous inspiration and surrender. And as he sang, he knew that he was in love with—*dearly* loved—Rachel Yoder. Without a shred of doubt. She was the woman in his life, the one woman who could complete him, fill his heart with the kind of simple joy he longed for.

She was his heart-mate, and he longed to tell her so.

Slowing the car at Anderson's Bakery, he turned around and headed east again, past the sleepy hamlets of Witmer and Smoketown, away from Lancaster City to Bird-in-Hand. And he felt truly happy. Never so blessed with a realization in all his life.

————

The bishop's funeral wasn't such a sorrowful thing, really. Not for Rachel and her family. Many of the Plain folk in attendance had known Seth Fisher for well over fifty years—from the time he'd begun his leadership work in the area. Many, too, had already heard of his so-called transformation . . . at life's end, of all things.

Because she was so jubilant about her healing, Rachel had gone along with her parents to the funeral to pay her respects to the man whose death, in all likelihood, would bring change to the Amish church. On the way, they passed the intersection of the Crossroad, and she took in all the sights without a single qualm or jitter. In the future, they would save much time on buggy trips to Intercourse, Gordonville, and farther east to see friends and distant relatives. She had much to be thankful for.

Well over five hundred Amish mourners attended the funeral, held at the bishop's old farmhouse. Lasting three hours, the service was steeped in tradition and form. But it was the talk afterward among the People that encouraged Rachel most, just knowin' how fast the word was spreading 'bout Seth's salvation experience, as well as her sight regained!

Rachel spied Blue Johnny in the throng and was somewhat startled to see him. Still, he had every right to be here, and it made sense that he would come, really. After all, Seth Fisher had chosen *him* when Gabe rejected the status of powwow doctor more than forty years ago.

She excused herself from Mam and Annie, as they stood outside bundled up in layers against the elements, waiting for the coffin to be moved from the front room of the bishop's farmhouse to the long white porch—for viewing purposes. Dat and Levi stood nearby, giving her even more confidence.

Working her way through the crowd of mourners, she soon found herself standing near enough to whisper to the man who'd repeatedly pursued her to pass on his healin' gifts. "Excuse me."

Blue Johnny turned and looked at her, his face not recording surprise, but rather glee. "Well, if it's not Rachel Yoder. Now . . . didn't I say you'd come lookin' for me someday?"

"You may have said it, but that ain't why I'm here." Rachel looked him straight in the face, praying silently for wisdom. "I've been healed by the power of God. I don't need evil powers to make me see. And I believe you, too, must surely be searchin' deep down in your heart for the truth . . . just like most everybody else I know 'round here." She inhaled, holding her breath for a second, then pressing on. "Seth Fisher got delivered of the devil's gift before he died. And if you don't believe it, you can talk to Rosemary, his widow." She stopped and pointed toward the house, to Seth's frail wife just now coming out onto the porch. "Just ask Rosie what God told the bishop on his deathbed."

His dark eyes grew more serious. "I've heard tell—bits and pieces— of what went on. Hard to believe a simpleton could influence a mighty man like that, I daresay."

"Well, the Lord says in His Word, 'A little child shall lead them.' So I s'pose then you hafta have that kind of childlike faith to enter the kingdom of heaven."

His head tilted a bit to one side, and by the somber look on his haggard face, she wondered if he might be paying some heed to what she was sayin'. "Jesus can set you free of powwowing, too. You don't hafta die in your sins, Blue Johnny. You can turn your back on what the devil's been after you to do all these years."

He blinked his eyes like he was right nervous now. "Been hearin' this all my life from one Bible-thumper or another. Thing is, most folk look on me and my black box as a powerful-good miracle-worker." He lifted his hand to scratch under his hat. "But never has an Amishwoman talked to me the way you are."

Rachel shook her head. "I'm not a preacher, if that's what you're thinkin', but I'm servin' the Lord in whatever way I can. If talking to you 'bout God and His Word is part of that callin', well, then, I'm ever so glad to do it."

Blue Johnny grimaced, saying nothing.

The bishop's body was being brought out in a long poplar coffin, wider at the shoulders and tapered on the lid. Time for the final viewing.

"I'll be prayin' for you, Blue Johnny."

"Praying . . . for me?" His eyes were pools of wonder.

Rachel nodded. "Jah, I will."

He didn't offer a smile but gave yet another dip of his bushy-haired head.

———————

No one was home when Philip returned to the Amish B&B. And though he tried the door and found it to be open, he nevertheless chose to remain outside until the Zooks and Rachel returned. He sat on the front porch for nearly thirty minutes, his feet and hands growing numb with cold, so he returned to his car, waiting with great anticipation.

Glancing at the digital dash clock, he decided to give Rachel and her family another half hour. If they didn't arrive home by then, he would leave a note for Rachel. *I must talk to you, my dearest*, it might say. He would post it in plain sight on the storm door—so either Benjamin or Susanna would be sure to notice it as they entered. He would be taking a risk of such a note ever finding its way into Rachel's hands, though. She might not be told of his message at all.

Sitting in the luxury of his warm car, he thought back to various conversations with Rachel, especially their last dinner together, when they'd discussed their differences at length. He considered his life as a future Amishman. Would he miss the many technological conveniences he was accustomed to? Would the Plain life be stimulating enough for his active mind? And what if he tired of the simple ways—would he long to return to the big city, regretting his decision to join the Anabaptist community?

But no, there was only Rachel for him—she was the answer to his heart's cry. Plain or not, she was his sweetheart. And whatever it took, he would leap the chasm that had separated them.

Don't make my mistake, Adele had warned, referring to herself and Gabe Esh. So Philip had benefited greatly from Adele's story—not to err and miss out on his heart-mate. He *was* ready to take the plunge to simplicity, tranquility, and devotion—the biblical aspects of a life "set apart," the very things that had called to him since coming to Lancaster County, where his heart had turned back to God in total abandon.

Philip breathed a prayer, all the while picturing himself settled in the Bird-in-Hand area, working the land, possibly; helping his neighbors harvest crops, assisting his beloved in her blindness, witnessing of God's grace and love, writing on assignment—a Christian publication would be a welcome change—and growing old gracefully and happily with Rachel by his side. And, the Lord willing, he would father many children and lead each of them to the foot of Calvary's cross.

Yes, there was no longer any mistake about it. He had come home.

Tables had been laid with plates and utensils for the shared meal—cold cuts of beef, hot mashed potatoes and gravy, various kinds of fruit, and coffee—following the burial service. After they served the men and teenage boys first, as was their custom, Rachel made sure there was room for Lavina to sit next to her. Women and children ate last, while the men stood 'round outside in the barn and outbuildings, comparin' notes on mules and upcoming auctions and whatnot.

"Looks to me like God answered your prayer," Lavina said, clasping Rachel's hand.

"Jah, He truly did."

Lavina's head was bobbin' up and down. "He's ever faithful, as Adele would say."

Leaning over, Rachel hugged Annie and noticed her missing front tooth. "Ach, when's the new tooth comin' in, do ya think?" She pointed to the tiny gap.

Annie's tongue did a gut job of feelin' for the new tooth. Suddenly, her eyes grew big as can be. "I feel it, Mamma! My big-girl tooth is on its way down."

Lavina and two of Rachel's sisters, Lizzy and Mary, laughed out loud at Annie's cute comment about the "big-girl tooth." Her sisters' tittering, especially, encouraged Rachel and gave her hope that a mended relationship might be forthcoming. Now that her sight had returned, maybe her siblings and their families wouldn't stay so far away. Maybe they'd understand, too, that she wasn't *narrisch*—crazy—or under the sway of some spell. She had faith—jah, even confidence!—that in time, her companionship with all her siblings would steadily improve. All eleven of them!

Meanwhile, she would pray and ask the Lord how to minister to dear Lizzy, first of all. Trust the Lord to show her older sister His grace and forgiveness, how He had brought Rachel to a clear understanding of the powwow "gifting" and its false belief system. In turn, Lizzy might pass on the knowledge to her youngest, the rambunctious and often impulsive Joshua. For now, Rachel would believe the Lord for divine wisdom to know what to say—and when.

"Did your New York guest leave already?" Lavina whispered during dessert.

"Right away this mornin'."

"Before your sight returned to you?"

"No . . . after."

Lavina's mouth dropped open. "Then . . . he *knows* 'bout your healing?"

She shook her head slowly, glancing 'round the table, hoping no one was paying them any mind. "I just couldn't tell him, Lavina."

"Well, why not?"

"'Cause I thought I was doin' the right thing not to let on. I . . . oh, Lavina, I wanted him to care for me whether I was blind or not."

"So you didn't learn nothin' from Adele and Gabe, I guess."

Heart aching, Rachel felt her confidence dwindling. When did Lavina come to be so outspoken? She just didn't know if she could abide this sad, lost feelin' that had come upon her at the older woman's reproach.

"You love him, I know ya do, Rachel. It's all over your face."

"But it's best this way" was all she could bring herself to say.

Twenty-Five

❖ ❖ ❖

The sky was beginning to streak bright golds and reds due to a myriad of clouds. Rachel watched from her vantage point in the buggy, enjoying the ride home. Never again would she allow herself to take her eyesight for granted. God did a wonderful-gut thing, giving it back. She couldn't keep from looking—no, starin'—at clouds, trees, farmland, neighbors' houses, even colorless plank fences.

Winter had always had a feel of silence to it, the cold seemin' to gobble up near all the sounds, 'cept for boots gnawin' away at crusty blankets of snow and horse hooves clapping against hardened roads. And there were the occasional shouts of glee from children playin' "Crack the Whip" on the pond. All of it, Rachel felt she was seeing and hearing for the very first time.

"We had a right gut turnout for the bishop's services," Dat spoke up in the front seat.

Mam nodded. "I think lotsa folk came out of curiosity, in a way."

"What do ya mean?" Dat sounded awful serious.

"Well, you know, all the talk of Seth's salvation going 'round. Some might've thought one of the preachers would stand up and give an account of the bishop's final words or suchlike."

"Seems to me they should've."

Mam sighed and Rachel could hear it from the backseat. "Word's travelin' faster than ever these days."

"Jah, and a few had heard of *my* news," Rachel chimed in. "I have a feelin' somebody must've gotten on the phone and called around."

Mam craned her neck and smiled real big at her. "Couldn't keep such a thing as my daughter's recovery to myself, now, could I?"

She hoped Mam felt the same 'bout the bishop's change of heart, wantin' to spread the word. 'Cause far as she was concerned, that was the best miracle of all.

"Well, what the world!" Dat said as they came down Olde Mill Road toward the house.

Rachel had been taking in the view on the opposite side of the carriage, gazing at just 'bout anything she laid eyes on, while Annie kept a-huggin' her. But when she turned, she was shocked to see Philip's car parked in the designated guest area, with Philip himself inside! She remained silent, though her heart beat so hard, she was perty sure Mam would hear it up front.

Annie jumped out of the carriage as soon as the horse stopped. "It's Mister Philip!" she said, running through the snow. "He's back . . . again!"

"Looks like we might be gettin' ourselves an Englischer son-in-law, Mam," Dat joked.

"Now, Benjamin, don't jump to conclusions." Mam turned 'round again, but this time she reached for Rachel's hand. "Your pop and I wouldn't be opposed to such a thing . . . in case you wondered. We'll help him turn 'round right . . . Plain and all."

Still, Rachel remained speechless. Philip had said good-bye already. Why on earth had he come back?

Walking hand in hand with Annie, he hurried over to the buggy. "I've been waiting for you, Rachel," he said, the biggest smile on his handsome face.

"Mamma . . . look who's here!" Annie said, grinning and showing her missing tooth.

Rachel set her gaze on his countenance, the first she'd seen him up close. Her eyes followed his hairline, took in the rich hues of his thick, light brown hair, his cheekbones and fine nose, his mouth. Philip was a treat for the eyes, all right, but it was his spirit that had attracted her first of all. She would never forget that.

"We'll be goin' inside now," Mam said loud enough for all to hear, 'specially Annie, who didn't take too kindly to the idea. But she went anyway.

Dat dallied a few seconds longer, tying up the horse. Then he skedaddled off, without so much as a glance over his shoulder.

"Rachel?" Philip's eyes searched hers, narrowing as in disbelief. "Can it be . . . that you can see?"

She nodded. "I didn't know if it was wise to tell you before."

Not waiting a second longer, he climbed into the buggy and found his way to her seat. "When did your sight return?" he asked, sitting next to her.

"While you were saying good-bye. It took me by surprise, I must say . . . that's why I kept my back to you . . . didn't tell you."

His smile was warm and earnest. "I wondered why, but I understand now."

"Why did you come back?"

"Because . . . I love you, Rachel. I couldn't leave without telling you." He reached for her mittened hands. "I've loved you ever since our first day together . . . in Reading."

She gazed on him, beginning to tremble, not with fear but emotion. "But how can this ever be?"

"I want to be Amish, Rachel. I want to live the simple life . . . with you and Annie."

She knew if she tried to speak, the words would come out too squeaky . . . too high. She fought back the tears—swallowing hard over the lump in her throat—her heart overjoyed.

"All my life," Philip continued, "I've felt something was missing, Rachel. It was your lifestyle—your Lord—I was searching for." His smile said more than a thousand words. "And I was looking for *you*."

"Oh, Philip . . ." Rachel's heart knew the answer before he ever posed the question here, under the covering of the winter sky and the carriage top. "*Ich liebe dich*, Philip—I love you, too!" She fell into his warm embrace, tears of happiness clouding her sight.

"I want to do things properly, according to your ways . . . should I ask your father for your hand?" Philip asked, all seriouslike, as they gazed on each other's faces.

She smiled at the notion. "The People don't do that sort of thing, but if you want to, that's just right fine." And the more she thought on it, the more she realized Dat might honestly like the idea.

So Philip did just that, and Dat took to it with ever such delight, followed by Mam's jovial well-wishing. Her father explained the rules of courtship, and when they told Annie the news, she jumped up and down for the longest time. But nobody seemed much annoyed by it, least of all Rachel and Philip.

Twenty-Six

❖ ❖ ❖

Philip could hardly keep up with Adele's many questions when he called her on his cell phone. She wanted to know when all this "excitement" had taken place, when he and Rachel were to be married, where they would live, and had he told his family yet. Most of all, she was delighted "beyond words."

"I have money stashed away for a down payment on a farmhouse," he told her. "Rachel and I haven't set a wedding date yet, but you'll be one of the first to know when we do. As for my family, I'll tell them on New Year's Eve. We plan to 'pray in' the year together at our—*their*—church."

"Now . . . how on earth will you make the transition to Plain life?"

She was being the Adele he'd come to know and love, asking pointed questions, sounding like an interviewer! Yet the dear lady had his best interests at heart, he knew that.

"I believe I've weighed every possible aspect of Amish life over the past three months. How hard can it be for a man who despises big-city life? Besides, I won't have to give up my car, Rachel says." He paused, more sober now. "I've longed for this sort of change since my first visit to Grandpap's cottage in Vermont. And Rachel, well . . . you know how very precious *she* is!"

Adele's laughter was warm and reassuring. "You're going to have a wonderful life, Philip. May the Lord bless you both."

They chatted a little longer. Then he said he would keep in touch. "You'll hear from me again soon. About the wedding, especially."

"You call when you can, and please tell Rachel I send all my best. May God give you lots of little Bradleys. Oh, and if you wouldn't mind, tell Rachel to pass on the word to Lavina that I received her color copies of Gabe's artwork."

"Gabe was an artist?"

"Evidently. The drawings Lavina sent are from his childhood," she told him. "Remember, his name means 'God is my strength,' so we should have expected him to be multi-talented, right?"

Philip liked that. Adele had a terrific perspective on life these days. So much had changed for the dear woman who had lost so much, only to help Philip and Rachel find their way. "I'll talk to you soon."

"Happy New Year, Philip. Remember, God is ever faithful."

Ever faithful . . .

Rachel went to the kitchen phone and dialed up Uncle Amos—his business phone in the woodworking shed. 'Course, he'd hafta run into the house and get Esther on the line. But it was worth the inconvenience, for sure and for certain.

At long last, she heard Esther's voice. "Can you and Levi come over tonight?" she asked.

"For goodness' sake, Rachel. You sound nearly breathless. Are ya all right?"

She took a slow, deep breath so she could get out the words without faltering. "Philip Bradley came back. He loves me, Esther. And I love him. Ach, I'm ever so happy!"

"Well, what do you know 'bout that!" There was no hesitation. "We'll be right over."

Rachel hung up, gettin' that awful giddy feeling. But mixed in with the giddiness was a prevailing peace. She thought of a favorite verse in Philippians: "And the peace of God, which passeth all understanding, shall keep your hearts and minds through Christ Jesus."

Rachel returned to the front room and stood near the fireplace, rubbing her hands together, thankful that Dat had a blazing fire goin'. When she was warmer, she moved to the windows and looked out at the gathering dusk, rising amidst snow-powdered pines, truly thankful for God's goodness and grace.

Philip went to stand with her at the window. "Our friend Adele approves."

"I had a feelin' she might."

"And she sends her blessing." He reached for Rachel's delicate hand, looking deep into her beautiful brown eyes. "Do you remember how Gabe signed his illustrious postcard?"

Rachel nodded cheerfully. "'Soon we'll be together, my love.' That's how he signed off."

"You remembered."

"How could I *forget*?"

Happily, they embraced, then turned to peer out at the sky, now dotted with stars and a near-full silver moon. Winter's wind had blown away the imposing buildup of clouds, making way for a clear and radiant twilight. The future was just as bright.

Epilogue

❖ ❖ ❖

I've begun to think our life theme must surely be God's faithfulness. My dear Philip refers to Adele's words often, even 'round the farm, in the seemingly incidental things. Jah, God's hand is ever so evident in our lives.

Of all things, just days before our wedding, Lavina offered to rent us her big farmhouse. She said she never needed such a large place. Well, it's three times bigger than *we* really needed. But that's just fine, 'cause not too long after we were settled in, Adele's doctor said she didn't need to be in a nursing home anymore. "Come make a home with us," we told her. So Philip, Dat, and I went up to Reading and moved her and her few belongings to our place.

We're one happy family, and Adele and Lavina live in the Dawdi Haus, built onto the southeast side of the main house. They look after each other like cheerful older sisters, and they tend to us like two doting *Grossmutters*.

Lavina's decided she wants to will over her house and part of the land to us before she dies. 'Course, we ain't lookin' forward to it anytime soon, but till that day comes, Philip's workin' the soil with Lavina's older brother and cousin. And he seems to love every minute of it.

Our baby's due in a few weeks, and Philip's first choice in a name for a boy is Gabriel. Adele thinks that would be "just lovely." Lavina too. Annie's counting the days till she's no longer an "only-lonely" child, as she puts it. I keep myself busy cooking, canning, and crocheting infant clothes and cradle afghans for our first little Bradley.

My sight is just as clear as ever, and the nightmares are less frequent now. I am grateful for the dark valley the Lord allowed me to walk through. Now I can truly empathize with other hurting souls. Believe me, I've had a gut many opportunities to talk to folk 'bout the Lord. It just seems one door after another keeps opening up for me.

For Philip, too. He's writing a short story collection, set in Amish country—puttin' all his new experiences as a Plain farmer into it. Honestly, he sold his computer, printer, and whatnot and seems ever so content to write longhand on the antique rolltop desk he bought at Emma's. The desk reminds us all of Gabe's postcard to Adele, which she still happily displays in her room.

Philip's parents and sister have already come to visit. They're always welcome here, and his young niece, Kari, is so attentive to Annie. There's just too many bedrooms in this great big house. One day, I believe, we'll have them all full up with children, though. Lord willin'.

Thou shalt see thy children's children. . . . Ach, Jacob surely must be smilin' down on us.

Last I heard, Smithy Lapp's courting a widow lady over in his own township. Seems to me that makes better sense. 'Course, who am *I* to be talking 'bout staying in home territory for a life-mate! Thing is, Philip and I know God put us together. Plain and simple.

At day's end, no matter the weather, we take long walks and watch the sunset, or at least the sky and the farmland stretching out on either side of us. Philip calls it the "best relaxation therapy" he's ever known.

We've had gut fellowship with several young couples at our Beachy Church. A group of the men have come alongside Philip and taken him under their wing. Hardest thing for me to get used to, at first, was Philip's coarse whiskers. Now his beard's nearly as soft as goose down. He fits right in 'round here, too. Perty soon, no one'll ever know he was "fancy" at all.

The Crossroad will forever serve as a reminder of God's grace and mercy in our lives. Every time we pass through, we think of how God has blessed us.

Esther and I have joyfully returned to writing letters the old-fashioned way. It's a nice change, even though I did enjoy hearing her voice on the tapes. When we get really homesick for each other, we just pick up the telephone. She, too, is expecting again—possibly twins this time!

As for the new bishop, Mam says he's much more open to the People reading their Bibles, even encourages them to buy the newly translated Pennsylvania Dutch New Testament. I rejoice daily at the things we see God doing here.

Another wonderful-gut thing is happening. Not only do Lizzy's and

Mary's families come to visit—even show some interest in having a Bible study—my brothers, Noah, Joseph, and Matthew, are beginning to warm up to us, too. Still, I'm hoping for the day when *all* us Zooks can have a big get-together. Maybe Philip and I will have it here at Lavina's place. . . .

Annie's a busy bee at school her first year, and she's lookin' ahead to helping Philip—she calls him Pop—gather pumpkins here right soon. We'll hafta show him how to make apple cider, too, while we're at it.

Powwow doctoring continues in the area, though people are beginning to associate it with voodoo and black magic. So the word's getting out, thanks to our pastors, as well. And, of course, Gabe Esh who got all this started so long ago. It seems that God has allowed us to stand on the shoulders of those who've gone before us—those who've been godly examples.

A few months back, Blue Johnny moved away, we heard, and so far no one's stepped forward to take his place. We pray daily for our community, that the People will be willing to walk the road to Calvary's cross and find healing for body, mind, and spirit.

Yesterday, Mam dropped by with some patterns for crib quilts. I liked the Lone Star best. So she and I, along with Lavina and Adele, are gonna have us a little quiltin' bee next week. Annie will sew her very first stitches in this coverlet for her new brother or sister.

After years of enduring darkness and pain in a cocoon of my own making, it's ever so gut to gnaw out of the protective covering—through the scars—and open my new wings. Some days they're a bit fragile, even doddering, but one thing I know for sure and for certain, the Lord has daily granted me a "speckle of pluck." Not a full measure of confidence just yet, but I'm trusting for that as I take one flitter of my new wings, a day at a time.

Author's Note

Divine protection—"underneath are the everlasting arms"—and Spirit-directed intercessors, who prayed even in the wee hours, made it possible for me to complete this, my most recent journey of faith.

I am also grateful to the Lancaster County residents who assisted me with research for this book and its prequel, *The Postcard*. Graciously, they reject any acknowledgment, as is their Plain custom, yet I appreciate their willingness to share.

My study of the life of Helen Keller ignited the inspiration for my character Rachel Yoder and her reaction to suffering a conversion disorder, causing blindness. In addition, I owe a debt of gratitude to the research assistance of Amy Watson, manager of Library Information Resources for the Helen Keller Archival Collection.

On some small scale, I was able to understand the world of the visually impaired due to my study, as well as incorporating information from the American Foundation for the Blind.

As always, my husband, Dave, shared equally in the joys and sorrows of this venture into Amish tradition, and I am delighted to call him "first editor."

Much appreciation to Gary and Carol Johnson of Bethany House Publishers, as well as my faithful editors, Barb Lilland, Anne Severance, and the entire BHP team. Special thanks to Jane Jones and Barbara Birch who read the manuscript for accuracy. I also wish to thank two of Jacob J. Hershberger's former students who shared their recollections of the late Amish Mennonite bishop, whose devotional columns in *The Sugarcreek Budget* of Ohio ("Lynnhaven Gleanings") inspired the subplot for this book, as well as *The Postcard*.

Big thank-yous to Auntie Em's Antiques & Gifts of Monument, Colorado!

The book *Gifts of Darkness* is purely fictitious, though based on actual writings by Amish church members and clergy.

Many blessings to my readers, who inspire me daily with letters and cards. I pray your hearts have been made receptive to God's redemptive love—lives set free—by the message of this book.

Sanctuary

To
Clyde and Susan,
our dear friends in
Connecticut.

Part One

God is our refuge and strength,

a very present help in trouble.

PSALM 46:1

One

❖ ❖ ❖

S he had hoped this day would never come.

Trembling, Melissa James returned the phone to its cradle and hurried to the stairs. She grasped the railing, nearly stumbling as she made her way to the second-floor bedroom. Her heart caught in her throat as she considered the next move. Her only option.

You can do this, she told herself, stifling a sob. *You must. . . .*

Quickly, she located an overnight case. The piece of luggage had been packed years before—in the event of such an emergency—wedged between other travel paraphernalia, high on the top shelf of their closet.

Melissa's mind reeled with the memory—the flat, yet familiar voice on the phone just now. The restrained urgency in his words. Her breath quickened, heart faltering.

Tossing a few items of makeup and hair accessories into the overnight case, she grabbed her stationery and pen. Frantic as she was, she would never be able to forgive herself if she did not take time to write a quick note. *That* much, at least, she owed her husband.

Weeping softly, Melissa penned the saddest words she'd ever written. How does a young bride bid farewell to the man she has loved for three perfect years? The man who had altered the course of her life for better. He'd softened the blow of her past, brought purpose to her future. Ryan James, whom she loved above all others.

She stared at the note, caught between life and love, wishing . . . longing for a resolve far different from the one she must choose. Signing the note, she placed it on his oak dresser, propped up against the brass lamp. Ryan was sure to find it there.

Snatching up her overnight case and purse, she rushed into the hallway. Her head whirled with unanswered questions: *What to do? Where to go?*

On the stairway landing, tall windows overlooked the backyard and the cove beyond. Melissa caught sight of the rose garden—*their* glorious garden, now in full bloom—bordered by the stone walkway and blue hydrangea bushes. Each delicate rose petal and leaf was bathed in sunbeams, their beauty mocking her, adding to her sorrow.

Downstairs, she peered tentatively through a tiny window in the entryway. Hand on the doorknob, her breath caught in her throat. *Don't panic!* she told herself.

No time to waste . . . still, she couldn't leave. Heart pounding, Melissa turned, facing the living room one last time. Was it essential to keep Ryan in the dark about her desperate need to flee? Shouldn't she run to his office, tell him the truth, and urge him to go with her?

Squaring her shoulders, Melissa walked to the back of the house. She paused to take in the enclosed sun porch, deliberately memorizing each detail—the fragrance of roses, the pillowed loveseat, the hanging ferns in two opposite corners, and the various knickknacks, souvenirs of their stateside travels. She recalled the intimate, loving words shared, the soothing backdrop of ocean waves lapping against the wide shoreline. This sun-drenched room where Ryan often held her in his strong arms, tenderly stroking her hair as they stared at the wide expanse of sea and sky. Where the dreamy music of Debussy lulled them into a world of serenity and joy—that place where evil cannot harm those who love.

The lump in her throat threatened to choke her. What precious memories! Too many to rehearse, in light of her present peril. Yet she lingered, refusing the urgency that threatened to overwhelm her. She allowed her gaze to wander to the gray-weathered dock, where impatient sea gulls perched on posts, waiting for handouts. To the sailboat, *Mellie*, christened with her own nickname, wrestling with low waves. To the cove and out to Block Island Sound, Fishers Island, and the wide blue of the Atlantic Ocean beyond.

Stricken, she turned toward the living room, where rays of light shimmered on Daisy's satiny coat, their sleeping golden retriever. "Good-bye, sweet girl," she whispered. "I'm going to miss you."

Opposite the sofa, a red-brick fireplace with rustic wooden mantel boasted numerous framed memories. Hand trembling, Melissa reached for a recent photo, recalling Ryan's pose in front of the historic Stonington Lighthouse. He was a slender, yet muscular man, twenty-seven years old, with sun-bleached brown hair and cinnamon eyes. Distinguished cheekbones shaped his tanned face, forming his warm and compassionate expression. Anyone, upon first meeting him, was drawn to his disarming manner. Just as she had been.

Good-bye, my darling. . . .

Shuddering anew, she pondered his response to her note. How grieved his dear, handsome face, his tender eyes. Undoubtedly, he would be shocked.

Resisting the impulse to take the photo with her, she returned it to the mantel, glimpsing the wall prints of Monet's *Water Lilies* nearby. Then her eye caught yet another piece of art. Seemingly out of place in a room dominated by French design, the picture depicted Christ holding a lamb. Printed below the image, the tender phrase: *"Come to me all ye who labor, and I will give ye rest. . . ."*

Melissa had never attended church as a young girl, yet she had felt compelled to purchase the print in New London last year. The picture had offered a strange respite from the underlying dread that defined her life, even these recent wonderful years with Ryan.

If only someone were able to push her backward in time to that childhood place of innocence where good, kind people ruled. Folk like dear Mr. and Mrs. Browning—her nurturing neighbors—and Grandpa and Nana Clark, her beloved maternal grandparents. Snap a finger, and there'd she be.

Time to go! She caught herself, the urgency returning. Melissa made her way back to the kitchen and peered cautiously through the window. After a time, she determined that it was safe to emerge. She opened the back door and dashed across the breezeway to the garage.

Inside, she locked the outer door and quickly slipped into her white Toyota Camry. Her hand shook as she reached for the remote, attached to the sun visor. She pressed the button, and the garage door rumbled open. For a split second she wondered what she might do if she were suddenly approached, made a prisoner in her own car.

Dismissing the terrifying prospect, she started the engine and backed the car into the driveway, glancing over at the splendid home, second thoughts haunting her.

It was then that she noticed Daisy shuffling onto the breezeway, mournful eyes watching her—almost pleading. Poor thing must've heard her leaving and followed her out through the doggie door. She resisted the urge to rush to Daisy's side, reassuring her that everything was all right. "I'm so . . . sorry," she murmured.

Melissa adjusted the mirror, then looked over her shoulder out of both habit and necessity. All clear . . . so far. Without delay, she pulled into the narrow street, past the gray-weathered waterfront homes and spacious front yards of her neighbors. Dozens of familiar landmarks—private piers and yachts, and Latimer Reef Light in the distance—all linked to her brief fairy-tale life.

Too good to be true, she thought as she sped down the street.

All she had ever dreamed of—the fulfillment of her lifelong hopes and wishes—grew more distant with each passing mile, then vanished into the moist sea air.

Two

❖ ❖ ❖

Five minutes to closing.

Ryan leaned back in his leather chair, hands laced behind his head, watching the markets close. No less than six computer screens lined the table along the right wall of his office, monitoring live information on stocks, bonds, options, and futures. He had a stake in all kinds of speculative vehicles, but he was *not* a jack-of-all-trades-master-of-none. As an investment manager for New England Asset Management, specializing in stock options and financial futures, Ryan's aggressive portfolio had more than doubled his clients' money during the past year.

He transmitted his orders for the market open tomorrow, then shut down the system. Drained of emotion, he rubbed his bleary eyes. He was not so much spent from watching monitors all day as he was weary of life, of the endless pursuit of the American Dream. Were it not for Melissa, his wife, living might have seemed nearly pointless. She was the one and only reason he wanted to get up in the morning, the reason to struggle through each day, the incentive to return home at night. Making money—loads of it—had become, for him, immensely overrated. Having someone like Melissa in his life was the true reward for his labors.

His spirits brightened when he considered the evening stretching out before them. Tonight he planned to surprise Mellie with lavender Damask roses, heavy with the fragrant aroma of spicy fruit. His wife appreciated the fine art of communicating with flower colors and arrangements. She, an avid reader of such English novelists as Jane Austen and the Brontë sisters, had enjoyed introducing him to the obscure customs of Victorian courtship.

He had debated between yellow and coral, ultimately deciding on the color that represented their marriage: lavender, which meant "love at first sight," Mellie had explained. And how true for them. The first time he'd laid eyes on her, he was finished.

Typically on Friday evenings they dined at Noah's in Stonington Borough. After a rich dessert, they often walked past the old lighthouse to Stonington Point, overlooking the harbor. Holding hands, they would revel in the sunset from their spot on Dubois Beach, sometimes prolonging the moment by sitting awhile on the massive boulders jutting out into the breakers.

But tonight, for a nice change, Ryan would take her to the Fisherman Restaurant, in the nearby village of Groton Long Point. Following dinner, when they were satiated with superb seafood cuisine, he planned to present a small white box with the words *Northern Light Gems* engraved in gold lettering. He could scarcely wait to see the look on her face. He would place the pearls around her neck, then happily kiss away the tears. The smallest expressions of love always seemed to take her by surprise.

He smiled at the thought and gazed at the silver-framed 4×6 desk photo of Mellie. He never tired of this picture of his young wife. Only twenty-four at the time, she was wearing a light blue T-shirt and tan shorts, her golden brown hair flowing unfettered about her shoulders, complementing her creamy-smooth complexion. He'd snapped the photo on their first anniversary a little over two years ago.

To celebrate that first milestone, they'd returned late in the day to the Watch Hill, where they had exchanged wedding vows. The sunset mingled purple with pink, and she had been mesmerized by the ocean's reflection of the scene. In the midst of her wonderment, she glanced back at him to share the moment. And Ryan had caught her pose, just as she smiled, capturing the perfect blend of her personality: her eager embrace of nature and her gentle spirit with a little twinkle in her eye.

Closing the necklace case, he slipped it into his coat pocket, taking care to lock his executive desk in the middle of a spacious office. The office, located on the second floor of a large converted Victorian house, stood a mere block from the Mystic River Bridge on Route 1.

In the reception area, Margaret Dyson, a plump fifty-five-year-old woman with gray-peppered brown hair, rapidly clicked the keys of her computer. Bernie Stanton, the boss, was sheltered in the confines of his own office on the other side of the lobby. A grim man who barked military-style instructions at the beginning of the day, Bernie often beat a hasty retreat to his own lavishly decorated domain. Only occasionally did he emerge to welcome clients, usually those of renowned affluence.

Marge tolerated Bernie's sour behavior because, as she succinctly put it, "He pays well. If it wasn't for your fresh and friendly face, Ryan, I'd be looking for a cheerful boss."

Ryan, on the other hand, didn't mind Bernie's temperament. He clearly remembered a time, not so long ago, when Bernie was known to smile, long before pressures of work had consumed him, destroying Bernie's marriage of thirty-five years in the process. More significantly, Bernie appreciated Ryan's investment savvy, delegating most of the important investment decisions to him.

"That's it for me," Ryan announced to Marge, closing the door to his office. "Any plans for the weekend?"

"My grandson Brandon's visiting from New Haven," she replied without looking up. "We're headed for the seaport . . . again." She grimaced.

"Why don't you talk him into going to the beach instead?"

"What, and lose most-favored-grandma status? No thanks." Marge smiled and turned to Ryan, a knowing look on her face. "Hey, it's tonight, eh?"

"Got it right here." Ryan tapped the necklace case in his pocket.

"Expensive enough, I'll bet?"

"Would've paid more."

"My, my. Aren't we still in love." Marge winked. "By the way, isn't your college friend coming out this weekend?"

"Denny flies in tomorrow. Providence airport."

Marge nodded, obviously remembering his friend. "Still talks a lot about church?"

"Denny's a good man, just a little overboard about religion."

"Sees a goblin in every closet?" Marge chuckled.

"More like a devil in every heart."

"One of those extreme types."

"Yeah. Hellfire and brimstone and all that."

"You could use a little church yourself," Marge said, making an impish face.

Ryan forced a smile. "Don't start."

"By the way," she replied, changing the subject, "now that you're in the habit of buying jewelry, let me remind you—Secretary's Day is coming up."

"You mean the usual paperweight won't do?" Ryan gave a smirk.

Marge laughed heartily at that, and they continued their banter. Ryan was anything but stingy, and Marge knew it. Last year, to celebrate Secretary's Day, Ryan had convinced Bernie to send Marge, her daughter, and grandson to the Bahamas for a five-day reprieve. Overwhelmed with gratitude, Marge had sent daily postcards to the office until she returned bearing souvenirs and gifts. Tanned and refreshed, she had taken one look at the pile of work on her desk and frowned mischievously. "Miss me?"

"Does a fish miss the sea?" Ryan had replied.

He smiled at the memory and reached for the doorknob. "Don't get any ideas about another vacation. We almost fell apart here without you."

Marge nodded. "Takes a man of character to admit how much he needs his secretary."

"An honest man," he said softly, waving good-bye. He was glad to hear Marge chuckle, basking, no doubt, in the pride of indispensability.

———

Ryan parallel parked in front of Mystic Florist. There he picked up Melissa's rose bouquet, hurried back to the car, hoping to miss the traffic jam at the drawbridge, and headed east on Route 1. But his timing was off. The light changed to red and he heard the loud whistle as the Mystic River drawbridge began to rise. He was sure to be stuck in traffic for a good ten minutes, at least. Tapping the steering wheel, he thought ahead to Denny's scheduled arrival tomorrow.

Dennis Franklin was an unusual specimen. A bachelor, Denny had played college football and *nearly* made the pros. Had it not been for a minor knee problem, his best friend might have wound up playing for the Denver Broncos. Instead, Denny had worked for a while in security before landing a teaching job in a Denver high school. Quite a comedown for some guys, but not for Denny.

His thing was religion now. He attended church three times a week, even conducted street meetings on the weekend in Denver ghettos. A big man—six feet five—Denny commanded respect wherever and whenever he opened his mouth.

Melissa liked Denny. During his last visit, she'd peppered him with questions. Naturally, the preacher-man was happy to oblige. Though Ryan had never admitted it, Melissa's obvious interest in religion made him uncomfortable. Much to his relief, she'd dropped the discussion once Denny left for home, and things soon returned to normal.

Waiting for the boat traffic to pass and the drawbridge to be lowered, Ryan thought about the weekend ahead. In the past, he'd enjoyed discussing philosophy and religion with Denny. But lately, Denny's incessantly exuberant, sometimes obnoxious, attitude had finally gotten to him. Not in a bad way. In fact, Denny's arguments had become . . . more intriguing. Perhaps it was time to settle whether or not Christianity had merit. To let Denny make his case, then dismiss it once and for all.

The drawbridge settled into place, and cars began to move slowly across in both directions. Ryan drove less than a mile to Lord's Point— their home—in silence. Built along the beach, the house was a cedar-shingled two-story cape. Thanks to Melissa, the yard boasted a smorgasbord of flowers—pansies lining the walkway, marigolds against the house. Fuchsia baskets hung from the eaves. A paradise of color.

Ryan parked his SUV beside the small one-car garage, reached over to the passenger side, and seized the bouquet for Mellie. Daisy, her usual eager self, met him at the kitchen door. "Hey, girl!" He stooped to pet the oscillating dog with his free hand.

Daisy barked her welcome, panting as she followed Ryan to the kitchen.

Placing the flowers on the counter, Ryan reached for the large vase in the cupboard and set about arranging the bouquet. When he finished, he stepped back to admire his handiwork.

Satisfied, he called to Melissa. "Sweetheart, I'm home." He poured water into Daisy's bowl and scooped dog food into her dish, waiting for Melissa to emerge from one room or another. Daisy scrambled over, nudged Ryan aside, and began gulping the food with loud chomping sounds, the sides of her golden body contracting with each voracious swallow.

"Easy girl. There's more where that came from."

Ryan headed for the sun porch where Melissa often curled up with a book or her diary. On occasion, she set up her easel, creating lifelike paintings of flowers and ocean scenery, as well. The room, graced by plump-cushioned wicker chairs, was dominated by a wall of windows facing the ocean. Melissa, however, was nowhere to be seen.

Ryan checked the downstairs level. The pool table, centered in the room, was surrounded by Melissa's framed floral paintings. Despite his frequent encouragement, she refused to hang them upstairs on the main level, claiming she wasn't ready for "prime-time" exposure.

Calling to her again, he strolled to the laundry room, expecting to hear his lovely wife humming to herself as she folded clothes. Instead, the room was deserted, the laundry appliances silent, empty.

Back upstairs, he wandered through the house to the backyard, where Melissa often tended her garden. The smell of salt and seaweed mingled with the wail of a distant sea gull. Across the yard to the south, George, their retired neighbor, puffed on a cigar and raked his own small portion of the sandy beach, obviously frustrated with the recent storm deposit of fresh seaweed. George nodded casually, then went back to work.

Ryan did not find Melissa sitting on the dock, her feet dangling off the edge, feeding the resident swans that often showed up for dinner. Nor was she napping in their tiny sailboat, docked to the pier, as he'd once discovered her on a lazy afternoon—having fallen asleep to gentle, shifting waves.

Ryan trudged up the slope to the garage, Daisy trailing close behind. Opening the door, he poked his nose inside. The space for Melissa's car was vacant.

"Why didn't you tell me, eh, Golden Nose?"

Daisy looked up as if to say, *You didn't ask.*

Ryan chuckled. Melissa was probably out running an errand somewhere. That was all. There was something strange about her being gone at this hour, though. On a Friday especially. He knew how she despised rush hour, liked to be home *before* he arrived for their weekend together.

He climbed the deck stairway leading into the house and went to the master bedroom. He showered in preparation for the evening, sure she would be back when he emerged.

As he dressed and fumbled with his shirt collar and tie, his gaze fell on the dresser. A note was propped against the lamp. Reaching for it, he scarcely recognized the scribble as Melissa's. Certainly, this was not her usual flowing script.

He held the note, read the hurried message.

The growing dread turned to panic.

Three

❖ ❖ ❖

S he'd gotten a jump on late-afternoon traffic. Interstate 95—the fast lane—was exceptionally wide open, yet she rejected the urge to speed. Not one to push her limits, not while driving, Melissa kept her focus on the roadway and her rearview mirror.

She did *not* relish the thought of encountering the hubbub and congestion of New York's rush hour, though she and Ryan often took this route to one Broadway show or another, to the theater district. Always on the weekend when traffic seemed destined to crawl.

Unable to peruse the road atlas at the moment, she contemplated from memory an alternate route through the city. In the past, when considering her options should she ever need to escape, she had never fully settled on where she would go. Any number of places might offer a safe haven until someone recognized her, caught up with her . . . again. She hated to think of running. After her brief sojourn in Connecticut, she was, once again, a fugitive among strangers.

She turned her thoughts to Ryan, her dear husband and best friend. What was he doing now? Reading her scrawled note, wondering just what sort of woman he'd married? How she missed him. The emptiness, the isolation, was nearly unbearable. With each mile, the hollow feeling swelled, seeping into even the most insignificant crevices of her soul.

She glanced in her mirror. Nothing out of the ordinary. Only cars, dozens of them. None whose drivers looked familiar.

Breathe easy, she told herself. She had to calm down. Just how long she might be gone from husband and home, she did not know. She had planned ahead, though, withdrawing enough money—now hidden away on her person—to coast for several months or more. Ryan wouldn't have minded. Her husband was a highly resourceful businessman, seemed to have a knack for turning everything he touched into gold. *The Midas touch*, their friends often joked.

From the earliest days of their marriage, she and Ryan had never wanted for anything. Just days before their wedding, he'd told her that she could work . . . "but only if you care to. We can easily make it with one income, if you prefer to stay home." So to work or not to work had been entirely her choice.

She had grinned back at him, their discussion turning to the all-important decision of who was to cook and clean house if she did choose to find a job. At the time, she wondered if he was hinting, hoping for a baby right away. But the topic of children hadn't come up. In fact, there was never any dialogue about their future offspring. Actually, though, she was glad they'd had this rather unspoken pact. Now, at twenty-six as she ran for her life, the thought of having a toddler in tow was anything but pleasant.

Adjusting the mirror, she studied the car directly behind her, straining to see the vehicle behind *that* car, as well. She recalled, as a girl she'd often wondered about her father's obsession with his rearview mirror. The notion that he was a fidgety driver seemed to hang in her memory. How old *was* she the first time she mentioned something to him? Seven . . . maybe a little younger?

Anyway, Daddy had been deep in thought as he drove her to school. Hers was a small private school on the outskirts of town, Palmer Lake, Colorado. The Montessori school, where she studied music, art, and creative play, was an elite institution. The place was staffed with good, solid instructors—"the best educators money can buy," Daddy often said. But he never boasted about having money. Not to anyone. Melissa never suspected in those days that she and her widowed father were well-off.

Changing lanes, she remembered a particular drive to the school. "What's wrong with the mirror, Daddy?" she'd asked. Usually a warm and gentle man, he had seemed fairly perturbed by her question and surprised her with staid silence. He continued to peer into the mirror, touching it many times, especially at the red lights along the way. She had not pressed it further.

Some things are best left alone, she now decided, making a turnoff the road in front of a police station to consult her road map. If someone, by chance, *were* tracking her, the pursuit would have to cease at least for now. A wise move, and she congratulated herself for it. She had not given careful thought to stopping for food, drink, and other necessities. After all, police stations were few and far between when you needed them.

Four

❖ ❖ ❖

Ryan sat on the edge of the bed, dumbfounded. Staring at the note, he tried to make sense of Melissa's message.

Dearest Ryan,
    I have no choice but to leave now. I can't explain why. Please trust me . . . don't look for me. And try not to worry.

I love you,
Melissa

Ryan raked his hand through his hair and reread the note, desperately seeking the comprehension that evaded him. *What on earth was happening? What was she thinking?*

His mind raced back to this morning when he'd kissed her good-bye. Nothing in Melissa's sleepy smile nor her tender kiss had indicated that she was troubled or . . . *what? That she was contemplating leaving me?*

Ryan shook his head, as if trying to shift his brain into high gear. Had something occurred between then and now? He rose and stumbled to the closet, searching for signs, clues. As expected, Melissa's wardrobe dominated the closet—dresses, slacks, blouses, skirts, jeans, and sweaters. Shoes galore. Nothing seemed out of place.

Then he noticed the top shelf, where various seasonal handbags and two fanny packs were neatly stowed. An empty space indicated an overnight case was missing. So she'd taken *something* along.

He descended the stairs to the living room and began to pace the floor, massaging his already tense shoulder muscles. He read the note again, attempting to read between the lines.

I have no choice but to leave now. . . .

Now? Did that mean she might return? And if so, when?

I can't explain. . . .

If she had to leave, why not explain? Why leave him desperate and wondering miserably?

Quickly, Ryan ticked off the typical reasons why a woman left a man. He was positive there was no other man in her life. She was not fleeing an abusive marriage. . . .

So had she lost her ability to think clearly? Was *that* it? He'd read of cases where people suddenly—sometimes overnight—lost their capacity to reason, to think. In a panic, they ran away, only to be found later, wandering the streets in a strange fugue, whispering of phantom strangers. But Melissa had exhibited no sign of a nervous breakdown, stress, or encroaching mental illness.

Suddenly, he recalled their weekend plans with Denny. Now totally out of the question. Denny just couldn't come, not with Melissa gone—running from some real or imagined terror.

Thoughts wavering, Ryan picked up the phone and dialed.

Denny tossed several pairs of jeans into the duffel bag, headed to his closet, and removed four T-shirts. Nearly all the shirts had Christian phrases or Scripture verses printed on them. He packed his clothing, wondering how to prepare for New England's fickle weather. Summers were normally hot in Connecticut, even toward the end of August, but more recently, Ryan had said, they had been plagued with days of unrelenting cloudy, cool weather. *"Unusual for paradise,"* Ryan had joked.

Denny threw in a sweatshirt and a couple pairs of shorts, just in case. Hopefully, sultry beach weather awaited him. He could use a few days of sunny relaxation.

Along with his Bible, Denny was taking a copy of C. S. Lewis's *Mere Christianity.* Last time Melissa had involved him in a deep discussion of the claims of Christ. He had been pleased to find her far more receptive than he would have guessed. But the newly purchased book wasn't for her. She wasn't interested in—didn't require—either logical or philosophical reasoning as to faith. Ryan, however, lived in the skeptical world of *prove it to me.* But the bigger question remained: Would Ryan even read the book? Doubtful.

Denny packed it anyway, in case the subject came up. He grinned. With him, the subject of Jesus *always* seemed to come up. It was unavoidable, impossible to remain silent about something that mattered so much to him. Even with strangers he met on the streets, Denny usually brought up the matter of Christ—delicately. Well, as delicately as possible for a man his size.

There were times when he regretted not getting into professional football. Not because he still craved fame or money, but because of the missed opportunity as a sports pro to influence souls for the kingdom.

Presently, he spent after-school hours and weekends with troubled teens, many who literally lived on the street. There was no greater joy than to roll up his sleeves, get down and get dirty—and make a difference in the life of a needy boy or girl. Helping with food and shelter. Offering a listening ear. Truly caring about their problems.

But lately he felt exhausted, needed time to reflect, to recharge. This chance to fly to the East Coast and hang out with Ryan and his wife had come at a most opportune time. Besides, this getaway would give him time to think through some of his own issues, especially his relationship with Evelyn and the possibility of marriage.

Denny dialed his bedroom phone and reached Evelyn Reed on the second ring.

"Are you packed yet, handsome?" she asked after she heard his greeting.

Hearing her voice was like coming home. She worked nearly around the clock at Denver's Children's Hospital as a nurse, the ideal career for her, a woman with a nurturing and gentle soul.

It didn't hurt his feelings that Evelyn liked to refer to him as *handsome*, even though he knew he wasn't *that* good-looking. For one thing, he was slick bald. The fact that she *thought* he was attractive was all a red-blooded American male like Denny needed to know.

"I'm having second thoughts," he replied grimly.

"About going?"

"About leaving you behind."

"I'll be fine, you big lug. It's only for a few days, right?"

"Suppose so."

She was silent for a moment, then—"I'll be praying for you, Denny. And for your friends Ryan and Melissa, too, that everything goes well."

They chatted a bit longer before he said a reluctant good-bye, hung up, and finished packing. He hadn't left town yet, and already he missed her.

The phone rang again.

Denny pounced on the receiver. Probably Evelyn calling back. "Hey, hon . . ."

"Uh . . . Denny, it's Ryan."

"What's up? Change your mind about my visit?" Denny joked, aware of the hesitancy in Ryan's voice.

"Well . . . actually, yeah."

Denny frowned. "Hey, I was just kidding."

"I'm not. Listen, this isn't going to be a good weekend, after all."

"That's cool." Then, sensing an ominous heaviness in his friend's voice, quickly added, "Everything okay there?"

Ryan sighed audibly. "Not exactly."

"What's wrong, man?"

Denny was stunned to learn about Melissa's disappearance. "Did you guys have a fight or something?"

"No, listen . . . uh, I need to get going. Sorry, we'll talk later."

"I'll call back tonight, okay? You've got me worried."

Ryan hung up abruptly, leaving Denny puzzled. Ryan and Melissa were the "perfect couple." What could have gone wrong?

Denny pushed the suitcase to the other side of his bed. Promptly, he lowered himself to the floor, kneeling like a schoolboy, and began to pray.

———————

Ryan disconnected with Denny and considered his next course of action. He tried to put himself in his wife's shoes. *Where would I go if I were Mellie?* he wondered.

He considered getting into the car and driving around to look for her, just to be doing *something*. But he thought better of it. He needed to be near the phone—in case she called.

Daisy padded to Ryan's chair, rested her chin on his knee, and whined softly. Ryan rubbed her golden fur and her floppy ears for a minute, then picked up the phone, dialing Melissa's best girlfriend, Alice Graham. *Ali.*

She answered on the third ring, and Ryan explained the situation as matter-of-factly as he could. Ali's reaction was utter shock, disbelief. "This is nuts. She left a note?"

Ryan read the note to her, which brought a little gasp. "I can't believe this," she whispered.

"The two of you were together for lunch today, right?" he pressed.

"Yeah . . ." She paused. "Oh no . . ."

"What?"

"I don't know . . . it didn't make sense to me at the time, but now—"

"What happened?"

"At the restaurant. We hadn't even finished eating, and . . . she just suddenly wanted to get going. Said she wasn't feeling well, so she got up and left, just like that. Left me sitting there alone. She seemed a little pale. I called later to check up, but she wasn't home."

"What time was that?" Ryan asked, his heart slamming the walls of his chest.

Ali seemed to hesitate. "I guess around two o'clock or so."

Ryan blocked out the rest of the conversation. Melissa . . . *sick?* Why hadn't she told him? What *had* happened today?

Five

✦ ✦ ✦

The highway had become a long and monotonous box—a rectangular shape, as though the pavement stretching out before her were the base; the blue of the sky, the top; the lush, green barrier of trees and underbrush, the sides.

Melissa scanned the radio, searching for something soothing. She chose an oldies station with frequent news updates featuring snarled traffic up and down I-95 along the eastern seaboard. Such gridlocks were apt to put her in a dire position—stalled. She simply could not afford the risk of entrapment.

So she listened intently for reports of serious snags on the major roads leading into the Big Apple. Populated areas were best, she'd decided. After all, a driver could lose herself in the mayhem of rush hour. And in an emergency, attention could easily be diverted elsewhere. Calculating a host of worrisome thoughts, she weaved in and out of traffic as afternoon hurtled toward evening.

Any day but Friday, Melissa thought. Yet, it wasn't as if she'd *planned* to leave on the worst traveling day of the week. Being mid-August posed another problem—last-minute family vacations. The northbound lanes were crammed, bumper to bumper, with cars, vans, and buses headed for the shore.

She thought of the beach at Napatree, near Watch Hill, Rhode Island, where she'd first met Ryan more than three lovely years ago. Had it already been that long?

Glancing at her watch, she took note of the date: August seventeenth. In more than one way, the final full month of summer was extraordinary. Her father would have celebrated his forty-eighth birthday this month, had he lived.

She gripped the steering wheel. She hadn't thought of her dad's birthday in years. And why, on the day of her mad dash away from the evil that tormented her life?

Trying to refocus her attention on driving, she shifted her weight slightly, eyeing the cruise control button. Should she set it in this congestion? Wouldn't it just be a matter of time before she'd have to brake, throwing the setting off? Why bother?

Leaning her head back slightly, Melissa forced herself to relax a bit. Traffic in her lane had slowed to a crawl. *To think I met Ryan in the month of Daddy's birth*, she mused. And yet, in the selfsame month she was leaving everything that was ever good and true.

A never-ending screen of trees and wild ferns on either side of the road appeared to close in on her. Inching her car forward, she noticed the ceiling-sky beginning to fade from its sapphire hue as the sun prepared for its slow dive over distant hills to the west. At times, the pavement itself seemed to disappear as additional vehicles vied for space.

More than once, she was tempted to use her cell phone to call Ryan. Oh, to hear his voice—the notion both thrilled and terrified her. She dared not succumb to temptation. Cell phones were dangerously susceptible to tracing.

By now Ryan would have made a myriad of phone calls to their neighbors, to Ali, and to the florist shop where she was employed. He may have already reported her missing to the police. Calling home was out of the question. The hazard was too great.

She ought to think about settling in somewhere for the night. Somewhere out of the way where she could make her next call from a safe phone. On the other hand, she didn't want to put herself in a more precarious spot—leaving the highway, getting off the road and into a rural area where she could easily become a sitting duck. She'd have to wait until after sundown.

Daddy always waited for nightfall, Melissa recalled. Yet she'd never consciously realized this fact as a girl, in spite of the many road trips they'd taken together. She remembered, very clearly, one night when she and her father had set out to visit Grandpa and Nana Clark, her mother's parents. Though she had never known her mother, who passed away when she was two, Melissa loved to visit her only living grandparents. And Daddy never seemed to mind driving the winding, mountainous roads over Loveland Pass, through the long Eisenhower Tunnel, then past Vail and Glenwood Springs, to Grand Junction. They sang campfire songs as they drove. Sometimes, they kept track of out-of-state license plates. And Daddy had his own songs, too. Silly little tunes he made up at will. On occasion they talked of his fondest memories of her mother, though for the most part, he shied away from things too sentimental. Or too painful.

It was nearly six o'clock when she spotted the exit sign for New Rochelle, New York. She would allow herself a very brief stop at the city nestled on the north shore of Long Island Sound in Southern Westchester County. Just long enough to gas up and purchase a few snacks and something to drink, at "The Queen City of the Sound"— inspiration for Broadway's former smash hit *Ragtime* and home to both Robert Merrill, opera star, and Norman Rockwell, America's popular artist.

Melissa knew the place well. She and Ryan liked to poke around in the shops that lined historic Main Street, where fruits and vegetables could be purchased in the same vicinity as children's toys and athletic apparel.

Glancing in her rearview mirror, she surveyed the car directly behind her. A blue sports car. Hadn't she noticed it earlier? Back near Fairfield, maybe?

Changing lanes, she stepped on the accelerator, but the blue car sped up, nearly on her bumper now. Instantly, her throat closed up. She was being followed, just as she feared!

Keep your cool!

Anticipating the exit, she rejected the urge to use her turn signal. Yet the blue Mustang veered into the far right lane just as she did. She strained to see the driver's face in her rearview mirror. If she could just manage that without causing an accident.

She was about to focus on the man's face when she heard the driver in the next lane blare his horn. A good thing, too, for she nearly plowed into the car in front of her, halfway to the end of the crowded exit ramp.

"Watch where you're going!" the driver hollered, leaning out the window.

"Sorry . . . sorry," she murmured. Her mouth was cotton as she waited, stuck between the Mustang behind her and the car ahead. Seconds seemed to tick by in slow motion. She double-checked the automatic locks in her car. Twice.

Gradually, the backed-up ramp eased a bit. At last she negotiated a sharp right-hand turn, and as she did, the Mustang roared around her, speeding off in a different direction. *False alarm.*

Heart still hammering, she located the nearest gas station and turned in. She leaned back and closed her eyes, willing herself to calm down.

Daddy had said he *needed* the sleeping tablets and that she must always remember to leave them on his nightstand before bedtime. And she had obliged, never forgetting.

Often she had wondered how the tablets made a person feel. At times she had held the tiny round pills in her hands, peering at them, holding them up to the light. Trying to see into them. Did they make your legs and arms tingle before you felt nothing? What parts of your body went numb first? Your feet, legs, arms? What caused such small pills to work? Most of all, why did Daddy need medicine to put him to sleep? She had never asked.

Her father was a compassionate man, more than generous with his hugs. He encouraged her to snuggle up on the sofa with him while they spent part of each evening reading aloud from her cherished picture books or school reading assignments. But tender words came more clumsily. "Mellie, be safe," he'd say each time she left the house for school or Girl Scouts or wherever. Never once did he call after her, "Have a good time," or "Enjoy yourself."

It was always: "Be on your guard. Watch yourself." His consistently serious tone rendered apprehension to her young heart, as did his sober eyes. Not until years later, having been told the full story of her father's fate, did Melissa fully comprehend the significance behind his warnings. Sadly, by that time, the man she'd called Daddy had been deceased for more than a decade.

Melissa purchased her snack items and pumped a full tank of gas, then hurried to the safety of her car. On the road, she kept watch for any vehicle trailing her, for any driver who might look suspicious. Even recognizable.

Juggling her sub sandwich, she managed to drive, though it was a challenge due to the ongoing bottlenecks as she neared the vicinity of each shoreline city or town. The closer she came to the Bronx, the more clogged the traffic. Was everyone in New England driving to the city for the weekend? Never had she seen so many vehicles on a Friday evening.

Thankfully, the day was beginning to cool down. She switched off the air conditioning and turned up the radio. A rambunctious announcer was crowing the high temperature for the day—"eighty-nine degrees." Hotter than usual, true, though coupled with higher than normal humidity, the day was classified "a doozy."

In more ways than one, she thought.

Waves of grief threatened her composure as she relived the morning's startling encounter—at a restaurant, no less—followed by the urgent phone call and her desperate escape.

The DJ kept talking about the weather, and she tried to listen, hoping to crowd out the events of the day. "Temps are bound to decrease as summer begins to wind down to fall," the announcer said. "Now, that's *one* thing you can count on."

One thing to count on . . .

Not much in life was reliable. Changing weather, hurricanes, high and low temperatures. In the course of things—of life, overall—what did it matter? What did *anything* matter?

Suddenly, she thought of dear Nana Clark, living in the hot, semi-arid region of the country—Colorado's western slope. How long since she'd visited her mother's family? Not since before her father died. She scarcely recalled the actual year, much less the event. Nana and Grandpa hadn't come to the funeral. Too frightened, perhaps. Who could blame them? They'd sent cards and letters, and there were occasional phone calls, too, during the years she'd lived with Mr. and Mrs. Browning. After college she'd disconnected from everyone, her Colorado relatives and friends included. Missing her grandparents and the Brownings, she wished she might have kept in touch somehow.

Flicking off the radio, she exhaled loudly, frustrated and angry with the way life had turned on her. If she were a religious woman, she would ask God for help about now. The way she saw it, praying was for dutiful folk who hadn't completely messed up their lives. People like Ryan's friend, Denny Franklin.

Oh no! The realization that Denny was planning to fly in tomorrow hit her. She shook her head, amazed that she'd spaced out his visit. Yet there was no choice in the matter.

Surely Ryan would call off the visit with Denny, wouldn't feel like entertaining his Bible-packing friend. He would be hurt, put in such an awkward position, having to tell Denny his wife had vanished.

The silence in the car trickled out through the cracks, and she was aware of the sounds of tires on the highway, the color and make of the two cars directly behind hers. A gray sedan hung back a bit, the third car in the current lineup.

The eerie dirge of dusk settled in about her. Once the sun was down, things would change for the worse. Darkness always hampered her behind the wheel—not that she suffered from night-blindness. Things just became very different after dark.

Melissa finished her snack and soda, making an attempt to stay focused, to keep her mind on her driving. A tug-of-war ensued. Wanting, *needing* to concentrate on the road and the types of cars around her, she found that her unruly mind wandered far afield. The struggle was in the way of a dream, a vision of sorts. A fanciful scenario of ''what ifs'' and tenuous ''if onlys.'' In truth, nothing she could have done would have altered the outcome of this day. Or of her life, really.

Indulging in imaginary games would easily take up a good portion of the trip. If she chose to go beyond Manhattan for the night, that is. New Jersey, Delaware, Maryland . . . where would she stop? When she tired of the driving, as well as her over-scrutiny of the past, present, and future—she might put on one soothing CD after another, humming all the while, just as she often had while traveling by car with her father.

The closer she came to New York's magnificent skyline, etched against the gray of smog and humidity and accompanied by millions of twinkling lights, the more she was tempted to check in at one of the Times Square hotels. Overnight, perhaps. Long enough to make her next phone call and get some much-needed rest.

She glanced at the corridor of trees lining the highway in the fading light. Was it her imagination? Were the leaves beginning to turn slightly? She fought the urge to stare at their beauty.

For the first time, she was going to miss the autumn glories of New England. Thinking ahead to the annual harvesttime festivities, she caught her breath, recalling Ryan's suggestion that they drive up to Vermont in mid-October. ''We'll make a three-day weekend of it . . . over Columbus Day,'' he'd said just last week, paging through the current Innkeepers' Register. And together they had decided on an elegant village inn at Ormsby Hill in Manchester, former residence of Robert Todd Lincoln's friend and law partner.

They wouldn't be going together . . . or at all now. Another disappointment for Ryan.

She choked back tears, struggling to see the road. How could he forgive her, spoiling their romantic plans this way? Destroying their Camelot?

Her idea to "get lost" in the teeming masses of Manhattan seemed perfect as she drove south toward the Whitestone Expressway, keeping her eyes peeled for the turnoff to west I-495. Halfway through the Queens Midtown Tunnel, she spotted the gray sedan again. A Buick. Trailing her by a distance of three vehicles, the car was nearly out of the perimeter of her rearview mirror. She was conscious of the lane changes the driver continued to make nearly every time *she* negotiated a turn.

Don't panic . . .

Resolving to remain composed, she purposely shifted lanes once the tunnel dumped out to East 36th Street, though she was cautious, mindful of the heavy traffic. The gray car slowed, but seconds later, blinked over and merged into the right lane, on her tail.

Several blocks later, traffic came to a full stop. Unable to accelerate, she was paralyzed in her lane; *all* options were blocked. The gray Buick, only two cars away, was too close for comfort.

At Madison Avenue, the Pierpont Morgan Library—an Italian Renaissance-style palazzo—seemed even more imposing than she remembered, with its pair of identical stone lionesses guarding the grand gated entrance. She shuddered as she stared at them and the monstrous building behind. But in doing so she was able to steal a glance in the vicinity of the silvery car through her outside mirror.

Melissa gasped. She recognized the square face, the man's fierce, raptorial eye. The familiar white tuft of hair on the left side of his otherwise thick head of dark brown hair—his peculiar trademark—confirmed her worst fear. The same man she had seen earlier today had followed her all the way from Mystic.

She fought to think clearly as she drove. The pulse in her chest and the heat surge to her head made planning difficult. Though she knew her way through Midtown well, making a decision under this kind of pressure—where and how to make the slip, get out of sight, even make a run for it—was beyond her ability at the moment. Penn Station was within five miles, but to get there she'd have to abandon her car and get

away on foot, then catch a train out of town. She didn't trust herself on
the street, not this far from the train station. The possibility of flagging
down a cab occurred to her as the cars began to move again. Out of the
question on a Friday night. No, she'd sit tight, hang on to the vehicle
she so desperately needed to take her to safety.

Call the minute you get to a safe place, the whispered phone warning
rang in her ear.

The Buick sedan signaled to change lanes, passing the car behind
her. It crept up, now side by side with hers. She dared not glance to her
left, dared not look. Not now.

Mellie, watch yourself, her father's voice echoed from the grave.

The light turned abruptly red at the next intersection. Tires
screeched, horns blared. What would she do if he forced her over?

She opened the glove box, eying the small black container of Mace,
a disabling liquid. If necessary, she wouldn't hesitate to use it. But she
did not want to allow the man to get *that* close.

Caught in a gridlock of taxis, cars, and limos, she strained to see if
the street was marked one-way. The minivan in front of her blocked her
view. She thought of turning the wrong way, or even running a red light
at some point. Maybe she'd try to get stopped by the police. But no,
matter what happened to her, no matter how many police she encountered, the gray sedan would keep showing up. The driver would merely
circle the block and pick up her trail eventually.

To her right, the gaping mouth of an underground parking garage
enticed her, wooed her into its depths. Momentarily, she considered the
possible escape route. But no, it was too constrained and concealed. She
must stay out of dark places, remain in the open, where people were
near. Where the populace could be witnesses . . .

Six

❖ ❖ ❖

Lela Denlinger looked out the window as she finished her supper. She enjoyed the last few crumbs of apple pie, then drank the remaining sips of her coffee. A bit more lonely than she'd felt in ever so long a time, she stared out across the meadow at the neighbor's barn, a lantern light a-shining for all its worth from an open door at its east end.

Her brother and his wife and their baby had come for a three-day outing from Virginia, leaving just after breakfast this morning. She'd spent the morning redding up after them—washing sheets, dusting, and whatnot. After such a lovely visit with her dear ones, the house seemed almost too quiet.

"What'll you have me do now, Lord?" she whispered in reverence, trusting her heavenly Father's ability to provide for her every need. But, being the sort of woman she was, she liked to offer a helping hand. 'Course, the Creator of the universe didn't need her assistance—any child of God knew that. Still, she wanted to be available, put herself on the altar of sacrifice, if that was what the Lord might indeed have in mind.

Clearing off the kitchen table, she set about carefully washing and drying each dish. As she wiped each of the counter tops and the table clean, she began to sing. "O Master, let me walk with thee, in lowly paths of service free. . . ."

Eager for a bit of cheer to fill the empty house, she put one of her favorite praise and worship CDs into the stereo and sat down with her Bible, devotional book in hand. She liked to read in the early morning, upon first awakening, feeding her heart and mind on God's Word. But today, as gloomy as she felt, she decided she'd have her quiet time twice.

Nothing at all wrong with that. Why, her own sister, who was church-Amish and lived down the road apiece, often did the same thing. "'Tisn't a thing to boast about," Elizabeth would say, just a-smiling and as merry as you please. "Reading what God has to say, no matter what time of day or how often, is a blessed thing, Lela."

And of course she agreed. Far be it for her to argue such a fact. She and Elizabeth were as close as any two sisters could be, though they didn't entirely see eye to eye on church membership, she being Mennonite and Elizabeth embracing the Amish tradition of her husband. Yet both were "homegrown" Pennsylvania Dutch girls, lived so close they could run barefoot back and forth between each other's houses, helped each other do spring and fall cleaning, and most everything else a body needed. The biggest difference between them was that Elizabeth married young, at nineteen, and had herself a fine, growing family already at twenty-seven. Lela was nearly thirty-one, come next week. Never married. 'Course, if the Lord brought someone along who loved her just for who she was, well . . . then, she wouldn't have to think twice 'bout that.

She'd heard the whispers—"maiden lady"—already at church and family gatherings but wouldn't let on that it bothered her. Though, of course, she was becoming just that in the eyes of her community. Still, she held on to a glimmer of hope that someday, in God's perfect timing and will, a godly man might come into her life.

Turning her attention to the devotional book, she found cheer and comfort in the verses found in chapter four of First Peter. "And above all things have fervent charity among yourselves: for charity shall cover the multitude of sins." Reading on, she was unusually moved by the words: "Use hospitality one to another without grudging. As every man hath received the gift, even so minister the same one to another, as good stewards of the manifold grace of God."

Hospitality . . .

Lela had never been one to show the slightest hesitation when it came to opening either her home or heart to family and friends. Even strangers. Habits of generosity were learned early among her people. She, along with her six brothers and sisters, had been taught that the importance of giving comes not from having much or little, but whether one's spirit is at home in community. She recalled Papa loaning his farm equipment to anyone who asked, Mama taking plates of hot food out to the hobos who stopped by. Best she could remember, they always chopped wood in exchange for the meal. Yet Mama liked to go all out, baking her best buttermilk biscuits, hot dumplings, and gravy to satisfy their hefty appetites. 'Course, she and Papa always kept Scripture tracts on hand to pass out, too, along with the food.

Lela's older brothers exhibited generosity in many ways. Often they helped, whether called upon or not, to raise a barn alongside their Amish neighbors. Her sisters were both willing to baby-sit free of charge, least till their own babies came along.

What really bighearted thing had she done lately? Closing her Bible, she felt led to pray about possibly opening her home, maybe renting out her spare room for a little bit of nothing, so eager she was to be a blessing to someone in need.

"Lord, I trust you to handpick the very soul you would send my way," she prayed in the stillness of the house.

———

Tired and scared, Melissa searched for a way to make the break. With her heart racing, she had difficulty considering what to do next. The gray car was parallel to hers.

What do I do now?

Anything to stop this madness.

The light turned green at last, but she must continue to wait while the cars in front of her inched ahead.

Move! She wanted to scream at them. *Just please move!*

At last the intersection gave way, and the cross street was in full view. All clear. She gunned the accelerator, turning a screeching hard right. As she did so, perspiration broke out, dampening her hair on the back of her neck. She heard honking and assumed the Buick was attempting a right-hand turn in the wrong lane, but she kept her attention on the cars ahead of her. No time to look. She must keep moving. Quickly.

At the very next street she made another fast right, onto another one-way street, now heading east. She was going in circles, but she didn't care. She would drive recklessly if necessary. She would escape the man. In order to survive, she *had* to. History was not going to repeat itself. Not this day.

Melissa looked back over her shoulder, saw a glimpse of gray, and realized the stalker had somehow made the turn. Angry and frightened, she wondered why he hadn't leaped out of the car, tried to drag her away when he had the chance. What was stopping him?

Keep moving, something in her head prompted her.

But where to go? She didn't care to be followed all night. And there was the matter of fuel. When would either of them run low on gas and need to make a stop?

What bizarre maneuverings, either in heaven or on earth, had transpired to put the two of them together in the same restaurant earlier today? What had brought him to the small town of Mystic? Was it just a coincidence? Or had it taken him literally three years to catch up with her again?

She could kick herself, thinking back on her suggestion to go to S&P Oyster Company, a restaurant overlooking the Mystic River and drawbridge downtown.

Ali had other ideas. She wanted to grab a sandwich and soda at a deli or pop in and out of Bee Bee's Dairy. "That way we can stroll past the boats along the river walk while we eat," Ali had said. But, no, Melissa had insisted they go "somewhere and sit with a view of the water."

Forcing herself to concentrate, Melissa saw that Lexington Avenue was coming up ahead. Suddenly a middle lane opened. Melissa's car shot forward, securing the position. Then she spied a police officer directing traffic at the intersection. His presence did nothing to alleviate her fears. The lights were out, and only a few cars were being allowed through at a time.

Just great, she thought, her hopes for making a break dashed. Frustrated, she pulled her hair back away from her face. The officer stood tall and lean in the middle of the busy junction, sporting a navy blue uniform, matching hat, and pristine white gloves. His shoes appeared to have been spit-shined. He was methodical in his approach to directing traffic, motioning only five or six cars through the intersection at a time; turning, moving, arms at a perfect right angle, as though performing a ballet. The man's precise attire and movements fleetingly reminded her of her father and some of his colleagues from the past.

Marking time, she glanced at the gas gauge. She had enough to get her a long, long way from here. If she could just move.

What had possessed her to come this way, through Manhattan on a Friday night? What had she been thinking?

A few more minutes of waiting, and at last it was her turn. She was relieved when the gray sedan was held back, not permitted to go through.

Now's your chance. Go!

Keeping her momentum, she floored it and turned right, past numerous skyscrapers, heading south now. Glancing in her rearview mirror, she saw a large service truck blocking the previous intersection.

Yes! She laughed out loud. From here, it was a straight shot to East 32nd Street and the Empire State Building. This wide street would lead her to the Lincoln Tunnel eventually. Certainly, it was the long way around, but, hey, this was freedom's way!

High with exhilaration, Melissa had a strong feeling she was home free. Well, not home exactly. Never home . . . maybe never again.

Seven

❖ ❖ ❖

Elizabeth King gathered her little ones around her. "We best be thinking 'bout a present for Aunt Lela," she told them after evening prayers. "Her birthday is next week, and you know how much she loves gettin' homemade gifts from each one of you."

Four towheaded youngsters nodded their heads. Mary Jane, age seven, grinned up at her. "I'll be makin' her a perty doily for her hope chest."

Not to dampen her daughter's spirits, Elizabeth wondered how she might focus on the doily and not Mary Jane's comment. "Well, if I were you, I'd make it white."

Her daughter seemed pleased with the suggestion. "Gut idea, Mama. White goes with anything."

The other children talked about making drawings and maybe some birthday cookies. Then, after a bit, they kissed and hugged their parents and headed off to bed.

All but Mary Jane. Being the oldest, sometimes she spent a few extra minutes with Mama before bedtime. "I'm sorry if I said somethin' out of turn," she whispered.

"Meaning what?" Elizabeth asked as they sat near the wood stove in the kitchen.

"Well, you know . . .'bout the hope chest." Mary Jane, eyes blue as the sea, stopped and took a childish deep breath. "'Sposin' Aunt Lela won't be marryin' anytime soon."

Elizabeth hugged her girl. "We don't know that for sure, now do we?"

Shaking her head slowly, Mary Jane's eyes were wide as ever. "Do ya think God has a husband out there somewheres for her?"

Elizabeth didn't rightly know. 'Twasn't something she and Lela had talked about for the longest time. Far as she knew, her older sister was fairly content in her singleness. She didn't especially seek out social outings or places that widowers would frequent. And honestly, widowers were about the only available men Lela could be thinking of now, considering her age.

"A husband for Aunt Lela?" Elizabeth repeated.

"*Jah*, Mama, that's what I'm askin'." Eager for a response, Mary Jane had the beginnings of a frown.

"I guess that's a task for the Good Lord," was all she said. But knowing her eldest as she did, the girl would be asking again. And again.

Mary Jane was becoming much more aware of things here lately. "You've got yourself a youngster who's mighty perceivin' of folk," Elizabeth's mother had said a few days ago.

That, she knew, was mighty true. Being the oldest of four—so far—Mary Jane wasn't such a handful, really. She was just interested in people. Same as Elizabeth herself.

"Time for bed," she said, shooing her darling toward the stairs. Morning came awful quick around here, especially with the second cutting of alfalfa upon them. Thaddeus would want them all up milking cows, helping in general, come five or so tomorrow.

Before she turned out the gas lamp in the kitchen, she slipped to the dark living room and peered down the road toward Lela's little brick house. She wasn't surprised to see the lights still on downstairs, as her sister often retired hours later than Elizabeth and her family. No need for her to get up with the chickens, after all. Wasn't like she was a farmer's wife.

But the thing that did surprise her was seeing the lights a-blazing in the second-floor bedroom, Lela's spare room. *Whatever is she doing in there?* Elizabeth wondered. Surely Lela had cleaned up after their brother and family left this morning. She kept a very tidy house, her sister did, so it wondered Elizabeth what still needed to be done. Especially at this hour.

"Comin' up to bed?" Thaddeus called to her softly.

"Be right there, dear." She pressed closer to the window and stood gazing down the narrow road, pale in the light of a quarter moon. "Dear Lord, please watch over my sister, Lela. And, if it be thy will, bless her with a nice husband," she whispered into the windowpane.

Only a shard of the moon was visible when Melissa spotted the bill-board just after the exit ramp to Keamy, in New Jersey. A wide sign, well lit, touted Lancaster County, Pennsylvania, as the heart of Amish Country—*where time stands still.*

"Exactly what I need," she whispered to herself. "A place locked in time."

She'd heard bits and pieces about the area, mostly about the attractions such as Dutch Wonderland and the Amish Village. Ali and her husband had spent an entire weekend a few years ago shopping the outlet malls, a big draw for tourists. They'd returned home full of talk about horse-drawn buggies and folks walking around in Plain clothing that "would make your head spin," Ali had said.

"Like how?" Ryan had said, laughing, not sure if she were joking or not.

"The men grow beards—no mustaches—and they wear dark trousers with tan suspenders and white shirts . . . and straw hats," Ali explained.

"How do the women dress?" Melissa asked.

"Long, dark, caped dresses and aprons, with little white netting caps called prayer coverings."

Melissa hadn't known what to make of it then, but she'd listened intently. "I've heard of prayer caps," she'd said softly. "Hutterite women wear them, too."

Ali didn't seem to know or care much about other Plain sects, but she was eager to chat about her encounter with the horse-and-buggy people. "You should see how cute the children are!" her friend had said, describing the way the girls wore their hair parted down the middle, "without bangs at all," and braids wrapped around their little heads.

Melissa hadn't been so interested in hearing about "the peculiar-looking people" Ali had talked about, and certainly not all the gawking her friends must've done while in Lancaster. But such a place *did* appeal to her. She longed for quietude, at least for the night. First, she must acquire a motel, then find a telephone.

For the first time since she'd left Connecticut, she dared to relax a little. A small sense of tranquility lulled her. But only for a time.

Southeast of Trenton, near Holland on Route 276, she glanced in her rearview mirror. There it was again, the undeniable outline of a Buick sedan, coming up close.

Her heart sank. *How did he find me?* Melissa was aghast, overcome with both dread and disappointment. Renewed panic rushed through her veins, charging her body with needed adrenaline.

She'd memorized the highway options earlier, before the sun sank low in the sky, before it was too difficult to reach for the map and study it as she drove. There were two distinct routes available. She could remain on this interstate highway and link up with Route 202 eventually, or follow this superhighway to another multilane artery, onto Route 30, passing through Exton and Gap, wending her way to her final destination.

In way over her head, she felt helpless. She was caught in the grasp of the greatest horror she'd ever known. But she would not give up without a fight.

Daddy's girl to the bitter end. . . .

She refused to let herself unravel. "Please, God, help me," she murmured, wondering now, as she drove pell-mell, if God cared at all. "If you're really out there somewhere, help me."

The sound of the Buick bumping her car made her scream. Melissa stomped on the accelerator, flooring it, exceeding the speed limit. This was life or death. Her car roared out ahead, momentarily leaving him in the dust. But she knew the Buick had more power than her car.

Sure enough, seconds later, he was within yards again. Only now they were speeding nearly out of control.

This is crazy, she thought. *We're both going to lose it.* She spied the cell phone. She'd been warned not to use it, but she had no choice. She had to get help.

Wham! The Buick bumped her again, just as she reached for the phone. The jolt stunned her, lurching her dangerously to the right. She grabbed the wheel with both hands, turned hard to the left, narrowly missing the ditch, but she'd overcorrected and the car began to spin.

Melissa slammed on the brakes, creating a squealing sound, knowing in seconds the Buick would ram her. But she had no choice. It was either stop or flip over.

Her car careened violently, completing nearly a full circle. Out of the corner of her eye, she saw the Buick swerve into the ditch to avoid a collision. The man fought to control his vehicle, flying past her. He gunned the engine, and the Buick leaped from the ditch in front of her.

The sound of an explosion jolted her to full alert. The gray sedan jerked and leaned stiffly, pitching *back* into the shallow ditch. At a dead stop now, dazed and confused, she stared at the listless car. *What . . . what now?* And then she knew. He'd blown a tire!

Struggling through her tears, she slammed her foot on the accelerator and passed the Buick just as the man opened his door. Instead of an angry face, he leered at her, grinning widely, as if taunting her.

It didn't matter. She was safe . . . for now.

Miles later, still shaking, Melissa made the turnoff to Highway 202. Even if the man changed his tire speedily, he would never find her on this road, never guess where she was headed. To Amish Country—the land that time forgot.

Heading into Lancaster on Route 30, she spotted some restaurants— Miller's Smorgasbord and several others—still open, serving hungry tourists. Motels were plentiful on either side of the highway. Limp and exhausted, Melissa was briefly tempted by a vacancy sign in front of the Steamboat Inn. *Not remote enough*, she thought.

The pressure was beginning to lift. The clench of her jaw had begun to lessen; her shoulders ached but were not nearly as tense as before. She was going to survive. At least, for today.

At the junction of Routes 30 and 222, she followed the road leading north, toward Eden. *Sounds like a pleasant place*, she thought, wondering where all the Plain folk lived. Were they scattered around the county . . . where?

Stopping at a fast-food place, she took a chance and went inside to stretch her tingling legs and to purchase a sandwich and a cup of coffee, inquiring of the clerk about lodging. "Do you know of any inns or B&Bs off the beaten track?"

"Plenty of places to stay around here," the young woman said, smiling. "What exactly are you looking for?"

"Something quiet, away from the noise."

The clerk nodded. "Well, since you're already headed this way, why don't you drive along Hunsecker Road, just up the way apiece. You'll see the sign where to turn. I think you'll find a good many places to stay. Even some private homes with rooms for rent."

"By the week or the day?"

"Whatever you'd like, I suppose. It's coming up on the end of the summer, so you shouldn't have a bit of trouble finding something."

She thanked the woman and hurried back to the car, food in hand.

Wooden boards rumbled as she slowed the car and drove over the Conestoga River via a covered bridge marked "Hunsecker Mill Bridge" on her map. Occasional small openings in the sides of the bridge brought in the slightest bit of light.

Once out in the open, she could see stars winking down at her through the willows and other large trees along the road. She thought again of Ryan's plans for a romantic getaway in Vermont. Columbus Day weekend was the ideal time to travel deep into New England autumn.

Melissa recalled the smell of woodsmoke permeating the crisp, dry air, the crackle of leaves underfoot. They liked to strike out into unpopulated and wooded areas, enjoying a daylong hike into the nearby Green Mountains. One of their favorite things was simply walking in the woods, amidst cinnamon ferns and the colorful undergrowth. There they held hands and talked freely. Always they discovered secluded gardens of milkweed and black-eyed Susans, gurgling streams, low stacked-stone walls, and spicebush swallowtail butterflies. Nature was tangible in such settings, and now, more than ever, she would miss their Vermont experience terribly. But her leaving had altered more than their plans for a romantic weekend. Now *everything* was different.

She might have missed the homemade sign, propped up between the mailbox and the little red flag, if her headlights had not shone directly on the words *Room for Rent*, in big, bold letters.

Pulling cautiously into the driveway, Melissa sat there with the car idling, giving her full attention to a tidy front-gable brick cottage. The land stretched out on either side, dwarfing the house somewhat. When she shut off the ignition, she could hear a host of crickets chirping through the car window. What peace! She longed to sit still, staring up at the expanse of sky and the sliver of a moon.

The front porch light beckoned to her, and she saw that a lovely grapevine wreath with blazing scarlet sage interspersed with ivy and other greenery made for a quaint greeting. Several lamps were still lit throughout the whole house.

Is it too late to knock? she wondered.

Melissa checked the time on the dashboard and saw that it was nearly nine o'clock. She hesitated, thinking how she would feel about company at such a time—*if* she were still at home. But the sign on the mailbox seemed to indicate a vacancy, and now that she looked, there was a sign in the front window, as well.

Getting out of the car, she hurried up the porch steps, realizing she needn't rush anymore. She was fairly safe here on the back byways of Lancaster County. She lifted her hand to ring the bell when the door opened and a woman, not many years older than Melissa, greeted her with a warm smile. "Hello, there," the Plain woman said. "Are you looking for a room?"

"As a matter of fact, I am," Melissa replied, noticing the small netting-type cap, the hair bun beneath, the high neckline, tucked bodice, and long, flowing dress with tiny lavender flowers. The very garb Ali had been so eager to discuss. "I might be staying only one night, if that's all right."

"Oh yes . . . 'Course you can stay as long or as short as you please." The screen door was opened to her and she was welcomed inside. "Please, just make yourself at home."

"Thank you." Melissa felt strange, not knowing the woman's name, but she didn't ask. Instead, she followed the slender brunette up the stairs, where she was shown the spare room and agreed to take it. She was surprised at the price. Thirty dollars per night, including breakfast. The lovely room would be offered at a discount if she decided to stay longer.

"My name is Lela Denlinger," the cheerful woman said.

"I'm Melissa." She gave only her first name, purposely. "I suppose you have a telephone?" she asked, hoping she hadn't stumbled into an Amish household where phones were taboo.

Lela smiled, pointing to the phone in the kitchen. "Oh my, yes, and you're welcome to use it anytime. My home is your home . . . for as long as you choose to stay."

Well, *this* wasn't the sort of reception she'd expected. Relieved, Melissa hurried to the car for her single piece of luggage. "I pack very light," she explained when Lela eyed the overnight case.

"Feel free to help yourself to anything you find in the refrigerator," Lela offered.

More perks than Melissa ever expected. The more she chatted with Lela, the more she genuinely liked the cottagelike retreat, as well as its owner. She'd stumbled onto a haven, of sorts. A sanctuary at last.

She waited until the house was quiet, grateful that Lela had left a lamp on in both the living room and the kitchen. At last she had access to a "safe" telephone. Digging into her pants pocket, she found the important number and dialed.

Then to her acute frustration she reached only an answering machine. "Please leave a message at the tone or dial my pager at this number—555-0097," the recorded voice directed.

Well, I guess it's better than nothing, Melissa thought. In the dimly lit kitchen, she spoke clearly into the phone, reading off the rather faded number printed on Lela Denlinger's telephone. Hanging up, she sighed, feeling bone tired, weary . . . but at peace, strangely enough.

Eight

❖ ❖ ❖

Ryan awakened Saturday to the distant cry of sea gulls. Morning light slipped into the room between the horizontal blinds, signaling the end of an arduous night. His sleep had been fitful, real rest elusive. The clock radio beamed the time: 5:33. Any hope of further slumber evaporated as he glanced at Melissa's side of the bed. How many times had he awakened that night, searching for her, only to experience fresh disappointment each time his brain registered her absence?

Slipping into his robe, he tightened the belt and went downstairs to make coffee. Morning ritual. Daisy followed him into the kitchen, then disappeared through the doggie door while Ryan ground coffee. The hum of the percolator disturbed the stillness, mimicking the sounds of a normal day. Yet today was anything *but* normal.

As he fully awakened, his mind began to race again, as he thought of Melissa out there somewhere, running away, running from . . . *what?*

Daisy lumbered back through her door and set her expectant gaze on Ryan. Padding to her food dish, she sniffed a little, disdaining the unappetizing crunchy breakfast. She slinked gloomily into the living room and located the spot where a future sunbeam was sure to find her.

Ryan poured his coffee, sipped, grimaced, and poured the entire contents down the drain. He headed upstairs to shower, reliving last night's flurry of activity and phone calls, having finally phoned the police. Around nine o'clock, two policemen had sauntered to the door as if they had all the time in the world. Once inside the house, they poked around and asked the standard formulaic questions. When they saw Melissa's "good-bye letter," their shared glance said it all.

For the next hour the tenor of the discussion changed dramatically.

Instead of initiating a rapid search for his wife, they began to treat Ryan as a *suspect*.

Struggling with frustration and worry, Ryan patiently endured their insinuating questions. Finally, one of the policemen stated outright, "There's no sign of foul play, Mr. James. People are free to come and go as they wish. Unless of course . . . you haven't told us everything."

Ryan was glad to see them leave. They glibly promised to "keep an eye out," then strolled out the front door, presumably to get on with real police business. He was on his own.

Later Denny called back as he had promised and insisted on flying in anyway, to be the proverbial good friend in this "time of trouble." Ryan had felt somewhat relieved, but in the end it didn't matter whether Denny came to visit or not. Only Melissa's safe return could bring him comfort now.

Before getting into the shower, Ryan turned on the water, adjusting the hot and cold, then grabbed the cordless phone receiver and placed it above the shower frame.

Just in case.

Several times during the night, Melissa had awakened, breaking out in cold perspiration. Each realization of her situation brought a fresh assault of fear. Now, muddled and confused, she pieced together yesterday's events. The unexpected encounter at the restaurant in downtown Mystic, her ultimate desperate flight.

She struggled to sit up in bed, but only briefly. Her head throbbed with the least exertion. *What must Ryan think of me?* she wondered, sinking back against the pillows again. *He must be desperate with worry.* On more than one occasion she had been tempted to call him but had resisted.

It was then that she thought of corresponding with Ryan by e-mail. That should be safe, shouldn't it? The notion gave her hope, though only a flicker. She remembered reading news accounts of on-line virus creators and senders—there must be ways to trace such offenders. If the authorities could locate hackers, then she, too, could be found. Her spirits sank.

In the distance, the sound of horses' hooves tapping the pavement piqued her curiosity. And yet another . . . what was *that* sound? She strained, listening. Such a familiar yet foreign sound—the unmistakable rattle of carriage wheels.

What on earth?

She sprang out of bed, taking no time to bother with slippers. Standing in the dormer window, she peered down at the road below and was amazed to see a horse and buggy hurrying along. Where were they headed at this hour?

Melissa glimpsed the driver—a young woman in a dark dress and apron, wearing a little white cap on her head—with a girl at her side, dressed similarly. She guessed they were Amish, the peace-loving sect Ali and her husband had so enthusiastically discussed after visiting here.

It's a real-life Jane Austen movie, she thought, momentarily pleased at the sight. She stood in awe, watching the carriage and horse until they disappeared from view.

Turning from the window, she inspected the room by dawn's light. The bed—surely an antique—was framed by a large brass headboard and footboard. Nearby, the bold scale and fine patina of the cherry bureau reminded her of a dresser owned by Nana Clark. She recalled how thrilled Nana had been to discover such a "find," for her grandmother adored antique furniture.

Sighing, she went and sat in the floral chair in a cozy nook, complete with built-in bookshelves and a gleaming brass floor lamp. The room was even more spacious than her own at home. Tucked way at one end of the room was a second sleeping area, where a single bed nestled behind hand-painted flowery curtains of gentle yellow and lavender. A small wicker table, painted solid yellow, anchored the sitting area.

Leaning back, she felt her muscles relax against the chair. In spite of her anxiety, she knew she'd made a good choice by coming here. After a time she reached for one of the many books behind her and, thumbing through, discovered the author to be a Mennonite minister. So was Lela also a member of the conservative group? Curious to know more about Plain tradition, she read several chapters before returning the book to its shelf.

Then, tiptoeing back to the bed, she sat down, staring at the rag rug beneath her feet. How had she stumbled upon such a whimsical cottage? And what of Lela Denlinger? The woman had been unusually friendly, welcoming Melissa as though an anticipated guest, even family. Was this typical for Plain folk?

The sound of further *clip-clops* enticed her back to the window. Below her, several buggies, spaced as if by an invisible hand, made their way down the road in front of the house. An undeniable calm swept over her as she watched, and for a moment, she felt safe. Safe, for the first time since yesterday morning when Ryan had kissed her good-bye.

Safe . . .

All too quickly, she recalled the startling circumstances by which she had come to this idyllic setting. She washed and dressed for the day, wondering when the phone would ring for her.

Nine

❖ ❖ ❖

Denny boarded the 747 bound for Providence, Rhode Island—the second leg of a flight originating in Denver—having changed planes in Atlanta. He was greeted by a smiley brunette flight attendant who offered an array of magazines. Denny patted the pocket Bible in his shirt. "Came prepared," he said, offering a smile.

"I can see that," she replied glibly and continued greeting the incoming line of passengers.

Denny struggled down the narrow aisle, maneuvering his large frame to a row midway through the plane. When he located his seat, he frowned and checked his boarding pass. He was fairly certain his travel agent had booked an aisle seat. A big man, Denny *always* requested aisle seating.

Bummer, he thought, sighing. *Maybe God has a reason. . . .*

Walking with the Lord had taught him one thing. Those who endeavored to live in Christ could expect the unexpected. No accidents for a Christian. Even the smallest irritations turned out to reveal God's marvelous intentions.

Denny squeezed into the middle chair between the aisle and window seats. Watching the remaining passengers find their spots, he replayed last night's conversation with Ryan. Denny had called back about ten o'clock and learned that Melissa was still missing.

"I'm coming anyway," Denny had declared. "You need help with this, man." To his surprise, Ryan had agreed, but Denny suspected his buddy was overcome with worry, too drained to protest. So be it. He assured Ryan he'd rent a car and spare him the two-hour round trip. But Ryan had insisted on making the trip personally to meet Denny at the airport.

Closing his eyes momentarily, he thought of Evelyn, missing her. He hoped she'd wait up for his call later that evening.

He was roused from his reflection when a morose-looking, pimple-faced teenager, clad in torn jeans and a soiled T-shirt, moped his way to Denny's row. Mumbling, the kid pointed to the window seat next to Denny. Denny smiled, struggled out of his seat and into the aisle, allowing the boy to pass.

Hot diggity! Denny thought. Reclaiming the middle seat next to the boy, he settled in once again, ready to strike up a conversation with the surly one. About that time, an elderly woman tapped him on the shoulder. In her hand she held the ticket to the aisle seat. "Care to switch?" she said, eyeing his giant frame with amusement.

"Thanks, but I'm fine," Denny said, returning a smile. "I'm smaller than I appear in person."

The kid next to him snorted.

"But you need room for your legs, young man," the woman insisted.

"They fit me fine," Denny told her. "They're collapsible."

"Okey-dokey," she said in a singsongy voice and plopped down in the aisle seat. "You're a funny one."

"Thank you, ma'am."

One minor disaster averted. Now on with the adventure. He bided his time, waiting for the right moment. As the plane taxied down the runway and took to the air, the moment arrived. The kid was gripping the armrest, his face a gray-green. Unmistakably, the boy was terrified. *Fear of flying.*

Denny leaned over and whispered, "Don't be afraid, man. God won't let anything happen to us."

The boy's eyes jerked open. "What?"

"We're cool," Denny said casually. "My number's not up yet, and since you happen to be on my plane, your number isn't up yet, either."

"How . . . do *you* know?" the boy muttered.

"Call it a hunch," Denny quipped. "Besides, there's a reason you're sitting next to me."

"Who *are* you?"

He grinned at the kid. "I'm your new best friend."

Frowning, the teen met Denny's gaze, then a slight grin emerged. They bantered back and forth, and in short order Denny worked his disarming wit on the kid. The fear began to dissipate, the shoulders relaxed, and the boy slowly opened up.

The breakthrough came when Denny revealed that he'd scrimmaged with John Elway at training camp. The walls came tumbling down. They talked football for a solid hour before Denny directed the discussion to more serious things.

He learned that the boy's name was Michael and that he'd been in and out of foster homes his entire life. Michael was returning from a visit with his estranged mother in Atlanta who, after two days, could hardly wait to be rid of him. She'd put him on an early flight back to his most recent foster family.

Denny listened as the kid talked. Prayerfully, he sized up the situation, not surprised at all by Michael's armor of rage. But the sword of salvation was stronger. Denny would cut through the rejection and pain with God's awesome love.

When the flight attendants came around with lunch, Michael was ready for some good news for a change. God had already prepared the way.

By the time the plane approached the runway, Denny had indeed made a new friend. Young Michael listened with rapt attention as Denny opened his pocket Bible and presented the Gospel.

"Oh . . . man. This is so . . . well, out there," Michael replied. "I need time to think it through."

"That's cool. Maybe we could hit a youth service somewhere while I'm in Connecticut," Denny replied.

"Church?" Michael frowned.

"Sure, wouldn't hurt to try it. At least once."

Michael considered this, then replied, "I didn't think this was gonna lead to *church*."

Denny understood. "I've been there, Michael. Church is just a place where people like you and I hang out. Like a gang—only for believers."

Michael snickered, but he seemed to respond to the unconventional explanation.

Their conversation ceased as the plane's wheels slammed, then bounced against the runway. The passenger to Denny's left—the lady in the aisle seat—leaned over. "You're quite the 'Billy Graham,' young man," she said without looking up from her needlepoint. "Can't say I've ever heard anything quite like it."

"I just show up, and God does the rest."

"Okey-dokey," she replied, putting her needle aside. She reached for the gate information in the seat pocket in front of her, obviously nervous. Maybe she was worried that Denny might start in with her about God and church.

He chuckled. *Double duty.* The woman had overheard the entire conversation. *And God's Word does not return void,* he thought joyfully.

Before deplaning, Denny and Michael traded phone numbers. The rest was in God's hands. Reluctant to bid farewell to Michael, Denny grabbed his own luggage and stuffed the pocket Bible in the kid's hands. "Take good care of it, okay?"

"Sure." The boy's eyes shone with gratitude, his earlier surliness gone.

Next challenge: Ryan and Melissa.

Ryan stood near the catwalk, waiting. Denny emerged soon enough, and Ryan was struck again by his friend's large and muscular build, wrapped in gray slacks and a red-and-blue polo shirt, topped off by that perpetual exuberance. The image of the Jolly Green Giant came to mind. Sans the green, of course.

They greeted each other as only good friends do, though pretending they were meeting under normal circumstances. "So . . . you've still got all your hair," Denny commented with false chagrin, releasing Ryan after a bear hug. "Uh! Wait a minute!" He pretended to examine Ryan's head. "I see some signs of hope . . . an emerging bald spot."

Ryan chuckled. "In your dreams."

"You know, it's an insult to flaunt that hair when you're around follicly challenged people like me."

"How do you think *I* feel?" Ryan shot back good-naturedly. "Standing next to you, I look emaciated."

"Jealousy will get you nowhere, my friend," Denny replied, releasing his grip.

They shared a good laugh and headed directly to the parking lot, since Denny preferred to carry on his luggage. No need to put up with baggage-claim madness.

Locating the SUV, Ryan opened the back and tossed Denny's bag inside. They negotiated the noncongested parking area, heading for the highway. Ryan steered the Bronco onto Interstate 95, southbound.

Small talk occupied their attention, at least for several miles, but the unspoken concern over Melissa created tension in the air. It was Denny who finally broached the subject heavy on Ryan's mind. "Did Melissa finally call?"

Ryan shook his head. "Still waiting." He picked up his cell phone. "All my calls are being forwarded to this."

"Any new ideas since we last talked?"

"No. I've called everyone I can think of—including the police."

Denny sighed audibly. "What're you going to do now?"

"Nothing I *can* do, but wait."

"Did she ever pull this kind of thing before? Just up and leave?"

Ryan hesitated. "Well . . . yes. Before we were married."

"Really?"

"She got spooked or something. I didn't know where she was for a couple days."

Denny looked surprised. "What happened?"

Ryan shrugged. "She finally called. And we worked everything out."

Denny didn't say anything for a moment. "Has she run off since you've been married?"

"Just that one time."

"Ever threaten to?" Denny persisted.

Ryan turned to his friend. "C'mon, Den, cut me some slack here."

Denny said nothing.

Eventually, Ryan's apologetic tone ended the silence. "Sorry. Guess I'm a little on edge."

"My fault. I'm like a bull in a china shop sometimes," Denny replied. "She'll call soon." He turned to look out the window, quiet for a moment, then—"I sure missed the trees here."

"I miss *your* mountains."

"Missed your ocean, too," Denny added.

"And your desert sand."

Denny laughed. "Yeah, right!"

"Just trying to keep up," Ryan replied. Denny grinned back. But as the miles passed, a subdued mood prevailed, and for the remainder of the drive to Lord's Point, neither said another word regarding Melissa. Ryan, however, thought of little else.

Ten

❖ ❖ ❖

R yan resisted the urge to hope. Melissa would *not* be waiting for him, sitting on the back steps when he arrived home from the airport with Denny. Foolish thought. But then again . . . what if she *were?*

He imagined the moment clearly, as if the vision might materialize by the sure force of his will. Pulling into the driveway, he'd catch a glimpse of her. Denny might point and grin at Ryan. "Well, whadaya know!"

Mellie might stand timidly, brush off her jeans, and watch him leap out of the car. Their eyes would meet and then . . . all hesitancy would melt away as they embraced like lost lovers who hadn't seen each other in months.

"I'm so sorry," she'd whisper over and over, asking his forgiveness for creating such a silly misunderstanding. He would hold her face in his hands, gently kiss her sweet lips. "Shh, my darling. It's okay now, everything's okay." All would be forgiven and their short nightmare—a mere twenty-four hours—would soon become a blip on the screen over the next fifty years or more, a lifetime of love.

Not normally given to flights of fancy, Ryan sighed. As they turned the final corner, their home appeared, and he drove into the driveway. His chest tightened in anticipation, hoping for a miracle. But Mellie was not waiting on the porch.

The cliché *It doesn't hurt to hope* crossed his mind. But he dismissed it, discouraged. *Yeah, it does hurt. Hurts a lot.*

"You okay?" Denny asked.

He caught his friend's expression of concern. "I'd better check on things in the guest room. Clean sheets, stuff like that." One more reminder of Mellie's absence. She would have been the one to prepare the room for Denny's stay.

"There's a bed, right?" Denny joked.

Ryan chuckled. "And some new paintings, too. Mellie was eager for you to see them. In fact, one of them is yours to take home. It was supposed to be a surprise."

"When did she—?"

"Finished it about a month ago." Ryan registered Denny's uncertain look. "She wanted you to have it—a special gift."

"Sure, man. Just seems so . . . weird."

Weird, all right, thought Ryan as he grabbed Denny's bag and led the way up the brick walk to the house. He was strangely aware of Melissa's flowers, well tended and blooming profusely. The lawn, edged and well manicured, was a mere backdrop for the colorful array.

Daisy was barely able to contain herself with delight, meeting them at the door and following close on their heels as they headed upstairs. Down the hall, past framed pictures recording their happy days, Ryan led his guest to the back room—Melissa's pride and joy. A breezy seaside retreat, nestled under the eaves, the roomy place was set up for their occasional guests, as well as another showplace for more of Mellie's art.

The bed, angled against two white-paneled walls, was draped with an airy comforter that resembled old-fashioned mattress ticking. Abundant pastel blue and cream-colored pillows vied for attention against the white wooden headboard. Windows on either side of the bed appeared wider, with louvered shutters that opened flat against the walls. Mellie's idea. She thought the room seemed larger by emphasizing the diagonal line.

Starfish, spray-painted white, stood along a plate rail a third of the way down from the pale blue ceiling. A see-through white birdcage graced the room as walls sang with Mellie's floral paintings.

One of her best paintings hung to the left of the dresser—a young woman surrounded by rosebushes, growing wild on a grassy mound near the beach-bordered ocean.

Denny seemed drawn to the image, gazing at the art as he inched closer. "This one's for me, isn't it?"

Ryan nodded. "She wanted you to take the ocean home with you."

Denny raised his finger to the canvas, delicately tracing the faint symbol in the clouds, a product of the shadows and light, "Is this—"

"She thought you'd appreciate it."

"Beautiful," Denny replied, transfixed by the unmistakable outline of a cross.

"I only wish she were here to present it to you herself."

Silence reigned for a moment. Then Ryan gestured toward the north-facing window overlooking the garage. "Not much of an ocean view, I'm afraid."

Denny shrugged. "The whole *house* has an ocean view. The beach is what . . . twenty paces away?"

"About that." Ryan opened the closet, showing Denny the available space and extra hangers. "Make yourself at home."

"Won't take me long to unpack." Denny was staring at the painting again, seemingly reluctant to take his eyes off it. Then he turned a worried look on Ryan.

"What is it?" Ryan asked.

"Shouldn't we go looking for her?"

"Where?"

"I don't know . . . but somewhere. Aren't you worried?"

Ryan sighed. "Of course I am. But where do we start? She has one friend, Ali, and she doesn't know anything. Mellie's mother died when she was young. Her father abandoned her, left her to be raised by a neighbor. No one knows where he is now. No other living relatives."

"No other friends?"

"Not here. None that she talked about," Ryan replied.

"Didn't she have some favorite places?" Denny sat on the bed, gingerly testing the box springs.

"A few. Watch Hill . . . Napatree. We never took you there last time you came out. I met her there, in fact."

"Why don't we check it out?" Denny persisted. "Take your cell phone along."

Ryan forced a smile. "We could do a late lunch."

"Hey, I do lunch," Denny chuckled.

Ryan closed the door, leaving his friend alone in Mellie's blue-and-white paradise.

Denny opened his suitcase, removed his toiletries—shaver, deodorant, and toothbrush—and placed them in the bathroom. One look in the mirror, and he knew another shave was in order. Plugging in the razor, he registered how quiet the house seemed this time, so empty without Melissa's eager presence. Not that she was larger than life, no. She just had a warm and welcoming way about her, a knack for making a person feel at home. Last time, she'd gone overboard to make him feel comfortable, even going so far as to arrange her menus around his preferences. Yet in spite of Melissa's obvious gift of hospitality, her outgoing nature, something had seemed amiss. At times she had struck Denny as . . . somewhat secretive. Just today Ryan had said of his wife that she had no living relatives, practically no friends besides Ali.

No friends or acquaintances from the past? Her estranged father out there somewhere, never bothering to contact his only daughter. Seemed strange.

He finished shaving, splashing on some aftershave, still absorbed in his overactive imagination. Melissa's leaving surely pointed only to a lover's spat—she and Ryan had simply had a misunderstanding and needed a few days to sort things out. That was all.

Suppressing his curiosity, he put away his shaver and finished unpacking.

––––––––

The last thing Lela wanted to be was pushy, but her Connecticut houseguest looked a little peaked this morning. "Would you care to eat lunch with me?" she asked. "There's plenty here, and I'd like the company. No extra charge." She let out a little chuckle, altogether glad she'd opened her door last night, in spite of the hour.

Melissa smiled back faintly, then rose from the sofa in the sitting area just off the kitchen. "I'd love to have lunch with you. Thanks."

Grateful for the positive response from her first boarder, she thought Melissa's face seemed downright thin, her eyes, though clearly blue, were drawn and pain ridden. She had been surprised when Melissa had not packed up and left this morning, as she had indicated she would. Lela overlooked the check-out time, and along about breakfast, Melissa mentioned that she was expecting a phone call and would it be all right if she stayed on a bit longer.

Glad for the company, Lela had agreed that Melissa could stay on another night, or for the extra hours she needed. "Don't worry about paying for half a day or whatnot. It's no trouble to me."

Obvious relief spread over Melissa's face, giving her cause to sigh. But, then, of all things—and on such a heavenly summer day, too—she had gone and curled up on the love seat in the corner of the room, sitting there all morning, just a-gazing out the bay window that faced westward, toward the area of Hunsecker Mill Bridge.

What could possibly weigh so heavily on her heart that she would sit nearly lifeless that way? Lela wondered. Was Melissa holding her breath for the telephone to ring? She *had* kept her eye on the kitchen phone a lot, no question. Seemed so awful downtrodden, too. Even despairing. So much so, Lela had thought of offering her a Scripture or a prayer.

She guessed Melissa to be no more than twenty-five. Maybe a bit older, though it wasn't always easy to tell. She wore a tasteful amount of makeup and the typical attire that modern women seemed to feel comfortable wearing these days. *Designer jeans*, yes, that's what they were called, Lela was fairly sure. And a T-shirt that had some writing on it, but she hadn't bothered to stare long enough to see really. Anyway, the girl from Connecticut had the look of—how should she say?—an up-to-the-minute woman. And it appeared that she was married, according to the wedding band and diamond ring on the fourth finger of her left hand. A married woman traveling alone? This idea was most foreign to Lela.

There was something else, too. Something she hoped she was wrong about; but Melissa appeared to be in some kind of trouble. The girl was more than anxious. Lela's concern for her guest increased considerably when Melissa asked to park her car "somewhere else."

"Where . . . do you mean?" she'd asked, confused, wondering why the driveway area outside the house wasn't just fine for a short time.

"Is there an out-of-the-way place?" came the strange request.

She hadn't had to think much about such a question. Why Melissa wanted to hide her car, Lela had no idea. "Well, I suppose you could drive on over to my sister and brother-in-law's place."

Melissa seemed eager. "How far from here?"

"Just up the road apiece, to the next farmhouse. I'll call up to the barn after lunch. That way I'm sure to catch somebody." She hadn't bothered to explain that Thaddeus King, her brother-in-law, though raised in the Old Ways, had joined a church with less conservative Amish folk. He enjoyed his newfangled conveniences, such as a radio—"helps calm the cows at milkin'"—as well as a telephone in the barn.

"Thanks." The color suddenly returned to Melissa's cheeks.

"Well, first I'll have to see if there's room for a car in their old shed." She didn't go on to say that Thaddeus might not want such a thing as an automobile hidden away on his property, being that he and Elizabeth still preferred horse and buggy for their main transportation.

But that sort of thing wouldn't make any difference to a fancy *Englischer*, probably.

Melissa stared out at countless acres of alfalfa, and, in the distance, verdant and rolling hills toward the south ridge. To occupy her mind, and out of courtesy, she offered to help Lela prepare lunch but was quickly turned down. Not rudely, though. She couldn't imagine the owner of this country cottage exhibiting anything but genuine courtesy.

Lela was the epitome of hospitality, the gracious hostess, in spite of the fact that Melissa was a paying guest. Lela had presented a lavish breakfast, so abundant that Melissa had felt almost too full. So she was content to simply while away the morning gazing out at the tranquil sweep of field and trees, waiting for the phone to ring.

Eleven

❖ ❖ ❖

Tendrils of English ivy, trained along the windows in the kitchen, was the perfect touch for the dining area. Melissa marveled at such a unique window treatment. Something she had never thought of doing. "What a great idea," she told Lela.

"I decided there was no need for curtains in this room," Lela explained happily over homemade chicken noodle soup and grilled cheese sandwiches.

"You could be an interior designer," Melissa remarked. "Who would've thought to eliminate the need for curtains by using strands of ivy?"

"Well, I've always loved natural light." Lela smiled, glancing at the windows. "Even as a girl, I liked to bring the outside in."

"I know the feeling."

They ate in silence until Lela remarked, "There's really no need for privacy what with the courtyard out back, you know."

"And all those beautiful trees."

"Oh yes, I do love my maples."

Melissa had a sudden urge to share her tree-hugging experiences. College years had spawned impulsive behavior. Yet she'd saved some enormous ponderosa pines in her lifetime and was proud of it. Taking another bite of her grilled cheese, she decided against the urge to reveal too much about herself. She must use caution.

Still overly anxious about her car, Melissa asked Lela when she might be able to move it.

"I'll call my brother-in-law as soon as the table is cleared off and the dishes are washed and dried." Which she did promptly and without accepting Melissa's offer of help.

"Hello, Thaddeus," Lela said when he answered.

"Well, how *are* ya, Lela?"

She filled him in quickly, so as not to call too much attention to her suspicions. After all, Melissa was sitting right across the room, curled up on the same sofa as before. "I have an overnight guest who needs a place to put her car. Somewhere out of the way," she told him.

"That's no problem. She can park it in our shed for the time being." Thaddeus fell silent for a second, then asked, "When didja decide to take in boarders?"

"Just last evening."

"Does Elizabeth know anything 'bout it?"

"Well, not yet she doesn't."

He sighed into the phone, probably mulling things over.

Before he could question her further, she said, "Then you won't mind about having a car parked in the shed?"

"Don't mind if it ain't too awful long," said Thaddeus.

"We'll be on over, then."

After hanging up the phone, she invited Melissa out on the front porch and pointed to the sprawling farmhouse up the way. "My sister and her family live over there. Her husband, Thaddeus, says it'll be all right to put your car in their shed."

"Thanks, Lela. This means a lot to me." Melissa pushed her hair behind her ear and turned toward the house. "I'll go in and get my car keys."

When she returned, Melissa asked Lela to ride along.

"Well . . . that's nice of you, but I don't mind the walk." She didn't want Melissa to think she was hesitant to trust her. But she wasn't sure if she ought to. The younger woman *was* a stranger, after all.

"Please, I insist," Melissa said. "You're doing me a big favor, and I'm very grateful."

Papa had often said if a person was gracious—thankful—you could most likely trust him or her. Melissa certainly was that. "All right, I'll ride there with you."

Melissa's eyes widened. "So, it's okay? I mean, you're allowed to?"

She laughed softly. "Of course, I may ride in a car. I'm not Amish, if that's what you're thinking."

"I couldn't be sure," Melissa said with a grin. "I'm not at all familiar with the customs here. I've heard there are many varieties of Plain folk."

"That's for sure," she replied, not wanting to go into all that just now.

They drove together, Lela in the front seat, telling Melissa where to turn into the long dirt lane. "See that sign there—says *Amish Quilts & Sundries*—that's where you turn. Then keep going till you come to the barnyard."

Melissa did just that. And when the car came to a stop, Elizabeth and the children came running out to greet them. "Here comes my sister and her brood. They'll be more than happy to meet an Englischer. They probably haven't seen or talked to a modern lady like you in the longest time."

When Melissa didn't seem to understand, Lela explained further. "In Plain circles, if you're not Amish, you're viewed as an outsider—an Englischer."

"Oh," said Melissa.

Lela wasn't at all certain if the woman eager to hide her car had any idea that she was actually considered worldly in the eyes of Elizabeth and the youngsters gathered round. But, really, she was more concerned how Elizabeth and Thaddeus would react to her taking in strangers as boarders.

Melissa was careful not to stare at Lela's Amish relatives. She recalled seeing from her bedroom window this morning the dark dresses and little white caps on the women riding in the horse-drawn carriages. But now, as she encountered the lineup of bare feet and the long brown dresses and black aprons worn by Lela's sister and her girls, and the peculiar black trousers, suspenders, and cropped hair on the boys, she felt terribly awkward. Still, their rosy cheeks, bright eyes, and genuine smiles soon captured her heart, and she felt strangely warm. Accepted.

"Melissa, this is Elizabeth King, one of my three sisters," Lela said, introducing them. "Elizabeth lives the closest of all my siblings."

"Hullo," said the soft-spoken woman. "Nice to meet you."

The children were next, beginning with Mary Jane, followed by Timothy, Linda, and John, the baby.

When Elizabeth invited them inside for lemonade and cookies, Melissa felt herself tense up. "Do you mind if I put my car in the shed first?" she asked, feeling the urgency to hide the vehicle from prying eyes as soon as possible.

"Not a'tall," Elizabeth said, exchanging curious glances with Lela.

Relieved, she scurried off to the car and pulled it forward, noticing an Amishman motioning to her. Tall, blond, and exceptionally tanned, the man nodded and smiled as she drove her car into the shed. Getting out, she called her thanks to him, deciding that he must be Elizabeth's husband.

"Name's Thaddeus King," he said, extending one hand and removing his straw hat with the other. "Are you new to the area?" He held his hat flat against his chest.

First question . . . How many more? she wondered.

"New England's my home." That was enough.

"Just passin' through, are ya?"

How far would he press?

She turned and scanned the farmland with her eyes. "I'd heard about Lancaster County from friends of mine. I wanted to see it for myself." Not entirely true, but this would have to suffice.

"Well, then, Lela will just hafta bring you over again sometime. We'll show you all around the farm."

She didn't have the heart to tell him she wouldn't be staying *that* long. Yet he seemed kind enough. Helpful, too. Still, people like Thaddeus made her feel uncomfortable. She just didn't know how to take him. Was he as considerate as he seemed?

"Slide over just a little," Elizabeth said, waving her hand at young John. "Your auntie can scarcely squeeze herself in."

"Oh, I'm fine," Lela said, giving John a quick hug. "There's plenty of room."

They were assembled in her sister's big kitchen, all of them, sitting around the long trestle table. Mary Jane helped her mother carry plates of cookies to the table. And there was a tall pitcher of fresh lemonade, the kind Elizabeth was known to serve her guests.

From across the table, she eyed Melissa, who seemed entirely out of place, what with her blue jeans and trendy T-shirt. Lela hoped the fancy woman didn't feel uncomfortable.

"Care for some chocolate chip cookies?" Elizabeth offered a plate of warm treats, all smiles.

"Thank you" was all Melissa said. Silently, she reached for a single cookie, displaying rust-colored fingernails. Several flashy rings, too— two on each hand. Her Connecticut boarder was clearly well off, wearing diamond-studded rings.

She tried not to dwell on such thoughts. The Lord was sovereign, giving good gifts to whom He saw fit. It was not her place to judge. Yet she wondered what Melissa was all about. The woman renting her second bedroom seemed as *naerfich*—nervous—as anybody she'd known. Why so?

The walk back to Lela's cottage was pleasant enough, though Melissa felt uneasy about being out on the open road. So vulnerable. Too accessible . . .

Even with Lela at her side, she felt the old apprehension settle in. Wild strawberry vines grew in the grassy ditch and occasional roses bordered the road. The setting reminded her of some of Ryan's favorite haunts in New Hampshire and Vermont, where winding narrow roads led to delightful destinations such as ancient covered bridges and cider mills. The song of many birds gave her courage, sounds reminiscent of her New England home by the sea.

Home . . .

Ryan was and always would be her home. Where he was, there she longed to be. He had found her at a time when she was lost, disconnected from the world. Young and terrified, she had welcomed his love, making his heart her home.

I have to let him know I'm safe, she thought. *He deserves to know that much.*

She walked a bit farther, reluctant to strike up another conversation with Lela. The smell of honeysuckle, the abandoned road, the patchwork land as far as the eye could see—all this offered her a chance to catch her breath. Desperately, she needed to soak in the serenity, because the minute the phone call came, most likely she would be on her way.

"Such a pretty day," Lela commented.

"Yes."

"I dislike staying indoors on days like this."

She wondered what Lela did for a living. Surely she worked somewhere. "Do you rent out your second bedroom all year long?"

"I suppose I would if someone needed it" came Lela's quick reply. "But I just got the notion yesterday to put out my room-for-rent sign."

Melissa was taken aback by this information. "So I'm your first renter?"

"God dropped the idea in my heart," Lela surprised her by saying. "Yes, you're the very first."

"Well, I'm honored."

Lela continued. "I'd been reading my Bible and praying, asking the Lord what I might do to help someone in need."

Melissa hardly knew what to say. Hadn't *she* herself made a prayer to God last evening, as well? A reckless one, at best. She'd asked God to help her get away from that monster in the gray sedan.

"I do believe God answered my prayer," Lela added.

And mine, thought Melissa.

"You believe in Him, don't you?"

The question was completely unexpected. She thought how she might answer. Lela's face was indeed earnest—the good woman was waiting for an honest response. She deserved as much.

"I'm not much of a prize for God, I'm afraid," she admitted softly.

"Well, now, you don't have to be," Lela said. "The Lord doesn't look on your heart and expect it to be neat as a pin. That's what *He* wants to do for you."

She wondered how a stranger could know anything about the state of her heart. Broken was the best word to describe her heart at the moment. Wounded and bleeding.

"The Lord loves you, Melissa. Just as you are."

She didn't feel she had to respond to Lela's comment. Instead, she focused on the bungalow with its gingerbread and wooden posts along the front porch, in the near distance. They made the turn at the bend, and the flower gardens arranged in perfect symmetry around the front yard came into view. Parallel rectangular beds divided by a flagstone walkway marked the path to the house. Black-eyed Susans bloomed en masse in a mixed perennial garden, outshining the other flowers.

"Is there taxi service out here?" she asked, not weighing the consequences.

"Well, I suppose there is, yes." Lela looked puzzled. "Why do you ask?"

She knew she owed the woman an explanation as to why she wanted to call a cab when free transportation—her own car—had just been concealed in Thaddeus King's shed. "I have a quick errand to run," she said. "I wouldn't want to bother your sister and husband again."

Lela's eyes widened. She was clearly confused.

Quickening her pace, Melissa worried that she'd missed her phone call.

"Are you in a hurry?" Lela asked as they approached the sidewalk leading to her house.

"Just a little." She stopped to admire the garden, hoping Lela wouldn't pry.

"Shall we cut some flowers for a bouquet?" Lela suggested, her voice higher in pitch than before.

Picking flowers in Lela's garden would be a delightful experience, but she wanted—*needed*—to send an e-mail to Ryan, risky as it was. She had to make contact with him, even though she'd been warned against doing so. He would receive the message on Monday morning when he turned on his office computer. She'd use his personal e-mail address at work.

"I'll take a rain check on the flowers," she said, hoping she hadn't offended her kind hostess. She could hardly wait to call a cab and get to town, locate a place to rent some Internet time. A short message would soothe some of Ryan's pain.

Love always finds its way home, Mrs. Browning used to say. Now, fondly recalling the woman who had served as her second mother, Melissa was surprised to have forgotten the often-repeated words. Remembering gave her permission to follow through with her plan, despite the perplexed look on Lela's face.

Something's awful wrong, Lela thought as she watched the yellow taxicab pull away. She thought of calling Elizabeth and confiding her growing concern about the woman who'd rented her spare bedroom. One minute Melissa wanted to hide away her car, or so it seemed. The next she was willing to pay good money for a taxi to drive her all the way into Lancaster. Well, she didn't care to think what a pretty penny such a trip might cost. Yet, why did she care? She'd encountered strangers a-plenty through the years. None as scatterbrained and restless, however. Just what Melissa's story was, she didn't know.

Suddenly, out of the blue, a strange feeling of foreboding clouded Lela's mind. A feeling of . . . *what?* Fear? Danger? Puzzled by her own emotions, Lela went immediately to her bedroom, closed the door, and knelt beside her bed. "Lord, I don't understand why Melissa is here. But I know you have a purpose in this. . . ."

She continued to pray for her guest, but the inexplicable fear only deepened in her heart. The fervency of her prayer increased in response, and she stormed the gates of heaven with her petitions for help and peace, until Lela felt like Jacob of old, who had wrestled with an angel.

She lost track of time as she interceded. And gently, quietly, the psalm came to mind: *The angel of the Lord encampeth round about them that fear him, and delivereth them.* A ray of hope pierced the darkness, and with it came renewed peace of mind. Ready to let the quiet embrace her, Lela collapsed on the bed, exhausted.

Twelve

❖ ❖ ❖

He stared at the screen of the small portable computer, took another drag on his cigarette, then ground the butt into the table. Sitting in a motel room specifically designated for non-smokers, he waited patiently for the modem to dial the number. He had all the time in the world.

Once the connection was made, he punched the keys, bringing up the Global Positioning Satellite Tracking Web site. He entered his password, ID, and the vehicle control number. Seconds later, he had what he wanted: a detailed local street map and a red star blinking beside the street address.

He smiled, lit another cigarette, then clicked the screen through several windows, cross-referencing the street address with a name.

Thaddeus King, 1135 Hunsecker Road, Lancaster, Pennsylvania.

"Gotcha, Missy James," he whispered, his smile turning to a full-fledged grin. The state-of-the-art tracking device—a transmitter—on the woman's Toyota Camry, about the size of a paperback book, weighed less than half a pound. Attached beneath the vehicle magnetically, it linked to the car's own battery system and harbored a NASA-developed stealth antenna. Undetectable to the casual observer, even a car mechanic could be fooled, assuming the small box performed a computerized automobile function. Accessing the United States Government Military Global Positioning Satellites, the device transmitted its exact location within thirty feet of accuracy.

What would I do without my marvelous toys? he thought, recalling the startled look on Melissa's face when he found her just outside Trenton, New Jersey, after she'd managed to elude him in New York. Finding the woman had been easy. A quick call to his GPS tracking service operator had alerted him to her location on Route 30, heading west, even reporting the Camry's precise speed at the time: sixty-seven miles per hour. Simple as that. *And now . . . she must feel safe again*, he thought, chuckling to himself.

Secure as a mouse in a cat's paw.

He was about to disconnect when the thought occurred to him to double-check the history of the transmitter—determining *each* specific location of the car during the past twenty-four hours. Clicking on *history*, he discovered Melissa's vehicle had *not* been parked at the King residence very long, little more than a few minutes. The first significant stop in Lancaster County—Friday night—had been a restaurant on Route 222, followed by another stop at 702 Hunsecker Road, overnight.

"Thought you could lose me . . ." he muttered.

He cross-referenced that location with the name/address software. Within minutes another name materialized: *Lela Denlinger.*

So . . . that's where you're hiding.

Closing the GPS Web site, he disconnected the modem from his laptop, then attached a portable telephone scrambler to the phone handset. Although he enjoyed taking chances, his partners were the nervous types. Without the aid of a scrambler, they would insist on speaking in elaborate Russian code, indecipherable to the most skilled translators.

Two short rings, then—"Yeah?" a gruff, apathetic voice answered in his native tongue. "Got something?"

"Found her."

The voice spewed profanity. "What are you waiting for?"

"Relax. We'll have what we want by tomorrow."

"What about the husband?"

"Oblivious," he replied.

"Then finish this . . . once and for all."

He hung up the phone and smiled once again. At times his work was pretty dull. Then there were times like this, when the thrill of the chase filled his soul with macabre delight.

Thirteen

❖ ❖ ❖

Ryan and Denny drove along scenic Route 1 toward Westerly, Rhode Island, and Watch Hill. Turning south on Watch Hill Road, they burrowed through a wooded and affluent neighborhood until the road became Bay Street, bordered by tourist shops on the left and a boat-congested harbor on the right.

Slowing, they turned right into a small parking lot and parked the SUV facing the dock. They sat for a moment, watching the tourists. In the harbor, moored sailboats rocked with the gentle waves. Sea gulls flew overhead, catching a warm air current and drifting lazily like paper airplanes.

Ryan gestured toward the Olympia Tea Room. "That's the place."

They got out, stretched their legs, and crossed the street. Entering the restaurant, they walked through glass doors into a crowded room dominated by dark wood and straight-back booths set in the middle of a checkered floor. Smaller booths bordered the walls near the windows.

They were greeted by the hostess, a pixie-faced brunette, who led them to a spot near the window. Settling into their seats, they waited for a waitress to serve water and deliver menus.

Ryan pointed toward the far end of the room, where the ceiling appeared to be made of wine glasses. "Four years ago, Melissa was over there wiping the counter. First time I saw her."

Denny twisted in his seat, eyeing the bar and wooden stools at the end of the room. "Proverbial love at first sight, across a crowded room?"

Ryan remembered the day as if it had happened *yesterday*. Melissa's hair had been pulled back from her forehead and done up in a bun. She'd glanced at him quickly. . . .

"For a split second, our eyes met, and it seemed as if we already knew each other," he recalled.

Denny nodded and added glibly, "So you just *happened* to walk in here, instantly fell in love, and got married twenty-four hours later."

Ryan concealed a wry grin. "No . . . actually it was Bernie's idea."

"Your boss?"

"Yeah, he liked to eat here. Told me about this waitress he'd met. He was impressed with her and wanted to hire her as his secretary. Before we hired Marge, he sent me out here to talk Melissa into applying for a job."

"What happened?"

Ryan chuckled. "Well . . . for one thing I discovered Melissa doesn't type."

"Whoa . . . strike one." Denny laughed. "So the secretary thing fell through. But in the meantime, you fell in love."

"Who's telling this story?"

"Okay, okay." Denny put up his hands. "I'm listening."

"I didn't ask her out right away."

Denny frowned. "Why not?"

"I don't know. She seemed reticent at first. Afraid of her own shadow."

"Didn't seem so shy to *me*."

Ryan considered this. "She trusted you."

Denny stared at him, then grinned.

"So how did *you* win her over?"

"I just kept coming to the restaurant. Asked to be seated in her section. Asked her lots of questions about herself."

Denny nodded. "And?"

"She answered some of them." He forced a smile.

"I think I might've given up."

"I did," Ryan admitted.

Denny seemed surprised.

Their conversation was interrupted when the waitress came to take their order.

Afterward, Ryan observed the activity in the room—tourists and locals. His buddy looked out the window until the waitress returned with their meals. Ryan took one look at the chicken dinner and promptly lost his appetite. At Denny's encouragement, he attempted a few bites, mostly watching Denny eat. *Old friends are the best friends*, Ryan thought.

Eventually, Denny grew silent, studying him from across the table as if biding his time, waiting for the right moment to probe deeper.

They drank their coffee, and the tension mounted. Denny fixed on him an expression that conveyed, *I'm really sorry to have to ask you this.*

Finally, Ryan said, "Why don't you just say it and get it over with?"

Denny smiled apologetically. "You know me too well, ol' buddy."

Placing the coffee cup on the saucer, he felt uneasy. Denny's expression was serious, yet his manner seemed nonthreatening. "Last time I visited, I was bowled over by Melissa's generous hospitality." Denny's voice trailed off.

"She knows how to make someone feel . . . comfortable."

"And yet . . ." Denny continued, "the more I talked to her, the more she seemed to be . . ." He stopped, hesitating once again.

"Go on," Ryan urged.

"Well . . . she seemed to be hiding something."

Ryan shrugged. "Like I said, Mellie has a hard time trusting people. I think it has something to do with her past, with her father abandoning her."

Denny nodded agreeably, a glint in his eye. "You said you gave up on her. What did you mean by that? Did you stop visiting the restaurant?"

"You're really interested in this romance stuff, aren't you?"

"Just trying to help."

"None of this has anything to do with why she left," he found himself saying.

"So, humor me, Ryan. What do we have to do besides wait? Tell me the whole story. Start at the beginning."

Sighing audibly, Ryan felt tense. "All right, you asked for it. I'll even take you to our beach."

"Now you're talking."

They paid the bill and left the restaurant, crossing the narrow two-lane street. Ryan touched the cell phone in his pocket.

Beyond the parking area, they made their way toward a sandy ridge. Napatree Point lay in the distance. The shoreline was part of a long, narrow cape, jutting into Long Island Sound. On a clear day, you could see out past Fishers Island.

Temperatures had risen in the past hour, but sea breezes made the heat bearable. Scattered low-lying clouds hovered at the horizon line as Ryan hiked up a knoll. There, he and Denny peered at the ocean below. Ryan gestured to the stone jetty to their left, and they worked their way through the sand past wild rosebushes, then crossed a small section of the beach before picking their way across the boulders and rocks stacked methodically to create a breakwater.

When they reached the end of the quay, Denny appeared breathless with wonder, staring at the ocean as if he'd never seen it before. "Melissa told me about your wedding. This must be the place."

"We came here one evening. Said our vows before a minister we found in the yellow pages, then tossed white and red rose petals into the ocean."

"Rose petals?" Denny asked. "Another secret meaning?"

"Mixed together, they mean *unity*." He pointed to the west, to the beach that extended toward Napatree Point. "Mellie and I used to come here all the time."

Denny shaded his eyes, following Ryan's gaze. Several families played in the sand, tossing beach balls just a few yards away. A German shepherd barked and scampered around in a frenzy of delight as he chased a Frisbee thrown by a young boy. Farther up the beach, teenagers fished from the shoreline.

"C'mon, let's go closer to the water," Ryan said as he led the way.

Away from the rocks, they removed their socks and shoes and headed toward Napatree Point, struggling to walk through the porous sand. As they did, Ryan pointed out the driftwood, seashells, wild rosebushes, sea birds—all the ingredients that gave the beach front its character.

At last he turned to Denny and forced a smile. "When we married, I believed Mellie would open up more in time. And she did . . . in a way. In her *own* way."

Denny regarded him thoughtfully. Ryan turned to gaze out at the ocean, lost in the past, as the waves crashed against the shore. They stood for several minutes before Ryan spoke again, as if speaking from the past, removed from a distance in time.

"I still remember the day I found her here. . . ."

The day had been unusually windy from the start, the sun slipping in and out of clouds. Ryan had arrived at the Olympia Tea Room on a Friday, traveling from Mystic, where he worked. Several weeks had passed since last stopping by the restaurant. He had decided to back off a bit. Melissa, most likely, wasn't interested in romance. At least not with him. Time to move on.

He marveled at how little he knew of her. She liked flowers and art; never spoke of parents, nor brothers and sisters. And she hailed from Minnesota. That was the extent of it. A couple of months of conversations—sometimes a smile.

So what was he doing back here? *Wasting my time,* he thought, as he stood in line waiting to be seated. Finally, Suzie, the hostess, greeted him. She smiled at him as if he were a long-lost friend.

"Hey, stranger," she said. "Haven't seen you for a while."

He'd smiled sheepishly. "Been busy."

"Too busy to eat?" She laughed. "Listen . . . I'm sorry Melissa isn't working today."

Just as well. Then Suzie said something that got his attention. "Melissa was asking about you the other day."

He sucked in a breath, trying to act nonchalant. "Oh . . . really?"

Her smile broadened. "Yep." Then she added with a mischievous glint in her eye, "She really *loves* to paint at the beach." She nodded her head to her left, toward the public beach area, out beyond the parking lot. "In fact . . . she spends lots of time there. Especially on her days off." Suzie grabbed a menu. "Nonsmoking section?"

"How 'bout I come back later?"

Suzie smiled knowingly. "Good idea."

Taking the hint, he left the restaurant, making his way to Napatree. Climbing the rim, he searched the beach front and . . . sure enough, Suzie was right. There was Melissa, sporting a yellow sundress, a refreshing change. She was walking barefoot in the sand at the edge of the water. He spotted a tripod several yards back, supporting a wide easel. One white swan, on a sea of glass, was the focal point of the painting.

Still with her back to him, she tossed pieces of bread to a lone swan, who lunged for each bite. Watching her, Ryan was taken with her beauty, her shoulder-length, sun-touched hair flowing freely in the wind. Unaccustomed to seeing her hair like this, he observed her movements. Tanned and lovely, she leaned playfully toward the swan in response to the bird's fluid movements. The agile animal had met its match.

Ryan made his way down the hill and sat in the sand, pretending to contemplate the ocean. The beach was relatively unpopulated. Only a dozen or so people. Some jogged by the sea. Others played ball or sat on beach towels in the sand.

He waited, enjoying the moment. Eventually, Melissa reached the end of the little bag of food she had with her and held up her empty hands in apology. The swan waddled off for greener pastures. She crumpled the bag, carried it back to the beach, and tossed it into the community trash can. Then she stopped to scrutinize her painting, picked up a brush and dabbed some additional blue on the calm sea. She stood back, cocked her head as she peered at her work. Seemingly satisfied, she returned the brush to the palette and strolled toward the ocean, her ankles soon enveloped in the incoming tide. Her profile was now visible to him as she gazed toward the horizon with obvious wonderment. A gust of wind had the nerve to assail her, but she shook her head defiantly, clearing her face from errant strands of hair and pinning down her tresses with one hand.

With the sun on her face, illuminating her near-angelic features, she turned bravely to the zephyr. Smiling, she closed her eyes dreamily, as if lost in the ocean's beauty.

As he watched from his spot in the sand, Ryan thought he saw tears on her face, although he couldn't be sure. She brushed her cheek with the back of her hand, opening her eyes and squinting against the sun.

After a time she seemed tired and turned to head back to her easel. At that moment she spotted him. Butterflies took flight in his stomach as he registered the recognition in her face, embarrassed to have been caught mid-worship.

She broke into a full smile as he rose to meet her.

"Hi!" she said enthusiastically. "I didn't see you. How long have you been here?"

"Not long," he replied, mustering his best casual smile. "Nice painting."

"Thanks. Did you see the *real* swan? I've lived here three months, and I haven't seen anything like it." Without pause, she began packing up her palette and brushes.

"I hope I'm not interrupting your work."

She shook her head. "I've been painting for hours, so . . . no." She removed the canvas, then folded the tripod. "Sit with me?" she asked, sitting down on the beach, demurely crossing her legs. Ryan joined her as they faced the ocean together.

She turned to look at him. "I'm glad you came. Haven't seen you for a while." She broke into another grin. "Suzie must've told you I was here."

He let out a short, nervous laugh. "You must get a lot of guys asking for your number."

She shrugged and removed the canvas. "It happens. Just not the *right* guys." She wrinkled her nose. "Sorry. I'm not usually such a flirt."

Surprised by her openness, Ryan wondered what had happened to his shy, reticent waitress. "You don't have to flirt with me."

"Why's that?"

He wanted to say, *Because you had me from the first day I saw you. . . .* But he didn't. He just shrugged, tongue-tied.

She laughed softly, elbowing his arm. "You're kind of shy."

Humored by the irony, Ryan replied, "You wouldn't think so . . . if you knew me."

"I hope to have that chance," she said, not missing a beat.

He turned to face her, but she looked away, toward the clouds, at the fragments of sunshine peeking through. "I love New England, but I wish it were sunnier here," she remarked.

"More like Minnesota?"

She pushed a strand of hair behind her ear, then regarded him mischievously. "You remembered."

"I listened," Ryan replied.

"Actually, Minnesota isn't consistently sunny, either." Then she paused. "So . . . do you remember my nickname, too?"

"Sure . . ." He paused, too, for effect.

"Well?"

"It's Mellie."

"Wow! I *am* impressed."

Their attention was distracted by a large sailboat, traveling south toward the outer ocean. "Have you been sailing yet?" he asked.

"No, but I'd *love* to go. Do you sail?"

"Yeah, but you can't go with me, you know. You shouldn't trust strangers," he said with a wink and a grin.

She nodded, as if giving his remark serious attention. "Well then, we'll just have to go sailing on our *second* date." She raised her eyebrows. "What do you say?"

"Confident, aren't we?" He liked her spunk.

"Just hopeful." Her expression turned more serious and she appraised him gently, her eyes a soft blue green. "I *didn't* trust you at first, you know. I don't trust most people."

"Can't blame you for that," he said softly. "Why did you change your mind?"

She grimaced a bit. "It's silly, I guess."

But he prodded her, had to know.

She was coy but met his gaze as if searching for an appropriate response. "Maybe it was . . . your eyes." She bit her lower lip, stifling a giggle, gauging his expression.

He laughed. "You're flirting again."

"Maybe."

A knowing look passed between them, and Ryan realized he'd succeeded at last. He had won her over. Their natural rapport, so-called love at first sight—a bit of a sputter initially—roared into full-blown romance. From that moment on they became inseparable.

A few months later, after a whirlwind courtship, they married on the stone pier, just before sunset.

Ryan finished their love story, waiting for Denny's reaction.

Tossing a pebble into the water, Denny stood and brushed sand from his slacks. "Why the sudden change in her behavior?" he asked skeptically.

"I never knew exactly. She just decided to . . . trust me."

Denny nodded, apparently lost in thought. Then—"Maybe you should've wondered if you could trust *her*. You knew so little about her."

"Maybe so." He waved his hand nonchalantly. "Ready to go?"

"Sure."

Ryan led the way back, plodding toward the stone pier. They climbed the ridge and headed back to the car.

Reaching the Bronco, Ryan unlocked the car, but Denny leaned on the door without getting in. "Listen, I didn't mean to pry, okay?"

"Yeah, you are a bit on the nosy side," he quipped, looking back toward the ridge. *Their* beach.

"So what's the next step in finding Melissa?" Denny asked, doing it again.

"If I haven't heard from Melissa by Monday, I'll report her credit cards and cell phone. Hopefully trace her location."

Denny frowned, reaching for the car door. "I guess I'm not very good at this waiting game."

He had to smile. "Sure you are. You've waited years for me. You know—Christianity and all?"

They got in the car. "I'm *still* waiting," Denny said.

"See? You have the patience of a saint."

"You're quoting Revelation, my pagan friend." Denny grinned and shook his head in mock disgust.

Ryan was glad to be heading home as he pulled out of the parking space and onto the road. There was little left to be said as dusk delivered a panorama of color. Perhaps a sign of hope. . . .

Fourteen

❖ ❖ ❖

Ryan checked the digital clock on his nightstand. 4:21. In a couple of hours, dawn. He pushed on his pillow, turning away from the window, struggling to recall what day it was.

Sunday . . .

His friend, Denny Franklin, was sleeping down the hall in the guest room. Daisy was . . . where? Sitting up, he peered around the dimly lit room. He spied the dog sprawled on the floor, her head draped over one of Ryan's slippers.

Sleep on, girl.

Melissa, on the other hand, was probably holed up in a motel somewhere. Did she miss him? Was she lonely?

Mellie . . . call me. Pick up the phone, let me know you're okay.

An image flickered in his memory, and stumbling out of bed, he located Melissa's note on the dresser. Holding it again, he relived the first moment of discovery, two days ago. He lay on the bed again and pushed back the covers, feeling as if *he* were the one awakening in a strange motel, in an unfamiliar town. . . .

Daisy roused a bit and pattered over to the edge of the bed. Placing her paws on the mattress, she hesitated as if reconsidering the height.

"Come on, girl," Ryan replied, patting the bed. "S'okay."

Suddenly confident, Daisy burst from the floor, landing awkwardly on his stomach.

"Umph!"

The dog went straight for his face, blanketing him with sloppy saliva. He covered his face with his hands, protecting himself from the barrage. "Too early to play," he said. "Go back to sleep."

Daisy stopped and began to whine. Following her gaze to Mellie's side of the bed, Ryan felt renewed sadness. "I know, girl. I miss her, too."

Still whimpering, Daisy snuggled into the cavity at his side, and Ryan stroked her fur, attempting to comfort his pet. Yet his own fears remained undiminished.

———

Melissa sat at the window watching the rising sun wink through the trees. Birds twittered in a large oak tree just outside the window, and beyond Lela's abode, farmers finished up early-morning milking, no doubt their stomachs rumbling for breakfast.

Having slept more soundly than the previous night, she felt better. Hiding her car away had served to lessen her worries, and she'd written her message to Ryan at last—a loving memo that told him she was safe. He would be somewhat relieved, she knew, though he would still wonder where she was and why she had left him.

Relax now, she told herself, still wondering why the expected phone call had not come. Returning from town yesterday afternoon, she'd inquired of Lela if there had been any calls or messages. "Not once has the phone rung," Lela told her, removing two plump pies from the oven.

Concealing her disappointment, Melissa climbed the stairs to her rented room. The weekend was possibly the holdup. Surely by Monday she would hear something. For now she ought to use this time to unwind, take advantage of the gentle setting, this quaint society of people, seemingly set in the middle of the nineteenth century.

Reaching up, she slid back the Priscilla curtains slightly, seeing the many horse-drawn carriages going up the narrow lane—more of them than yesterday. Quite a parade of them, heading . . . where? To a common church building, perhaps. At breakfast, she would ask Lela where Amish folk went en masse.

Here she was, the second day away from home. Lela had seemed agreeable about allowing her to stay another night. In fact, she assumed that Lela was enjoying the company, since she seemed to be going out of her way to serve hot meals, home-baked goodies, and delicious cold drinks. For a woman thirty-something, it seemed strange that she had no work outside the home. So the extra income was surely welcome.

Kneeling beside the chair, Lela folded her hands in prayer. "Dear

Lord, please make me a blessing to my houseguest this day." On behalf of her additional concerns, she prayed about her great-aunt's ill health, a friend's pending marriage, and a second cousin's need for direction in ministry. She also breathed a prayer of thanksgiving for God's abundant blessings. The earlier sense of doom had vanished completely.

Her father had taught her and her siblings to lift high the name of the Lord in gratitude for all He had done in their lives and in the lives of those around them. "We must never live unto ourselves," he would often say. "Yet we must surely recognize what a blessing our heritage is, a privilege, really, to serve the Lord."

"Now, Pop," her mother would sometimes chide him, "we aren't any better for being Plain than the next person."

"Well, now that's the truth," Papa might say. Yet Lela felt her father was a little bit proud of his spiritual heritage, the fact that for more than four generations, there were God-fearing Mennonites on both sides of the family tree.

All well and good, she thought, getting up from her morning prayer. Yet she knew the importance of a person yielding his or her heart to the Savior—a personal relationship—not relying on the faith of others who'd gone before. With all her heart, she yearned for God and His ways. She longed to be a servant, as the Lord was to His own disciples while here on earth. In spite of her meager means, she wanted to be a giver, as well.

She remembered a poem Mama had taught her as a child, about the camel. He kneels in the morning to take the burden upon his back and kneels again in the evening to have it removed. Her prayer ritual went something like that, too, she sometimes felt. Not that she was weighed down with the cares of life like some folk, no. But she was a willing vessel, prepared to lay down her life if need be to show love for others. "Shake me, Lord. May I hurt for my neighbor who may not know your saving grace," she often prayed.

Today she wept on her knees. "Help me build bridges to a lost world . . . beginning with Melissa."

The dear girl was clearly perplexed, suffering. When Melissa had inquired about phone calls, Lela was sure she saw grave concern in the blue eyes. Who or what was the woman afraid of? And what was so urgent as to keep waiting for a call, not to mention hiding her car?

Sometimes in the past twenty-four hours, just thinking on it, Lela was tempted to give way to fear herself—having such an apprehensive person in the house. Truth was, she'd prayed Melissa into her care last Friday evening. So without a shadow of doubt, she knew the Lord had sent the woman her way.

———

Hours later, sleep coming in snatches, Ryan slipped out from under the covers, leaving Daisy to nap in the bed. Tossing his robe aside, he showered, dressed, then headed down the hall, looking in through the partially open door to Denny's room. Bed made . . . room empty. Denny was an early riser. He found his friend sitting in the living room, reading his Bible.

"Are you up for some church after breakfast?" he asked, expecting Denny to fall off the sofa in shock.

"That's *my* line," Denny said, eyes wide. "You're not messing with my head, are you?"

"What else do we have to do today—besides wait by the phone?"

"Say no more." Denny grabbed the phone book, flipped through the yellow pages under churches.

Ryan headed to the kitchen to cook breakfast—fried eggs, German sausage, and whole-wheat waffles—the sort of food he and Melissa rarely ate. They preferred whole-grain cereal and fresh fruit. Healthy fare.

"What about the Village Church . . . in Groton?" Denny called from the living room. "Okay with you?"

"Whatever you decide." Typically, on other occasions when Denny had come to visit—if Melissa was around, that is—no one had suggested attending church. But this time things were so up in the air, it didn't matter to Ryan how they spent the day. To some degree time had ceased. He was merely marking it, hour by hour, till Mellie contacted him.

Unaccustomed to the aroma of rich food, Daisy whined incessantly, begging for a bite. Ryan resisted Daisy's pleading, and sat down to eat. Denny, however, gave in, tossing Daisy a taste of sausage after Ryan nodded his reluctant consent.

"You have to know, she'll get fat," he cautioned.

"Maybe, but she'll love me for it," Denny replied. "Besides, after I leave, you can put her back on a diet."

Daisy nuzzled her head into Denny's leg as he rubbed her neck.

Then she lifted her paws to his lap—a household no-no—glancing at Ryan as if to gauge his response.

"See, she loves me best," Denny said, giving Daisy a full rubdown.

"She craves people food. You just happen to be the delivery boy."

"No-o," Denny cooed at Daisy. "You love me for my mind, don't you? Want to come home with me and have people food every day?"

Ryan chuckled. "You're corrupting my dog."

"Sorry, chief."

"Would you care to go with me to the Mennonite meetinghouse today?" Lela asked her guest, serving up hot scrambled eggs and bacon.

Melissa looked up from the table, a rather startled expression on her face. "Well, I . . . I don't know." Then, quickly, "No. I'd better stay here."

"To wait for your phone call?"

Nodding, Melissa spread rhubarb jelly on her toast. "Any other Sunday . . ."

"Just not today?" she said, hoping Melissa might elaborate.

"I wondered . . ."

"Yes?"

Melissa paused, frowning, before she continued. "Where were all the horses and buggies headed this morning?"

"Up mighty early, were you?"

"The clip-clopping of horses' hooves awakened me just after dawn." Melissa's face was drawn and serious, though she seemed a bit more rested than before. "I didn't count them, but there were far more than yesterday."

"Ah yes, I know just what you mean." She reached for her coffee cup and leaned back in her chair. Glancing up at the ivy vines encircling her windows, she explained, "It's Sunday-go-to-meetin' in Lancaster County, which means many of my Amish neighbors are heading out to house church."

"You mean they attend church at someone's house?" Melissa seemed altogether surprised at this revelation.

"Two hundred and more in some cases." She explained how the Old Order folk removed various partitions in their living rooms, making it possible to accommodate that many church members. "Same with

Amish weddings and funerals. They make room for their people. The Plain folk are a close-knit bunch."

Melissa nodded, but there was a faraway look in her eyes.

"The horses and carriages were hurrying off to worship services all over this area," she added. "'Tis a common sight every other Sunday morning, round here." She went on to say that the Old Order Amish have what they call "off Sundays," when they don't gather for preaching but spend the day reading their German and English Bibles, visiting and resting.

"Do your sister and husband ever have house church?" asked Melissa, gaze intent.

"Sometimes. With so many folk per church district, a family doesn't have preaching service too often. But I think they're due to have a meeting at their place here pretty soon." She rose, went to the pantry, and looked on the back of the door at the calendar. "Yes, next month. September ninth, in fact."

Melissa was quiet for the longest time, then—"I really liked your sister."

"Elizabeth?"

"She reminds me of someone from my childhood." *Mrs. Browning's housekeeper,* she thought.

"Elizabeth's a sweet girl, and she loves her family, as anybody can see."

"She must have a little store back behind the house," Melissa remarked.

Chuckling, Lela replied, "Oh my, does she ever. Suppose you saw the sign."

"I couldn't help but be curious."

"Well, if you stay on another day or so, I'll be happy to take you over, give you a look around the country store." Lela sighed, thinking she ought to stop talking so awful much and eat her breakfast. She didn't want to be late for church. "Elizabeth and I keep the store well stocked with all sorts of handmade items."

"So, you work for Elizabeth—making things?"

She nodded. "Quite a lot of crocheting and sewing, and sometimes I make quilted pillow shams and bed coverings to match."

"Then, you're an artist," Melissa said.

She felt her cheeks get warm. "Well, now I wouldn't go that far."

"But you *are!*" insisted Melissa. "I love to paint flowers, the sea. I like to think of myself as an artist, too."

"What else do you like to do—for hobbies, I mean?"

Melissa sighed, getting that distant look in her eyes. "Making scrapbooks is one of my big interests, but it's been a long time since I worked on anything new."

Noting her wedding band, Lela wondered how much she should ask. Wouldn't want to pry where she ought not to.

"My husband enjoys our vacation scrapbooks," Melissa said, opening up the subject Lela was curious about.

"Where do you like to go together . . . on vacation?"

"Vermont and New Hampshire, especially. We get off the main roads and stay in small towns. Go exploring, I guess you could say."

She might've posed another question, but just then, the phone rang. Melissa let out a startled sound, locking eyes with her, but Lela put her guest at ease. "I'll get that," she said, rising up from the table.

Turned out the call wasn't for Melissa, but for Lela. "Do you want a ride for church?" asked Sadie Nan, her church friend. "My brother's in town from Indiana. I thought the three of us could go out to eat after, if you don't have other plans."

Paul Martin . . .

She'd heard through the community grapevine that Paul's wife had passed away, leaving him a widower with a young son.

"Well, I don't . . . know, uh, really." She disliked stumbling around like this. Not with Melissa sitting across the room, no doubt wondering what had her so flustered all of a sudden.

"Oh, please say you'll come, Lela. We'll have the *best* time. Besides, my brother's been asking 'bout you."

She would've said, "What's he asking?" but held her tongue. No, it would never do for Paul and Sadie Nan to show up at her door, what with Melissa here. Still, she was more than curious about Paul. Just why was he in town anyway?

Looking out the window, she could see the sun shining nice and bright. Looked to be a pretty day. "I believe I'll ride my bike to service," she managed. "Maybe another time."

"Okay, but I'll hold you to it," Sadie said.

"I'll see you at church."

Melissa tried to ignore the phone conversation going on uncomfortably near. She stared out the wide windows that comprised a good por-

tion of the west wall in the dining area of the kitchen. Today, while Lela
was at church, might be a good time to do some exploring. At least, she
might venture out past the patio courtyard directly behind the windows,
near the low stone walls where pink and purple clematis spilled over
native stone, to the perennial borders and herb gardens and tall hedges
so characteristic of English gardens. A rose-covered pergola reminded
her of the years spent with Mrs. Browning, the gardener extraordinaire
who'd mothered her well into college.

Turning back to her coffee and the delicious "sticky buns," she
glanced up to see Lela's face turning a bright pink, brown eyes glistening. She was sputtering like a schoolgirl. Well, what was this? Did Lela
have a boyfriend?

She continued to observe as the phone conversation ensued. From
what she could gather, someone was inviting Lela somewhere, and now
she was declining. Why Melissa cared at all about any of this, she didn't
know. Sure beat racing around on the highway, though, trying to ditch
the contemptible man who'd tried to bump her off the road. He probably would have killed her—if he had gotten close enough.

The area behind the house beckoned her, and she found herself gazing with longing, eager to stroll around the grounds. She spied what she
thought was a sundial centered in a bed of snow-white and rose-colored
alyssum. Leaning forward, then getting up, she moved to the window
and peered out. Yes, it *was* a sundial! She favored the sundial above all
the garden trappings in her own backyard retreat.

She knew well the rewards, the pleasures reaped from spending time
in one's garden. Of all her hobbies, frittering away the hours doing the
quiet, contemplative work of pruning, digging, weeding, planting,
watering—all the necessary tending required—gardening was her thing.
She often wondered if her years with Mrs. Browning had fostered such
a love, wondered if her own mother, long deceased, might not have had
a green thumb, as well. From her own enthusiasm for lovely plants,
flowers, and shrubs had come her passion for painting. Daddy hadn't
seemed all that fond of her childish sketches, but as she grew and her
interest changed, he'd shown considerable amazement for her watercolor
renderings, especially of roses.

"If you'll excuse me, I better see to cleaning up the kitchen," Lela
said when the phone conversation ended.

"Let me help," Melissa said, remembering her manners. "In fact, why don't you go and dress for church. I'll finish up here."

For a fleeting moment she thought Lela was going to reject her offer, but then the big brown eyes softened. "That's thoughtful of you. Thank you, Melissa."

"Please . . . call me Mellie," she said all of a sudden.

Lela nodded, all smiles. "Well, sure I will. How nice of you to say so."

Going to the sink, Melissa turned on the hot water. "Have a good day," she said softly.

"You too." Lela turned to go, then paused. "If for any reason your phone call is delayed, feel free to stay on, all right?"

She was taken aback by the woman's generosity. "I'll keep that in mind, thanks."

Mutual admiration society, she thought. All this gratitude exchanged. Well, it *was* a lovely reprieve from the nightmare she'd experienced two days ago. To think she may have found a trustworthy friend in this Plain woman. . . .

In no time the kitchen was spotless, the place mats shaken over the sink and replaced at the table. With one purpose in mind—she would give herself permission to relax all day—Melissa hurried to the back of the house, to the four-season porch overlooking Lela's backyard garden. Sure, it was the Lord's Day, as Lela had so aptly put it, but the day was also Mellie's. She would guard the notion, see to it that nothing marred the next carefree hours.

Fifteen

❖ ❖ ❖

When Ryan pulled into the Village Church parking lot, the area was so crowded he had to back out and park across the street. The church building itself was a white colonial—classic New England architecture—complete with columns and a tall steeple.

They entered through the large double doors to the sound of hymn singing. A young woman greeted them with a smile and offered each of them a bulletin. Denny told her they were visiting.

"Welcome—and make yourself at home," she said. "I think you'll like it here."

"I'm sure we will," Denny replied quickly, with a sidelong glance at Ryan.

Heading into the sanctuary, Ryan wondered how he would survive an hour of dull religiosity. He was only doing this for Denny, who seemed thrilled to have his company.

He sat through a few hymns and some brief announcements. Then the pastor told a story about Jesus meeting a woman at a well, adding humorous anecdotes and personal illustrations. To Ryan's surprise, he found the sermon rather interesting. No protracted conjecture on theology, no demands for money, not even a hint of condemnation.

After the service, while driving back to Mystic, Ryan said little. The minister's words echoed in his mind: *Drink the living water . . . and never thirst again.* He wondered what Mellie would have thought of the sermon, knowing the answer instinctively. She would have enjoyed it.

Yet in the past few years, he'd given little encouragement to her religious preference. Hadn't she purchased the picture of Christ, so out of place in their living room? She'd also painted the cross in Denny's painting—this, very recently. Yes, she was definitely inclined in that direction.

"How'd you like the sermon?" Denny asked, interrupting Ryan's reverie.

"Short and sweet."

"You're hopeless," Denny moaned. "Did you hear him recite Melissa's favorite quote?"

Ryan nodded, remembering her framed poster of homeless people standing in a soup kitchen line. Under the picture was the caption *The mass of men lead lives of quiet desperation.* Last year Mellie had decided to read the book *Walden*, sometimes even reading aloud to him.

"So you must think religion is the answer to man's feelings of desperation," he replied, glancing over at Denny.

"Not religion—"

"And not *everyone* feels desperate, right?"

Denny paused. "Listen, I didn't come here to pound away at you— not this weekend. I mean. . . . what with Meliss . . . and everything, maybe this just isn't the right time."

"I'm a big boy," Ryan said. "Answer the question."

"About desperation? Okay. I disagree with you. I think *everyone* feels some degree of underlying despair. We just call it by different names. I mean, not everyone's thrashing around in a miserable state. But most of us do seem to be dissatisfied, discontented. And another thing . . . we're all *addicted*."

"Addicted," Ryan echoed flatly.

"Yeah. It goes hand in hand with discontent. We're addicted to having *more*. Getting more. More with a capital *M*. But *more* is never enough. We're like rats on a treadmill. We never catch up with the cheese, but we keep chasing it anyway. We spend our whole lives running after something—anything—to give us fulfillment, to satisfy our longing, our insatiable desire. We think more money, new loves, more notoriety will finally make the difference."

He stared out the window for a moment before continuing. "More of anything *never* satisfies, because ultimately we're looking in the wrong place. Most of us grow old thinking that feeling lost and lonely is simply a part of being human . . . but it isn't."

"*Some* people seem pretty happy," Ryan objected.

"Are they? *Really* happy?" Denny's voice trailed off. "The rich and famous often come to the end of their lives still feeling lost and unfulfilled. It's not money or fame that satisfies, Ryan. It's Christ who offers the *more* we're all seeking—the water that quenches our spiritual thirst."

Ryan shook his head. "But most Christians don't act like they're drinking living water."

Denny shrugged. "We only get little sips, here and there. Brief glimpses of eternity. Not the full deal—yet. But, ah . . . those glimpses."

"So how is any of this proof of Christianity?"

"Well . . . think about it. As human beings, we have complex physical and emotional needs. All those needs have a corresponding fulfillment. You might say that experience has proven to us that if we *need* something, fulfillment of that need exists somewhere, somehow. For example, our bodies need nourishment to survive, which proves the existence of food and water. We need oxygen to breathe, which proves the existence of air. We need light and warmth, which proves the sun exists. We desire to procreate, which proves the existence of sex. We get lonely simply because friendship and community exists. But even with all these physical and emotional needs satisfied, we *still* feel unfulfilled. Why? Because we have a deeper spiritual need—a need for God. And that, my friend, proves the existence of a Creator."

"Now you're sounding like Socrates," Ryan said.

"Would our spiritual need be the single exception—our one need that *doesn't* have a corresponding fulfillment?" Denny asked. "That seems unlikely. Let me put it another way: If it's proof you want, proof is in the pudding—in the *tasting*. Come to Christ and you'll find the evidence."

"But people need the evidence *first*, don't they?" Ryan said, adjusting his grip on the steering wheel.

"Most people don't need proof per se. They need to be *willing* to repent. The demand for evidence is often a smoke screen for hanging on to sin. For every reason I give you, you can find another objection. If you *want* to believe, you'll find my reasons are sufficient—even *compelling*. If you *don't* want to believe, no amount of logic will convince you."

"Back up a sec. That's where you lose me, Den. The *sin* part. Remember our college philosophy class?"

"Sure, I spent years recovering."

"We were taught that sin is a myth," Ryan said.

Denny grimaced. "So you're saying that evil is simply—"

"Ignorance," Ryan interrupted.

"Most skeptics argue that evil and suffering disproves the existence of God. But you're telling me evil doesn't even exist?"

"Of course it exists. But as a human race we can do *better*. Better psychology. Better treatment centers. Better schools. The worst evil we commit is telling our kids how bad they are. If we loved our children unconditionally, imparting genuine self-esteem, our so-called sinful behavior disappears."

"I agree with you, but only to a point," Denny said. "Sin goes much deeper into the human psyche, far beyond superficial behavior. As a human race we're sunk in moral depravity. We're bad to the bone. And that's *why* we experience such desperation and insatiable longing. Because our sin separates us from God. We need *divine* redemption, not better schools or psychological Band-Aids."

Steering the car into the restaurant parking lot, Ryan replied, "I'm sorry, Denny. It's just not working for me."

"Which part?"

"The whole thing."

Green fields, dotted with black-and-white cows, widened out to meet the sky to the north. Silhouettes of windmills and silos punctuated the landscape, and flocks of crows flew overhead, like great dark clouds.

Melissa paused at the screen door, a slight shiver running down her back in spite of the warm day. Set against the gray slate floor and white clapboard walls, the cozy porch tempted her to remain in the confines of its protection. She *was* safe here. How ridiculous to think otherwise.

Opening the screen door, she ventured out. She wished she had her palette and a canvas. Her eyes embraced a myriad of colors and textures—Cleome spider flowers, their slender stems rising four feet high, topped with a deep pink crown. Amassed in a bold grouping that ran along the stone walkway from the house, the tender annuals withstood the sun's strongest rays during summer. This she knew from her growing-up years at Mrs. Browning's house.

Stepping down into the garden area, she felt as if she were wandering back to that familiar place in faraway Colorado. . . .

"Come here and look at this, Mellie dear," Mrs. Browning called, motioning her to the rows of golden yarrow growing near the birdbath.

She scurried across the yard, blades of grass cool beneath her bare feet. Always, she was interested in seeing what Mrs. Browning was up to, what new bud or blossom she'd discovered. The woman was a master gardener, and everyone in the small town of Palmer Lake knew it.

People would stop by or call for gardening advice, sometimes bringing a feeble vine or distressed cutting to her for help. Melissa had seen Mrs. Browning work miracles with her green thumb.

This woman her father had chosen to raise her, as designated in his will, was vivacious and full of energy when she worked in her garden. But housework didn't thrill her, and Mr. Browning, at one point, decided to hire a housekeeper, who made short order of the dusting and vacuuming, much to Mrs. Browning's delight. "All the more time to talk to my flowers," she said, going about her business in the yard.

"What'd you want to show me?" Mellie squatted down near the yarrow.

Mrs. Browning's eyes shone. "Just imagine what fun we could have drying these naturally."

"What for?"

"Oh, we can use them for crafts, you know, for presents."

She liked the idea and followed the woman to her rose gardens, where twenty different varieties bloomed, a difficult task in such a dry climate. Yet Mrs. Browning persevered, adding mulch and fertilizer, installing a drip hose, and as always, whispering her sweet talk.

Mr. Browning stopped to listen when his wife spoke of another "very special rose garden" in the southernmost section of the yard.

"That one's in memory of your father," Mrs. Browning said, pointing to the garden plot, reminding Melissa once again. "How your daddy loved his pure white roses," she said, leaning down to breathe in the sweet fragrance of dozens of ivory-colored blossoms.

"White roses stand for silence and innocence," Mellie said, remembering all that her father had taught her of the language of flowers.

"And secrecy, too, don't forget," Mrs. Browning said. "White roses have more than just a few meanings."

Mr. Browning was nodding his head as if to reinforce the importance of it all.

"More than any of that, always remember how much your father loved *you*, dear." Mrs. Browning gave her a little hug, then went about her work.

Always remember . . .

Lela was ever so glad for partly cloudy skies, a reprieve from the typical dog days of August, as she pedaled her bicycle to the meeting-house down the road. Less than a mile away, the church was accessible either by foot or her favorite mode of transportation, her old ten-speed bicycle. The exercise was good for her, and besides that she liked to talk to God as she rode.

Arriving at the small brick structure, she parked her bike near the side door and hurried into church, feeling terribly uncomfortable knowing that Sadie Nan and her brother would be arriving any minute. She'd first met Sadie during elementary school days, both girls having attended the Amish-Mennonite school two miles in the opposite direction, over on Snake Hill Road.

Sadie's brother was a year older, a student at the same school. For a time, he seemed to care for Lela. So much so that during their last years of high school, she began to expect a marriage proposal from her dear Paul. Around that time a new girl with strawberry blond hair and a coquettish grin caught his fancy, coming between them, dashing Lela's hopes. Never interfering to save their relationship, she followed her mother's example of a submissive attitude and quiet spirit, and several months after Paul's graduation, rumor had it that he'd married the blond girl and moved to Indiana.

"Plenty more good fish in the sea," Sadie had offered in an attempt to comfort her. "You'll see."

Wounded in spirit, Lela's heart was so broken she never cared to hope for another love. She poured herself into her singleness, helping her siblings with each new babe as the little ones came along, tending to her gardens, and sewing her fine stitchery to put food on the table and tires on her bicycle. Thankfully, her house was paid for, the result of her oldest brother's wise investment. Another brother paid her yearly property taxes and the utility bill each month, so she was quite content to work for Elizabeth, helping keep the shelves stocked with handmade goods at the little country store. The money from her larger-ticket items—such as the quilted coverlets and pillows—easily paid for phone bills and groceries, with money left over to give to the Mennonite missions and benevolence fund at church.

On the left side of the church where the women sat, she found a spot next to several cousins, happy to be surrounded by loving faces. She bowed her head in prayer, asking the Lord to anoint their minister's sermon, that he might break the Bread of Life so needed for the week ahead. She prayed for wisdom and help from her heavenly Father regarding any possible encounter and renewed friendship with widower Martin.

And she prayed for Melissa, who'd decided to stay at home, waiting for a phone call. "Touch her with your grace and love today," she whispered, then felt the Holy Spirit prompting her to pray further. "Please send your ministering servants—angels—to watch over Melissa . . . over *both* of us. In Jesus' name, amen."

Ryan and Denny drove to Noah's in Stonington Borough and ordered halibut for lunch. Later they stopped in at the Stonington Lighthouse, built in 1823 on Stonington Point. The stone tower—thirty feet high—had once supported a lantern with ten oil lamps and silver reflectors. Denny appreciated the maritime history, commenting on the numerous relics from Stonington's whaling and sealing ships.

They spent the afternoon watching a preseason game between the Patriots and the Bengals. Ryan tolerated the game while Denny phoned his girlfriend on Ryan's cell phone, keeping the main line free in case Melissa called. They chatted for a good half hour, then Denny made another call to some kid he'd met on the plane.

Meanwhile, Ryan paged through several of Melissa's recent journals, reading her latest entries, searching for clues. *Anything.* He opened the scrapbook she'd recently finished of last year's trip to Manchester, Vermont. Picture after picture of peak foliage. Besides painting, Melissa loved the creative process of making scrapbooks. "The preservation of family history," she liked to call it. Every one of their vacations was imaginatively detailed for posterity, including ticket stubs, pictures, and brochures.

He couldn't handle even a few minutes of this self-induced torture. Setting the vacation scrapbook aside, Ryan's depression deepened. His single strand of hope—that Mellie would eventually call—was beginning to unravel. He'd expected her to phone him within a few hours of her leaving. But the hours were turning into days.

Ryan walked out through the sun-room door, following the short path past Melissa's rose garden to the dock, all the while replaying events from the past several weeks.

The sun had already set. Denny was napping in front of TV news. The moon's silvery glow cast an eerie reflection on the ocean stillness, accompanied by a corresponding sense of endlessness.

Most men lead lives of quiet desperation. . . .

"You don't know the half of it, Mr. Thoreau," Ryan whispered, sitting on the dock with his legs dangling over the edge. Minutes later Daisy joined him, padding across the sun-bleached wood to nuzzle his back.

He hugged his dog. Then, facing the vast sea, Ryan recalled the day he'd proposed to his darling girl, their subsequent private wedding ceremony on Watch Hill, and her tear-streaked face when he'd kissed her.

"I'm so happy," she'd whispered with upturned face, eyes shining. "I wish today would never end."

"I won't let it end, Mellie," he'd promised, only to fail.

Sixteen

❖ ❖ ❖

Russian-born Dima Ivanov had been abandoned as an infant on the doorstep of an orphanage. Left in a crib for weeks on end with no attention and scarcely enough nourishment to survive, he'd suffered the kind of neglect that has been known to breed severe psychological disturbances, even psychopathic tendencies. At least, that's what his sympathetic psychiatrist had told him when he was sent to a Psikhushka, a psychiatric hospital for troubled youths. Secretly, Ivanov regarded his lack of conscience as a *gift*.

Escaping from the Russian institution, he lived on the streets of Moscow, joined a gang, and made money through scams and extortion. Bred from the deep pain of abandonment, anger dominated his every waking moment. The pleasure of settling a grudge became so empowering, he craved the thrill of revenge.

Ivanov was only twenty-one when he escaped the state police and stowed aboard a commerce ship bound for America. Once in New York, he took the American name "Jim" Ivanov, practiced his English compulsively until his accent was only slight, and joined forces with two other Russian exiles.

Thirty years later Dima kept close protective ties with his *krysha*— homeland compatriots who sent him their dirty cash for laundering. And though they had lackeys to do the dirty work, Dima was a reckless man. He enjoyed implementing the day-to-day details of his criminal operations. Especially . . . *enforcement*.

Ivanov and his "partners" ruled their underworld through the twin powers of *fear* and *greed*. In the Russian homeland, bribery was a way of life. But in America, bribery was much more difficult. Dima and his men were required to pay more for criminal complicity, to select their criminal participants more carefully, and to be more persuasive.

So they bribed policemen who were struggling to feed their families on low wages. They bribed judges, jealous of exorbitant attorney fees, eager to exchange favorable rulings for briefcases full of cash. They located dishonest corporate executives and bribed them for insider corporate information. Lastly, they bribed disgruntled bank officials in exchange for laundering their Russian cash.

Ivanov insured the preservation of his criminal operations through the judicious use of fear. His numerous greedy participants, including the fools they couldn't bribe, were taught the consequences of noncompliance. Dima had been arrested countless times, but never had a jury convicted him. Witnesses either disappeared or jurors dissented in terror.

Now, at two o'clock in the morning, Dima surveyed the Denlinger home, barely visible in the distance. Satisfied that the situation was benign, he worked his way through the pasture to the dirt road where his gray sedan was parked and drove to within half a mile of Lela Denlinger's home. With the aid of binoculars, he spotted the gleaming porch light populated by mosquitoes and moths.

Inside the cottage, Melissa James lay sleeping, the single offspring of the man who had humiliated him in California, the scene of Ivanov's *only* failed operation. He had taken out his revenge on the man, but Dima's rage was not spent.

His pulse quickened, nerves heightened as addictive fixation set in. He placed the binoculars on the console and caught his breath, overwhelmed by his need for retribution. First, he would get her to talk; then when he had learned the location of the money, he would enact his revenge.

Focusing his binoculars, he swept the surrounding area, assuring himself again of his safety. Earlier, he'd considered approaching the small house from the back. Such caution seemed unnecessary. In fact, there was no reason why he couldn't simply park the car on the street, stroll up to the front door, and slip inside.

Setting the binoculars aside, he patted his shirt pocket containing the Sodium Pentothal, also known as truth serum. While it didn't guarantee complete "truth-telling," the drug effectively unhinged the recipient's inhibition.

His left coat pocket contained a bottle of a nervous-system drug designed to stop the heart—undetectable in an autopsy. And finally,

under his left shoulder, his holster concealed the 10mm Glock pistol—
his weapon of choice, equipped with a silencer. Unlikely he'd need the
gun tonight. These women would be frightened into compliance with a
nasty stare.

Show time.

Focusing the lenses on the Denlinger house for one last look, he gave
a sharp intake of breath.

He whispered a curse, putting down the glasses, attempting to make
sense of it.

He put the binoculars to his eyes again, squinting and frowning.
Sure enough, two men lumbered about the front yard of the Denlinger
cottage. Both were blond and bearded, wearing straw hats, tan suspenders, and wide-legged black trousers. *Amishmen*, he thought, profoundly
irritated. He continued to watch them from a distance as they roamed
about the front yard, seemingly performing chores. The more he
watched, the more confused he became.

What were they doing at this time of the night? Was there some
strange custom that compelled these Amishmen to work while others
slept? Shifting in his seat, he decided to wait them out. Eventually, they
would leave.

Dima awakened suddenly with a jolt and looked at his watch. 3:30
A.M. Grabbing the binoculars, he focused on the house, deeply relieved.
The Amish farmers were gone at last.

With no time to waste, he shoved the car keys into his pocket,
reached for the door handle, and climbed out. The night was softened
with starlight and a large splinter of a moon. The echo of crickets
mingled with the distant bark of a dog. Wearing tennis shoes, his steps
were muted, yet he walked with purpose, creating the appearance of a
local on his way home.

Less than a block from the house, he stopped short, dumbfounded.
The Amishmen had suddenly returned, busy with indiscernible tasks.
Staring at the men in frustration, Dima considered his options. He could
return to the car and come back tomorrow or proceed with his plan.

In the end, greed decided for him. He'd waited for years for this
moment, and he mustn't wait any longer, no matter the human casual-
ties. He lifted his right foot in an attempt to move forward but nearly
stumbled, his legs unpredictably weak, like jelly. Recovering his bal-

ance, a wave of unexplainable anxiety washed over him.

Standing on the narrow sidewalk in the early hours of the morning, he stared at the men, trying to get a grip on his own ridiculous reaction to these strange, nocturnal farmers.

What's the matter, Dima, losing your edge?

Angry with his mental weakness, he patted his holster and quickened his pace to the house. He was within a few yards of the gate when his arms began to shake uncontrollably, then his legs. Fear embraced him so completely that each step was an enormous effort.

When he reached the gate at last, he slumped against it, then turned his back on the Denlinger house, hyperventilating. Against his better judgment, he drew his gun out in the open, barely able to hold the weapon in his sweat-drenched palms. Raising the gun, he turned toward the Amishmen.

They stood motionless, their hands at their sides, watching him, their expressions deliberate, serious, almost grieved. Facing their penetrating gaze, he felt like a deer caught in the headlights of an oncoming car, unable to turn away.

Then something peculiar happened. Unfamiliar emotions began to click through his awareness like dominoes in a chain reaction.

Shame, guilt, conviction . . . ending with a final emotion long since dormant through decades of denial—the proffer of *acceptance.* Something he'd last felt as a child sitting across the table from the compassionate psychiatrist, as the doctor tended him with comforting words. *"Let me help you, Dima. I care about you. . . . You are safe here. . . ."*

For a brief, mysterious moment, he felt drawn to these men, as if they held the answers to the anguish that had driven him to a lifetime of revenge.

He shuddered, and the gun slipped through his fingers, bouncing against the concrete sidewalk. He fell to his knees, scrambled for it, finally grabbed the weapon with both trembling hands. In that moment, his anger returned, but all resolve had vanished. Stumbling to his feet, he backed away to the sidewalk, then bolted in an all-out sprint for his car.

Taking one last glance up the block at the Denlinger house—the Amishmen were gone—he shoved the gearshift into drive. Seconds later he squealed a narrow U-turn in the middle of the block and sped down the street, not caring what sort of commotion he created.

Seventeen

❖ ❖ ❖

I vanov composed himself during the drive toward Connecticut. Confused and shaken by the events of the night, he wondered just what had happened at the little house on the deserted lane. But his mind remained vacantly unaware, as if he were just now coming out of a trance.

He considered turning the car around, waiting for daylight, and making another attempt to approach the house. But thinking of the Denlinger home and the Amishmen caused a cold sweat to break out.

No matter. Ivanov was a resourceful man. In a few hours he'd be back in Mystic, Connecticut. It was time for a surprise visit with Melissa's husband.

————

Silently, Ryan slipped out the back door, methodically working his way around the gardens to the peaceful cove, coffee cup in hand. The steam curled and rose into the unseasonable coolness of early morning as gray-backed terns flitted about.

In the distance, the sea was pewterlike—a stunning contrast to last night's moon-dappled waves. Their sailboat, *Mellie*, shifted with the gentle lapping of waves, air still as death. Just as sunbeams winked over the horizon—a show of gold on Fishers Island Sound—an unexpected gust came up. He turned his face toward wind and sun, experiencing the dawning of a new day, a sunrise that held little hope.

Slowly draining his cup, he considered his next course of action. Three raucous terns interrupted his thoughts, swooping toward the dock and landing on posts. Waiting.

She's not here, he thought. *Come again another day.*

Overwhelming sorrow encompassed him anew, and he turned back toward the house. Where the rise leveled off, he paused to look at the sundial, the focal point in Mellie's miniature rose garden. Abundant with peach-colored thimble-sized blooms, each twelve-inch plant nearly smothered itself in tiny but perfect rose blossoms. Mellie had chosen this classification of rose because of its undemanding nature. "Anyone can grow these," she'd said, laughing out loud as they worked together.

The color, peach, had been Mellie's idea. "A peach-hued rose is delicate and stands for admiration. Its Victorian Era meaning was 'Please, believe me,'" she gaily informed him as they planted each one.

"'Believe me' . . . about what?" he'd played along.

"Oh, *you* know." She stood, wiping her brow and grinning her irresistible grin.

Playfully, he'd run to her, held her close, and whispered, "Believe that I'll love you for always?"

She nuzzled against him silently. Then, stepping out of his embrace, she pointed to the circular bed where the sundial would eventually stand at center stage—*their* rustic sundial discovered in New Hampshire at the Americana Celebration Antiques Show months later.

The horizontal stone dial was etched with the equation of time, boasting a metal gnomon and, at the center, a single rose. He recalled her squeal of delight at finding such a prize, and on the drive home, she spoke of nothing else. "We own a true masterpiece," she'd said. "Nearly as ancient as mankind itself."

"Pretty profound," he'd teased. "Sounds like you're a poet today."

Mellie had laughed with glee, snuggling close to him in the car, humming a happy song and reliving their day in New Hampshire. "Can we go back sometime soon?" she asked.

"Just say the word." He would take her to the ends of the earth and beyond if she so desired. Whatever brought a smile to Mellie's face was worth any amount of hassle, aching feet, and empty wallet.

Returning to the house, he was met with sounds of Denny banging around in the kitchen. Apparently, his guest had decided to cook.

"So . . . you didn't like *my* eggs?" Ryan mocked.

"Don't make me answer that," Denny shot back. "I value your friendship." He dipped his head beneath the counter, searching for the frying pan, no doubt.

"Over there." Ryan pointed to the wide drawer under the range and left his friend, going to the living room to phone the office. He left a short message for Marge. "I'll be a half hour late today," he said, recoiling at what awaited him upon his arrival at work—having to fill Marge and Bernie in on Melissa.

When Denny called him to breakfast, Ryan was pleasantly surprised with the results. Denny had whipped up creamy omelets and plenty of bacon. The food was good, albeit lethal.

"A few more meals like this and I'll be dead by next year," he said, picking up his fork.

"Admit it. You like it." Denny grinned.

"That's the problem. I should get back to granola and fruit." He bit into his toast. "By the way, I have to make an appearance at the office, for a couple hours at least."

"Not a problem." Denny tossed a bit of egg Daisy's way. The dog seemed to inhale it in one sniff. Wiping his hands on a napkin, Denny regarded Ryan uncertainly.

"I thought she'd call by now," Ryan said flatly. "I guess it's time to pull a trace on her credit cards and call the cell phone provider. I'll do that from the office. You gonna hang around here?"

"Sure," Denny replied. "I'll read a little. Maybe I'll look around a bit, if you don't mind."

"Make yourself at home, Investigator Franklin." Ryan rose to clear off the table. Together they loaded the dishwasher and wiped the table.

———

Ryan marched through the anteroom door to a cheerful secretary. Marge grinned, eyes sparkling.

"What's that look?" he quizzed her.

"How was your weekend with the preacher man?"

He exhaled audibly. "You know . . . we could all use a little church around here."

"Oh my. He *is* getting to you."

He shrugged. "Any calls?"

"Bernie left you a note."

He felt a surge of disgust, grabbed the folded note paper, and hurried to his office door.

Marge called after him, "Say, I almost forgot. How did Melissa like the necklace?"

"Don't ask." Not ready to broach the subject, he closed the door to his office. Seated at his desk, he removed the key from his pocket and turned the lock, opening the drawers. He rubbed his face with both hands. Already he felt drained, wished he could turn around and go home—forget the day.

A flick of a central switch and all computers and monitors in the room buzzed to life. He glanced at his watch. Twenty minutes till the market officially opened. Premarket was already in full swing. Clutching Bernie's note, he cringed. The stock tip was comprised of a mere four letters—a basic stock symbol—*the* stock for the day.

He'd come to despise this aspect of his job. Utilizing the keyboard at his desk, Ryan accessed information on the Internet for the stock's recent technical pattern and the company fundamentals. Last Friday the stock had closed at 98½. Contacting his market maker electronically, he placed an order to short twenty thousand shares.

Then, glancing at the corner of his home page, he saw what he had somehow missed upon first booting up. A single e-mail message—originating from his own address. *Strange.* Assuming it was a mistake, his finger involuntarily reached toward the delete key. But just before touching it, instead he clicked the icon.

The note was from Melissa.

Ryan,
   I had to let you know I'm okay. Someday soon I'll make you understand. I promise.

                              Miss you terribly,
                              Mellie

He kicked himself mentally. Why hadn't he realized she might send a note via e-mail? At least he was relieved to hear that she was safe. Also that her leaving wasn't about *them.* But if not, then what?

Lela thought surely she had time to dash over to Lapp's General Store, less than half a mile away, before midmorning chores. Hezekiah Lapp never turned away early-bird shoppers, even up to an hour or so before the store officially opened at nine o'clock of a morning.

She was planning a special dinner at noon for Melissa, who'd been in a strange slump before breakfast. The phone call she had been eager for had simply not come.

Some rhubarb tapioca and Mama's old-fashioned chicken loaf with pimentos and melted butter might help, she thought.

But she'd run out of a few of the necessary ingredients and decided, since it was another nice day, to bicycle down to the store bright and early. The sky was bluer than yesterday, hardly a cloud, though she could see some building up on the horizon to the north. Still, she was ever so glad to be running errands on behalf of a wounded soul.

Arriving at Hezekiah's grocery shop, she parked her bike in one of the parallel spots, putting the kickstand down. A shiny blue car was parked at the end of the row. She entered the store, the tinkle of the bell greeting her.

"Hullo there, Lela," called Hezekiah. "I see you're out right early today."

She smiled back. "Need some pimentos for dinner," she replied, spotting another customer, a man whose back was turned to her, in the bulk foods aisle.

"Let me know if I can help you find anything," Hezekiah said, glancing over at the man. "And you, too, sir."

That's when she noticed the familiar profile, though it had been quite some time since she'd laid eyes on Paul Martin. Nevertheless, he was as handsome today as he had been back in high school. Her heart twitched a bit at the memory of those long-ago days. The demise of their love, due to the woman he'd chosen over her. Deceased now. The irony of it all.

Refusing to stare, she kept busy with her search for the items she needed. Paul was only a small part of her past, a truly happy memory if one left out the way things ended between them. 'Course, now, what with Sadie Nan eager to play matchmaker, well, she just didn't know what to think about such a thing. And yesterday, after church, Sadie had tried mighty hard to catch Lela's eye. Yet she would have nothing to do with Paul's sister's scheming. The fact of the matter was, she didn't like the thought of playing second fiddle to the fancy blond girl who'd claimed him as her husband. Dead or not.

"Well, my goodness, is that you, Lela?" She heard his voice, and something in her froze.

Turning, she gave him a cordial smile. "Hello, Paul."

"I'd hoped to visit with you yesterday after church, but you slipped out before I could—"

"What brings you to Lancaster?" she broke in.

Tall and ruddy, he looked at her with shining blue eyes. His light brown hair was cropped around his ears, cut and styled as though he'd never grown up in a strict Anabaptist community. Still, she found his meekness appealing. "I'm here on business," he replied.

Somewhat relieved, she wondered how long he would stay, though she had no intention of asking. For sure and for certain, Sadie Nan would be all too eager to fill her in.

"I hope you'll consider having dinner with me." His voice was gentle, his eyes sincere. "I know I don't deserve a second chance."

What was she to say? Spurned in her youth, here was the man who'd rejected her for another. "That's awful kind of you," she said softly.

"May I call you sometime?" He wasn't mincing words.

"I don't know . . . how I feel about that," she confessed.

He smiled down at her, waiting.

"And . . . I'm real busy with a boarder presently."

"Oh?" He seemed surprised to hear it. "I didn't know."

Because she was *not* in dire straits, definitely not, she didn't want him to think she was vulnerable, in need of a man. "God nudged me in that particular direction just recently," she said, revealing nothing about Melissa or the young Englischer's desperation.

"Well, then, I'm glad to hear it." He stepped back, smiling his winning smile. "My sister tells me you're well."

"Yes, and you?"

"Very well, thanks."

She hesitated to inquire of his wife's fatal illness. The subject seemed rather untouchable. "I'm sorry to hear of your loss."

"Thank you, Lela. How generous of you to say so."

To think otherwise would have been erroneous on his part. Surely, he must have known how very painful their breakup was for her.

"God bless you, Paul." She said it quickly, turning away to tend to her shopping.

Eighteen

❖ ❖ ❖

Settling onto the couch in the sun-room, Denny was glad he'd brought a long-sleeved shirt. A hint of fall hung in the air, though he knew the day would most likely warm up. After all, this was Connecticut.

He read the newspaper for a few minutes but had trouble concentrating. His gaze drifted to the corner of the room, where Melissa's easel stood poised, the initial stages of a floral painting on display.

Thinking back to his first visit with Ryan and Melissa, he recalled his earliest impression of Ryan's wife: she was simply beautiful. Further conversation more than confirmed his initial reaction. Not only was Melissa very attractive, but more important, she had a warm personality and a sweet spirit.

He'd announced to Ryan in her presence, "You definitely married *up*, my friend."

Ryan had laughed. "You aren't telling *me* anything."

Melissa only blushed, slipping her arm through Ryan's.

He also remembered the morning Ryan ran off to the grocery store, leaving him alone with Melissa in the sun-room. They had exchanged small talk until he broached the subject of faith, discovering her to be open and receptive to spiritual things. While he painted word pictures for her of a loving, personal God, she perched on her stool, painting her oceans and listening intently.

"That sounds so . . . intriguing," she replied, seemingly sincere. In answer to her questions, he used Scripture, to the best of his ability. Melissa was definitely searching.

Eventually, Ryan returned with several pints of frozen yogurt. After that singular moment, no other opportunity to discuss spiritual matters with Melissa had presented itself. Yet something about that day stuck in his memory. He had been talking about growing up in Colorado, then switched gears to inquire of her home state, Minnesota. Usually candid, Melissa had turned elusive. At the time he'd dismissed it, thinking perhaps she was uncomfortable discussing her childhood.

To a history and geography buff, Denny found it strange that Melissa was uninformed about the basic facts of her own state, as if ten thousand lakes, enormous mosquitoes, harsh winters, even outlandishly high state taxes were somehow foreign to her. Now, with Mellie on the run, the incongruity of their previous discussion haunted him.

Several scrapbooks were lined up along the top shelf of the bookcase. He reached for them and, one by one, perused the pages—mostly pictures of Melissa and Ryan at scenic or historic sites in New England, intermingled with poses at the beach or in front of quaint B&B's.

He examined each picture carefully as if something in Melissa's face, her expression might reveal something important. He was unsure what he was looking for, but he had a peculiar feeling about the whole situation.

The jangle of the phone interrupted his musing. He rushed to the living room in search of the portable. Finding it, he answered, "Hello? James residence."

"Denny—" Ryan's voice.

"What's up?"

"You're not going to believe this. Mellie sent me an e-mail message."

Denny breathed a sigh of relief. "Where is she?"

"She didn't say, but she's all right."

Still confused by Melissa's secrecy, Denny did not reply.

"Well . . . I wanted you to know," Ryan said. "See you later."

"Later," Denny said and hung up, puzzled, then headed back to the sun-room. Melissa was safe. *Thanks, Lord.* Carefully, he placed the scrapbooks back on the shelf, determined to focus on other matters. But a smaller album, tucked back in the corner, caught his attention.

Let it go, man, he thought. *She's okay.*

Something urged him on. He thumbed through the pages, a single photo to each album leaf. The small scrapbook contained childhood photos of Melissa. Photos of a giggling girl riding her bike, posing shyly next to a woman who was possibly her teacher, walking with several other girls on a pathway beside a small lake, opening Christmas pres-

ents. The excitement in the small child's innocent smile touched his
heart. He was about to close the album when he noticed something
slightly different about the final page. He felt its thickness—bulkier
than the others. *Why?*

Clumsily, Denny poked the page protector, creating a gap for his
thumb and forefinger to explore. Sure enough, another photo lay hidden
between. Carefully, he pulled it out and studied the birthday picture. A
current of energy shivered down his back.

The photo was of Melissa blowing out candles on a cake. Denny
squinted to count them. Eight. Beside her, an older man stood nearby,
probably Melissa's father, his hand resting protectively behind her
chair. Neither Melissa nor the man in the photo caused him concern.
Directly behind Melissa was a window, and through it a grove of trees.
And not just any kind of trees. These were *aspen trees.*

Aspens didn't grow in Minnesota. They thrived at higher elevations,
typical of Colorado. Even more disturbing was the color of the foliage.
The aspens had turned *golden* . . . an autumn birthday. . . .

Denny tapped the photo. His mind flashed back to a phone conversation he'd had with Ryan last spring. For her birthday, they'd gone out
past Fishers Island in their sailboat, taking along a "catered picnic
lunch," a surprise from Ryan. But Melissa's birthday was supposedly in
mid-May, not fall. *Is that why this photo was hidden?*

Must be an explanation, he thought. After all, why would anyone lie
about their birth month? For that matter, why fib about your home
state? The more he thought about it, the more it bugged him.

Wandering through the living room, he looked out the back window
and checked his watch: 10:15. Ryan would be home in a half hour. He
recalled his friend's invitation prior to heading off to his office. *Make
yourself at home, Investigator Franklin.*

He knew Ryan's filing cabinet was just off the family room, downstairs. Hurrying for the stairs, he felt a twinge of chagrin. Was he
crossing a line? Maybe.

Flicking on the light, he swept past the pool table to a tall black
cabinet standing against the far wall. He reached for the top drawer and
tugged. Unlocked, it slid open easily. He began to work his way through
the multitude of alphabetized files. The label *Personal Information*
caught his eye, and he opened it, finding Ryan and Melissa's marriage
certificate. Examining the document, he found nothing unusual.

He continued his thorough search until he spotted what he had been looking for: Melissa's birth certificate and social security card. Reading the certificate, he noted the newness of the document and the word "reissue" at the bottom.

Birth Certificate
Louis Weiner Memorial Hospital
Marshall, Minnesota

This certifies that
Melissa Leigh Nolan
was born in this hospital
at 2:21 P.M.,
on Saturday the 7th day of May A.D. 1975.

According to the document, Melissa was born in Marshall, Minnesota. The superintendent of the hospital had signed on the appropriate line, as had the attending physician. Below their signatures, Denny saw something that gave him pause. *Family History.* Mother's and father's full names, their birthplaces, and birth dates.

The question nagged at him: Was her birth certificate valid? Denny was somewhat familiar with the process of personal identification in the U.S. and knew that birth certificates were widely considered to be the basis of identity. Before God had nudged him toward becoming a teacher, Denny had worked as a security officer for a high-profile law firm—his size had made it seem a natural career choice. During that time, he'd heard of people wishing to escape some crisis who assumed a new identity by either forging a birth certificate, which was risky, or having a new certificate issued in the name of someone who died at a young age, thus assuming that person's identity. With a fake birth certificate, all the other pieces of identification could be obtained, including social security number, driver's license, even passport.

Anyone could verify the authenticity of a forged birth certificate by calling a local agency where records of local births were maintained. A forgery was detectable in minutes; the agency would simply have no verifying records of the forgery. But the assumption of a deceased person's identity was more difficult to trace. After all, that birth certificate would be registered in a local county office. Unless the country cross-referenced birth certificates with death certificates, this kind of assumption of identity usually went undetected.

This is absurd, Denny thought. *Who am I kidding? Would Melissa actually fake her identity?* Unassuming and sweet, the young woman's only real crime was fleeing her home, leaving behind a mysterious note.

He came close to dumping everything back into the file and just forgetting the whole thing. But Denny couldn't walk away, not knowing for sure. Closing the filing cabinet, documents in hand, he trudged up the steps to the main floor. From the kitchen phone, he dialed Information.

"What city?" the operator asked.

"Marshall, Minnesota."

"One moment, please."

A few seconds later, another operator's voice—"What listing?"

"The county records division, where birth and death records are kept."

"Just a moment." A computerized voice read the number, then immediately connected. The phone rang. . . .

"County recorder. Gwen speaking."

Denny identified himself and told the clerk what he was looking for: the birth and death record of a Melissa Leigh Nolan, born in 1975 at Louis Weiner Hospital. He could hear her keyboard clicking in the background. "Mr. Franklin? We have the record of her birth but not her death."

Denny thanked her and hung up. He sighed. Maybe he was wrong after all. Maybe Melissa was who she said she was—Melissa Nolan, born in Marshall, Minnesota, in 1975. Denny chuckled. *I must have a bad case of overactive imagination.*

But he wasn't finished with his follow-up. If a person died outside their home county, the place of birth may not have the death record, even if cross-referenced. One more lead to follow . . .

Birth history. The mother and father. Ryan had told him that Melissa's mother had passed away and that her father had abandoned her to the care of a neighbor. But was the story true? One way to find out.

He dialed Information again, feeling increasingly stupid. He checked his watch again: 10:30. When the operator in Marshall, Minnesota, came on the line, Denny read the names directly off the birth certificate. "Bill and Georgia Nolan, please."

Silence prevailed while the operator's computer searched for the listing. "I show no listing for Bill. . . . I have a William—"

"Let's try that."

Denny was connected, and he could hear the phone ringing.

"Hello?"

"Yes, I'm trying to locate a Bill and Georgia Nolan."

"Well, my name's Bill, but there's no Georgia here. Wife's name is Betty."

"Oh, sorry to bother you," Denny replied, discouraged. *Time to let it go.*

"But I know just about every Nolan in the area."

"Yes, sir, well, thanks—"

"We had a Georgia Nolan, now that I think of it. Lived across town from us. Let me think . . . yeah, I think her husband's name was Bill. Like mine. But I'm thinking they moved away."

"Oh." Denny wasn't sure how to proceed. "I was hoping to get some information concerning their daughter."

"Daughter, you say?" The man paused, then—"Hey, the wife just walked in. Let me ask her if she remembers anything about the family."

He heard muffled voices in the background. Bill Nolan had covered the phone with his hand. In a moment he was back on the line. "Well, the wife remembers 'em better'n I do. She says their daughter lives in Minneapolis somewhere."

"Mr. Nolan, I've taken enough of your time—"

But Bill went on. "Guess their *other* daughter died real young. Didn't even make it to school age."

Denny shuddered at this revelation. "Do you happen to know her name?"

"Here, you talk to the missus."

Betty got on the phone and began chattering away as if Denny were an old friend. "Bill doesn't pay much attention to people—not like I do. I remember Georgia Nolan real well, but they moved away years ago. What a tragedy! I don't think she ever recovered."

"Excuse me?"

"From little Melissa's death," she said almost reprovingly. "What a wonderful child. I can remember her from our church nursery. Used to substitute teach for the regular teacher on Sundays sometimes. Too old now for youngsters, though."

"Where did their daughter die?"

Betty paused, considering Denny's question. "You know," she began again, "I don't think it was here. Near the Twin Cities, I think.

We heard about it, though, through friends in the church. Snowmobile accident. Can you imagine that?"

Eventually Denny hung up, after suffering through Betty's lengthy recollections of the other Nolan family. Enough information to know he'd found the truth. Melissa Leigh Nolan of Marshall, Minnesota, born in 1975, died *years* ago. Ryan's wife had obviously assumed her identity and obtained a copy of the birth certificate. The information left Denny reeling. Questions continued to plague him. Who was Ryan's Melissa? But more importantly: Why had she taken on the identity of another?

Folks who assumed false identities were running from something in their past, either from creditors . . . *or from the law*. What was Melissa running from?

Denny returned the folder to Ryan's filing cabinet and was closing the drawer when he heard the sounds of the upstairs back door.

Ryan was home.

Nineteen

❖ ❖ ❖

Denny climbed the stairs in time to witness Daisy's jubilant reunion with her master. Struggling to keep his composure, Denny stood silently in the doorway.

Ryan tossed his keys on the kitchen counter and crouched to rub down his over-eager pet. "It's too nice out to hang around here."

Ryan's gloomy demeanor of the weekend had faded somewhat. Having received the first bit of good news in days, his friend seemed hopeful . . . and now Denny had to deliver more bad news.

Giving Daisy another pat, Ryan said, "We could hit a donut shop."

"Sure, whatever." Wasn't his place to throw a damper on things.

They drove past Ryan's office building and over the drawbridge. A banner, still advertising last weekend's Annual Mystic Outdoor Art Festival, extended across West Main Street. Ryan mentioned that Melissa often entered her work in the juried show.

Not this year, he thought. *Maybe never again.* "So how did everyone at the office take it . . . about Melissa?" he ventured.

Ryan begged the question. "I haven't told them yet. Thought I'd wait till tomorrow. Who knows? Maybe she'll be back by then."

Not sure how to open a can of worms, Denny fell silent. He was fairly certain that Melissa was never coming home. "Did you check back with the police?" he asked finally.

Ryan shook his head.

Denny struggled with his knowledge of the situation. What would Ryan think of his snooping around in his files, calling record bureaus of vital statistics? Even so, he couldn't just leave his friend in the dark. Ryan would *want* to know the truth, wouldn't he?

They found a parking space on Water Street, then walked toward West Main.

"There's a little coffee shop Melissa liked to visit. In fact, Brad Short, the owner, is a client of mine."

"A coffee shop owner has money to invest? Thought you guys took only *rich* clients."

"Let's put it this way: Brad doesn't run a coffee shop because he needs the revenue."

"Family money?"

"Exactly."

The storefront boasted signs welcoming the coffee drinkers of the world. Inside, the owner, an older man with silver-gray hair and white apron tied around his waist, stood at attention behind a chest-high glass counter. He was preoccupied with a trio of giggling girls trying to decide which of the many delicious donuts to choose from behind the polished glass.

Spying Ryan, Brad nodded and gave a knowing snort. "Hey there, money man, I'll be right with you." He turned back to the group with an impatient look. "Ladies, what'll it be?"

"We'll have three of those," said one of the girls, gesturing toward the glazed donuts.

Denny and Ryan waited for the young women to divide up the sale, then rummage around in their tiny purses. Placing his hand on Ryan's back, Denny leaned over and said, "Listen, man, we need to talk. Somewhere private."

Turning to face him, Ryan's expression was one of bewilderment. "Something wrong?"

"Could be" was all he said.

Ryan frowned, glancing about the room. "Private enough?"

Surveying the shop, Denny noticed several patrons at one large table. Smaller tables for two were available near the back corner. "That one's fine," he said, moving toward the rear.

"Sure you don't want anything?" Ryan called to him.

"Some coffee. Make it black." He took the chair facing the windows while Ryan ordered. Outside he saw tourists clambering about, hauling their purchases in large shopping bags.

Over near the counter, the teenagers moved on as Ryan greeted the owner, making small talk. He overheard snippets of the conversation. Brad was saying something about the outrageous payroll taxes and how hard it was to get quality help.

"How's the market?" Brad asked. Then, without waiting for an answer—"Hey, I got a question about the last portfolio statement your office sent out."

"Problem?"

"No, no. Just curious. By the way, how's that wife of yours?"

Ryan covered well, casually sidestepping Brad's innocent queries, but Denny noticed that his demeanor changed, shoulders slumped. Ryan soon brought two coffees and several donuts on a tray. Sliding the tray onto the table, he sat down with his back to the front door and took a quick sip of coffee. "Speak to me, my friend."

Denny sighed.

"Hey, you look like you're carrying the weight of the world."

"I think I am." Forging ahead, Denny said, "You told me you didn't know Melissa very well when you married her."

Ryan regarded him curiously. "So? What's the point?"

"I have a feeling she's not coming back."

"What do you mean?"

"Maybe I should start at the beginning—"

"Good idea," Ryan said.

Denny began with an apology for poking his nose into their personal files, then about finding the hidden photo. He removed the picture from his shirt pocket and handed it to Ryan, pointing out the aspen trees "in fall colors."

Ryan seemed alarmed initially but said nothing.

Denny pushed ahead to Melissa's birth certificate, revealing what he'd learned during his calls to Marshall, Minnesota. He shared the exchange with Bill and Betty Nolan, too, the startling disclosure of Melissa Leigh Nolan's untimely death at age five.

Staring blankly, Ryan remained silent, but his jaw dropped and his face suddenly paled. He sighed deeply, as if gathering enough strength to speak. "You're saying that Melissa lied about who she is?"

Denny nodded respectfully. Telling Ryan had been harder than he'd imagined. He felt his friend's anguish, the sting of disbelief. "She assumed the identity of a child who died years ago," Denny managed to say.

"How do you know you're not mistaken?"

"Well, we could follow up with the death certificate, contact the parents of the original Melissa . . . verify their story."

Ryan shook his head, defeated. "No . . . actually . . ." He stopped, eyes glistening. "I suppose I shouldn't be too surprised at anything, after all this.'' He shrugged, unable to continue.

How many hits does a guy have to take? Denny felt lousy being the one to deliver the blow.

A tray fell, clattering to the floor. They turned in unison to look. A long line of customers, eager for donuts and varieties of coffee, stretched nearly to the door.

The girl behind the counter came around sheepishly, bending down to clean up the mess on the floor. "Oh man . . .'' she said, evidently embarrassed by her clumsiness.

"Just let it go,'' the owner hollered from another room.

Flustered, the young clerk straightened and scurried back behind the counter to take orders, then filled them single-handedly.

"Nice guy, this client of yours,'' Denny interjected, feeling sorry for the poor girl.

"A little rough around the edges'' was Ryan's distracted comment.

Observing the clerk's attempt to juggle the crowd, Denny's gaze zeroed in on a middle-aged man sauntering in the doorway, wearing gray slacks and a white shirt. Standing in line, the man made a furtive sweep around the room, stopping at their table. Then he turned away, a look of recognition on his face. *Strange*, thought Denny, who was particularly struck by the lone tuft of gray in the man's full head of dark hair.

He returned his attention to Ryan. "Has anyone ever contacted you about Melissa?''

Seemingly preoccupied, Ryan shook his head. "No. Listen—''

Just then, Ryan's pager chirped. He pulled the pager off his belt, scrutinizing it, then finding his cell phone, he punched in a couple of numbers and waited. "Cover twenty thousand shares immediately,'' he barked. When he was finished, he shook his head. "I need some air. Let's take a walk.''

Finished with coffee, they rose from their seats well after the man with a splash of silver in his hair had strolled out the door.

"Take it easy,'' Ryan called to the owner.

"Hey, don't I wish!'' came the crusty reply.

Outside the donut shop, Ryan turned suddenly. "I forgot, Brad had a question. Can you wait a minute?''

"No problem.''

"See you in a few minutes.'' Ryan hurried back inside.

Waiting, Denny leaned up against the glass window, watching the hustle and bustle around him. Tourists gawking and shopping, young mothers pushing baby strollers, traffic backed up.

Everyone seemed caught up in the movement downtown, everyone except himself . . . and the man he'd seen earlier in the shop, now across the street, casually drinking his cup of coffee. For no particular reason, Denny felt wary of the man. But he dismissed his unexplainable caution and went back into the shop, where Ryan and Brad were chatting at the far end of the counter, going over some figures on a piece of paper.

Ryan spotted Denny and nodded.

"Take your time." Denny poked his thumb toward the door. "I'm going to check out the gift shop up the street."

"Yeah, sure. I'll meet you there."

Denny headed up the sidewalk, trying to shake his apprehension. But he had an odd feeling that he was being watched. He covered half a block before peering over his shoulder again. The man had disappeared. Denny scanned the area, wondering how the man had slipped away so quickly.

Relax, Denny thought, ignoring his sense of foreboding. *Stop playing detective. You've done enough harm for one day.*

He resumed his mission to buy a gift for Evelyn. *Something "New England,"* Denny decided. *She'll like that.*

Twenty

❖ ❖ ❖

I don't know when I've eaten food this delicious," Melissa noted after the last bite of the noon meal.

"Well, thank you." Lela, sitting opposite her, smiled. "I wanted to cook up something extra special for you."

Lela was perhaps one of the sweetest women Melissa had ever known. The fact that the Plain woman was past thirty and not yet married was astonishing. The truth was, the hostess had everything going for her—great cooking skills, gardening talent, a well-kept home. Why hadn't she married? Any reasonable man would find Lela Denlinger an excellent choice.

But Melissa knew little of the dating and courtship practices in the quiet community, and she wasn't about to ask. She *did* recall the blush of embarrassment on Lela's face, the slightly flustered speech, just yesterday morning. So did she have a man friend after all?

Their conversation turned to Elizabeth and Thaddeus and their little ones. Lela, it seemed, adored her nieces and nephews. She was also quite fond of Elizabeth. "We had the most interesting childhood," Lela said. "Always together, till school issues separated us. But, nevertheless, we had our evenings . . . and the summers."

"What happened at school?"

"Elizabeth began dating Thaddeus, a young Amishman, so she dropped out of higher education, so to speak, preparing to follow in his Old Order ways." Lela explained that the Amish stop educating their young people after eighth grade. "Since Elizabeth was well past that level, she decided to honor her fiancé."

"She quit school for Thaddeus?"

"To please him, you know."

Melissa hadn't heard of such a thing. Women's rights had been the top issue in college. The notion of a woman giving up her plans for a man was foreign to her.

"Did Elizabeth ever second-guess her decision?" she asked.

"Never, so far as I know." Lela paused. "But, then, Thaddeus has always been a good, kind man. He and Elizabeth became the best of friends, even before their marriage. Still are, I suspect."

Best of friends . . .

She'd always viewed herself and Ryan that way. And they *had* been close friends, in spite of their occasional disagreements. The commonalities between them made up for other things. They both loved dogs—Daisy was proof—and they enjoyed their quaint abode on Lord's Point, the sea, the sailing, and all that the prime cove-front property afforded.

How she missed being there, Ryan at her side. By now he would've read her e-mail message, and he would know she was safe and sound. She wondered how he'd reacted. Did he long to return a note to her? Did he . . .

She couldn't follow in this vein of thought. Lela was dishing up dessert. Time to continue their visit, try not to think about the phone over there on the counter, the telephone that was much too silent today.

"Would it be possible for me to visit Elizabeth's little store?" she asked, accepting the rhubarb tapioca dessert and a warm-from-the-oven coconut oatmeal gem—a delicious cookie.

"Oh sure." Lela beamed, her eyes bright. "We can go over after bit."

She wasn't sure how soon "after bit" was, but she would be ready whenever the time came. "I'm curious about the type of quilts you make to sell."

Lela nodded. "I'd be ever so happy to show you some of my patchwork upstairs, if you'd like."

Anything to kill some time. She wasn't exactly thrilled about the idea of examining piecework, quilting, all of that. But she was curious about Lela's simple life in Amish country. The young Mennonite didn't own much, though her home was nicely furnished, her wardrobe pleasant, if plain. She hadn't cared or bothered to learn to drive a car, didn't own one either. Lela's greatest joy seemed to come from within. She had an amazing sense of herself, not so much self-assured as she was settled. At peace.

They worked side by side in the kitchen, and at one point, Lela began to hum a tune. The melody offered a reprieve from Melissa's angst, if only briefly.

While drying dishes, she made a decision. If her contact had not returned her phone call by two o'clock Eastern Daylight Time, she would phone him again. This waiting was impossible. She had to know what she was to do next. For both her sake and Ryan's.

Lela's sewing room was a tiny spot situated under the garret. Wall shelving accommodated many spools of colorful thread and other sewing notions. An electric sewing machine was positioned under a window, and there was a table on the opposite wall for cutting out patterns. She also had a small bookcase, where she kept extra tracts and devotional books. The room was her "quiet place."

"As you can see, it's small but efficient," Lela said, showing Melissa around.

Melissa was most interested in the quilted goods, and Lela was eager to oblige, showing her the original pattern. "I've used this to make hundreds of pillow shams," Lela said.

Marveling at the tiny quilting stitches, Melissa found herself enjoying this creative side of her Mennonite friend—a common thread that tied her to this woman and brought more than a small measure of comfort.

When the two women set out later in the afternoon, the road to Thaddeus King's farmhouse was deserted. It was paved, but only a two-lane, and that hardly wide enough for cars to pass each other. The stretch of road was ablaze with the westerly sun, its dips and turns accented by tall, lovely trees scattered here and there along the wayside.

When they neared the large clapboard house, Melissa noticed three of the King children at play in the side yard. School evidently was not yet in session.

"Baby John's probably down for a nap," Lela commented, pushing a strand of hair under her prayer bonnet. "I daresay Elizabeth's taking full advantage of the quiet house, cleaning and baking and whatnot."

Melissa was a little surprised that Lela seemed to know her sister's schedule so well. "Isn't it hard to keep up with four children?" she said, as they made the turn into the Kings' dirt lane.

"Not so hard, really. Elizabeth knows how to make the children mind. Besides that, Mary Jane and Timothy help the younger two. The more children, the less work a mother oughta have.''

The idea of the older ones assisting the younger children was something Melissa hadn't known, being an only child . . . and a half orphan for the first ten years of her life.

In the Jane Austen novels she loved, there was a hierarchy of duties among children, she remembered. She had no way of knowing where Plain people got *their* ideas, not having had contact with any of them before. She did find the ordering of domestic duties fascinating. Things ran like clockwork at both Lela's and Elizabeth's homes, almost effortlessly.

"We aren't perfect," Elizabeth said after greeting them and serving up some shoofly pie. "Don't ever think that." Melissa's awestruck comments had elicited the disclaimer.

Mary Jane came over and plunked down at the table across from her. "I sewed my first stitches just this mornin'," said the adorable child. "Wouldja care to have a look-see?"

"I'd love to," Melissa said, marveling at the girl's confidence. She herself had been lacking in such characteristics, especially at Mary Jane's tender age. The years following her mother's death had left her unsure of herself and her future. Her loss had been so deep that the mere act of getting up and off to school was a daily burden.

Mary Jane came back, face full of eagerness to show the straight stitches she'd sewn into a scrap of fabric. "Mama helped me," she whispered.

"Your mama's the best one for the job," Lela agreed.

Elizabeth waved her hand, as if the compliments were not accurate. "Ach, I can't take much credit, really. Mary Jane's a born quilter, I should say."

Lela grinned at young Mary Jane. "We know who's one of the best quilters around these parts, don't we?"

Mary Jane and Linda, her wee sister, nodded their heads. "And Mama makes wonderful-*gut* food, too," Linda, just four, said, her eyes growing bigger by the second.

Baby John began to cry upstairs, and Lela slipped away from the kitchen to get him. Bringing him down, she soothed him, rubbing his tiny back gently. She was so comfortable around little ones. Melissa wondered if being at ease with children was something a person had to be taught. Or were there women who took to it naturally, like both Elizabeth and Lela?

"The honor system must be in use today," Lela commented about the little store behind the house.

"Jah," said Elizabeth, "and so far nobody's seen fit to steal from us, which is right nice." She paused. "Oh, by the way, I forgot to tell you I sold another set of your quilted pillow shams first thing this mornin'."

"So you must be down to about three sets?" Lela walked up and down the kitchen with John nestled in her arms.

"What's left will go fast, I daresay." Elizabeth prepared a snack of applesauce for the baby.

"I best be getting busy, then," replied Lela while the children contented themselves with coloring at the table. "I oughta make up a batch more of them, fast as they go."

Melissa enjoyed watching the moments unfold, as if observing a scene from an old-fashioned movie. She was impressed with the children's good behavior, as small as they were. She found herself wondering what it would be like to have youngsters around her. Ryan might not be interested, as busy as he was. But if she taught her children to help take care of each other, as Elizabeth had, Ryan wouldn't have to be concerned over his hectic work schedule interfering so much. Now, thinking about the possibility of being a mother someday, she wondered why she'd never discussed the idea with Ryan. And why *he* hadn't broached the subject with her.

Allowing her hopes and dreams to run wild was a mistake. Most likely she was going to be a very lonely woman, and for a long, long time.

———

Elizabeth's store was a small but tidy portion of a shed, though it was as well organized as any shop Melissa had ever seen. There were quilted items such as pillows—square, round, and heart-shaped—on one long row, with prices pinned to each. Doilies, table runners, pillowcases, and linens of all kinds—each handmade—graced the Amish store. Kitchen items included potholders, mitts, and aprons.

There were crocheted sweaters and shawls of various colors for women, as well as sunbonnets in all sizes, some small ones for girls. Baby items—terry-cloth bibs with appliqués for both boys and girls, tiny hats, dresses, baby sweaters, booties, and blankets.

Above them, on a makeshift clothesline, were quilted wall hangings with appliquéd pictures prominently pieced in—a woman wearing a sunbonnet and hanging out her wash featured each small item of clothing hanging free, attached only at the very top. So clever.

"The '*Sundries*' part of the sign out front are *my* things," Lela said, laughing.

"Since Auntie isn't Amish," Mary Jane spoke up.

"I see," Melissa said, playing along. "But if she were Amish, what then?"

"The sign might just say *Amish Store*. Ain't so, Mama?"

Elizabeth nodded with a smile, straightening a pile of tablecloths, then moved to the area where faceless dolls were lined up on a shelf. "My youngest sister, Emma, makes these."

Going over to look at the cute little dolls, Melissa noticed that the boy dolls had tiny suspenders and black felt hats. "These look tedious to make."

"Oh my, are they ever," Elizabeth said. "I don't see how Emma does it, workin' all day long on 'em."

"She must have good eyes," Lela added. "I'd sure hate to have to fool with such wee things."

Mary Jane came over for a closer look at the dolls' clothing. She removed a hat from the boy doll's head and, inspecting it closely, said, "I think *I* could prob'ly sew up a hat like this someday."

"Jah, someday you will, dear," Elizabeth agreed.

Just then several cars pulled into the barnyard. Melissa felt the old panic return, but when the customers entered the little store, she realized they were harmless. Just tourists eager to load up on the "real thing," said one. They had come to buy souvenirs and Christmas gifts "to take back home."

"No one would believe this place exists," said another with a laugh.

Isn't that the truth? thought Melissa.

When they returned to Lela's home, Melissa asked if she could do a small load of laundry, since she'd brought so few clothes with her. Lela cheerfully obliged, and when the clothes were dried and folded, Melissa asked her to please check for phone messages. There were none.

Her spirits plummeted, but her impatience bolstered her resolve. *I can't wait any longer.* "Do you mind if I use your phone?" she asked.

"Not a'tall." Lela discreetly left the room, going to sit in the living room while Melissa made her call.

She removed a slip of paper from her pocket, then dialed quickly, hoping to get through this time. No more leaving Lela Denlinger's phone number on an answering machine. She needed answers—now. She wondered what Lela would think if she knew who Melissa was calling. Would the young Mennonite woman be frightened and ask her to leave?

She heard a click. "FBI," a male voice answered.

Finally . . . her contact.

"This is Melissa James," she identified herself. "Why haven't you—"

"Melissa? Where are you?" came the suddenly tense reply.

She paused, bewildered over his strained tone. "I left a phone number last Friday night. No one got back with me."

"We've been calling the entire weekend," he insisted. "Tell me the number again, in case something happens or we get disconnected."

Confused, Melissa held up the phone and began reading off Lela's phone number. "Wait." She stopped after reading the first three digits. She saw her mistake. In her haste she must have given the wrong number last Friday night.

Unbelievable. After all this time, they *had* been trying to reach her. She finished giving the correct phone number.

"Confirm the address."

Melissa told him, then paused. "I was followed, but I lost him."

The man exhaled loudly. "We've got to get you out of there."

"No . . . I'm safe here."

"Listen, your life may be—"

"I left my husband behind because you insisted I flee. You didn't answer my questions then, so now I'm asking again—why did I have to leave my home?"

"It was imperative you leave, Melissa. By your own admission, you may have been in imminent danger. Our nearest agent was an hour away. But now we must speak with you . . . in person."

Something was horribly wrong. Doom was palpable. She heard it in his voice.

Her stomach knotted up. She leaned hard on the counter, breathless with worry, waiting for her world to come to a complete end. "It's about Ryan, isn't it?" she said at last.

The agent ignored her. "We can be at your location within ten minutes."

"The truth," she said simply with resignation. "I must know about my husband."

Terrifying images swept through her mind. She recoiled in horror. The room began spinning like a time capsule. She was ten again, black-and-white police cars were flashing in front of Daddy's little house. A woman in a blue uniform gently but firmly sat her down, telling her that her father had gone to heaven. *What do you mean? I just saw him this morning. Daddy dropped me off at school. . . .*

The nightmare was happening again. She felt, for a moment, Mrs. Browning's loving arms about her, soothing her. *"There, there, dearie, I'm here. Your Mrs. Browning will see to you. . . ."*

See to you . . .

She shivered, thinking of the precious woman. But Mrs. Browning wasn't here to pick up the pieces of her life this time. Angrily, Melissa shook her head. Hot tears spilled down her face. She felt she might erupt with rage.

You told me Ryan would be safe! She directed her thought to the FBI agent.

Teeth clenched, anticipating the worst, she waited for the agent to continue. When he spoke again, his voice was softer, gentler, as if attempting to console her. "Melissa . . . I have some upsetting news. It's about your husband, Ryan James. . . ."

Twenty-One

❖ ❖ ❖

As God as her witness, Lela did not wish to eavesdrop on Melissa's phone conversation. Yet she *had* heard bits and pieces, and she was greatly troubled. Could it be that Melissa's husband was in danger? She refused to think the worst, though Mellie's angry words echoed through the house—"I must know about my husband. . . ."

Now Mellie was venting her anger into the telephone, shouting at whoever was on the line. Then a period of calm followed. Silence overtook the place.

Last came weeping. "No . . . no, it can't be. . . ." Mellie's voice carried into the small living room. "You must be wrong."

Not knowing what to say or do, Lela prayed silently. *Lord, please help Melissa with whatever it is . . . let me be a comfort.*

Suddenly, she heard Melissa shout into the phone, "I don't believe you! Just leave me alone!" Abruptly, she returned the phone to its cradle.

Worried, Lela rose from her chair. She went to the kitchen where the girl was sobbing inconsolably. "Mellie?" she whispered.

Making eye contact with her, Melissa stammered through her tears, "I need to get my car. I have to leave."

"Sure, Mellie, but are you . . . will you be all right?"

Melissa shook her head. "Nothing's ever going to be all right again."

Picking up the phone, Lela quickly dialed the number for Thaddeus King. Meanwhile, Melissa rushed upstairs, still weeping. Thankfully, Elizabeth answered on the second ring. Lela told her sister that Melissa would be over soon to get her car. She hung up just as Melissa reached the entryway with her overnight case, fumbling through her purse.

Approaching her, Lela prayed silently for divine guidance, observing Melissa's obvious frustration.

Turning to face her, with plaintive eyes, Melissa said, "I forget how much I owe you."

"Oh . . . well, it's thirty dollars per night. You've been here three nights total."

Melissa shuffled through a number of bills in her wallet—more money than Lela had seen in a long time—handing over five twenties. "This should cover it. Keep the change."

Meekly, she received the money. "Can I help you in any way?" Lela asked, her heart going out to the disturbed woman.

Tears welled up, and Melissa's lip quivered as she shook her head no. She juggled her overnight case and purse and headed for the door, then stopped abruptly, as if someone had spoken her name, calling her back.

Lela's own tears kept her from seeing clearly, yet she was hoping, perhaps, that the poor thing had changed her mind. Oh, more than anything, she wanted to help.

Melissa inched forward, making another attempt to exit. Yet once again she halted. Sighing ever so deeply, she set her overnight case down with some degree of resignation. Hugging herself, she seemed to stare past the door. Her expression changed from fear to grief. A pallor descended over her. "I can't go back. Can't *ever* go back," she whispered.

Seizing the opportunity, Lela reached out a hand. "Please stay longer, Mellie . . . as long as you like."

The young woman turned, her face a contortion of pain and sadness. Lela did what she knew best—she opened her arms to the hurting soul, and Melissa fell into them, sobbing without restraint.

After a time Melissa said she was tired and needed to lie down.

"May I steep some tea for you to take to your room?" Lela offered.

Mellie declined, desperation on her face. She made her way up the steps, slowly, methodically, lost in her anguish.

Thinking it wise to follow closely, Lela kept an eye on Melissa as the young woman went to the spare room, where she finally lay on the bed, breathing heavily.

"Oh, Ryan," whispered Mellie again and again. "Not you, too."

Lela pulled up the handmade quilt at the foot of the bed, placing it over Mellie's quivering body. The swollen red eyelids had closed, shutting out the world.

Watching over Mellie just now, Lela was reminded of the times she'd stood silently near the beds of her sleeping nieces and nephews. As if her presence were somehow consoling, though she took no pride in it.

When it seemed Melissa's breathing had slowed to a steadier rate, Lela felt the Lord prompting her to pray. She reached down and touched Melissa's arm lightly. *Father in heaven, please comfort this your dear one. Enfold her in your loving arms, for Jesus' sake. Amen.*

Sleep came at last. Lela left the room. She must phone Elizabeth right quick, let her know that Melissa would not be needing her car. Not just yet.

———

Periodically throughout the afternoon, Lela checked in on her guest, but Melissa, sleeping soundly, did not stir once. It was well past five o'clock when Lela made another round past the spare room. She found Melissa sitting at the edge of the bed, looking a bit groggy, a sad, lost look in her eyes.

"May I get some tea for you now?" she asked, tapping the door that stood slightly ajar.

Attempting a weak smile—perhaps trying to acknowledge Lela's generosity—Melissa's face was stony white. "I should go," she said blankly, "back to Connecticut."

Lela was filled with dismay. Melissa was in no shape to drive any distance, much less all that way. "I thought you said . . . you could never return."

Melissa looked up at her, eyes glistening anew. "You've been so kind to me, Lela. It wouldn't be right for me to stay longer."

"Well, why not?"

Melissa's eyes lowered. "My life's in danger. I can't put you in jeopardy. If I stay . . . he might find me."

"*Who* will?" Lela was stunned by Melissa's admission. Perhaps, though, the young woman was just confused. Lela sat on the bed, turning her gaze back to Melissa. "Does someone want to hurt you?"

Nodding, Melissa leaned her head into her fists, beginning to cry.

"Does that person know where you are?" she probed gently.

"I don't see how . . . but it's still too dangerous."

"I believe God will keep you safe here, Mellie. He is bigger than the evil around us," Lela said. "Our help cometh from the Lord," she whispered.

Melissa looked doubtful. "Can God stop bullets?"

Lela's breath caught in her throat. *What sort of trouble is Melissa in anyhow?* she thought, not letting on. Bravely she smiled. "Are you in some kind of trouble . . . with the law, I mean?"

Melissa smiled crookedly. "No."

"Should we call the police?"

"They'll do nothing. And he'd find me for sure."

"You'll be all right here till you decide what to do. We'll trust in the Lord."

"Why are you willing to take the chance?"

Lela felt the assurance rise up in her. "Truth is, I've seen the miracle-working power of God in this community."

Melissa's gaze held hers, as though searching, hoping for truth, then she shook her head, lying back on the bed. "God doesn't answer my prayers."

"Mellie—"

Melissa shook her head, then closed her eyes again, hugging herself tightly, as if hiding from the world. Lela reached down, pulled the covers over her guest, and left the room.

———

The next morning Lela knocked on Melissa's door. The door was ajar, and she saw that Mellie was up, sitting in a chair, pale and listless. "Were you able to sleep much at all?" she asked.

"I think so."

"What would you like to eat?"

"Only some juice, thanks."

Lela headed downstairs to fix breakfast. Maybe if Melissa smelled the food cooking, her nose would prod her stomach. How important that the girl keep up her strength. Especially being so emotionally overwrought.

Pouring batter into her waffle iron, she kept an eye on the eggs frying and bacon sizzling. She set the table, placing a small cluster of flowers in a vase for the centerpiece.

When the table was ready, she heard footsteps on the stair and caught a glimpse of Melissa coming through the kitchen, heading toward the sun porch. "It's another nice day," she called to her. "Go ahead, have yourself a look round the garden."

Melissa obliged and went outside. Lela could see her looking out over the pastureland to the east. She seemed motionless, quite forlorn.

After a time Lela carried a tray of freshly squeezed orange juice outside, offering some to Melissa, who accepted it graciously. "This may help to make you feel better," Lela said, hoping it would.

Their eyes met. "You remind me so much of . . ."

"Who?" Lela asked, curious to know.

"My best friend . . . Mrs. Browning."

Lela was glad to see Melissa coming out of her shell a bit. "Did you know each other from school?"

"No, she was lots older. She took care of me after . . ." She paused as tears filled her eyes. "My friend was like a mother to me."

"Where is she now?"

Melissa bit her lip. "I haven't seen Mrs. Browning in years. I used to talk to her about everything. I miss her so much."

"Some people say *I'm* a good listener."

Melissa nodded, her face drawn. "I know you are."

"I don't mean to pry, but if you feel like talking, I'm here for you. All right?"

The poor thing looked away, out toward the distant horizon. "I wouldn't even know where to begin," she said, her voice low. "I don't even know who I am anymore. I've lost my identity . . . and my husband in the same lifetime. Everything important to me is gone. . . ." Her voice trailed off and her shoulders shook with fresh waves of grief.

Lela was stunned, allowing her guest to sob out her pain. She wished she might comfort the poor girl, but she was unsure of what to do, considering Melissa's secrecy.

After a time she headed back into the house to check on the breakfast in the warming oven. Eventually Melissa followed and sat at the table, preoccupied as she reached for her cloth napkin and placed it solemnly in her lap.

Lela served up eggs and bacon, along with the waffles. "Sometimes when I need solitude, I take long walks," she said. "There's a beautiful place almost a mile from here. I call it my sanctuary, but it's not mine, really. Still, I can go and sit on the banks of the Conestoga River and talk to the Lord."

"Where is it?" Melissa asked.

"Did you come in by way of Hunsecker Mill Bridge?"

"Is that the covered bridge?"

"Yes, that's the one. Sometime, we'll go for a walk there."

Melissa seemed remotely interested. "I saw the bridge by moonlight last Friday evening. "

"It's mighty peaceful and lovely with the willows along the river," Lela added.

"I know that feeling of tranquility." Melissa had a faraway look in her eyes. "I had a place something like that, too, when I was a girl. Actually, it was Mrs. Browning's flower garden, the whole backyard of the house."

Lela was cautious, didn't want to pry into Melissa's past without permission. "Tell me about your best friend, if I may ask."

"Mrs. Browning . . ." Melissa began wistfully. "I was seven years old when my father, a widower, announced we were going to move to a small town in Colorado," she began. "It's hard to remember much about that time of my life, I was so young, but I do remember the over-all feeling I had—one of confusion. Why did Daddy have to take us away from everything we knew and loved?"

Lela sat silently, eager for Mellie to continue.

"It was difficult, relocating so hurriedly. And there was a great sense of urgency." She sighed, leaning back in the chair, reliving bits and pieces of her little-girl fears. "My father never explained the reason for the sudden change in our location. We flew to Denver the next night, leaving everything we owned behind at our home in Laguna Beach, California, except for a few changes of summer clothes and two of my favorite stuffed animals. My father said we could buy 'all new things' at our new home."

"How strange."

"Yes, but Daddy and I had each other. In a few short weeks, we settled into our little rental home in Palmer Lake, a place where everyone seemed to know everyone else. A quiet little town with friendly people. Folks there truly cared—teachers taught because they loved kids, not for the paycheck. Postal workers walked their route, stopping to visit along the way. And there was Mrs. Browning, who lived down the block from us—she and her husband became our good friends, our very best friends in the world."

The first time she'd met the British woman, Melissa and her father were choosing roses for the backyard at Algoma's Nursery, a small garden center on the outskirts of town. Mrs. Browning was also there, purchasing bedding plants. "Welcome to Palmer Lake," the middle-aged woman called across a table of pansies and petunias.

"Thanks," Melissa's father said. "Nice to be here."

At the time, Melissa found it interesting that the lady with a strong accent seemed to know they were newcomers. She tugged on her daddy's arm, whispering, "How's she know about us?"

He took time to explain that folks in a town this small knew who was a longtime resident and who wasn't. Melissa, all the while, watched Mrs. Browning's cart fill up with peachy pink roses. Missing their rose gardens in Laguna Beach, she was intrigued by the nice lady with creamy complexion, nut brown hair, and emerald eyes.

"Can we make more rose gardens, Daddy?" she asked, hiding behind her father.

"That's why we're here," he said, setting about picking out a number of hybrid tea roses, in a variety of colors, striking up a conversation with the cheerful woman, exchanging names and discovering that they were neighbors.

The next day Mrs. Browning and her husband, a sprite of a man, knocked on their door bearing gifts—strawberry shortbread and a box of chocolates. They were invited inside to chat, and from then on, Mellie was allowed to spend time with the charming couple.

Before their move, her father had been hesitant to let Mellie out of his sight. Here, in Palmer Lake, he seemed to trust people almost instantly. Especially Mrs. Browning. And Mellie was glad, because their neighbor was both fun and creative. Mellie fantasized that her deceased mother might've had similar qualities, though her father was reluctant to talk of his childhood sweetheart, now passed away.

Daddy always had time for me. . . .

She was especially fond of their after-supper hours. Curling up beside her father, Mellie listened intently as he read aloud, everything from *Heidi* to the classic fairy tales. Sometimes they watched favorite videos, always together.

Emery Keaton was outspokenly opposed to the violence so readily offered up on television. Having only one TV in the house, and a closely monitored one at that, kept Mellie somewhat sheltered during her primary grades.

One Tuesday, the week after school was out for the summer, she asked to go to the zoo. The day was exceptionally bright and warm for early June.

"Which zoo?" Daddy asked.

"I like Cheyenne Mountain Zoo best." She explained, in her little-girl fashion, that the walkways were steep and "very exciting." Meandering pathways, interspersed with flowers and foliage unique to Colorado, led them through the aviary, lion house, and outdoor bear exhibit. "Best of all, there's a great big monkey house." The tiniest monkeys always made her giggle. She liked the way they'd swing about, then turn and look down, eyes shining and mischievous, as if performing for her alone.

At the drop of a hat, Daddy took her off to the zoo. She never realized at that time just how financially well off they were. The fact remained, on a typical day her father rarely left the house. Occasionally, he did "run a few errands," but Mellie never knew precisely where his office was or if he even had one. Much of his supposed work took place at home, over the telephone. And after school, when she arrived eager to talk about the day, he was always there, waiting with warm eyes and smile.

There were frequent visits to the Brownings' home, as well. Mellie especially liked to wander about in the vast gardens beyond the house, thinking surely the place was much like, even patterned after, the "real" secret garden in the world of Mary Lennox and Misselthwaite Manor.

"Do you know the book?" she asked Mrs. Browning one day while the two of them weeded the small-blossomed roses Mrs. Browning called her "Joseph's Coat" masterpieces. Tricolored, they were low growing, similar to a small bush, their red, orange, and pink petals forming as sprays or clusters.

"Why, of course I do." Mrs. Browning, it turned out, had made a trip with her sister to see the rose garden in Maytham Hall, Kent, England—the source for the fictitious one, where the author lived during the late 1800s. Just as the garden in the story had a hidden entrance with a low arch and a wooden door, the real-life garden did as well. "I adored the book *The Secret Garden*, and I don't know of anyone who should say differently."

Books, flowers, and outdoors in general became the attachment by which the twosome explored the world and their relationship. By the beginning of third grade, Mellie liked to think of her neighbor as a relative of some kind. An aunt, perhaps. But when she'd gotten up her nerve to inform Mrs. Browning of her hope, the woman gently chided her, saying they were "the best of friends, yes," but Mellie shouldn't think of her as more than that.

Saddened for a day, Mellie sought out her father for advice on the matter. "She's as close as any relative might be," she insisted, thinking of Nana Clark, whom she hadn't seen in the longest time. "So why won't Mrs. Browning let me call her 'auntie'?"

Daddy was kind, understanding. "The truth is Mrs. Browning is your friend." He paused, looking over his glasses as he lowered his newspaper. "Isn't she?"

Mellie agreed. "My *best* friend."

"Well, then, I'd say you have more than a pretend relative in our neighbor."

"What do you mean?"

"To say that someone is your friend is a wonderful thing." Her father went on to explain that not just *anyone* might have such a title bestowed on them. He said that relatives were usually not chosen, only inherited, "except, of course, in the case of adoptions." But the truth of the matter was that her father believed in the beauty of true friendship. "If you find one or two close friends in a lifetime, that is all a person needs."

Promptly, she shared her father's opinion with Mrs. Browning, who said she couldn't agree more, and that was that. Mellie and Mrs. Browning *were* friends—a higher calling than any common aunt or cousin. They were gardeners and bookworms, too, and what was wrong with that?

Her father also liked to help their neighbors by working in Mrs. Browning's gardens, due to the fact that Mr. Browning's back sometimes gave him considerable trouble. The most and best he could do was dig with a shovel—bending over and weeding were definitely out of the question.

Mellie often volunteered her father's services, helping Mrs. Browning, who wasn't getting any younger. Her father liked to make up rhymes about flowers, especially roses, as he worked. This became somewhat of a game for the three of them. He began by chanting the first line of the rhyme, and Mellie would say the next, and so on.

Sometimes her father would see who could name the author of a particular quotation, including Mrs. Browning in the contest. "Who knows this one?" Daddy might say, eyes gleaming. "'There is no duty we so much underrate as the duty of being happy.'"

Mellie didn't have to think for long. The saying was one of Daddy's favorites. "Robert Louis Stevenson," she announced, glad to know.

"Never forget it, Mellie," Daddy said, nodding his head and looking at her with all the love in his eyes.

And they *were* happy those first few years. Happy—if it meant a young girl could run down the street and spend time learning the names of flowers with a fifty-year-old British woman and her ailing husband. Happy—if it meant going to the library in nearby Colorado Springs, hoarding fiction books by the dozens, reading aloud to either Daddy or Mrs. Browning whenever skies were gray or clouds surrendered rain. Truly, happiness was growing up under the cautious eye of an attentive parent, someone interested in every minute detail of her life. But their cozy paradise was soon to be shattered.

Twenty-Two

❖ ❖ ❖

The day was not unlike any other school day. Daddy made a hot breakfast and drove her to the Montessori School only a few blocks away. He always took her and dropped her off, no matter the weather.

With a wave and a smile he called after her, "I'll miss you, Mellie."

"See you this afternoon," she called back.

"Be careful." At every parting, he offered her a warning. The words rang in her thoughts. They had become his trademark. She must never forget. . . .

She didn't think much of it when two police officers arrived during afternoon recess. When they came in search of *her*, being escorted by the principal, she began to feel frightened. Never before had she encountered such serious-looking folk.

One of the officers was a lady with blond hair and gentle eyes. "Something's happened, Melissa," she said, squatting down. "We're here to take you home."

Uneasy, she followed them into the school building, gathered up her things, and headed toward the squad car. Her classmates were wide-eyed as she left, and she felt as if everyone was watching, which made her very nervous. She had not been a child who drew much attention to herself. She preferred to be left alone, always working independently of others, studying at her own fast pace. Today, being ushered out of the school by police unnerved her. She had no idea what was ahead.

Fear gripped her as they drove down the familiar street and neared her house, which was now surrounded by police cars. A long yellow strip encircled the property, but she did not see her father. And the squad car did not stop and let her out. Instead, the policewoman said they were "going to see Mrs. Browning."

"Where's my daddy?" she asked, starting to cry. "Why can't I go home?"

There was no answer, not at that moment. But soon, all too soon, she discovered the truth.

Mrs. Browning met her at the door, gathering her into her arms. "My dear, dear Mellie" was all she said.

A short time later, a lady—a social worker in a navy suit—arrived at Mrs. Browning's house. She was accompanied by a policeman, also wearing a dark suit. The woman sat with her on the sofa, patting Melissa's hand, which made the little girl very afraid.

"Where's my daddy?" she asked.

"There's been an accident," the woman said slowly, putting an arm around Mellie's shoulder. "Your father's gone to heaven."

"Daddy's *dead*?" She was overcome with grief. "How? Why?" she cried.

No words offered her comfort. She had need of answers.

But so did the social worker, it seemed. After the initial revelation that Daddy had indeed died, the woman quizzed her about her father. She was shown several pictures of men while the man in a suit stood in Mrs. Browning's doorway, observing.

"I've never seen any of them," she stammered through her tears. "And I don't know where Daddy works or anything about what you're asking."

Mrs. Browning sat nearby, a worried expression on her face. At one point she cut in, asking if the little girl couldn't be allowed to grieve for her father "alone and in private."

The social worker glanced over at the man. "Are we finished here?" she asked.

He nodded and the woman consented to end the interrogation. Mellie, relieved to see them go, flew into Mrs. Browning's arms. There she felt safe as her friend spoke in soothing tones for the longest time, stroking her head until Mellie had no more tears left to cry.

In the days following her father's death, Mellie stayed with the Brownings, after a scribbled will was discovered. A judge agreed to recognize it as the last will and testament, believing the appointment of guardianship to be "in the child's best interest, due to the preexisting bond." Grandpa and Nana Clark were not considered an option because of health and other concerns of aging.

Mellie continued her education at the private school, with funds from her father's life insurance policy. But she kept to herself more than ever. The other girls treated her differently; some of the boys whispered rumors on the playground. One of those rumors she overheard at lunch one day. "Mellie Keaton's dad was murdered."

She wanted to shout back at the boy, who had no business spreading such horrid things. But she felt helpless to say a word. The truth was, Daddy was dead, but she didn't know, not for sure, what had happened to end his life. She stayed awake at night wondering how it could be that her father had died "accidentally." What sort of accident had killed a grown man in his own home?

The only way to avoid the cruel talk by her classmates was to pretend to be ill on occasion, and for several mornings in a row, she missed school. Mrs. Browning never questioned Mellie's complaints of headaches or stomachaches. Though her temperature reading was usually normal, Mrs. Browning seemed to understand. So she spent some days being read to, enjoying homemade soups and teas, and in general, being looked after with great compassion.

"I always wondered how the Good Lord would answer my prayers, my yearnings for a child," Mrs. Browning confided one day when Mellie was suffering a throbbing headache.

"You did?"

"Oh, most certainly, dear." Mrs. Browning's smile stretched across her face. "You are the splendid answer to any woman's heart's desire."

Daddy had to die so Mrs. Browning could have a daughter, she thought innocently. *How strange.*

Later that week Mr. Browning said that he, too, "was very glad to have the honor of helping Mrs. Browning raise our girl."

So Melissa felt thoroughly loved and wanted, thanking God—if there was one—for allowing her to live with such fine, compassionate folk.

———

"Hickory, dickory, rose; the bug crawled up the stem," she chanted.

"The rose looked down and she did frown . . . hickory, dickory, rose," Mrs. Browning finished the silly verse.

Mellie burst into laughter, recalling the days when her father used to make up nonsense rhymes as they worked in the garden together.

On various occasions she had considered calling her guardian by the

name of "Mother," but with her parents deceased, she couldn't bring
herself to do so. Melissa had always thought of Mrs. Browning as a truly
dear friend. And, as Daddy had often said, "one or two close friends in
a lifetime, that is all a person needs."

Months turned to years, and her emotional recovery was slow. She
made friends with more classmates, groping through life, learning to feel
confident again. But her closest ties were to the Brownings and the life
they had crafted for her. Hours were spent in the gardens behind the
house, hours of deep thought and creativity. She liked to take her sketch
pad and pencils and sit near the bed of ivory roses, missing Daddy,
sometimes weeping. She threw herself into her drawings, illustrating her
father's beloved roses, perfecting her drafts as she worked on them, eras-
ing, reworking, and modifying during all her free moments.

Melissa also enjoyed the lake near the train tracks in town, where
she and her German friend, Howard Breit, her first high-school boyfriend, liked to feed the ducks. He was handsome, with hazel eyes and a
gentle spirit. They strolled around the lake together, Mellie doing most
of the talking. Compared to other boys his age, Howard was shy. He
spoke with a heavy accent, and his clothes, while always clean, were
never brand name. Howard was his own person, though reserved. Melissa had befriended him because he was a newcomer to the community
and didn't seem to fit in, especially at school. She knew that feeling all
too well. So their friendship blossomed.

"What do you want to do when you grow up?" she asked one
springtime day, their second year as friends.

He didn't know offhand, but he gave her his answer in time. It was
while they tossed bread crumbs to one particularly rambunctious duck,
he finally said, "I want to work at a job that makes good money."

"You're excellent in math, right? You could become a banker," Melissa offered.

Howard chuckled. "Yeah, I like numbers, especially with dollar
signs in front of them."

"You can help me with my algebra. Okay with you?"

He smiled, his eyes dancing. "Thought you'd never ask."

Mellie wouldn't have thought anything was amiss with Howard. He
was the nicest boy she'd ever known. He truly cared for her, didn't he?
Even took her home to meet his sister and his parents, went with them
to Denver several times to a play or to see the Broncos at Mile-High

Stadium, and once, out to eat down at the Village Inn in Monument, a few miles away.

One day, while studying at the library, Howard fixed her with a serious gaze. "You never talk about your father," he remarked.

She was silent, not prepared for the question.

"How did he die?" Howard persisted.

"I'd rather not talk about it," she said abruptly. Howard looked hurt, and she felt guilty.

Later, on the walk home, she tried to smooth things over. "I'm sorry . . . I honestly don't know how my father died."

Howard looked at her as if eager to pursue the topic. "Are the rumors true?"

She stared at the ground. "What are people saying, exactly?"

"That your dad was hooked up with the mob."

She was stunned. "That's the dumbest thing I've ever heard."

But Howard wouldn't quit. He continued to pry, until she broke into tears.

When they arrived at the Browning home, she left him on the front lawn, running up the steps and into the house. She couldn't bear to look back. Why had Howard taken this sudden interest in the most painful part of her life?

Later that week Howard called to apologize. Gladly, she forgave him, even invited him for dinner on the weekend. Mrs. Browning cooked an authentic German meal of onion soup au gratin, beef roladen, potato balls, butter twist rolls, and Black Forest cake for dessert.

During the meal, things seemed normal again, until Howard excused himself to the rest room. When he was gone for more than a few minutes, Melissa began to wonder. She found the bathroom door wide open and no Howard. Down the hall, she pushed open her bedroom door only to discover her friend digging through her desk drawers. "Looking for something?" she demanded.

Howard turned, startled. Caught red-handed.

"I think you'd better leave," she said angrily.

Without a single word of explanation, Howard fled down the hallway and out the door. While she continued to see him at school, she never spoke to him again. With Howard out of her life, she just assumed the strange occurrences would cease. But she was wrong.

At one point Mr. Browning realized that some of his mail was missing, especially various financial statements. He began to watch the street more closely. One day he discovered Howard Breit poking grimy fingers into the mailbox. Mr. Browning shouted to the boy, but Howard ran off. Frustrated, he called the Breit residence but got only an answering machine.

Immediately he reported the stolen mail to the police. In the end, the boy was threatened with a five-hundred-dollar fine. But the mail was never returned.

The very next month Mellie was shocked when their trash was strewn about the yard, as if someone had been searching through it. "Must be your Howard," Mr. Browning quipped. But Melissa was not amused.

Eventually Howard dropped out of school, and Melissa never saw him again. But even more troubling things began to happen. On the day of her driver's test, after sealing her chance of acquiring a driver's license on her sixteenth birthday, she noticed a man following her from the town of Monument to Palmer Lake.

During her senior year, she often felt she was being watched, especially when she headed for her car after school. Sometimes she wondered if she was being followed as she drove home. At first she chalked up the tension to the lingering creepiness she'd come to associate with Howard Breit.

Unwilling to trust a new relationship with any of the boys at school, she decided she wasn't going to miss out on her own prom. "Let's go together . . . in a group," she suggested to three other girls who were also without dates.

They danced and laughed the night away. But coming home late—in the wee hours—she felt she was being followed again. The back of her neck broke out in a cold sweat, and she wished she hadn't offered to drop off the others. On the drive back to the Brownings' little home, she felt vulnerable and alone.

Slowly making her way down the narrow road, she thought of diverting the other car by pulling into another residence. See what the driver might do. Not feeling particularly courageous, she pulled up in front of her father's former rental house—the darling home she and Daddy had lived in for such a short time. Her heart leaped up when she realized that the car had pulled in behind her and was parked at the curb.

Not thinking, she gunned her car forward, hightailing it down the street, so frightened was she. Her need for safety had led the stalker to her very door. She burst into tears when she was safe at last, trying to make sense of it to dear Mrs. Browning. "Someone's after me!"

"Oh, honey, not in *this* town. More than likely the driver was a bit soused, just trying to find his way home from the tavern, that's all. No, no, you're perfectly safe here. No need to worry." Mrs. Browning seemed so sure of it that Mellie dismissed the night's events as a figment of her own imagination. After all, she was quite tired, her head filled with the music and the handsome tuxedoed boys. Maybe Mrs. Browning was right. There was nothing to worry about at all.

———

Emery Keaton had set aside money for college in a trust fund for Melissa. After high school graduation in the fall, Mellie bid a fond but sad farewell to the Brownings, having enrolled in the Rocky Mountain School of Art in Denver. There she lost herself in the world of figure drawing, acrylic and watercolor painting, her greatest passion being landscapes and still life. The peculiar incidents of the past years faded as she poured herself into study, hoping to have her own art studio and gallery in the future, as both Nana Clark and Mrs. Browning had encouraged her to do. Nana, more recently in letters and phone calls. "Your grandfather and I are so proud of you, Mellie. Please keep in touch," Nana often said before hanging up. "We love you."

Love . . .

Where did love ever get you? Where did it lead . . . but to heartache?

In suffering the death of both her mother and father, and at such an impressionable age, she had lost a chunk of herself. What did she have to give another person when half her heart was buried six feet under?

Twenty-Three

❖ ❖ ❖

O n the evening of March twenty-first, during her final semes-
ter at the art school, Melissa received a phone call. She was
delighted to hear Mrs. Browning's voice, but her spirits
promptly sank when she was told the sad news. "Mr. Browning has
passed away just this afternoon, God rest him. I hated to tell you so late
in the day—"

"No, no, I'm glad you did."

"I worried that you might not sleep, Mellie."

"Forget sleep," she said, fighting back tears. "I'm on my way
home." She promptly left, and in less than forty-five minutes was turning into the driveway.

Mrs. Browning was glad to have her; Mellie was a comfort, too, it
appeared. Together they met with the funeral director to plan the local
memorial service. Mrs. Browning held up amazingly well, but then she
had always exhibited a cheerful spirit in the midst of trying times—one
of the reasons Mellie was drawn to her in the very beginning.

After the burial, it took several days to answer all the sympathy
cards and letters, thanking various friends and the Browning relatives
for flower sprays and other remembrances. Mellie was glad to help with
that particular chore, and while she was there, she also cleaned the little
house from top to bottom, even rearranging some of the furniture and
sorting through Mr. Browning's clothing and personal effects for donation to a Colorado Springs charity. Folks were generous with their con-
dolences, bringing in home-cooked meals.

Melissa wondered what Mrs. Browning would do now. "Will you be
all right here alone?" she asked, preparing to return to Denver the next
day.

"I shall be fine. Don't you worry one lick about me. I have my gardens in spring and my books in winter."

"Are you sure?"

"Absolutely" came the firm reply. "I have my friends, too, a host of them. They'll look in on me." Mrs. Browning nodded her head, though the sheen in her eye gave her away.

Not convinced she should leave her second mother, not now—not this way—Mellie promised to check in, even spend weekends in Palmer Lake. Which she did, nearly every weekend until summer break.

———

It was the day after graduation from art college. She was busy packing, hauling clothes and books and things out to her car. A middle-aged man approached her, came right up to her apartment steps.

"Are you Melissa Keaton?" He held up his badge briefly. "I'm Agent Galia, from the Federal Bureau of Investigation."

She nodded. "Yes . . . I'm Melissa."

What does the FBI want with me? At first she was startled, her memory jogged a little. The man seemed familiar, but, no . . . the more she studied him, the less she was sure. "Mr. Galia?"

"*Agent* Galia. I'd like to talk with you . . . about your father."

"My father?" Melissa said, confused, then gestured toward her apartment door. "Let's go inside."

He sat in a chair facing her on the couch and began to weave a mind-blowing tale. He told her everything, starting with her father's true identity. The news struck her like an actual physical blow. He said that her father had been a high level "accountant" for an organized crime group.

Her mind reeled. *So . . . the rumors were all true. Her beloved father—a criminal.*

"At one point, he turned informant," Galia continued. "With the help of the FBI, both of you had to be protected, hidden away under the Witness Protection Program."

"Hidden?" Her vague memory of their quick escape to Palmer Lake.

"You were *both* given new identities."

My real name isn't Keaton?

"Your father wanted out, but once a gangster, always a gangster," the agent said with a sigh. He went on to share information about her background, her life in Laguna Beach, even details about her ailing mother, who was "completely unaware of her husband's wrongful activity."

And then the agent got to the point. He studied her, eyes narrowed. "Just before he fled, your father stole eighty million dollars, had it wired to a secret account. He didn't even tell us—the FBI—about the money. And, unfortunately, after he testified he was found and killed. His death may have been an accident; he may have collapsed under severe questioning concerning the money. There was evidence of torture. Either way, once they found him, his people wouldn't have let him live."

Melissa pondered this, speechless. She hugged herself, feeling alone, empty. She simply could not fathom such a horrible death. She was saddened anew.

Galia's expression was empathetic. "I'm deeply sorry about your father."

"I always wondered . . ." She fought the tears. "I never knew how Daddy died."

He sighed, as if reluctant to continue. "The money was never recovered. Overnight, eighty mil vanished into thin air."

"Eighty million dollars?" They had lived like anyone else, renting the little house down the street from the Brownings, scraping together enough money to buy rosebushes and occasional ice cream treats. Except for her private school instruction and the fact that her father was often at home, she never thought of them as more than middle-income folk.

"This is news to me," she managed, her voice sounding far away, even to her own ears. "I have no idea. There *were* some strange things going on several years ago." She remembered Howard's dishonesty, the mail incident followed by the trash episode. She told the agent about the day of her driver's test and the night of her prom—how a man had followed her both times. "He scared the living daylights out of me!"

Galia shook his head with disgust. "The kid was probably paid to snoop around. These are evil people, Melissa. Your father was a part of them, I hate to say. We have reason to believe they are presently on *your* trail. That's partly why I'm here today. This issue must be settled, once and for all, not only for your safety, but also because, rightfully, that money belongs to the U.S. government. Eighty million would go a long way toward efforts to eliminate organized crime."

"Are you saying that you think *I* know where the money is?" she asked.

Galia nodded. "Your father was a smart man. There's no question in our minds—he would have made provision for the money to be salvaged in the event of his demise."

Her father may have been smart but apparently not enough to protect his own life. She was aware only of monies that had been earmarked for her schooling, though a far cry from eighty million dollars. And she told him so.

"Think hard about it, Melissa. As long as the money is missing, your life is in danger." He put his note pad away and took out his business card. "I'll visit you again tomorrow. Meanwhile, here's my number. Call me if something comes up. The slightest clue may be helpful."

Just as the agent started for the door, something occurred to her. "How do you know the mob hasn't already recovered the money?"

Agent Galia smiled. "Good question. I'm afraid I can't answer that directly. But we know for sure they have not. That's all I can say for now."

Rattled, she accepted his card, twisting it in her fingers. When he left, she stood at the window, watching. *How can any of this be true?* she wondered. *My father . . . a criminal?*

Agent Galia strode down the sidewalk toward his car. She stood, still as a stone.

Eighty million dollars . . .

By late morning Melissa *had* thought of something. Not the location of the money but about Mrs. Browning's safety. She didn't want anyone, not even special agents, harassing her dear friend. In her hurry to pack, however, and in the midst of the shocking revelation, Melissa had misplaced the agent's card.

Looking in the phone book under the government pages, she located the FBI's Denver office. Quickly, she dialed the number.

"FBI," a male voice answered.

"May I speak to Agent Galia, please?"

"One moment." A pause. "I'm sorry, but no one by that name works in our office."

"But he was just *here*."

"When was that, miss?"

"Just this morning. He came to my apartment."

"I'll check on Colorado listings." He was gone for less than a minute. "We have no record of any Agent Galia working for the FBI in this state, or anywhere in the country, for that matter."

Shaken, she pondered the strange information. "I don't understand."

"Has someone talked to you, claiming to be an FBI agent?"

"Yes." She gave her name and the gist of her conversation with the man claiming to be Agent Galia.

"I'll send someone out immediately."

Melissa was boxing up her dishes when the agent arrived. Her mind was in a frenzy of worry. *How can I trust anyone?*

She heard the bell ring and answered it. Another serious-looking gentleman, wearing a black pinstripe suit, stood before her, similar in appearance to the previous man in both demeanor and attire. When he had displayed his badge with the name "Agent Walsh" in plain view, she invited him inside, where he questioned her about "Agent Galia."

This is like a sitcom, she thought. *Only too ridiculous.*

The agent pulled out a photo and showed it to her. "Is that the man?"

"Yes," she breathed, feeling a pang of alarm. "That's Galia."

"His real name is Ivanov," Walsh replied. "He's been arrested before and brought to trial, but nothing sticks. It appears you may be in grave danger, Miss Keaton. I've been given authorization to reveal the complete story regarding your father. Typically, we would never confirm the existence of an informant . . . even to his own family."

When Agent Walsh described her father's involvement with the mob, all the details were the same—everything except for the money. He said nothing at all about the eighty million dollars.

When she revealed this information, Walsh was astonished. "Your father *was* a shrewd man," he acknowledged. "What we'd call a slick operator. I guess I shouldn't be surprised at all."

This character assessment was far from comforting.

"The Witness Protection Program was necessary for you and your father—for your survival," Walsh explained. "Your father had testified in court to no avail. The fear-ridden jury refused to convict, resulting in a hung jury. The Justice Department case against the organized crime group collapsed, and there were no additional witnesses to provide the evidence needed. Further investigation conducted through the years has been fruitless."

She listened, amazed at the information. "So without an 'informant' there was no case?"

Walsh nodded. "That's how Ivanov operates. Those he can't bribe, he terrorizes. Those he can't frighten, he eliminates. After your father's death, the FBI dropped out of the picture. Mistakenly, we assumed you were safe. But your father never told us about any money. In fact, that would have been a clear violation of our agreement." The agent paused. "But now we have something—impersonating an FBI agent is a crime. We need to pursue this."

"What do you mean?"

"Ivanov was going to return tomorrow, right?"

She nodded, fear gripping her in fresh waves.

"The next visit likely would not be a friendly one. In all probability, he would drop all pretense, resorting to more cruel means of obtaining information." His eyes softened. "It's a good thing you called us."

A dark shiver ran up her back.

"If we can find Ivanov, we'll arrest him and try him with *your* testimony. Can you locate his so-called business card?"

Within ten minutes she found the imposter's phone number. Agent Walsh dialed the number on his own cell phone and reached a Denver hotel. The man had already checked out. Instantly, the lead had vanished.

"We'll have to wait . . . watch for him. We can set you up temporarily, try to lure him out again."

"I'm not your bait," she broke in firmly. She thought of Mrs. Browning and her grandparents. How would they feel if she, too, just happened to die from an "accident"? Hiding out hadn't helped her father in the end. Ivanov had found him. Now they knew where *she* was. . . .

"We need your testimony, Miss Keaton. We have a chance to catch the man who killed your father. "

"I'm sorry, but you don't seem to protect your informants very well."

"Miss Keaton—"

"And nothing will bring my father back," she replied coldly.

Walsh glanced at the floor, shaking his head as frown lines wrinkled his brow. "You have no idea who or what you're dealing with—just how treacherous these people can be. If Ivanov finds you again . . ." His voice trailed away.

"You mean that I might end up like Daddy," she said accusingly.

The agent looked embarrassed. "If he thinks you know something about the eighty million—more specifically, where it's hidden . . ."

Walsh seemed at a loss for words. "Melissa, if you won't help us, we can't force you," he continued. "Off the record, if you wish to be safe, your best bet is to find a way to drop off the planet. Go where you can't be found."

He offered his personal contact number. "If you change your mind . . ."

She accepted his card. "Will they bother my friend, Mrs. Browning, my legal guardian?"

Hesitating, Walsh said, "I seriously doubt it. These guys operate in the shadows."

That was some comfort. But only a little.

She contacted a private investigator, doing exactly as the FBI agent had advised. The PI, in turn, gave her a quick lesson on the art of disappearance: Find someone who has died and assume their identity.

Melissa recalled an acquaintance at the art institute whose sister had died at a very young age. The deceased girl's name had been Melissa, as well; born in Marshall, Minnesota. Perfect.

After purchasing a short auburn wig, she attempted to make a radical change in her appearance. Only to save her life. She left in the middle of the night by taxi, checking in at a nearby Denver hotel, leaving behind her car and an apartment filled with her packed belongings. Mrs. Browning and others would think she was kidnapped for sure, but there was no other way.

While at the hotel, she was able to obtain a fake birth certificate and a new social security number. In a matter of days, she was Melissa Nolan, from Marshall, Minnesota, having appropriated the other girl's vital data. Miss "Nolan" paid cash for her plane ticket to the East Coast, traveling by car to Westerly, Rhode Island, where her father had often visited. There she began her new life.

In New England she established residence close to her waitressing job at the Olympia Tea Room in Watch Hill, discarding the wig and heavy makeup. But the pain and deep disappointment regarding her father and his criminal involvement remained, torturing her night and day.

Was there one good person left in the world? Whom *could* she trust?

She had abandoned her life in Colorado, leaving all that was precious to her, never having the chance to make good on her hopes and dreams of establishing her own art gallery. All this for a peaceable life. At least she was safe here in Watch Hill.

Twenty-Four

❖ ❖ ❖

L ela shifted in her chair, eyes fixed on Melissa. "So how was it
you came to meet your husband?" she asked.

"I'd always felt we were *supposed* to meet, if you know what
I mean," she said, recalling wistfully that moment in time.

Some people were simply born gregarious. Ryan James was one such
person. She'd first noticed him at the restaurant, stopping in for breakfast or lunch, about a week after she began working as a waitress at the
Olympia Tea Room, one of the nicest places a person might ever expect
to work or dine. Though a far cry from the world of painting she had
planned for herself, the tip money alone more than paid for her rent and
groceries. So, for the time being, she was set financially.

"It's only temporary," she explained to the tall and handsome man
when he asked why a bright girl like herself was waiting on tables.

He took her answer in stride, steering their conversation to other
things, speaking of his brokerage firm, "in Mystic . . . ever been there?"

She hadn't. And she had no intention of leaving the protection of the
cozy small-town feel of Watch Hill. Not even when he offered her a job
as receptionist was she interested in broadening her horizons. She was
still getting her bearings, acclimating to the name Nolan instead of Keaton, reminding herself that her birthday was no longer in mid-October
but rather early May. She'd also falsified her life story to exclude the
Brownings and, most importantly, her father's dealings, telling Ryan
that her mother had died when she was a baby and that her father abandoned them shortly after. As far as the handsome broker knew, she'd
grown up in a small town in Minnesota, where winters crept in stiffly
on the heels of autumn, where folk took long walks to cool hot tempers
instead of resorting to domestic violence, where curling up with a good

book or touring an art museum in the big city of Minneapolis was the rule, not the exception.

Week after week Ryan came to the restaurant, ordering full dinners over the lunch hour, no doubt to keep her coming back to his table, she came to realize. They talked, snippets of conversation here and there, when she brought his salad, more coffee, the dessert. Over time they got to know each other, though she'd never sat down across from him at the table, secretly longing to. She even wished he might ask her out, yet not knowing if she could follow through with a solid romance, the kind her heart longed for.

So she'd backed off, changing her work schedule, sending him an unspoken message. Suzie, however, kept her appraised of his comings and goings. More "no shows" than before. Must be that he was taking the hint, backing away from what might have been.

"The day Ryan found me on the beach was really amazing," Melissa said. She told Lela of the wild roses, dyed both red and white by genetic origin, growing in nodding rows near the shoreline. Scent so fragile, yet alluring, she ran to them, eager to embrace their beauty . . . uncultivated and free. Here they flourished where one would least expect such robust blossoms, recipients of wind and weather, competing for attention with the enormity of the indigo sea. Minuscule distractions, no doubt, to the swell and pounce of breakers, the dash and spray of tide, and the salty bouquet of the deep. For Melissa, these roses held a special meaning, all the same. Delicate and lovely, they grew amidst smelly seaweed and polluted sand, like an innocent child surrounded by evil.

"I was so glad to be off work," she said. "Tired of carrying trays and serving impatient customers."

She had set up her tripod a few yards from water's edge, determined to paint as long as she pleased. Here, along the shoreline of her favorite beach, she settled in for the duration, happy for the leisurely flow of the day. Be it sailboats, seaweed, or sea birds, she would paint to her heart's delight. Whatever captured her fancy.

Heaven knows she needed a day like this, after what she'd gone through to find her way to safety and tranquility. Yet she'd left all that was dear behind. Never sparing time to say good-bye to either her grandparents or Mrs. Browning, she'd flown off to her new life, like a warbler's migration. A season of change, in all respects. Yet the season was rife with summer, heart-stoppingly picturesque in every way.

A swan caught her eye. The gentle creature must have crossed the ridge, perhaps followed her here. She picked up her brush and made wide, broad strokes, composing the vision of grace before her on canvas. Oh, to share this moment with Mrs. Browning. More than ever, she missed the dear lady, having only been in Rhode Island for three months. Not a single day passed that she didn't think of the woman, reliving the good days, the happy times, before everything changed. The ivory color of the swan reminded her of Daddy's favorite roses—white as the moon.

"The farmer in the dell," she sang, remembering her father's nonsensical response. *Farmer's stuck in the well* . . .

How many times had she and Mrs. Browning laughed over that one? And all the other ridiculous, meaningless rhymes Daddy created as they tilled and weeded the rose gardens at both the Browning house and their own. This couldn't be the same Daddy that . . .

Sighing, she knew if she recalled the memories for too long, she'd wind up weeping. Not today. Not here where the beach seemed to belong to her and her alone. Where a friendly swan had decided to pose for her, lingering near the shoreline, having waddled or flown over from the harbor, no doubt.

She focused on the gossamer whiteness, its feathers a high sheen in the luster of sun and half shadow. The sinuous movements intrigued her, and leaving her palette and canvas, she wandered out near the water, pulling bread crumbs from a small sack she'd brought with her, flinging the morsels. She laughed softly, coaxing the exquisite bird closer . . . closer.

In afternoon's light, she stopped to listen, absorbing surf and sound, enthralled by the idyllic moment. She thought no more of her father, of loved ones, of her daring dash to safety. She put all of it behind her, caught up in the rapture of the swan, its tantalizing poise and amity beguiling her.

How long she remained there, feet stuck in wet sand and the ebb and flow of tide, she cared not. Her very existence she celebrated in that sweeping moment, when nature and beast reached into her very soul. She was alive! She'd survived the ordeal of her past. In one brush stroke of fate, she had been made new. The time had come to submit, give in to love fully.

Turn over more than one leaf at a time, she told herself.

She must, as this swan did, acquiesce to both sun and shade. Allow the sky, as broad and lucid as heaven, to spread its canvas of blue, red, or gold above her; it mattered not. And the handsome young man who continued to pursue her, stopping by the restaurant to make supposed small talk over soup and sandwiches, was a big part of it. So why not? She had every reason to cease worry and enjoy life for a change, without fear.

This was *her* time, at last.

———

Melissa soon discovered Ryan sitting there in the sand. Not knowing how long he'd been there, *watching her*, she thought back to her inter- action with the swan, blushing at her spontaneity. Nevertheless, Ryan had found her, observing her delight over the lone swan, soaking up the sunshine, rejoicing in her newfound life.

She had been wary of the dashing man since they'd met. Unwilling to trust, unsure of herself; too vulnerable, perhaps. This being the first time she'd ever gone so far from home, she felt she had better look out for number one. For too long now she had been looking over her shoul- der, half expecting to come face-to-face with more of the insanity.

Something real changed in her that day at Napatree. It may have been the manner in which Ryan spoke to her, taking his time to let the moment unfold. Or perhaps it was that she sensed he was trustworthy after all. All the same, she'd met a man who, like herself, longed for a profound and meaningful companionship. Not just the flirtatious here- today-gone-tomorrow type of thing. No, Ryan James was solid as gran- ite. And sure. She felt she could bet her life on him.

They began dating, falling into the swift current of a serious rela- tionship. They saw each other regularly, nearly every day. She shared her love of art, told him about the secret meaning of roses, reciting the various hues and classifications. Before too many weeks they became engaged—she, accepting a ring, and Ryan pressing to set a wedding date.

But one morning she freaked and left her fiancé wondering what had happened to her. She'd awakened from a terrifying dream. A nightmare that involved the remnants from her past as Melissa Keaton, a dream so real, she nearly fell to her knees in prayer. Her father was being tied to a chair, asked repeatedly the same question: *"Where is the money?"*

He refused to reveal a thing to the men in the room, the living room where bedtime stories had been lovingly told to Mellie, where she had laughed and romped and played with her darling father, the very room that had become their refuge from the universe. That day their home had been violated, her faith in all things good and true shattered. And now her dreams were menacing reminders of what she was trying to escape.

I can't let them touch Ryan, she thought, throwing clothes into a suitcase. She felt she must be crazy to fall in love with someone normal, someone who was innocent to the malevolence that lurked in the shadows, threatening to find and devour her. No, she would not let them hurt Ryan, too.

So she fled, "losing" herself for two days in the city of Providence, where she could easily hide, crying herself to sleep, knowing she had given up all hope of happiness. And she would have followed through, sneaked back to Watch Hill and packed up the few items she called her own, never to see Ryan again. She would've done so had she not missed him so desperately. Not only missed him but longed to be his wife, to start anew, to put the past behind her. This she decided the afternoon of the second day, phoning Ryan at his office in a panic, weeping . . . sobbing her apology.

Soon after, they planned a private wedding on a ridge of rocks jutting out into the ocean. To the cry of sea gulls, they sealed their love, tossing rose petals into the water below. The setting sun splashed reds and golds onto the blue canvas overhead, a ceremonious canopy. And Melissa Leigh Nolan took Ryan's hand and his last name, embracing the covering of his love. Forever. . . .

Twenty-Five

❖ ❖ ❖

T he waterfront house lay at the far end of the road, set apart
from the other homes by ample landscaping and trees. Hand in
hand, they strolled up the stone walkway, Ryan grinning from
ear to ear. Melissa wasn't quite sure why her husband had brought her
here, having picked her up from the florist shop, her new workplace,
and whisking her off to Lord's Point. "Whose house is this?" she asked,
innocent as to what Ryan had planned.

"Ours." He opened the door for her.

She was amazed at the spaciousness, the open, light feeling as she
stepped over the threshold and into the home facing the water. "You're
kidding, right?"

Leaning against the door, he folded his arms over his chest. "I
bought it with you in mind."

She had no reason to distrust him; he'd never lied to her before. "But
we don't have money set aside. . . ."

He caught her and pulled her close, kissing her lips. "We have
money you know not of," he teased. Then, turning toward the kitchen,
he led her through the house. "So what do you think?"

What did she think . . . well, she could scarcely get the words out.
"The truth?"

"And nothing but."

Standing in the middle of the sun-room, windows wide and wonderful, she claimed the place immediately for her art studio. "I love this
room," she whispered, tears threatening to blur her vision. "Are you
sure . . . this is really ours?"

"Every square inch." Ryan crossed the room to her. "Wait till you
see the backyard."

She'd already glimpsed the garden area, the rolling lawn, and the private dock not many yards from the back door. Together they meandered about the place, pointing out perfect locations for various flower beds and Melissa's dream come true—her very own rose garden. *I'll have gardens like Mrs. Browning's*, she thought, relishing the idea, wishing above all she could share the truth of her past with her dear husband.

On several occasions she'd started to tell him, but each time decided to wait. Once, while Ryan was watching a television program depicting the dealings of the Mafia, he had laughed out loud, discouraging her further. "Is this for real?" he said, obviously surprised at the facts presented by the commentator. So Melissa withdrew, waiting for the right moment, which never seemed to come.

They moved in promptly, decorating the house from a seemingly bottomless account Ryan said he was glad to share with her. "Been saving up for something like this for a long time," he told her.

She was frugal in her decisions, however, choosing colors and fabrics, furnishings that met her liking. She included Ryan in the decision-making process, though he wanted *her* to do as she pleased. He made it very clear that this was more her home than his, "only because I know you're an artist and a woman." She had let him sweep her into his arms at that remark. "Women have a knack for making a house much more than just a place to hang a hat," he whispered, his face buried in her hair.

Laughing, she freed herself, reaching for his hand and taking him upstairs. "I want you to see where I've hung some of my paintings."

He obliged, and she was proud to show him the canvas displaying the friendly swan. "I thought this wall was best for it," she said.

"It is." He paused, studying the painting.

"Remember that day?"

He drew her near to him. "How could I forget?"

So the framed canvas remained in the hallway, across from the door leading to the master bedroom. "You can't miss it, coming and going."

"It's perfect," said Ryan. "Like you."

The Amtrak train to Manhattan was always prompt, and that day Ryan ran ahead, glancing over his shoulder to see that she was close behind as they approached the platform. They had planned a weekend in the city, making the rounds of various art museums. "It's your birthday, so we'll do what you enjoy today."

May seventh—her first encounter with the new birth date. Disorienting at best. Having been accustomed to an autumn celebration for as long as she could remember, the springtime event fell flat.

"What's wrong, honey? Aren't you having a good time?" Ryan asked as they grabbed a salad at a nearby deli.

She couldn't bring herself to tell him that the day was an ordinary one, in fact, *not* her birthday at all. The whole situation seemed rather silly now that she felt perfectly safe as Ryan's wife, living in an out-of-the-way place like Lord's Point. Their home was nestled on a promontory, bordered by Quiambaug Cove and Fishers Island Sound. The cape was sparsely populated, a plus for someone yearning for peace.

"I'm fine," she answered, presenting him with her most endearing smile. "What a fabulous place to celebrate a birthday." She considered the little girl, Melissa Leigh Nolan—the *real* girl—long-since buried. Not only had she stolen the child's name and birth date to escape to freedom, to a life worth living, she had chosen to continue the lie. Playacting, of sorts. But what else was she to do?

It was a Friday morning in mid-August when her good friend Ali Graham called Melissa at work. "Can you get away for an hour or so?" Ali had asked.

Melissa knew she could. Her boss recognized a loyal worker when she saw one. Melissa was certainly all that and more, a conscientious florist's assistant.

"It's been forever since we've had salad and a good face-to-face," Ali said, using their catch phrase.

"A face-to-face, eh?" She laughed, glad her friend had called. "I'll meet you there."

S&P Oyster Company, located beside the drawbridge, was crammed with hungry noontime patrons. Melissa gave her name to the receptionist and was told the wait would be "about ten minutes." Okay with that, she and Ali chatted, catching up on each other's lives. She noted the maroon awning above the outside deck, where small white lights twinkled over flower boxes, night and day.

Expansive windows on the entire west side of the restaurant looked out to the river. Private yachts and the *Mystic Belle* were docked nearby.

The Sabino, a steam-powered passenger vessel, formerly an island steamer in Casco Bay, Maine, transported tourists to and from Mystic Seaport, a maritime museum.

"Did you and Ryan get to the outdoor art festival last weekend?" Ali asked.

"Wouldn't miss it. Great stuff."

Ali said that she and her husband had gone to Boston for a play. "Sometime the two of you should go with us."

"Sounds like fun." Melissa felt a bit overwhelmed by the crush of the crowd waiting for tables. "Maybe we should go somewhere else to eat," she commented.

They were about to leave when her name was called. They followed the hostess down the step to a table for two near the window, overlooking the water. Once seated, she said, "Glad we stayed?"

Ali agreed. "With a waterfront seat? Sure am."

They quickly ordered from the menu, glad for the opportunity to visit.

Midway through lunch, Melissa noticed a man seated across the room from them. Curious, she stared at him. His angular, square chin and piercing eyes drew her attention. Then it came to her.

"Ivanov," she whispered. Here, on *her* turf, was the man who'd claimed to be with the FBI in Denver, using the name Galia.

"What?" Ali said, obviously confused.

Melissa watched him a moment longer. She didn't think he had seen her. But it was only a matter of time before he did. She turned in her seat, shielding her face from his view.

Now what?

"Are you okay?" Ali asked, frowning.

"I don't feel good. I . . . I'd better leave."

Ali looked worried. "I'll drive you."

"No." She rose from her seat, grabbing her purse. "I'll see you later. I'm sorry."

"Mellie . . ." Ali called after her.

Outside, she stood across the street, waiting . . . watching the entrance. From her position she could see the entire restaurant. Several couples emerged during the few moments she waited. But Ivanov did not.

When she could wait no longer, she turned and headed up the street toward her parked car. *How foolish of me!* she thought as the realization

of her precarious situation sank in. Why did she have to handle things
herself? Her way?

At home she wasted no time locating the business card for the FBI's
Agent Walsh, the kind man who had offered her protection back in
Denver. The man whom she had not so politely refused.

Fingers shaking, she dialed the agent. Thankfully, he remembered
her. "I wondered what had happened to you," said Agent Walsh. "You
were going to keep in touch."

Quickly, she told her story, that for three years she'd been living in
the Mystic area under an assumed identity. "But today I saw Ivanov at
a restaurant downtown. I don't know what to do."

"Did he see you?" he asked, his voice suddenly tense.

"I'm not sure."

"I don't like the sound of this. And I don't believe in coincidences.
Do you think it's possible he followed you to the restaurant?"

"I just don't know. How could he have found me?"

"That's what troubles me," the agent replied. "Think carefully. Did
he follow you home?"

"I don't think so. I waited for him to follow me out of the restaurant,
but I didn't see him come out."

The agent sighed.

"Should I call the police?"

"That may not be the best course," he replied. "That would only
make you an easy target. This man is very dangerous. Unfortunately, I
don't have an agent in the area right now. Let's go over this again. . . ."
He asked her a few questions, starting with her address, whether she
had kept in touch with her old friends and relatives, and whether or not
she had ever married.

"My husband works for New England Asset Management," she told
him.

A sudden pause. "Melissa," he said, his voice rising slightly. "You
must do exactly as I say."

The terror, that all-too-familiar response, rose in her chest, blocking
her lungs, making it difficult to breathe or to think.

"You must leave the area immediately . . . don't say a word to anyone."

"I don't understand."

"We have no time to debate this, Melissa. Find a safe place, a *new*
location. Make sure you're not followed. When you arrive at your

destination, call me again. Do not use your cell phone, except in an emergency."

"What about my husband? I can't just leave him."

"Your husband will be safe. Trust me."

"But—"

"Listen to me," he said, his voice adamant. "Your life is in grave danger. I'll explain everything when you call."

She hung up, nearly hysterical, found her overnight case, and scribbled a note to Ryan. Saying good-bye to their dog, she hurried to the car.

Once on the highway, she gave in to her fear and desperation. More than that, though, was her concern for Ryan's safety.

"You poor thing," Lela said, brushing tears from her eyes. "What you've been through."

Melissa had surprised herself by sharing so much. Yet now, looking into the face of the Mennonite woman, she knew Lela would keep her secrets, guard the truth. In the very core of her, she knew.

"When you called the FBI agent yesterday, what did he tell you . . . about your husband?" Lela asked, her eyes compassionate.

Melissa folded her arms at her waist, holding herself against the sadness that swept over her. How could she voice the words? Breathing deeply, she leaned forward, revealing the startling information. "Ivanov wasn't the only reason I had to leave Connecticut."

"Whatever do you mean?" Lela frowned.

Melissa shook her head, tears falling fast. *Just like Daddy* . . . "It's about Ryan," she whispered, then stopped, unable to speak.

Lela touched her arm gently. "What is it?"

Struggling with the reality, she said softly, "Ryan is—is one of *them*."

"I don't understand." Lela's frown seemed to encompass her entire face.

"Ryan works for the same people who killed my father."

Part Two

It is only with the heart that one can see rightly;

what is essential is invisible to the eye.

ANTOINE DE SAINT-EXUPERY

Twenty-Six

❖ ❖ ❖

The dawn was bright, the sky clear. Mystic River flowed effortlessly toward the ocean. Several ducks waddled to the edge, hoping for handouts. Ryan had none to give as he leaned against the railing, hours before he was expected to arrive at work.

He had come to Mystic River Park, as he often did, to ponder the past few days. To question how everything had gone so wrong; how he might make it all right again.

"Hey, Mister Ryan."

He turned to see Stevie, a brown-haired boy, holding two fishing rods in his right hand and a tackle box in his left. Several months ago they'd met at this very spot. Ryan had bantered with Stevie, and the lonely boy had haltingly invited Ryan to fish with him. Since then it had become an oft-repeated event.

Ryan smiled at him. "Haven't seen you for a while."

"I've been here. Every morning," his young friend replied with a slight tone of reproach.

"Sorry. Been busy."

"Too busy today?"

"Give me that pole, young man. Let's wake up the fish."

Stevie broke into a grin. All was forgiven. Together they attached their bait and tossed the lines into the water. They fished for over an hour, enjoying each other's company, talking about guy stuff.

"Catch anything?" someone said behind them. Ryan turned to see Jim Ivanov leaning up against the retaining wall.

Ryan was surprised to see him. "Thought you were coming next week."

Jim shrugged, staring at the water. "Something came up."

"Bernie know you're here?" Ryan asked.

"Not yet."

"Have you had breakfast?" Ryan asked, making small talk.

He glanced at Stevie, whose face was crestfallen. He twitched the fishing line.

Ivanov ignored Ryan's question. "You going to be in the office today?"

"For a few hours. Have to take a friend to the airport this afternoon."

"I need a meeting with you and Bernie. Say about nine o'clock?"

Ryan frowned. "Is there a problem?"

"Nah," Jim replied casually, walking away.

"That guy's creepy," Stevie said once Ivanov was out of earshot.

"He just doesn't have any friends to play with," Ryan said.

Stevie giggled, pulling back on his fishing pole.

"God will help us," Lela whispered as early-morning rays danced on the kitchen wall. She bowed her head, thinking of Melissa, still asleep upstairs. "Dear Lord, I stand on the promises of your Word. I rest in your care, confident of your mighty power. Thank you. Amen."

Mellie's words echoed in Lela's mind: *"You're in danger if I stay here."* She felt the slightest shiver of fear again. But she remembered the Scripture: "The angel of the Lord encampeth round about them that fear him." Renewed peace flooded her heart. She was doing the right thing, encouraging Melissa to stay put. Whatever danger lurked outside her doors, God was in control. Both she and Mellie were safe.

Melissa had not slept well. Her thoughts whirled with memories of the man she had believed in, trusted, and married. How could it be that her beloved husband was in league with the same group who'd taken her father's life? Part of her rejected it, disbelieving that her support system, all wrapped up in one wonderful man, could have been false.

She recalled one event after another where Ryan was true and good. Always forthright and decent. Never once had she doubted him or suspected that he might be less than honest in his business dealings or with her. She wished she could phone him and ask him for herself, yet she dared not.

Pushing back the covers, Melissa rose to face the window. She stared past the curtains to the sky, blue as a robin's egg. Ryan's words came back to haunt her. *"I have money you know not of,"* her husband had playfully teased her when first they'd gone to Lord's Point to see their house. At the time she'd wondered about his comment, but only for a flicker of a moment. The shine in his eyes, that spontaneous look of expectation and joy, had erased even the slightest hint of doubt.

Finally, she had to face something she hadn't thought about in years. *Eighty million dollars.* Where *was* it? If only she knew the answer to that, perhaps then, and only then, would this nightmare cease. As long as men like Ivanov suspected she knew where her father had holed away eighty million dollars, as long as they were watching her every move, she would never be truly free.

Does Ryan know about the money? Melissa wondered. *Did he trick me into marrying him, hoping I might reveal something someday? Has everything about our marriage been a lie?*

———

Marge was at her desk when Ryan entered the reception area. "Mr. Personality is in town," she whispered grimly.

Ryan smiled. "Yeah, I know."

Her eyes darted toward Bernie's office. "They're in there."

"Hmm." Ryan headed for his own office and began preparing for his daily trading routine, turning on his wall of monitors.

Several minutes later Marge peeked in. "Bernie wants to see you— ASAP." She jerked her head toward Bernie's office, giving Ryan a look that said, *Pretty weird, eh?*

Ryan stood up quickly, trying to remember the last time Bernie had called him to the executive office. He followed Marge across the reception room to the door with the words *Bernard Stanton* etched in gold.

Ryan rapped twice on Bernie's door and opened it. Immediately to his left, Ivanov stood up. "Have a seat." Ivanov gestured toward his now vacant chair, as if it were *his* office Ryan was entering. "I'll leave you two alone for a moment." The client slipped out.

Ryan quickly appraised the seat that Ivanov had just vacated, choosing instead to sit in the chair opposite Bernie's desk. Glancing at his boss expectantly, their eyes met, then Bernie dropped his gaze to his hands, rubbing them together, as if preparing a speech.

"You wanted to see me," Ryan ventured.

Bernie didn't speak at first, allowing an uncomfortable silence to fill the room. A room nearly twice the size of Ryan's office. The floor, covered in deep forest green carpet, accented the mahogany bookcases and desk that the boss seemed to hide behind. *No wonder he escapes here every day*, Ryan thought fleetingly. *It's a paradise.*

Bernie stood tentatively, turning his back on Ryan to look out his tall windows. It was obvious by his awkward movements that the older man was deeply troubled. The ever-lengthening silence only served to unsettle Ryan's nerves.

Ryan frowned. "Everything okay, Bernie?"

His boss turned to face him, tracing his finger along his desk.

"Did we lose a client?" Ryan asked, thinking of Ivanov.

Bernie sat down again, steepling his fingers. He paused again. "Do you have any idea what we've been doing here all these years?"

"What do you mean?"

Bernie met his gaze. "Don't play games with me. I'm talking about our *business* . . . those stock symbols I feed you from time to time."

Ryan, loath to voice the words, replied softly, "Insider trading."

Bernie snorted, dropping his hands to the desk and giving Ryan a look of disgust. "For starters, yeah. Throw in money laundering, and you've got a better picture. Don't say you didn't figure *that* out years ago. If you didn't, then you're not as smart as I give you credit for."

Ryan had tried to ignore the occasional suspicious nature of their transactions. "It was none of my business," he replied, hoping Bernie would drop it.

"Why rock the gravy boat, eh?" Bernie stood tall, considering Ryan cynically. "You've been well paid to look the other way."

"What's your point?" Ryan asked.

"I'm getting to that." Bernie angled his head toward the reception area and lowered his voice. "First off, Ivanov isn't just a client. He *owns* us."

Bernie's admission sent shock waves through Ryan. "He *what?*"

Leaning forward, his boss continued. "He and his partners run an extensive interstate network. Our company, New England Asset Management, is only a front, with a few *real* clients tacked on to make things look legit." Bernie dropped his gaze to the desk again. "And . . . do you remember a little more than three years ago, when we were interviewing potential secretaries?"

Ryan shifted in his seat, uncomfortable with the direction the conversation was taking.

"I sent you out to Watch Hill to interview Melissa for the job," Bernie said. "Did you think I'd merely picked out a cute waitress and decided to hire her as office dressing? Truth is, Melissa's *father* used to work for Ivanov. I figured the best way to keep an eye on her was to have her work for us. We never expected you to *marry* her."

Ryan's mind reeled with Bernie's rapid-fire revelations. *Keep an eye on her.* . . .

Before Ryan could respond, a single knock came at the door. Ivanov ambled in, carrying a coffee mug. He sat down and fixed Bernie with a smug smile. "My turn?"

Bernie shrugged and pulled out a handkerchief, mopping his brow.

Ivanov chuckled, seemingly aware of the crackle of tension in the room. He picked up the story without missing a beat, his slight Russian accent becoming more conspicuous. "Your wife's father and I were business associates. Then one day he got cold feet and betrayed me. He was an *izmyenik*—a traitor."

And then it came to Ryan, as if putting the pieces of a puzzle together. This "truth session" had to do with Melissa's disappearance. "Where's my wife?" he asked, sitting forward abruptly.

"Don't jump ahead of me," Ivanov said, taking a long drink of coffee before continuing. "Quite an amazing thing, you know. What's the word for it—irony?—that Melissa would flee from Colorado, hoping to hide from me, and instead she ends up here in Connecticut. In my own backyard! The gods do smile on me."

Ryan stared at the arrogant man with growing fury and frustration. Denny's tortured revelation about Melissa's fake identity now made complete sense. His wife had been hiding from Ivanov.

"You seem to have left out a few important details," Ryan said.

"Yes, it seems I forgot the most important part. Your wife's father stole my money, and I want it back," Ivanov replied matter-of-factly.

"Well, ask him for it," Ryan replied.

Ivanov exchanged glances with Bernie. "I'm afraid the man's a little indisposed at the moment."

Ryan barely concealed a shiver of fear.

Ivanov smirked, as if registering Ryan's realization. "You catch on fast." He took another measured sip of coffee, seeming to enjoy the power he wielded. Lowering his mug, he looked at Ryan with false sympathy. "Your wife spotted me at a restaurant last Friday. I was hoping to have a friendly conversation with her. Instead she took off like a frightened gazelle. Luckily, I was able to track her down again."

"Where is she?" Ryan demanded a second time, his voice deliberate and controlled, unlike his emotions.

"She's fine," he said. "But I need your help—"

Ryan came uncorked. "You terrorize my wife, and now—?"

"I want my money . . . is that too much to ask?"

"And you think Melissa knows where it is?"

Ivanov smiled broadly. "Of course she knows."

"If you're so sure, why'd you wait so long to approach her?"

"Good question. Frankly, at first, I had my doubts about her. I briefly considered the possibility that she had no knowledge of the money or its whereabouts, unlikely as that seems to me now."

"She never said anything to me—"

"My point exactly," Ivanov said. "She didn't say *anything* about her past at all, did she?"

Ryan said nothing.

Ivanov looked amused. "Don't feel too bad. She lied to both of us. And that's what finally persuaded me that she was hiding the money."

"That's a big leap in logic," Ryan muttered. "I want no part of this fantasy."

Bernie shook his head sadly. "There's no getting out, Ryan."

Ivanov changed the subject abruptly. "Do I understand correctly that your parents reside in Montana? Your dad goes to town on Friday afternoons . . . helps a friend restore a '57 Chevy."

Ryan was beginning to comprehend.

"Sundays, they attend the community church, always sit in the fourth pew, in front of their neighbor, Doris Chandler, who annoys your mother with her constant chattering. Need I continue?"

"Need I be impressed?" Ryan said.

"Be convinced. I have friends everywhere." Ivanov cocked his head.

"You're threatening my family."

"I'm explaining the stakes."

Ryan fell silent. Ivanov added, "You might as well know the full story. Your wife's been in touch with the FBI. She knows you work for me."

Ryan frowned in disbelief.

Ivanov smirked. "My dear boy, if it walks on two legs . . . I can bribe it. I've got enough Feds on my payroll to start my own federal police force. How do you think I found Melissa's father?"

"What do you want from me?"

"Talk sense to your little woman. Lay out the red carpet of reason," Ivanov said calmly, as if explaining the theory of physics. "We don't have much time. If the Feds put her under their protection—*poof!* she's gone. Later, she betrays you in court, taking the rest of us down, too. Of course, I won't let that happen."

Ivanov's eyes turned cold as he leaned over to make a point. "Mr. James, witnesses have a way of disappearing long before they ever testify in court."

The evil truth registered in the Russian's merciless eyes. Ryan took a deep breath and exhaled. "Let's cut to the chase, shall we?"

"By all means," Ivanov said.

"Why don't you question her yourself? Why do you need me?"

Ivanov stared back at Ryan, and for the first time since he'd entered Bernie's office, his confidence seemed to falter. His face paled briefly, then he recovered his bravado. "I figured that you, as her husband, might be more . . . persuasive."

Ryan considered Ivanov's odd response. "And why should I believe you won't harm her once we find your precious money?"

Ivanov broke into a resounding guffaw. "Because I *need* you, James. You've made us exceedingly rich. You're like the goose laying the golden eggs. If I ruffle your feathers you might stop."

"You have a strange way of putting things."

"We're starting over, bringing you fully on board. Are you with us or not?" Ivanov demanded.

Ryan caught Bernie's eye, which registered an unmistakable look: *Don't be a fool.* . . . Ryan hesitated. The silence spun out agonizingly. Finally he nodded. "All right."

Bernie gave his own sigh, apparently relieved.

"Good man." Ivanov made an open gesture with his hands that encompassed the entire office. "I don't understand much of what you do here, but some of my financial people want to take a look at your files."

"My files?" muttered Ryan.

"We want to expand your responsibilities when this is over. And, of course, you'll make far more money." Ivanov stood, brushed off his coat, and extended his hand to Ryan.

Ryan shook it, as if sealing an ordinary business deal—not a life-and-death decision to save Mellie's life.

To Bernie, Ivanov scoffed, "You worry for nothing. This went well." He got to the door and turned back to them. "They'll give you a call, Ryan. You won't meet here, of course."

Ryan watched Ivanov swagger out.

Twenty-Seven

❖ ❖ ❖

E ast Main Street was crammed with vehicles waiting for the
drawbridge, allowing early-morning boat passage down the
Mystic River. Ivanov stared at the line of cars. *Commoners,* he
thought, despising them. *Dull, pathetic mortals. . . .*

He sneered, recalling his conversation with the weak-minded but
easily manipulated Bernie Stanton. *Like taking candy from a baby.* He
especially reveled in the pathetic expression on Ryan James's face as
Ivanov expertly led him down the long narrow path that would eventually lead to execution.

And to think I waited so long for this pleasure, he thought, remembering how, three years ago, he had sent his lackeys to place the transmitter
under Melissa's car. Then his men, posing as city utility workers, had
placed bugs in the living room of the beach-front home, as well as in the
sailboat. Finally, to insure complete surveillance, they monitored all
telephone and cell-phone communications. All this to snag the moment
when Melissa might reveal to Ryan the truth about the money.

But nothing had been revealed, so Ivanov decided to stir the pot. He
allowed Melissa to spot him at the restaurant, taking great pleasure in
her scramble for safety. Then he'd tracked her movements, following
her, curious to discover her final destination. Perhaps she might even
lead him to the money. But she hadn't.

No matter. Ivanov was finished with his elaborate spy games. In a
few days, thanks to naïve but desperate intervention from her beloved
husband, Melissa would reveal where her father had hidden eighty million, which, by now—if properly managed—should have quadrupled in
value.

He held little trust in the whole bunch of "money-handlers," that echelon of society that controlled large sums of drug and extortion money. But Ryan had made a tremendous amount of money for the network through his legitimate activities, and his partners were reluctant to part with their "star" trader.

Ultimately, though, desire for revenge had trumped his greed. Ivanov had convinced his partners to analyze the trading methods contained in Ryan's computer records. They'd consented, and the last brick was in place. Time to eliminate the "goose," since the golden eggs could be purchased elsewhere.

Revenge! How sweet it would be, and to take it out on the daughter of the very man who'd made him out to be a fool, along with the underling who'd married her.

Ryan was shaken as he stared at the row of monitors in his own office. When a knock came at his door, the sound seemed but a distant echo. Slowly the door opened and Marge poked her head around. "Need anything?"

He didn't reply at first, then asked absentmindedly, "Has Bernie left for the day?"

Marge nodded. "That guy had some weird effect on both you *and* Bernie. Why don't you just drop him? Who needs clients like that?"

Looking up at her, as though in a dream, he watched her enter the room tentatively.

"Ryan?"

"I'd better head out," he managed to say. "Denny's at home, waiting for a ride to the airport."

"Hey, I'm worried about you," Marge said quickly.

His mind a fog, he forced a laugh. "Don't be."

"See you tomorrow?"

He ignored the question and reached down to twist the key to his desk, locking up for the day. That done, he shut down the bank of screens.

––––––

Denny stroked Ryan's dog, then carried his suitcase outside, tossing it into the trunk. He waited for Ryan to emerge from the house, holding the wrapped painting, the gift from Melissa.

A few more hours and he'd see his Evelyn again. Never in his life had he missed anyone so much. Coming to Connecticut, he'd hoped to help Ryan, but in the end he'd only made matters worse, it seemed.

Ryan eventually ran out to the car, wearing jeans and a blue golf shirt. He gave Denny a halfhearted smile, and they settled into the car for the drive to the airport.

"I left you a book," he told Ryan, "in case you feel like reading."

"Sure, thanks," Ryan muttered.

"I wish things could have been different," Denny said softly, determining whether he should press further. Denny waited a moment, then continued. "I also wish we could have prayed together . . . about this whole mess."

Ryan snorted. "And what would *that* accomplish?"

Neither of them spoke for a time; then Denny said, "Hey, pal, what's going on . . . besides the fact that you're worried sick about Melissa?"

"Sorry, I'm not in a party mood."

"No . . . it's more than that," he persisted.

"C'mon, Den—"

"Let me say this. I'm your friend, Ryan. We've been through a lot together. I know when things aren't right."

Ryan looked at him. "What do you want from me?"

"What aren't you telling me? Why did Melissa *really* leave? Help me out here."

Ryan shook his head as if disgusted but remained silent. Denny looked over at his friend, feeling the sadness that emanated from Ryan like relentless ocean waves. And then it came to Denny as if a whisper from a still, small voice. The thought didn't make complete sense, but he plunged forward, almost desperately, taking a stab in the dark. "God can forgive anything, Ryan."

His friend frowned, obviously surprised. "What're you talking about?"

"It doesn't matter what you've done."

"You think I ran her off?"

"Of course not."

"Then what?"

"I don't know. . . ." A Scripture floated into Denny's mind. "Remember the sermon on Sunday?"

Ryan said nothing, looking ahead to the road.

"'Come to me all you who labor and are heavy laden, and I will give you rest.' That's what it's about, Ryan. Repentance. Forgiveness of sin.

Peace of mind. Freedom from guilt. That's the gospel. You don't need proof. You need grace. And it doesn't always make sense, but it's free. It's not for good people. It's for sinners—"

"You're a broken record. You're stuck in one place."

"Yes, I am," Denny replied.

"Just *who* do you think I am?"

Denny pondered the question, then said, "I'm not sure anymore."

Ryan shot an angry look at him. "I have no use for your God. Melissa's lost and He can't find her."

Denny caught the expression in Ryan's eyes—the hurt and guilt, mingled with something new: *bitterness.* He'd seen the same look countless times on the streets of Denver's inner city. "Don't let time run out for you," he finally urged.

When they reached the airport, Ryan drove to the gate, braked, and got out. Denny went around to the back of the car, carrying the painting from Melissa. He watched as Ryan opened the trunk, removed the suitcase, and placed it firmly on the cement. "Still friends?" Denny asked, extending his hand.

Ryan offered no response but shook hands as if finishing a deal. "Take care, Denny," he replied, with a tone of finality.

His heart heavy, Denny picked up his bag and walked into the building alone. Once inside, he looked over his shoulder, through the glass windows, intending to wave good-bye, but Ryan had already sped off.

Daisy was exuberant, running to Ryan as he came into the house.

"Not now," Ryan snapped, tossing his keys on the kitchen counter. The dog dropped back, cowed by the unaccustomed rebuff.

Making his way to the living room, where the wide windows overlooked the cove, Ryan erupted in a fit of anger, grabbing the first thing he found—a pewter vase—and hurled it at the window.

Crash! The glass exploded, jagged shards landing on the carpet and the floor of the porch outside. Several fragments sprinkled onto Melissa's unfinished painting.

Daisy whined and scampered back, obviously stunned by the outburst.

Immobilized, Ryan stared at the bay through the broken window and, in a moment, felt Daisy whimpering next to him. She squatted down, nervously clawing at his ankle.

"I'm sorry," he said, his eyes shifting to Mellie's painting.

He was startled by the jangle of the phone and answered it, expecting Ivanov. The call was not from the man who made his blood boil, but rather from his mother in Montana.

"Ryan?" she said. "I'm surprised to catch you at home. I was calling to thank Mellie for the lovely birthday card. How's everything?"

Composing himself, he felt chagrined at the damage he'd caused to his own home. With forced calmness, he replied, "Fine, Mom. How are you and Dad?"

"Oh, your father hasn't complained in the last hour, so I guess he's all right." She laughed softly. "We received your check. Can't say how much we appreciate your help."

"Forget it, Mom. . . ." His voice trailed off.

"How was your visit with Denny? Such a nice young man."

"He left for Colorado a few hours ago."

"Did he like Mellie's painting? She told me all about it."

"Yeah, he liked it. Uh . . . Mom, I need to get going."

"Oh, sure. But may I talk to Melissa real quick? I want to thank her—"

"She's not here at the moment. I'll talk to you soon. Take care of yourself, okay?"

Ryan said good-bye and hung up, then placed both hands flat on the counter, breathing deeply, his mind a jumble of emotions. He stared at the broken window and then at Mellie's painting, marred by his own rage—a fitting symbol of their fairy-tale existence.

Rehashing the past, he recalled the first time, years ago, when Bernie had approached him with a questionable trade. At the time, he'd vacillated, torn between making more money than he'd ever dreamed of— that, or taking the high road. Something inside him, a core of decency and honor, told him to quit his job and pack his bags. But greed had a stronger, louder voice.

Bernie was right. Ryan had been paid very well to look the other way. But he'd never known . . . *this*—the extent of the evil empire that controlled his workplace. And yet his own thirst for money had brought him to this place. Now he was in too much trouble to get out. The very lives of his wife and parents depended on what he did next.

How can Mellie ever forgive me? he thought grimly.

Twenty-Eight

❖ ❖ ❖

Evelyn met Denny at the airport, and after they embraced and engaged in small talk for a while, he filled her in on Ryan's plight. "It's a sad situation," he said as she drove him to her home.

"I've been praying for them . . . and for you, too, while you were there," Evelyn said, looking exceptionally beautiful in a denim skirt and matching blouse.

"Thanks, I appreciate that," he said, meaning it.

"Well, I hope you're hungry," she said as they entered the front door of her town home. "I made dinner for you."

"You're always thinking of me." He took her in his arms once again. She giggled with delight, then headed off to the kitchen.

"Mind if I check my phone messages from here?"

"Make yourself at home," she called back over her shoulder.

He reached for the portable phone in the living room and dialed the number. Punching in his code, he listened to the usual smattering of hang-ups and unimportant calls, until he heard something disturbing. "Denny? It's me, Melissa. . . ."

Sitting down, he listened with interest to the rest of the recorded call. At the end she had given a number where she could be reached. Quickly, he hung up. Then, using his phone card, he dialed Melissa before he forgot the number.

When Evelyn wandered into the living room, he covered the mouthpiece with his hand and whispered, "Melissa." Evelyn's eyes grew wide.

But it wasn't Melissa who answered. When he identified himself, the woman said, "I'll go get her."

Soon he heard Mellie's familiar voice. "Denny, is it you?"

"Hey, where are you?" he asked. "Have you talked to Ryan? He's worried sick." He glanced over at Evelyn. She was sitting across from him in a chair, her hands clasped as if in prayer.

"I need to talk to you, Denny," Melissa said.

"I'm listening."

For the next few minutes, Melissa wove quite a tale on the phone, as unbelievable as any he had heard. Coupled with what he'd learned of her while in Connecticut, he was dubious. He suspended his judgment, nevertheless, long enough for her to finish her side of the story.

"Melissa . . . I'll be honest with you. I'm having some trouble believing any of this."

She paused. "I guess I shouldn't expect you to believe me" came her soft reply.

"You're saying that Ryan's a member of a Russian Mafia group? How do I wrap my brain around that?" He didn't want to shut her out, because it was obvious that Melissa needed someone to talk to. But it sounded like Melissa was a couple of eggs short of a dozen.

Melissa sighed into the phone. "I've lived this nightmare for so long, I've forgotten how mind-boggling it probably sounds."

Denny was uncertain how to proceed. Silently, he breathed a prayer heavenward, asking God for guidance. Organizing his thoughts, he realized he may have jumped to some conclusions. He recalled his conversation with Ryan as they drove to the airport, his own suspicions. *What aren't you telling me? Why did Melissa really leave?* he'd asked Ryan. Then it came to him . . . the mysterious man at the coffee shop. Was there more to him than met the eye?

He looked at his fiancée, her eyes compassionate and understanding. He sensed she was praying, too. Then, slowly . . . deliberately, she mouthed the words "Believe her."

Melissa was sniffling into the phone.

Denny nodded. "How can I help you, Melissa?"

Marge was putting away her purse and keys the next morning when Ryan arrived at the office. She seemed reticent to meet his gaze.

He mumbled a quick "Hello" and walked to his office, leaving his door ajar.

For the hours that followed, neither of them engaged in their usual offhand bantering. In fact, they scarcely spoke at all.

Just before noon, when Marge delivered several documents, he was standing at the window, watching traffic cross the bridge. His computers were deathly still. At midday, no less.

He sensed her behind him and turned, forcing a smile.

"May I get something for you? Coffee, maybe?" she asked.

"I've never asked you for coffee. You know that."

"Well, I certainly don't mind if—"

"Thanks, anyway."

She slipped back toward the reception desk just as his phone rang. Fifteen minutes into the conversation, Marge poked her head in his door again.

He covered his receiver. "Yes?" he whispered, offering her an expectant look.

"I'm sorry to interrupt," she said. "But your friend Denny Franklin's on the other line."

"Denny?"

She nodded. "He says it's urgent . . . sounds worried."

He's calling to apologize, he thought. *Or to preach some more.* Ryan was put off. "Tell him I'm busy," he said.

Looking rather bewildered, Marge nodded and turned to leave.

Ryan uncovered the receiver and spoke at last. "I can meet you tomorrow morning, ten o'clock."

"Blue Waters Motel. Come alone," stated the voice on the other end.

"Alone . . . of course," Ryan said and hung up.

Twenty-Nine

❖ ❖ ❖

There were two phone calls in the afternoon. One from Elizabeth, inviting both Lela and Melissa for supper tomorrow evening. "It's your birthday, ya know," her sister reminded her. "Oh my, I nearly forgot."

Elizabeth chortled. "Now, how on earth can you forget your own birthday?" She paused. "So you'll be comin', then?"

Without consulting Melissa, Lela agreed that they would. Thinking of the dire situation Mellie was in, she was tempted to ask for prayer from Elizabeth and Thaddeus. But she kept her peace, knowing full well that one thing could lead to another. Best this way, keeping Mellie's confidence, not sharing one iota with a soul, though she knew beyond a shadow of a doubt that she would be talking to her heavenly Father, who sees and knows and cares.

The second call came from Paul Martin. "I was hoping to catch you at home, Lela," he said, not waiting long for her response. "A little bird told me it was your birthday tomorrow."

Now, who could that be? she wondered, guessing it was Sadie Nan.

"Would you like to join me for dinner somewhere?" he asked. "You know—to celebrate."

She found it almost humorous that the man—this man who'd left her for another—was nearly pleading with her to spend time with him. Offhand, she'd thought of inviting him to Elizabeth's tomorrow evening. *Safety in numbers*, Mama always said, growing up. Paul *had* been a friend of the family, a close friend at that. Years ago. She resisted the urge, knowing it was not her place to extend the invitation. "Do you mind if I get back with you on this?" she said, finding her voice.

"Why, no, not at all."

They went on to chat about the fair weather and the good sermon yesterday. Small talk, to be sure, but Lela sensed the undertow of interest. Keen interest, at that.

"If it suits, you may call me later this evening," she said.

Indeed, she had a plan.

"I daresay my sister's in over her head with that fancy boarder of hers," Elizabeth confided in Thaddeus while the two of them swept out the milk house.

"Now, we don't know that for sure, do we?" her husband chided. "Best wait and see what happens. Who knows but maybe the Lord's in it, just like Lela seems to be thinkin'."

"Jah, maybe you're right. After all, it's not like Lela's the impulsive kind. She lives her life pleasin' to God, follows His leading in most everything she does." Elizabeth thought of one aspect of her sister's life—the part that left hardly any room for a husband. True, Lela had been hurt something awful by Paul Martin, back when. Elizabeth couldn't blame her sister for choosing the single life, wholly committed to the Lord God Almighty.

Thaddeus broke into her thoughts. "What gets my goat, though, is this car we're hidin' out over here."

"I'm not surprised you feel that way."

"Then Lela calls up to say the fancy woman's coming to get it, only to call back in a minute that she isn't." He shook his head, then scratched under his straw hat. "Seems to me, that woman she's got livin' over there doesn't have the slightest idea what she wants, no how."

Elizabeth had to chuckle. "'Least we won't hafta be hiding anyone else's car in our shed, jah?" She thought of their Amish neighbors farther up the road, whose son had been caught hiding his automobile behind a tree in his father's own pasture. 'Course somebody got wind of it and blew the whistle on him, hauling the young fella in before the brethren. Since he hadn't joined church yet, hadn't taken the oath before God and the membership, he was spared a shunning. Still, she wondered what anybody would say or think if they knew about the shiny white car veiled by the wide planks of aging wood in their own shed.

If Lela's plan didn't set well with Paul, that, of course, was his prerogative entirely. But she *did* think she would ask Elizabeth to invite him to supper tomorrow evening. If he decided to do so, sharing a meal with the family gathered there, he'd have to behave like a gentleman. 'Course, having known Paul well before, she didn't see how that should be a problem at all. The man hadn't committed a sin by becoming a widower. But, then again, a woman of her circumstances couldn't be too cautious.

While Mellie slept, Lela phoned Elizabeth and had to laugh a little when her sister decided it was a "wonderful-gut" idea, Paul coming for the birthday meal, and all.

In Melissa's dream, she was a little girl again, preparing a flower bed for planting. "Mellie, Mellie *not* contrary, how does your garden grow?" Daddy chanted.

"Water and sunshine and everything fine . . . that's what makes rose gardens grow," Mellie answered.

Mrs. Browning was tickled at the two of them. "Goodness' sakes, you ought to jot down some of those silly sayings."

"What for?" Mellie asked.

"Why, for posterity, that's what," Mrs. Browning said, looking pert and sweet in her work apron.

Daddy stopped his raking, smiling down at little Mellie as she reached for a fat brown worm he had uncovered, dangling it in midair. "She'll forget just like we all do when we grow up."

"I'm *never* growing up," Mellie insisted.

"That's right," said Daddy, laughing, then resumed his raking.

"And I'll never forget either," Mellie vowed.

When she awakened, her thoughts flew to Ryan. Heartbroken at the thought of her husband's double life, she wept, realizing that she was never going back to Lord's Point.

Never again to be held in Ryan's arms, talking and sharing into the night to the music of Debussy's "Claire de Lune." Never again would she laugh as he comically scrutinized her artwork too closely, or bask on the sun deck of their little sailboat. Never again. . . .

Not only was Paul Martin on hand at the Kings' house, but his young son Joseph was there, too, playing a game of checkers with Timothy King. Indeed, Lela felt peculiar arriving *after* Paul, coming into her sister's back door along with Mellie, seeing him there already. She tried to ignore the awkwardness of the situation, greeting him and going out of her way to introduce Mellie.

"Very nice to meet you," Paul said, extending his hand to Melissa.

"She'll be staying on with me . . . indefinitely." She felt she ought to be straightforward with Paul, in case he decided to call on her at home sometime. Having Mellie there was also a deterrent, perhaps, a safeguard against something romantic developing too quickly.

"Are you enjoying yourself here in Lancaster County?" Paul asked Melissa, offering a smile.

Nodding, Mellie said, "Very much, thanks."

Just then Elizabeth rang her tiny dinner bell, and the children scurried to the kitchen to wash up, taking turns as they lined up. Lela enjoyed watching her nieces and nephews, as well as young Joseph, vie for the soap and, later, the hand towel. She quickly dismissed any notion of becoming the towheaded boy's new mama. No, she mustn't set herself up for more pain, though it was clear Paul's adoring gaze was hard to avoid.

Best be careful not to lose my heart again, she thought. Besides, no one asked—not once during the meal—just how long Paul was scheduled to be in town. No one inquired of the business that had supposedly brought him home, either. So she steeled her emotions, praying for divine guidance, quite unsure of herself all round.

When the birthday cake was brought out, Lela delighted in discovering that her sister had baked a lemon cake with rich chocolate icing. Not at all in the typical Amish style, but definitely Lela's favorite dessert and one their mother often made in her own Mennonite home. "Why, thank you, Elizabeth," she said, looking around the table at the dear faces surrounding her. "And thanks to each of you for helping me celebrate this day."

Young Mary Jane excused herself, along with Timothy and Linda, and they headed for the front room. John, the baby, sat in his high chair, waving a spoon. Lela figured they were up to something. And they were. Her nieces and nephew returned, bringing homemade presents. Mary Jane's was a white doily; Timothy and Linda had made colorful drawings of cows and barns. To top things off, Elizabeth brought out a platter of whoopie pies.

"Don't you think we've had enough sweets for one day?" Lela said, smiling across the table at the children.

"Ach, how can that be?" Timothy answered, reaching for the plate of goodies.

"All right, then." Lela was ever so pleased.

Melissa could not have counted the times she noticed a loving exchange, eyes glowing, between Elizabeth and Thaddeus King. They were obviously very much in love and quite content with their happy brood of four. She was also well aware of Paul Martin's excessive courtesy and attention toward Lela, who was seated across from him and his son. Ardent interest, yes. So *this* was the man, no doubt the reason for Lela's blushing cheeks on the phone the other day.

Observing both couples, her heart ached anew for Ryan, con artist and smooth talker though he had turned out to be. Yet part of her longed to know, from his lips, the truth.

When the time came to say their good-byes, she wondered if she ought to make herself scarce, leave ahead of Lela, giving the woman ample opportunity for a proper send-off. But, no, Lela wouldn't hear of it, implored her to wait "and we'll walk home together."

"Please, allow me to drive you," Paul said, his hands resting on little Joseph's shoulders. "I would be very happy to see you both home."

Melissa was careful not to smile at the man's insistence, though he was not unpleasantly so. She rather liked him, and was fairly convinced that Lela did, too.

In the end Lela gave in, and they rode the ridiculously short way home—Lela in the front seat, Melissa in the back, next to Joseph.

"We're moving back to Lancaster," the boy said suddenly.

"You are?" Melissa asked. "And where is it you live now?"

"Alone . . . all alone, in Indiana." The child's voice was so pathetic, she wondered if he had been coached by his father.

Melissa fully expected Paul to comment at this point, but he directed not a single remark toward the backseat.

Wondering when she might hear Lela's take on the celebration—particularly this guest—Melissa hoped they might have opportunity to walk to the covered bridge before dusk. She stared up at the sky, glad there was still plenty of light. More than an hour left before nightfall.

———

"Let's walk down to Hunsecker Mill Bridge," Lela suggested to Melissa after saying good-bye to Paul and his delightful son. "Now's a good time for me to show you my own personal refuge."

"That's what *I* was thinking." They laughed, both a little surprised that they were thinking along the same lines. "A walk is a good idea."

"Yes, and Hunsecker Bridge is a lovely spot at dusk." Lela's face still felt warm from her encounter with Paul, but she hoped Mellie hadn't noticed. "You'll see what I mean when we get there."

"I can hardly wait."

It never occurred to Lela that they might be in any danger, walking the back country roads. The way she saw it, if the Lord God of heaven and earth couldn't take care of the two of them here *today*, what good was it to trust in Him for things eternal? They would have their nice stroll down the road to the covered bridge and the lovely grounds surrounding it—evil mobsters, or no.

"I'm glad you shared so openly with me yesterday," Lela said as they walked. "Believe me, what you told me about your past won't go anywhere but to the throne of grace."

Melissa didn't respond, keeping pace with Lela's quick step.

"The weather's not bound to be this pretty too much longer," she said to change the subject. "Around here we often get sudden changes of weather, least expected."

"In late summer?"

"That's right." She went on to explain that sweater weather would soon be upon them, and that maybe they should look for a handmade sweater or cape for Melissa to wear. "Or I can have Elizabeth make you one."

"That's nice of you, but I'll manage just fine."

"Maybe you'll feel comfortable going in to town now and then." Lela paused, wondering if she should say more. "'Spose I could go along with you, show you to the best stores and whatnot. But only if you want to."

"Sure, I'll go sometime."

Lela smiled. "You seem much better, more relaxed now."

Mellie nodded. "I don't know why, but I'm beginning to feel very safe here. I'm glad to be staying on."

Breathing a prayer of thanksgiving, Lela said, "I'm ever so glad to hear it."

"Your birthday was extra special this year, I do believe."

Lela couldn't help but laugh. "Oh, dear me, I hope it wasn't written all over my face."

"And . . . Paul's," Mellie ventured. "He's your—special friend, right?"

"He *was*, but that was a long, long time ago . . . before he married someone else." Lela sighed, not realizing till this minute just how much she'd hoped to open her heart to Mellie, seeing as how the younger woman fully understood the pain of rejection and disappointment. Strange as it seemed, a delicate yet common thread seemed to bind the two of them together.

They sat along the grassy banks of the Conestoga River, the covered bridge spanning the water to their left. Birds twittered here and there as the sun made its slow tumble through the trees toward the unseen horizon.

"So it appears that Paul Martin has come back for me, now that he's a lonely widower," Lela said, glad for the solitude here and the opportunity to share openly with Mellie.

"'Love always finds its way home.' That's what Mrs. Browning used to say."

Lela didn't know what to think. "Easier said than done, I 'spose."

Mellie was quiet for a while, then—"I think I know what you mean."

Silently, they soaked up the beauty of their peaceful surroundings. Not speaking, yet joined in complete empathy.

"I did love Paul, very much," Lela said softly.

"I'm not surprised. He seems like a nice man."

"Paul was the joy of my life, but when he chose someone else to devote his life to, a good part of me died, I'd have to say," she confessed.

Mellie said she could understand that nothing could fill the void. "Nothing ever will."

"Well, now, that may be where we're different," Lela spoke up.

"How do you mean?"

Lela hugged her knees through her long dress. "After Paul and his wife left the area, I felt all my hopes were dashed to pieces. But very soon afterward, I decided to lay down my burden . . . at the feet of Jesus." She told Mellie how she'd grown up in a conservative Christian home, how her parents had instilled various worthwhile character traits. "My father liked to think he was passing down 'good gifts' to his children. Things like purity, generosity, sincerity . . . you know."

Mellie nodded. "My father encouraged me the same way, but we never attended church. Neither did the Brownings, but they were good people."

Lela was careful not to sermonize, yet she felt Mellie's heart was opening to spiritual truth. "Church attendance is all well and good, but walking with Jesus every day makes life joyful, even in spite of the pain of disappointment."

"I talked about this with someone once," said Mellie thoughtfully. "When my husband's friend Denny Franklin came for a visit. He always seemed so happy and full of life. I guess I'm searching for what both you and Denny have."

"Today's as good a day as any to find it," Lela said softly, turning to face her new friend. "Wouldn't you like to give your burdens to the Lord who loves you?"

Tears sprang to Mellie's eyes, and she gripped Lela's hand. "Yes. . . ." she said. "That's exactly what I want to do."

An easier witness she'd never given. Lela was more than happy to lead Mellie in the sinner's prayer. There, amidst the flowing green willow boughs and the rush of the Conestoga River, Melissa James became a child of God. And Lela Denlinger her elder sister.

Melissa brushed tears from her eyes, thankful despite the circumstances that she had found her way to Lela's little house. Grateful that the Mennonite woman had cared enough to bring her to this sacred moment.

She thought of the picture of Christ the Good Shepherd, the one hanging in Ryan's and her living room, and as she did, she followed the river's current with her eyes, drinking in the tumble of water over rocks, mossy banks profuse with wild flowers, and thick ivy cascading about. She celebrated the moment, breathing in the freshness of the air, allowing the sound of finch and swallow to cloak her in this tranquil place.

At last, I belong to God, she thought, yearning to share this divine peace with Ryan. Yet knowing she could not.

Thirty

❖ ❖ ❖

Before dawn, Lela Rose dressed and began sewing more pillow shams for Elizabeth's country store. Nothing fed the spirit like working with one's hands—baking bread daily, mending and sewing, putting up pickles and preserves, tatting pretty edges around ordinary-looking pillow slips, and the like. She hummed and prayed as she worked, anxious to catch up a bit, for she'd fallen behind on any number of house chores since Mellie's arrival. Still, she wouldn't have traded the hours and days spent with her boarder-turned-friend. Leading the young woman to the Savior had been the highlight of Lela's year. Oh, the light in Mellie's eyes as she sat there in the grass, having just opened her heart to Jesus!

"Thank you, Lord, for planting all this in my heart," she whispered. It had become very clear to her, the reason for Melissa James's arrival last week. She recalled the prayer she'd prayed, how eager to serve she had been. And she'd felt compelled to make the advertising signs to rent her spare room. So much good had happened because she had been willing, unafraid to branch out from her comfortable and familiar life. And with God's help she would continue to share the love of the Lord Jesus.

Somewhat unexpectedly, she thought of little Joseph Martin. Surely, the bright-eyed boy must be as lonely as he sounded in the car, awful lost without his mother. 'Course, Lela would not allow herself to become romantically involved with Paul merely for the sake of his son, no. But there was no harm in thinking about the boy. For how she loved children, and Joseph would certainly be easy to love, given his sweet manner and seemingly obedient ways. Who couldn't fall in love with a child like that?

She thought of her own nieces and nephews, Elizabeth's children, as well as her other siblings' children. A growing number to be sure, yet she continued to remember each one with a crisp one-dollar bill on their birthdays, a tradition she'd started years ago when her oldest brother's first baby was born.

Yes, for one reason or another she was beginning to have a mighty good feeling about Paul's renewed affection for her. Didn't know precisely why that was, except that she'd given it over to the Lord. Now, it was up to Him to work His will and way in their lives.

Mellie awakened with such an overwhelming urge to call Ryan, she could scarcely think of anything else. But Agent Walsh's startling revelation continued to trouble her. Denny had called back to say that Ryan had refused his phone calls. If she wanted to hear the truth from his lips, she'd have to talk to Ryan herself. She had secretly wondered how any of it could be true, though she mourned the statement as if it were. Her darling—on the side of evil? How could that be?

All the endless days stretched ahead. The years—interminably long and lonely. Having enjoyed Lela's young nieces and nephews so much, she entertained a strong desire to have a baby of her own. With Ryan sharing her joy, the rebirth of their union, perhaps. And for the first time in years, she longed to celebrate her actual birthday in the fall, in October, the month it *ought* to be observed.

She reminisced of autumn's pungent flavors, of pumpkin carving, home-baked pies, and dried cornstalks propped up on the front porch, accompanied by a scarecrow or two. Christmas, too, soon followed. The best thing about Christmas, she decided, was that it was forever predictable. The lovely sound of traditional carols, the icy-sweet smell of falling snow, brightly colored packages beneath the tree, good will to men. Twigs of evergreen decorating a window, where glowed a new, tiny spruce tree, glittering with frosty flakes and white lights—their own first Christmas tree, she recalled. Ryan had taken the tree outside on the day after Christmas and planted it in the backyard, where it continued to thrive to this day.

She and Ryan painstakingly decorated their long dock each year at Lord's Point. Stringing strands of white lights along the pier, they tied sprigs of greenery with red bows here and there. Their parties were festive get-togethers. There was music and dancing and good food, always catered.

How would Ryan celebrate this year? Or would he celebrate at all?

Knowing him as she did, she wondered if he'd feel so lost and alone that he might merely endure Christmas. She ached with the thought of him missing her so. On the other hand, perhaps she didn't know the real Ryan James. Perhaps she never had. . . .

Glad to have caught up a bit with her sewing, Lela dusted the front room, going over the mantel with a damp rag. She wiped down each of the tiles surrounding the fireplace, singing hymns of praise. Carefully she dusted each shelf of her pine corner cabinet, lifting out the various china cups and saucers. Some of the nicest pieces she owned. Having given up the notion of a hope chest long ago, she had to smile at herself. Paul Martin's return to Lancaster certainly had stirred things up in her.

Dismissing the thought, she decided to offer tea, along with some raisin bars she'd baked yesterday—a recipe Elizabeth had shared with her recently—to the five ladies who would be coming this afternoon for the weekly Bible study. She couldn't help but hope that Mellie might join them, too.

What a good time we'll have together, she thought, taking the dust rag outside and giving it a good shake.

She was quite beside herself to see Paul Martin's car parked in front of her house, and here he came with a handful of red roses bobbing their heads as he made his way to the gate and up the walkway. "I hope it's all right to drop by," he said. "Just wanted to say hello again." He seemed slightly self-conscious, glancing down at the flowers, then holding them out to her like a schoolboy.

Their fragrance was so tempting, she leaned forward and breathed in their aroma before even greeting him. "Oh, they're lovely! Thank you, Paul."

He stood tall and lean before her, his eyes enormous, their blueness astonishing. "May I talk with you, Lela?" he asked.

She hesitated, glancing up the street, unsure of herself. At last, she said, "Come on around to the back. We'll sit on the porch."

Placing the long-stemmed roses in a vase on the small table, she sat in her white wicker rocker. Paul found a spot in the cushioned settee. She wondered what had brought him here to her today, but she waited, hoping he'd strike up the conversation.

"I hope you won't think it bold of me, but I'd like to tell you about my life . . . outside the Mennonite community—the years I spent in Indiana, while I was married."

She didn't reply to this at once but waited, her hand resting on the uneven wicker weave of the rocker. He waited, too, and after a little while, she said, "It must've been a bit difficult for you, so far from family and the church you'd grown up in."

"That's not the half of it." He sighed, leaning forward for a moment, then back again. "I was warned not to marry my wife. More than a handful of folks said I'd live to regret it, leaving my Plain roots behind. My own mother said I ought to 'think twice about marrying an outsider.'"

Lela didn't know what to make of this. She was ever so uncomfortable hearing such things. She rubbed her hands against the arms of the rocker. Yet she had not the heart to stop him.

His face was earnest, eyes sincere. "My life changed radically the day I married. I did my best to make my wife happy, working hard to give her the things she desired. To the best of my ability, I loved her, yet nothing I ever did seemed good enough."

He paused, staring out across the yard toward the tall trees that formed a border between the gardens and the pastureland beyond. "When Joseph was born, our lives were taken up with a new baby and all the extra duties required. Soon after his birth, my wife became seriously ill. I tended to both her and our son until the day she passed away."

"I'm sorry things were so difficult."

"Well, it seems I've been making mistakes all my life. God allowed me to follow my own path for a time. Thankfully, I have my Joseph."

Her heart went out to him, this man whom she'd loved so dearly. "You've come through a dark tunnel, suffering so. But Joseph *is* a wonderful child. God knew what would bring a smile to your face."

Leaning forward, he covered her hand with his. "You always knew what to say to cheer me, didn't you?"

She smiled. It was true. She'd known how to treat him special, all right.

His voice came softly then. "I've come to ask your forgiveness, my dear Lela."

"Oh, Paul, I forgave you a long time ago."

He was still for moment, then released her hand. "I've been praying about the second chance God has given me—us—if that meets with your approval."

She gave him her most assuring smile, though she could not say just now whether Melissa's staying on with her might possibly put any thoughts of romance on hold.

"Red roses stand for true love," Melissa told Lela when she'd arranged the roses in a larger vase and placed them on the kitchen table after Paul had departed.

"Well, now, is that so?" Lela said.

"Absolutely. Ask me about any rose color and its meaning. My father taught me all about them." Even now, the thought of him both stung and sustained her. Like thoughts of her own true love. . . .

Lela hurried about the kitchen, cleaning up from lunch, but Mellie could see the woman's gaze straying often to the red roses.

————

When the women arrived for the scheduled Thursday Bible study, Lela felt nearly giddy with joy. Sadie Nan seemed to notice and came into the kitchen, eyeing the bouquet. "Did my brother happen to stop by today?"

Lela was discreet—after all, the other women were only a few steps away, visiting in the living room. "Well, now, what do *you* think?"

"You mustn't play games with me." Sadie Nan scolded jokingly. "Aren't the roses from Paul?"

Pulling her aside, Lela lowered her voice. "I had a most interesting visitor this morning."

Sadie's eyes lit up. "Well, I do declare. When's the wedding?"

"Let's not rush things, now, all right?"

"What's to rush . . . you've got so many years to catch up on. Don't be waitin' too long, you hear?"

Lela hugged Sadie Nan. "We just might get to be sisters after all."

The other woman grinned. "I'd like that very much."

Lela went back to pouring tea while Sadie Nan arranged the raisin bars on a plate. "Your boarder, Melissa, seems mighty hungry for the things of the Lord."

"Yes, she's just become a Christian. Yesterday evening, in fact."

They talked briefly about how to include Mellie in their church and community events. Yet Lela never once divulged the circumstances by which Melissa had come to Lancaster County. Neither did she say how the fancy Englischer's staying on might actually put Paul's hopes and plans on hold.

Thirty-One

❖ ❖ ❖

R yan turned his vehicle into the parking area of the small motel, located several miles west of New London, and pulled to a stop in front of room #12. The place was a flat concrete structure with the typical neon sign out front and a number of cars parked nearby. Not a trash motel, by any means, yet a second-rate meeting place, to be sure.

He sat for a moment, then grabbed the satchel containing his digital financial files and got out of the car. Quickly, he knocked on the door. It opened slowly, revealing a tall, muscle-bound man wearing a solemn expression. Behind him, two other men sat at a small table, their suit coats bulging from hidden shoulder holsters.

At the back of the musty room, another man emerged from the bathroom, drying his hands on a towel. It was obvious to Ryan who was in charge. The man approached him with a smile, extending his hand. Nodding, he shook hands. Pleasantries seemed pointless now.

The man introduced himself as *McGuire*. "You know, like the baseball player," he said with a wink. He clasped his big hands together, as though eager to get started, gesturing to the table. "Have a seat."

One of the men locked the door, crossed his arms, and stood in front of it, legs spread, like a sentinel guard. The other guy sat on the bed, across from them. Ryan eyed them nervously. *You've seen one too many gangster flicks, pal,* he thought.

"Well . . . Mr. James," McGuire said once they were seated, the tone in his voice suddenly somber. "Where shall we begin?"

———

One of the many facets of morning, Melissa had realized in the past few days, was her ability to cling to that delicate interval of time between sleep and awakening. One could appeal to the memory, relive a past precious moment at will. This day, she longed to experience again the Christmases spent with Daddy at the Brownings' home in faraway Colorado. Through the mist of preawakening, the scenes burst into her brain like sleet skipping against the pavement. . . .

Christmas was the smell of gingerbread cookies baking in the Brownings' kitchen, the tempting aroma of bacon, eggs, and sausage. Nearly every December twenty-fifth morning, Mellie and her father were invited to share a mouth-watering brunch with their neighbors. And what a spread it was. The tangy smell of freshly peeled tangerines filled the house, even as Mellie entered the Brownings' home, hand in hand with Daddy.

They walked the snowy sidewalk that led from their house to their neighbors', only a short block away. Before ringing the doorbell and being greeted with "Merry Christmas!" Mellie liked to look for the lights in the front window. Mrs. Browning loved to decorate in a rather big way, putting up a small tree in each room of the house. All except the living room, where a tall spruce often dominated one corner.

This tree captured Mellie's attention first and foremost. Taller than Daddy, and most beautiful, it was decorated with ornaments illustrating Clement C. Moore's poem "The Night Before Christmas." Dancer, Prancer, a sleigh, and even tiny mice embellished the tree, nestled inside a large red drum.

Mr. Browning pointed out the fact that each ornament was hand painted, and Mellie went over to inspect them, seeing if she might someday mimic such pretty things for her own tree. After she'd married her Prince Charming and had her own little house, of course.

But the large bouquet of white roses, sent over each year by the florist from Daddy, was most often the topic of conversation—just before time to dive into the presents piled beneath the tree. Mrs. Browning always made a big to-do about thanking Daddy for his "generous and handsome gift." Mr. Browning did, too.

Daddy winked at Mellie and pushed his nose into one of the elegant blossoms, breathing deeply of what he called "the perfect perfume." Mellie frequently followed suit, having to be boosted up to the table to smell the sweetness. "Anyone remember what white roses stand for?" Daddy said, a twinkle in his eye.

"Secrets!" Mellie clapped her hands, eager to see what wonderful gifts lay in store.

Each year her father repeated the same ritual. Mellie enjoyed the solid traditions, but given the chance, she would've chosen a bouquet of velvety *red* roses at Christmastime, or double red-and-white amaryllis blooms. Flowers with color made better sense on the Big Day. Yet Daddy insisted on the white roses, his favorite.

Plumping her pillow, Melissa decided that this Christmas would be far different from those of the past. *This year* she would find her way to a church, where the organ played "Oh, Come All Ye Faithful," and choirs sang "Joy to the World, the Lord is come!" This year, she knew the joy of such a heavenly coming. Embraced it totally. God had made himself real to her on the banks of the Conestoga River, with a little help from compassionate Lela. Yes, this year she would definitely commemorate the Holy Days in a new and different way. Although, perhaps in Daddy's memory, she would present a bouquet of white roses to her dear new friend.

"Wait a minute," she said to herself, throwing off the covers and getting out of bed. Until just this moment, she had never thought of her father's gift of white flowers and the talk of their *meaning* as anything more than a mere game. A new thought, impossible to shake, nagged at her brain.

Searching her memory for additional clues, she decided to break her own rule. Risking her false identity no longer intimidated her into silence. She must make a phone call to Mrs. Browning. After all this time, the sweet lady would probably think she was truly hearing from the grave.

Immediately after breakfast, Melissa called for a taxi and had the driver take her to the nearest pay phone. "Please wait for me," she told the cabbie. "I won't be long."

Dialing the familiar area code and phone number, she felt a resurgence of hope. If she could just figure out where the eighty million dollars were hidden, she could be free.

Free from the life of a fugitive. . . .

The phone rang several times before she heard the soft voice say, "Browning residence."

She gulped back the tears. "Please don't be alarmed, Mrs. Browning. It's Mellie."

There was silence for a moment, as if the line had become disconnected. Then Mrs. Browning spoke. "Oh, my dear child, whatever happened to you? I've worried for so long!"

Melissa wasted little time filling the woman in on the past several years. She said how very sorry she was for not saying good-bye, for not contacting Mrs. Browning at all. "There was no way I could reveal my whereabouts," she said.

"Are you safe now?" came the inevitable question.

"I'm all right, yes."

"How I've missed you, Mellie, my little lamb."

The choking sensation made speech impossible. At last she managed, "Someday, I promise, I'll come visit you." *When this nightmare is over.* "We'll have a long visit, just the two of us."

"Yes . . . yes, you do that."

"Do you still live in the same house?" Melissa asked.

"The very same."

"And your gardens . . . do you still grow roses?"

She heard the chuckle. "What would life be without flowers?"

"What about the white rosebushes? Is Daddy's flower garden still. . . ?" Melissa couldn't go on. Hard as she tried, her heart was in her throat.

"I shouldn't think of doing away with your father's favorite roses—never!"

Dare I say it? she wondered. It was imperative now. She had to know. "Can you get someone to dig up that garden . . . today?"

"Why, dearie, whatever for?"

She was at a loss as to how to make the woman understand. Plunging in, she told Mrs. Browning her strong hunch that there might be something buried "under Daddy's white roses."

"And what might that be?" came the vague reply.

"I don't know . . . something . . ."

"And . . . if I should find anything?"

"I'll call you back in a few hours."

"Whatever you say, Mellie." Mrs. Browning was clearly confused. "I'm doing this for you . . . whatever it means. . . ."

"Thank you, Mrs. Browning. Thank you so much."

———

Lela was certain that Melissa was up to something mighty important. The girl had sprung out of the house at first sight of the taxicab, nearly forgetting her pocketbook. For goodness' sake, she was in a hurry!

In less than thirty minutes Melissa had returned, her face flushed. She had been crying. "I'll be leaving the house in a few hours," Melissa told her as she came inside.

"For good?" Lela asked, hoping not.

"No, to make another phone call." Melissa explained that she didn't want to take the risk of calling from Lela's phone. "It could easily be tapped."

That concerned Lela, but only a little. God was powerful enough to wipe out a phone tap if necessary, to protect them. She fully trusted in the Lord God of Abraham, Isaac, and Jacob. "That's all right," she said. "You do what you must."

Lela returned to her sewing room and cut out several more large pieces of fabric for additional pillow shams. All the while, she either sang or quoted Scripture. "My heavenly Father sees the tiniest sparrow. . . . 'Fear ye not therefore, ye are of more value than many sparrows.'"

Melissa waited impatiently to leave the house again and get to a pay phone, but she wanted to give Mrs. Browning enough time to find or hire a neighbor to spade up the singular garden. It was past noon when she phoned for a taxi again. She was relieved to see that the driver was not the same man, and she played it safe and asked to be taken to a different pay phone, having inquired of Lela where another one might be.

Once there she looked about her cautiously, then closed the phone booth's doors behind her. Praying for God's help—that she could actually pull this off—she dialed Mrs. Browning's number.

"I'm glad you rang me again," Mrs. Browning said breathlessly. "I should say you knew what you were talking about, my dear."

"You found something?"

"A small metal box, and inside, a laminated piece of paper."

"Is there a number on the piece of paper?" she asked, shaking with anticipation.

"Yes . . . the name of a bank in Switzerland, the word *rose*, and an account number, to be sure."

"Please read it to me, very slowly."

She wrote down the number, reading it back for verification, then asked Mrs. Browning to burn the piece of paper. "Put it in the sink and light a match to it."

The dear woman promised to "see to it right away," without further question.

"I'll visit you soon," Melissa said.

"Very soon?" asked Mrs. Browning.

In her mind's eye, she remembered her second mother's smile. "It won't be long, I promise."

From where Elizabeth stood at the kitchen window, she could see their alfalfa fields shifting in billowy patterns, swaying in the breeze like sea green velvet. Out in the barnyard, Thaddeus and several other men from their church district gathered to cut the alfalfa for the second time this summer, since early June. When that chore was finished, the whole family would be going out to Ohio to visit with Elizabeth's second cousins. She could hardly wait to see her Mennonite relatives again. Wouldn't be but a minute before she and Cousin Henny would be all caught up in their chatter—"catchin' up on our lives," they'd tell the menfolk, and be off to the kitchen, exchanging recipes and whatnot all.

She turned back to making chow-chow ahead for the evening meal, hoping for some time to spend with Lela this afternoon. In the past week, since Melissa had arrived on the scene, Elizabeth had hardly had a chance to pay her sister what was coming to her from the country store. *I'll take her the money I owe her and some strawberry jam, too*, she decided, thinking back to the interesting birthday supper for Lela. She had a feeling there was most likely goin' to be a new member in the family, and mighty soon at that. She'd seen the way Paul Martin looked in earnest at her sister. Funny how the Lord God heavenly Father answered prayer, and sometimes so awful fast!

Melissa strolled down the road, alone this time, past Thaddeus and Elizabeth King's farmhouse, in a new direction. After the startling conversation—the discovery made by Mrs. Browning—she'd decided to go for a walk, taking Lela up on her offer of a cotton summer dress. The hem of the dress nearly skimmed her ankles as she walked, and she began to feel something like a Plain woman herself. As though she were living in a haven of sorts, far removed from the troubles of modern life.

Pondering the unearthing of her father's money, she recalled her previous phone conversation with Denny. He'd urged her to trust the FBI. But trusting was difficult. Yet what choice did she have? Ivanov would find her again, in just a matter of time. She had to do *something*.

A black-and-white warbler chirped his high-pitched solo, and Melissa smiled, glad for the distraction and for the way things had fallen into place so far today. She had spent the lunch hour over a hearty meal of apricot salad, ham loaf, and green beans, getting to know Lela even better. The woman was definitely in love, and Melissa was glad. Such a kind and caring person, Lela would surely be a good wife to Paul. Melissa had thought often of the little boy, the widower's son. A more precocious child she had never encountered, but then, she hadn't had much opportunity to engage herself with children. Never in college, and certainly not at the florist shop in Mystic.

Strangely enough, though, she could easily imagine herself caring for and raising children. Two, maybe, although Elizabeth King made child rearing appear almost effortless. Something about the Plain style of living made hard work seem altogether natural.

The countryside had a calming effect on her. She enjoyed every little wild flower, maidenhair fern, and tree along the way, the sky an appealing blue that reminded her of walks along the beach with Ryan and their golden retriever.

She was glad to be alone. Lela had taught her, through word and deed, that a little solitude each day was essential to good health and emotional well-being. Lela was big on having what she called a "quiet time" each morning. "Too many people are afraid to be alone with their thoughts," Lela had said just this morning. "There's always something—television, radio, family, and friends—vying for our attention, filling up the empty space, keeping us from feeding our inner person."

Melissa had never thought of it quite like that. Yes, she'd regretted not having her mother growing up, yet she'd had Mrs. Browning. She'd hated the thought of her grandparents living so far away in Grand Junction, but they were only a phone call away. She'd suffered great loss, it was true, but in spite of her loneliness, she had never learned to feel completely comfortable with herself. Until this day. The past and the future were eliminated as she breathed in the fresh air, infused with the subtle smell of alfalfa. Only the present remained as she talked to God, the first real prayer she'd prayed since her experience on the banks of the Conestoga River. "I'm not very good at this," she began. "But my friend Lela tells me that you listen and understand, that you hear the heart's cry of your children. I'm glad about that, because my heart's rather torn up these days." She prayed that God might change the souls of men like Ivanov, and she prayed for Ryan. "Help him find his way to you, Lord." But most important, she prayed for wisdom, as Lela put it—"Help me make the right decision."

She felt a peculiar lightness in her step. Her eyes were once again opened to the beauty around her. The euphoric flutter of a monarch butterfly caught her attention, and she walked more briskly, following its meandering path as it stopped to alight on shell pink pasture roses that covered a small slope. She was aware of the vivid, broad blossoms of the species roses, but she kept her gaze fixed on the butterfly's orange-brown wings, its black veins and borders, missing her palette and brushes. Orchard orioles and vivid goldfinches darted here and there, from one tree to another, as she made her way up the narrow country road—and she painted the picture in her memory instead.

Thirty-Two

❖ ❖ ❖

The phone rang late in the afternoon, after Elizabeth had dropped by for a short visit, bringing along peach and pineapple preserves, as well as some money she owed Lela for her many quilted pillow shams.

Melissa was curled up on one of the sofas, reading Lela's Bible, when the jangle made her glance up as Lela scurried to the kitchen.

"Denlinger residence." Lela paused, listening for a moment, then replied, "Who may I say is calling?" She came into the living room, eyes too wide, the phone cord trailing behind her. Lela covered the receiver with her hand and whispered, "You have a phone call."

"Who is it?" Melissa mouthed.

"Your husband."

A thousand questions spun through her mind, and renewed panic seized her. For a moment, she considered denying that she was here and bolting for the door.

"What do you want to do?" Lela whispered, still holding the phone.

Finding courage, she said, "I'll talk to him."

Lela's expression conveyed hesitancy, as if asking, *Are you sure?*

Melissa nodded, getting up, and taking the phone. "Hello, Ryan?" she said, a lump already forming in her throat.

"Mellie, honey . . . are you okay?"

"How did you know where to reach me?"

"Sweetheart, you must listen to me—"

"Please, answer *me*, Ryan. How did you know where I was?" She looked at Lela, who was standing near, arms folded, eyes closed. She appeared to be praying.

"The FBI," he replied softly.

Melissa's breath caught in her throat, and she reached for a chair to sit down. "I don't understand. How can that be?"

"There's been a huge mistake—"

"But . . . Agent Walsh said . . . no, don't do this, Ryan. Please don't lie to me." Tears welled up, and she fought the confusion and the fear.

"Don't hang up. Let me explain."

"I'm listening."

"Melissa . . . I *work* for the FBI as an informant. I'm on your side," Ryan said. "My job was to help the government break Ivanov's network. That's why I couldn't tell you the truth before. But it's over now. Ivanov and his crowd don't trust me anymore. That's why he showed up at the restaurant in Mystic last week. He was making a final play for your father's stolen money."

Her husband's explanation was, at best, astonishing. She struggled to understand. Even so, a new emotion surfaced. *Hope.* With all her heart she wanted to believe him. Was this the answer to her prayer on the road?

"I want to believe you," she said, her voice trembling, her heart longing for assurance. "But how do I know you're telling the truth?"

"You simply have to trust me."

"But I . . ." She was more confused than ever. She breathed deeply, contemplating his words.

"Mellie, I know everything about you and your past. This one time, you must trust me."

This one time . . .

"But you lied to me, Ryan. If what you tell me is true . . . all those years . . ."

"I was sworn to secrecy. That's different, isn't it?" He seemed to have an answer for everything.

But he was right on one count. She had never entrusted him with her deepest secret, and she'd made a terrible mistake, panicking after seeing Ivanov at S&P Oyster Company. Now she felt foolish. Her walls of suspicion were beginning to crumble. "I've missed you, darling. I'm so sorry," she whispered.

She heard him sigh. "I've missed *you*, Mellie. You have no idea."

"What do we do now?"

"First of all, we stop this madness. These people will never be satisfied until we settle the issue about the money. I know you don't know where it is, but—"

"No . . . I *do* know, Ryan."

A disturbing silence fell between them.

Then—"What did you say?"

"I figured it out," she said. "My dad put the money in a Swiss bank account."

"Do you have the account number?"

"That, along with the code word."

"Listen, Mellie, what's the nearest restaurant to you?"

She turned to inquire of Lela.

"The closest place is Best Western Eden Resort Inn," Lela said, eyes serious.

Relaying the information to her husband, Melissa felt nervous, yet excited about seeing him again.

"Meet me in the parking lot there, tomorrow morning at eleven o'clock. An FBI agent will accompany me. From there we'll go to the bank and transfer the money to the government, get things squared away once and for all."

She was glad he was taking charge of things. For too long she'd carried her burdens alone. "I'll see you tomorrow."

"It's going to be okay, Mellie. This nightmare will soon be over. At last we'll be together, and no secrets between us anymore." His voice was tender and sweet to her ears.

"No secrets," she whispered. "I love you, Ryan."

"I love *you*, sweetheart."

She hung up the phone, her heart lighter than it had been in *ever so long*, she thought, lapsing into Lela's quaint speech.

Thirty-Three

❖ ❖ ❖

Durak!—fool!" bellowed Ivanov as both he and Ryan replaced their receivers. "Why didn't you get the account number?"

Ryan looked surprised. "I thought she would suspect something. I'll call her back if you wish." He reached for the phone again.

"No," Ivanov spit out. "You're right." Then he paused, composing himself. "That was quite the performance. You're a better liar than I thought you were."

Sitting in the swivel chair, looking exhausted, Ryan leaned his elbows on the desk.

Ivanov began pacing the floor, rehashing his plans. Tomorrow they'd meet up with Missy James and take her to a Philadelphia bank. There they would transfer the money, not to the federal government, as Ryan had told Melissa, but to Grand Cayman and other offshore accounts hidden around the world. Once the money transfer was complete, he'd be on his way to the Caribbean for a much needed rest. He had a penchant for hot, balmy weather.

"Are we finished here?" Ryan asked rather impatiently.

"Got a plane to catch?"

Ryan regarded him coolly, then looked away.

"Betrayal doesn't set well with you, does it?" Ivanov said, feeling amused, and for one tantalizing moment, he visualized the look of terrified shock on both Ryan's and Melissa's faces when they discovered Ivanov's own treachery. He had no intention of letting them live, not once he extracted the money. *A two-for-one deal*, he thought. *I get both my revenge and the money.*

"I'll get over it," Ryan replied.

"Good man. You two can go on a second honeymoon when this is over. Plenty of time to charm your way back into her good graces," he said. Then he clapped his hands once loudly, rubbing them together. "Better get some sleep. We've got a busy day tomorrow."

———————

Melissa waited outside, standing by her car in the parking lot of the Eden Resort Inn. She anticipated seeing her beloved again. So much so that she'd scarcely slept, too excited at the unexpected turn of events.

At 10:55 she spotted Ryan's white SUV pulling into the parking lot. Catching a glimpse of him, her heart leaped up. She noticed the shadowy man in the backseat of the vehicle and assumed the FBI agent had come along, just as Ryan had said.

Rushing to the parked vehicle, she opened the passenger door. "Ryan . . . darling!"

He smiled tentatively, reaching for her as she jumped into the car. She snuggled next to him, returning his tender kisses. "I missed you so much," she whispered, tears blinding her. "I thought I'd never see you again."

She was startled by the sound of the car door slamming behind her. The FBI agent had gotten out and closed her door. Why? Confused, she turned toward the man, just as he slid into the backseat.

"Miss me, too?" he replied, leering at her.

She nearly choked. *"You?"* Horrified, she turned back to Ryan. "What's *he* doing here?"

Her husband's smile had faded. Yet something in his expression communicated compassion. "It's okay, Melissa. Let me explain."

"You tricked me," she said, the truth sinking in. She grabbed for her door, pushing on the handle with all her strength.

Locked.

"Melissa . . . please."

She pushed again, to no avail. Now Ryan's hand was on her shoulder. She twitched in horror, and he quickly removed it. Then, slumping against the door, she closed her eyes, overcome with both grief and terror. Helpless . . . defeated, she prayed. *Please, Lord, help me.*

Turning to Ryan, she unleashed her fury. "You said I could trust you!"

Ryan was silent, his eyes intense, yet empathetic.

"We're wasting time here," the man grumbled in the backseat. "I'll take the account number *and* the code word."

She stared at Ryan. "So . . . it's all about the money?" she blurted. "For that you betrayed me?"

Ryan shook his head. "You don't understand—"

"The number, please!" the man behind her roared.

Angrily, she shot him an icy look. "It's up here." She tapped her forehead.

Reaching into his coat, Ivanov withdrew a pocket-size notebook and tossed it over the front seat. "Write it down," he barked.

"And if I won't?"

"You should know the answer to that," Ivanov replied, his greedy eyes dancing with confidence.

She studied him, despicable man that he was. "And lose your precious money forever? I don't think so."

Ryan looked over his shoulder at Ivanov. "I'll handle this."

"By all means, work your magic."

Ryan reached for her hand, but she withdrew again. "Please, just do as he says, Mellie."

She glared at Ryan.

"All he wants is the money. Then we can be together again," Ryan reiterated.

She shook her head, her rage out of control. "No matter what happens, it's over between us."

Ryan flinched as if she'd slapped him in the face.

Ivanov asked again for the bank number, but she refused.

"Listen, Missy, I call the shots here." Ivanov pulled his jacket away from his chest area, exposing his gun holster. "I've had enough of your games, young lady. I'm willing to gamble that deep down you still love your husband. So . . . how would you like to become a very young widow?"

There was a flicker of fear in her husband's eyes. Relenting, she took her pen and began to write the account number on the small notebook. Finished, she handed it over to Ivanov. "How do you know I didn't just make up a number?"

"Melissa—" Ryan said.

"No, that's a very good question," Ivanov said. "Which is why we're all going to the Philadelphia bank together. Anything goes wrong—the account number's false—and I'm the instant owner of waterfront property. Follow me?"

She stared back at the monster. *How can this be happening?*

He kept it up. "When the wire transfer is complete, you go your merry way, with or without your husband. It's no concern of mine."

To Ryan, Ivanov snapped, "Get moving."

She couldn't help keeping her eyes on Ryan as he pulled out of the parking lot. His gaze, however, was on the road. Silence fell over the car as they drove out of the parking lot. Melissa prayed from her heart, *Lord, I trust you.*

———

When they reached the outskirts of Philadelphia, Ryan made a turn onto I-76, heading south. Within minutes they were in the congested downtown area. Ryan pulled into a parking garage connected to a bank, removing the parking ticket from the machine as they passed the entrance into a labyrinth of increasingly darker levels.

Melissa grew more nervous as Ryan pulled into an available space near the elevator.

"All right, you lovebirds, it's show time. We're getting out of the car and going inside," Ivanov said, glowering at Melissa. "*Without* drawing attention to ourselves. Catch my drift?"

Ivanov pulled the handle and kicked his door open. Once out, he opened her door. Ryan emerged from his side, and the three of them walked toward the elevator doors, Ivanov taking up the rear, glancing about the parking lot. They were alone. Seconds before the elevator opened, Ivanov grabbed Melissa by the shirt and shoved her against the concrete wall.

"Lord, help me!" she whispered sharply, catching her breath.

"Hey, easy!" Ryan yelled.

Ivanov shot him a loathsome look. Melissa caught Ryan's eye and saw deep concern etched in his face. Ivanov leaned close to her, his repulsive breath overpowering. "Anything happens in there, and Ryan doesn't walk out. . . ."

"I know what you're capable of," she said, looking at Ryan again. The muscles in her husband's jaw twitched. He returned her gaze but remained sadly silent.

"That's right. You *would* know," Ivanov taunted. "Your daddy made some very poor decisions. Wouldn't advise you to make the same mistake."

"You're not half the man my father was," she murmured.

Ivanov laughed at her comment. "Maybe. But I'm alive." He released her, removed his cell phone from his coat pocket, and punched in some numbers. "Yeah, we're here. Meet us at the fourth-floor elevator."

Ivanov hung up, gesturing to the open elevator. The doors swallowed them with a swish, and they soared to the fourth floor. She noticed the marblelike floors with low-growing plants in lovely urns and the occasional hibiscus tree in various corners. *All fake*, she thought. *It's all a façade.*

A man who appeared to be a bank officer arrived as they entered the hallway. His face turned ashen when he spotted Ivanov. "What are *you* doing here?"

"I'm handling this one myself. Too much on the line," Ivanov said.

Was he referring to the men who normally handled his criminal transactions? Melissa wondered.

The officer turned to face Ryan and Melissa, obviously scrutinizing them. "Relax," Ivanov muttered to him. "They're with me."

Melissa caught the knowing exchange between the bank officer and Ivanov. Why would Ivanov allow her to witness this event? Unless . . .

She dreaded the answer, knowing she was in grave danger.

"Follow me," the man replied, evidently peeved at Ivanov's indiscretion.

Ivanov grabbed Melissa's arm, and she and Ryan were led through an office area. Dozens of bank employees worked at well-polished desks. Unsuspecting souls.

They were ushered down a short hallway, then into a small windowless room. A lone computer perched on an executive desk. Several chairs lined the walls. Numerous wires ran from the computer to the right wall. Ivanov closed the door.

Melissa made a quick assessment of the situation and realized that her escape options were limited. This was to be the location of the money transfer.

"Have a seat," Ivanov ordered.

Ryan took the chair next to her. "Are you all right?" he whispered.

It was a little late for caring. "I think he's going to kill me," she said softly.

"Quiet!" Ivanov bellowed, causing the bank officer to jolt in his seat. He grabbed a chair near the wall and pulled it over to the desk, where he was able to oversee the phone call to Switzerland.

After a brief conversation, the officer recited the code word and account number she'd given to Ivanov. Moments later, the bank officer acknowledged, "The information is correct. They'll transfer the funds immediately."

Ivanov gave Melissa a look that said, *Lucky for you*. Then he reached into his pocket and withdrew another piece of paper. "Transfer the money to this account," he ordered the officer. "Others will disburse it from there."

The man in uniform glanced at Ivanov's paper and nodded.

The room fell silent except for the click of computer keys as the numbers were entered. A second bank officer opened the door and walked in. Ivanov whirled in his chair, a puzzled look on his face. "Gerald, I'm sorry to interrupt," said the second employee. "Can you take a moment to sign something for me?"

The officer making the transfer for Ivanov kept his focus on the screen. "Later. I'm busy at the moment."

Suddenly, six other men barged into the room, guns drawn. "FBI! Freeze, Ivanov! Don't move!"

In the midst of the melee, Melissa dove off her chair just as someone wrestled Ivanov to the ground. Three men restrained him, removing his gun and cuffing his wrists.

Stunned, she saw that Ryan was also being seized by two men who pinned his arms, shoving one high behind his back. She turned away, unable to watch.

"Are you okay?" a woman agent asked. "Let's get you out of here." She pulled Melissa quickly to her feet, taking her arm and guiding her toward the door.

Once safely in the hallway, she looked over her shoulder. Ivanov, his eyes flaring with fury, was being led away toward the elevators by half a dozen FBI agents.

"Come with me," the woman agent said, but Melissa resisted momentarily, watching as Ryan was also ushered away. For an excruciating moment, his eyes found hers, and a curious look of relief veiled his countenance. Then he was escorted down the hallway—the same direction that Ivanov had been taken.

"Are you ready?" the agent asked.

Tearfully, Melissa nodded, unable to speak. She submitted, turning her back on the sad scene.

The two agents flanking Ryan led him to a waiting vehicle. Ivanov, too, was being taken to a car, although a different one, parked directly in front of them.

At one point, Ivanov turned and glowered at his captors. "I'll be out on the street by tonight. You have *nothing*." But the agent shoved Ivanov into the backseat, cutting short his diatribe.

"Watch your head," one of the agents told Ryan as he ducked and lowered himself into the car. The door closed firmly behind him, and two well-dressed men slid into the front seat.

They pulled out of the bank parking lot onto the main street, which by now was filled with hundreds of spectators observing the commotion. Ryan lowered his head as the car maneuvered through the narrow streets.

Choosing to shut out the thrill-seeking crowds, Ryan's thoughts were of Melissa—and her alone. He recalled the pain in her eyes as she had been confronted with his betrayal. As long as he lived, he would never forget the look of disbelief on her face.

The car was void of all conversation as they drove past City Hall to Market Street, heading toward I-95. Several miles outside of Trenton, New Jersey, the driver pulled onto a side road and followed it for several miles to a deserted park. Veering right, they drove several more yards, stopping beside another dark sedan.

The driver turned and smiled at Ryan. "Tired of the cuffs?" The agent got out of the car and opened Ryan's door. He fumbled with the key to the handcuffs and unlocked them. "Better?"

"Much." Ryan got out of the car, rubbing his sore wrists.

The back door of the sedan opened. A man in a dark suit got out, adjusting his tie. Then the front passenger door opened, and another man stepped out into the sunshine.

It was McGuire. *FBI Special Agent in Charge* McGuire.

He walked over, extending his hand to Ryan. "I followed the whole thing on the radio. Excellent work."

Ryan shook hands, but he didn't share McGuire's obvious triumph. McGuire introduced his passenger as Agent Walsh with Organized Crime. Walsh and Ryan exchanged nods.

"How're you feeling? A little shaken up?" McGuire asked.

"How's Melissa?" Ryan asked.

"She's headed back to the Denlinger home. Want me to get her on the phone?"

Ryan considered this but did not relish the entire FBI force listening in. "I'll talk to her later."

McGuire shrugged. "She'll be told everything—that you had no choice in being a part of the sting."

"I betrayed my wife," Ryan replied. "We never gave *her* a choice. She was terrified."

Walsh spoke for the first time. "We needed her participation. You know yourself she wouldn't have played the game willingly."

"It was a judgment call for the good of the country *and* for her own personal safety," McGuire chimed in. "Ivanov will never bother her again. Not only that, but because of you and Melissa, we caught the men on the other end of the wire transfer. The entire network is sunk. We recovered nearly half a billion dollars. Once we threaten Ivanov with extradition, he'll turn on his Russian buddies in a heartbeat."

"Just like that?" Ryan struggled to comprehend.

McGuire smiled wryly. "These boys aren't the Italian Mafia—brotherhood, honor, loyalty, all that good stuff. Believe me, at this point, Ivanov will say or do anything to avoid going back to Russia. Even betraying his friends and family."

"Any evidence of . . . compromised agents?" Ryan asked.

McGuire laughed. "Like I said before, Ivanov was bluffing. Sure, we're investigating, but keep in mind, it's almost impossible to bribe an FBI agent."

"And my parents—?"

"Safe and sound. Another one of Ivanov's bluffs."

"What about Bernie?"

McGuire's expression changed. "We picked him up this afternoon. No resistance. He was resigned to his fate. If he sings a pretty tune, I'll recommend leniency."

"Just take me home," Ryan said.

"Whatever you say, partner." McGuire patted him on the shoulder as the three of them headed back to their cars.

Ryan's assigned driver, Special Agent Carlson, turned off the main highway, heading into Lord's Point. The car slowed as the road curved around toward the shoreline, then pulled into the driveway of the waterfront property. He gazed at the beautiful house and surrounding acreage. No longer did any of it belong to him.

In exchange for agreeing to testify in court, the government promised not to prosecute him for his complicity in money laundering and insider-trading crimes. Part of the deal included the forfeiture of his house and bank accounts—everything except for a few personal belongings.

All in exchange for his freedom. But freedom in itself held little appeal. Money and the possessions it afforded had long since ceased to interest him. Life without Melissa was hardly worth living.

By now she would know the truth about him, that he'd turned a blind eye to the shady dealings of his company. That he had *not* been an informant for years, as he'd told her on the phone. He'd merely made a quick deal to save his own skin. On top of everything, he had tricked her into participating in a dangerous sting.

"No matter what happens, it's over between us." Her words echoed in his mind, spoken in the motel parking lot in Lancaster County in the midst of his "betrayal."

Agent Carlson parked the car, and Ryan led the way into the house. Tonight he was scheduled to sleep at a city hotel, where the FBI could keep an eye on him. Tomorrow a moving van would haul away the remainder of his personal effects. Presumably, Melissa would have the same opportunity to sort out her belongings.

Where he would ultimately reside, he had no clue. The FBI was calling the shots now. They would select his next home and his new identity, until he was to be called to trial. While most informants were held in jail awaiting trial, Ryan was an exception. As the government's star witness, he was to be held under house guard. Once the trial was over, he would be given the freedom to resume a normal life again.

As usual, Daisy was waiting just inside the front door. Carlson bent down to pet the golden retriever. "Good-looking dog."

Ryan said nothing, relieved that Daisy would be shipped out to his parents.

"How long will you be?" Carlson asked.

"A few minutes." He looked around the room, seeing only distant memories. How quickly things had changed in the space of a week. He regarded the wilting lavender roses he'd purchased for his wife and considered throwing them away. Dismissing the thought, he left them on the counter.

Hurrying upstairs, he packed a large suitcase full of clothes and a smaller one for toiletry items. When he was finished, he wandered down the hall to the guest room, noting the empty space on the wall where Mellie's painting for Denny had hung. *The Cross painting*, as Denny had so aptly termed it. The vacant wall space seemed forsaken.

He glanced at the bedside table, noticing the book *Mere Christianity*. Denny's doing. He reached for the book, deciding to pack it, as well. *I'm going to have plenty of time on my hands*, he thought, returning to the bedroom. Picking up his suitcases, he lugged them downstairs, where Agent Carlson stood as if guarding the front door.

Thirty-Four

❖ ❖ ❖

Climbing the stairs at Lela's for one last time, Melissa felt both emancipated and miserable all wrapped up in one confusing emotion. Her FBI escort, now waiting on the front porch, had assured her that Ivanov was behind bars. She was safe at last. At some point she would be free to live her own life. After the trial—whenever that might be.

She looked forward, with all eagerness, to flying to Colorado, where she hoped to renew her bonds with dear Mrs. Browning. Yet feelings of depression swept over her each time she thought of Ryan. Or recalled how he'd tricked her. *Betrayed* her.

"I hope I can keep in touch with you," she told Lela, paying up on the rent she owed, grateful once again for the comfort and serenity of the Mennonite cottage. Melissa knew now that the Lord had guided her steps, bringing her to the godly woman's home. "And thank you, Lela, for the Bible. I will treasure it, truly."

Lela nodded, touching her arm. "Rest assured, you're in God's safekeeping, Mellie. Remember that always."

She clasped the woman's hand. "Thank you for leading me to your God."

Lela's eyes were bright with tears. "He's *yours*, too. You are a child of the Father, to be sure."

She embraced the Plain woman quickly, then—"If for any reason you don't hear from me for a while, don't worry, all right?"

"You're in good hands. I know that."

With that, they said fond farewells, and Melissa joined the agent waiting patiently outside.

———

They stood gawking at the old shed in the dim light of early evening, wondering what on earth they'd do with an abandoned automobile. Beyond, in the two-story bank barn, one of the cows let out a low moan, weary of the day. Crickets burst forth with their timpani at dusk, mingling their sounds with the hum of katydids and other summer insects vying for solo time.

"I daresay we're stuck with four wheels and nary a key to start it up," Thaddeus said, taking his straw hat off and scratching the back of his head.

Elizabeth clucked a little. "Now why wouldja be thinkin' thataway?" she asked. "You aren't planning to take a little drive around the farm, now, are you?"

"Well, now, I think you oughta know your husband better'n that." He pulled her close, planting a kiss on her lips.

Both laughing now, Elizabeth asked, "Why do you think Lela's guest had to up and leave so awful fast, for goodness' sake?"

"Says Lela, she had important business to be tendin' to."

"Must be mighty important." She couldn't imagine leaving behind something that must've cost a pretty penny. Not at all. "Maybe Paul Martin can teach Lela to drive it . . . someday," she added.

"Could be that he will." Thaddeus had a right nice smile on his face. "Might be just the thing to get 'em close, you know. Teachin' a lady to drive, well now, that just might be the best idea we've had in a gut long time."

"I doubt Paul needs an excuse to get close to my sister," Elizabeth replied. "He seems ready to pick up the pieces, right where he left them so long ago."

Hurrying back to the house, she checked on her cabbage chowder. *Thank you, Lord, for this beautiful day, and for the folk who cross our paths*, she prayed silently as she and Mary Jane set the table.

Ryan tossed his bags onto the queen-sized bed of the motel room. Agent Carlson looked in momentarily through the open door. "If you need anything, I'm in the next room."

Ryan nodded, then scanned the sparsely furnished room. There was a TV in the far corner, a small table and two chairs near the window, a large dresser opposite the bed. His home for the night, perhaps longer. He sat on the edge of the bed and rubbed his weary eyes.

The phone rang and he reached for it cautiously. "Hello?"

It was McGuire calling to outline tomorrow's schedule. "You have a decision to make," he said. "You and the missus—are you going together or parting ways?"

Ryan didn't know the answer to that.

"She's not at the Denlinger home anymore," McGuire replied. "I'll have her call you. Let me know tomorrow what you two decide."

Ryan hung up, closed his eyes tightly, and tried to calm his still-taut nerves. Disjointed images of the day played through his mind. Ivanov's predatory eyes seemed to follow him everywhere—those little oval slits of evil, frenzied and desperate with the prospect of recovering "his" money.

Since the moment he'd seen Melissa again, Ryan had been deathly afraid that Ivanov would discover his duplicity and execute vengeance on both of them long before they reached the bank. The tension from that anxiety continued to reverberate. But most persistent was Melissa's tortured expression of disbelief. From a legal standpoint, Ryan had finally done the right thing by turning informant. The network had been crushed in one fell swoop, the money confiscated. The sting would go down as one of the biggest busts in organized crime. Yet the knowledge of it offered him scant comfort. After three years of harboring a deep dark secret, Melissa had finally trusted him implicitly. And how had he rewarded her?

With deception and betrayal.

Feelings of despondency overtook him as he grabbed his luggage, unzipping the side pocket where he'd placed the book from Denny. Intending to simply pass a few hours, he paged to the first chapter: *The Law of Human Nature*—the theme of his last religious discussion with Denny.

It was after eleven o'clock when Ryan closed the book and dropped it on the mattress next to him. The room was poorly illuminated by a single lamp on the nightstand beside the too-silent phone.

He got up and stretched his legs, walking over to the window. The beige curtains were tainted by the faint smell of cigarette smoke. Outside, the motel parking lot was half filled with cars and trucks, families on vacation, businessmen eager to get home. A small breeze through the screened window fluttered the curtains, bringing in the scent of impending autumn.

In only a few hours he had managed to read more than half of *Mere Christianity*—enough to know he was on the brink of something new. He'd expected Lewis's arguments on the subject to border on the ridiculous. Instead, the author presented flawless evidence for the truth of Christianity. The premise not only made sense but was intellectually compelling. But Ryan questioned his own judgment. After today's emotional events he was obviously vulnerable.

Ryan turned from the window, leaning against the sill. He stared at the phone before picking it up and dialing the number he knew by memory. It was just after nine o'clock in Denver, Colorado.

Two rings, then: "Hello?"

"Hey, preacher man."

Denny chuckled. "Well, howdy stranger. You finally called back."

"Sorry, Den."

"You okay, man?"

Ryan leaned back on the pillow and began to tell Denny all that had recently transpired. Denny listened, interrupting only to ask for clarification. When Ryan finished, Denny was initially silent, as if formulating his response.

"Melissa called me," Denny finally said, his tone serious. "Couple days ago. She needed . . . some advice."

Ryan considered Denny's revelation, wishing Melissa might have called *him.* "I guess I really blew it with her." Then changing the subject, he said, "I just read the book you left, most of it anyway."

"Yeah, what'd you think?"

"It's . . . actually convincing. But . . . considering everything, I'm obviously not thinking straight tonight. I need time to think things through."

"Maybe you're thinking clearly for the first time in your life."

"C'mon, Denny, it's a cliche: *Local man loses home, money, and wife. Gets religion.* Sound suspect?"

"Maybe. But then again, that could be a good place to start. Not to sound glib, but sometimes the bad things in our lives serve as catalysts to wake us up. After all, the atheist in the foxhole turns to God because his life has suddenly been reduced to the bare essentials."

Ryan chuckled to himself. Same old Denny—*Preacher Man.* "Well, I wanted you to know you won't be hearing from me for a while. Not until the trial's over."

"Bummer. So who's gonna be the best man in my wedding?"

"You're getting married?"

"You don't have to act so surprised—"

"I didn't say anything," Ryan protested.

"I heard it in your *tone*."

"You know . . . if you need someone to stand up with you, Daisy's always available. You two got along pretty well. In fact, you both shared something very deep and meaningful."

"Okay, this better be good. What deep and meaningful experience did I share with your dog?"

"Sausage and bacon, of course. Not to mention fried eggs."

Denny chuckled. "You're absolutely right. Greasy food *is* a deep and meaningful experience. Guaranteed to create bonds of friendship that last a lifetime. But I gotta tell you, Ryan, you don't sound like an atheist in a foxhole, anymore. You sound kinda chipper, in fact."

"Just needed a buddy-fix."

They bantered another few minutes before Ryan said good-bye, promising to visit the newlyweds when he had a chance. But his buoyed spirits sank the moment he hung up and looked about the cramped and stale-smelling motel room. Sighing, he looked back at the phone. The message light was as dim as the room. Melissa still hadn't called.

As the reality of the past few days set in again, a rush of silence seemed to inhabit the darkness of the room like a wind filling a vacuum. Accompanying the feeling of emptiness and isolation was the renewed sense of *struggle*. As if a war were being played out in his mind, tugging at the opposing sides of his reason, battling for control. Despite his apprehension concerning Melissa, he realized he had a decision to make.

"Maybe you're thinking clearly for the first time . . ." Denny had said.

Raking his hand through his hair, he recalled C. S. Lewis's succinct explanation of the human condition. Earlier he and Denny had discussed the nature of evil as a mere philosophical theory. But coming face to face with evil incarnate—in the form of an evil man—was a whole new ball game.

If complete and utter evil could exist in the form of a human being like Ivanov, surely goodness, on a far greater level, could also exist—in the form of God. In light of Ryan's recent experience, "depravity of man" was the only logical explanation for mankind's suffering and misfortune, a bad-to-the-bone wickedness that is beyond the reach of sheer education or human enlightenment.

The irony was that in the end, Ivanov himself was Ryan's proof of man's depravity. But a sudden realization sent cold shivers down his back, accompanied with a deeper feeling of remorse: *Ivanov—we're not so different, you and I.*

Slipping to the floor, he knelt, overwhelmed with a need for redemption unknowable to his human reasoning, longing for the forgiveness of his sin—yet beset with a lifetime of skepticism. A phrase ran through his mind—*where had he heard it?*—and he embraced it as his own: *Lord, I do believe . . . help my unbelief!*

Faltering, he prayed, a man at the end of his rope. Tears of anguish and sorrow followed. Eventually all inner resistance melted away, and he experienced something new. Something that until this moment he had only heard about but had never accepted as reality.

Rest for his weary soul.

The morning sun flickered through the curtains as Ryan tossed the last remaining items into his overnight bag and zipped it shut. Agent Carlson was waiting in the downstairs lobby. One more meeting with McGuire.

When the phone rang, he turned, staring at it. After a solid week of waiting, there was no doubt in his mind. The caller was Melissa.

Filled with apprehension, he realized anew that his wife might never forgive him. He'd have to make peace with that someday. Either way, this was the moment of truth.

He dropped his bags on the floor and picked up the phone.

Thirty-Five

❖ ❖ ❖

T he sunset seemed to linger longer than usual as Melissa made her way barefoot over the well-known ridge to Napatree Beach. Sighing with relief, she wondered how the sun would look as it set tonight. A spectacular array of color? Or a gentle whisper of muted tones, like the still lifes she favored?

Breathing hard, she made her way to the promontory, that high area where the point reached out like a finger into the water below. Angling up to the crest, she stood there scanning the shoreline, thankful to be here. With scarcely a breeze stirring, the pre-twilight atmosphere was still. Occasional clouds dappled the line separating sky and sea. The sun had a few more fluid minutes before it dipped into the deep, flinging its molten rays wildly into a burst of breathtaking hues.

Few beachcombers were left. Three or four seemed content to roam the wet sand, scavenging for shells and other debris. One girl had a burlap satchel thrown over her shoulder, filled, no doubt, with sea treasures.

Melissa's gaze focused on the very tip of the jetty, where large rocks were stacked to create a manmade dock of sorts. Shielding her eyes from the sun as it plunged toward the ocean, she could see the figure of a man sitting there facing the horizon.

It was Ryan, precisely where they had arranged to meet, his hands folded in a contemplative fashion. She felt a pounding in her head, matching the sound of the waters beyond, as she watched him, this man, seemingly a stranger, even though it had been scarcely more than a week since her frantic escape. So much had happened since then. Events from which many married couples never recover.

She smiled to herself. But they weren't just *any* couple. After Agent

McGuire's explanation of yesterday's events, Melissa had needed time to think. And to pray.

Slowly, carefully, she picked her way over the boulders, careful not to slip. Somewhere on the sandy hill behind them, FBI agents hovered near, watching like a sturdy angelic guard.

Just as she reached the end of the pier, the sun dipped past the horizon, shooting out sprays of purple and gold. Ryan turned as if on cue, hope reflected in his eyes, delight in his smile.

Three years ago she had promised to love and cherish this man. She would keep her word.

"Mellie," he whispered, gathering her into his arms.

Safe in the protection of his tender embrace, she felt the promise of a new beginning as husband and wife, under God.

Acknowledgments

With sincere gratitude we wish to acknowledge our editors, Barb Lilland, Anne Severance, and Carol Johnson, as well as the editorial staff and marketing team at Bethany House Publishers. Our special thanks to Clyde and Susan Gordon who cheerfully assisted with regional research, and to Dale and Barbara Birch who proofread the manuscript. The "wonderful-gut" help we gleaned from our Plain friends and contacts made all the difference.

We treasure the ongoing prayers of our family and friends, including John Henderson who kept us in stitches throughout the writing process. Many thanks to the faithful readers who offered thoughtful words of encouragement and love.

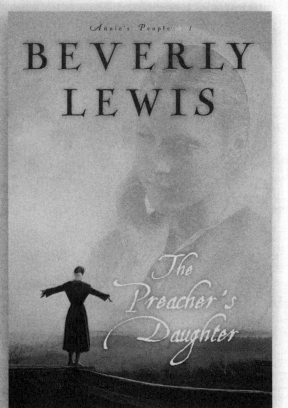
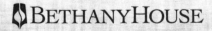

Explore the World of Plain People
Whose Lives Are *Not* So Simple

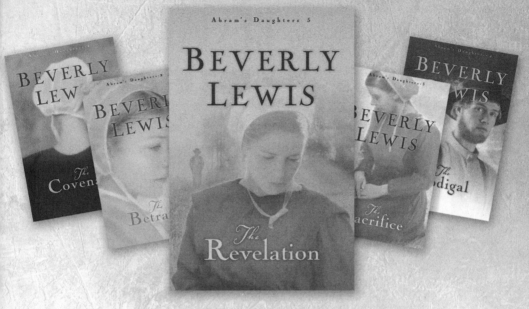

*"Lewis is a master of eliciting empathy for characters
caught in troubles of their own making.... The tension between [the
Plain people] and the encroaching English world is palpable."*
—Library Journal

New York Times bestselling author Beverly Lewis
brings to life the stories of ABRAM'S DAUGHTERS
in this series about a quaint Old Order community
whose way of life and faith in God are as enduring as
their signature horse and buggy. Or so it seems....

Join the hundreds of thousands of readers who
have made every book in this series a #1 Christian
fiction bestseller and discover for yourself the captivating charm of this Amish family.

ABRAM'S
DAUGHTERS
by Beverly Lewis

The Covenant
The Betrayal
The Sacrifice
The Prodigal
The Revelation

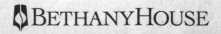

BETHANYHOUSE

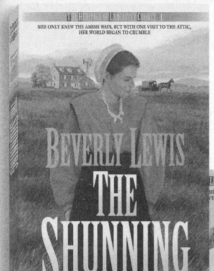